## Also by Stuart Gibbs

**The FunJungle series**
*Belly Up*
*Poached*
*Big Game*
*Panda-monium*
*Lion Down*
*Tyrannosaurus Wrecks*
*Bear Bottom*
*Whale Done*

**The Spy School series**
*Spy School*
*Spy Camp*
*Evil Spy School*
*Spy Ski School*
*Spy School Secret Service*
*Spy School Goes South*
*Spy School British Invasion*
*Spy School Revolution*
*Spy School at Sea*
*Spy School Project X*

*Spy School the Graphic Novel*
(with Anjan Sarkar)

**The Moon Base Alpha series**
*Space Case*
*Spaced Out*
*Waste of Space*

**The Charlie Thorne series**
*Charlie Thorne and the Last Equation*
*Charlie Thorne and the Lost City*
*Charlie Thorne and the Curse of Cleopatra*

**The Once Upon a Tim series**
*Once Upon a Tim*
*The Labyrinth of Doom*

*The Last Musketeer*

# STUART GIBBS

ILLUSTRATED BY **ANJAN SARKAR**

# spy camp

## THE GRAPHIC NOVEL

A **spy school** NOVEL

Simon & Schuster Books for Young Readers
New York London Toronto Sydney New Delhi

SIMON & SCHUSTER BOOKS FOR YOUNG READERS
An imprint of Simon & Schuster Children's Publishing Division
1230 Avenue of the Americas, New York, New York 10020

SIMON & SCHUSTER BOOKS FOR YOUNG READERS
and related marks are trademarks of Simon & Schuster, Inc.
For information about special discounts for bulk purchases, please contact
Simon & Schuster Special Sales at 1-866-506-1949 or business@simonandschuster.com.
The Simon & Schuster Speakers Bureau can bring authors to your live event.
For more information or to book an event, contact the Simon & Schuster Speakers
Bureau at 1-866-248-3049 or visit our website at www.simonspeakers.com.
Interior design by Lucy Ruth Cummins
The text for this book was set in Memphis LT Std.
The illustrations for this book were rendered digitally.
Manufactured in China
1122 SCP
First Edition
10 9 8 7 6 5 4 3 2 1
Library of Congress Cataloging-in-Publication Data
Names: Gibbs, Stuart, 1969– author. | Sarkar, Anjan, illustrator.
Title: Spy camp the graphic novel / Stuart Gibbs ; illustrated by Anjan Sarkar.
Description: First Simon & Schuster Books for Young Readers hardcover edition. |
New York : Simon & Schuster Books for Young Readers, 2023. |
Series: Spy school | Audience: Ages 8–12 | Audience: Grades 4–6 |
Summary: "Top-secret training continues into summer for aspiring spy Ben Ripley—
and so does the danger"— Provided by publisher.
Identifiers: LCCN 2021055680 (print) | LCCN 2021055681 (ebook) |
ISBN 9781534499386 (hardcover) | ISBN 9781534499379 (paperback) |
ISBN 9781534499393 (ebook)
Subjects: CYAC: Graphic novels. | Spies—Fiction. | Schools—Fiction. |
LCGFT: Spy comics. | Graphic novels.
Classification: LCC PZ7.7.G5324 Sp 2023 (print) | LCC PZ7.7.G5324 (ebook) |
DDC 741.5/973—dc23/eng/20211124
LC record available at https://lccn.loc.gov/2021055680
LC ebook record available at https://lccn.loc.gov/2021055681

For Ciara —S. G.

For Kenji —A. S.

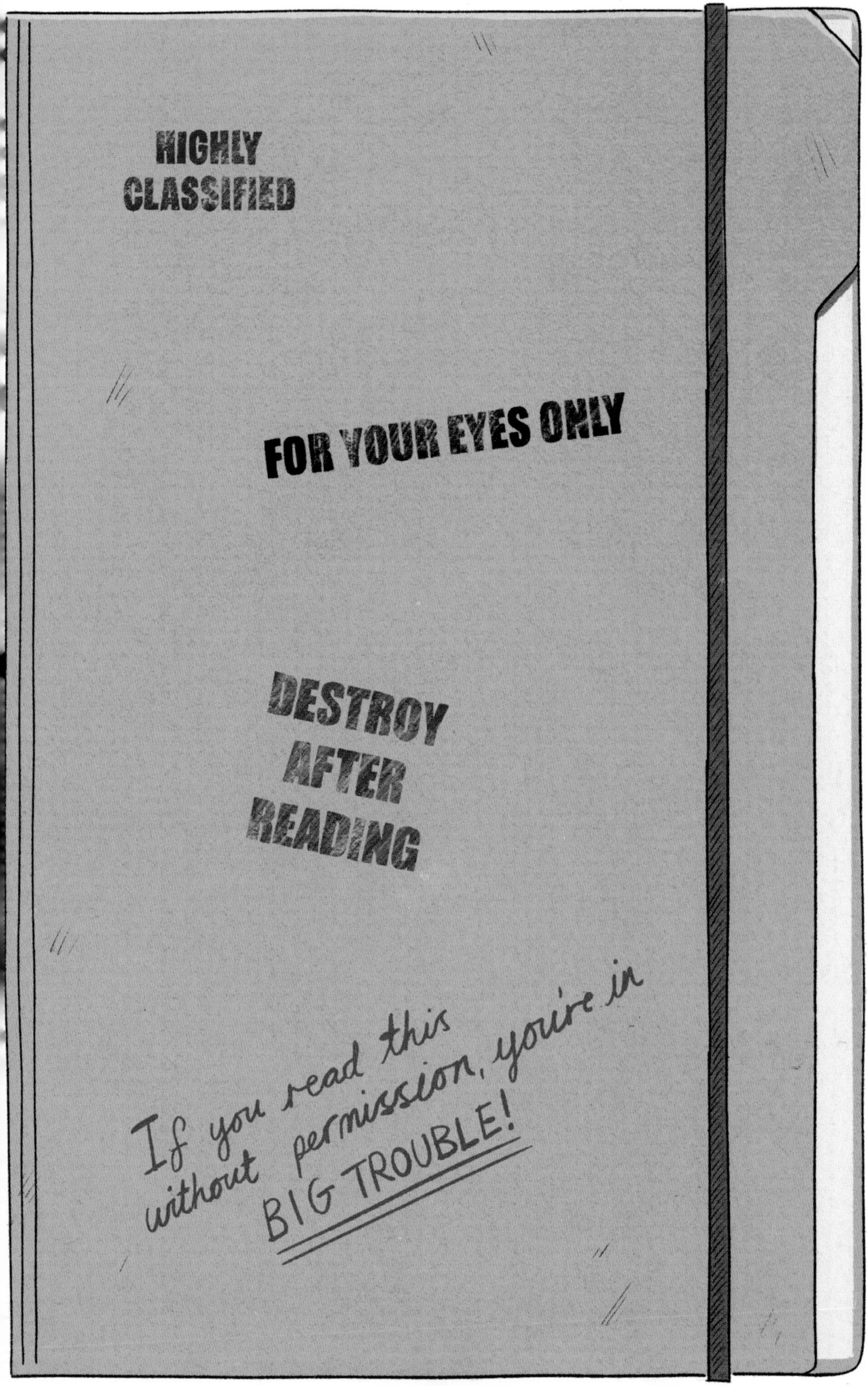
HIGHLY CLASSIFIED
FOR YOUR EYES ONLY
DESTROY AFTER READING
If you read this without permission, you're in BIG TROUBLE!

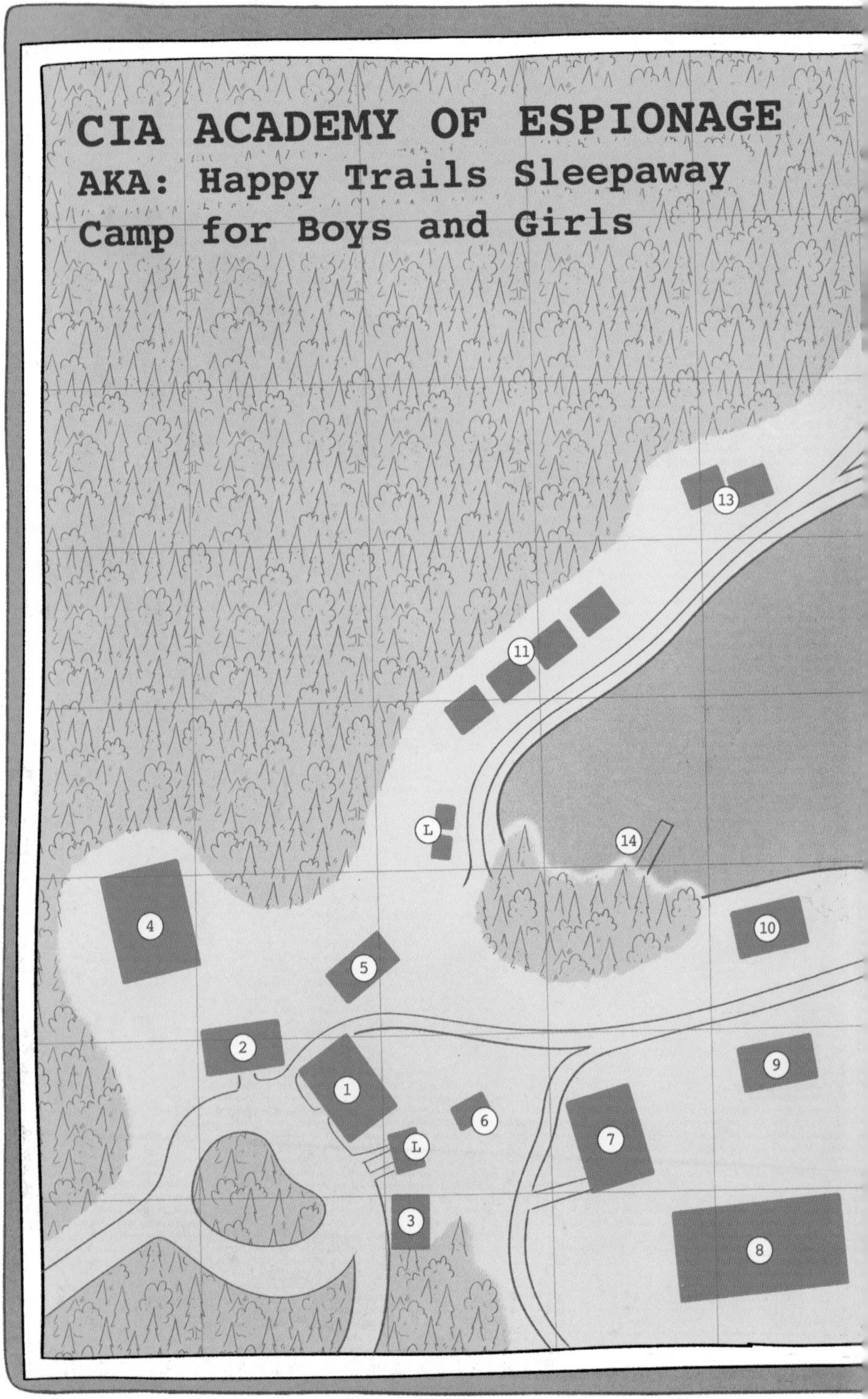
CIA ACADEMY OF ESPIONAGE
AKA: Happy Trails Sleepaway Camp for Boys and Girls
13
11
L
14
4
10
5
2
9
1
6
L
7
3
8

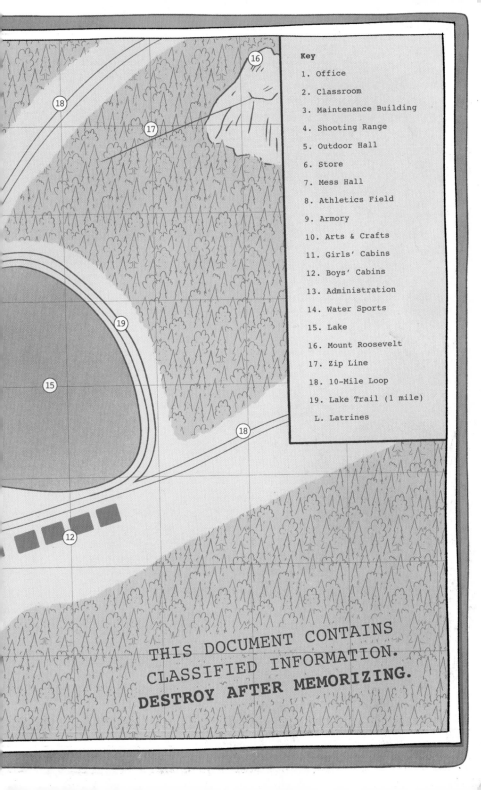

Key

1. Office
2. Classroom
3. Maintenance Building
4. Shooting Range
5. Outdoor Hall
6. Store
7. Mess Hall
8. Athletics Field
9. Armory
10. Arts & Crafts
11. Girls' Cabins
12. Boys' Cabins
13. Administration
14. Water Sports
15. Lake
16. Mount Roosevelt
17. Zip Line
18. 10-Mile Loop
19. Lake Trail (1 mile)
L. Latrines

THIS DOCUMENT CONTAINS CLASSIFIED INFORMATION.
DESTROY AFTER MEMORIZING.

**Name:** Benjamin Ripley

**Age:** 12 (but about to turn 13)

**Year at the academy:** First

**Code name:** Smokescreen

**Mental acuity:** Very intelligent. Level 16 math skills.

**Physical acuity:** Very little. Hopeless when it comes to weaponry. DO NOT let him have a weapon under any circumstances. It would be wise to not even let him use a fork in the mess hall.

Recruited to the Academy of Espionage five months ago as part of Operation Creeping Badger.

Although Ripley was secretely brought in as bait to lure a mole out of hiding, due to several unforeseen events, he wound up playing a larger role in the operation than originally expected.

As a result, he is the only person at the CIA to have ever had direct contact with the nefarious evil organization known as SPYDER. In fact, SPYDER actually tried to recruit him, although he turned them down.

Because Ripley started at the academy late in the year, he is a bit behind other students in his class and still may not be fully informed of all academy practices.

**Name:** Murray Hill

**Age:** 13

**Year at the academy:** No longer valid

**Code name:** Washout

**Mental acuity:** Not bad; very sneaky and underhanded

**Physical ability:** Embarrassing

Murray Hill flunked his first year at the academy and then spent much of his second year working as a covert mole for SPYDER. Thanks to Operation Creeping Badger, he was apprehended before he could blow up the academy and has now been incarcerated at the Apple Valley Reformation Camp for Delinquent Teens.

UNDER ARREST

**Name:** Erica Hale

**Age:** 15

**Year at the academy:** Third

**Code name:** Ice Queen

**Mental acuity:** Excellent

**Physical acuity:** Off the charts

Despite merely being a third-year student, Hale is easily the best student at the academy. This can be attributed, in part, to the fact that she is a legacy: The Hale family can be traced back to Nathan and Elias Hale, spies for the Colonial forces during the American Revolution. Thus, the Hales have been spying for the United States since before there was a United States.

Erica is adept in five forms of martial arts, can speak six languages and has familiarity with a great variety of weapons. However, her interpersonal skills are somewhat lacking. She is regarded by her fellow students (and much of the faculty) as cold, impersonal, and kind of scary.

She was integral to the success of Operation Creeping Badger despite the fact that she was not supposed to be a part of that operation at all.

**Name:** Agent Alexander Hale

**Age:** Classified

**Code names:** Gray Wolf, Alpha Dog, Blazing Stallion, Vengeful Lion

Alexander Hale has been a highly decorated agent for many years at the CIA and has served on dozens of operations in exotic locales around the world. He comes from a long line of agents and is the father of agent-in-training Erica Hale.

According to his most recent reports, he was integral to the defeat of SPYDER in Operation Creeping Badger.

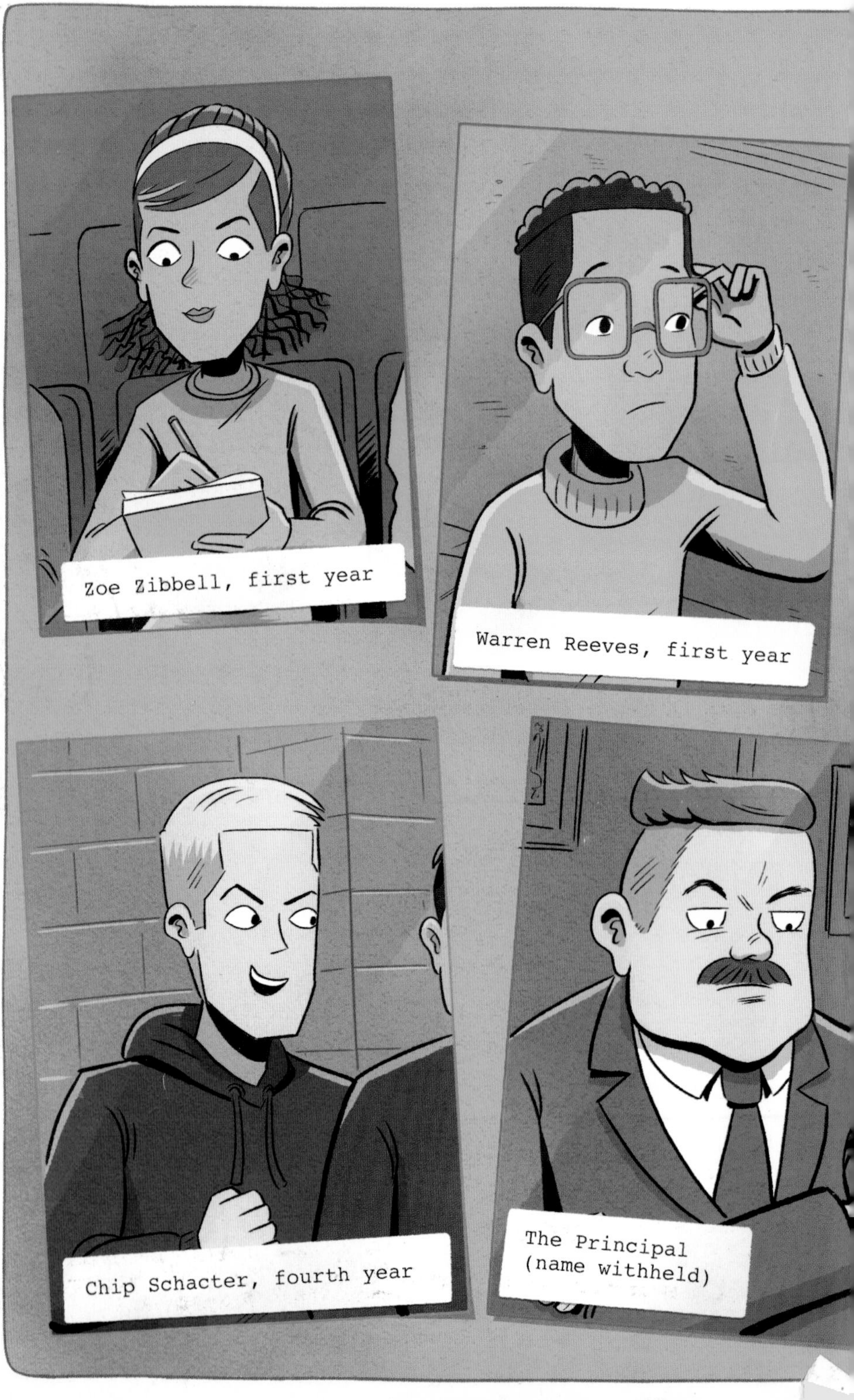
Zoe Zibbell, first year
Warren Reeves, first year
Chip Schacter, fourth year
The Principal
(name withheld)

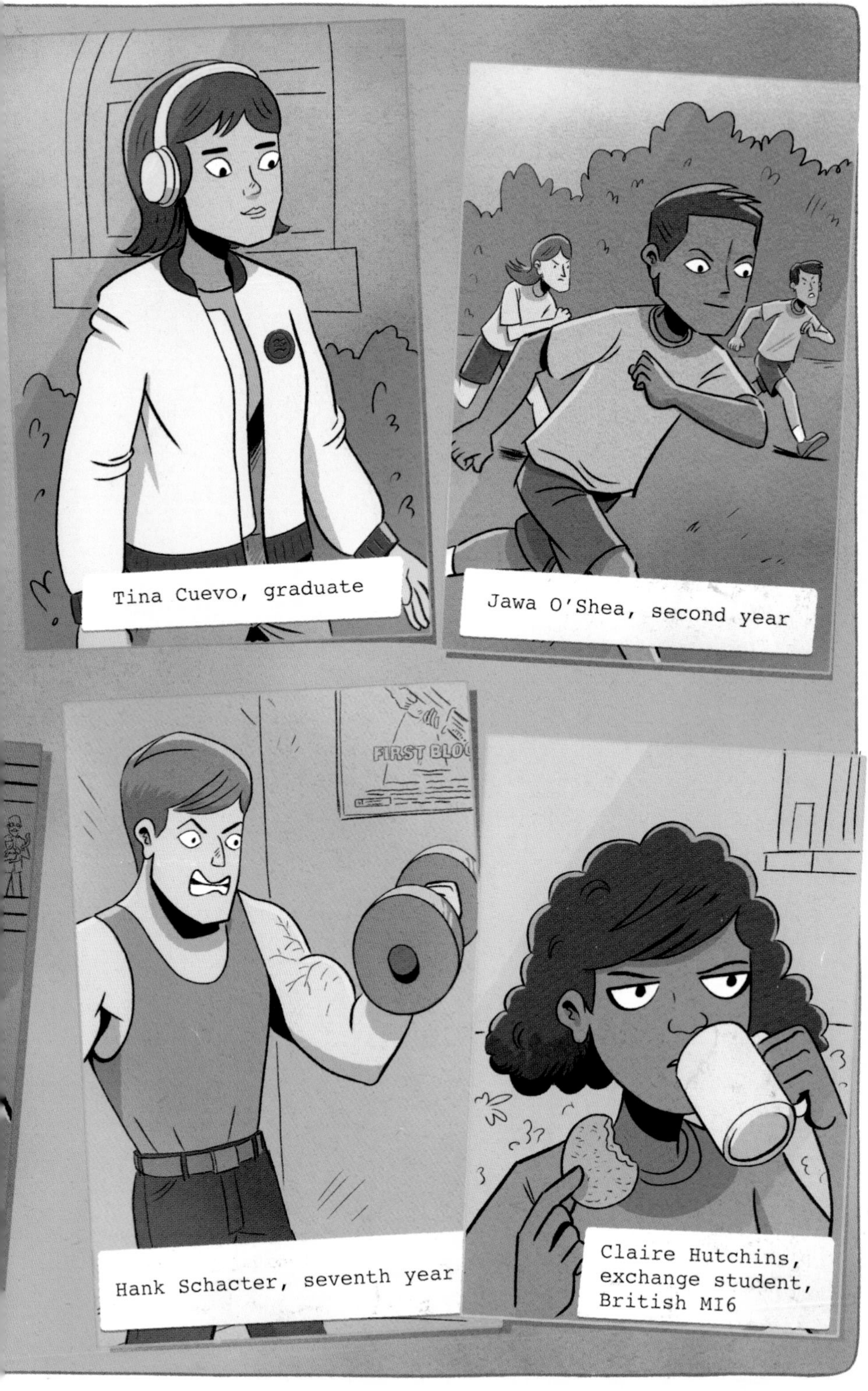
Tina Cuevo, graduate
Jawa O'Shea, second year
FIRST BLOO
Hank Schacter, seventh year
Claire Hutchins, exchange student, British MI6

From:
Office of CIA Internal Investigations
CIA Headquarters
Langley, Virginia

To:
██████████████████
Director of Covert Affairs
The White House
Washington, DC

Classified Documents Enclosed
Security Level AA2
For Your Eyes Only

Well, here we go again.

As you are probably aware, the events of June 10–16 of this year, in which
████████████████████████████████████ have warranted a
significant internal investigation. Once again, Mr. Benjamin Ripley, aka
Smokescreen, a first-year student at the Academy of Espionage, was involved.
The following pages are compiled from 54 hours of debriefings.

This episode, although not an official CIA operation at the time, is currently
being classified as Operation Angry Jackal. The events described indicate
a disturbing trend of ████████████████████ (
and ██████████████████ If Mr. Ripley and the others involved are to be
believed, we came perilously close to ██████████████████████
████████████

After these documents have been read, they are to be destroyed immediately, in
accordance with CIA Security Directive 163-12A. No discussion of these
pages will be tolerated, except during the review, which will be conducted in
a secure location at ██████████████████████ Please note that no
weapons will be allowed at said meeting.

I look forward to hearing your thoughts.

██████████████████
Director of Internal Investigations

Cc:
██████████████████
██████████████████
██████████████████
██████████████████

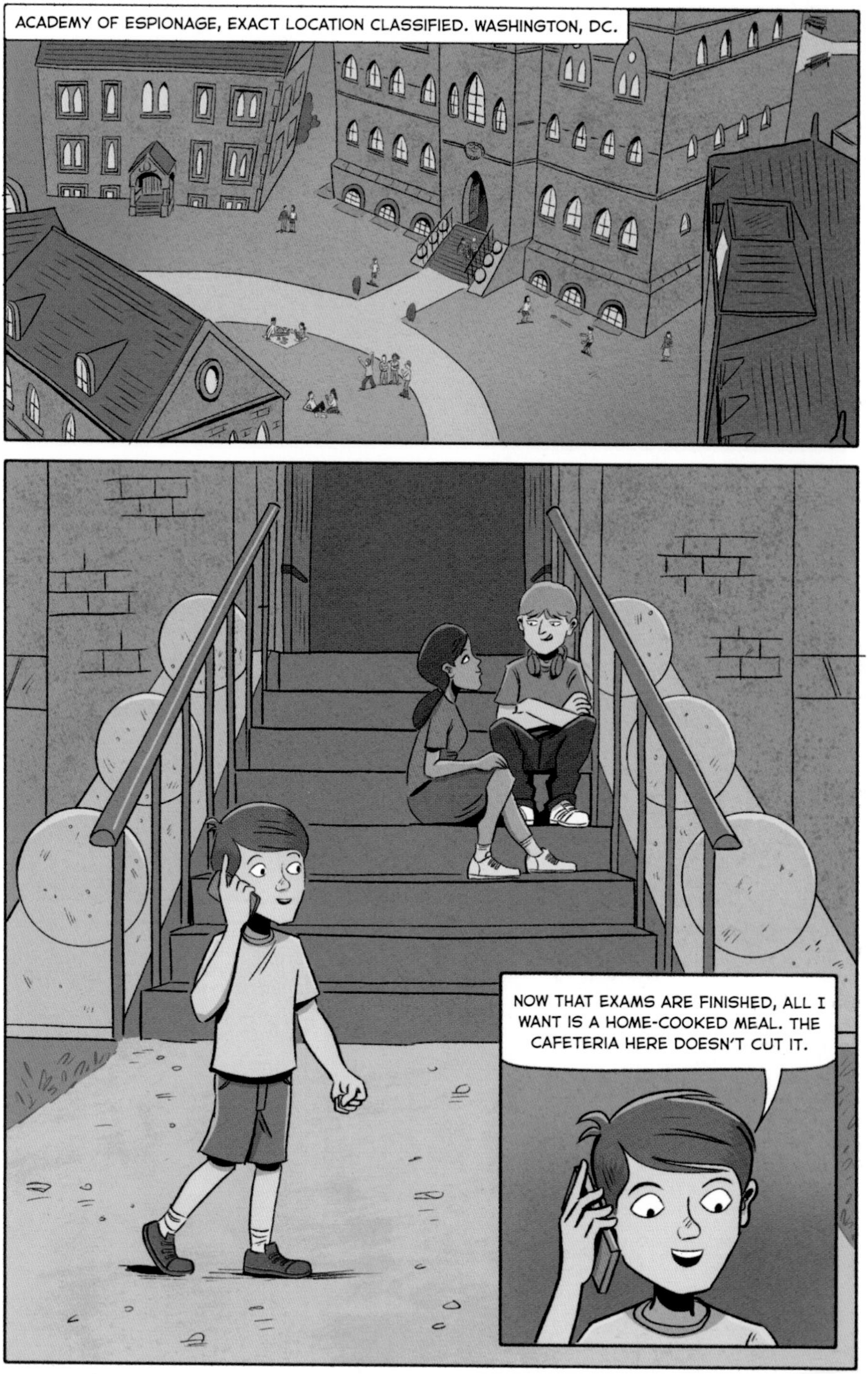
ACADEMY OF ESPIONAGE, EXACT LOCATION CLASSIFIED. WASHINGTON, DC.
NOW THAT EXAMS ARE FINISHED, ALL I WANT IS A HOME-COOKED MEAL. THE CAFETERIA HERE DOESN'T CUT IT.

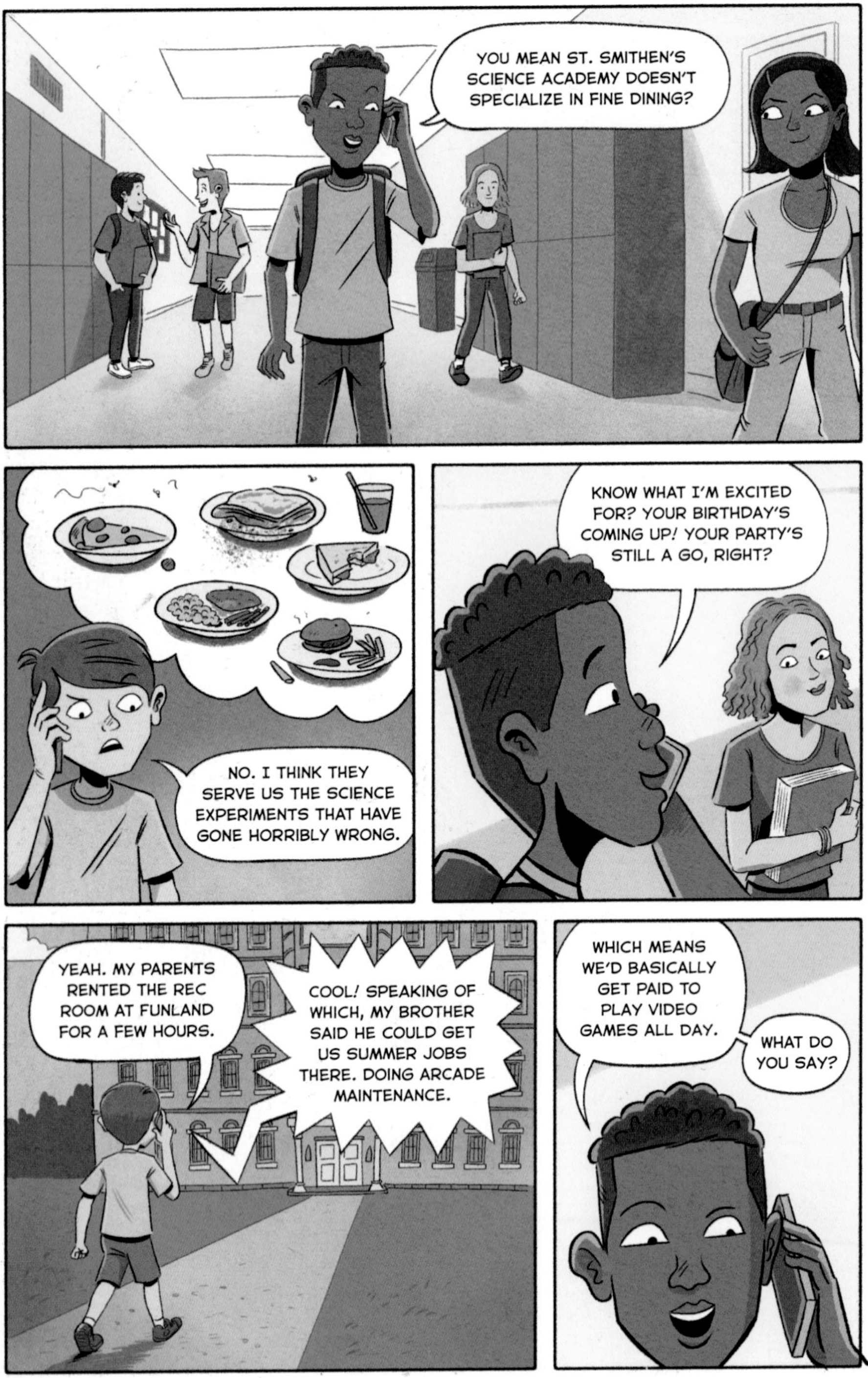
YOU MEAN ST. SMITHEN'S SCIENCE ACADEMY DOESN'T SPECIALIZE IN FINE DINING?
NO. I THINK THEY SERVE US THE SCIENCE EXPERIMENTS THAT HAVE GONE HORRIBLY WRONG.
KNOW WHAT I'M EXCITED FOR? YOUR BIRTHDAY'S COMING UP! YOUR PARTY'S STILL A GO, RIGHT?
YEAH. MY PARENTS RENTED THE REC ROOM AT FUNLAND FOR A FEW HOURS.
COOL! SPEAKING OF WHICH, MY BROTHER SAID HE COULD GET US SUMMER JOBS THERE. DOING ARCADE MAINTENANCE.
WHICH MEANS WE'D BASICALLY GET PAID TO PLAY VIDEO GAMES ALL DAY.
WHAT DO YOU SAY?

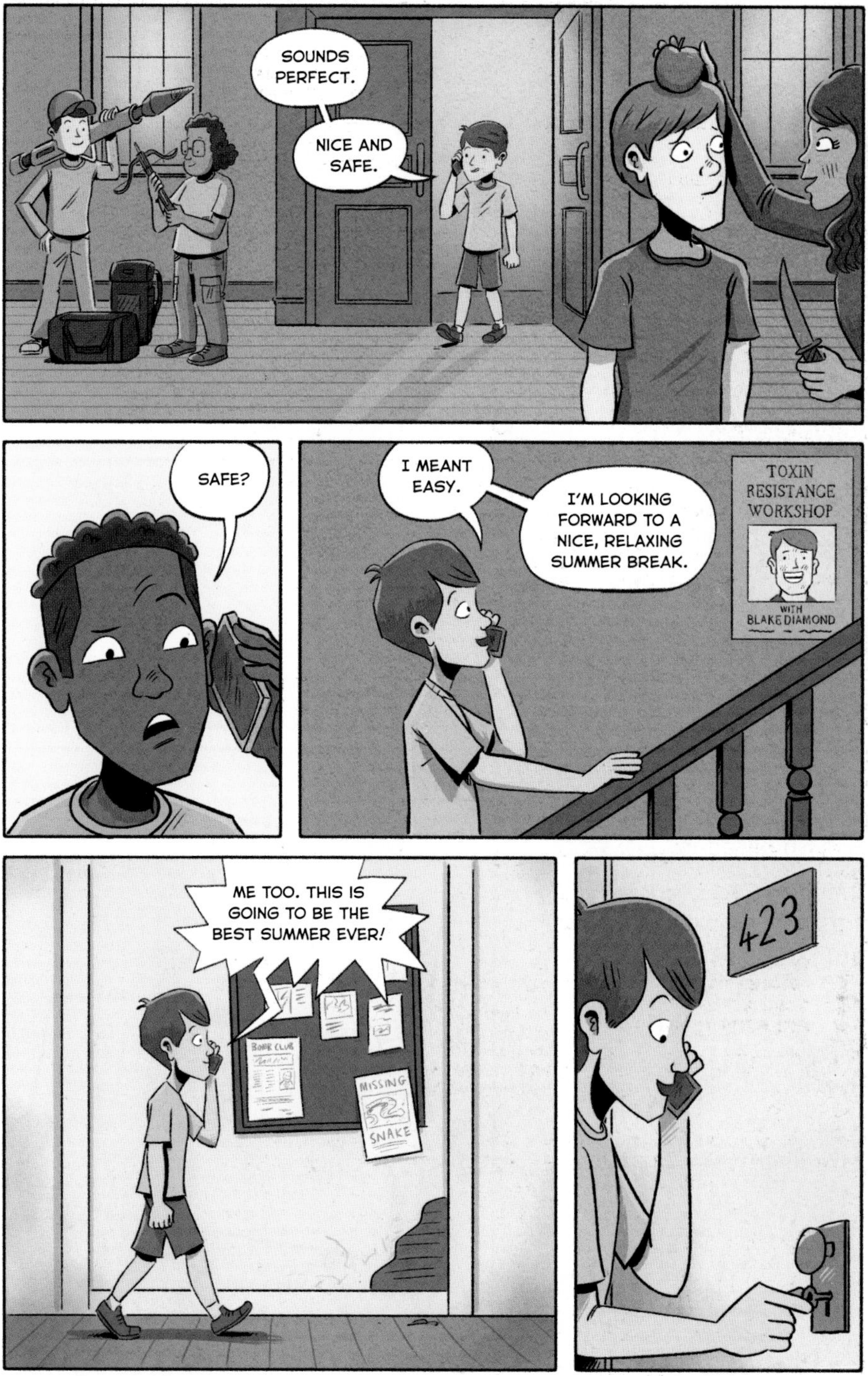
SOUNDS PERFECT.
NICE AND SAFE.
SAFE?
I MEANT EASY.
I'M LOOKING FORWARD TO A NICE, RELAXING SUMMER BREAK.
TOXIN RESISTANCE WORKSHOP
WITH BLAKE DIAMOND
ME TOO. THIS IS GOING TO BE THE BEST SUMMER EVER!
MISSING
SNAKE
423

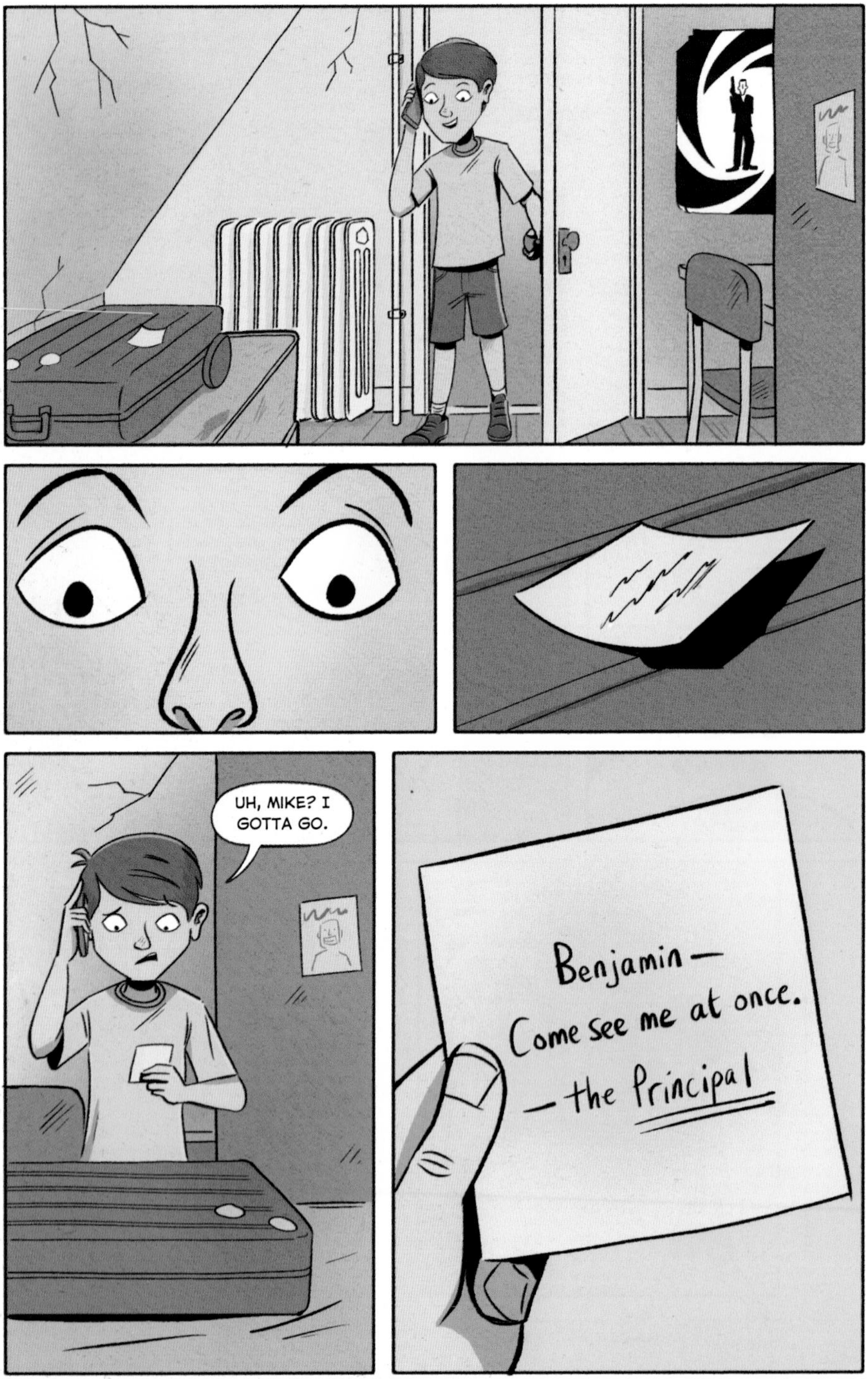
UH, MIKE? I GOTTA GO.
Benjamin—
Come see me at once.
—the Principal

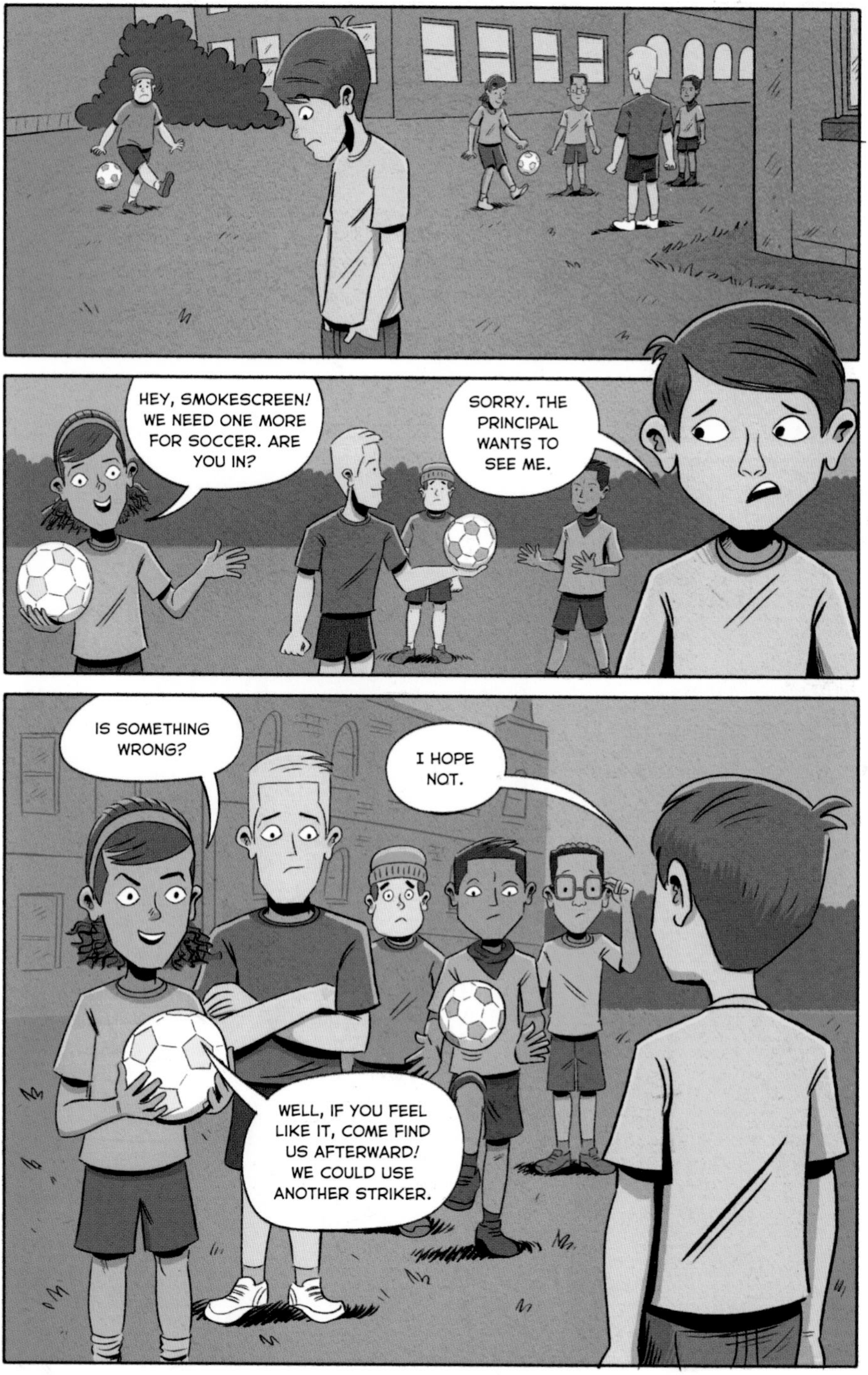
HEY, SMOKESCREEN! WE NEED ONE MORE FOR SOCCER. ARE YOU IN?
SORRY. THE PRINCIPAL WANTS TO SEE ME.
IS SOMETHING WRONG?
I HOPE NOT.
WELL, IF YOU FEEL LIKE IT, COME FIND US AFTERWARD! WE COULD USE ANOTHER STRIKER.

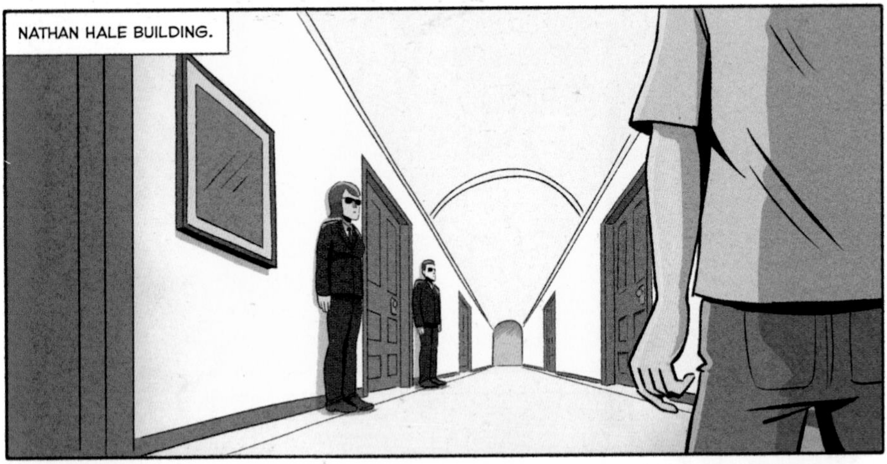
NATHAN HALE BUILDING.

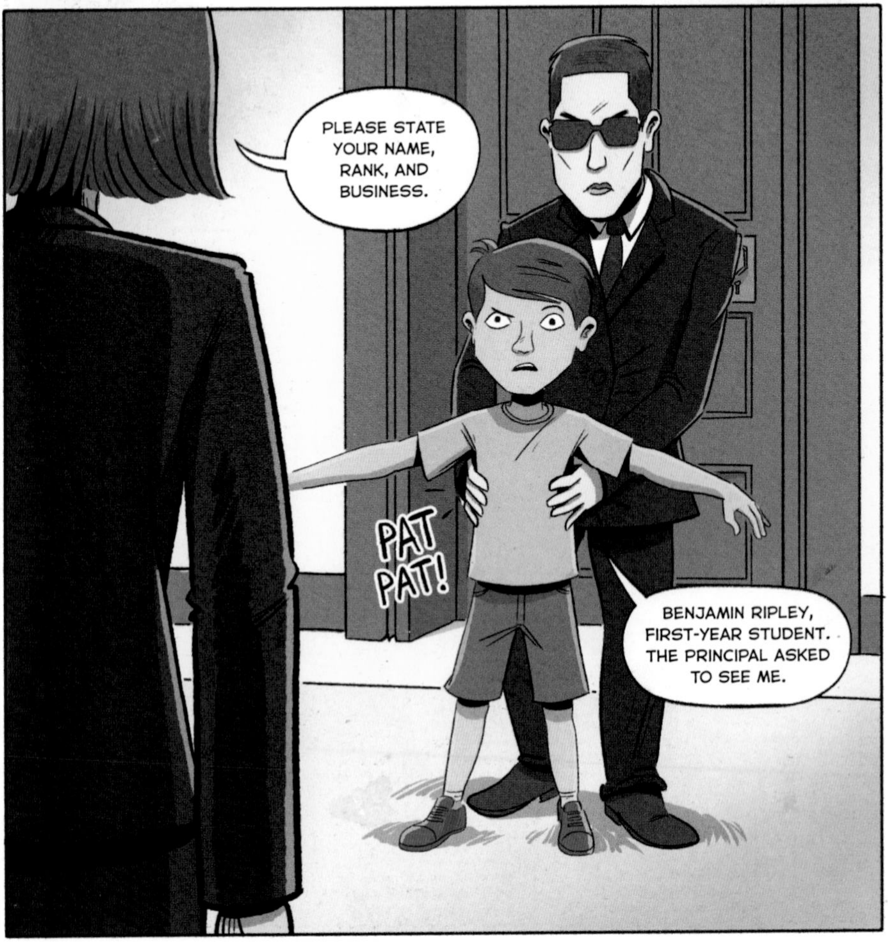
PLEASE STATE YOUR NAME, RANK, AND BUSINESS.
PAT PAT!
BENJAMIN RIPLEY, FIRST-YEAR STUDENT. THE PRINCIPAL ASKED TO SEE ME.

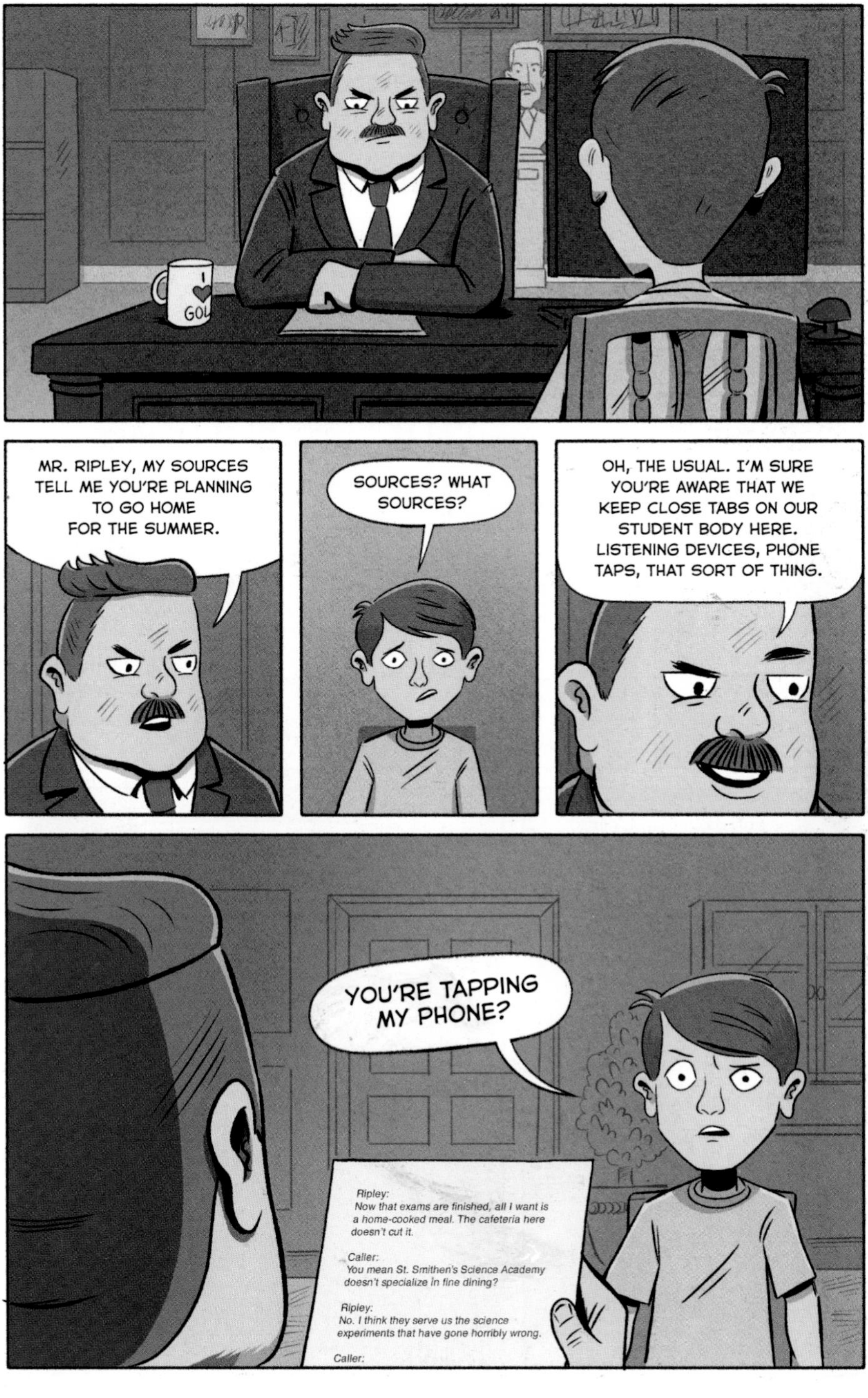
MR. RIPLEY, MY SOURCES TELL ME YOU'RE PLANNING TO GO HOME FOR THE SUMMER.
SOURCES? WHAT SOURCES?
OH, THE USUAL. I'M SURE YOU'RE AWARE THAT WE KEEP CLOSE TABS ON OUR STUDENT BODY HERE. LISTENING DEVICES, PHONE TAPS, THAT SORT OF THING.
YOU'RE TAPPING MY PHONE?
Ripley:
Now that exams are finished, all I want is a home-cooked meal. The cafeteria here doesn't cut it.
Caller:
You mean St. Smithen's Science Academy doesn't specialize in fine dining?
Ripley:
No. I think they serve us the science experiments that have gone horribly wrong.
Caller:

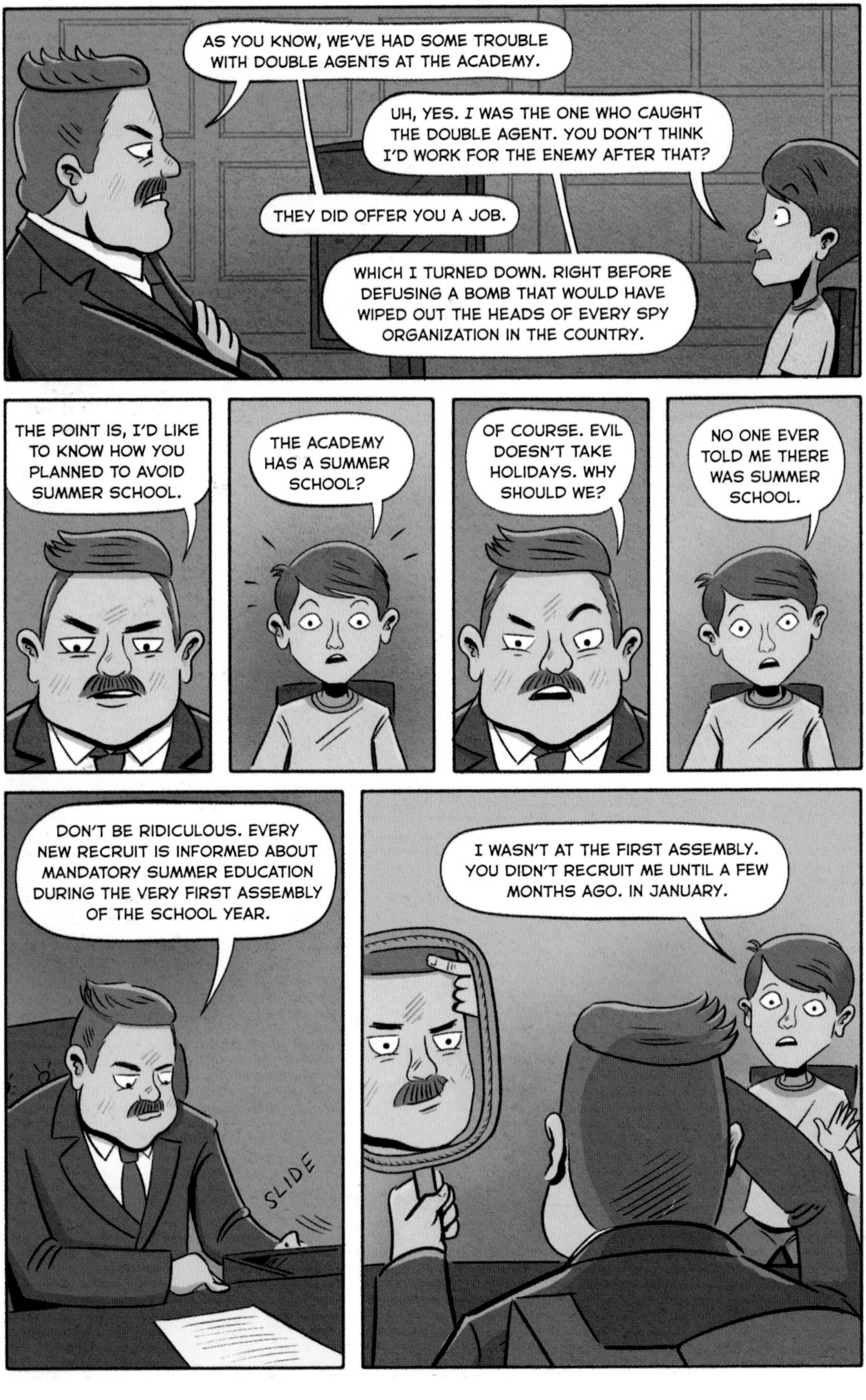
AS YOU KNOW, WE'VE HAD SOME TROUBLE WITH DOUBLE AGENTS AT THE ACADEMY.
UH, YES. *I* WAS THE ONE WHO CAUGHT THE DOUBLE AGENT. YOU DON'T THINK I'D WORK FOR THE ENEMY AFTER THAT?
THEY DID OFFER YOU A JOB.
WHICH I TURNED DOWN. RIGHT BEFORE DEFUSING A BOMB THAT WOULD HAVE WIPED OUT THE HEADS OF EVERY SPY ORGANIZATION IN THE COUNTRY.
THE POINT IS, I'D LIKE TO KNOW HOW YOU PLANNED TO AVOID SUMMER SCHOOL.
THE ACADEMY HAS A SUMMER SCHOOL?
OF COURSE. EVIL DOESN'T TAKE HOLIDAYS. WHY SHOULD WE?
NO ONE EVER TOLD ME THERE WAS SUMMER SCHOOL.
DON'T BE RIDICULOUS. EVERY NEW RECRUIT IS INFORMED ABOUT MANDATORY SUMMER EDUCATION DURING THE VERY FIRST ASSEMBLY OF THE SCHOOL YEAR.
SLIDE
I WASN'T AT THE FIRST ASSEMBLY. YOU DIDN'T RECRUIT ME UNTIL A FEW MONTHS AGO. IN JANUARY.

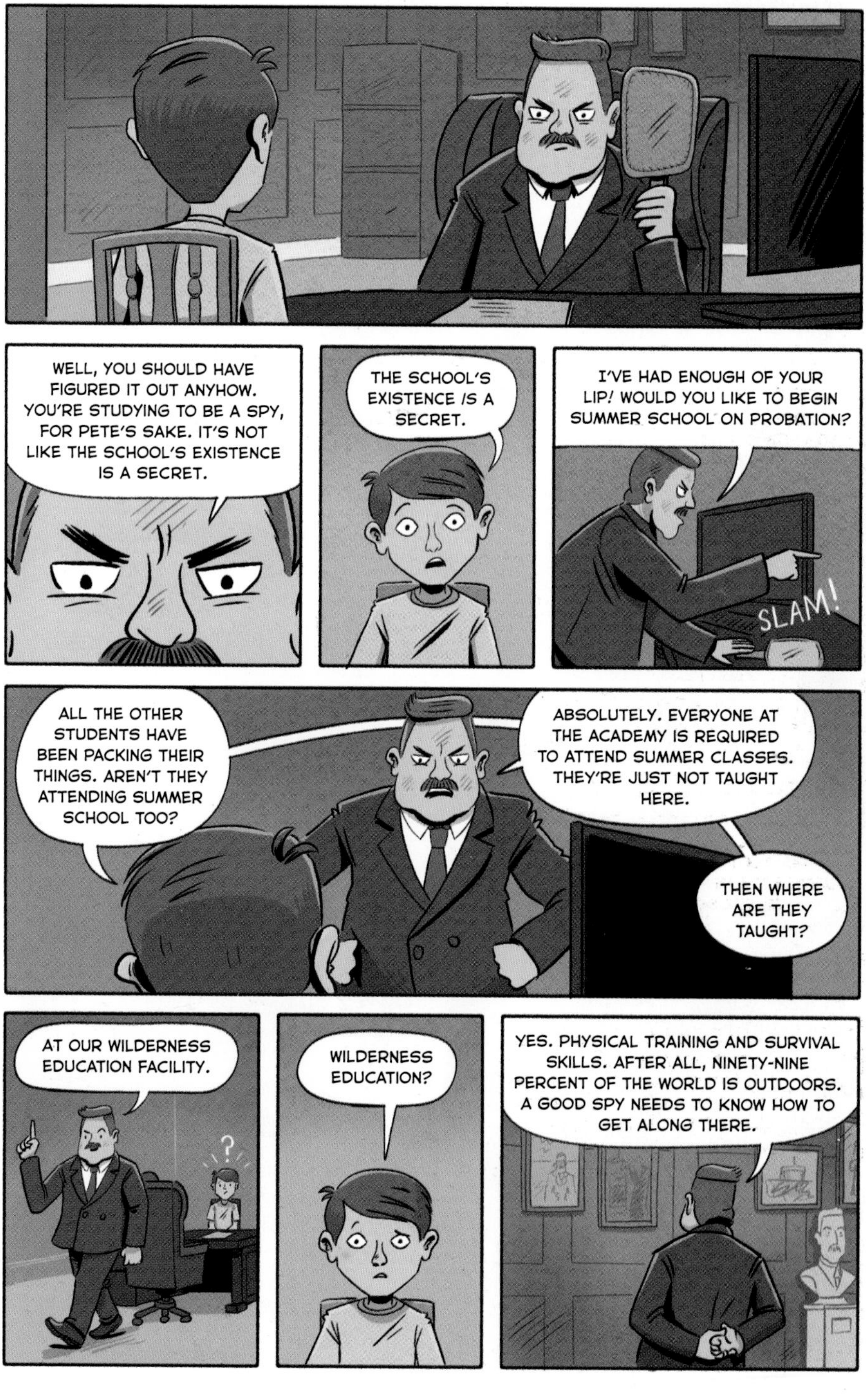
WELL, YOU SHOULD HAVE FIGURED IT OUT ANYHOW. YOU'RE STUDYING TO BE A SPY, FOR PETE'S SAKE. IT'S NOT LIKE THE SCHOOL'S EXISTENCE IS A SECRET.
THE SCHOOL'S EXISTENCE IS A SECRET.
I'VE HAD ENOUGH OF YOUR LIP! WOULD YOU LIKE TO BEGIN SUMMER SCHOOL ON PROBATION?
SLAM!
ALL THE OTHER STUDENTS HAVE BEEN PACKING THEIR THINGS. AREN'T THEY ATTENDING SUMMER SCHOOL TOO?
ABSOLUTELY. EVERYONE AT THE ACADEMY IS REQUIRED TO ATTEND SUMMER CLASSES. THEY'RE JUST NOT TAUGHT HERE.
THEN WHERE ARE THEY TAUGHT?
AT OUR WILDERNESS EDUCATION FACILITY.
?
WILDERNESS EDUCATION?
YES. PHYSICAL TRAINING AND SURVIVAL SKILLS. AFTER ALL, NINETY-NINE PERCENT OF THE WORLD IS OUTDOORS. A GOOD SPY NEEDS TO KNOW HOW TO GET ALONG THERE.

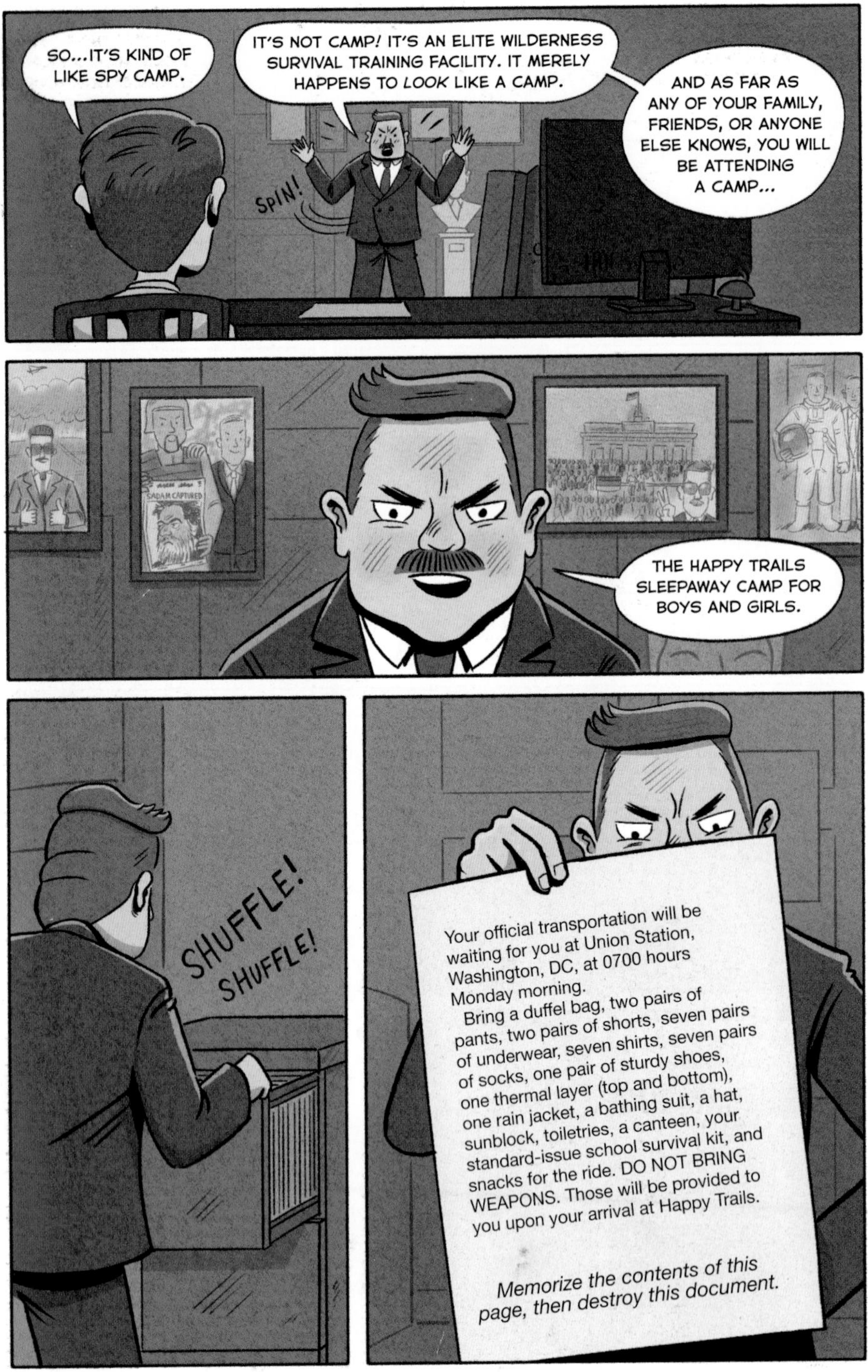
SO...IT'S KIND OF LIKE SPY CAMP.
IT'S NOT CAMP! IT'S AN ELITE WILDERNESS SURVIVAL TRAINING FACILITY. IT MERELY HAPPENS TO *LOOK* LIKE A CAMP.
AND AS FAR AS ANY OF YOUR FAMILY, FRIENDS, OR ANYONE ELSE KNOWS, YOU WILL BE ATTENDING A CAMP...
SPIN!
SADAM CAPTURED
THE HAPPY TRAILS SLEEPAWAY CAMP FOR BOYS AND GIRLS.
SHUFFLE!
SHUFFLE!
Your official transportation will be waiting for you at Union Station, Washington, DC, at 0700 hours Monday morning.
Bring a duffel bag, two pairs of pants, two pairs of shorts, seven pairs of underwear, seven shirts, seven pairs of socks, one pair of sturdy shoes, one thermal layer (top and bottom), one rain jacket, a bathing suit, a hat, sunblock, toiletries, a canteen, your standard-issue school survival kit, and snacks for the ride. DO NOT BRING WEAPONS. Those will be provided to you upon your arrival at Happy Trails.
*Memorize the contents of this page, then destroy this document.*

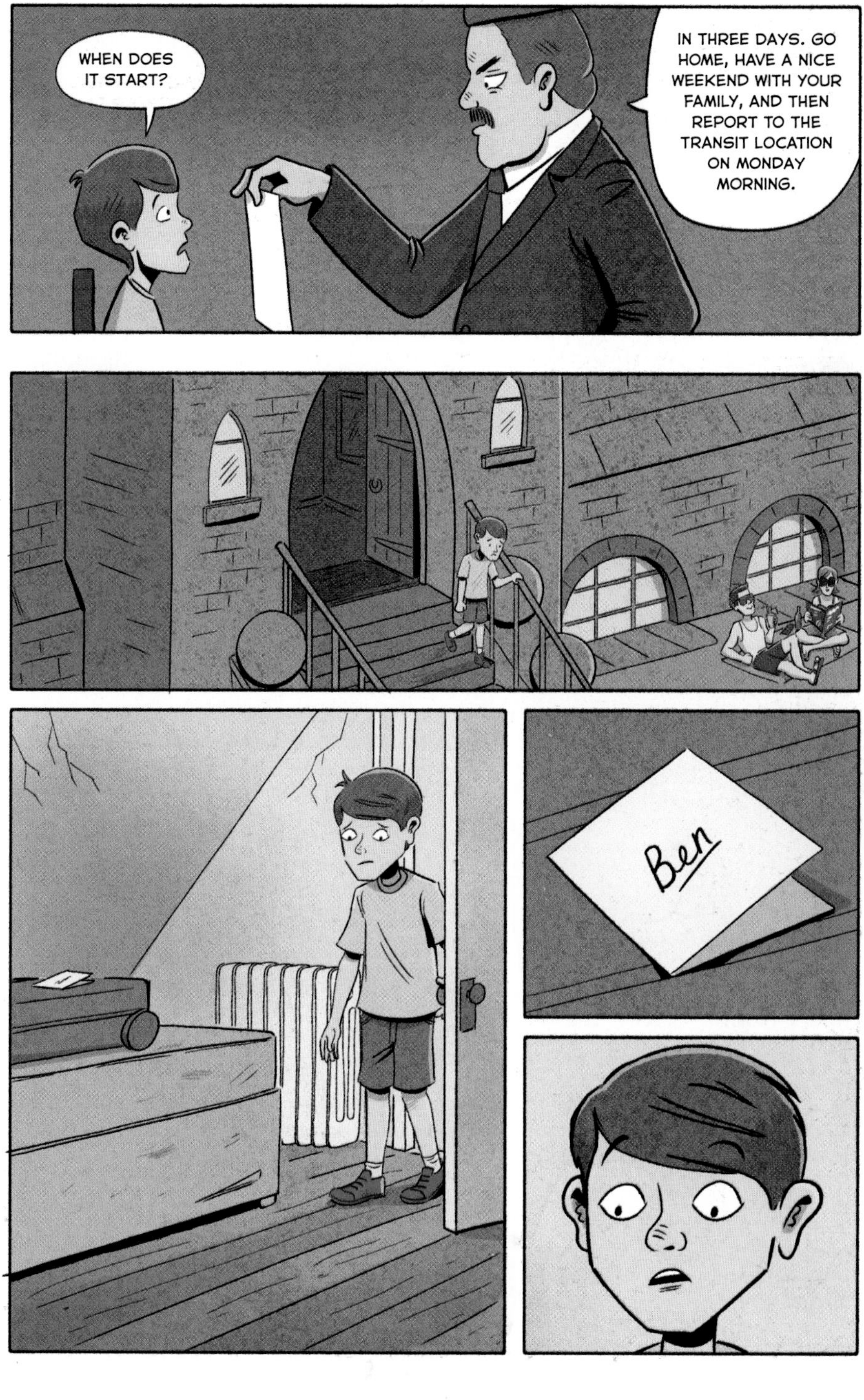
WHEN DOES IT START?
IN THREE DAYS. GO HOME, HAVE A NICE WEEKEND WITH YOUR FAMILY, AND THEN REPORT TO THE TRANSIT LOCATION ON MONDAY MORNING.
Ben

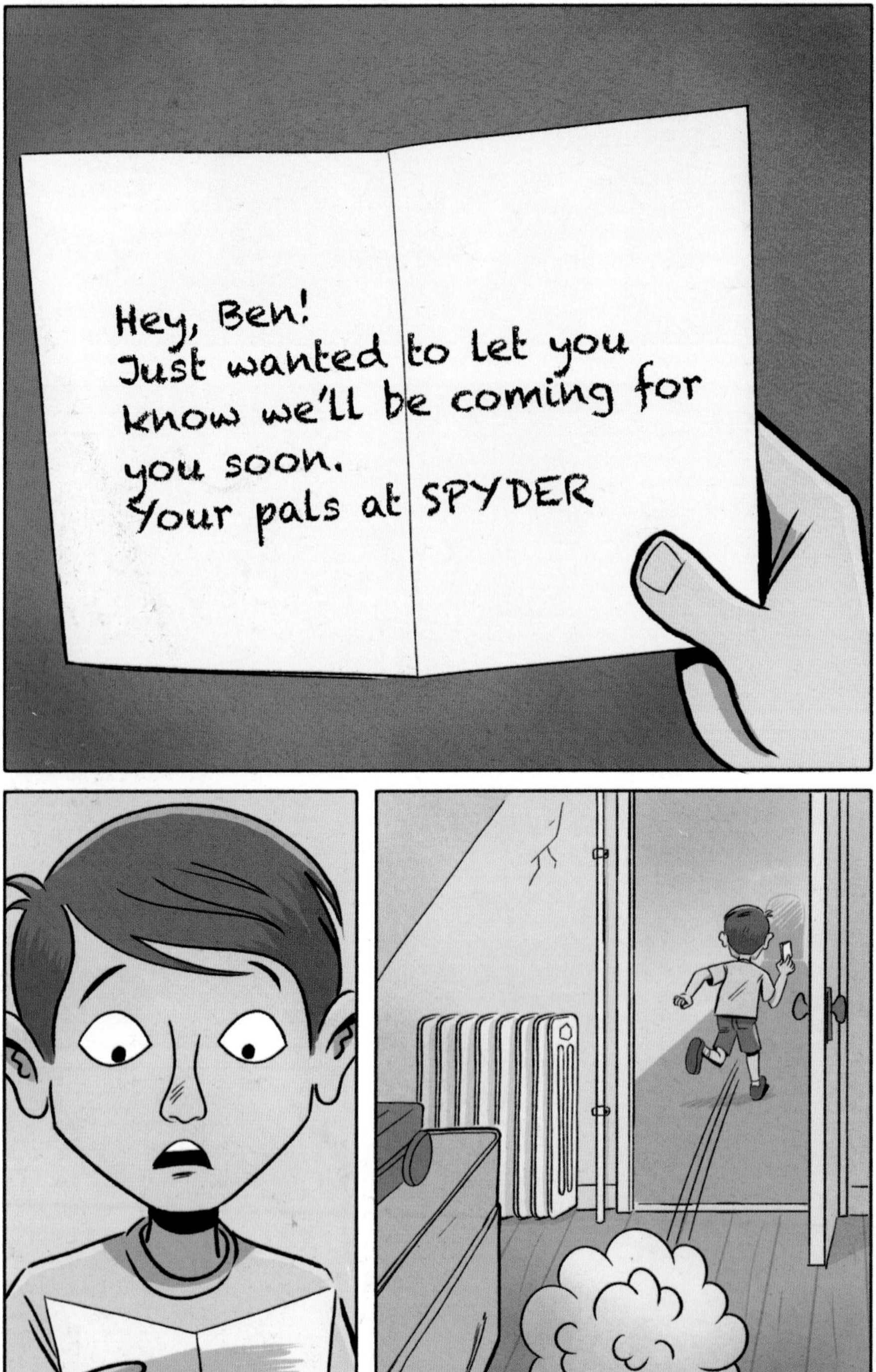
Hey, Ben!
Just wanted to let you know we'll be coming for you soon.
Your pals at SPYDER

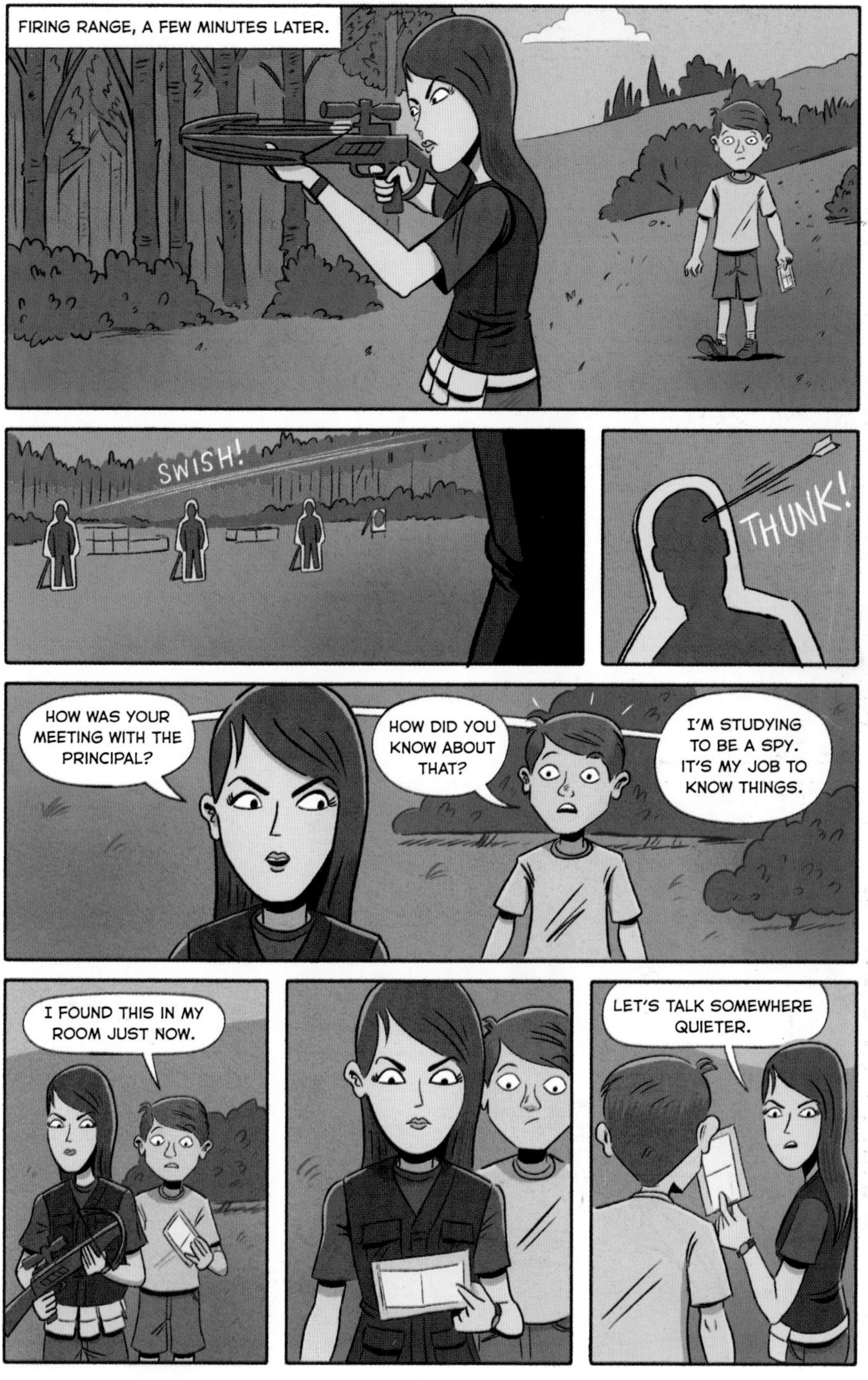
FIRING RANGE, A FEW MINUTES LATER.
SWISH!
THUNK!
HOW WAS YOUR MEETING WITH THE PRINCIPAL?
HOW DID YOU KNOW ABOUT THAT?
I'M STUDYING TO BE A SPY. IT'S MY JOB TO KNOW THINGS.
I FOUND THIS IN MY ROOM JUST NOW.
LET'S TALK SOMEWHERE QUIETER.

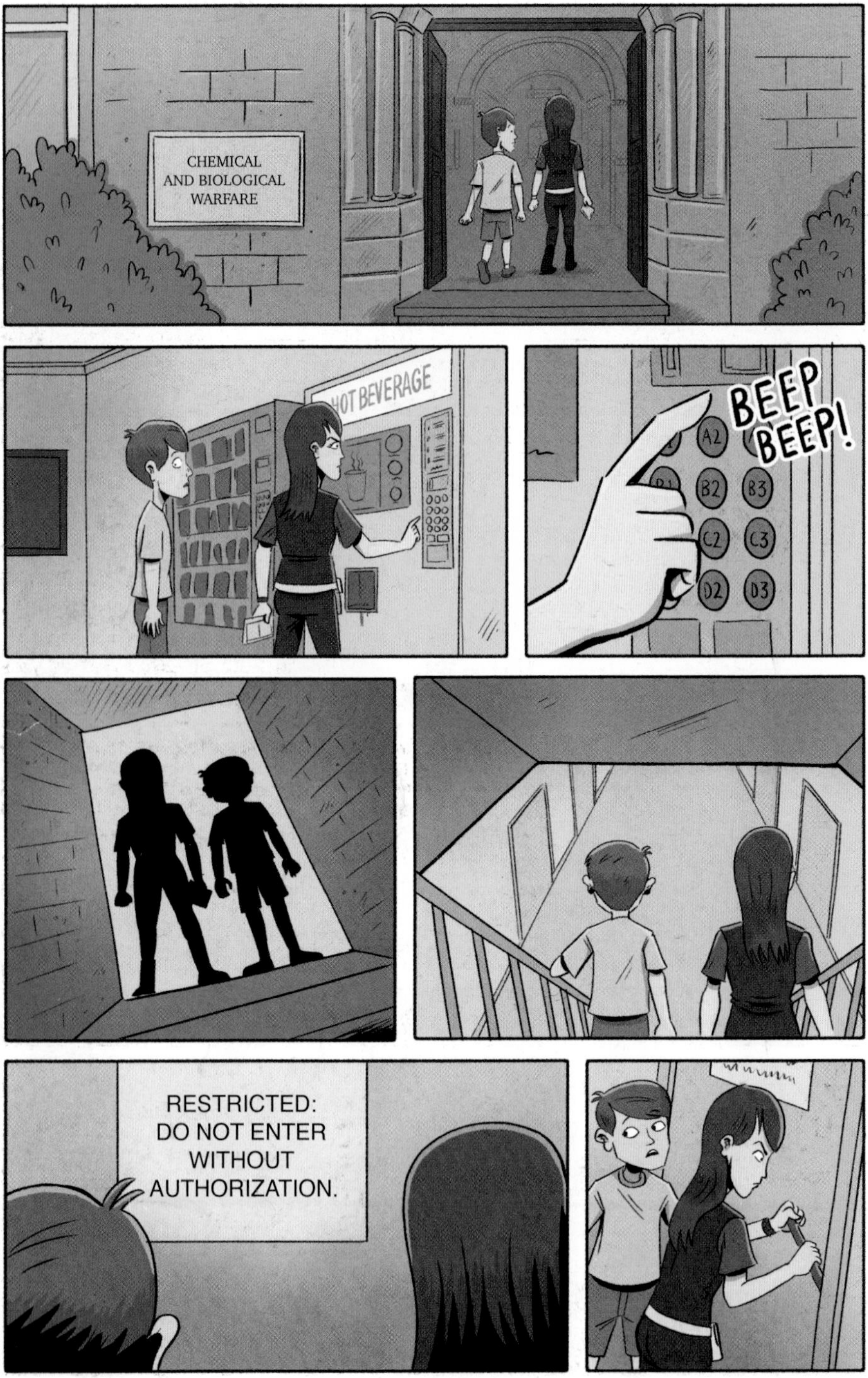
CHEMICAL
AND BIOLOGICAL
WARFARE
HOT BEVERAGE
A2
B2
B3
C2
C3
D2
D3
BEEP
BEEP!
RESTRICTED:
DO NOT ENTER
WITHOUT
AUTHORIZATION.

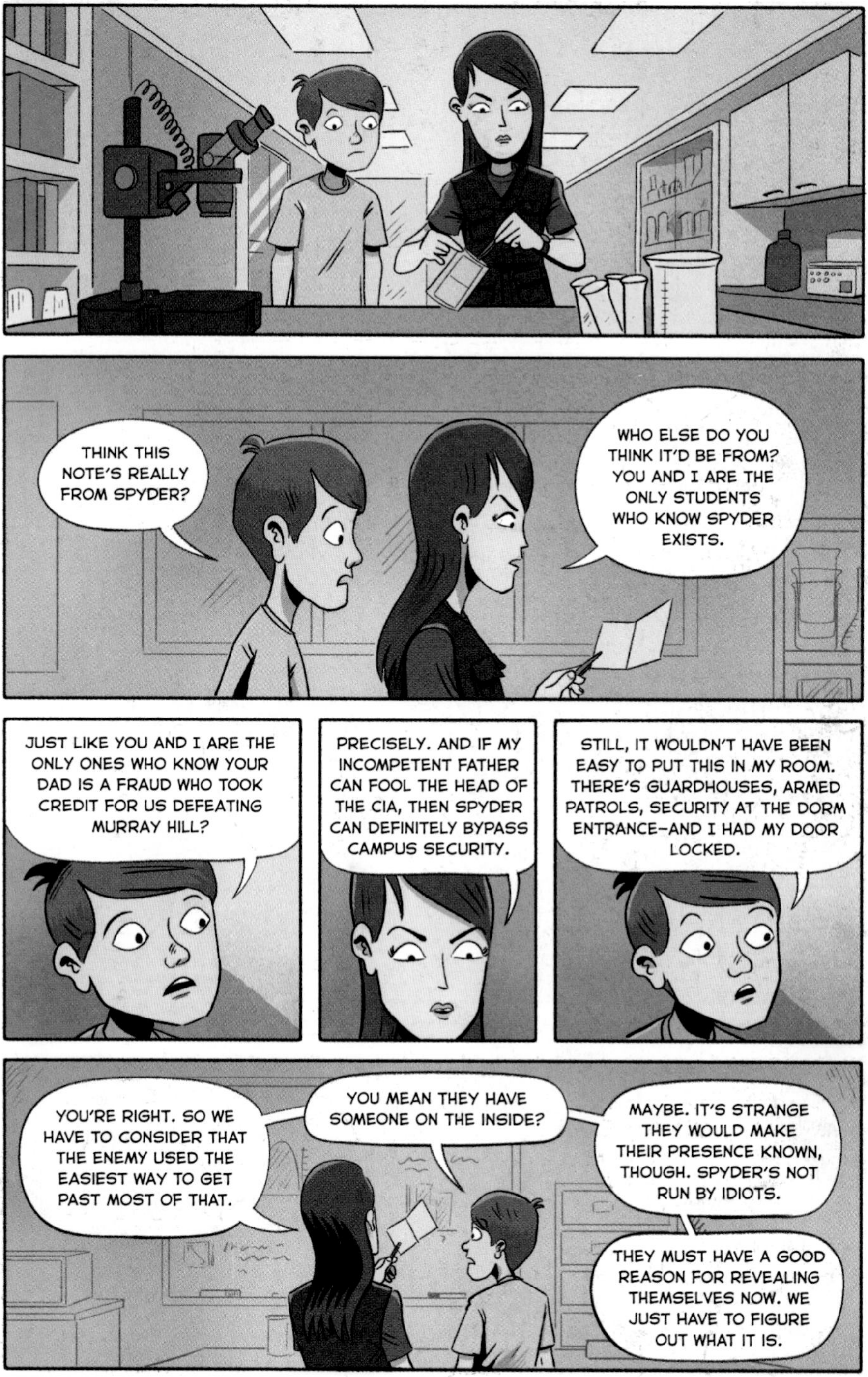
THINK THIS NOTE'S REALLY FROM SPYDER?
WHO ELSE DO YOU THINK IT'D BE FROM? YOU AND I ARE THE ONLY STUDENTS WHO KNOW SPYDER EXISTS.
JUST LIKE YOU AND I ARE THE ONLY ONES WHO KNOW YOUR DAD IS A FRAUD WHO TOOK CREDIT FOR US DEFEATING MURRAY HILL?
PRECISELY. AND IF MY INCOMPETENT FATHER CAN FOOL THE HEAD OF THE CIA, THEN SPYDER CAN DEFINITELY BYPASS CAMPUS SECURITY.
STILL, IT WOULDN'T HAVE BEEN EASY TO PUT THIS IN MY ROOM. THERE'S GUARDHOUSES, ARMED PATROLS, SECURITY AT THE DORM ENTRANCE—AND I HAD MY DOOR LOCKED.
YOU'RE RIGHT. SO WE HAVE TO CONSIDER THAT THE ENEMY USED THE EASIEST WAY TO GET PAST MOST OF THAT.
YOU MEAN THEY HAVE SOMEONE ON THE INSIDE?
MAYBE. IT'S STRANGE THEY WOULD MAKE THEIR PRESENCE KNOWN, THOUGH. SPYDER'S NOT RUN BY IDIOTS.
THEY MUST HAVE A GOOD REASON FOR REVEALING THEMSELVES NOW. WE JUST HAVE TO FIGURE OUT WHAT IT IS.

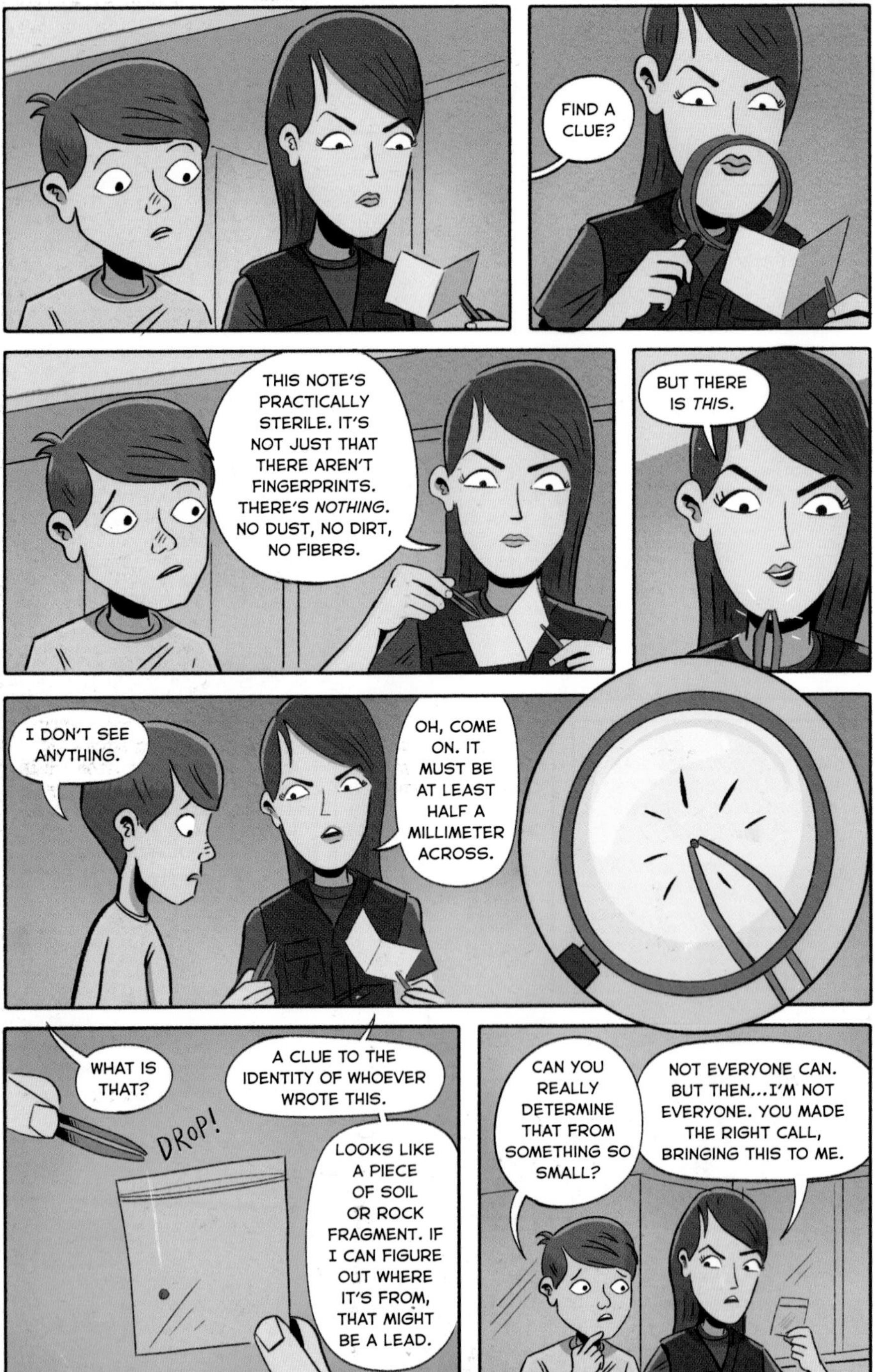
FIND A CLUE?
THIS NOTE'S PRACTICALLY STERILE. IT'S NOT JUST THAT THERE AREN'T FINGERPRINTS. THERE'S *NOTHING*. NO DUST, NO DIRT, NO FIBERS.
BUT THERE IS *THIS*.
I DON'T SEE ANYTHING.
OH, COME ON. IT MUST BE AT LEAST HALF A MILLIMETER ACROSS.
WHAT IS THAT?
A CLUE TO THE IDENTITY OF WHOEVER WROTE THIS.
DROP!
LOOKS LIKE A PIECE OF SOIL OR ROCK FRAGMENT. IF I CAN FIGURE OUT WHERE IT'S FROM, THAT MIGHT BE A LEAD.
CAN YOU REALLY DETERMINE THAT FROM SOMETHING SO SMALL?
NOT EVERYONE CAN. BUT THEN...I'M NOT EVERYONE. YOU MADE THE RIGHT CALL, BRINGING THIS TO ME.

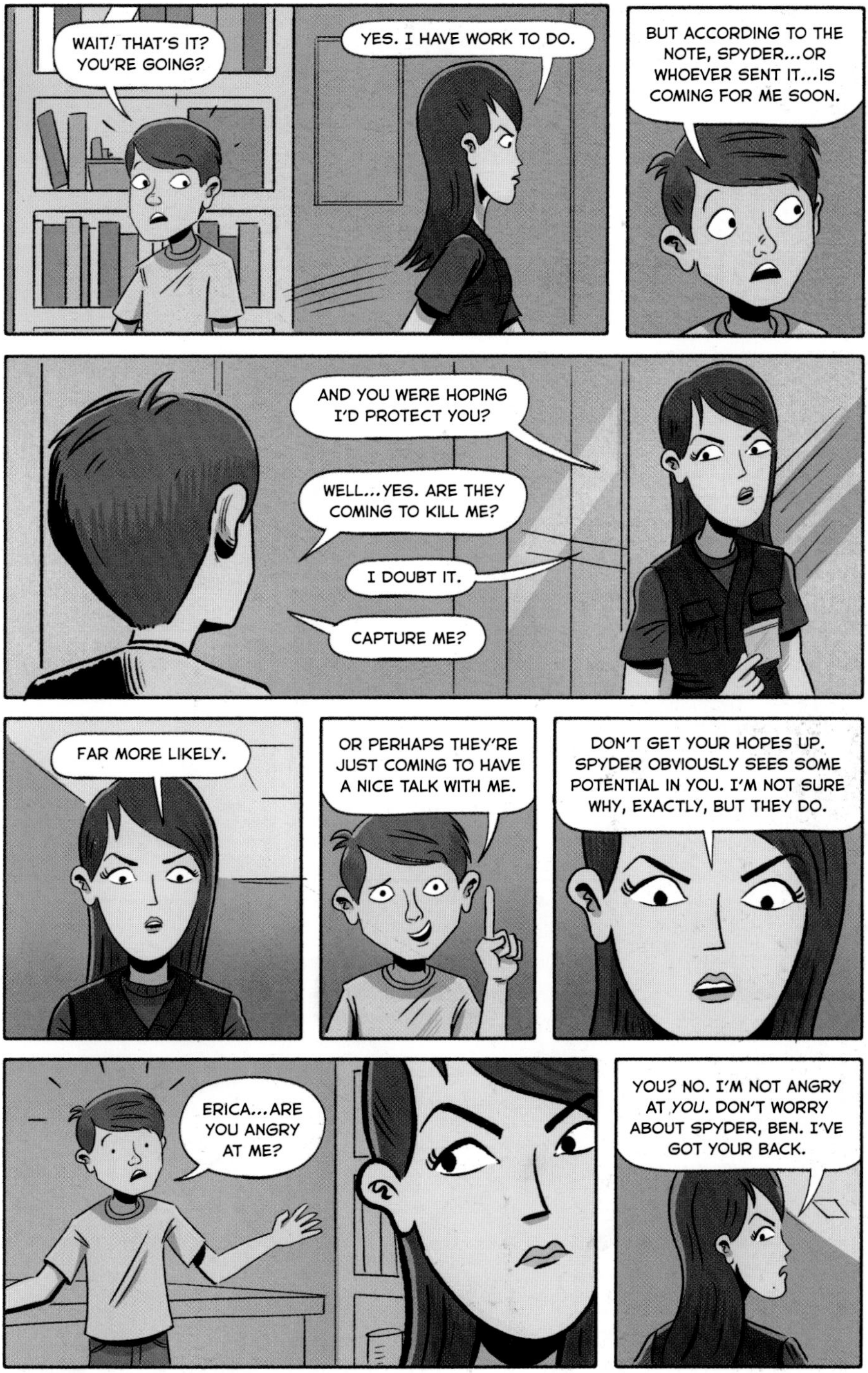
WAIT! THAT'S IT? YOU'RE GOING?
YES. I HAVE WORK TO DO.
BUT ACCORDING TO THE NOTE, SPYDER...OR WHOEVER SENT IT...IS COMING FOR ME SOON.
AND YOU WERE HOPING I'D PROTECT YOU?
WELL...YES. ARE THEY COMING TO KILL ME?
I DOUBT IT.
CAPTURE ME?
FAR MORE LIKELY.
OR PERHAPS THEY'RE JUST COMING TO HAVE A NICE TALK WITH ME.
DON'T GET YOUR HOPES UP. SPYDER OBVIOUSLY SEES SOME POTENTIAL IN YOU. I'M NOT SURE WHY, EXACTLY, BUT THEY DO.
ERICA...ARE YOU ANGRY AT ME?
YOU? NO. I'M NOT ANGRY AT *YOU*. DON'T WORRY ABOUT SPYDER, BEN. I'VE GOT YOUR BACK.

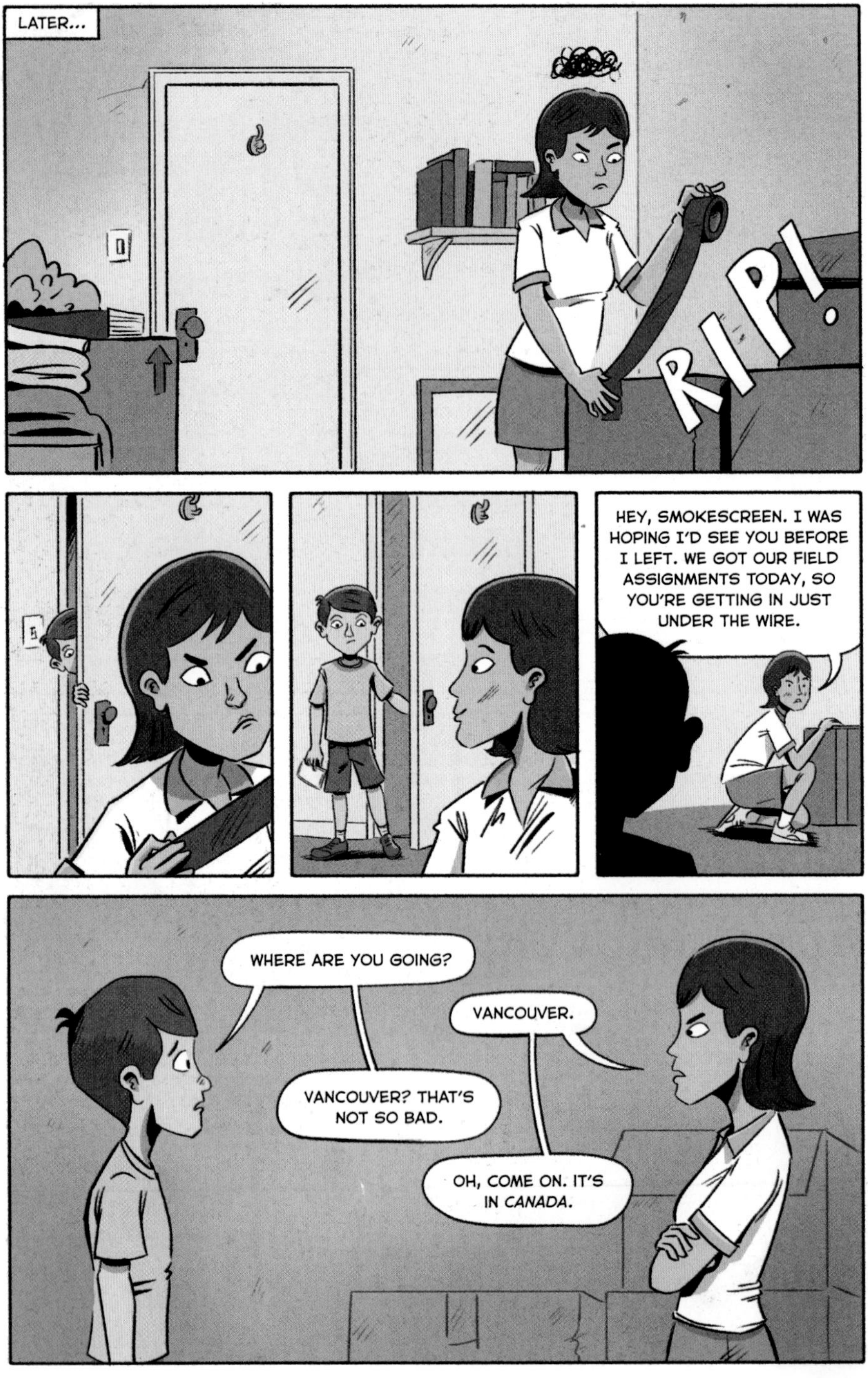
LATER...
RIP!
HEY, SMOKESCREEN. I WAS HOPING I'D SEE YOU BEFORE I LEFT. WE GOT OUR FIELD ASSIGNMENTS TODAY, SO YOU'RE GETTING IN JUST UNDER THE WIRE.
WHERE ARE YOU GOING?
VANCOUVER.
VANCOUVER? THAT'S NOT SO BAD.
OH, COME ON. IT'S IN *CANADA*.

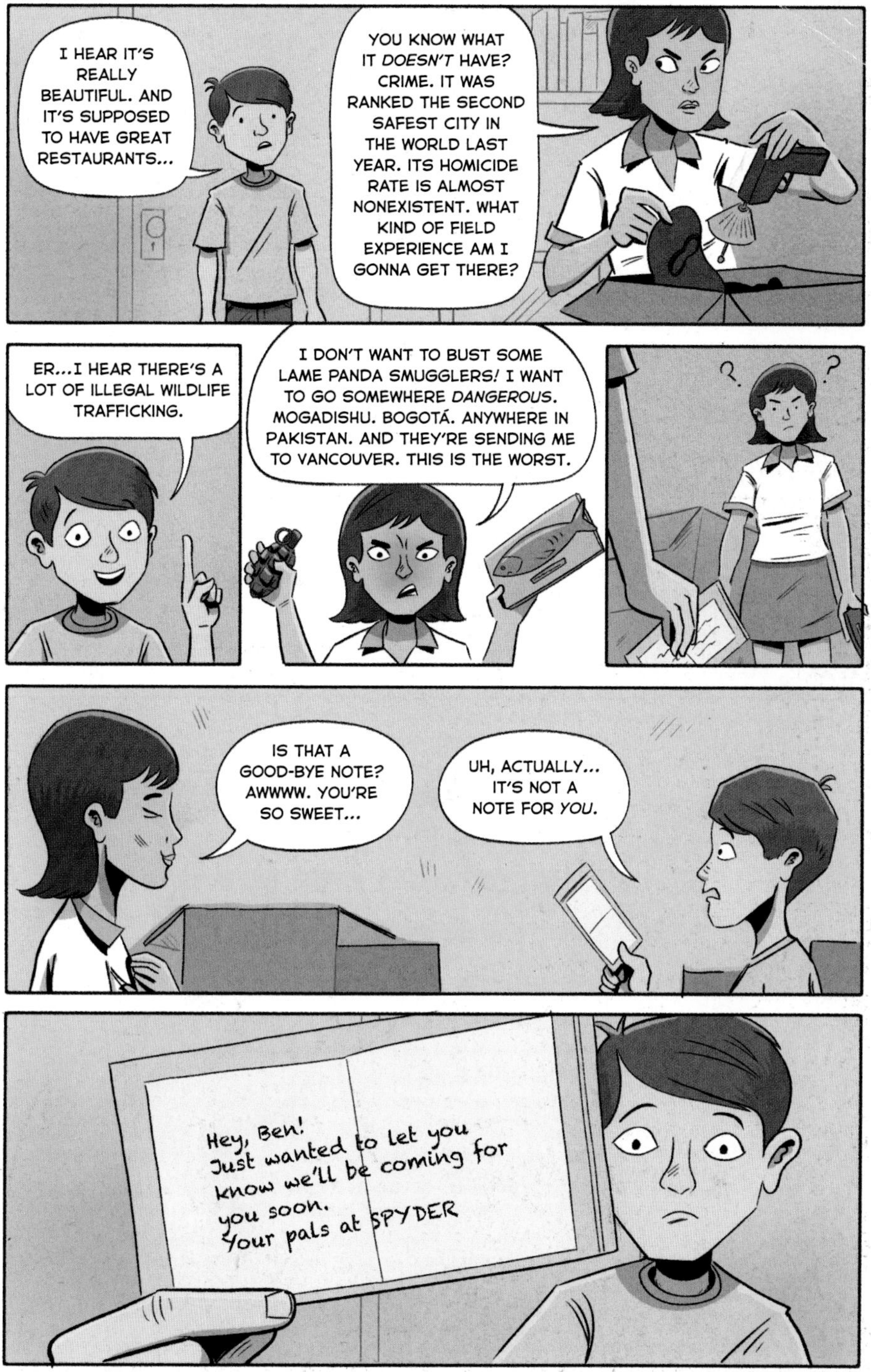
I HEAR IT'S REALLY BEAUTIFUL. AND IT'S SUPPOSED TO HAVE GREAT RESTAURANTS...
YOU KNOW WHAT IT *DOESN'T* HAVE? CRIME. IT WAS RANKED THE SECOND SAFEST CITY IN THE WORLD LAST YEAR. ITS HOMICIDE RATE IS ALMOST NONEXISTENT. WHAT KIND OF FIELD EXPERIENCE AM I GONNA GET THERE?
ER...I HEAR THERE'S A LOT OF ILLEGAL WILDLIFE TRAFFICKING.
I DON'T WANT TO BUST SOME LAME PANDA SMUGGLERS! I WANT TO GO SOMEWHERE *DANGEROUS*. MOGADISHU. BOGOTÁ. ANYWHERE IN PAKISTAN. AND THEY'RE SENDING ME TO VANCOUVER. THIS IS THE WORST.
? ?
IS THAT A GOOD-BYE NOTE? AWWWW. YOU'RE SO SWEET...
UH, ACTUALLY... IT'S NOT A NOTE FOR *YOU*.
Hey, Ben!
Just wanted to let you know we'll be coming for you soon.
Your pals at SPYDER

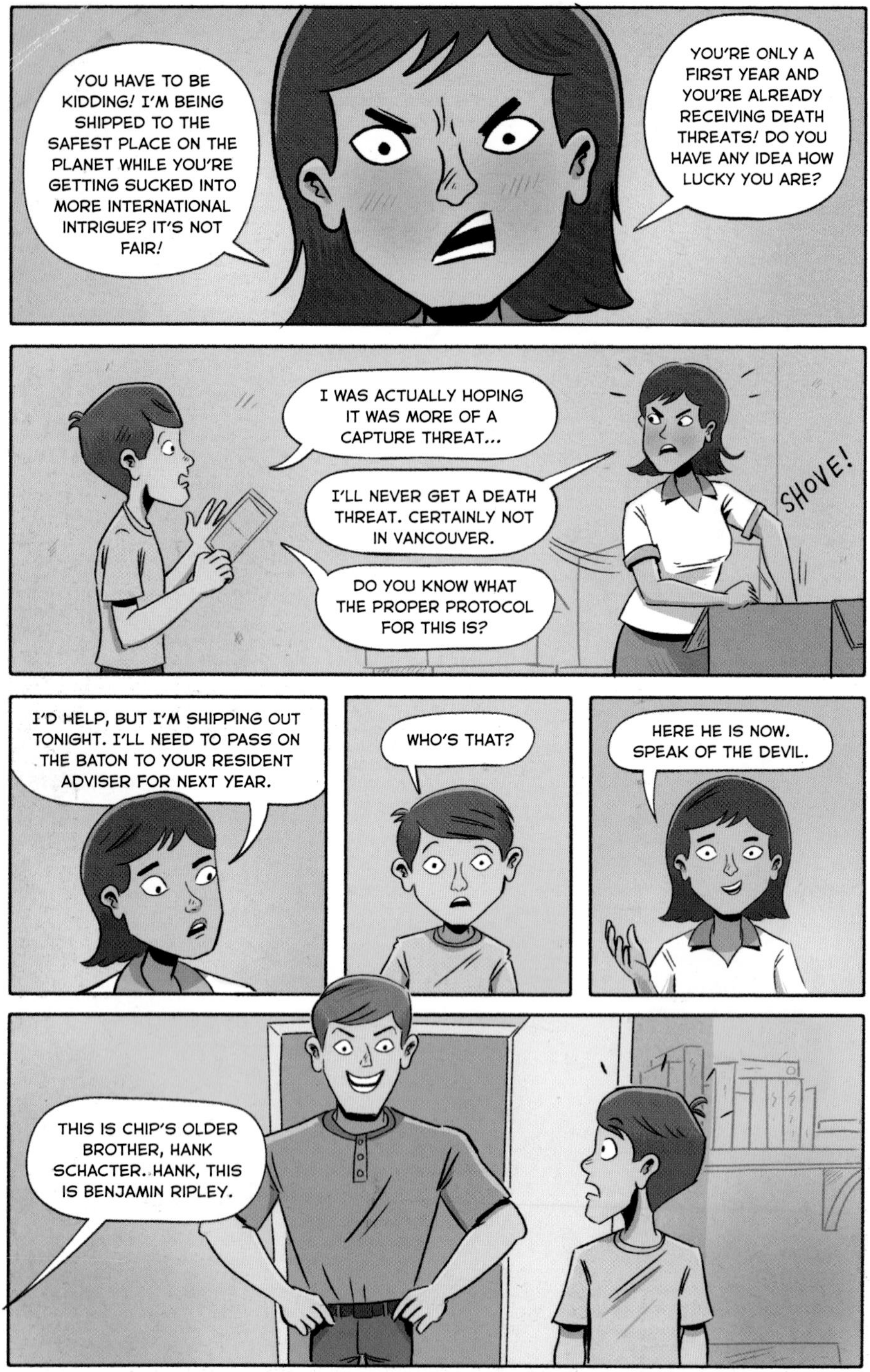
YOU HAVE TO BE KIDDING! I'M BEING SHIPPED TO THE SAFEST PLACE ON THE PLANET WHILE YOU'RE GETTING SUCKED INTO MORE INTERNATIONAL INTRIGUE? IT'S NOT FAIR!
YOU'RE ONLY A FIRST YEAR AND YOU'RE ALREADY RECEIVING DEATH THREATS! DO YOU HAVE ANY IDEA HOW LUCKY YOU ARE?
I WAS ACTUALLY HOPING IT WAS MORE OF A CAPTURE THREAT...
SHOVE!
I'LL NEVER GET A DEATH THREAT. CERTAINLY NOT IN VANCOUVER.
DO YOU KNOW WHAT THE PROPER PROTOCOL FOR THIS IS?
I'D HELP, BUT I'M SHIPPING OUT TONIGHT. I'LL NEED TO PASS ON THE BATON TO YOUR RESIDENT ADVISER FOR NEXT YEAR.
WHO'S THAT?
HERE HE IS NOW. SPEAK OF THE DEVIL.
THIS IS CHIP'S OLDER BROTHER, HANK SCHACTER. HANK, THIS IS BENJAMIN RIPLEY.

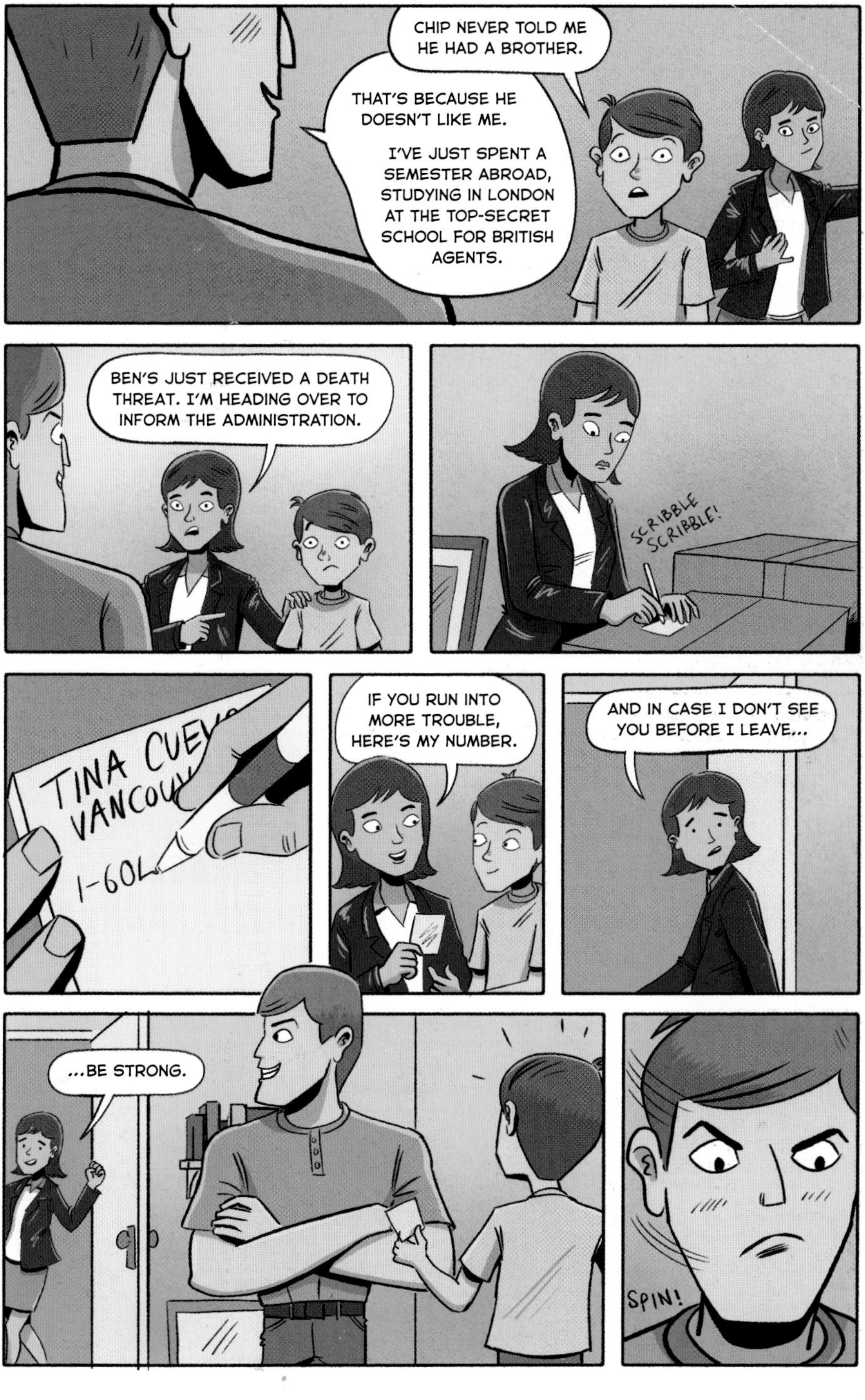
CHIP NEVER TOLD ME HE HAD A BROTHER.
THAT'S BECAUSE HE DOESN'T LIKE ME.
I'VE JUST SPENT A SEMESTER ABROAD, STUDYING IN LONDON AT THE TOP-SECRET SCHOOL FOR BRITISH AGENTS.
BEN'S JUST RECEIVED A DEATH THREAT. I'M HEADING OVER TO INFORM THE ADMINISTRATION.
SCRIBBLE SCRIBBLE!
TINA CUEV
VANCOU
1-60
IF YOU RUN INTO MORE TROUBLE, HERE'S MY NUMBER.
AND IN CASE I DON'T SEE YOU BEFORE I LEAVE...
...BE STRONG.
SPIN!

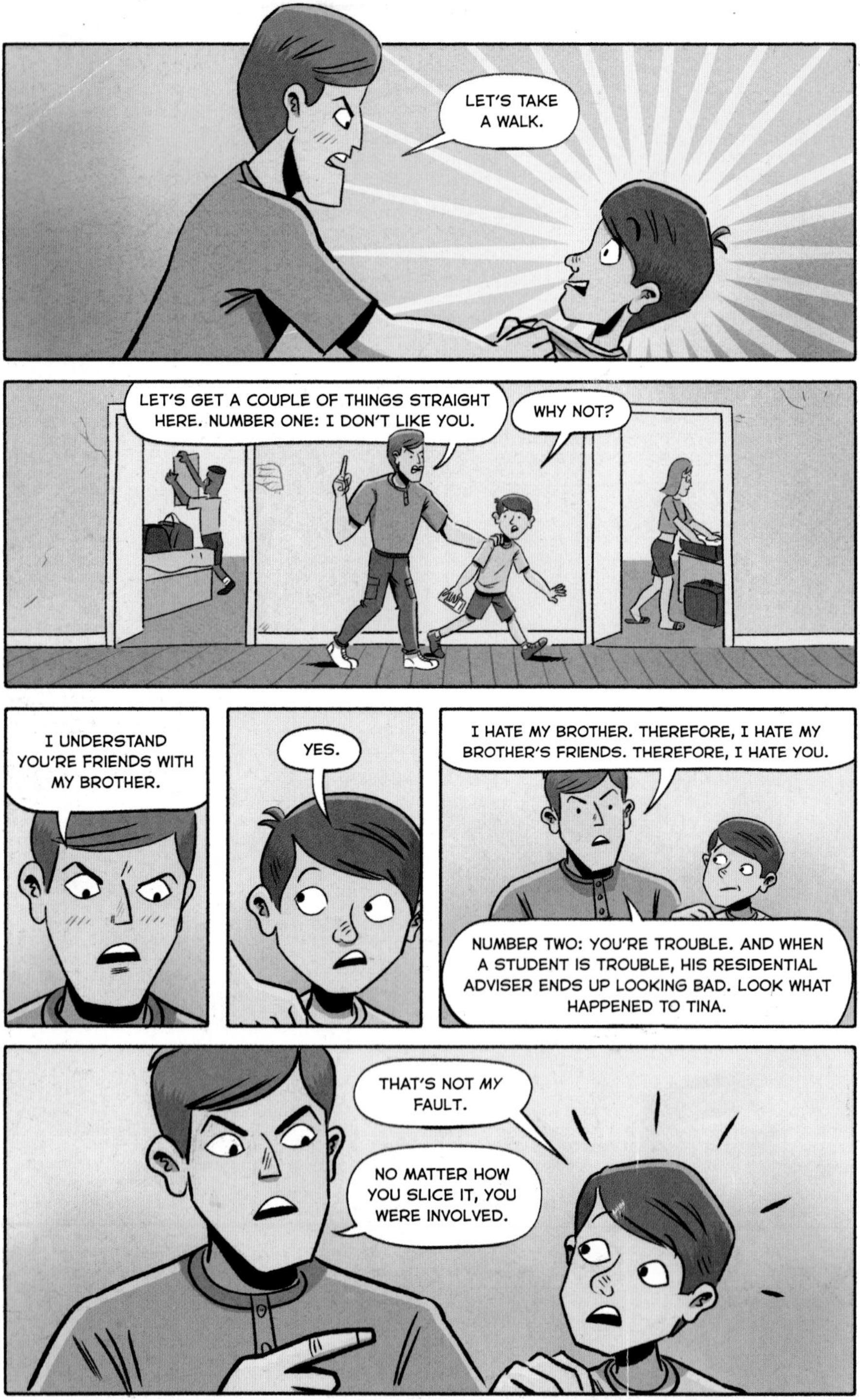
LET'S TAKE A WALK.
LET'S GET A COUPLE OF THINGS STRAIGHT HERE. NUMBER ONE: I DON'T LIKE YOU.
WHY NOT?
I UNDERSTAND YOU'RE FRIENDS WITH MY BROTHER.
YES.
I HATE MY BROTHER. THEREFORE, I HATE MY BROTHER'S FRIENDS. THEREFORE, I HATE YOU.
NUMBER TWO: YOU'RE TROUBLE. AND WHEN A STUDENT IS TROUBLE, HIS RESIDENTIAL ADVISER ENDS UP LOOKING BAD. LOOK WHAT HAPPENED TO TINA.
THAT'S NOT *MY* FAULT.
NO MATTER HOW YOU SLICE IT, YOU WERE INVOLVED.

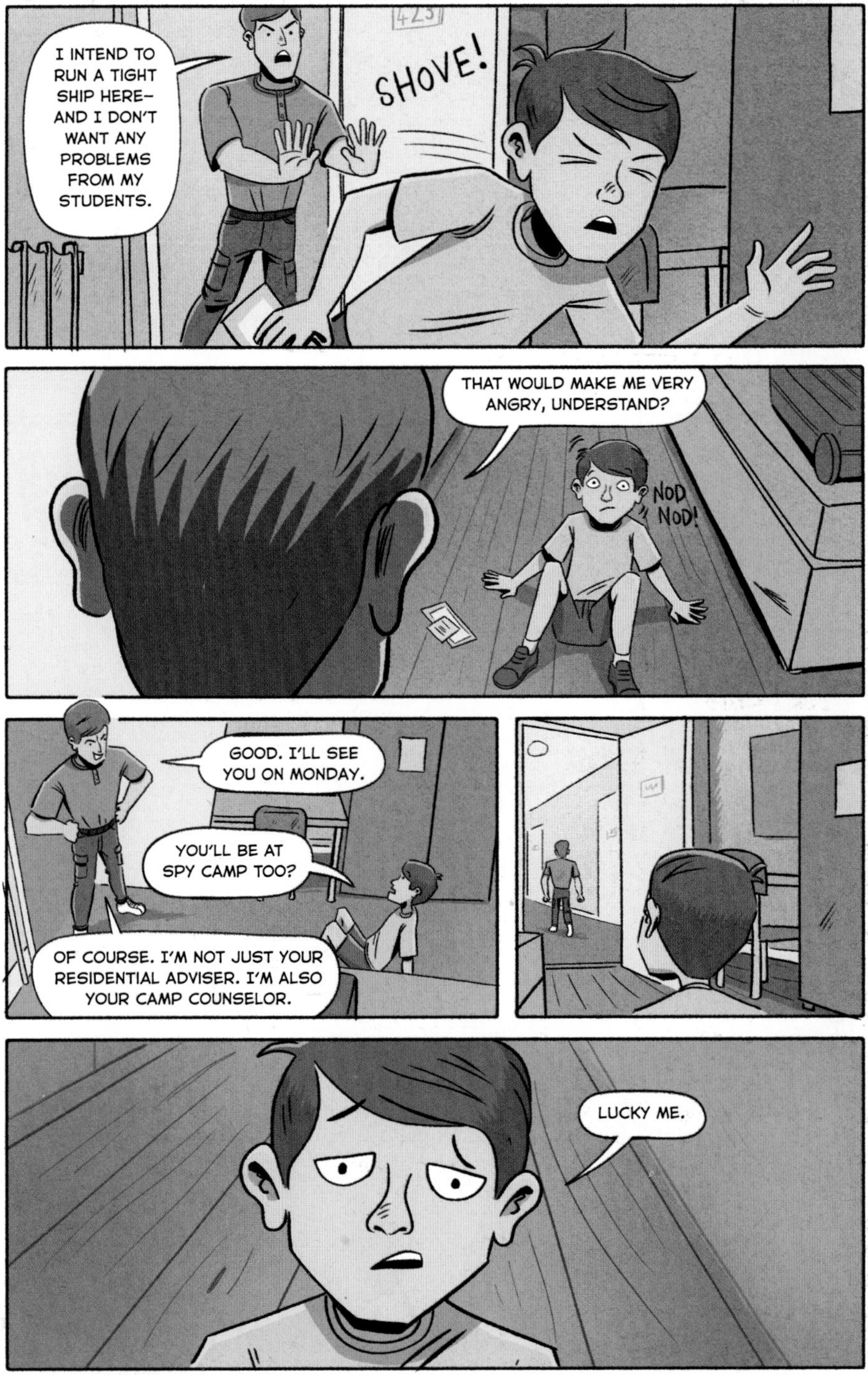
I INTEND TO RUN A TIGHT SHIP HERE—AND I DON'T WANT ANY PROBLEMS FROM MY STUDENTS.
SHOVE!
THAT WOULD MAKE ME VERY ANGRY, UNDERSTAND?
NOD NOD!
GOOD. I'LL SEE YOU ON MONDAY.
YOU'LL BE AT SPY CAMP TOO?
OF COURSE. I'M NOT JUST YOUR RESIDENTIAL ADVISER. I'M ALSO YOUR CAMP COUNSELOR.
LUCKY ME.

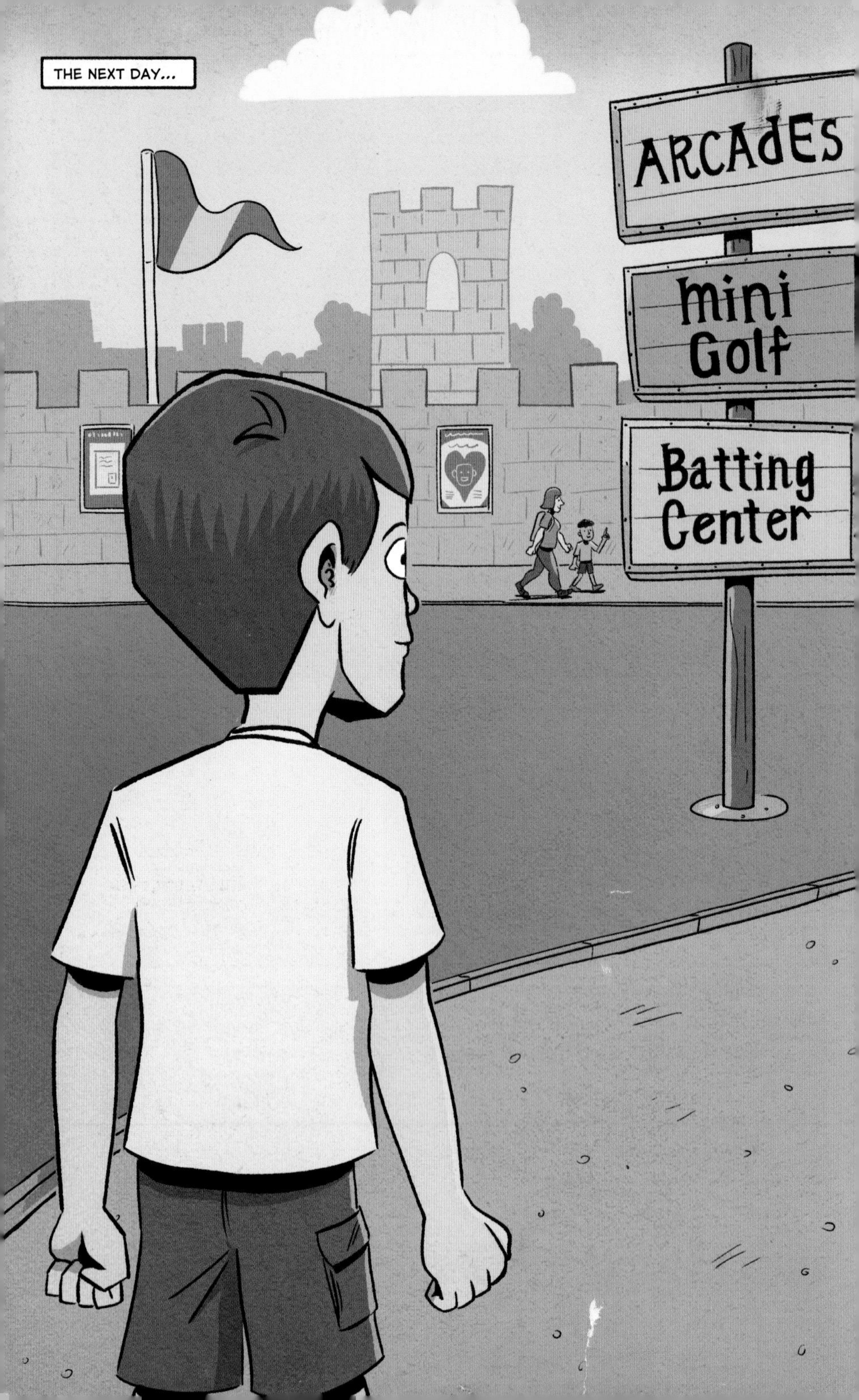
THE NEXT DAY...
ARCADES
Mini Golf
Batting Center

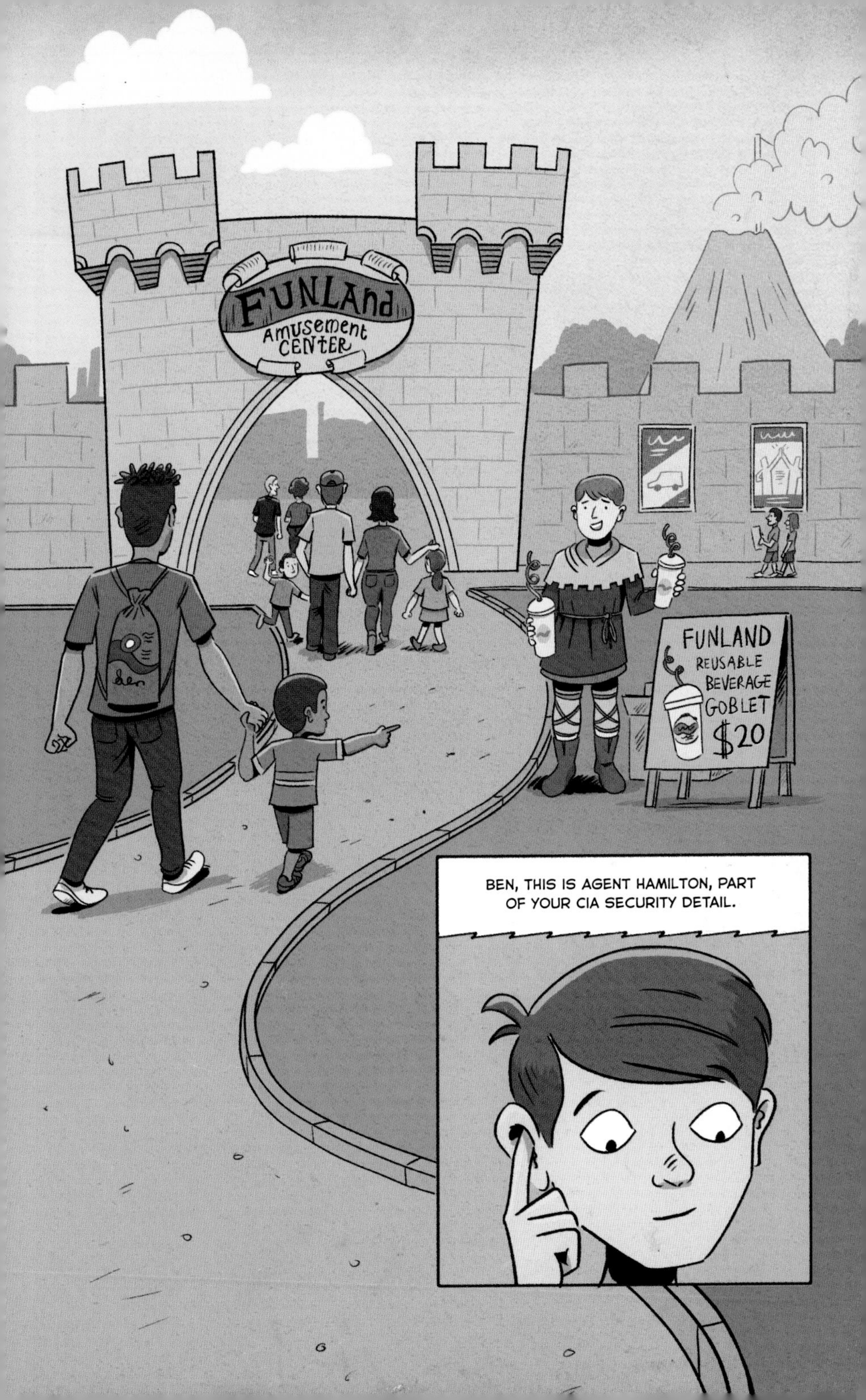
FUNLAND
AMUSEMENT CENTER
ben
FUNLAND REUSABLE BEVERAGE GOBLET $20
BEN, THIS IS AGENT HAMILTON, PART OF YOUR CIA SECURITY DETAIL.

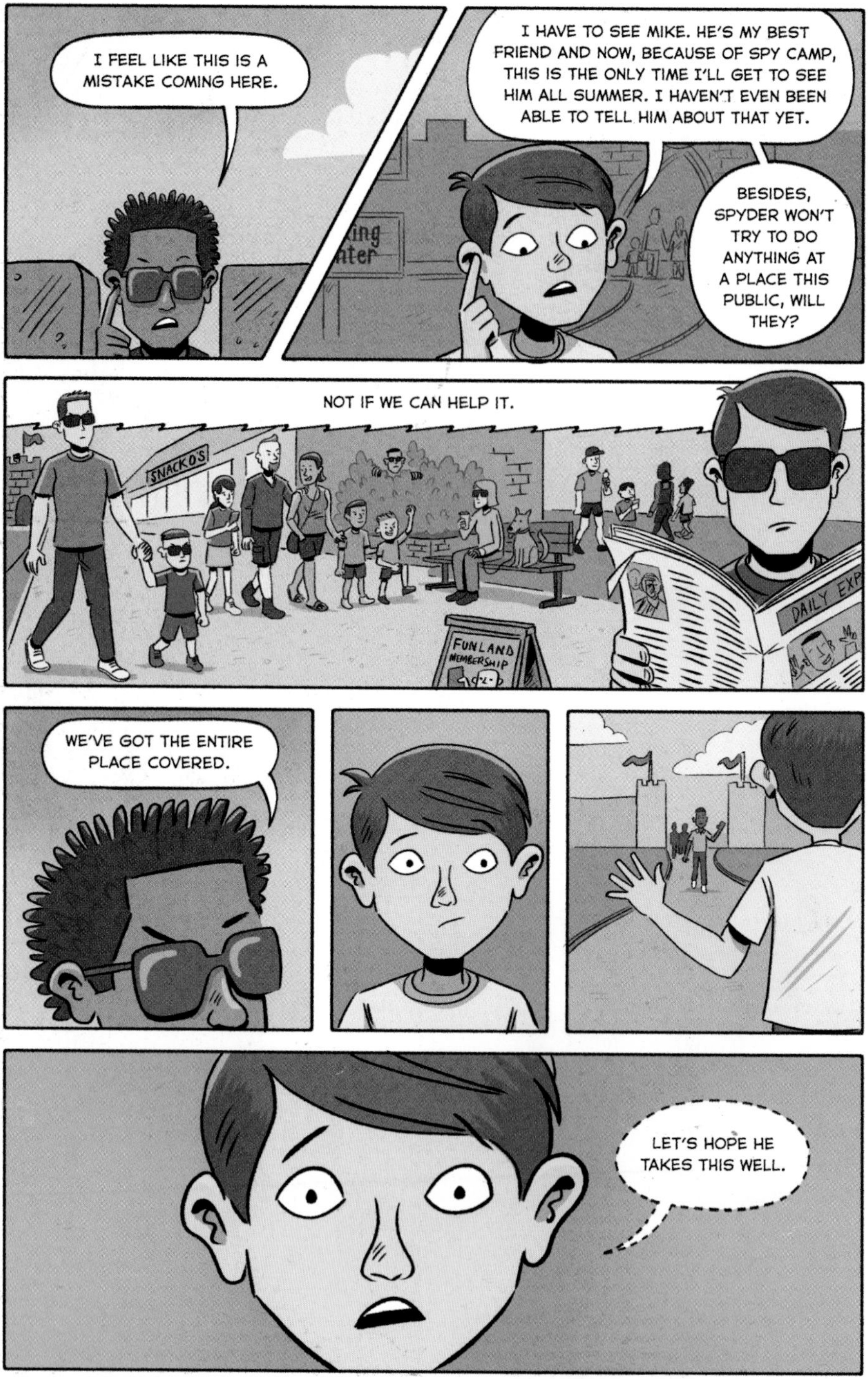
I FEEL LIKE THIS IS A MISTAKE COMING HERE.
I HAVE TO SEE MIKE. HE'S MY BEST FRIEND AND NOW, BECAUSE OF SPY CAMP, THIS IS THE ONLY TIME I'LL GET TO SEE HIM ALL SUMMER. I HAVEN'T EVEN BEEN ABLE TO TELL HIM ABOUT THAT YET.
BESIDES, SPYDER WON'T TRY TO DO ANYTHING AT A PLACE THIS PUBLIC, WILL THEY?
NOT IF WE CAN HELP IT.
SNACKO'S
FUNLAND MEMBERSHIP
DAILY EXP
WE'VE GOT THE ENTIRE PLACE COVERED.
LET'S HOPE HE TAKES THIS WELL.

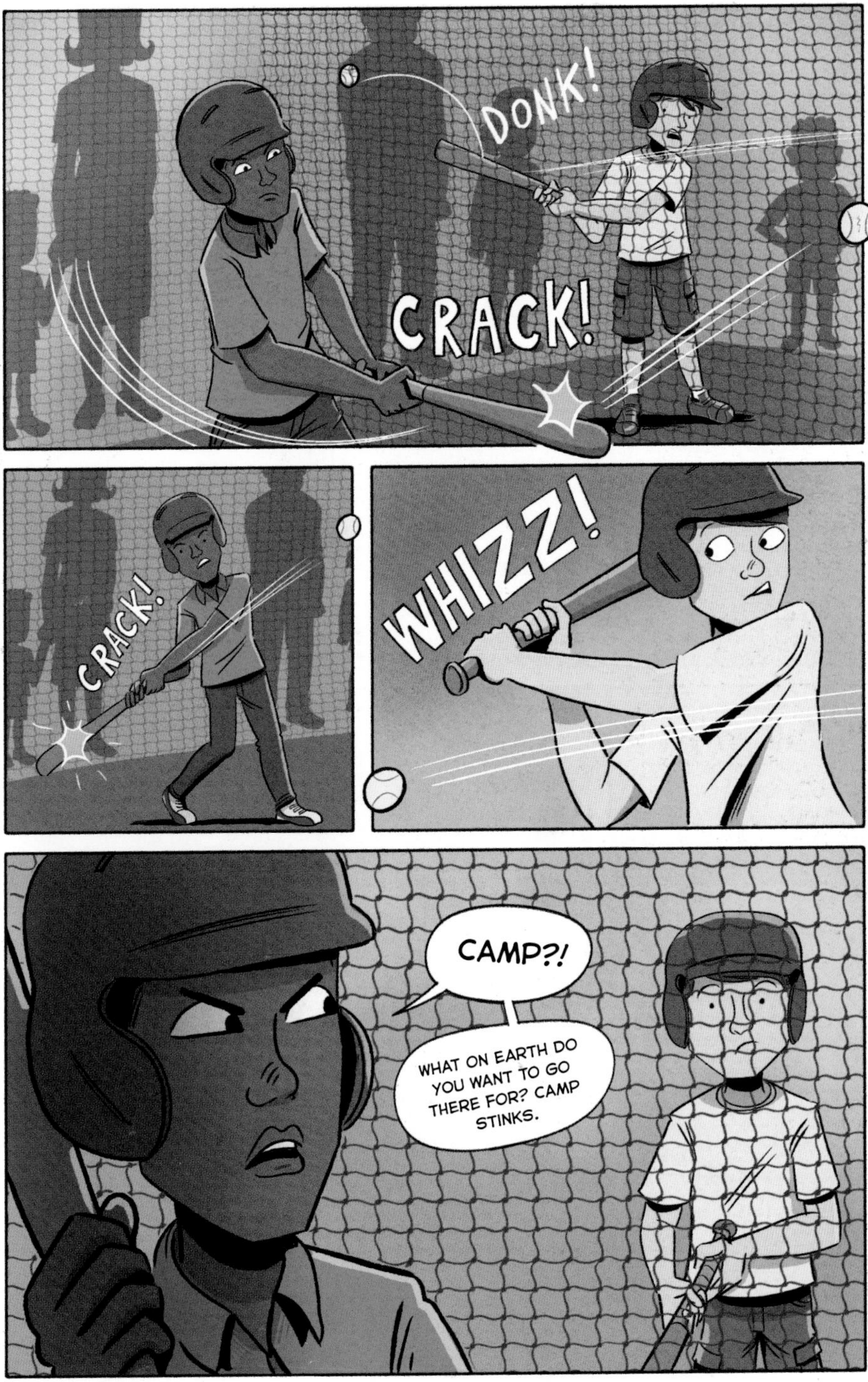
DONK!
CRACK!
CRACK!
WHIZZ!
CAMP?!
WHAT ON EARTH DO YOU WANT TO GO THERE FOR? CAMP STINKS.

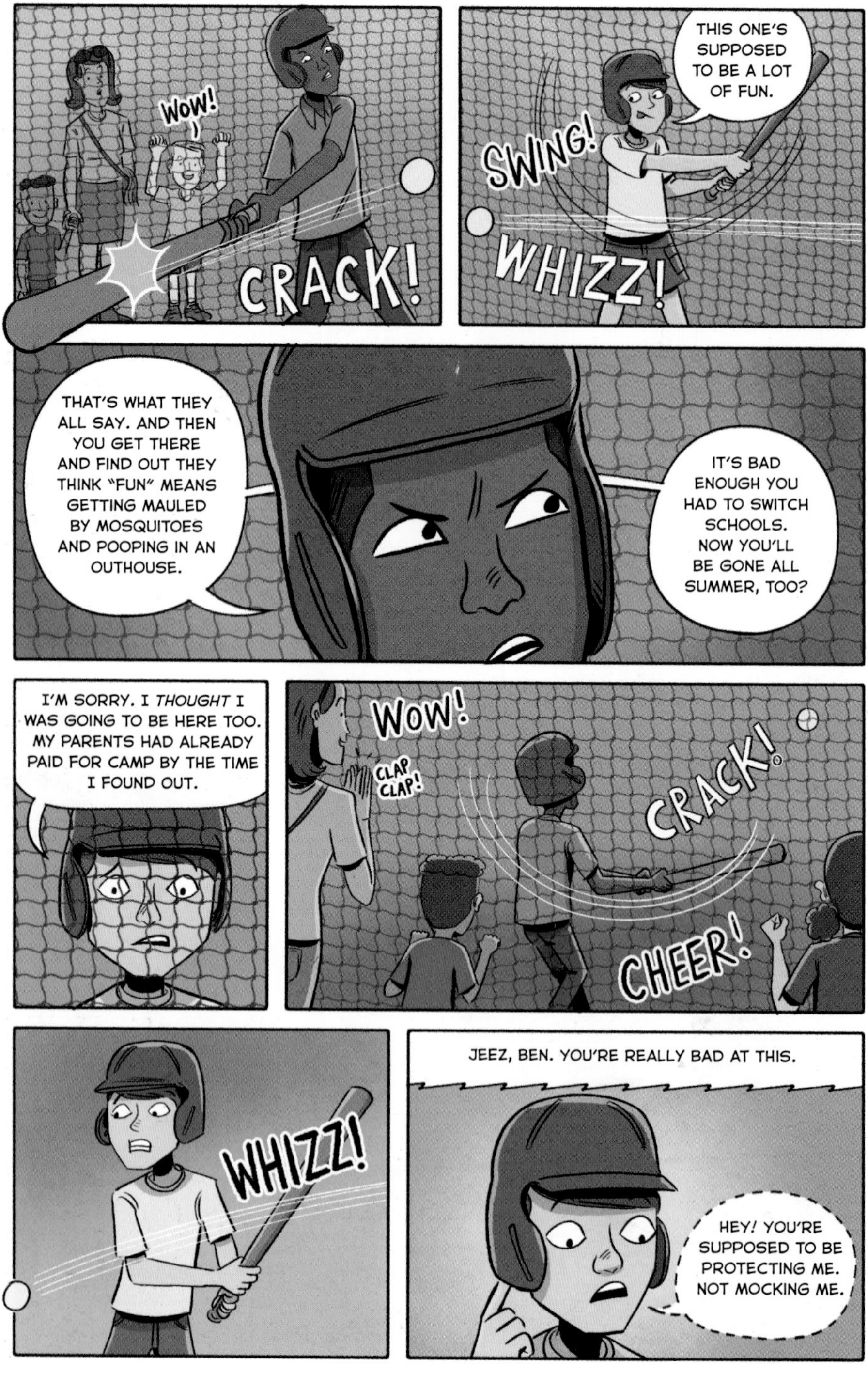
WOW!
CRACK!
THIS ONE'S SUPPOSED TO BE A LOT OF FUN.
SWING!
WHIZZ!
THAT'S WHAT THEY ALL SAY. AND THEN YOU GET THERE AND FIND OUT THEY THINK "FUN" MEANS GETTING MAULED BY MOSQUITOES AND POOPING IN AN OUTHOUSE.
IT'S BAD ENOUGH YOU HAD TO SWITCH SCHOOLS. NOW YOU'LL BE GONE ALL SUMMER, TOO?
I'M SORRY. I *THOUGHT* I WAS GOING TO BE HERE TOO. MY PARENTS HAD ALREADY PAID FOR CAMP BY THE TIME I FOUND OUT.
WOW!
CLAP CLAP!
CRACK!
CHEER!
WHIZZ!
JEEZ, BEN. YOU'RE REALLY BAD AT THIS.
HEY! YOU'RE SUPPOSED TO BE PROTECTING ME. NOT MOCKING ME.

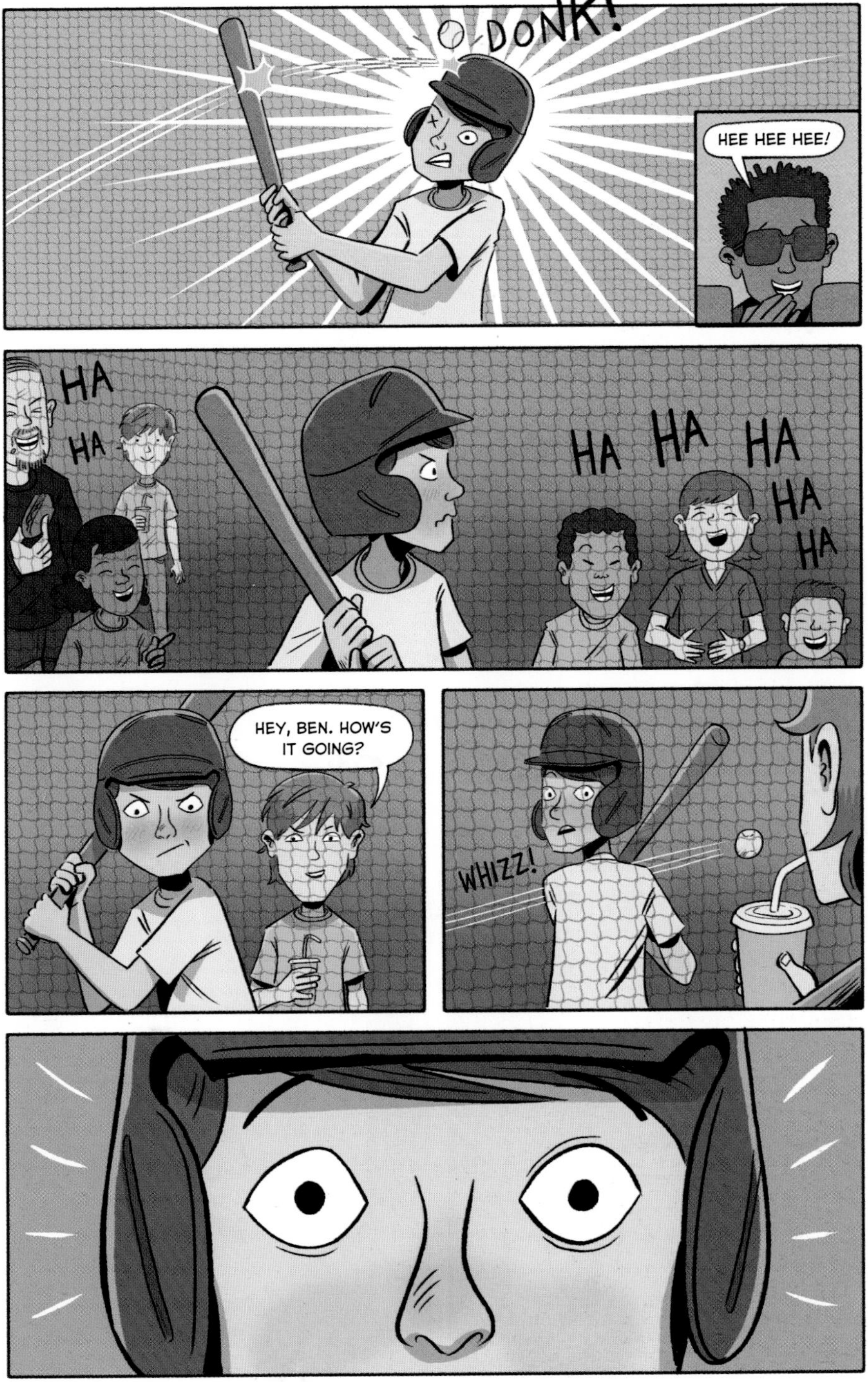
DONK!
HEE HEE HEE!
HA
HA
HA
HA
HA
HA
HA
HEY, BEN. HOW'S IT GOING?
WHIZZ!

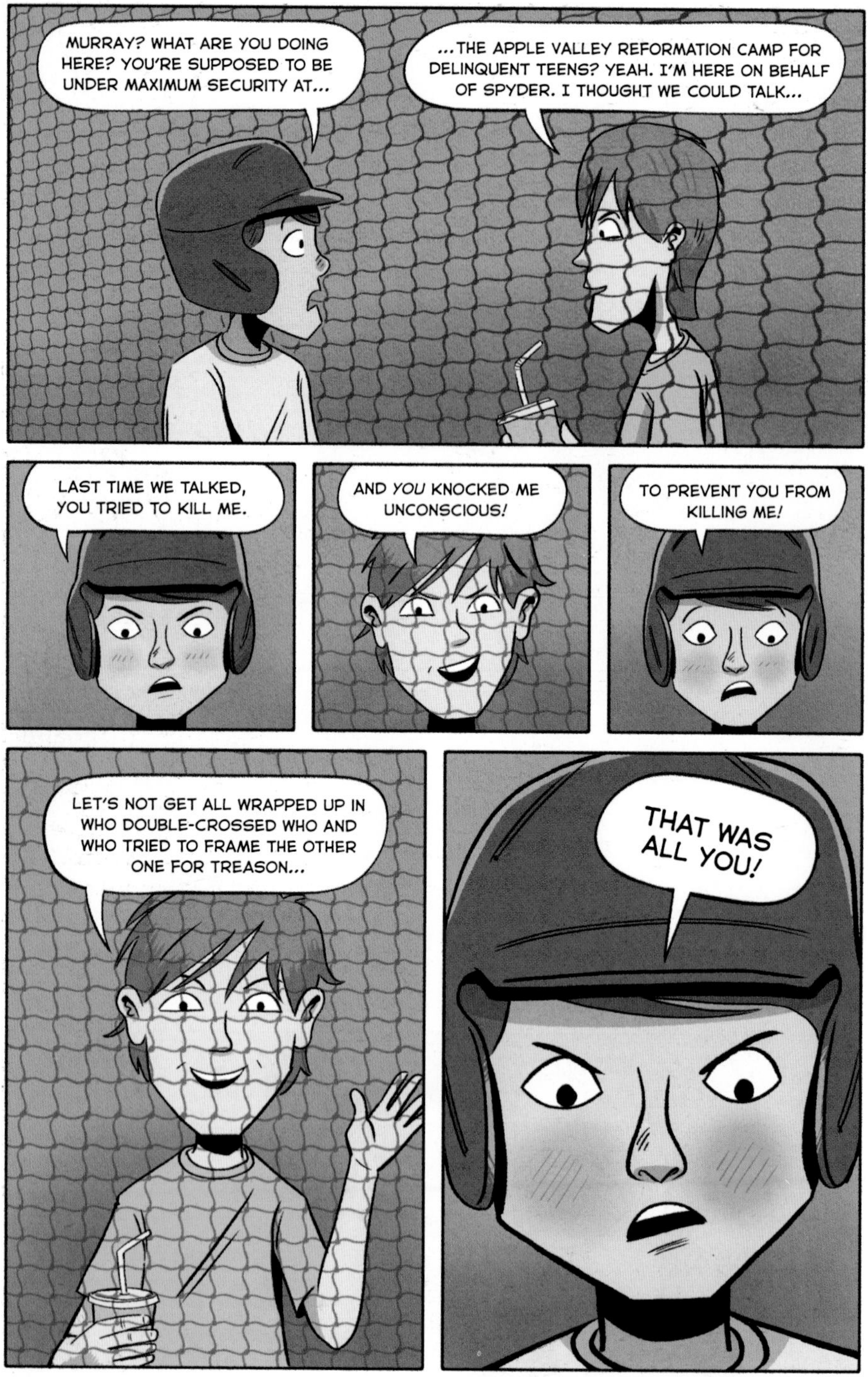
MURRAY? WHAT ARE YOU DOING HERE? YOU'RE SUPPOSED TO BE UNDER MAXIMUM SECURITY AT...
...THE APPLE VALLEY REFORMATION CAMP FOR DELINQUENT TEENS? YEAH. I'M HERE ON BEHALF OF SPYDER. I THOUGHT WE COULD TALK...
LAST TIME WE TALKED, YOU TRIED TO KILL ME.
AND *YOU* KNOCKED ME UNCONSCIOUS!
TO PREVENT YOU FROM KILLING ME!
LET'S NOT GET ALL WRAPPED UP IN WHO DOUBLE-CROSSED WHO AND WHO TRIED TO FRAME THE OTHER ONE FOR TREASON...
THAT WAS ALL YOU!

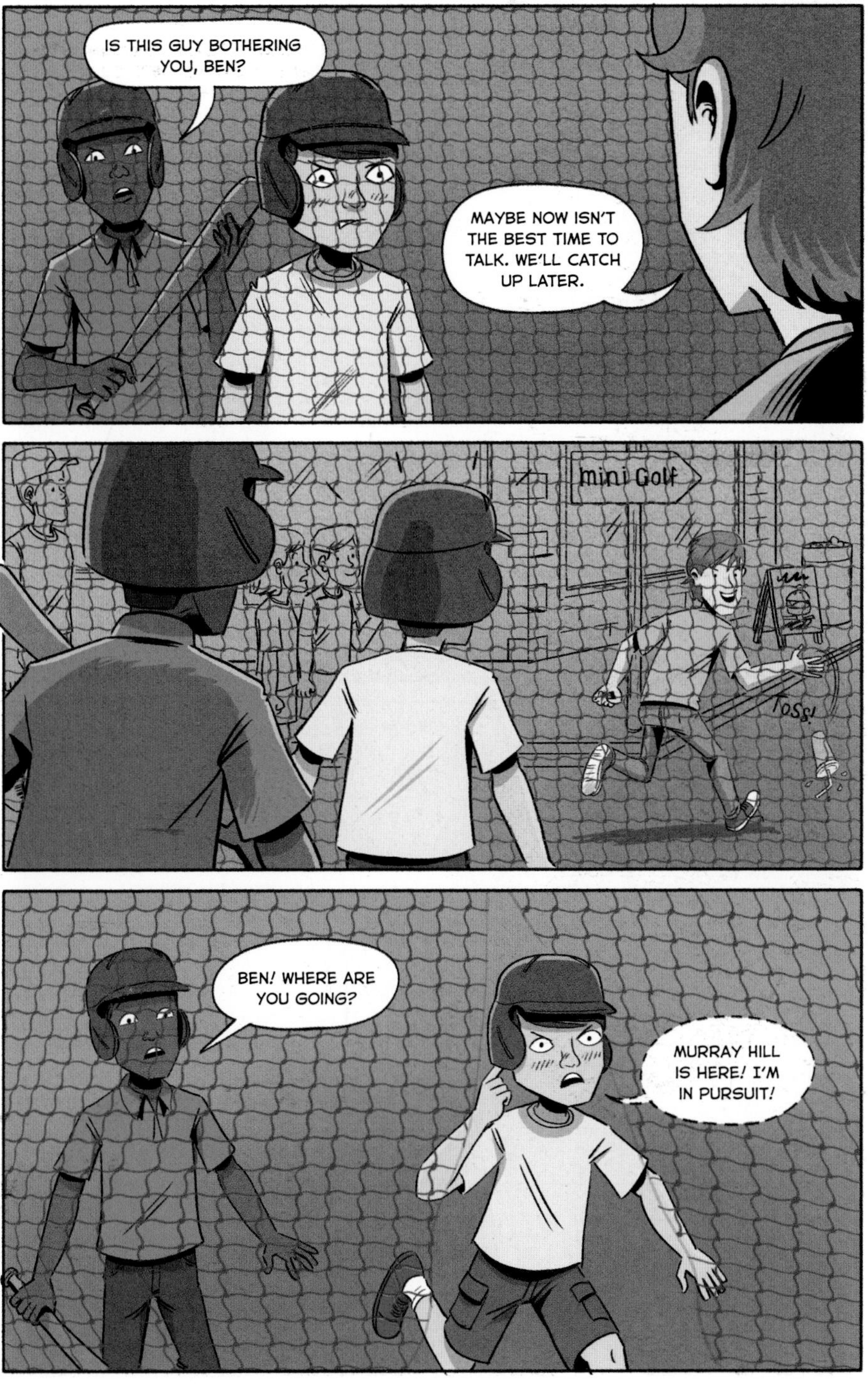
IS THIS GUY BOTHERING YOU, BEN?
MAYBE NOW ISN'T THE BEST TIME TO TALK. WE'LL CATCH UP LATER.
mini Golf
TOSS!
BEN! WHERE ARE YOU GOING?
MURRAY HILL IS HERE! I'M IN PURSUIT!

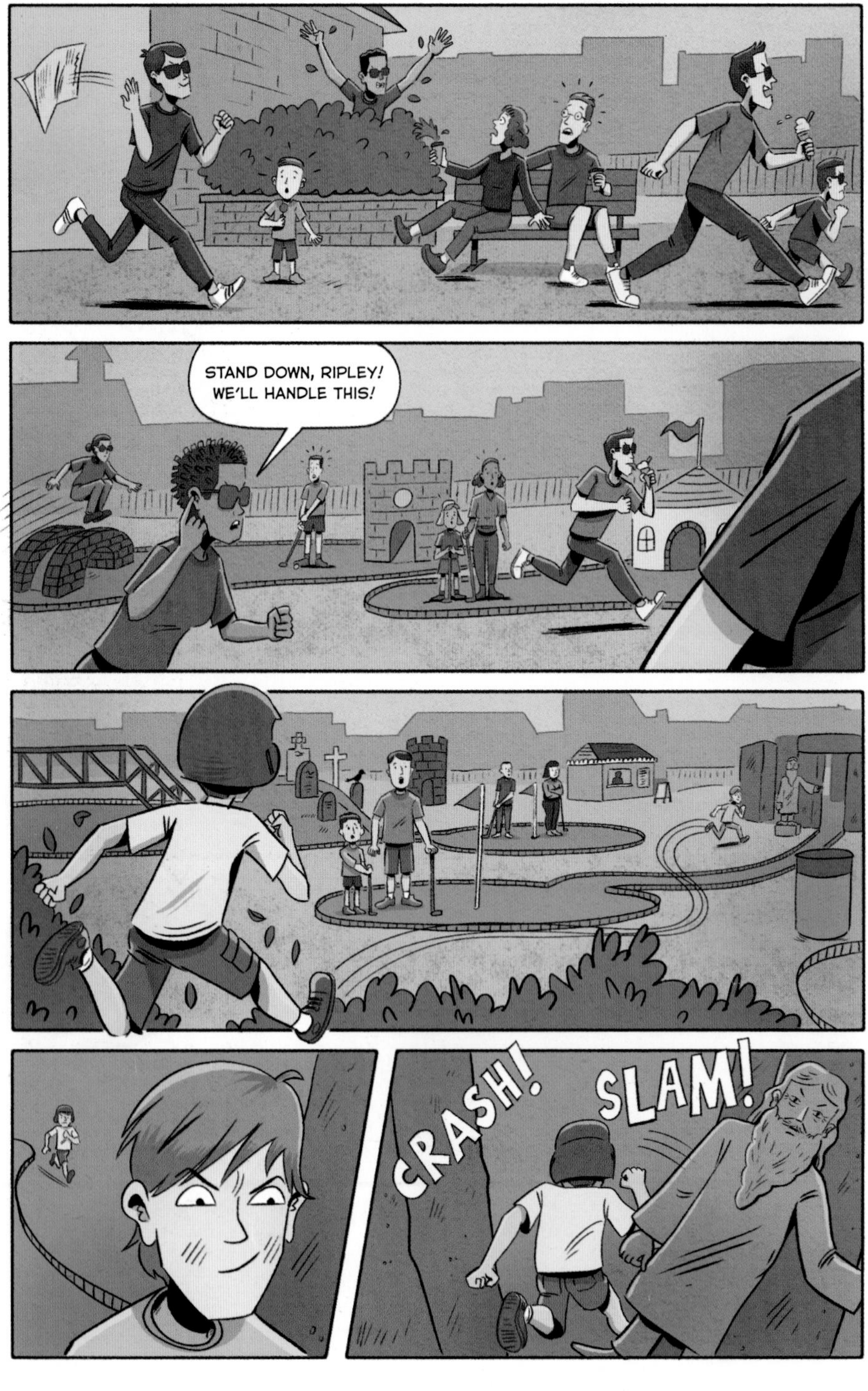
STAND DOWN, RIPLEY! WE'LL HANDLE THIS!
CRASH!
SLAM!

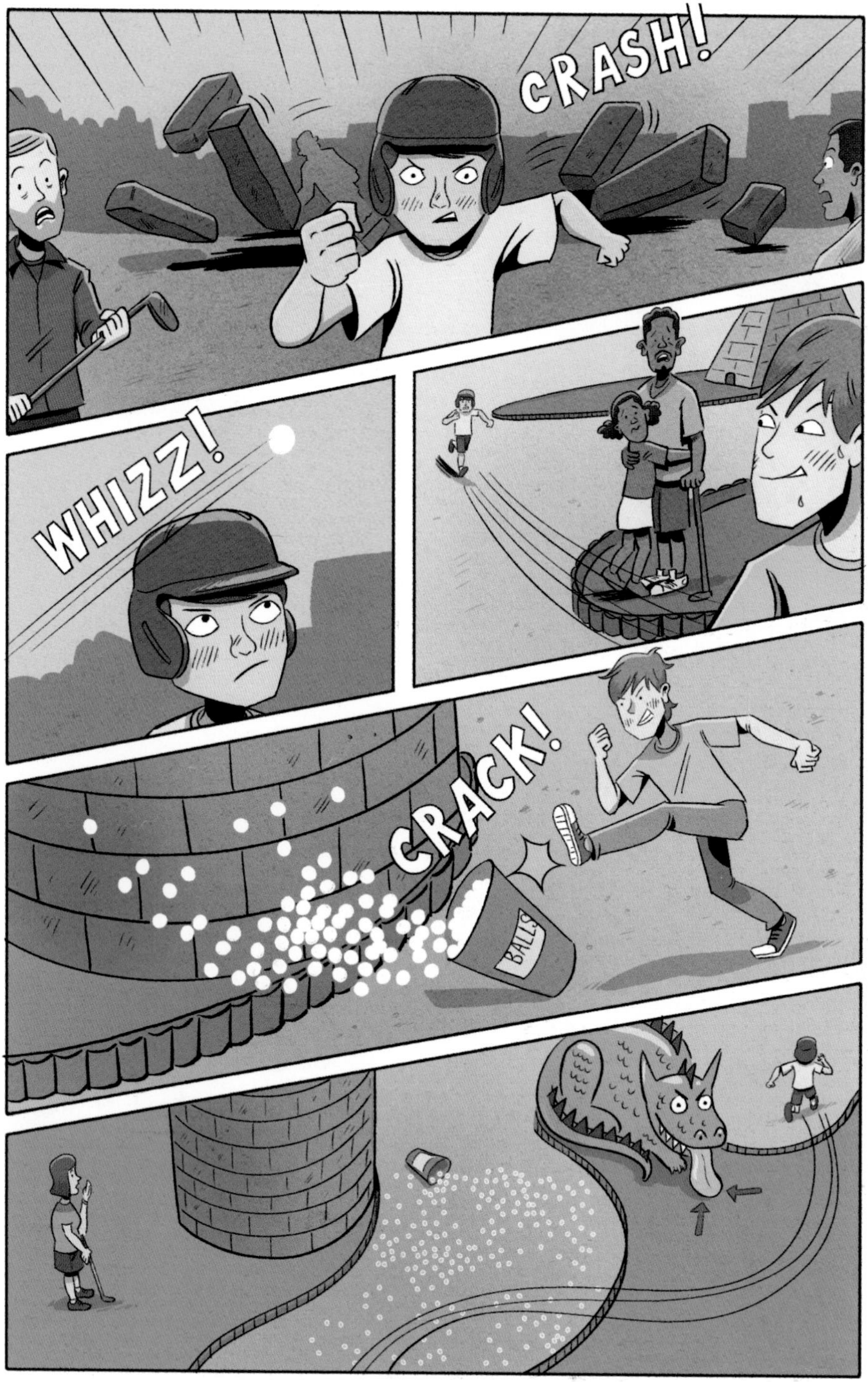
CRASH!
WHIZZ!
CRACK!
BALLS

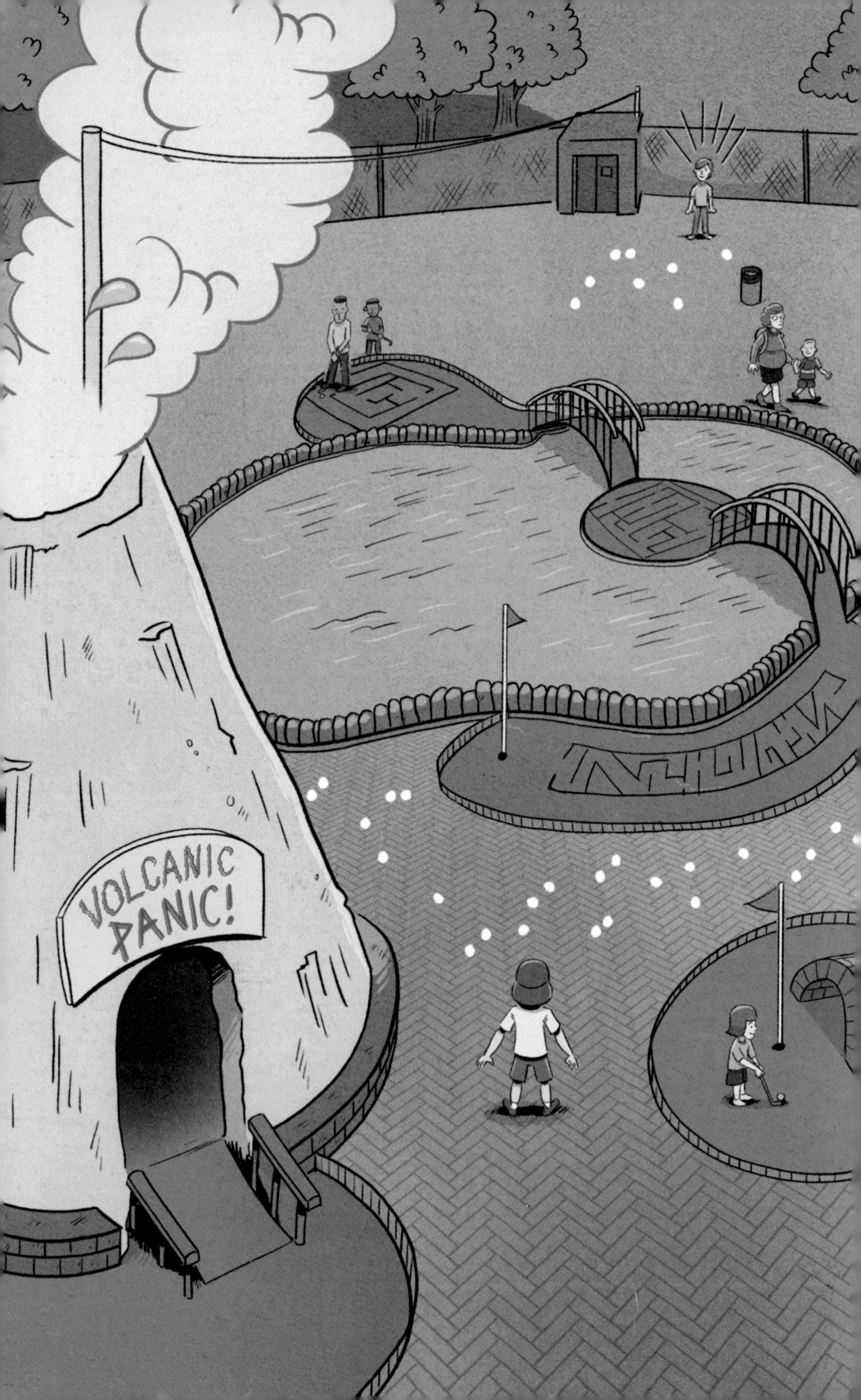
VOLCANIC
PANIC!

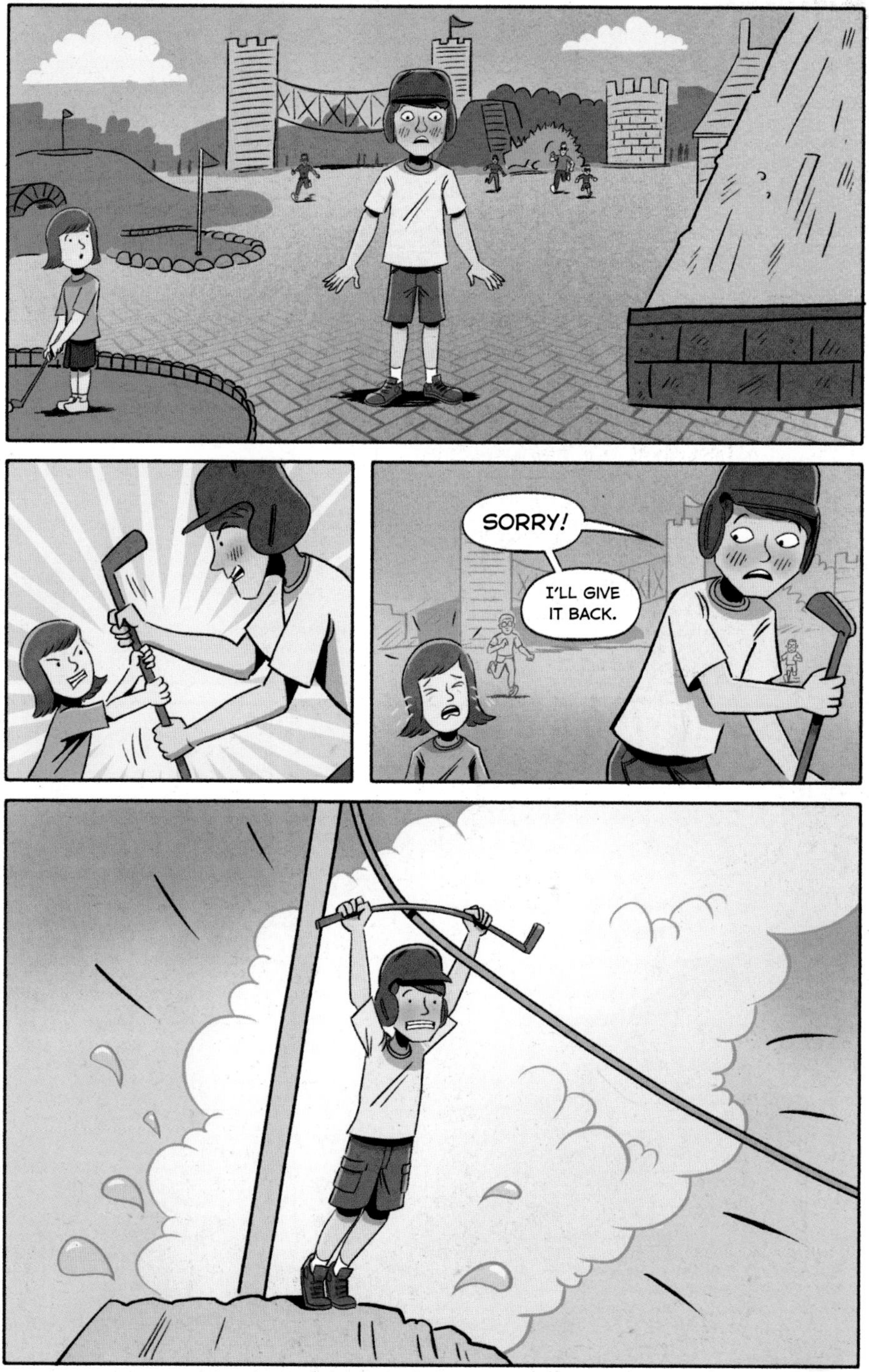
SORRY!
I'LL GIVE IT BACK.

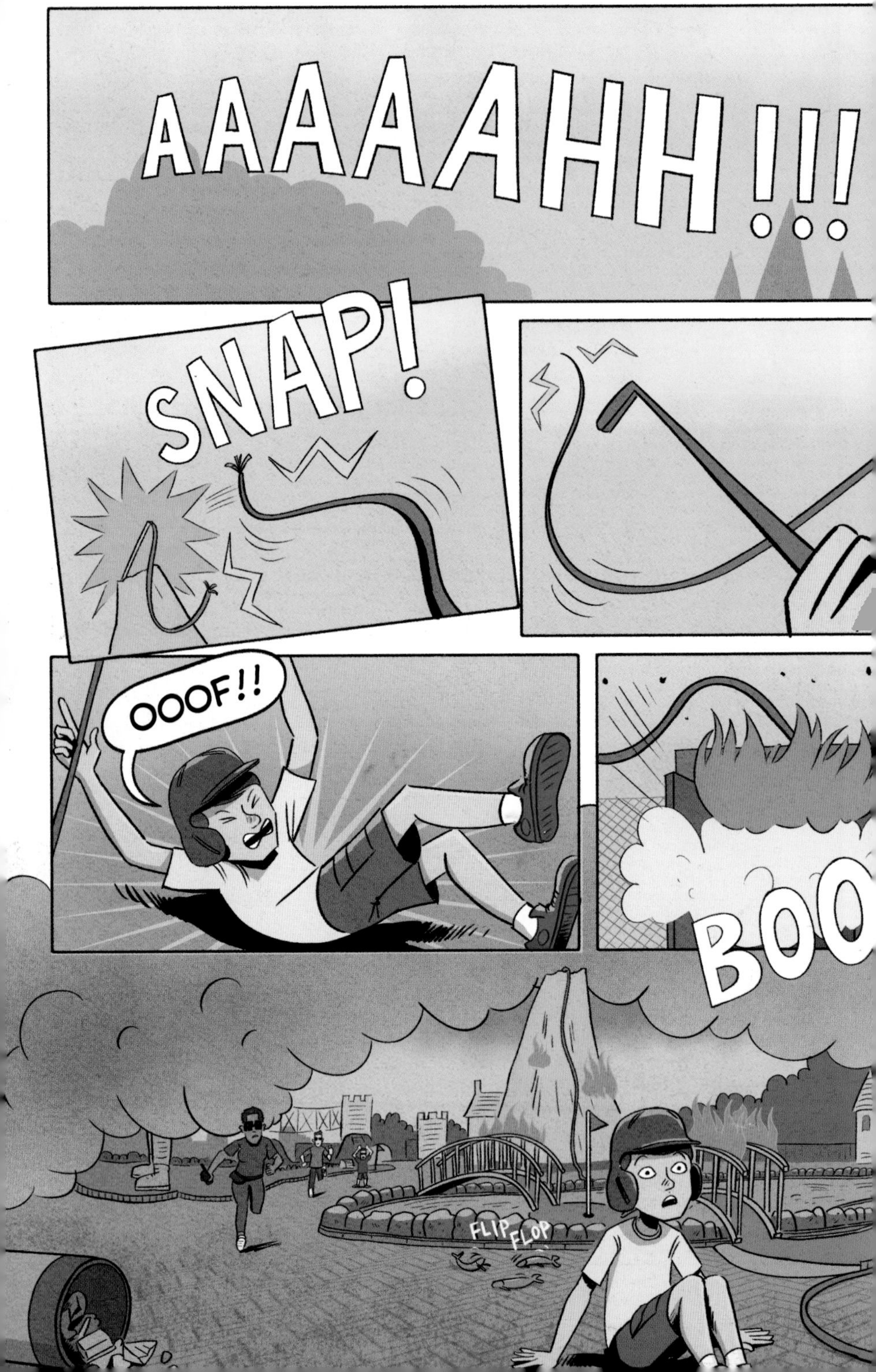
AAAAAHH!!!
SNAP!
OOOF!!
BOO
FLIP
FLOP

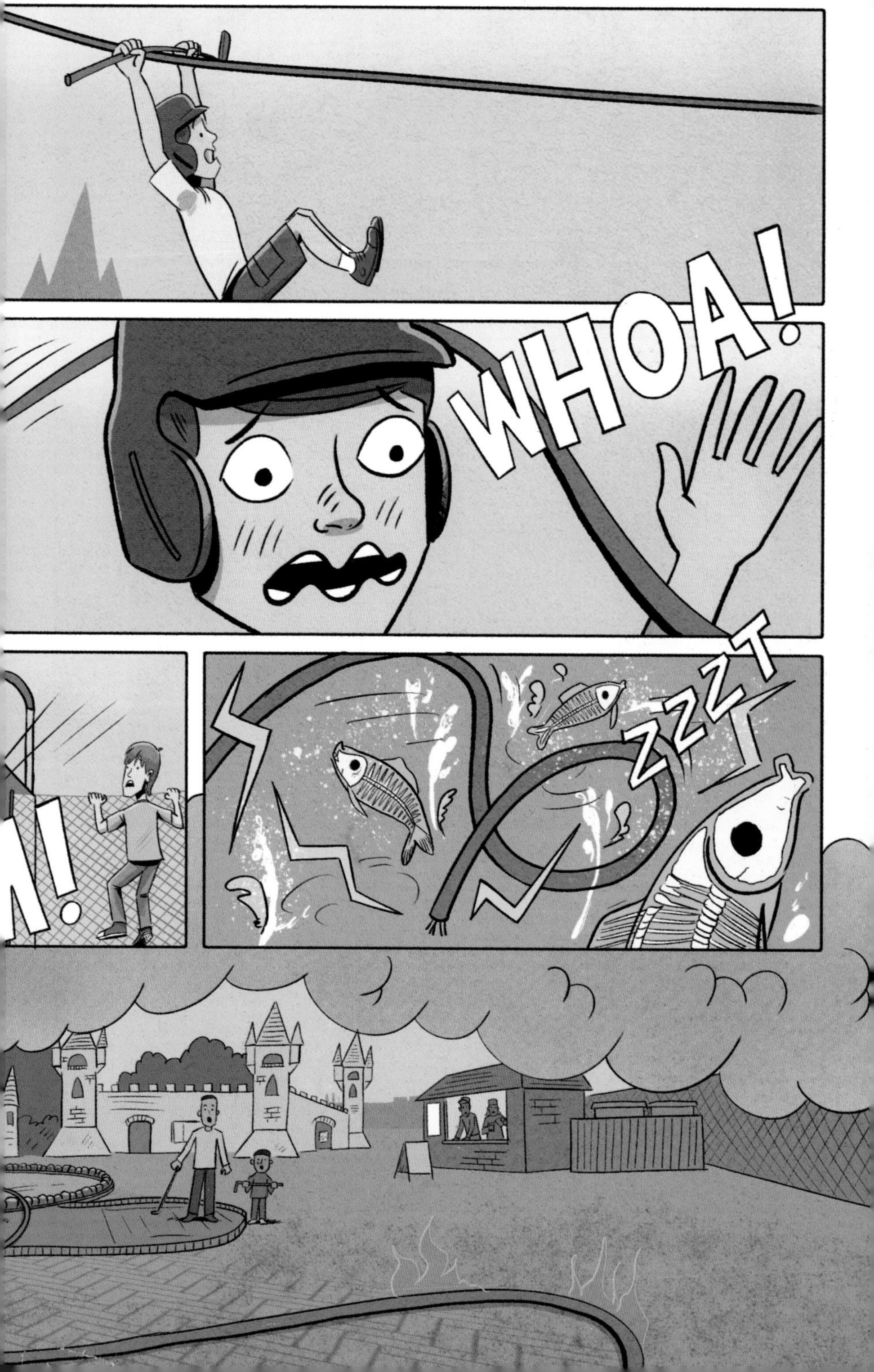
WHOA!
ZZZZT

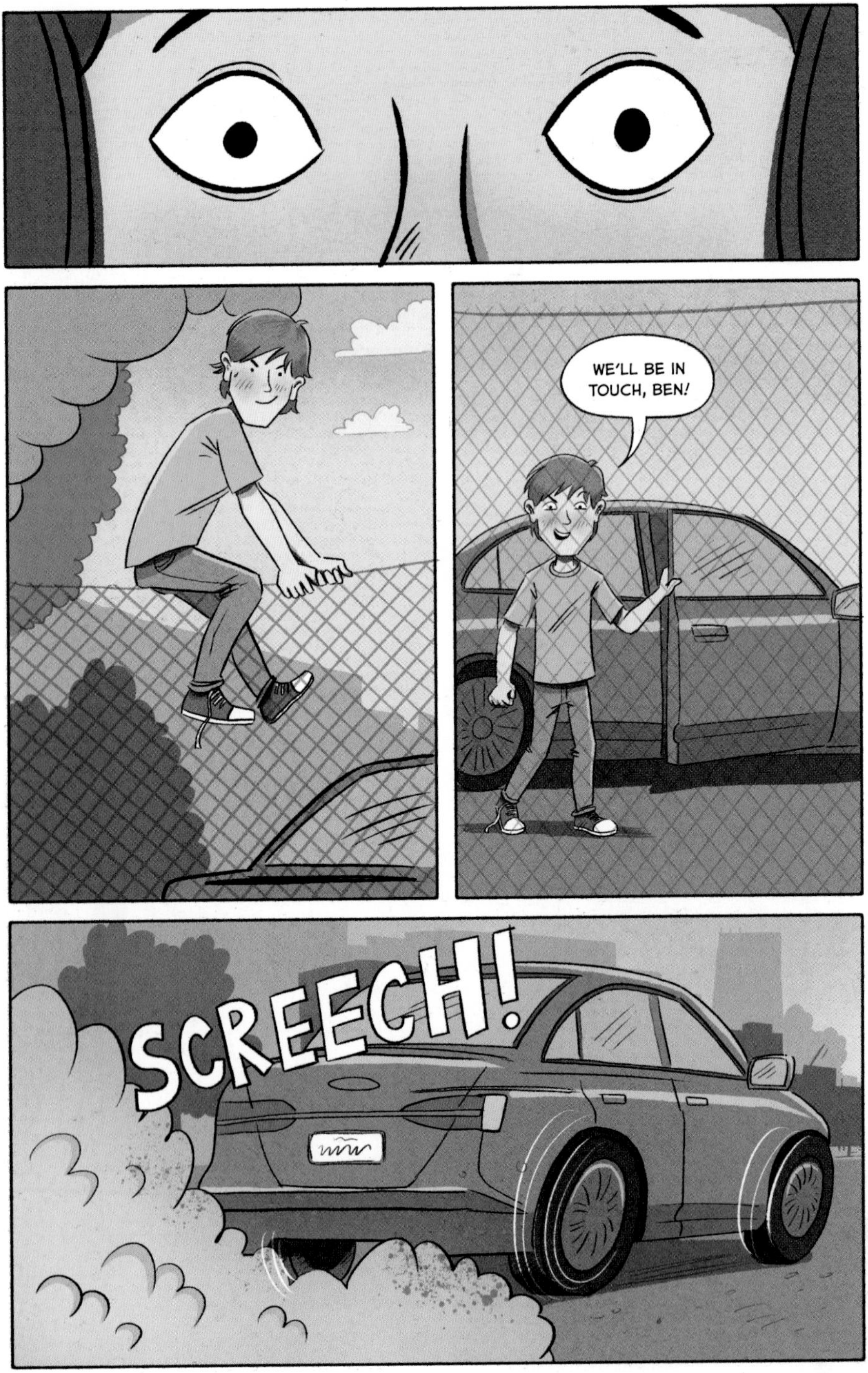
WE'LL BE IN
TOUCH, BEN!
SCREECH!

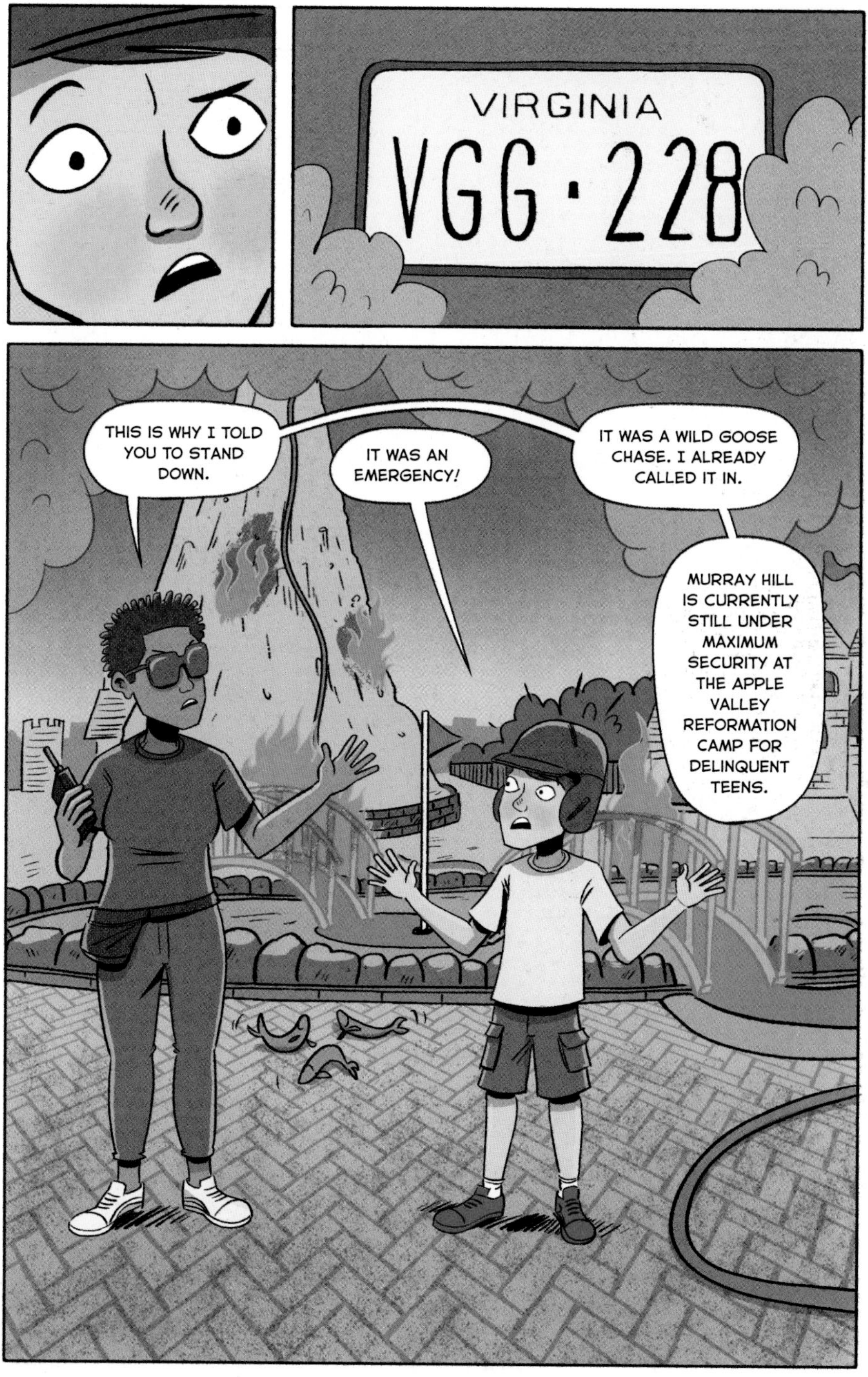
VIRGINIA
VGG·228
THIS IS WHY I TOLD YOU TO STAND DOWN.
IT WAS AN EMERGENCY!
IT WAS A WILD GOOSE CHASE. I ALREADY CALLED IT IN.
MURRAY HILL IS CURRENTLY STILL UNDER MAXIMUM SECURITY AT THE APPLE VALLEY REFORMATION CAMP FOR DELINQUENT TEENS.

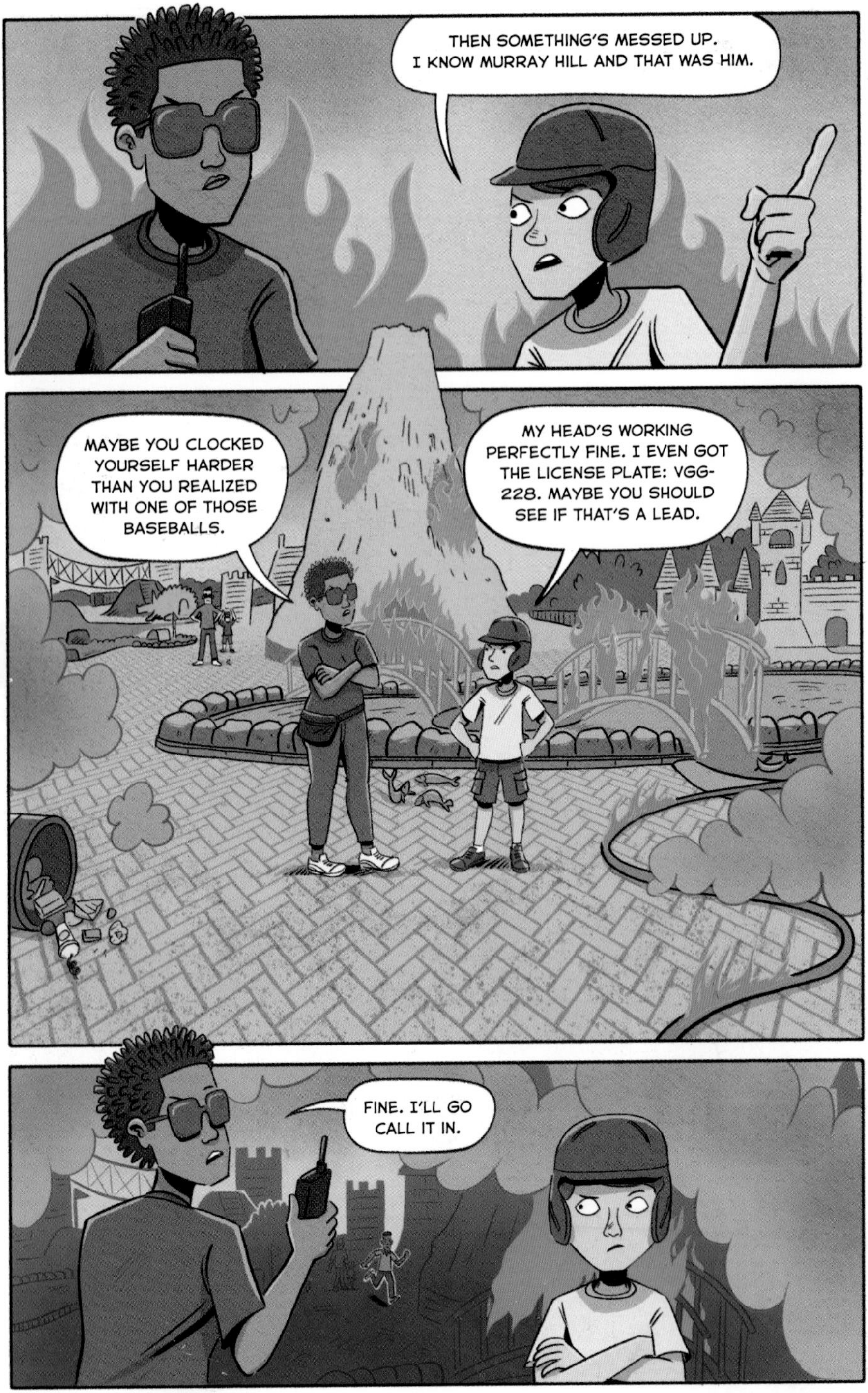
THEN SOMETHING'S MESSED UP. I KNOW MURRAY HILL AND THAT WAS HIM.
MAYBE YOU CLOCKED YOURSELF HARDER THAN YOU REALIZED WITH ONE OF THOSE BASEBALLS.
MY HEAD'S WORKING PERFECTLY FINE. I EVEN GOT THE LICENSE PLATE: VGG-228. MAYBE YOU SHOULD SEE IF THAT'S A LEAD.
FINE. I'LL GO CALL IT IN.

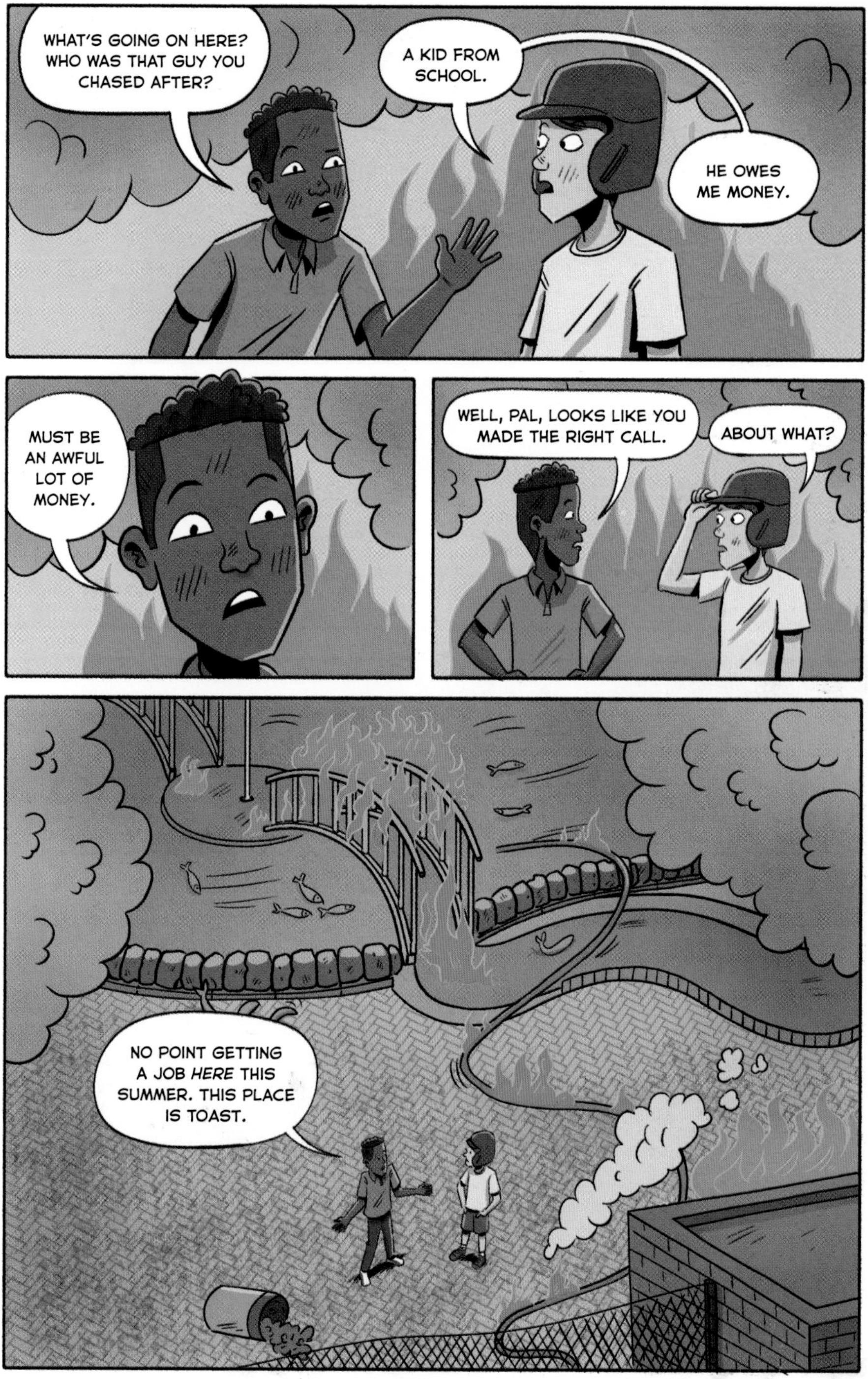
WHAT'S GOING ON HERE? WHO WAS THAT GUY YOU CHASED AFTER?
A KID FROM SCHOOL.
HE OWES ME MONEY.
MUST BE AN AWFUL LOT OF MONEY.
WELL, PAL, LOOKS LIKE YOU MADE THE RIGHT CALL.
ABOUT WHAT?
NO POINT GETTING A JOB *HERE* THIS SUMMER. THIS PLACE IS TOAST.

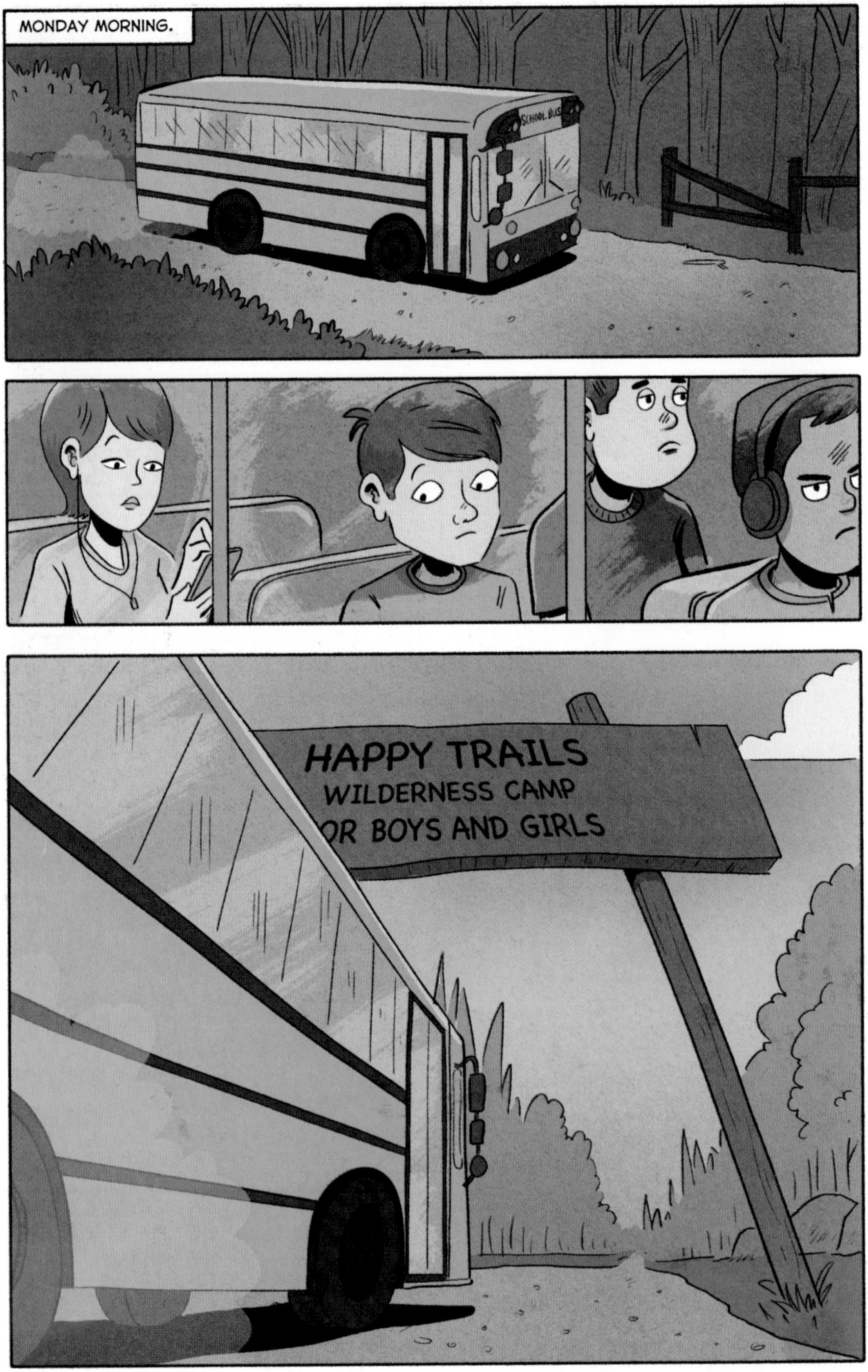
MONDAY MORNING.
SCHOOL BUS
HAPPY TRAILS
WILDERNESS CAMP
OR BOYS AND GIRLS

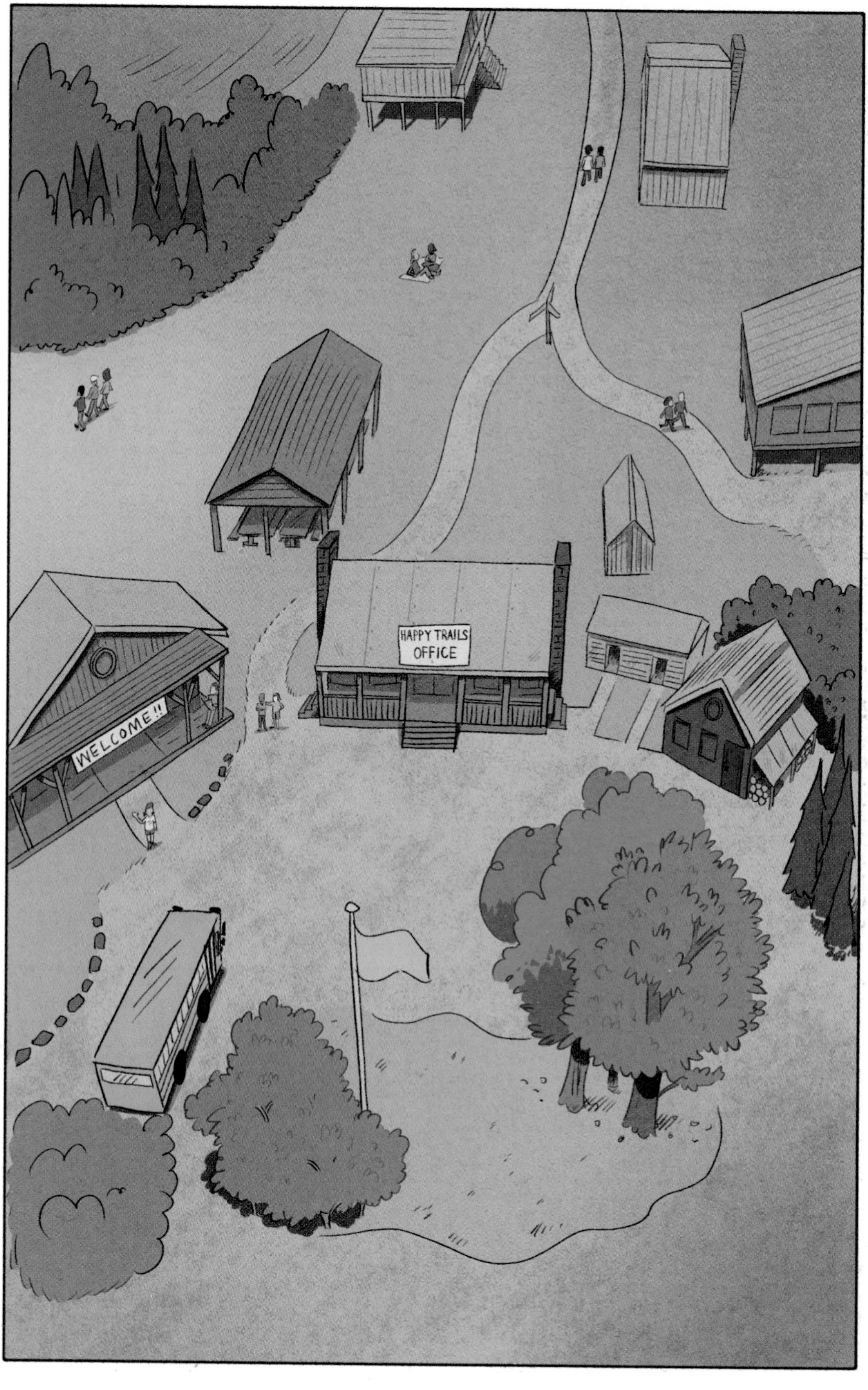
HAPPY TRAILS
OFFICE
WELCOME!!

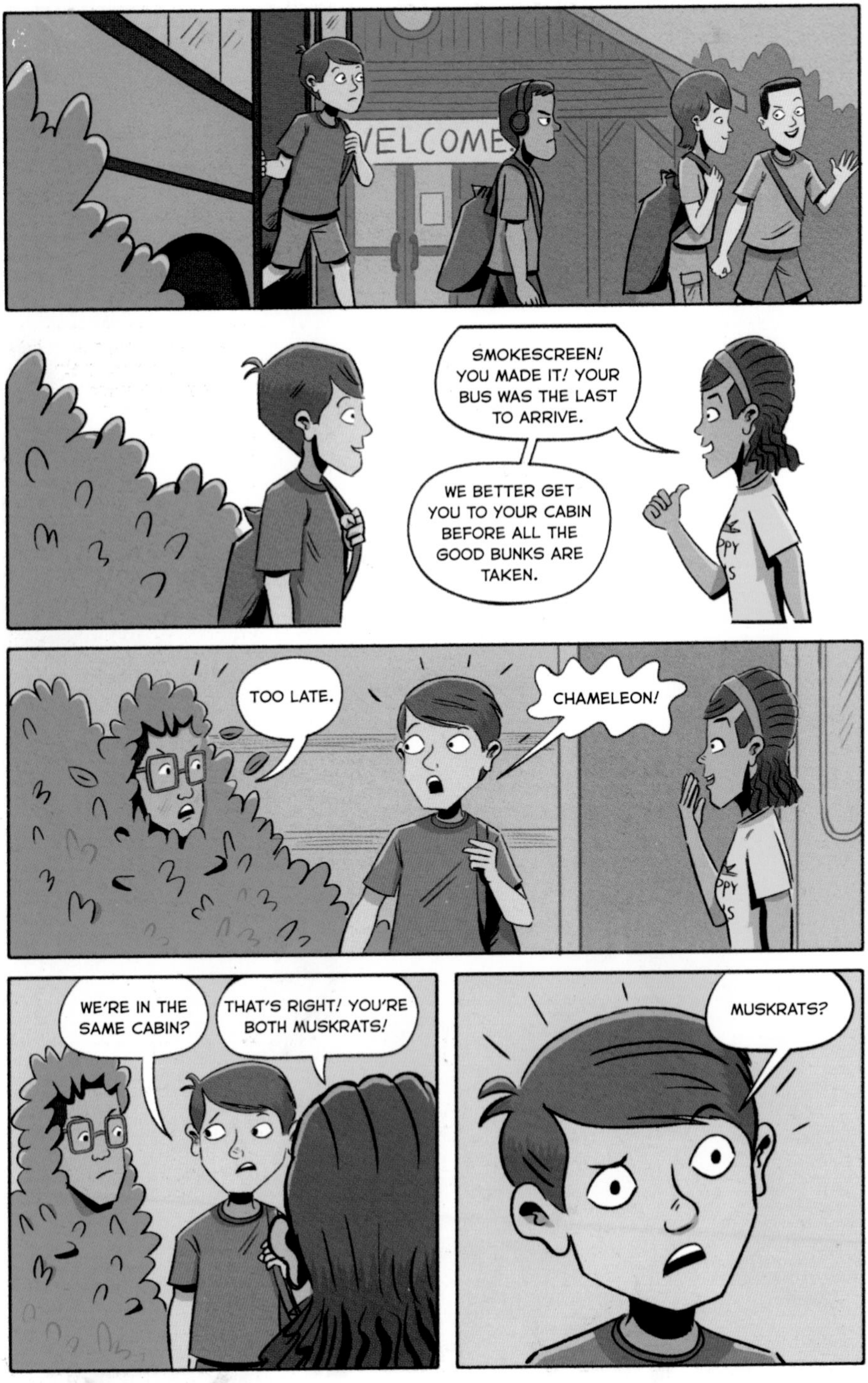
VELCOME
SMOKESCREEN! YOU MADE IT! YOUR BUS WAS THE LAST TO ARRIVE.
WE BETTER GET YOU TO YOUR CABIN BEFORE ALL THE GOOD BUNKS ARE TAKEN.
TOO LATE.
CHAMELEON!
WE'RE IN THE SAME CABIN?
THAT'S RIGHT! YOU'RE BOTH MUSKRATS!
MUSKRATS?

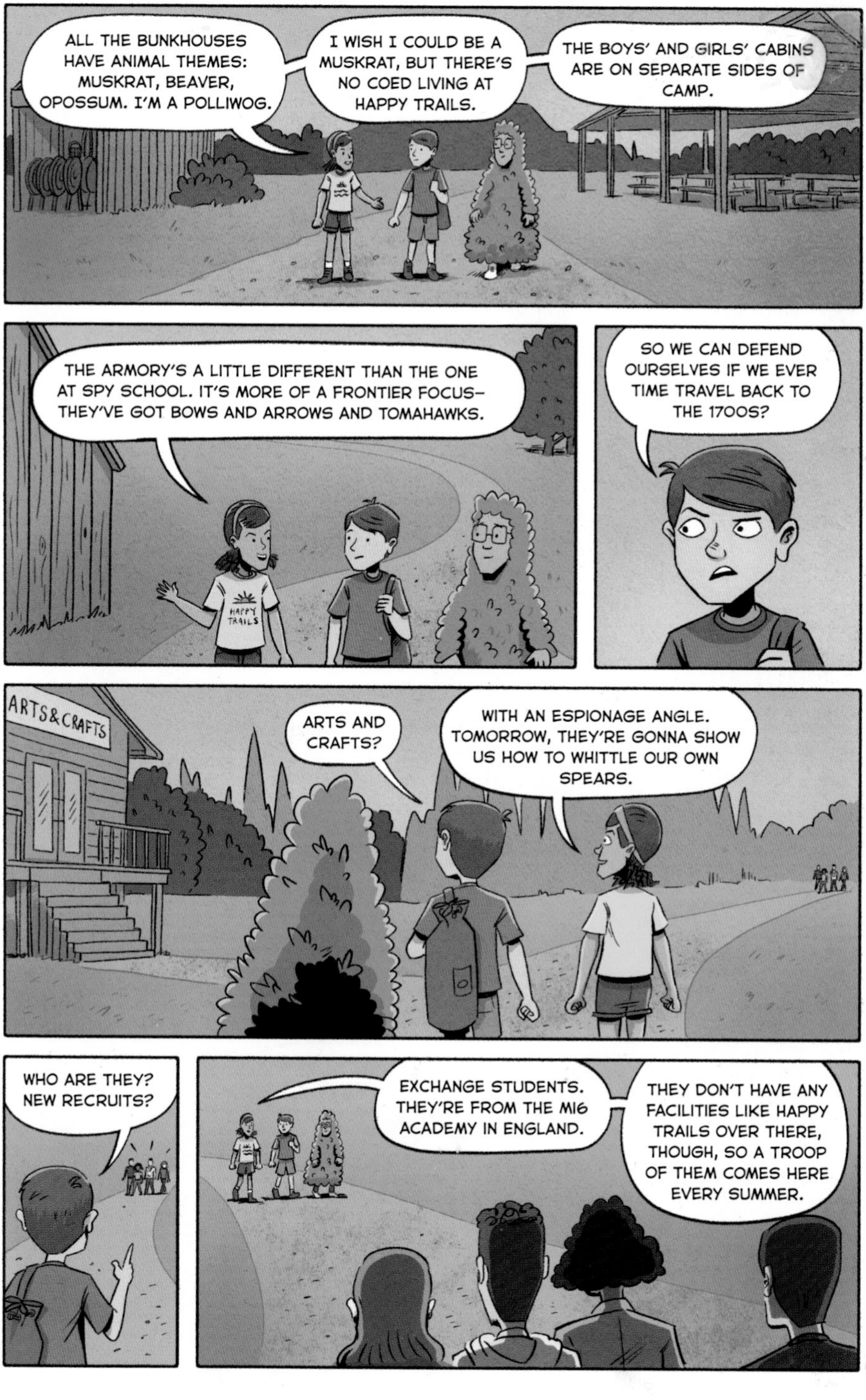
ALL THE BUNKHOUSES HAVE ANIMAL THEMES: MUSKRAT, BEAVER, OPOSSUM. I'M A POLLIWOG.
I WISH I COULD BE A MUSKRAT, BUT THERE'S NO COED LIVING AT HAPPY TRAILS.
THE BOYS' AND GIRLS' CABINS ARE ON SEPARATE SIDES OF CAMP.
THE ARMORY'S A LITTLE DIFFERENT THAN THE ONE AT SPY SCHOOL. IT'S MORE OF A FRONTIER FOCUS—THEY'VE GOT BOWS AND ARROWS AND TOMAHAWKS.
HAPPY TRAILS
SO WE CAN DEFEND OURSELVES IF WE EVER TIME TRAVEL BACK TO THE 1700S?
ARTS & CRAFTS
ARTS AND CRAFTS?
WITH AN ESPIONAGE ANGLE. TOMORROW, THEY'RE GONNA SHOW US HOW TO WHITTLE OUR OWN SPEARS.
WHO ARE THEY? NEW RECRUITS?
EXCHANGE STUDENTS. THEY'RE FROM THE MI6 ACADEMY IN ENGLAND.
THEY DON'T HAVE ANY FACILITIES LIKE HAPPY TRAILS OVER THERE, THOUGH, SO A TROOP OF THEM COMES HERE EVERY SUMMER.

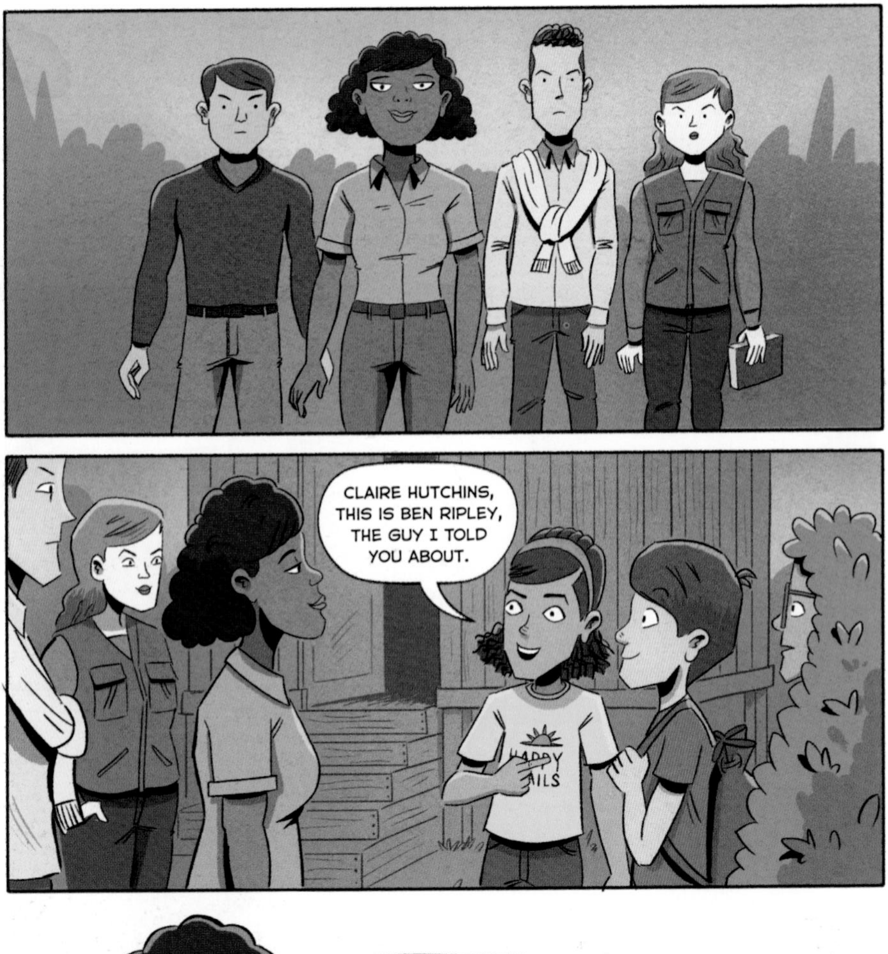
CLAIRE HUTCHINS, THIS IS BEN RIPLEY, THE GUY I TOLD YOU ABOUT.
YOUR REPUTATION PRECEDES YOU. IT'S A PLEASURE.
THE PLEASURE'S ALL MINE.

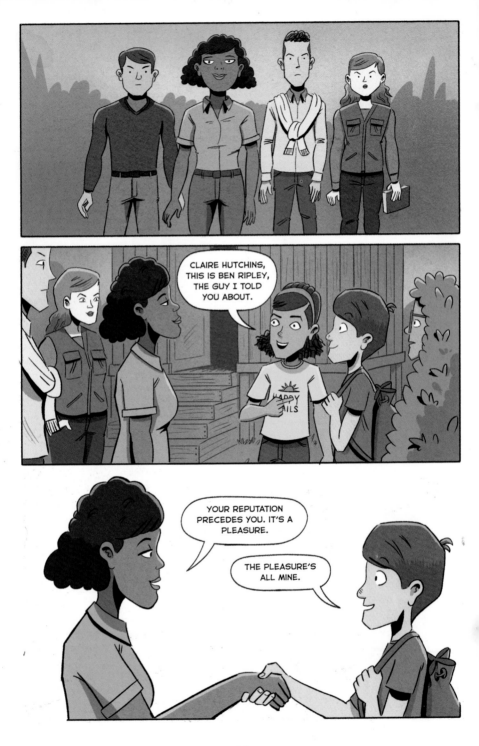

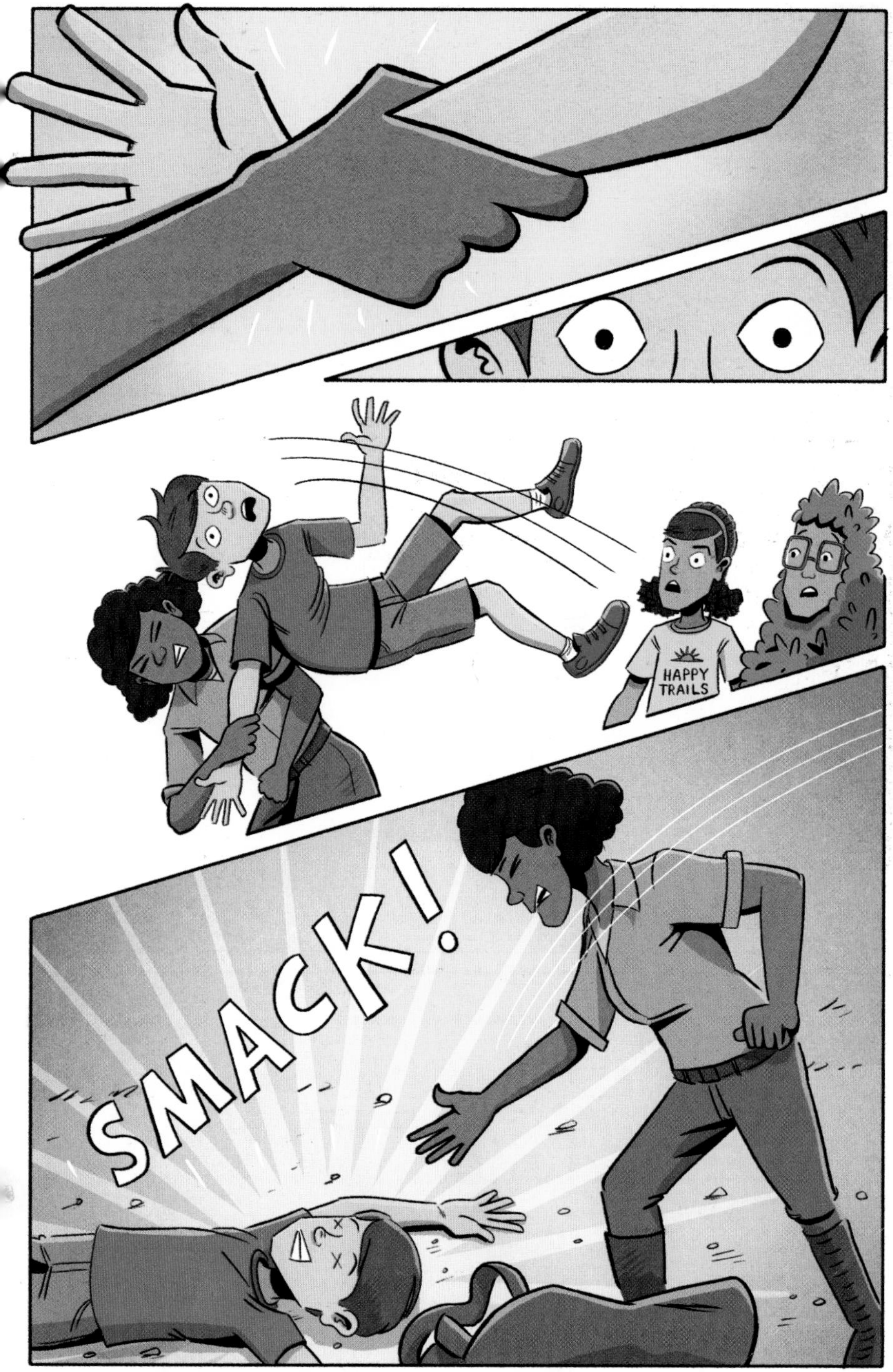
HAPPY TRAILS
SMACK!

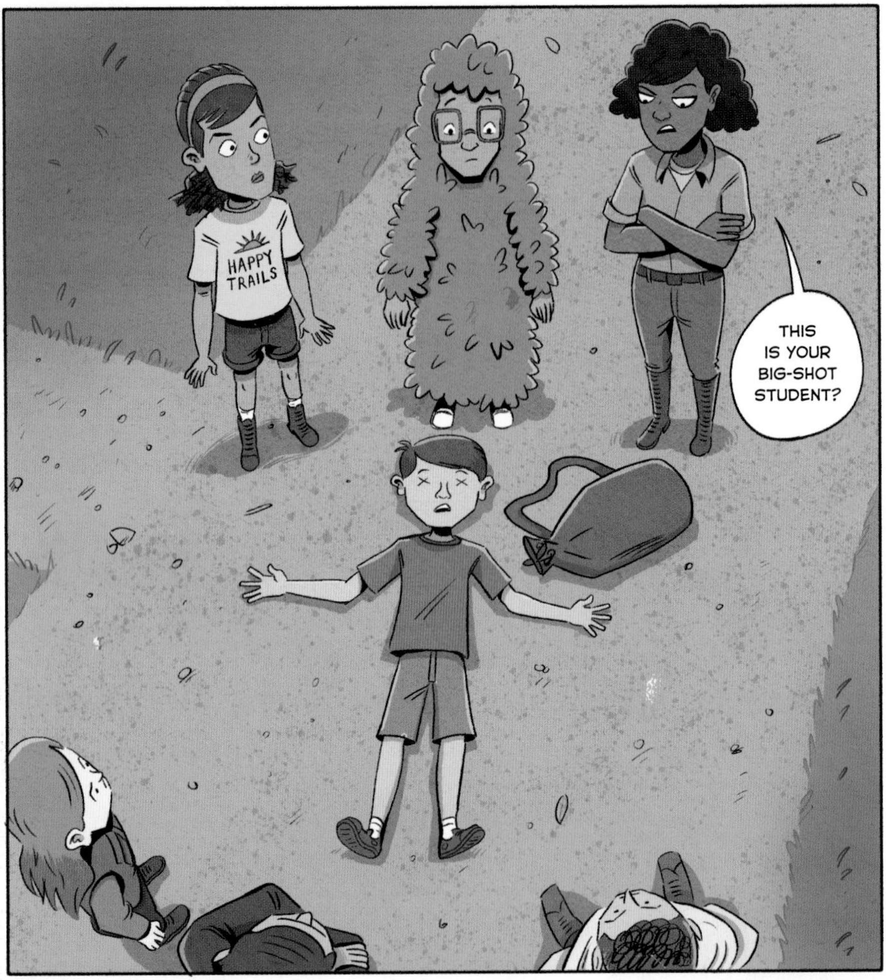
HAPPY TRAILS
THIS IS YOUR BIG-SHOT STUDENT?

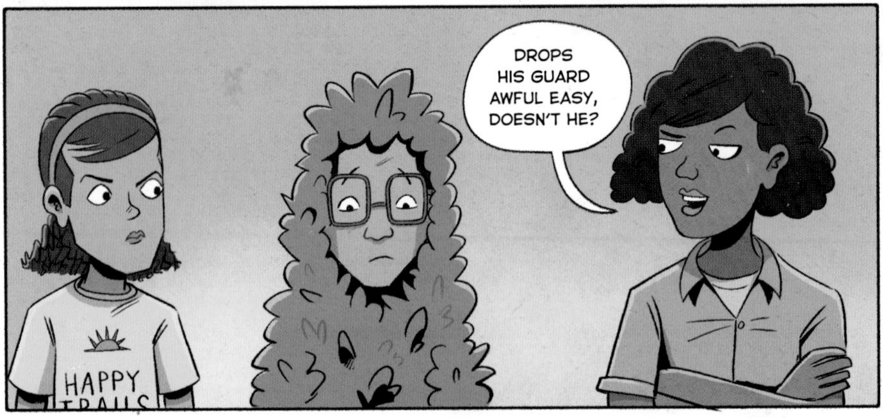
DROPS HIS GUARD AWFUL EASY, DOESN'T HE?
HAPPY

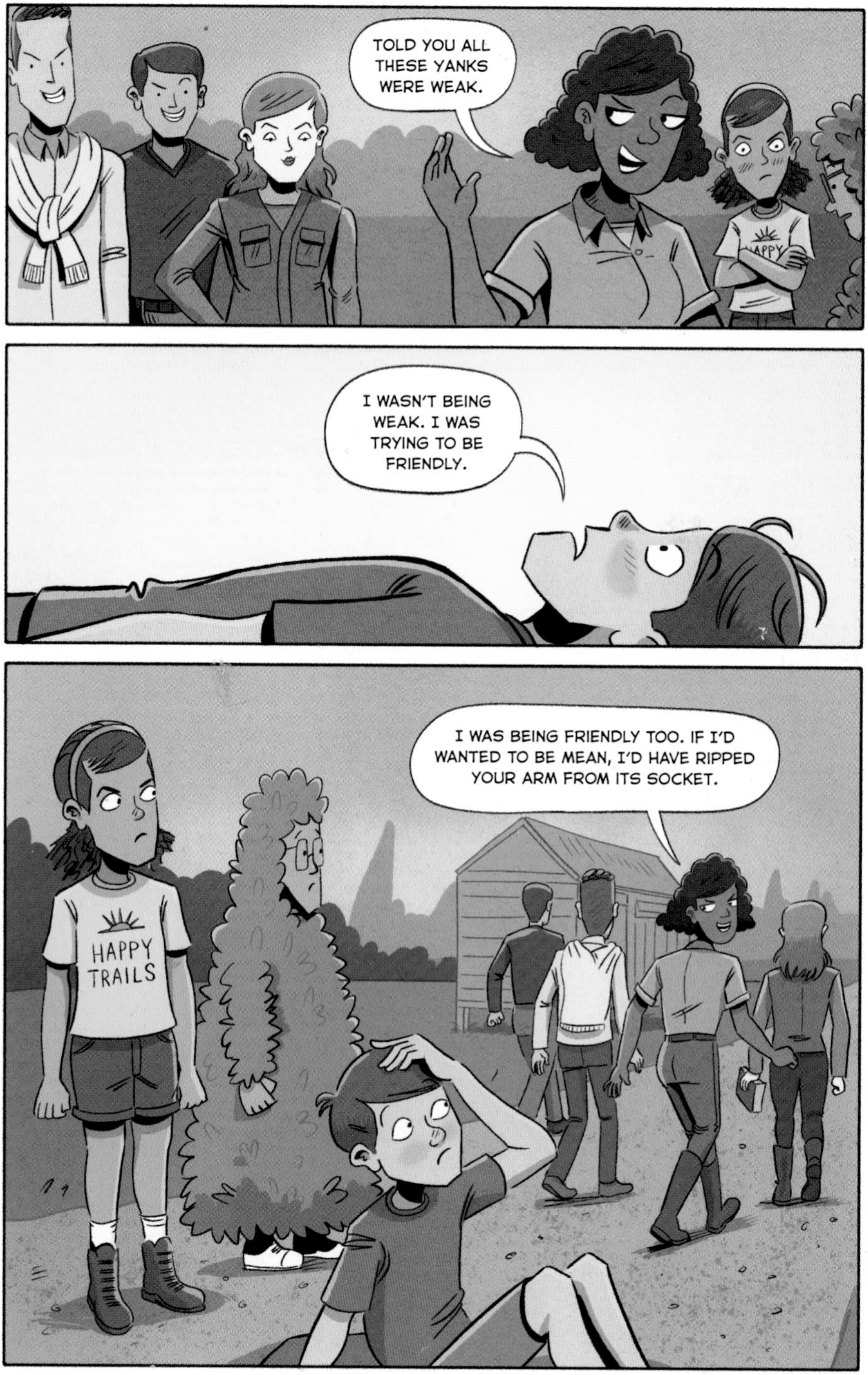
TOLD YOU ALL THESE YANKS WERE WEAK.
I WASN'T BEING WEAK. I WAS TRYING TO BE FRIENDLY.
HAPPY TRAILS
I WAS BEING FRIENDLY TOO. IF I'D WANTED TO BE MEAN, I'D HAVE RIPPED YOUR ARM FROM ITS SOCKET.

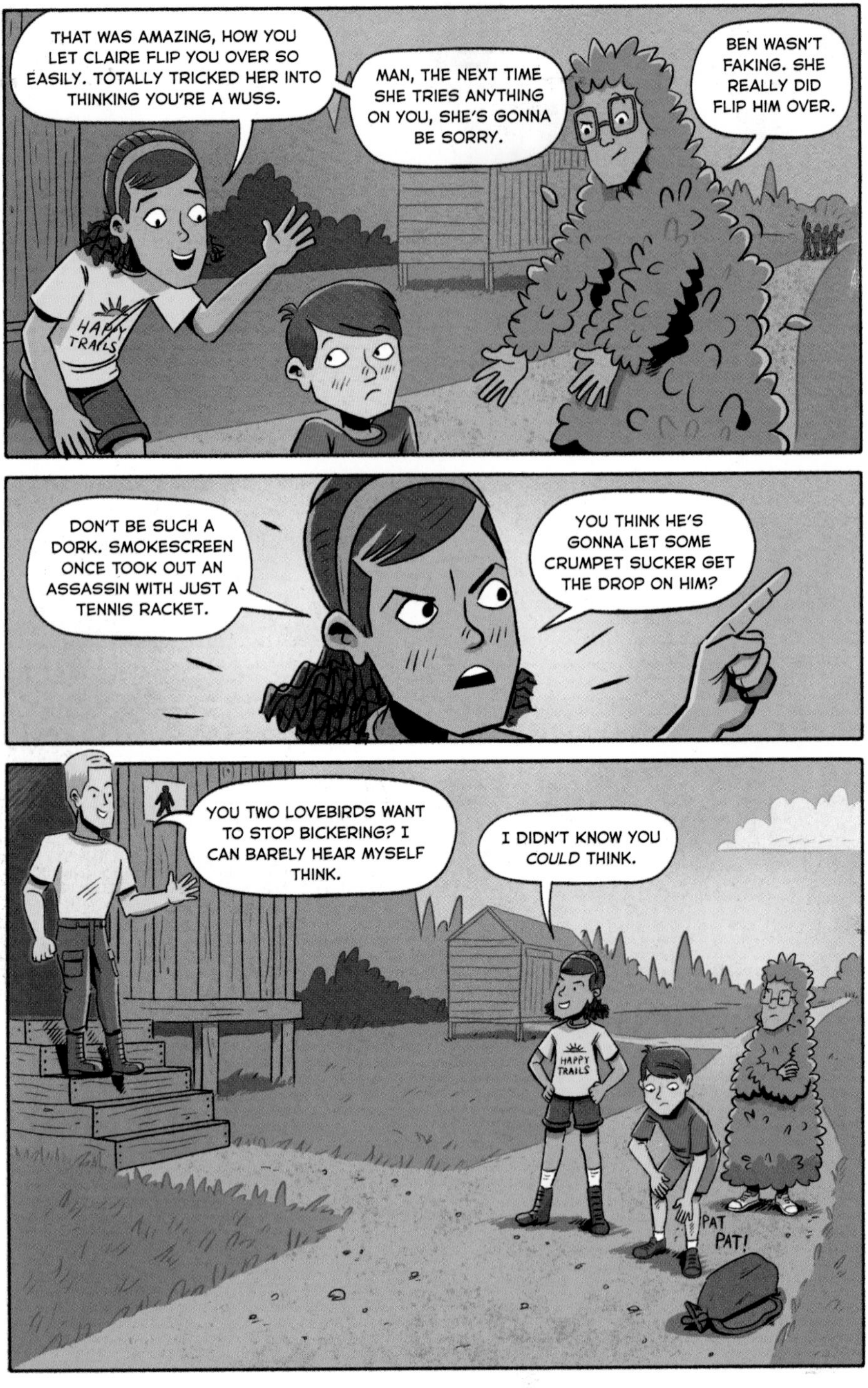
THAT WAS AMAZING, HOW YOU LET CLAIRE FLIP YOU OVER SO EASILY. TOTALLY TRICKED HER INTO THINKING YOU'RE A WUSS.
MAN, THE NEXT TIME SHE TRIES ANYTHING ON YOU, SHE'S GONNA BE SORRY.
BEN WASN'T FAKING. SHE REALLY DID FLIP HIM OVER.
HAPPY TRAILS
DON'T BE SUCH A DORK. SMOKESCREEN ONCE TOOK OUT AN ASSASSIN WITH JUST A TENNIS RACKET.
YOU THINK HE'S GONNA LET SOME CRUMPET SUCKER GET THE DROP ON HIM?
YOU TWO LOVEBIRDS WANT TO STOP BICKERING? I CAN BARELY HEAR MYSELF THINK.
I DIDN'T KNOW YOU *COULD* THINK.
HAPPY TRAILS
PAT PAT!

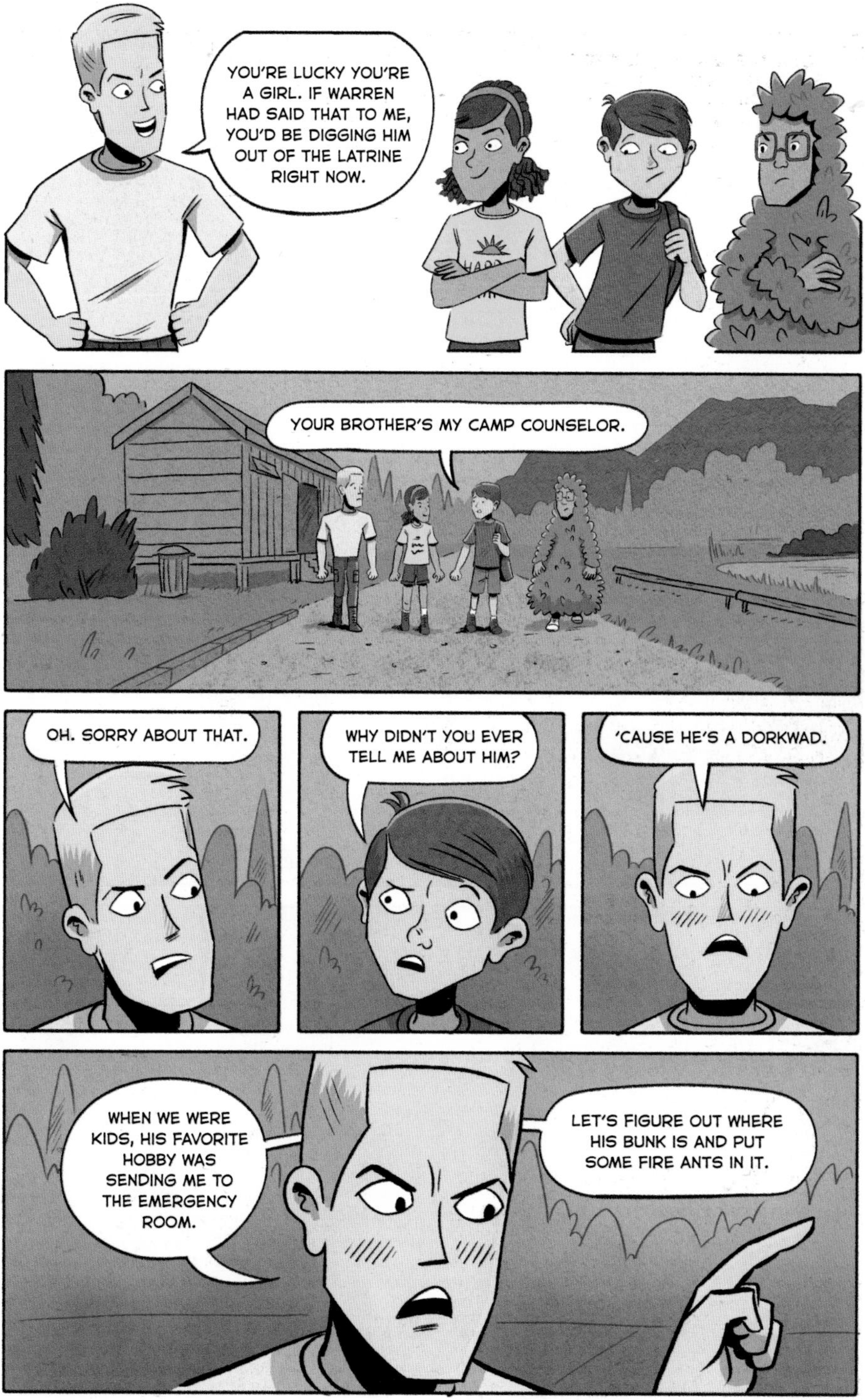
YOU'RE LUCKY YOU'RE A GIRL. IF WARREN HAD SAID THAT TO ME, YOU'D BE DIGGING HIM OUT OF THE LATRINE RIGHT NOW.
YOUR BROTHER'S MY CAMP COUNSELOR.
OH. SORRY ABOUT THAT.
WHY DIDN'T YOU EVER TELL ME ABOUT HIM?
'CAUSE HE'S A DORKWAD.
WHEN WE WERE KIDS, HIS FAVORITE HOBBY WAS SENDING ME TO THE EMERGENCY ROOM.
LET'S FIGURE OUT WHERE HIS BUNK IS AND PUT SOME FIRE ANTS IN IT.

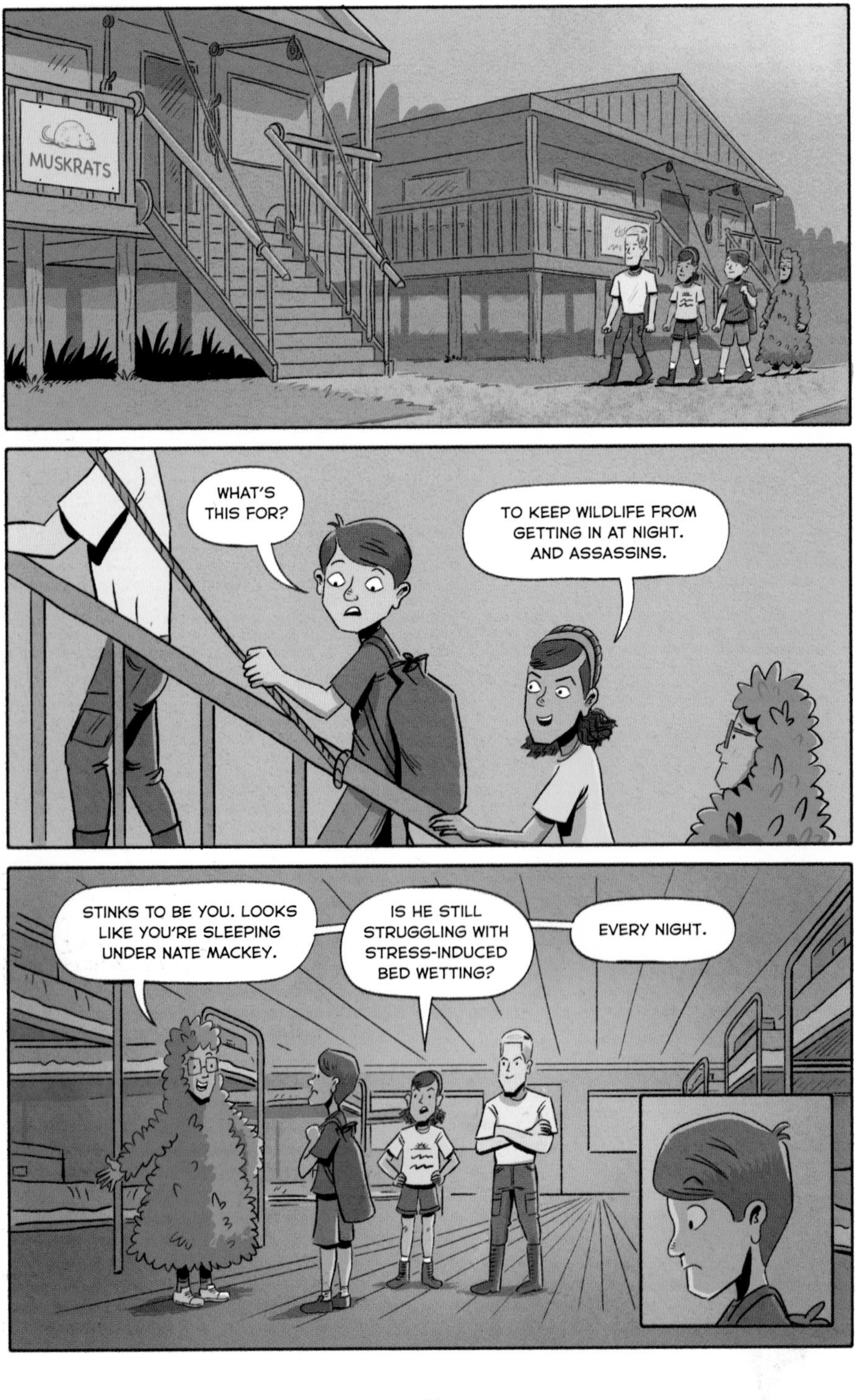
MUSKRATS
WHAT'S THIS FOR?
TO KEEP WILDLIFE FROM GETTING IN AT NIGHT. AND ASSASSINS.
STINKS TO BE YOU. LOOKS LIKE YOU'RE SLEEPING UNDER NATE MACKEY.
IS HE STILL STRUGGLING WITH STRESS-INDUCED BED WETTING?
EVERY NIGHT.

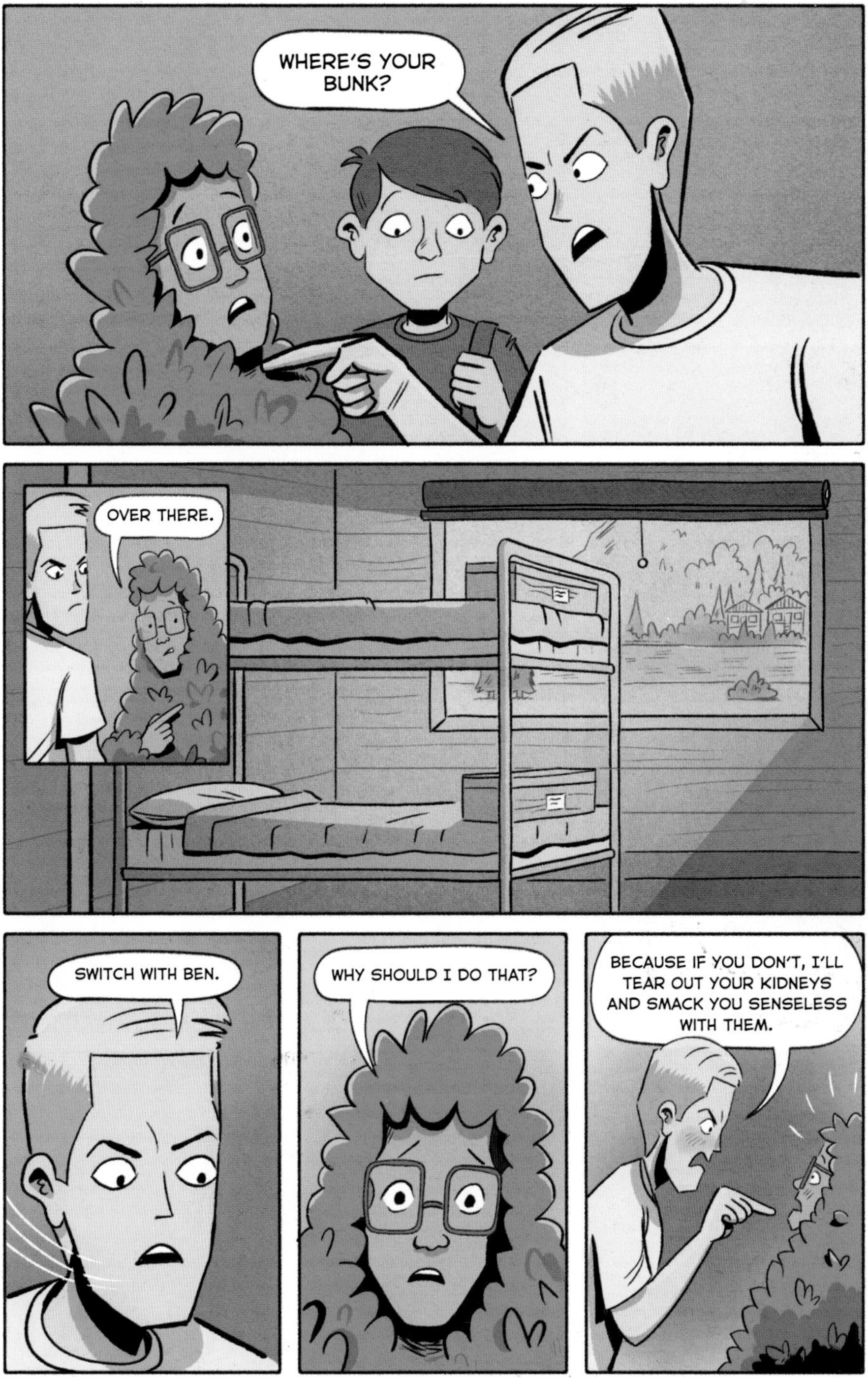
WHERE'S YOUR BUNK?
OVER THERE.
SWITCH WITH BEN.
WHY SHOULD I DO THAT?
BECAUSE IF YOU DON'T, I'LL TEAR OUT YOUR KIDNEYS AND SMACK YOU SENSELESS WITH THEM.

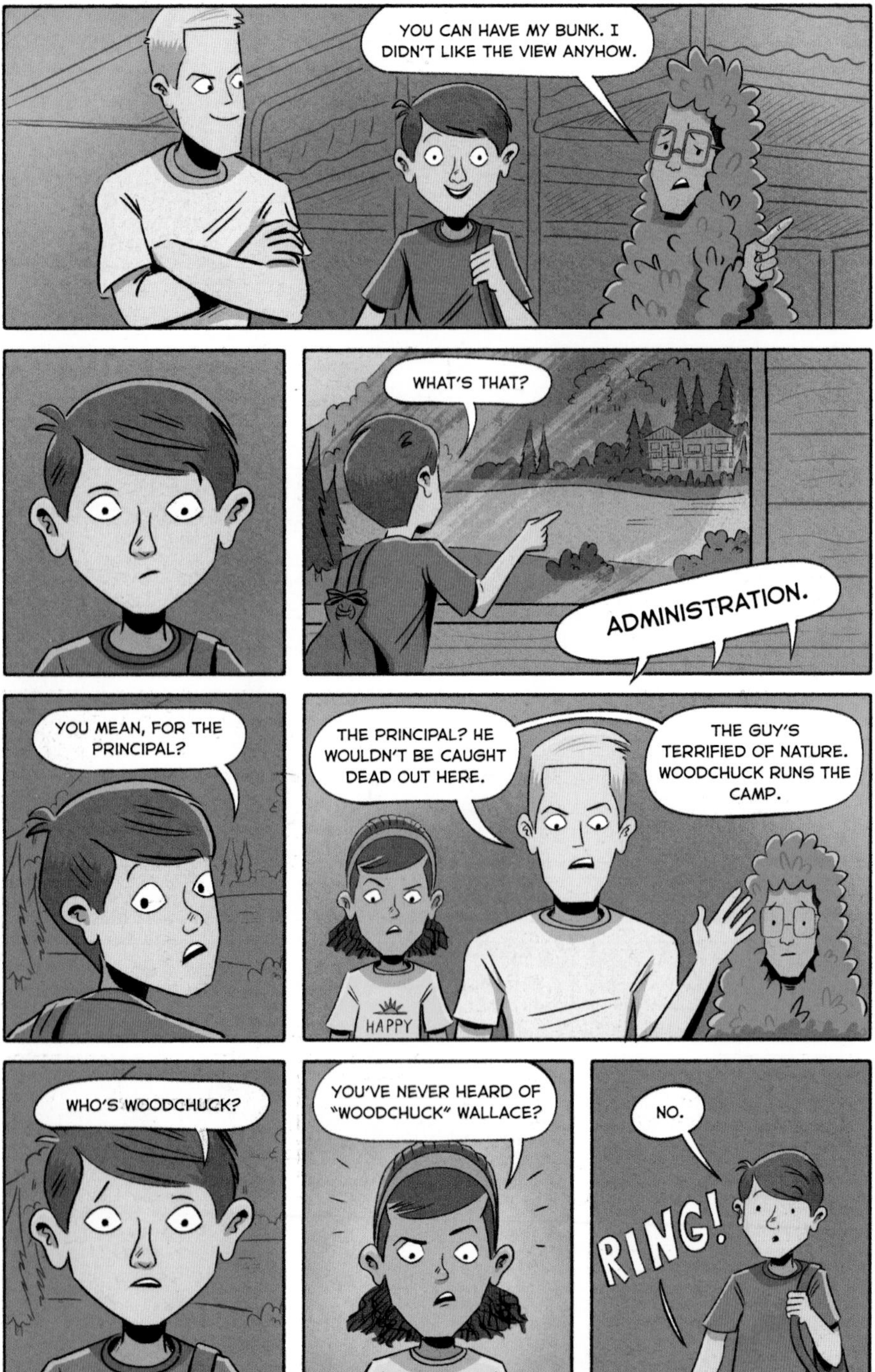

YOU CAN HAVE MY BUNK. I DIDN'T LIKE THE VIEW ANYHOW.
WHAT'S THAT?
ADMINISTRATION.
YOU MEAN, FOR THE PRINCIPAL?
THE PRINCIPAL? HE WOULDN'T BE CAUGHT DEAD OUT HERE.
THE GUY'S TERRIFIED OF NATURE. WOODCHUCK RUNS THE CAMP.
HAPPY
WHO'S WOODCHUCK?
YOU'VE NEVER HEARD OF "WOODCHUCK" WALLACE?
NO.
RING!

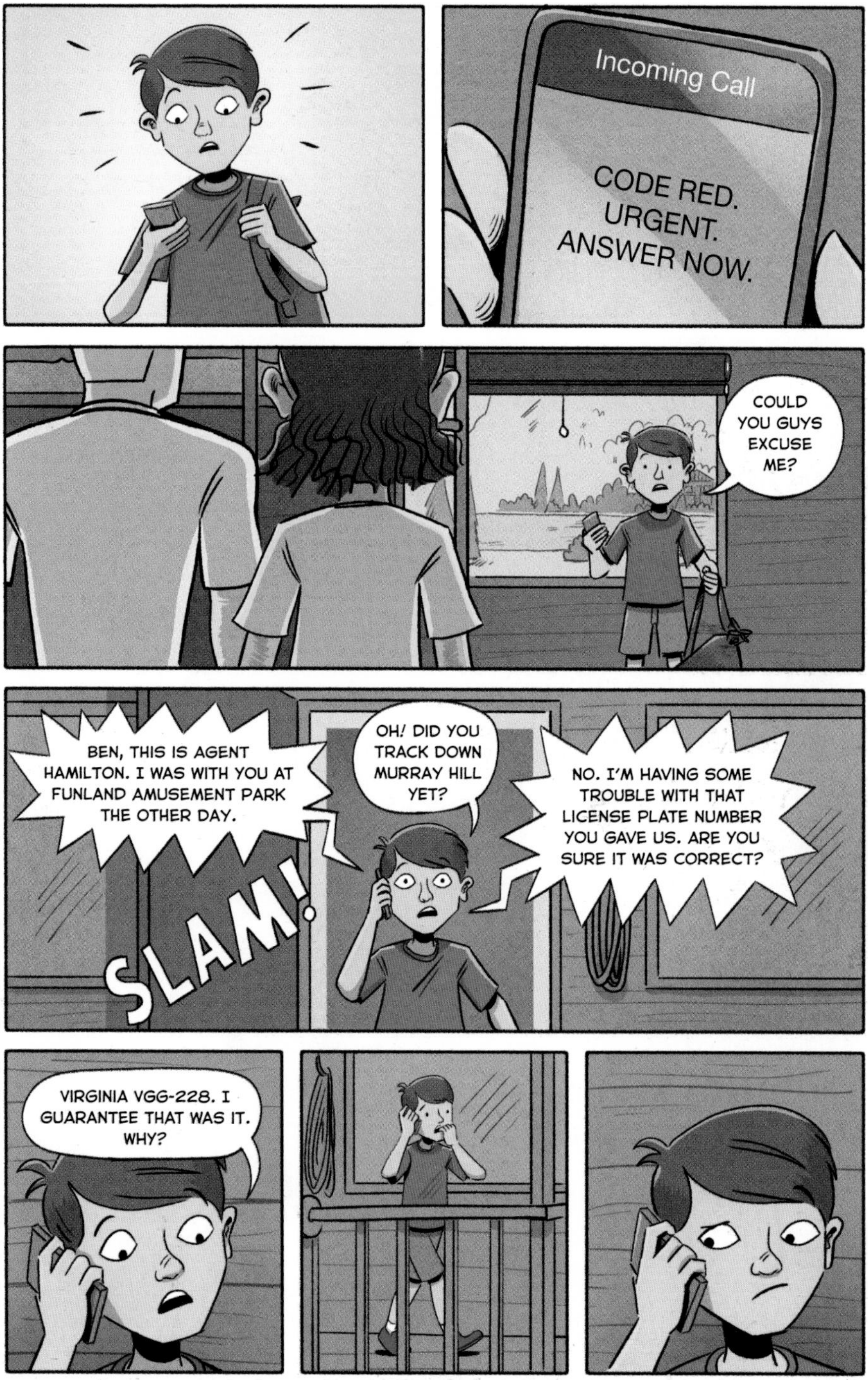
Incoming Call
CODE RED. URGENT. ANSWER NOW.
COULD YOU GUYS EXCUSE ME?
BEN, THIS IS AGENT HAMILTON. I WAS WITH YOU AT FUNLAND AMUSEMENT PARK THE OTHER DAY.
SLAM!
OH! DID YOU TRACK DOWN MURRAY HILL YET?
NO. I'M HAVING SOME TROUBLE WITH THAT LICENSE PLATE NUMBER YOU GAVE US. ARE YOU SURE IT WAS CORRECT?
VIRGINIA VGG-228. I GUARANTEE THAT WAS IT. WHY?

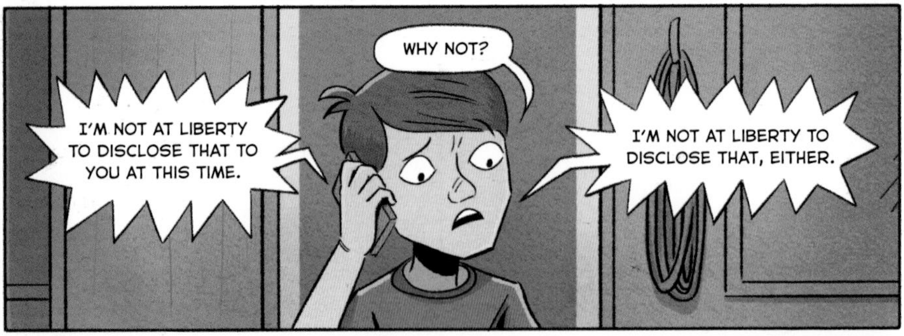
WHY NOT?
I'M NOT AT LIBERTY TO DISCLOSE THAT TO YOU AT THIS TIME.
I'M NOT AT LIBERTY TO DISCLOSE THAT, EITHER.

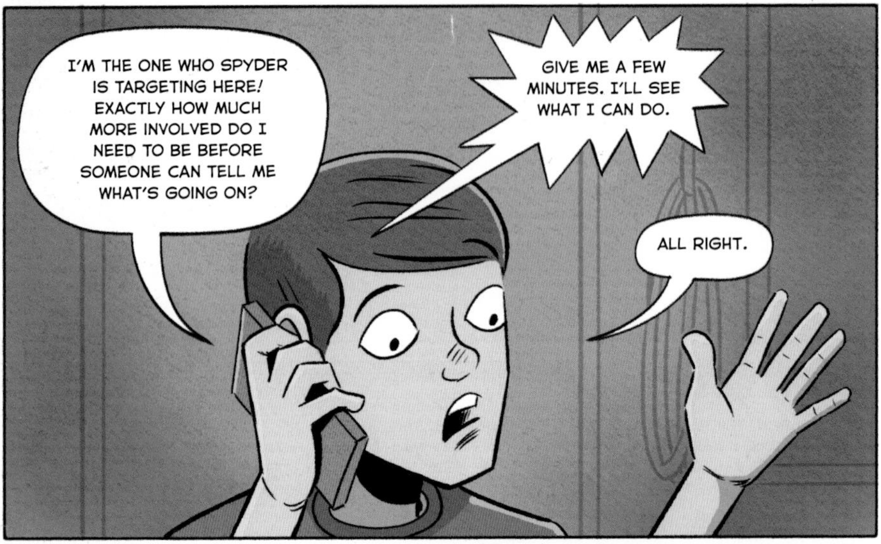
I'M THE ONE WHO SPYDER IS TARGETING HERE! EXACTLY HOW MUCH MORE INVOLVED DO I NEED TO BE BEFORE SOMEONE CAN TELL ME WHAT'S GOING ON?
GIVE ME A FEW MINUTES. I'LL SEE WHAT I CAN DO.
ALL RIGHT.

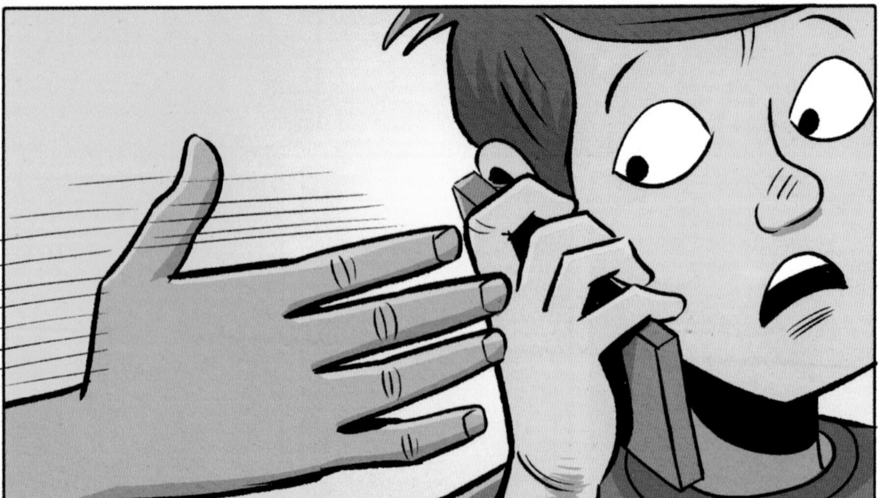

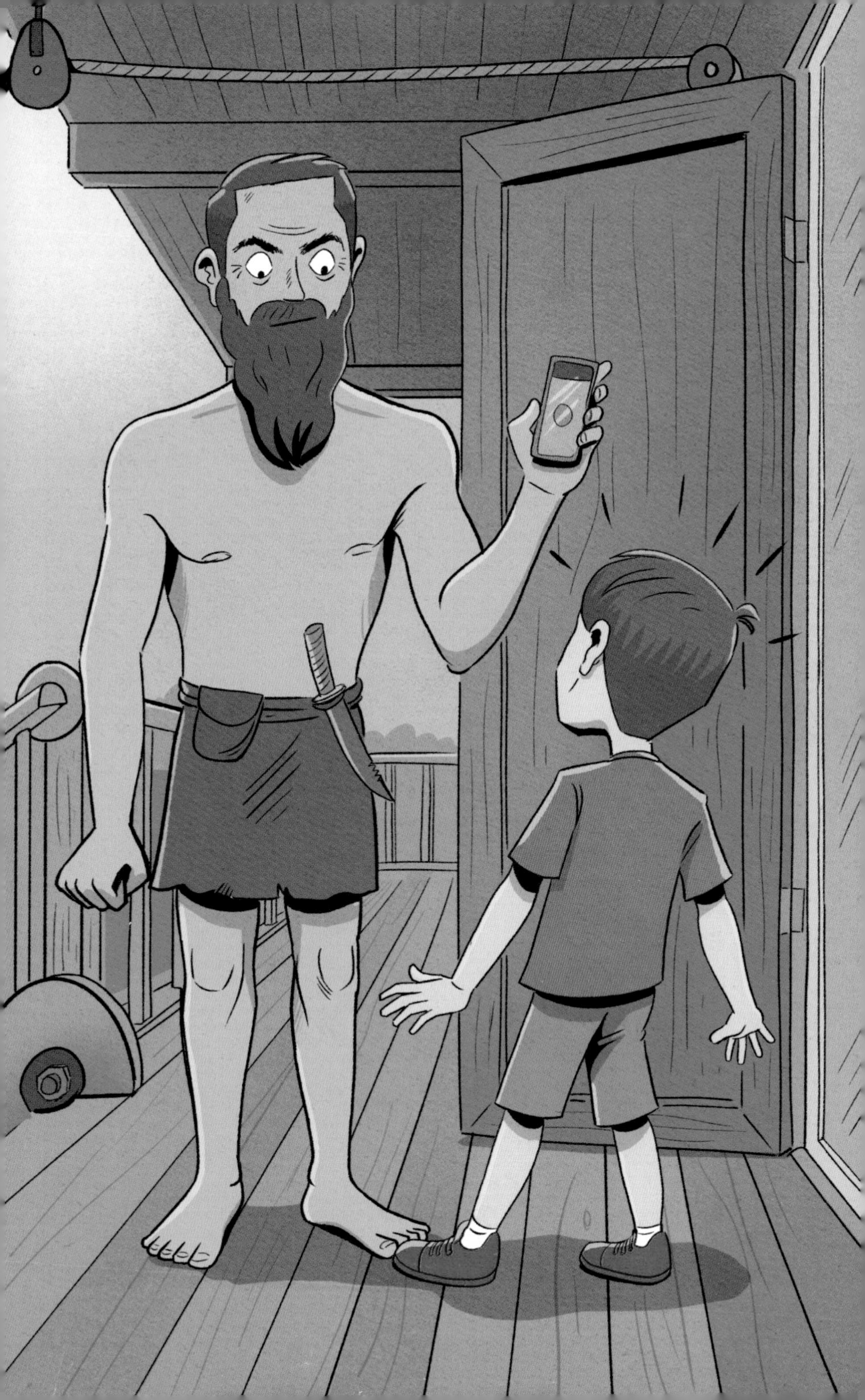

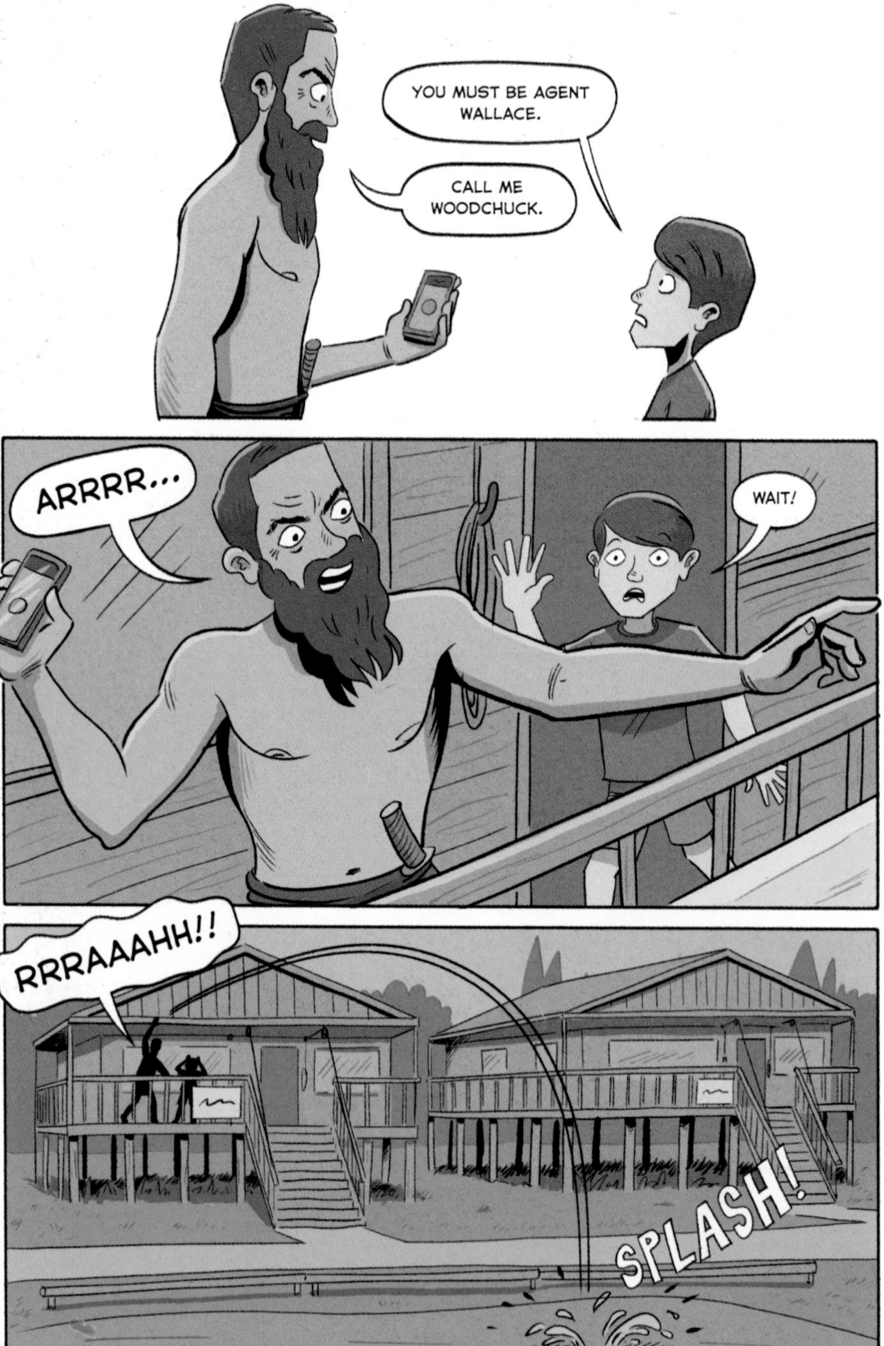
YOU MUST BE AGENT WALLACE.
CALL ME WOODCHUCK.
ARRRR...
WAIT!
RRRAAAHH!!
SPLASH!

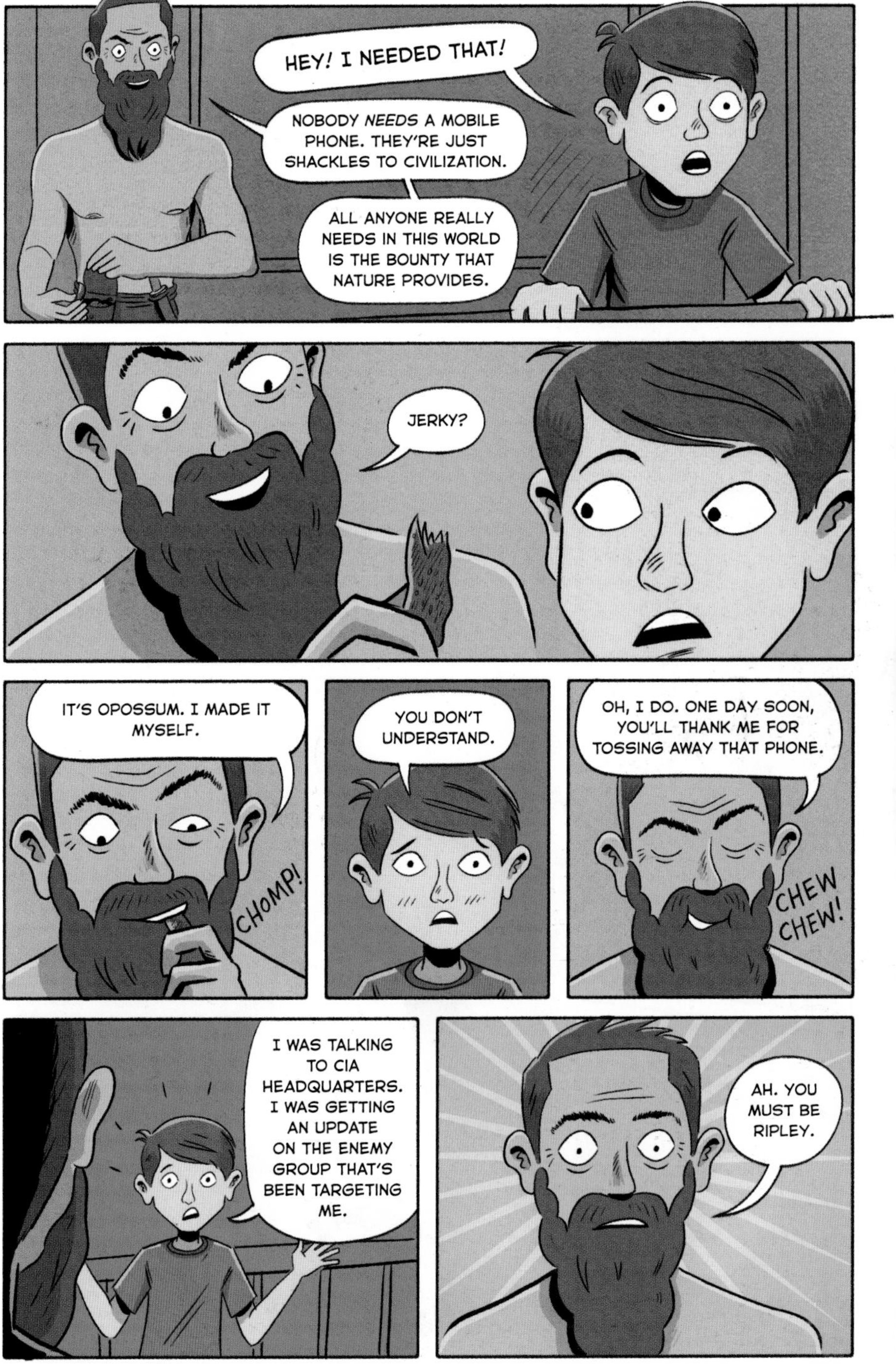
HEY! I NEEDED THAT!
NOBODY *NEEDS* A MOBILE PHONE. THEY'RE JUST SHACKLES TO CIVILIZATION.
ALL ANYONE REALLY NEEDS IN THIS WORLD IS THE BOUNTY THAT NATURE PROVIDES.
JERKY?
IT'S OPOSSUM. I MADE IT MYSELF.
CHOMP!
YOU DON'T UNDERSTAND.
OH, I DO. ONE DAY SOON, YOU'LL THANK ME FOR TOSSING AWAY THAT PHONE.
CHEW CHEW!
I WAS TALKING TO CIA HEADQUARTERS. I WAS GETTING AN UPDATE ON THE ENEMY GROUP THAT'S BEEN TARGETING ME.
AH. YOU MUST BE RIPLEY.

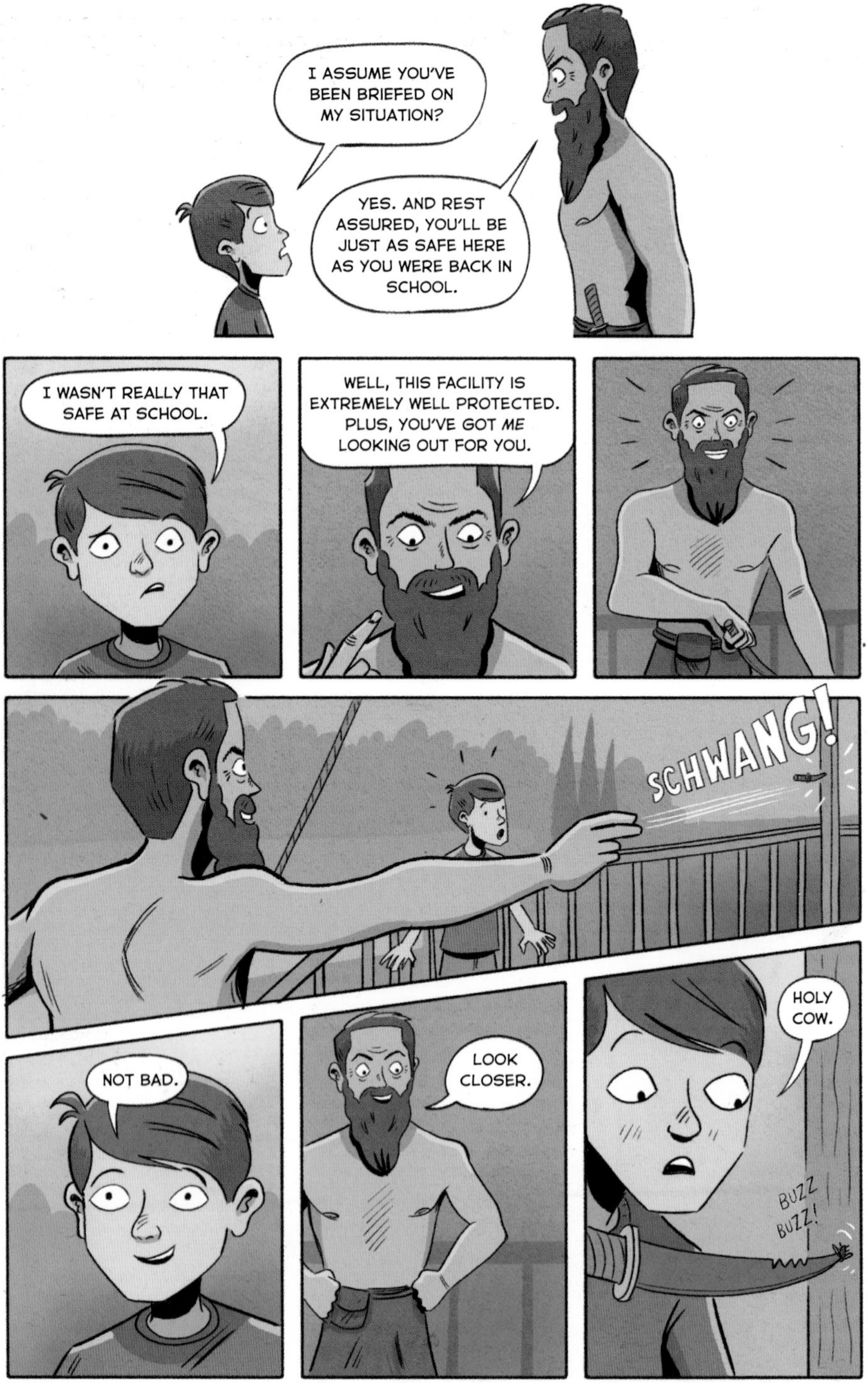
I ASSUME YOU'VE BEEN BRIEFED ON MY SITUATION?
YES. AND REST ASSURED, YOU'LL BE JUST AS SAFE HERE AS YOU WERE BACK IN SCHOOL.
I WASN'T REALLY THAT SAFE AT SCHOOL.
WELL, THIS FACILITY IS EXTREMELY WELL PROTECTED. PLUS, YOU'VE GOT *ME* LOOKING OUT FOR YOU.
SCHWANG!
NOT BAD.
LOOK CLOSER.
HOLY COW.
BUZZ BUZZ!

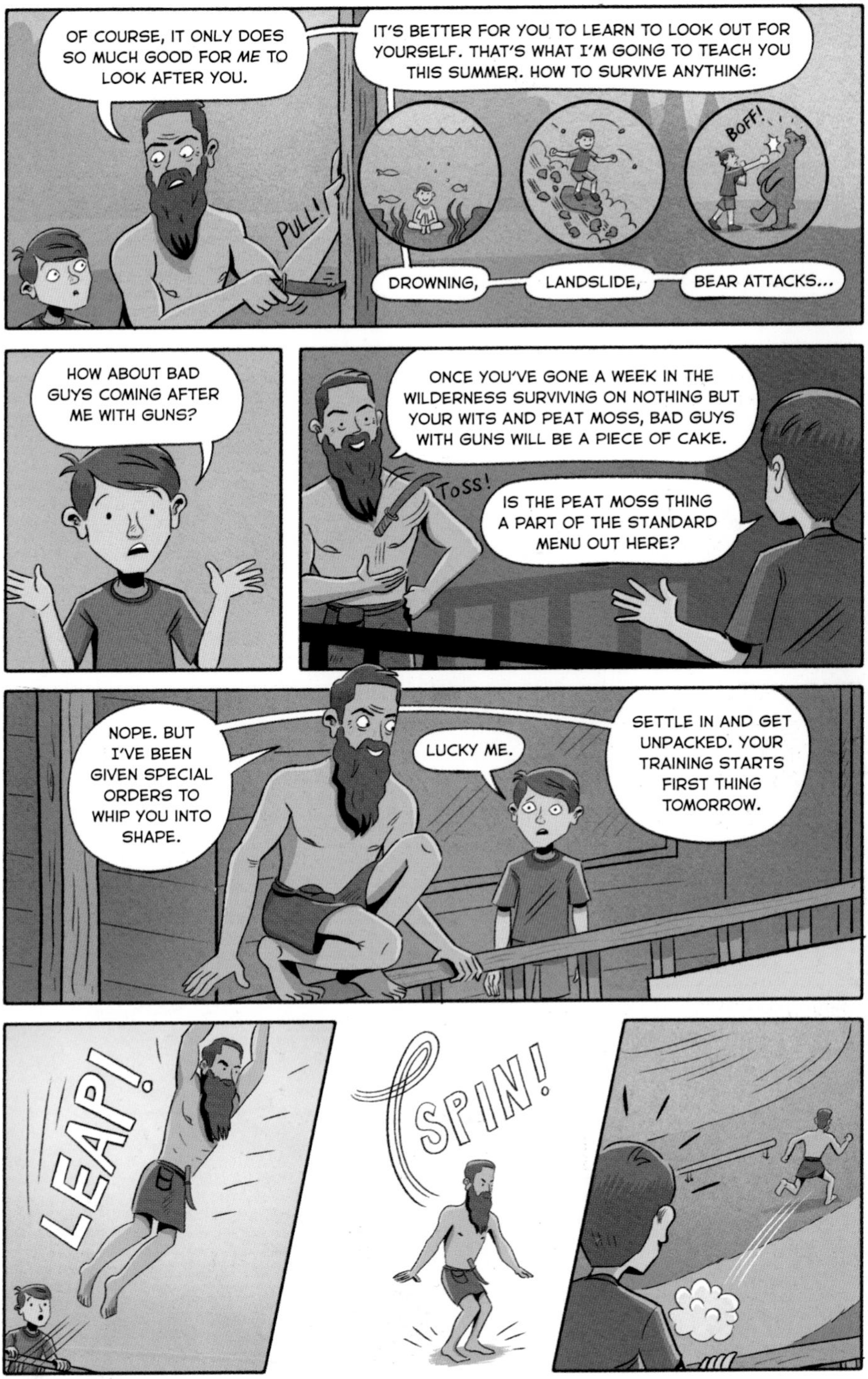
OF COURSE, IT ONLY DOES SO MUCH GOOD FOR *ME* TO LOOK AFTER YOU.
IT'S BETTER FOR YOU TO LEARN TO LOOK OUT FOR YOURSELF. THAT'S WHAT I'M GOING TO TEACH YOU THIS SUMMER. HOW TO SURVIVE ANYTHING:
PULL!
BOFF!
DROWNING,
LANDSLIDE,
BEAR ATTACKS...
HOW ABOUT BAD GUYS COMING AFTER ME WITH GUNS?
ONCE YOU'VE GONE A WEEK IN THE WILDERNESS SURVIVING ON NOTHING BUT YOUR WITS AND PEAT MOSS, BAD GUYS WITH GUNS WILL BE A PIECE OF CAKE.
TOSS!
IS THE PEAT MOSS THING A PART OF THE STANDARD MENU OUT HERE?
NOPE. BUT I'VE BEEN GIVEN SPECIAL ORDERS TO WHIP YOU INTO SHAPE.
LUCKY ME.
SETTLE IN AND GET UNPACKED. YOUR TRAINING STARTS FIRST THING TOMORROW.
LEAP!
SPIN!

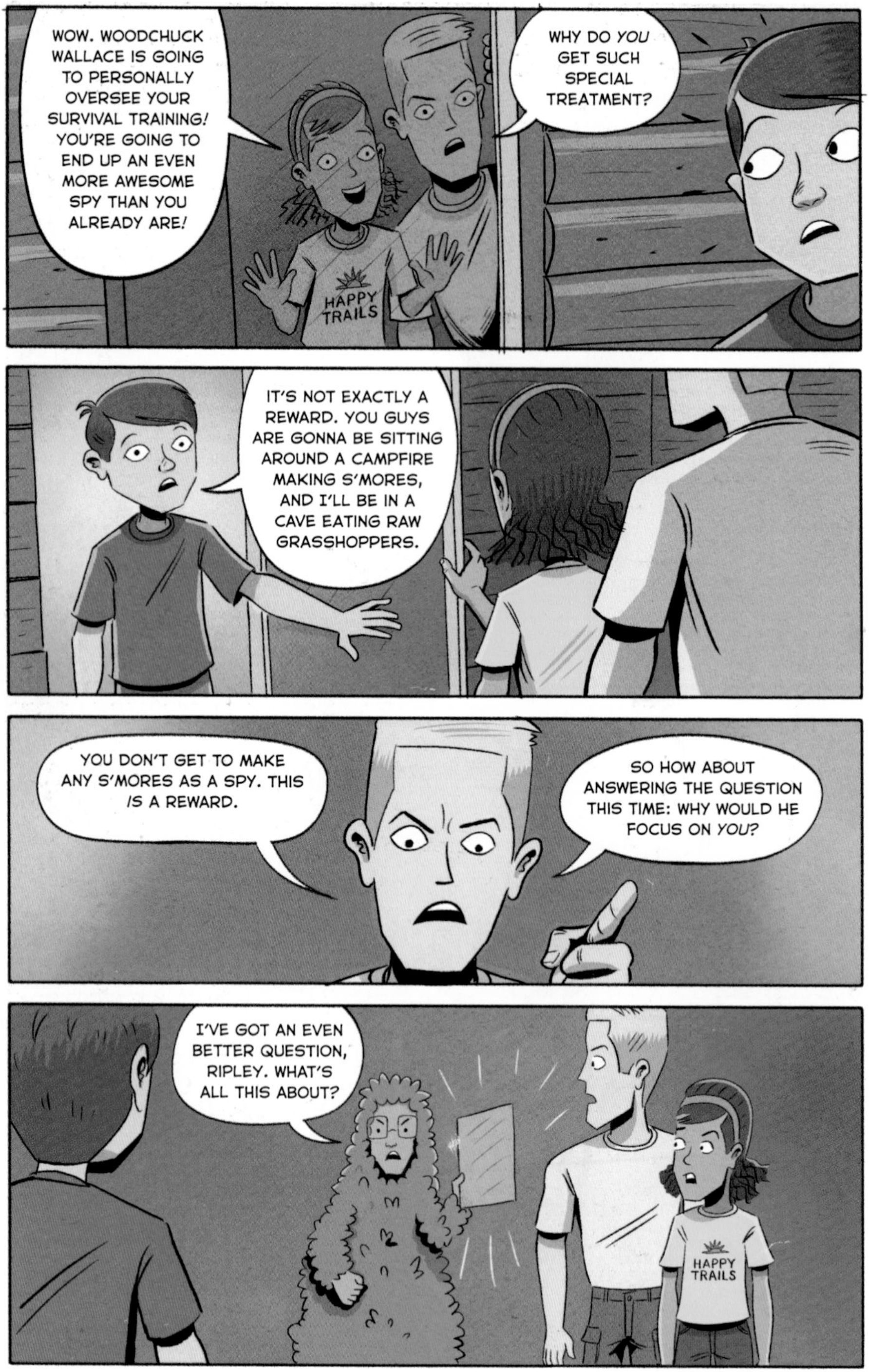
WOW. WOODCHUCK WALLACE IS GOING TO PERSONALLY OVERSEE YOUR SURVIVAL TRAINING! YOU'RE GOING TO END UP AN EVEN MORE AWESOME SPY THAN YOU ALREADY ARE!
WHY DO *YOU* GET SUCH SPECIAL TREATMENT?
HAPPY TRAILS
IT'S NOT EXACTLY A REWARD. YOU GUYS ARE GONNA BE SITTING AROUND A CAMPFIRE MAKING S'MORES, AND I'LL BE IN A CAVE EATING RAW GRASSHOPPERS.
YOU DON'T GET TO MAKE ANY S'MORES AS A SPY. THIS *IS* A REWARD.
SO HOW ABOUT ANSWERING THE QUESTION THIS TIME: WHY WOULD HE FOCUS ON *YOU*?
I'VE GOT AN EVEN BETTER QUESTION, RIPLEY. WHAT'S ALL THIS ABOUT?
HAPPY TRAILS

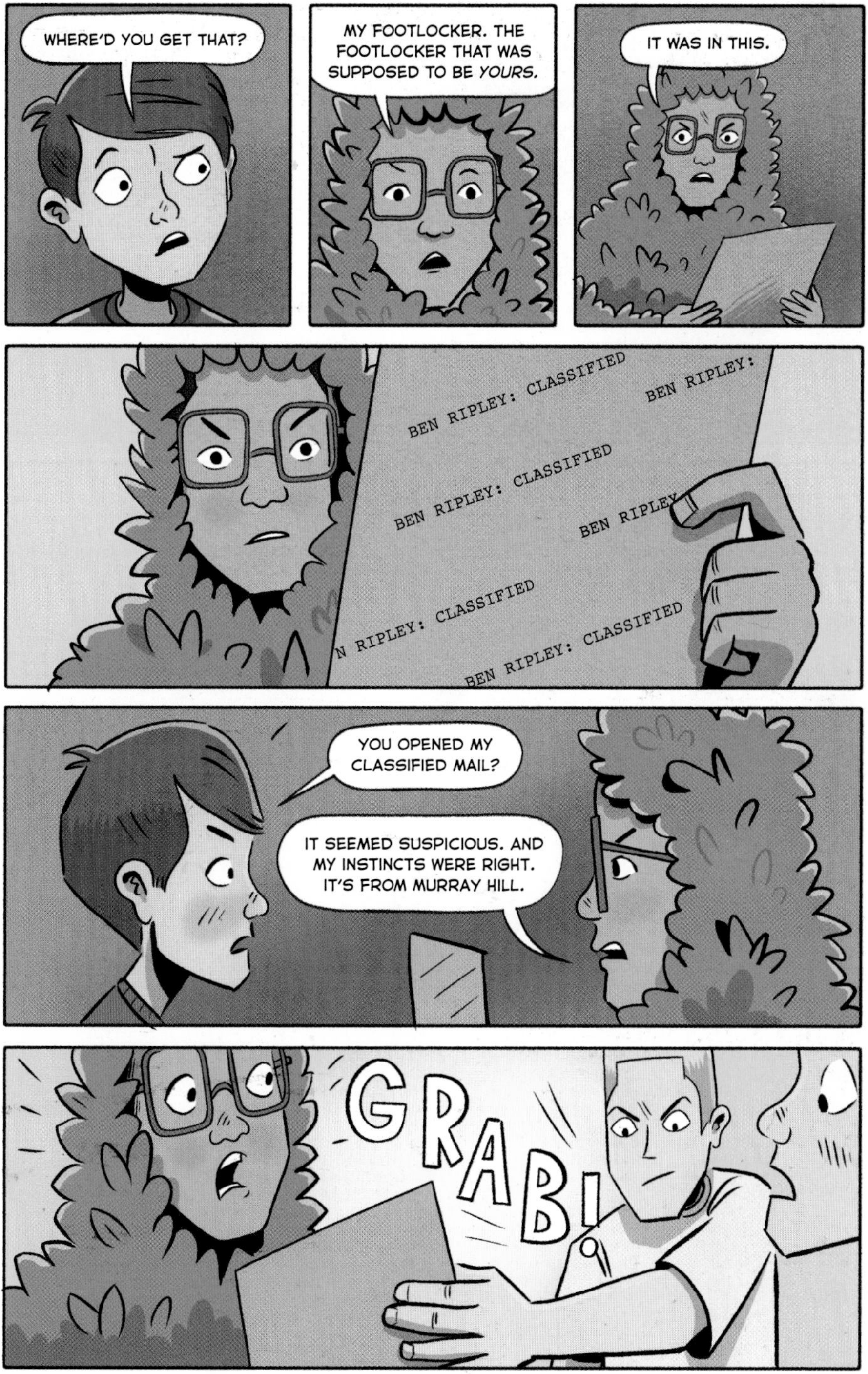
WHERE'D YOU GET THAT?
MY FOOTLOCKER. THE FOOTLOCKER THAT WAS SUPPOSED TO BE *YOURS.*
IT WAS IN THIS.
BEN RIPLEY: CLASSIFIED
BEN RIPLEY:
BEN RIPLEY: CLASSIFIED
BEN RIPLEY
N RIPLEY: CLASSIFIED
BEN RIPLEY: CLASSIFIED
YOU OPENED MY CLASSIFIED MAIL?
IT SEEMED SUSPICIOUS. AND MY INSTINCTS WERE RIGHT. IT'S FROM MURRAY HILL.
GRAB!

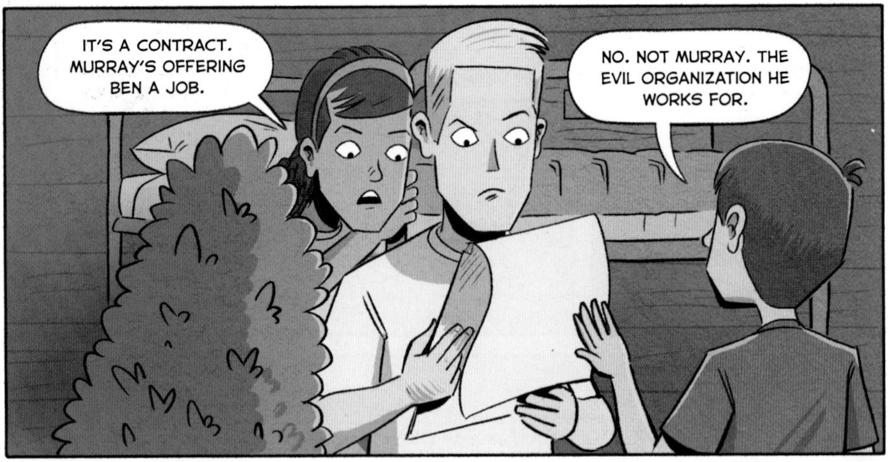
IT'S A CONTRACT. MURRAY'S OFFERING BEN A JOB.
NO. NOT MURRAY. THE EVIL ORGANIZATION HE WORKS FOR.

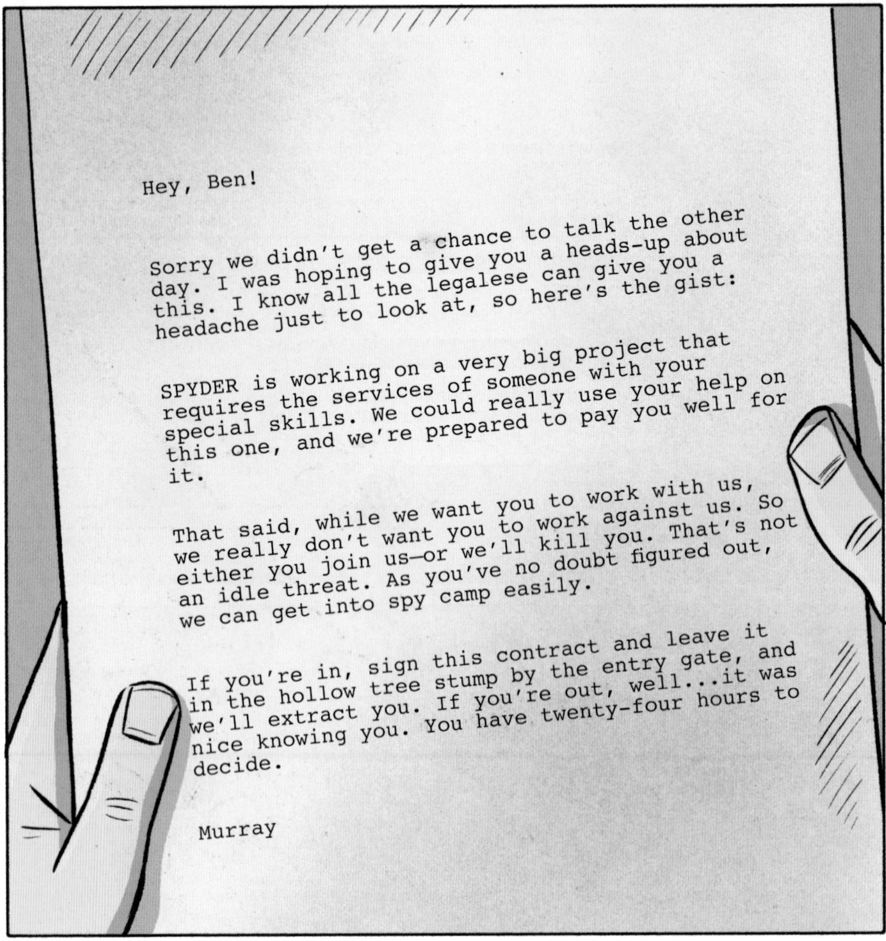
Hey, Ben!
Sorry we didn't get a chance to talk the other day. I was hoping to give you a heads-up about this. I know all the legalese can give you a headache just to look at, so here's the gist:
SPYDER is working on a very big project that requires the services of someone with your special skills. We could really use your help on this one, and we're prepared to pay you well for it.
That said, while we want you to work with us, we really don't want you to work against us. So either you join us—or we'll kill you. That's not an idle threat. As you've no doubt figured out, we can get into spy camp easily.
If you're in, sign this contract and leave it in the hollow tree stump by the entry gate, and we'll extract you. If you're out, well...it was nice knowing you. You have twenty-four hours to decide.
Murray

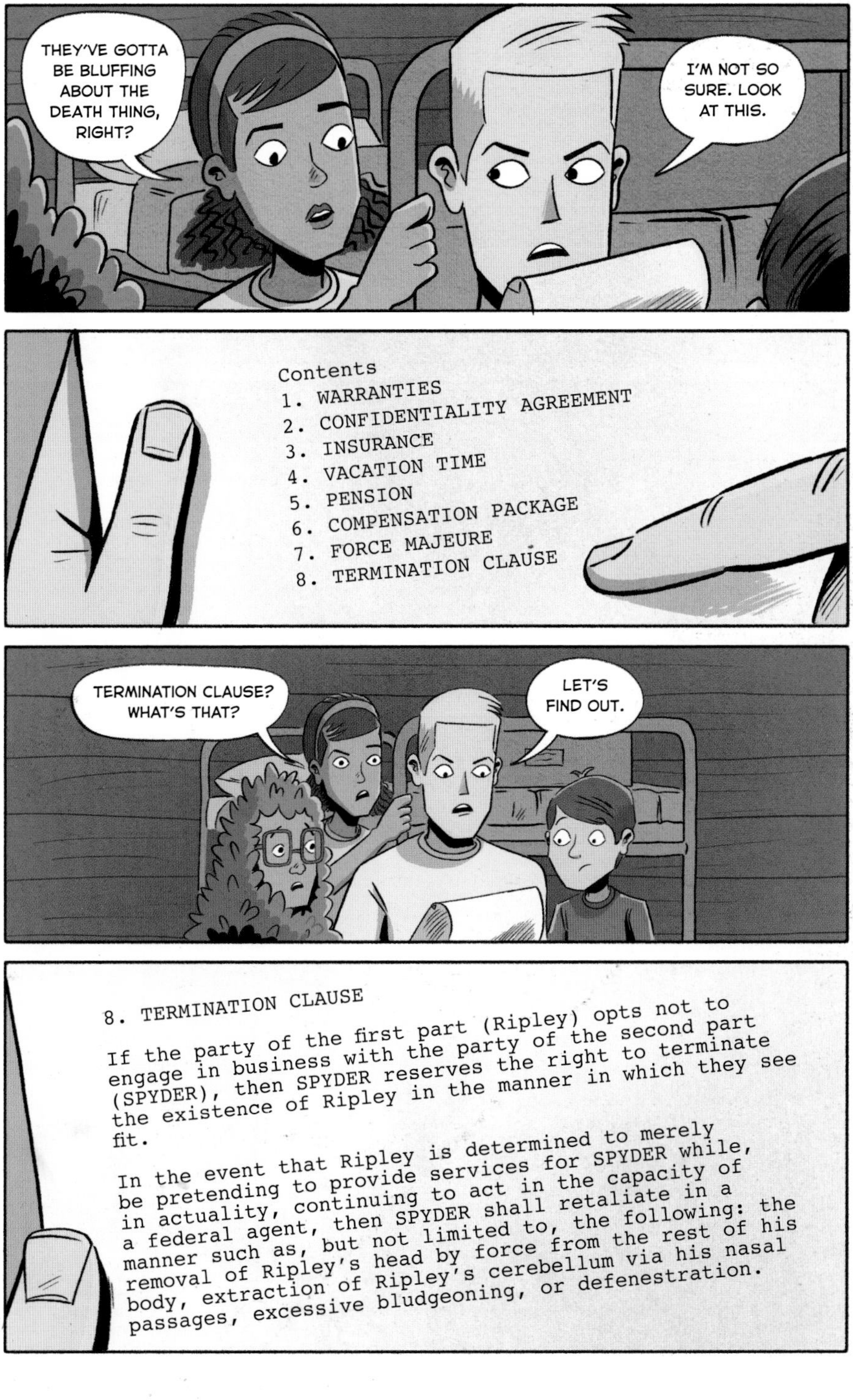
THEY'VE GOTTA BE BLUFFING ABOUT THE DEATH THING, RIGHT?
I'M NOT SO SURE. LOOK AT THIS.
Contents
1. WARRANTIES
2. CONFIDENTIALITY AGREEMENT
3. INSURANCE
4. VACATION TIME
5. PENSION
6. COMPENSATION PACKAGE
7. FORCE MAJEURE
8. TERMINATION CLAUSE
TERMINATION CLAUSE? WHAT'S THAT?
LET'S FIND OUT.
8. TERMINATION CLAUSE
If the party of the first part (Ripley) opts not to engage in business with the party of the second part (SPYDER), then SPYDER reserves the right to terminate the existence of Ripley in the manner in which they see fit.
In the event that Ripley is determined to merely be pretending to provide services for SPYDER while, in actuality, continuing to act in the capacity of a federal agent, then SPYDER shall retaliate in a manner such as, but not limited to, the following: the removal of Ripley's head by force from the rest of his body, extraction of Ripley's cerebellum via his nasal passages, excessive bludgeoning, or defenestration.

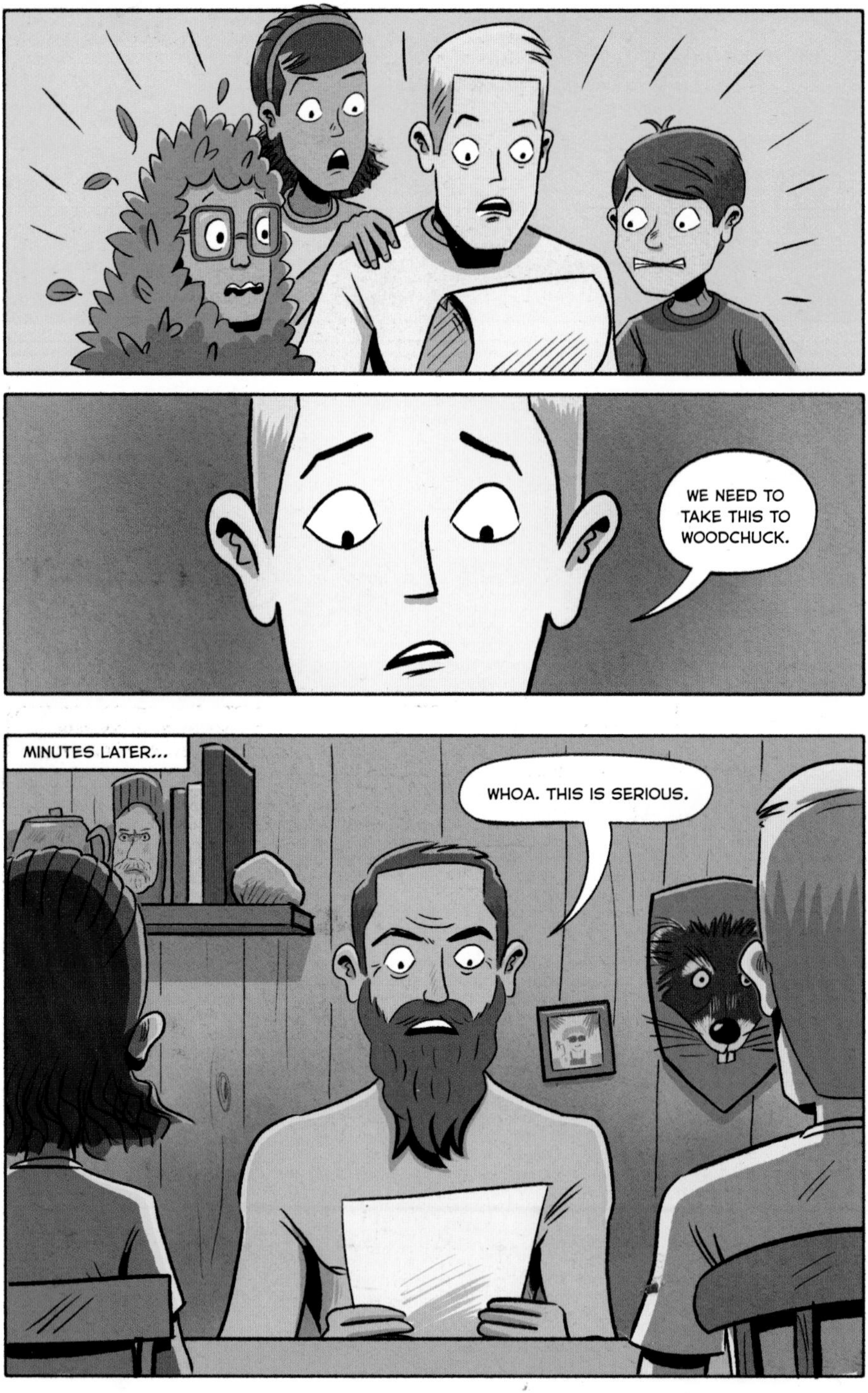
WE NEED TO TAKE THIS TO WOODCHUCK.
MINUTES LATER...
WHOA. THIS IS SERIOUS.

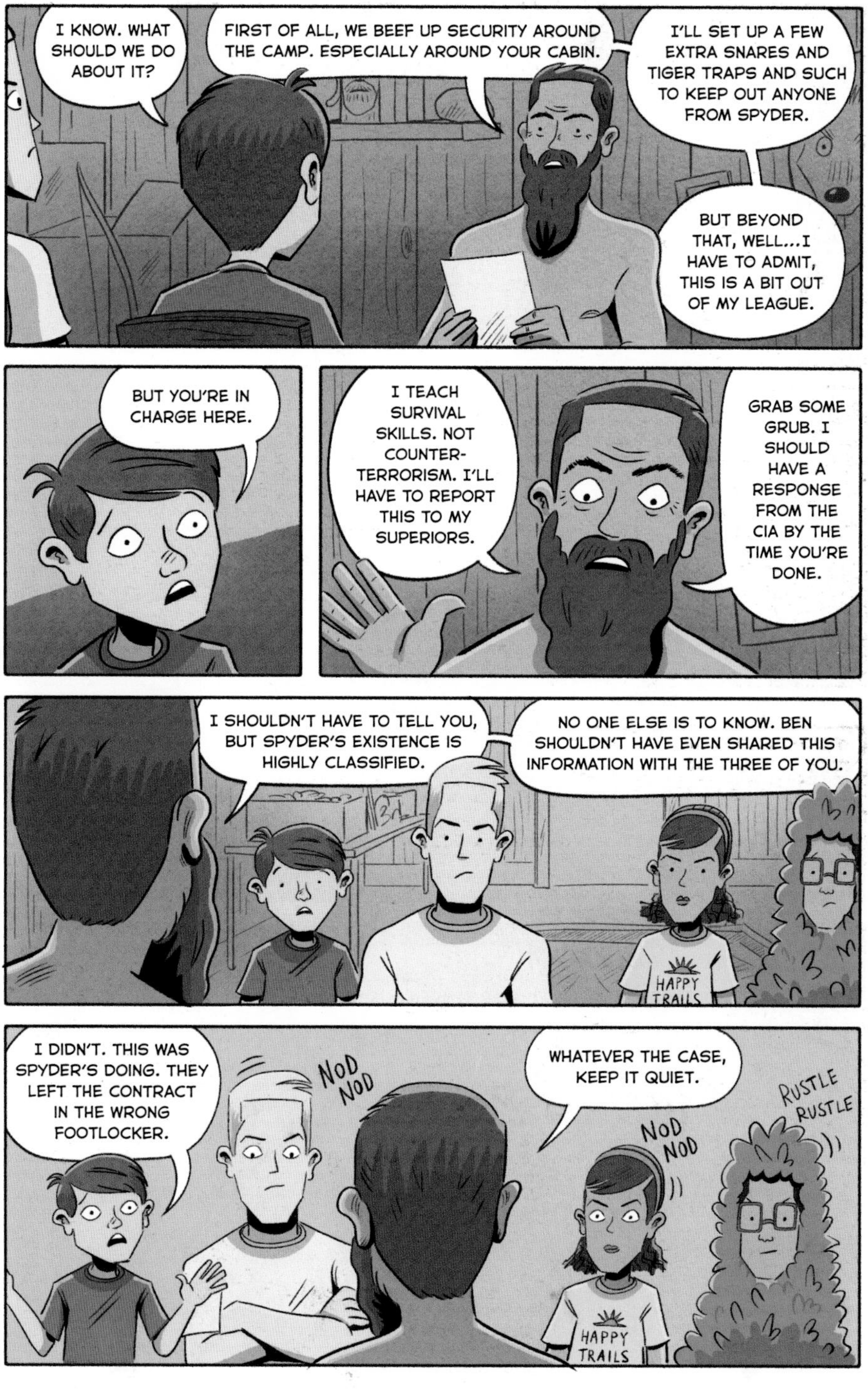
I KNOW. WHAT SHOULD WE DO ABOUT IT?
FIRST OF ALL, WE BEEF UP SECURITY AROUND THE CAMP. ESPECIALLY AROUND YOUR CABIN.
I'LL SET UP A FEW EXTRA SNARES AND TIGER TRAPS AND SUCH TO KEEP OUT ANYONE FROM SPYDER.
BUT BEYOND THAT, WELL...I HAVE TO ADMIT, THIS IS A BIT OUT OF MY LEAGUE.
BUT YOU'RE IN CHARGE HERE.
I TEACH SURVIVAL SKILLS. NOT COUNTER-TERRORISM. I'LL HAVE TO REPORT THIS TO MY SUPERIORS.
GRAB SOME GRUB. I SHOULD HAVE A RESPONSE FROM THE CIA BY THE TIME YOU'RE DONE.
I SHOULDN'T HAVE TO TELL YOU, BUT SPYDER'S EXISTENCE IS HIGHLY CLASSIFIED.
NO ONE ELSE IS TO KNOW. BEN SHOULDN'T HAVE EVEN SHARED THIS INFORMATION WITH THE THREE OF YOU.
HAPPY TRAILS
I DIDN'T. THIS WAS SPYDER'S DOING. THEY LEFT THE CONTRACT IN THE WRONG FOOTLOCKER.
NOD NOD
WHATEVER THE CASE, KEEP IT QUIET.
NOD NOD
RUSTLE RUSTLE
HAPPY TRAILS

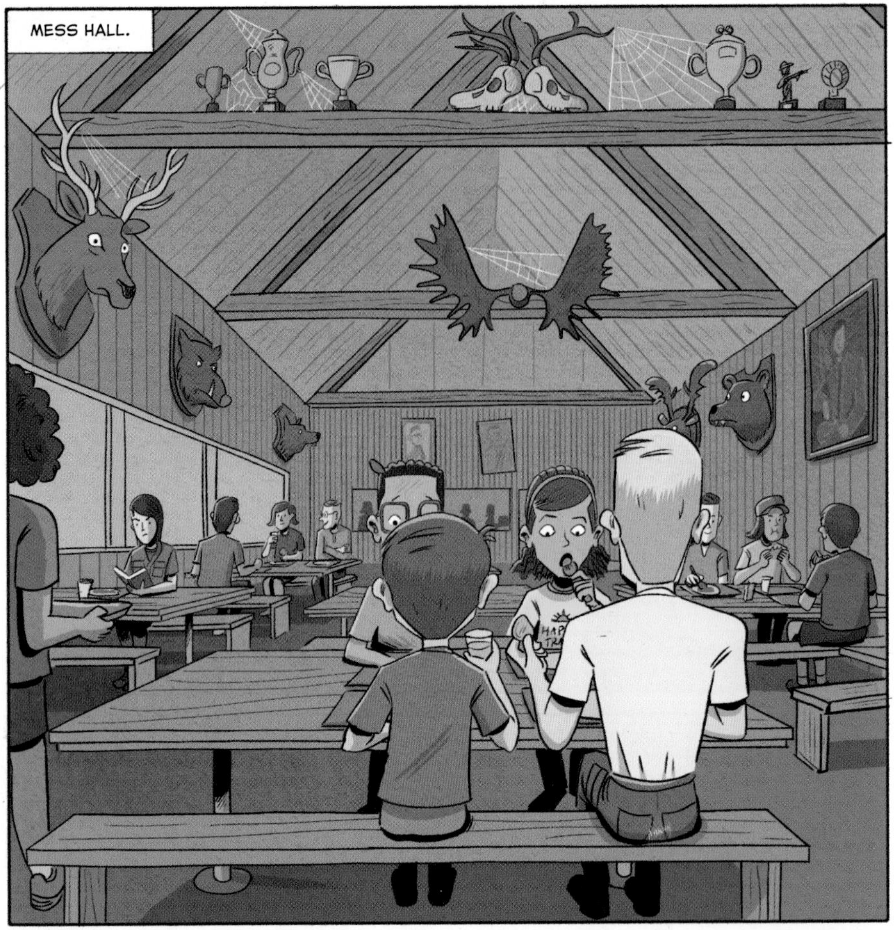
MESS HALL.
HAPPY TRAILS

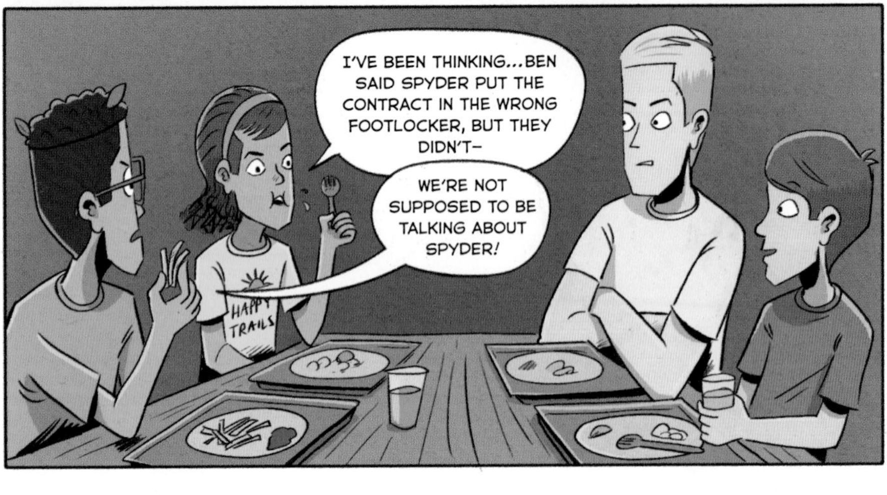
I'VE BEEN THINKING...BEN SAID SPYDER PUT THE CONTRACT IN THE WRONG FOOTLOCKER, BUT THEY DIDN'T–
WE'RE NOT SUPPOSED TO BE TALKING ABOUT SPYDER!
HAPPY TRAILS

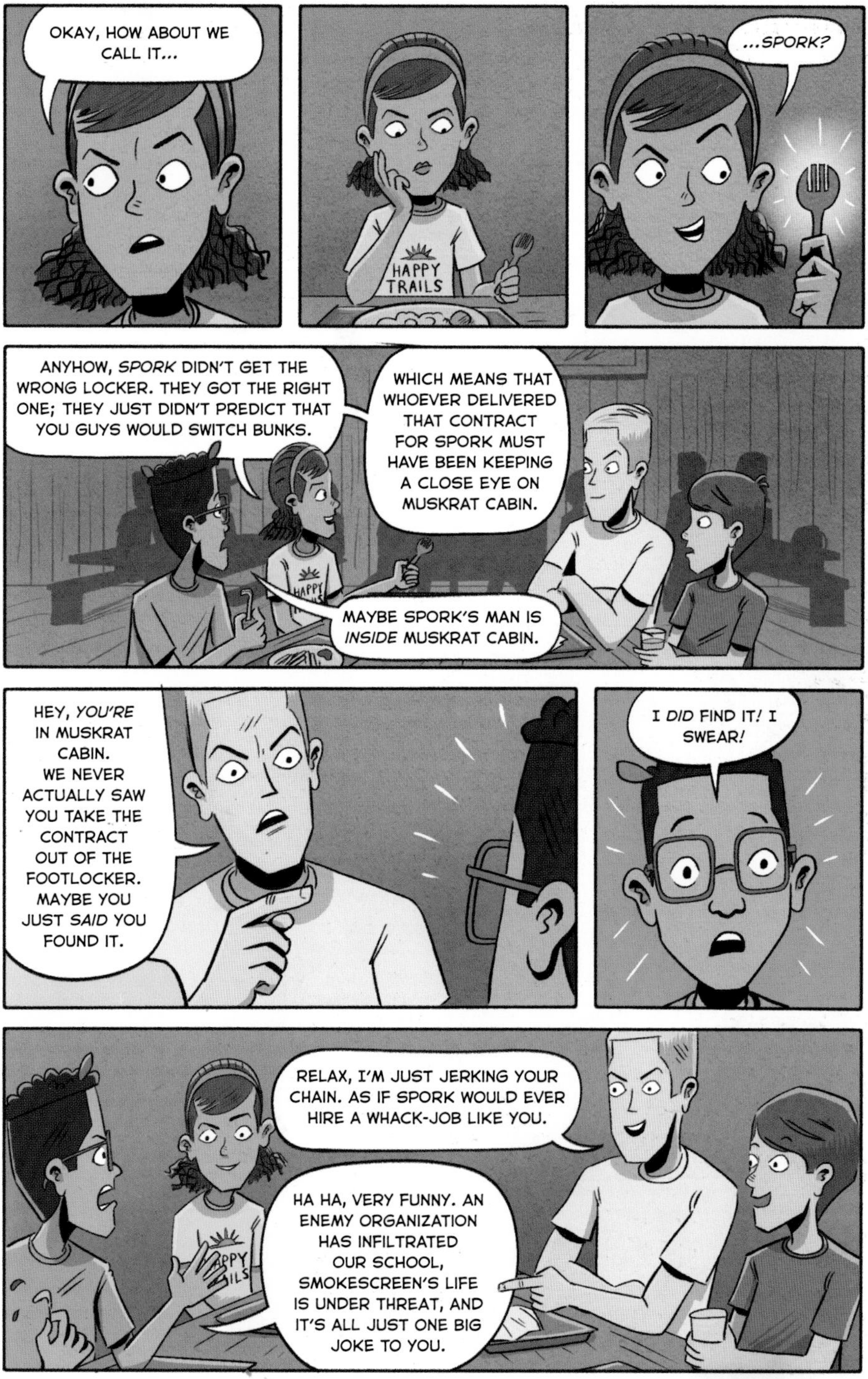
OKAY, HOW ABOUT WE CALL IT...
...SPORK?
HAPPY TRAILS
ANYHOW, *SPORK* DIDN'T GET THE WRONG LOCKER. THEY GOT THE RIGHT ONE; THEY JUST DIDN'T PREDICT THAT YOU GUYS WOULD SWITCH BUNKS.
WHICH MEANS THAT WHOEVER DELIVERED THAT CONTRACT FOR SPORK MUST HAVE BEEN KEEPING A CLOSE EYE ON MUSKRAT CABIN.
MAYBE SPORK'S MAN IS *INSIDE* MUSKRAT CABIN.
HEY, *YOU'RE* IN MUSKRAT CABIN. WE NEVER ACTUALLY SAW YOU TAKE THE CONTRACT OUT OF THE FOOTLOCKER. MAYBE YOU JUST *SAID* YOU FOUND IT.
I *DID* FIND IT! I SWEAR!
RELAX, I'M JUST JERKING YOUR CHAIN. AS IF SPORK WOULD EVER HIRE A WHACK-JOB LIKE YOU.
HA HA, VERY FUNNY. AN ENEMY ORGANIZATION HAS INFILTRATED OUR SCHOOL, SMOKESCREEN'S LIFE IS UNDER THREAT, AND IT'S ALL JUST ONE BIG JOKE TO YOU.

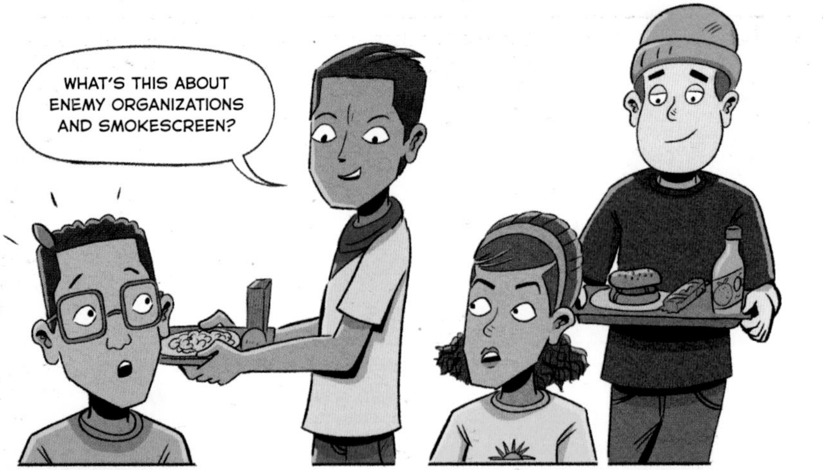
WHAT'S THIS ABOUT ENEMY ORGANIZATIONS AND SMOKESCREEN?

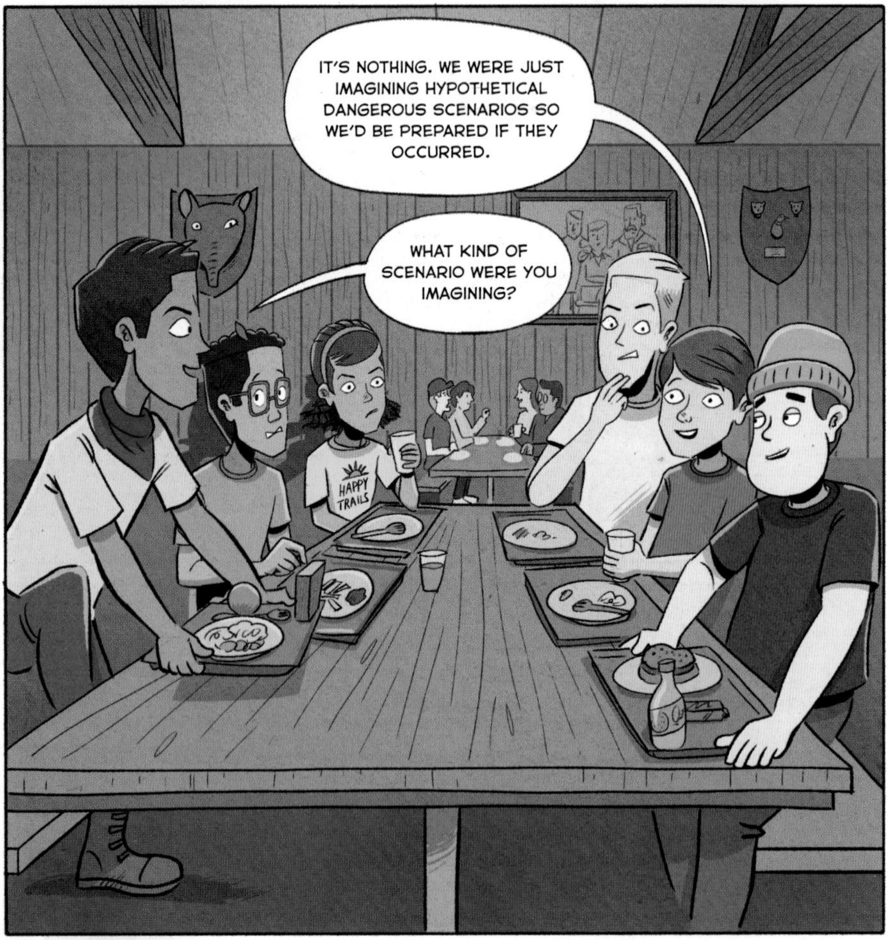
IT'S NOTHING. WE WERE JUST IMAGINING HYPOTHETICAL DANGEROUS SCENARIOS SO WE'D BE PREPARED IF THEY OCCURRED.
WHAT KIND OF SCENARIO WERE YOU IMAGINING?
HAPPY TRAILS

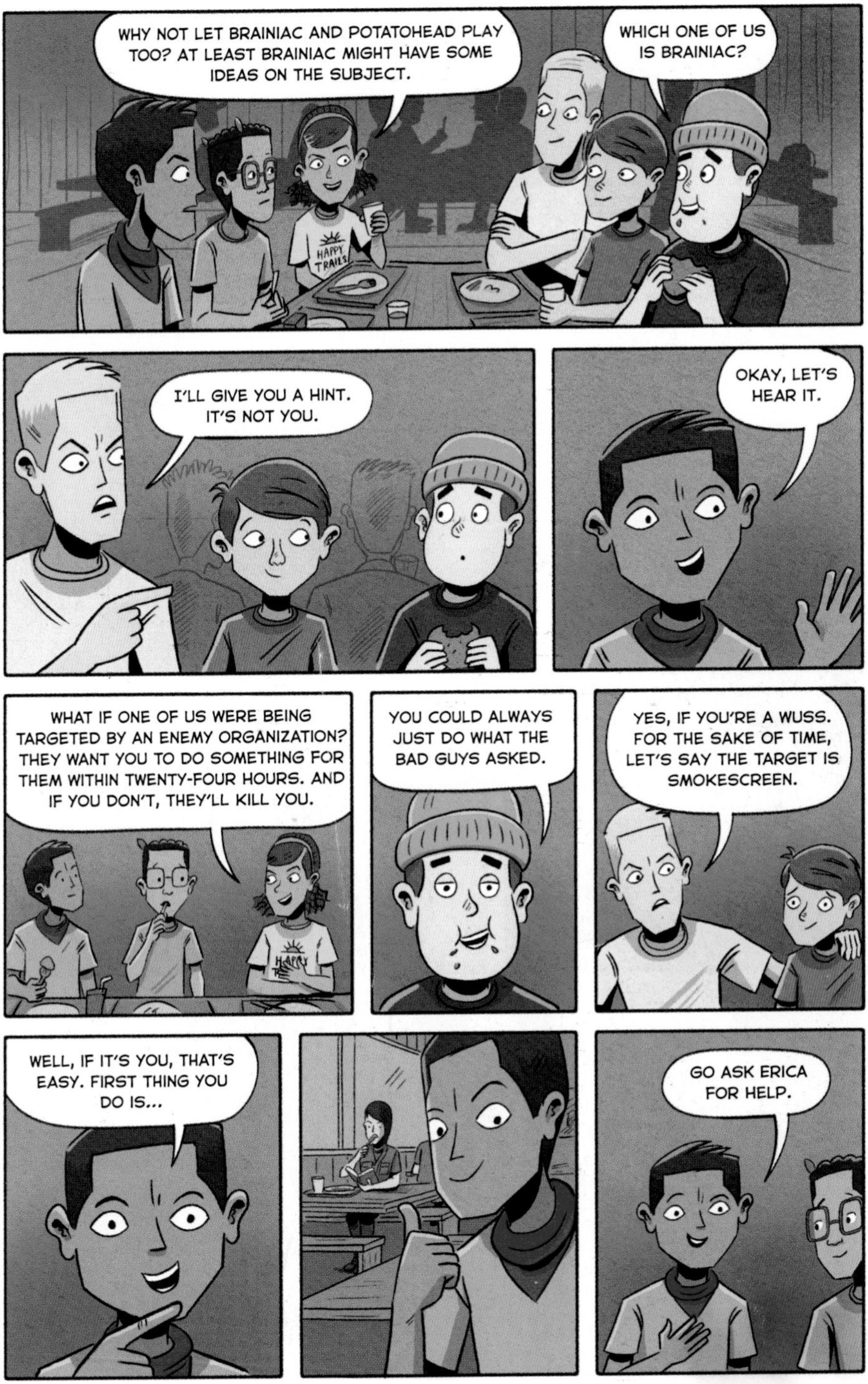
WHY NOT LET BRAINIAC AND POTATOHEAD PLAY TOO? AT LEAST BRAINIAC MIGHT HAVE SOME IDEAS ON THE SUBJECT.
WHICH ONE OF US IS BRAINIAC?
HAPPY TRAILS
I'LL GIVE YOU A HINT. IT'S NOT YOU.
OKAY, LET'S HEAR IT.
WHAT IF ONE OF US WERE BEING TARGETED BY AN ENEMY ORGANIZATION? THEY WANT YOU TO DO SOMETHING FOR THEM WITHIN TWENTY-FOUR HOURS. AND IF YOU DON'T, THEY'LL KILL YOU.
YOU COULD ALWAYS JUST DO WHAT THE BAD GUYS ASKED.
YES, IF YOU'RE A WUSS. FOR THE SAKE OF TIME, LET'S SAY THE TARGET IS SMOKESCREEN.
WELL, IF IT'S YOU, THAT'S EASY. FIRST THING YOU DO IS...
GO ASK ERICA FOR HELP.

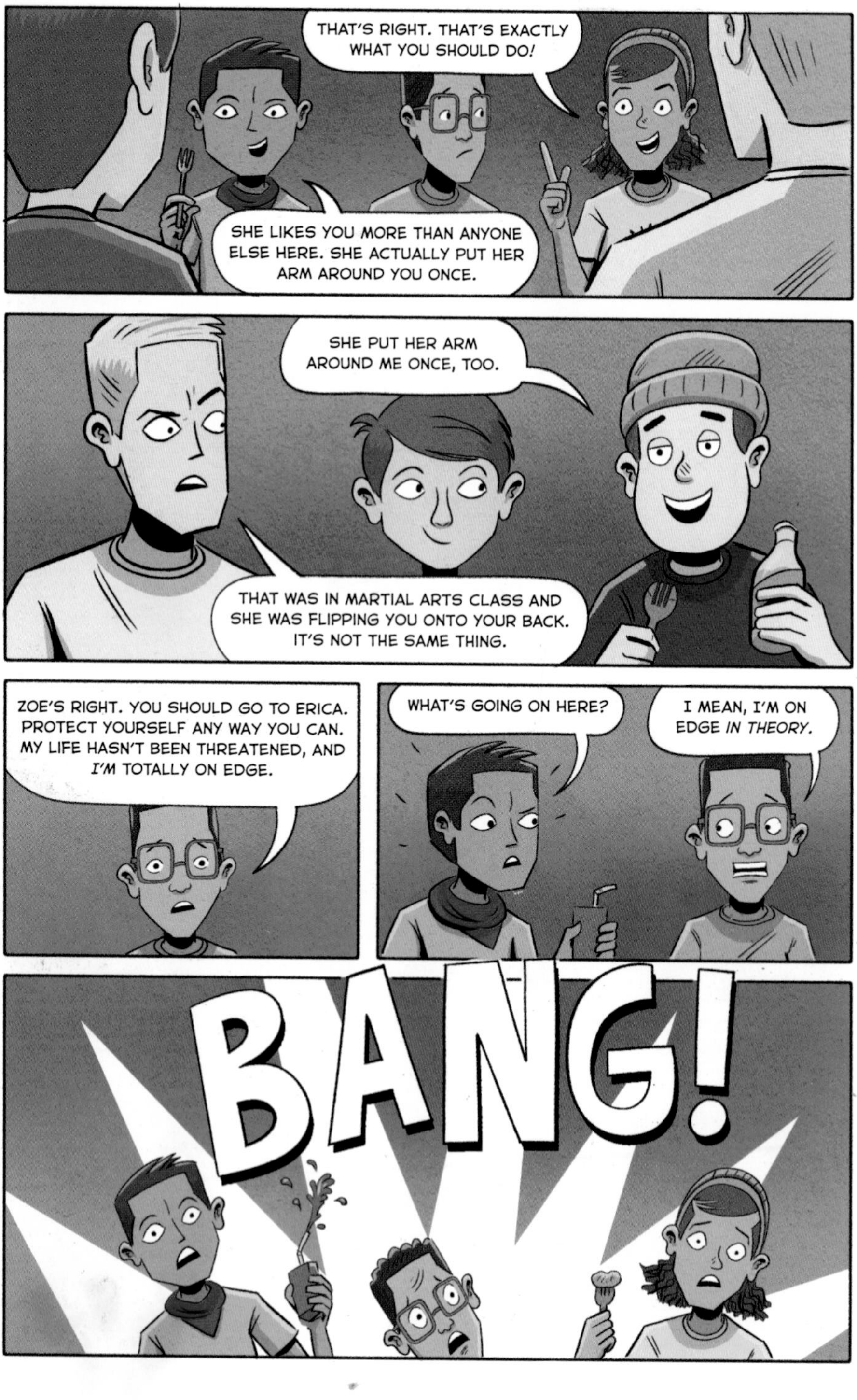
THAT'S RIGHT. THAT'S EXACTLY WHAT YOU SHOULD DO!
SHE LIKES YOU MORE THAN ANYONE ELSE HERE. SHE ACTUALLY PUT HER ARM AROUND YOU ONCE.
SHE PUT HER ARM AROUND ME ONCE, TOO.
THAT WAS IN MARTIAL ARTS CLASS AND SHE WAS FLIPPING YOU ONTO YOUR BACK. IT'S NOT THE SAME THING.
ZOE'S RIGHT. YOU SHOULD GO TO ERICA. PROTECT YOURSELF ANY WAY YOU CAN. MY LIFE HASN'T BEEN THREATENED, AND *I'M* TOTALLY ON EDGE.
WHAT'S GOING ON HERE?
I MEAN, I'M ON EDGE *IN THEORY.*
BANG!

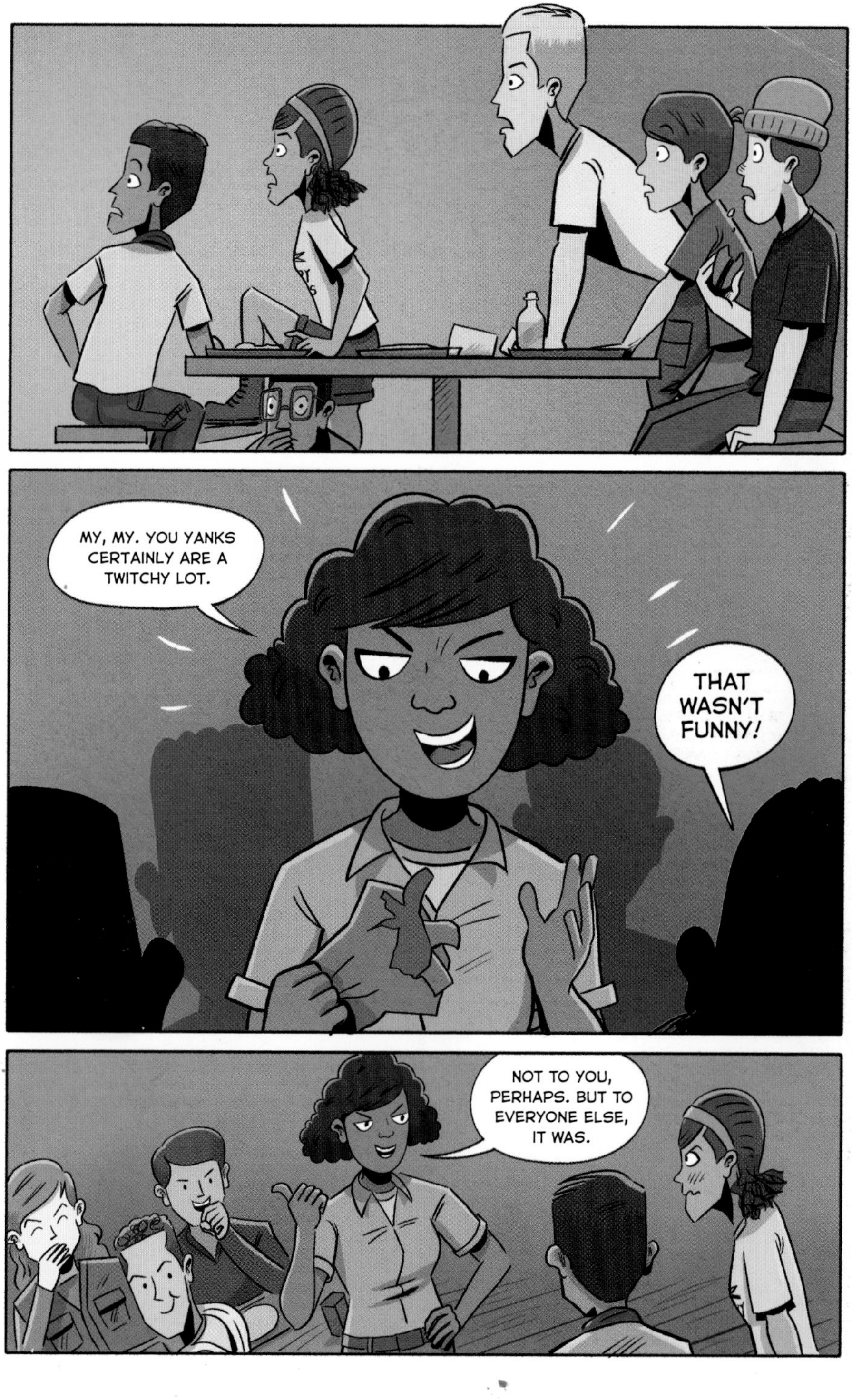
MY, MY. YOU YANKS CERTAINLY ARE A TWITCHY LOT.
THAT WASN'T FUNNY!
NOT TO YOU, PERHAPS. BUT TO EVERYONE ELSE, IT WAS.

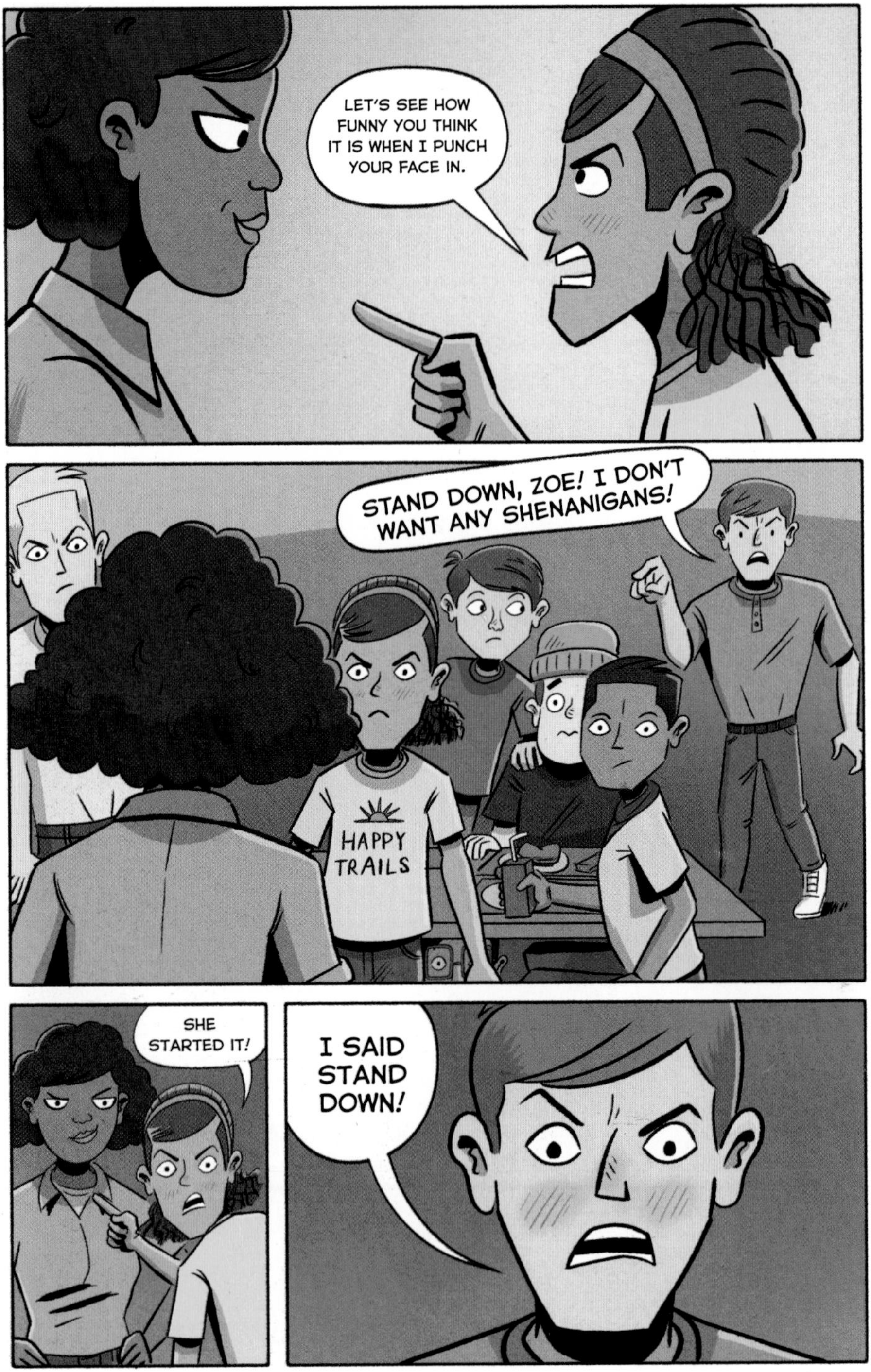
LET'S SEE HOW FUNNY YOU THINK IT IS WHEN I PUNCH YOUR FACE IN.
STAND DOWN, ZOE! I DON'T WANT ANY SHENANIGANS!
HAPPY TRAILS
SHE STARTED IT!
I SAID STAND DOWN!

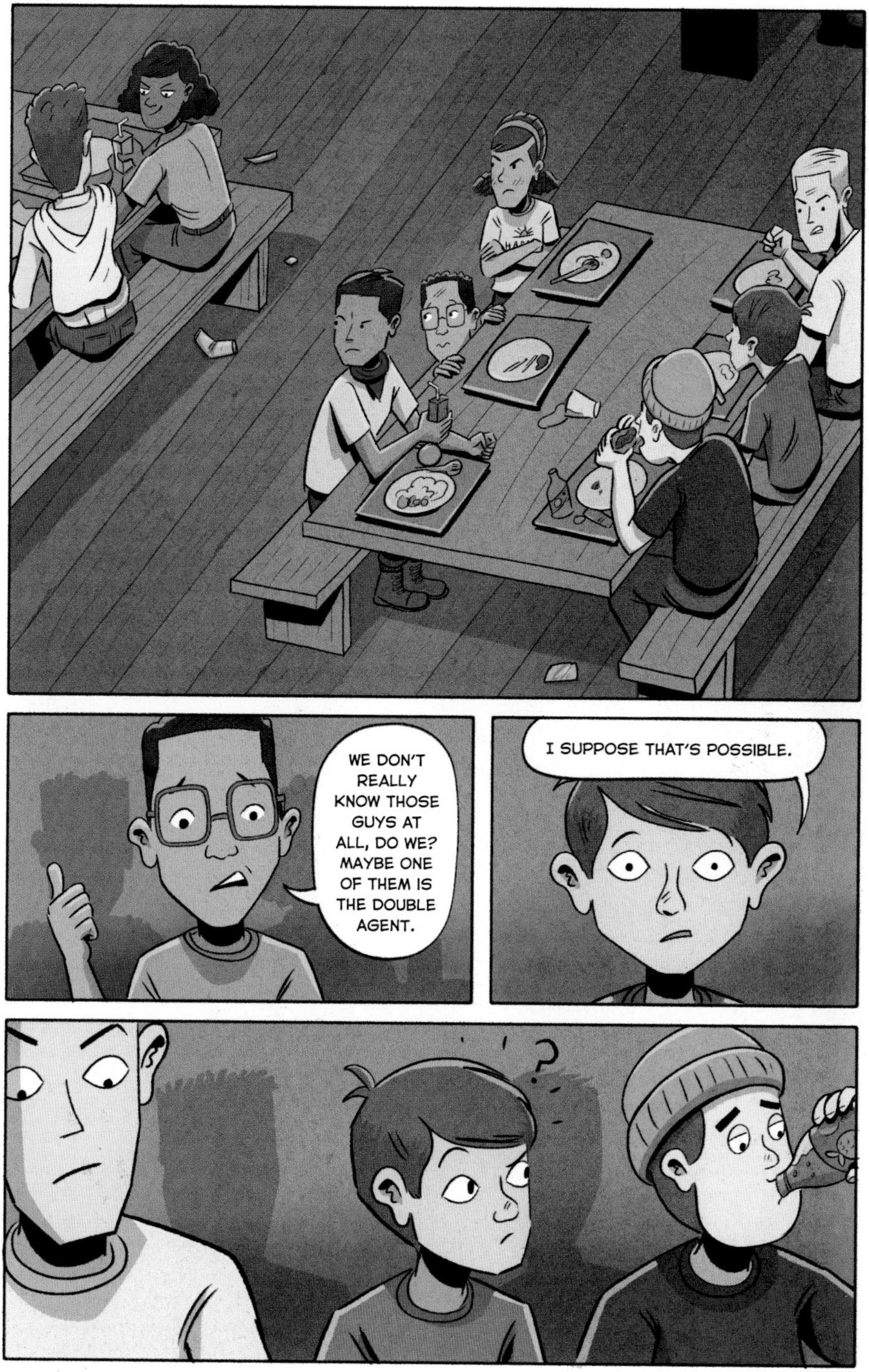
WE DON'T REALLY KNOW THOSE GUYS AT ALL, DO WE? MAYBE ONE OF THEM IS THE DOUBLE AGENT.
I SUPPOSE THAT'S POSSIBLE.
?

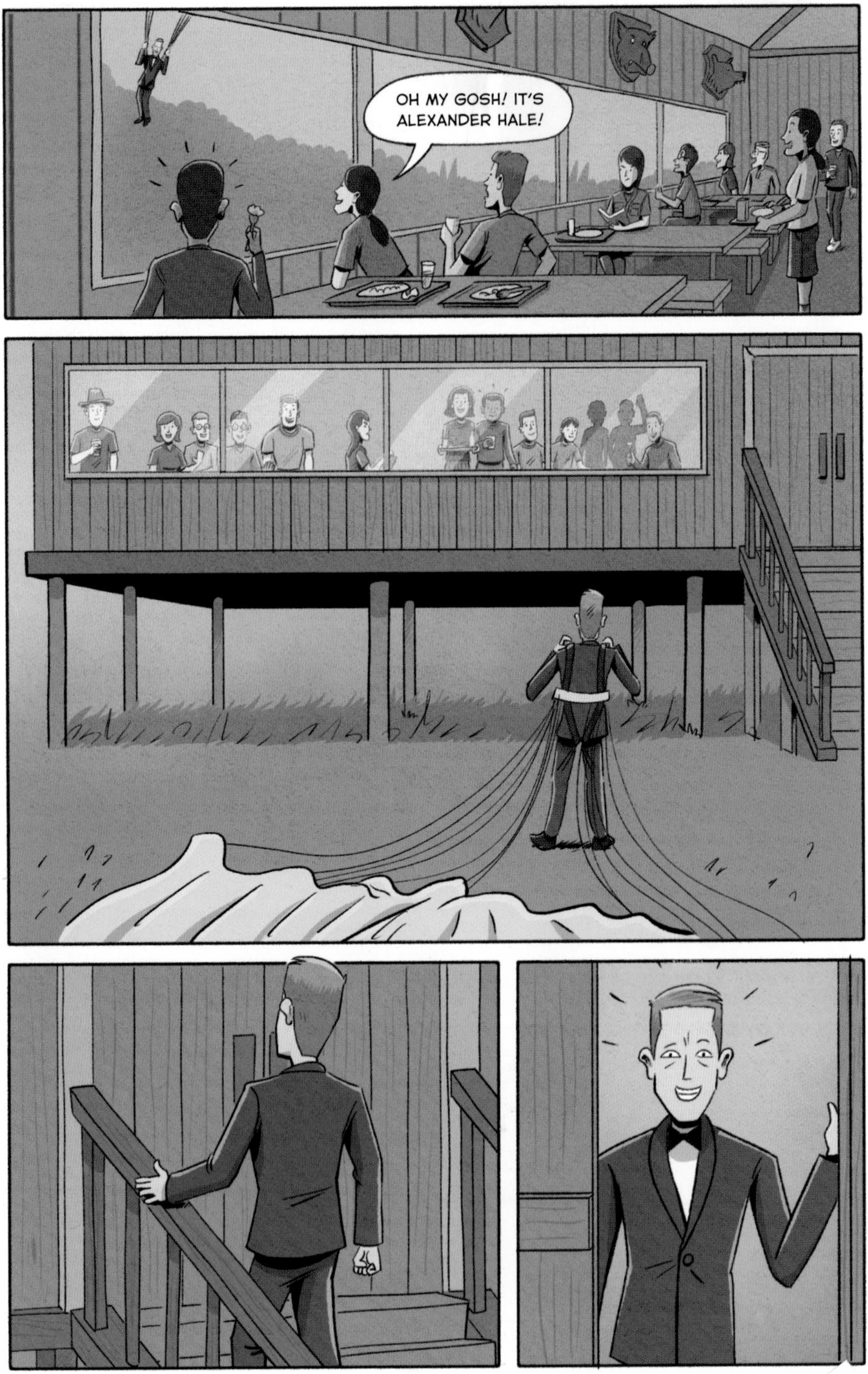
OH MY GOSH! IT'S ALEXANDER HALE!

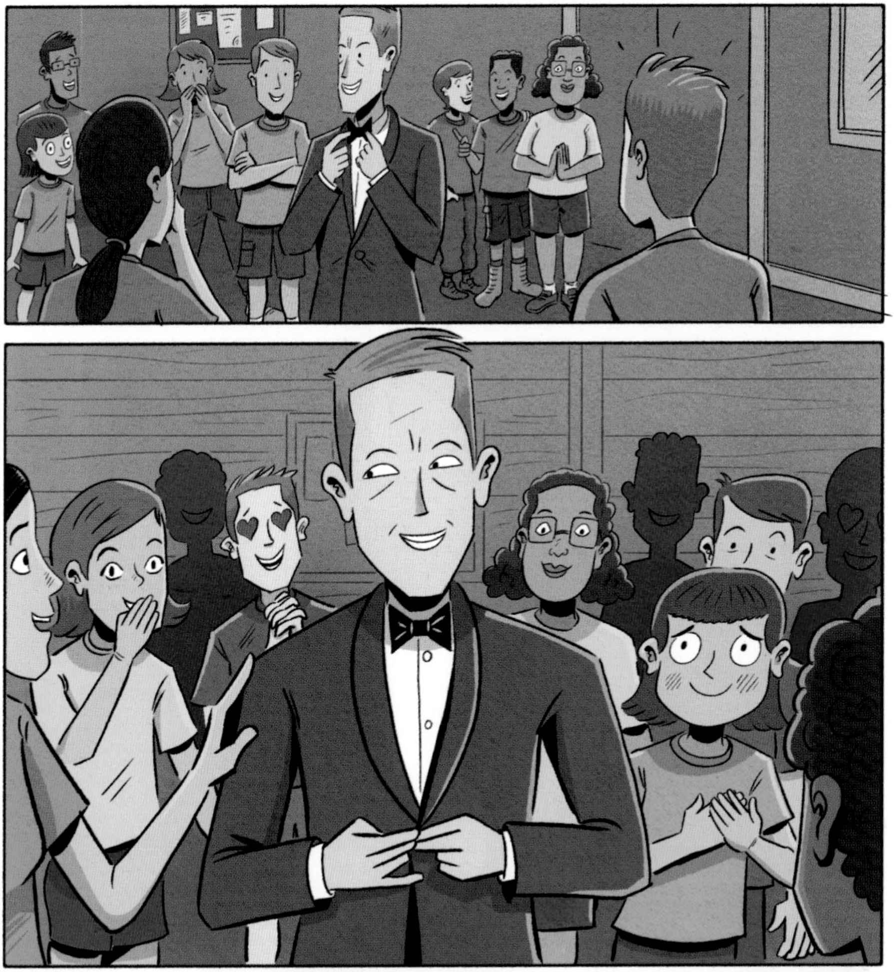

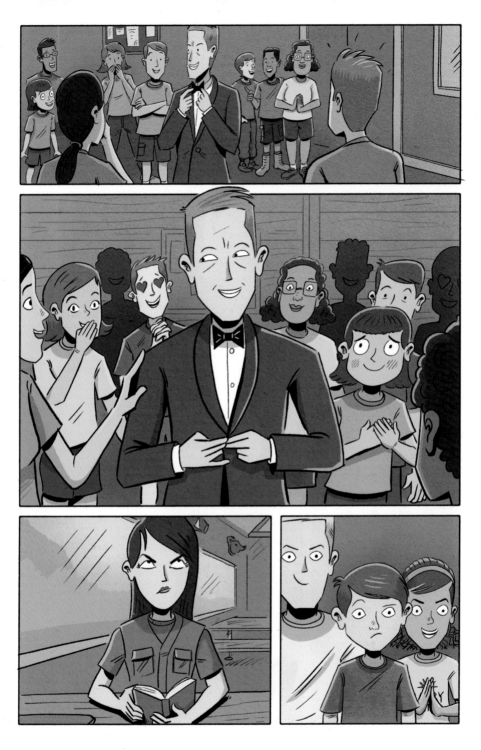

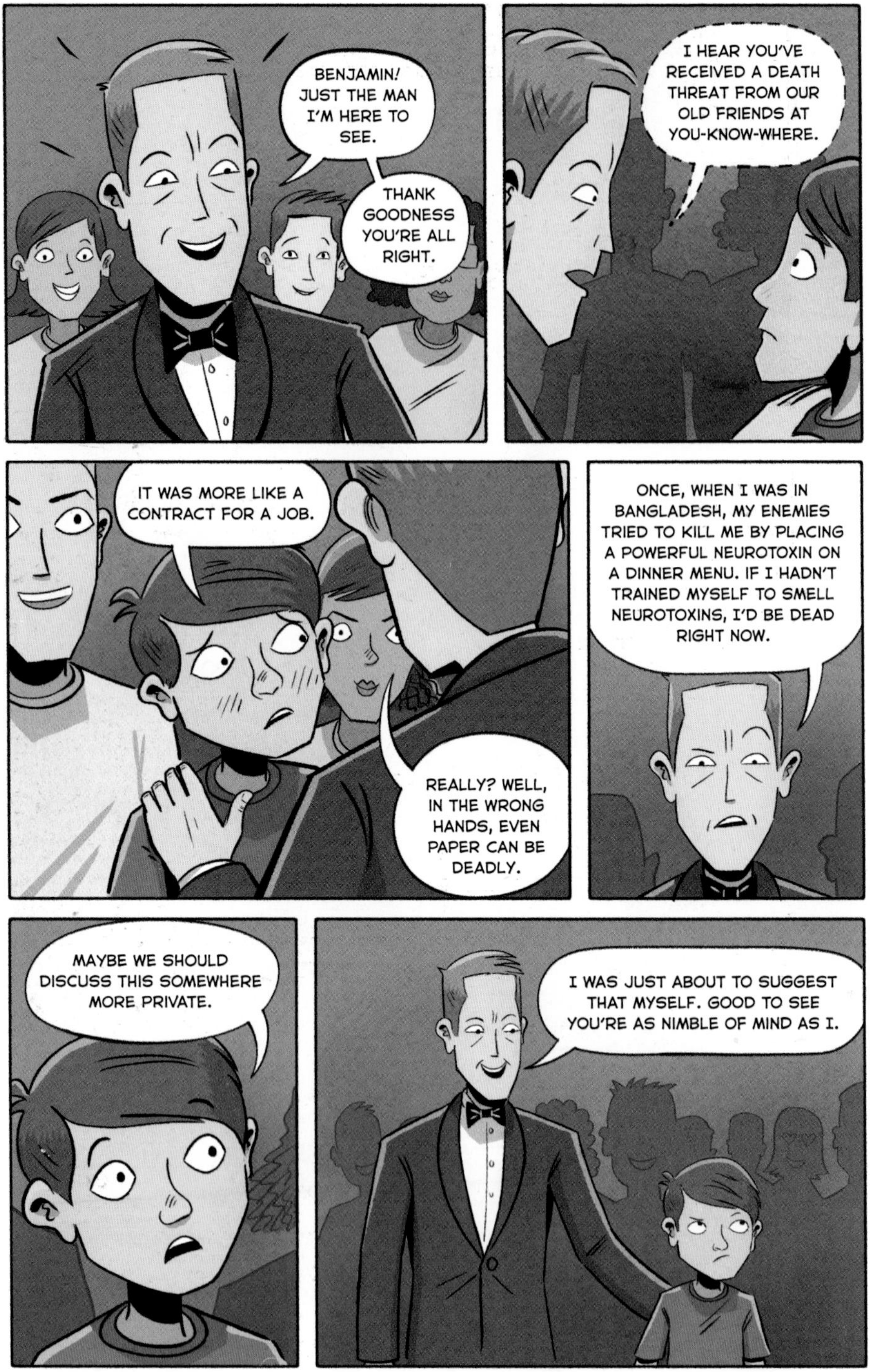
BENJAMIN! JUST THE MAN I'M HERE TO SEE.
THANK GOODNESS YOU'RE ALL RIGHT.
I HEAR YOU'VE RECEIVED A DEATH THREAT FROM OUR OLD FRIENDS AT YOU-KNOW-WHERE.
IT WAS MORE LIKE A CONTRACT FOR A JOB.
REALLY? WELL, IN THE WRONG HANDS, EVEN PAPER CAN BE DEADLY.
ONCE, WHEN I WAS IN BANGLADESH, MY ENEMIES TRIED TO KILL ME BY PLACING A POWERFUL NEUROTOXIN ON A DINNER MENU. IF I HADN'T TRAINED MYSELF TO SMELL NEUROTOXINS, I'D BE DEAD RIGHT NOW.
MAYBE WE SHOULD DISCUSS THIS SOMEWHERE MORE PRIVATE.
I WAS JUST ABOUT TO SUGGEST THAT MYSELF. GOOD TO SEE YOU'RE AS NIMBLE OF MIND AS I.

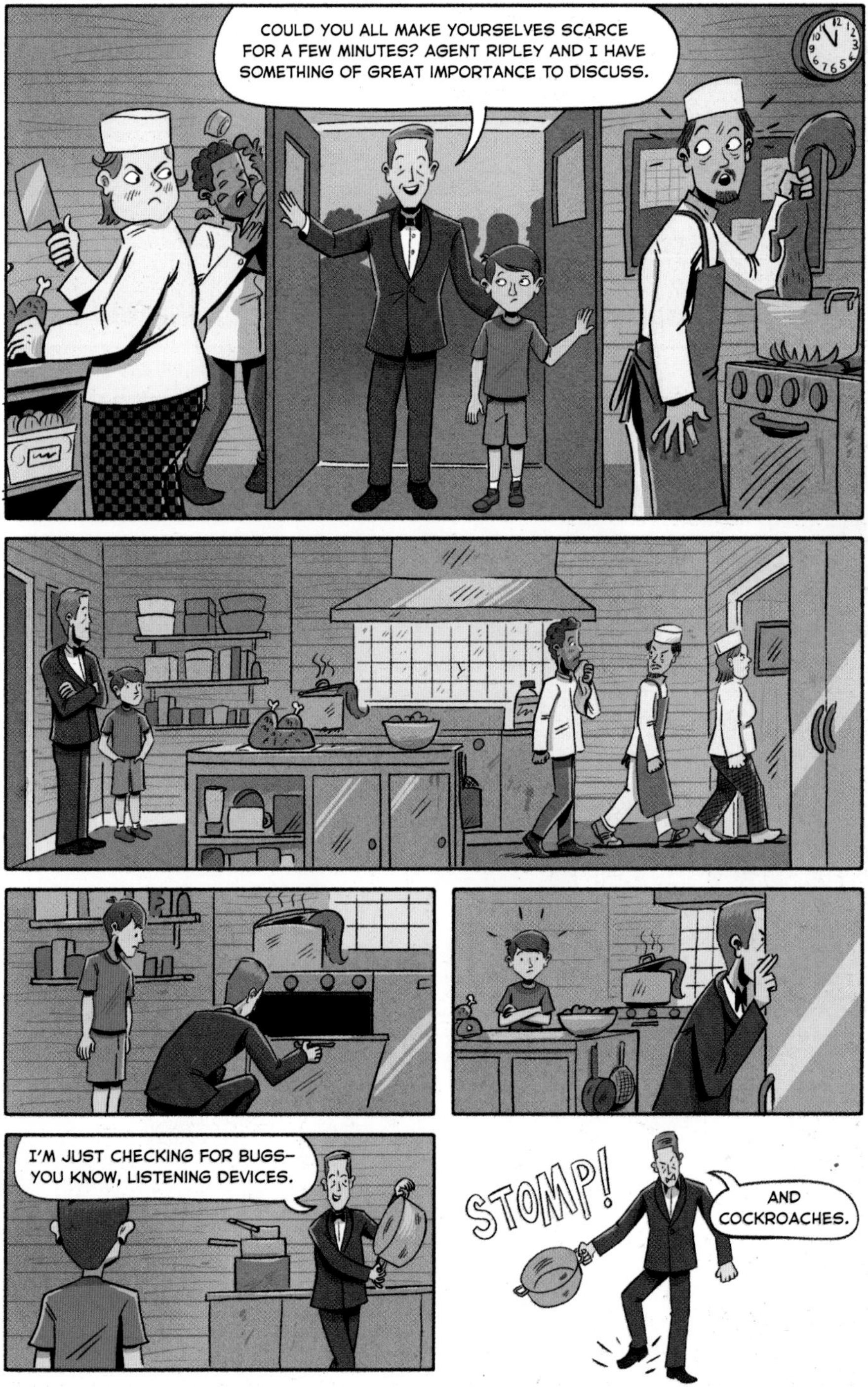
COULD YOU ALL MAKE YOURSELVES SCARCE FOR A FEW MINUTES? AGENT RIPLEY AND I HAVE SOMETHING OF GREAT IMPORTANCE TO DISCUSS.
I'M JUST CHECKING FOR BUGS— YOU KNOW, LISTENING DEVICES.
STOMP!
AND COCKROACHES.

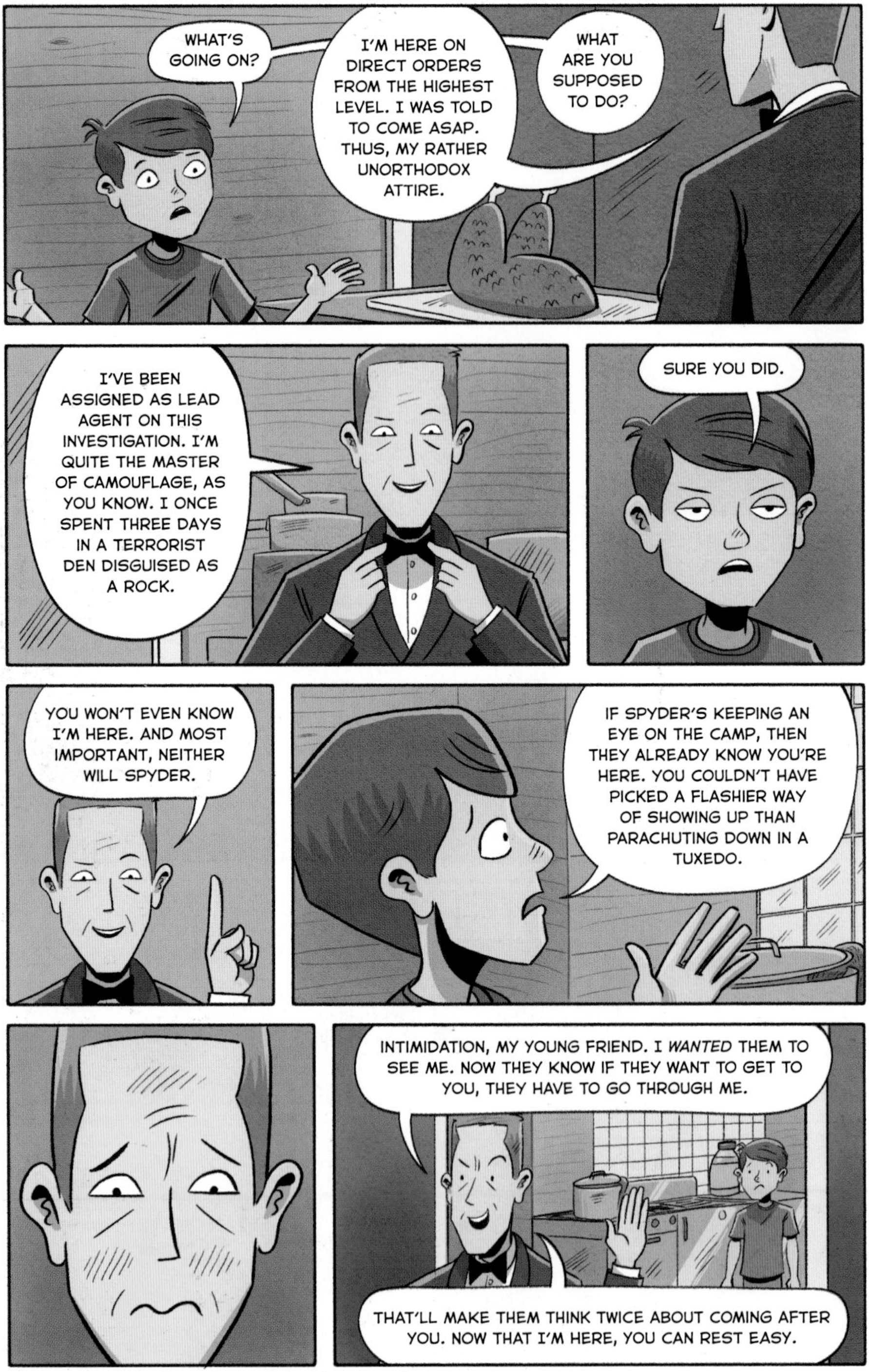
WHAT'S GOING ON?
I'M HERE ON DIRECT ORDERS FROM THE HIGHEST LEVEL. I WAS TOLD TO COME ASAP. THUS, MY RATHER UNORTHODOX ATTIRE.
WHAT ARE YOU SUPPOSED TO DO?
I'VE BEEN ASSIGNED AS LEAD AGENT ON THIS INVESTIGATION. I'M QUITE THE MASTER OF CAMOUFLAGE, AS YOU KNOW. I ONCE SPENT THREE DAYS IN A TERRORIST DEN DISGUISED AS A ROCK.
SURE YOU DID.
YOU WON'T EVEN KNOW I'M HERE. AND MOST IMPORTANT, NEITHER WILL SPYDER.
IF SPYDER'S KEEPING AN EYE ON THE CAMP, THEN THEY ALREADY KNOW YOU'RE HERE. YOU COULDN'T HAVE PICKED A FLASHIER WAY OF SHOWING UP THAN PARACHUTING DOWN IN A TUXEDO.
INTIMIDATION, MY YOUNG FRIEND. I *WANTED* THEM TO SEE ME. NOW THEY KNOW IF THEY WANT TO GET TO YOU, THEY HAVE TO GO THROUGH ME.
THAT'LL MAKE THEM THINK TWICE ABOUT COMING AFTER YOU. NOW THAT I'M HERE, YOU CAN REST EASY.

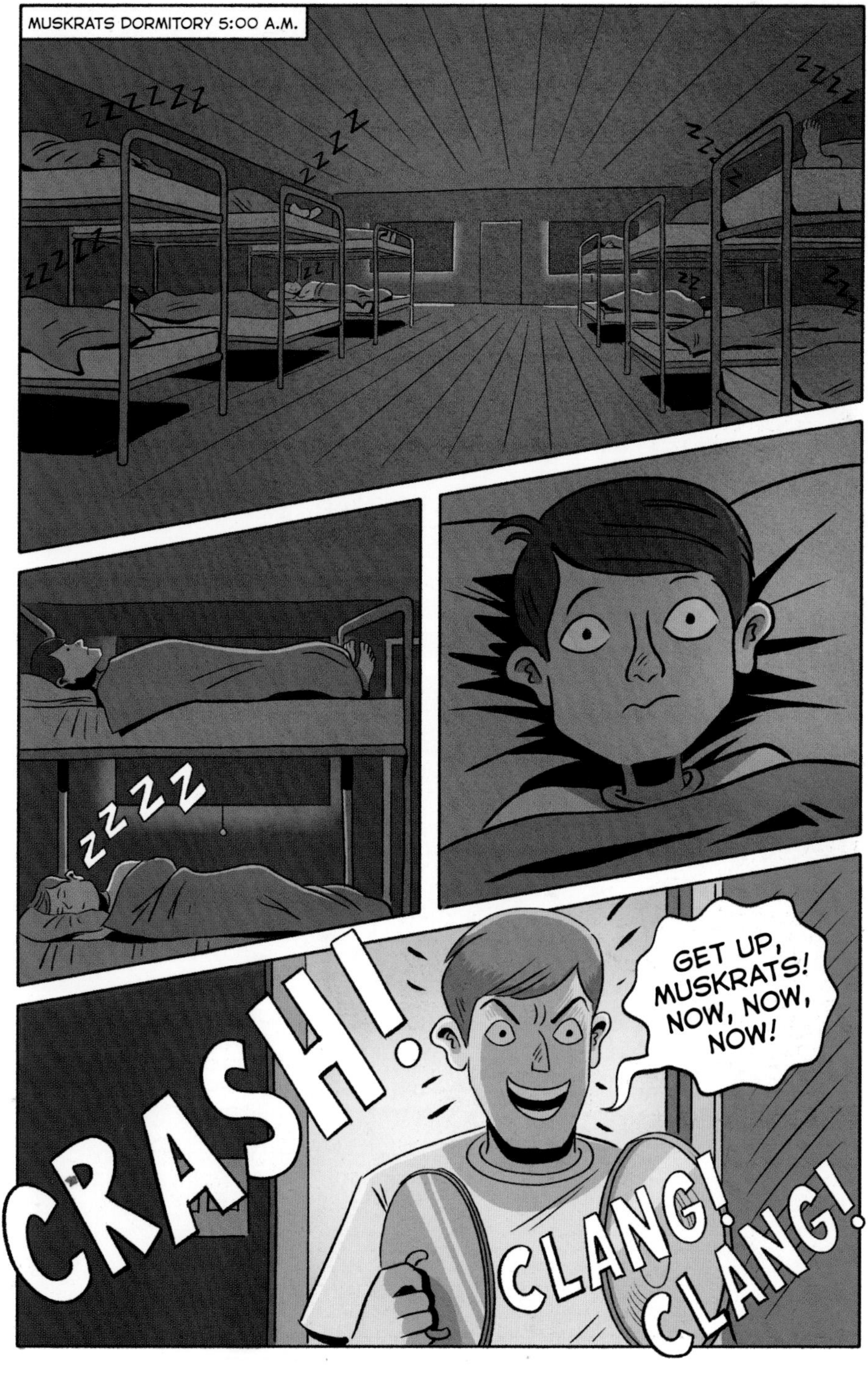
MUSKRATS DORMITORY 5:00 A.M.
ZZZZZZ
ZZZZ
ZZZZZ
ZZ
ZZZZ
ZZZZ
CRASH!
GET UP, MUSKRATS! NOW, NOW, NOW!
CLANG!
CLANG!

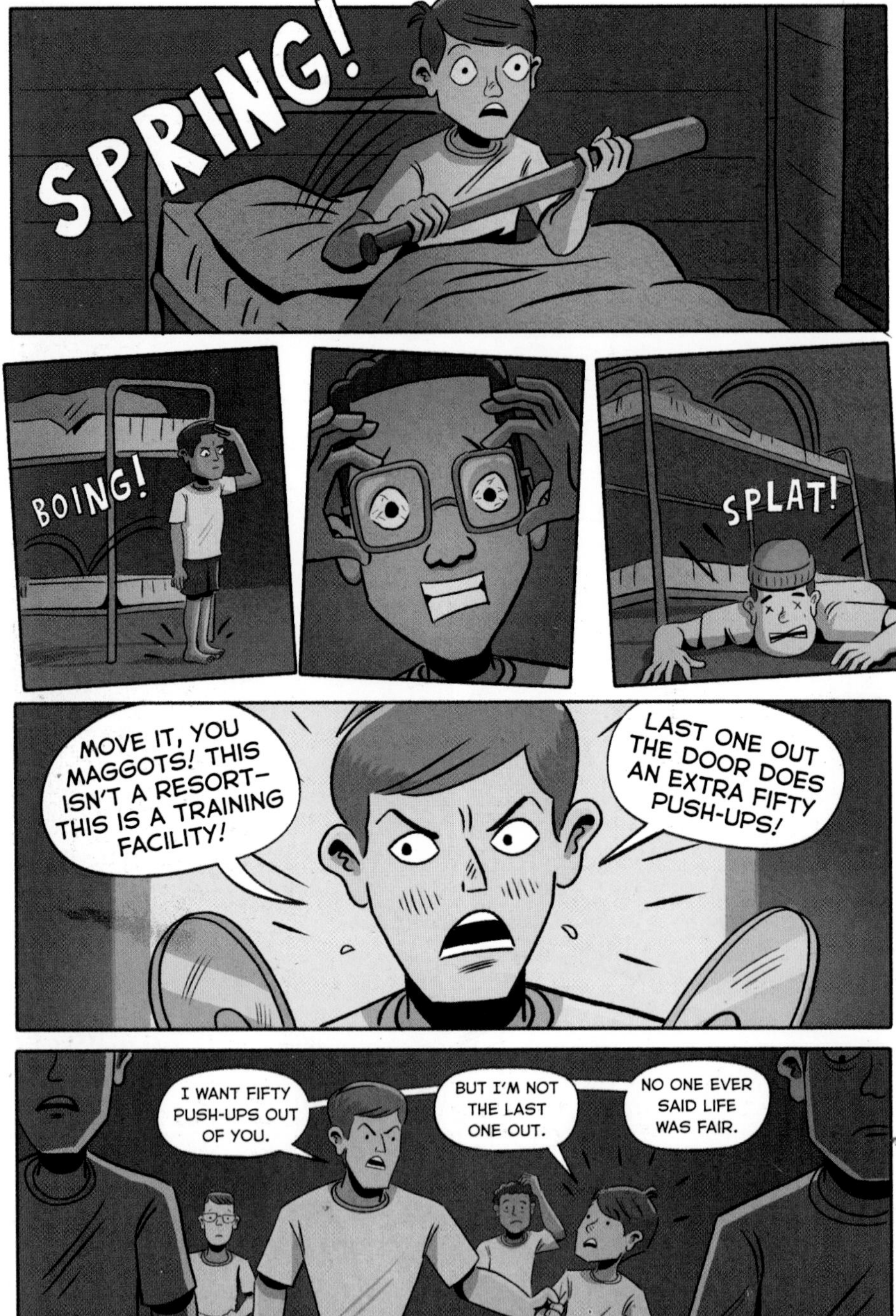
SPRING!
BOING!
SPLAT!
MOVE IT, YOU MAGGOTS! THIS ISN'T A RESORT— THIS IS A TRAINING FACILITY!
LAST ONE OUT THE DOOR DOES AN EXTRA FIFTY PUSH-UPS!
I WANT FIFTY PUSH-UPS OUT OF YOU.
BUT I'M NOT THE LAST ONE OUT.
NO ONE EVER SAID LIFE WAS FAIR.

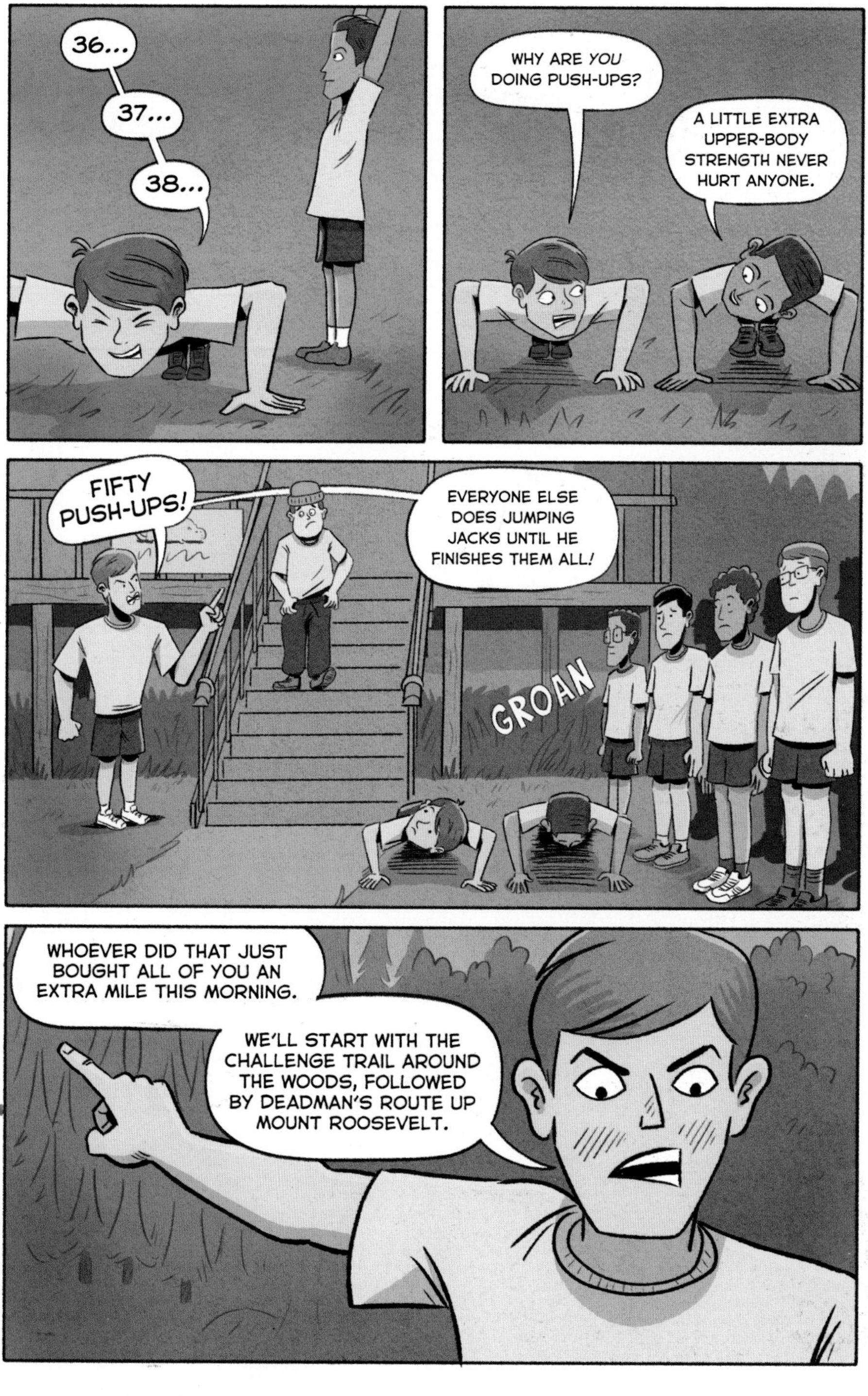
36...
37...
38...
WHY ARE YOU DOING PUSH-UPS?
A LITTLE EXTRA UPPER-BODY STRENGTH NEVER HURT ANYONE.
FIFTY PUSH-UPS!
EVERYONE ELSE DOES JUMPING JACKS UNTIL HE FINISHES THEM ALL!
GROAN
WHOEVER DID THAT JUST BOUGHT ALL OF YOU AN EXTRA MILE THIS MORNING.
WE'LL START WITH THE CHALLENGE TRAIL AROUND THE WOODS, FOLLOWED BY DEADMAN'S ROUTE UP MOUNT ROOSEVELT.

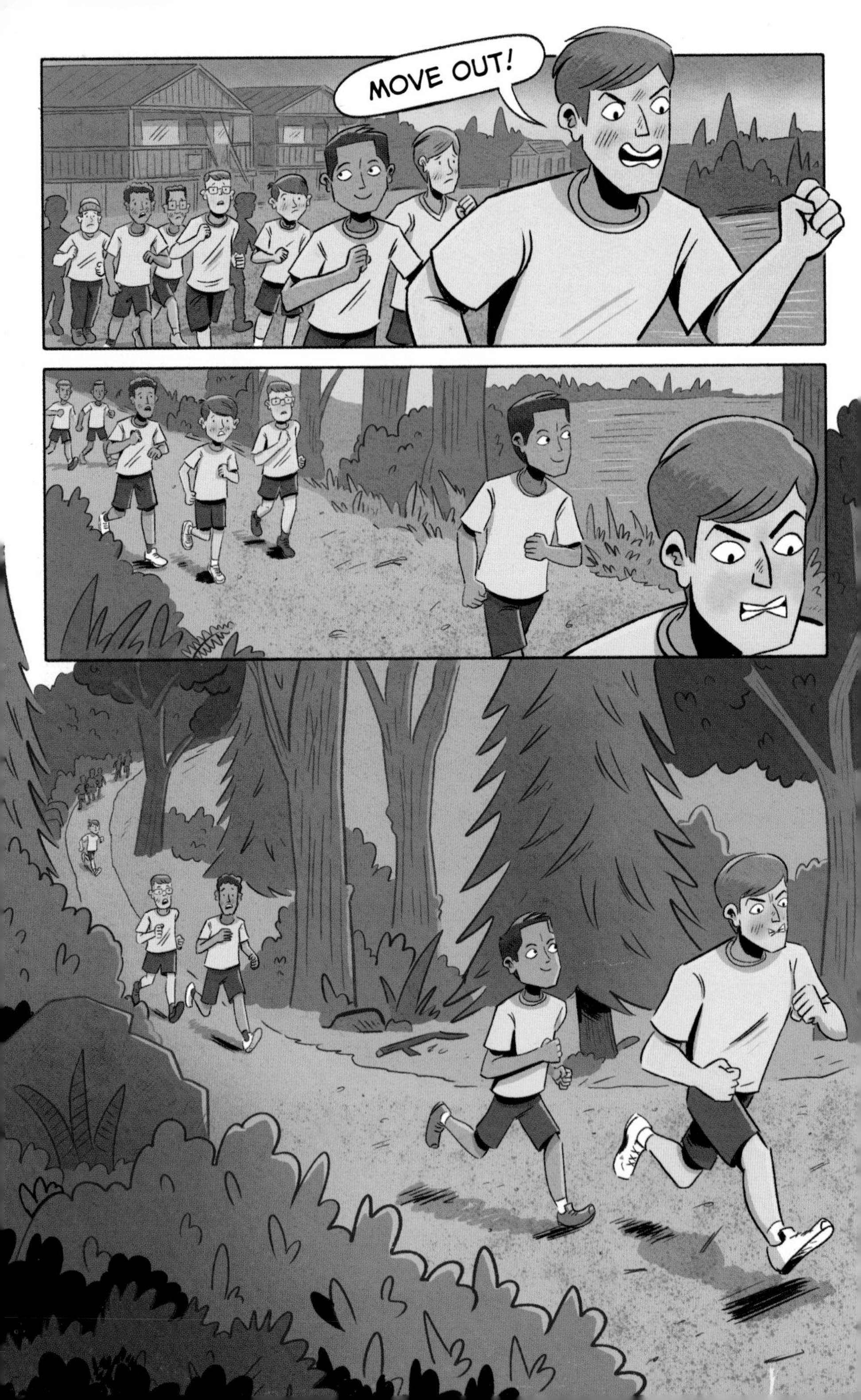
MOVE OUT!

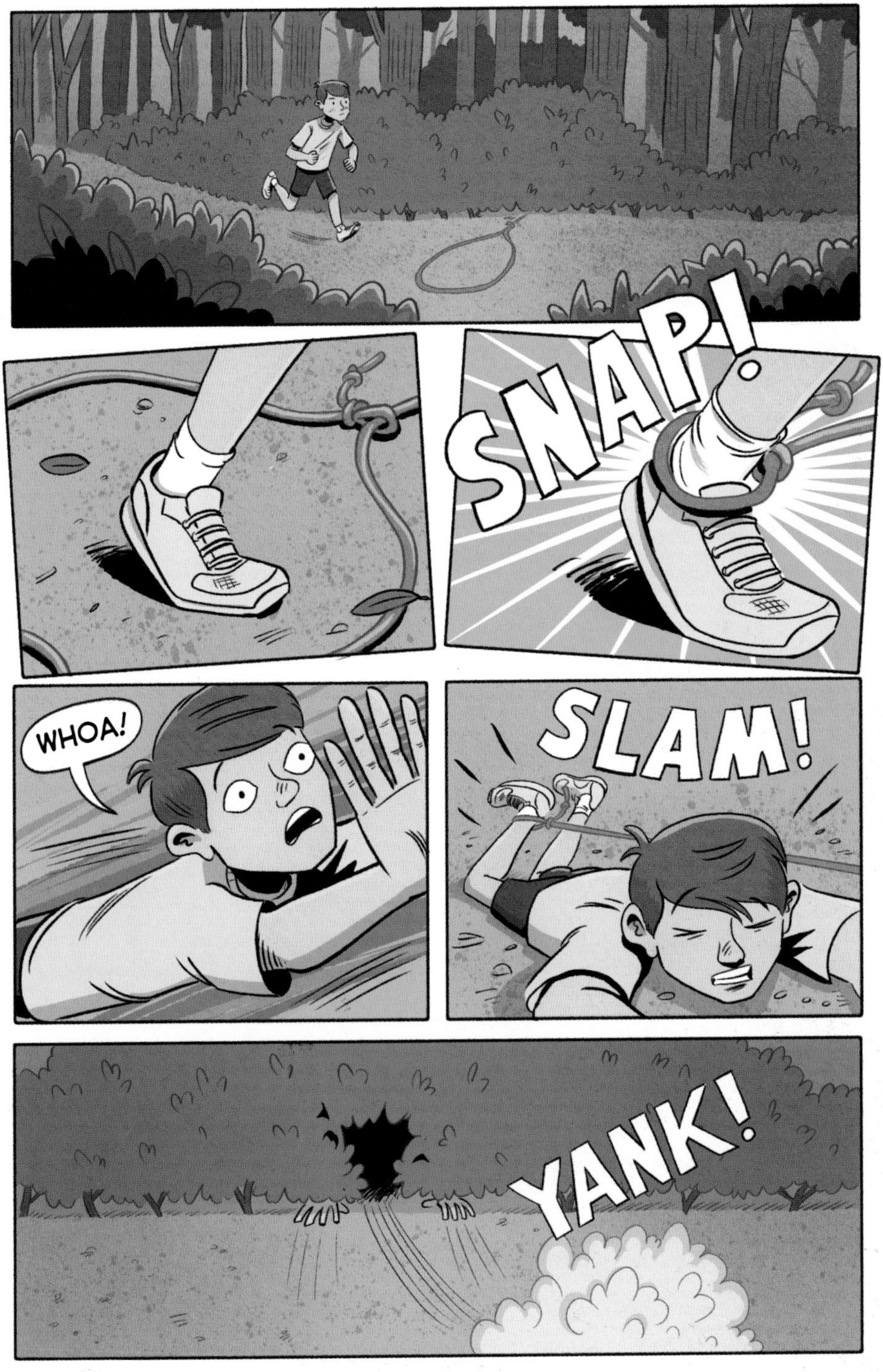
SNAP!
WHOA!
SLAM!
YANK!

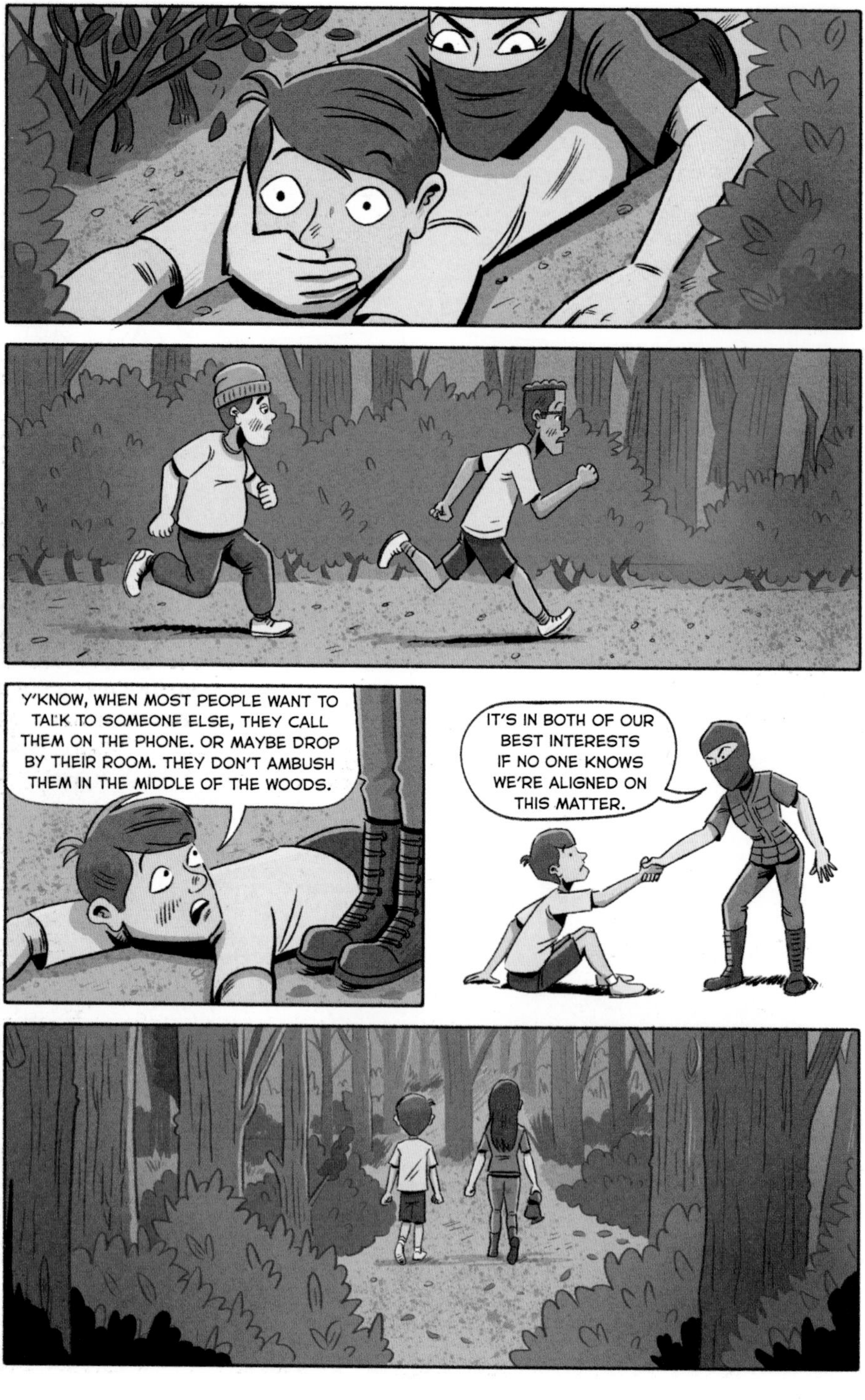

Y'KNOW, WHEN MOST PEOPLE WANT TO TALK TO SOMEONE ELSE, THEY CALL THEM ON THE PHONE. OR MAYBE DROP BY THEIR ROOM. THEY DON'T AMBUSH THEM IN THE MIDDLE OF THE WOODS.
IT'S IN BOTH OF OUR BEST INTERESTS IF NO ONE KNOWS WE'RE ALIGNED ON THIS MATTER.

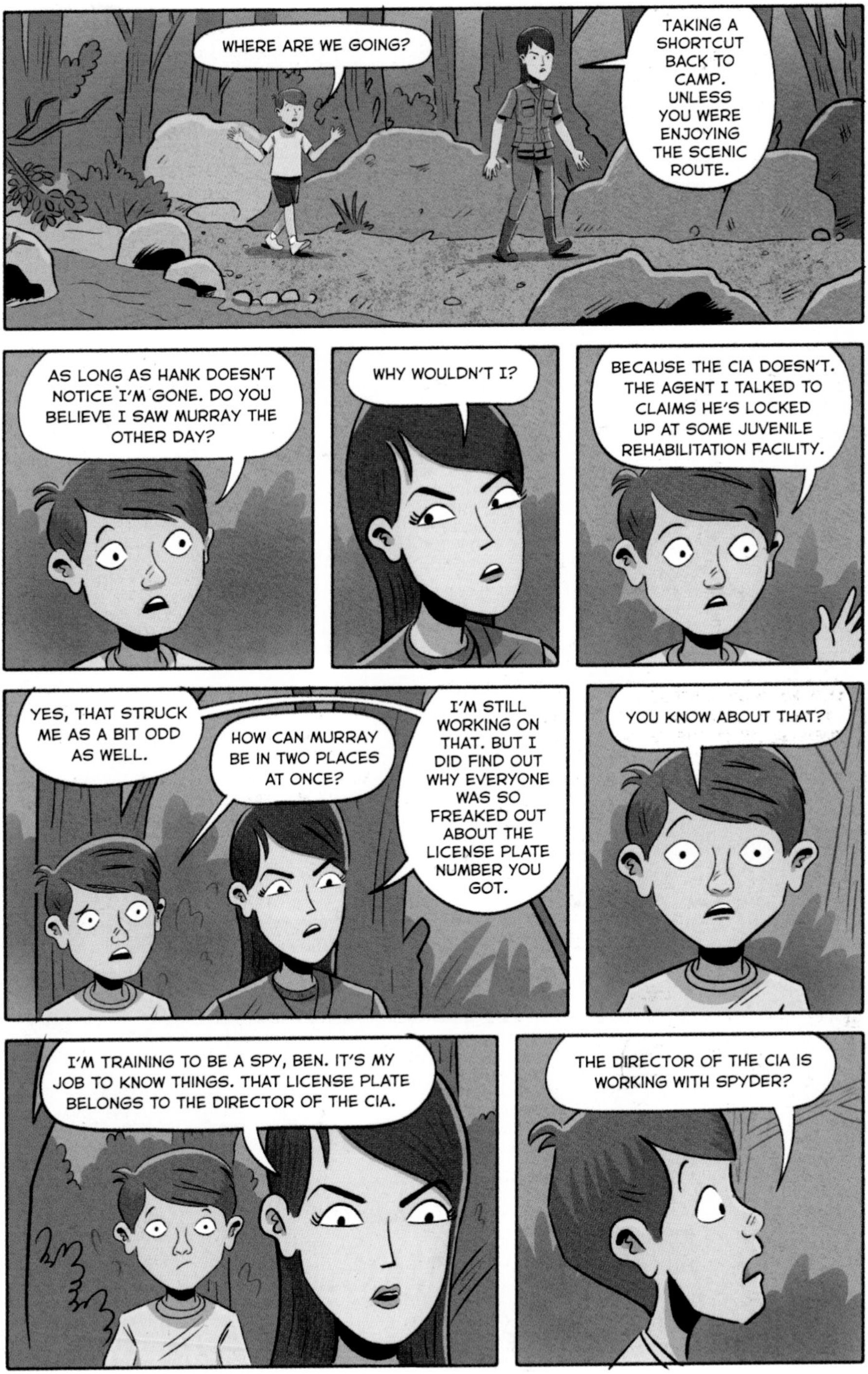
WHERE ARE WE GOING?
TAKING A SHORTCUT BACK TO CAMP. UNLESS YOU WERE ENJOYING THE SCENIC ROUTE.
AS LONG AS HANK DOESN'T NOTICE I'M GONE. DO YOU BELIEVE I SAW MURRAY THE OTHER DAY?
WHY WOULDN'T I?
BECAUSE THE CIA DOESN'T. THE AGENT I TALKED TO CLAIMS HE'S LOCKED UP AT SOME JUVENILE REHABILITATION FACILITY.
YES, THAT STRUCK ME AS A BIT ODD AS WELL.
HOW CAN MURRAY BE IN TWO PLACES AT ONCE?
I'M STILL WORKING ON THAT. BUT I DID FIND OUT WHY EVERYONE WAS SO FREAKED OUT ABOUT THE LICENSE PLATE NUMBER YOU GOT.
YOU KNOW ABOUT THAT?
I'M TRAINING TO BE A SPY, BEN. IT'S MY JOB TO KNOW THINGS. THAT LICENSE PLATE BELONGS TO THE DIRECTOR OF THE CIA.
THE DIRECTOR OF THE CIA IS WORKING WITH SPYDER?

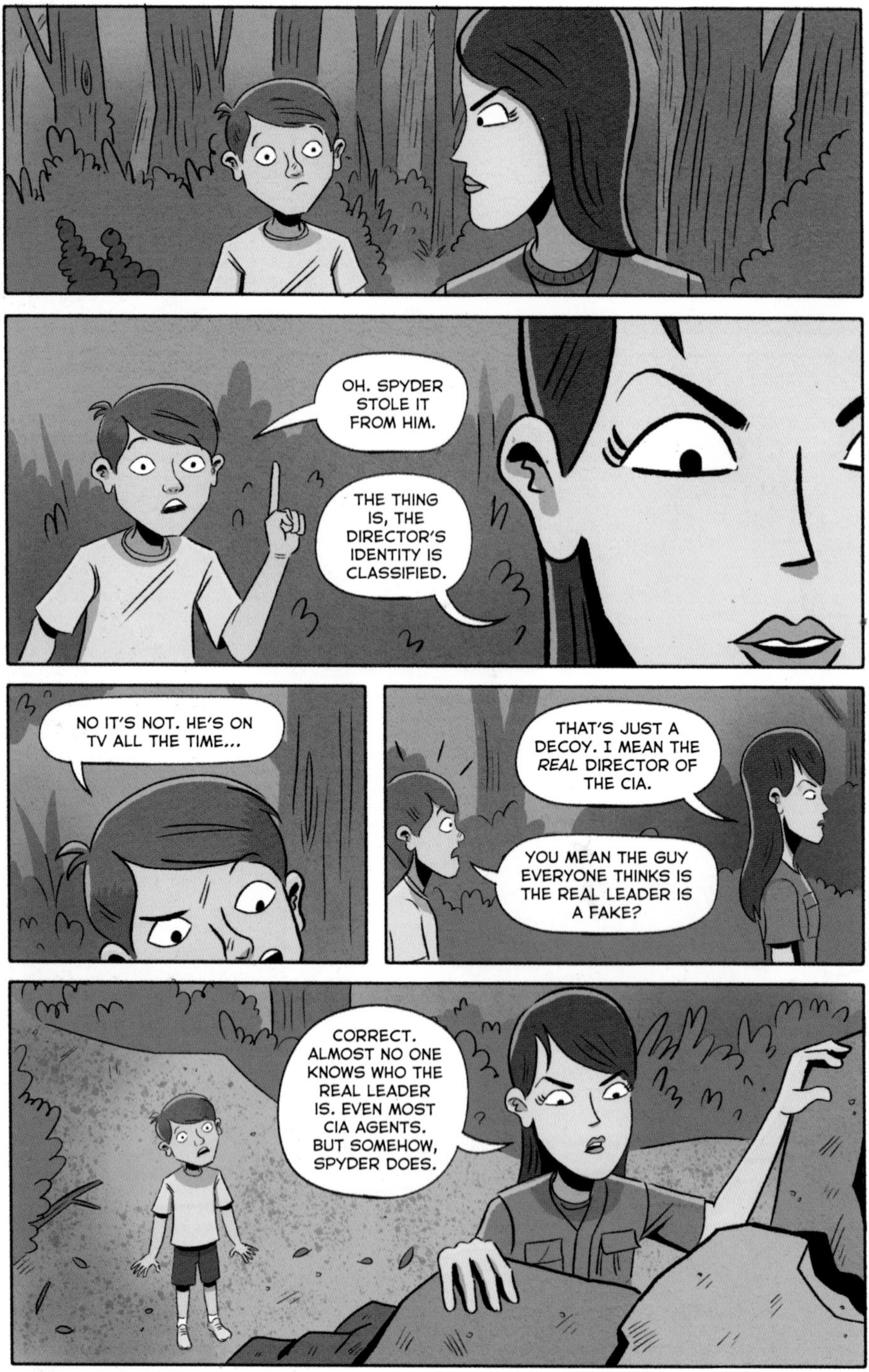
OH. SPYDER STOLE IT FROM HIM.
THE THING IS, THE DIRECTOR'S IDENTITY IS CLASSIFIED.
NO IT'S NOT. HE'S ON TV ALL THE TIME...
THAT'S JUST A DECOY. I MEAN THE *REAL* DIRECTOR OF THE CIA.
YOU MEAN THE GUY EVERYONE THINKS IS THE REAL LEADER IS A FAKE?
CORRECT. ALMOST NO ONE KNOWS WHO THE REAL LEADER IS. EVEN MOST CIA AGENTS. BUT SOMEHOW, SPYDER DOES.

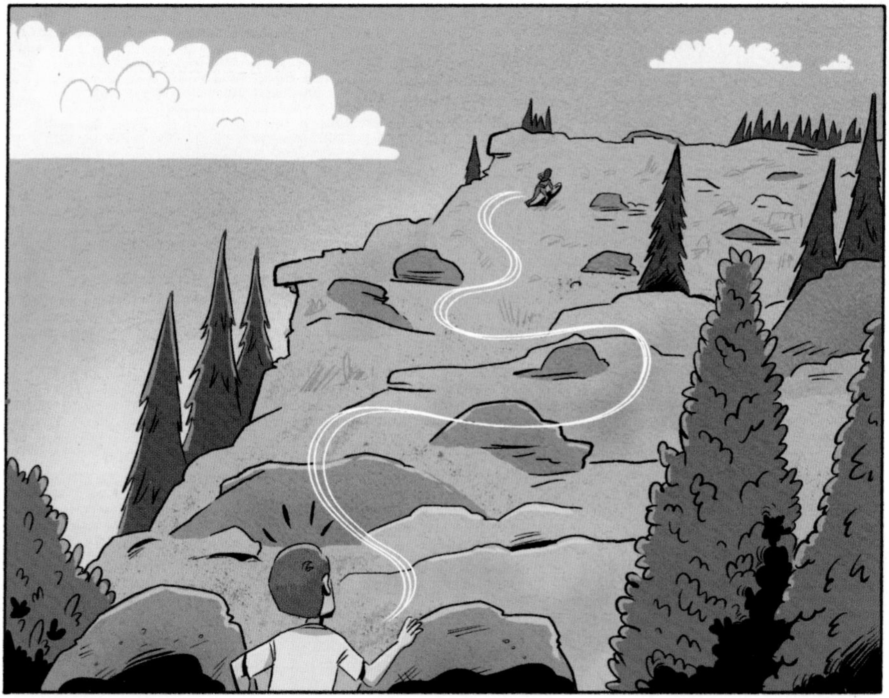

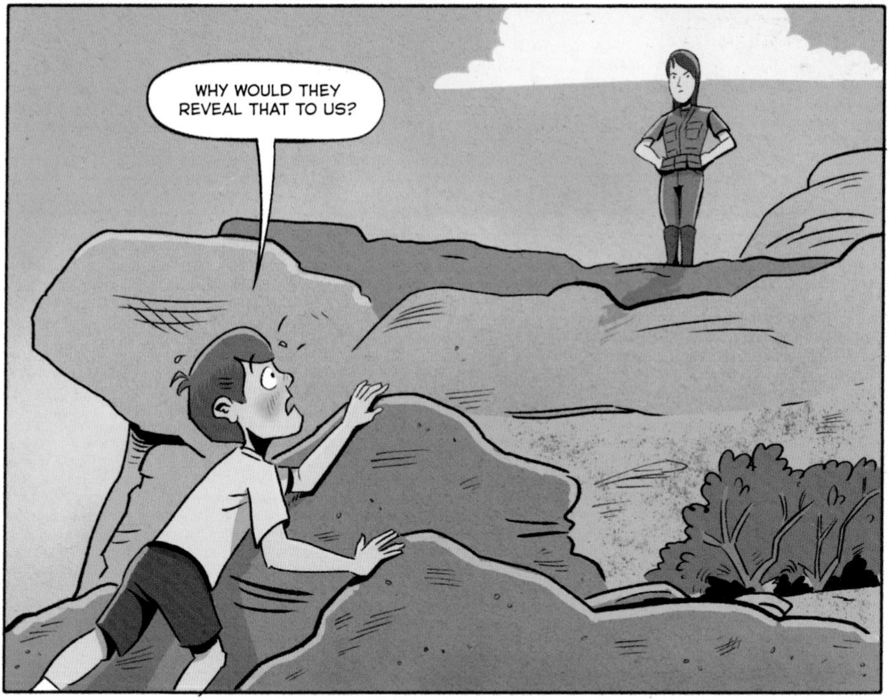
WHY WOULD THEY REVEAL THAT TO US?

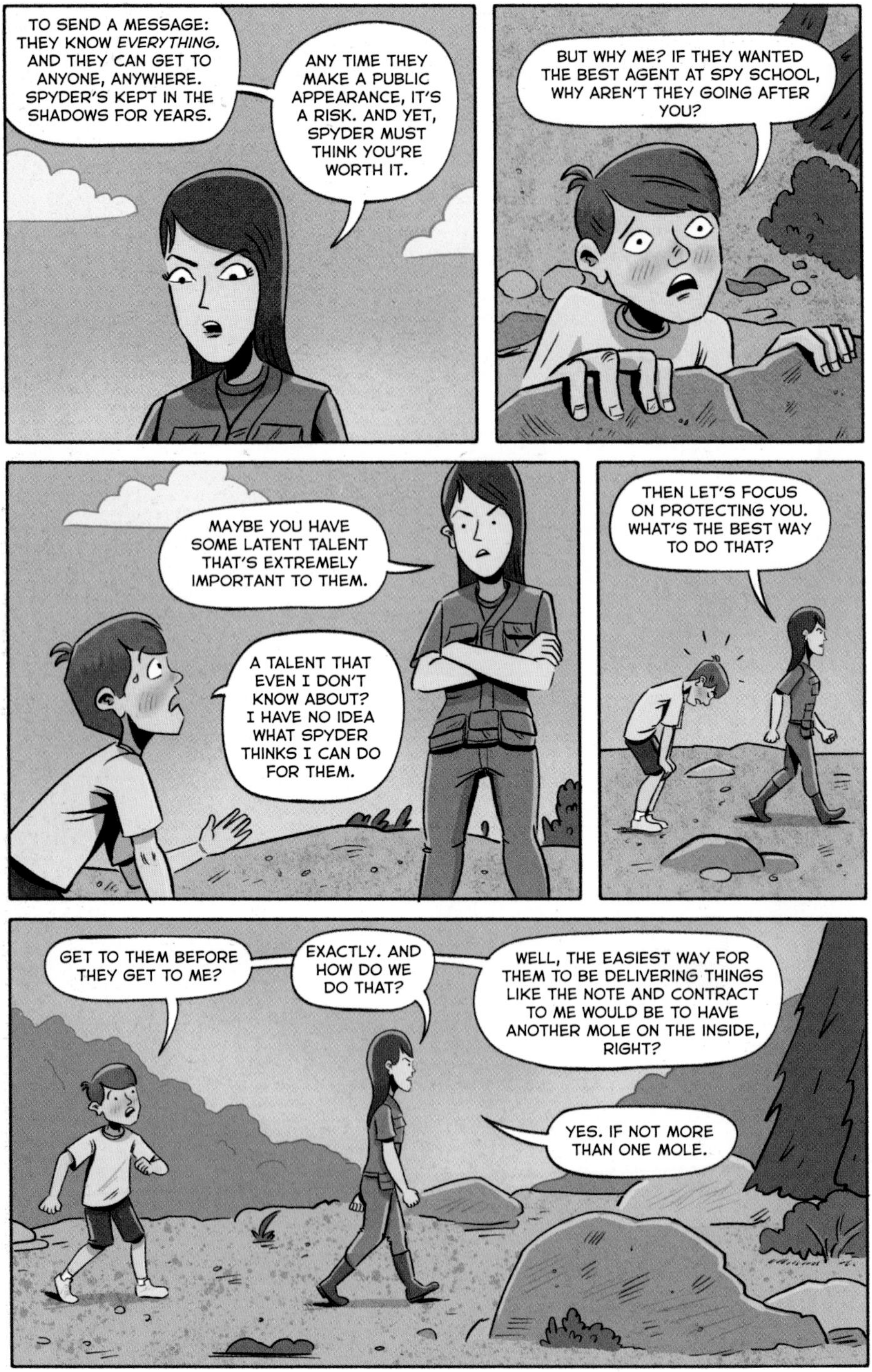
TO SEND A MESSAGE: THEY KNOW *EVERYTHING.* AND THEY CAN GET TO ANYONE, ANYWHERE. SPYDER'S KEPT IN THE SHADOWS FOR YEARS.
ANY TIME THEY MAKE A PUBLIC APPEARANCE, IT'S A RISK. AND YET, SPYDER MUST THINK YOU'RE WORTH IT.
BUT WHY ME? IF THEY WANTED THE BEST AGENT AT SPY SCHOOL, WHY AREN'T THEY GOING AFTER YOU?
MAYBE YOU HAVE SOME LATENT TALENT THAT'S EXTREMELY IMPORTANT TO THEM.
A TALENT THAT EVEN I DON'T KNOW ABOUT? I HAVE NO IDEA WHAT SPYDER THINKS I CAN DO FOR THEM.
THEN LET'S FOCUS ON PROTECTING YOU. WHAT'S THE BEST WAY TO DO THAT?
GET TO THEM BEFORE THEY GET TO ME?
EXACTLY. AND HOW DO WE DO THAT?
WELL, THE EASIEST WAY FOR THEM TO BE DELIVERING THINGS LIKE THE NOTE AND CONTRACT TO ME WOULD BE TO HAVE ANOTHER MOLE ON THE INSIDE, RIGHT?
YES. IF NOT MORE THAN ONE MOLE.

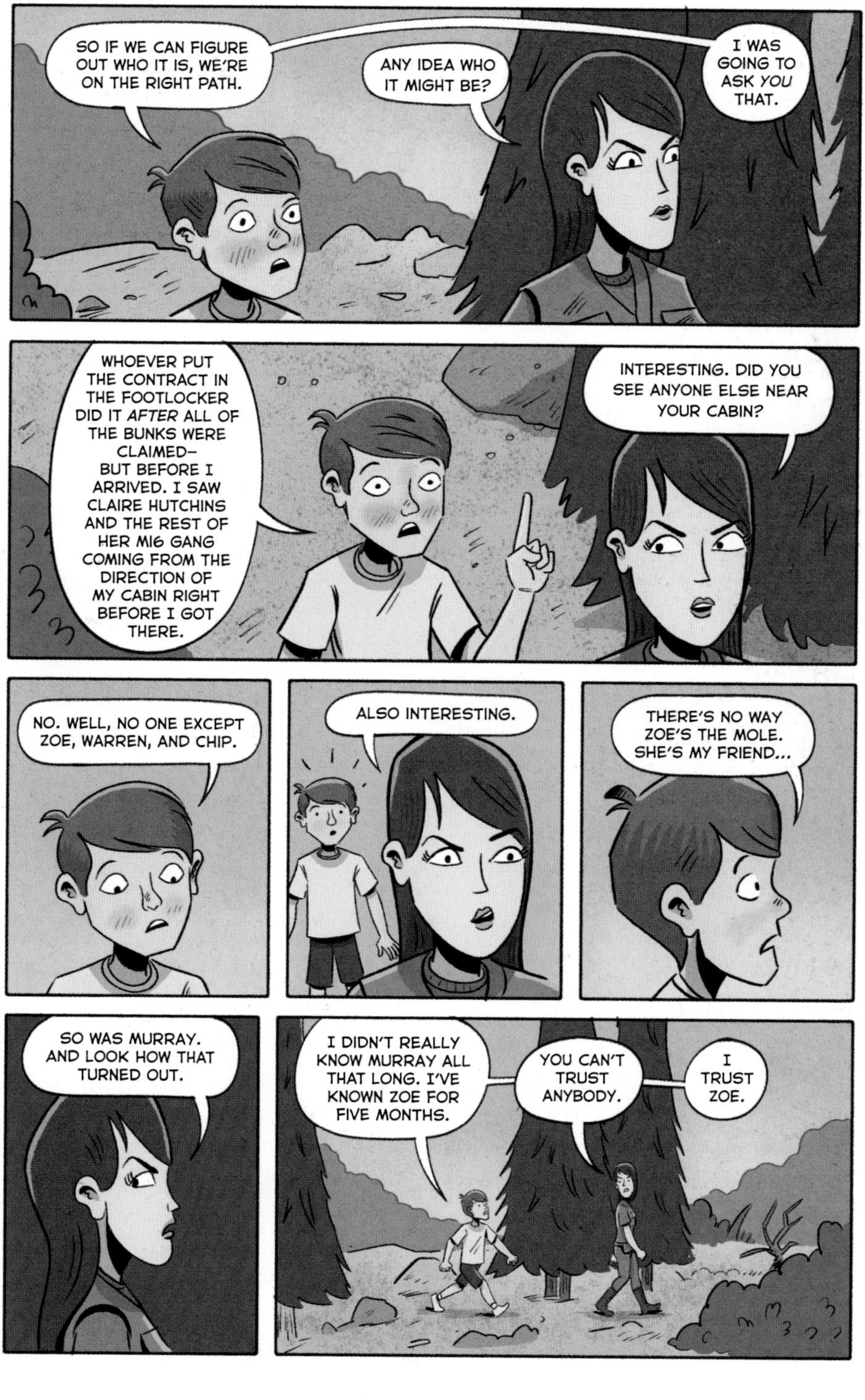
SO IF WE CAN FIGURE OUT WHO IT IS, WE'RE ON THE RIGHT PATH.
ANY IDEA WHO IT MIGHT BE?
I WAS GOING TO ASK *YOU* THAT.
WHOEVER PUT THE CONTRACT IN THE FOOTLOCKER DID IT *AFTER* ALL OF THE BUNKS WERE CLAIMED— BUT BEFORE I ARRIVED. I SAW CLAIRE HUTCHINS AND THE REST OF HER MI6 GANG COMING FROM THE DIRECTION OF MY CABIN RIGHT BEFORE I GOT THERE.
INTERESTING. DID YOU SEE ANYONE ELSE NEAR YOUR CABIN?
NO. WELL, NO ONE EXCEPT ZOE, WARREN, AND CHIP.
ALSO INTERESTING.
THERE'S NO WAY ZOE'S THE MOLE. SHE'S MY FRIEND...
SO WAS MURRAY. AND LOOK HOW THAT TURNED OUT.
I DIDN'T REALLY KNOW MURRAY ALL THAT LONG. I'VE KNOWN ZOE FOR FIVE MONTHS.
YOU CAN'T TRUST ANYBODY.
I TRUST ZOE.

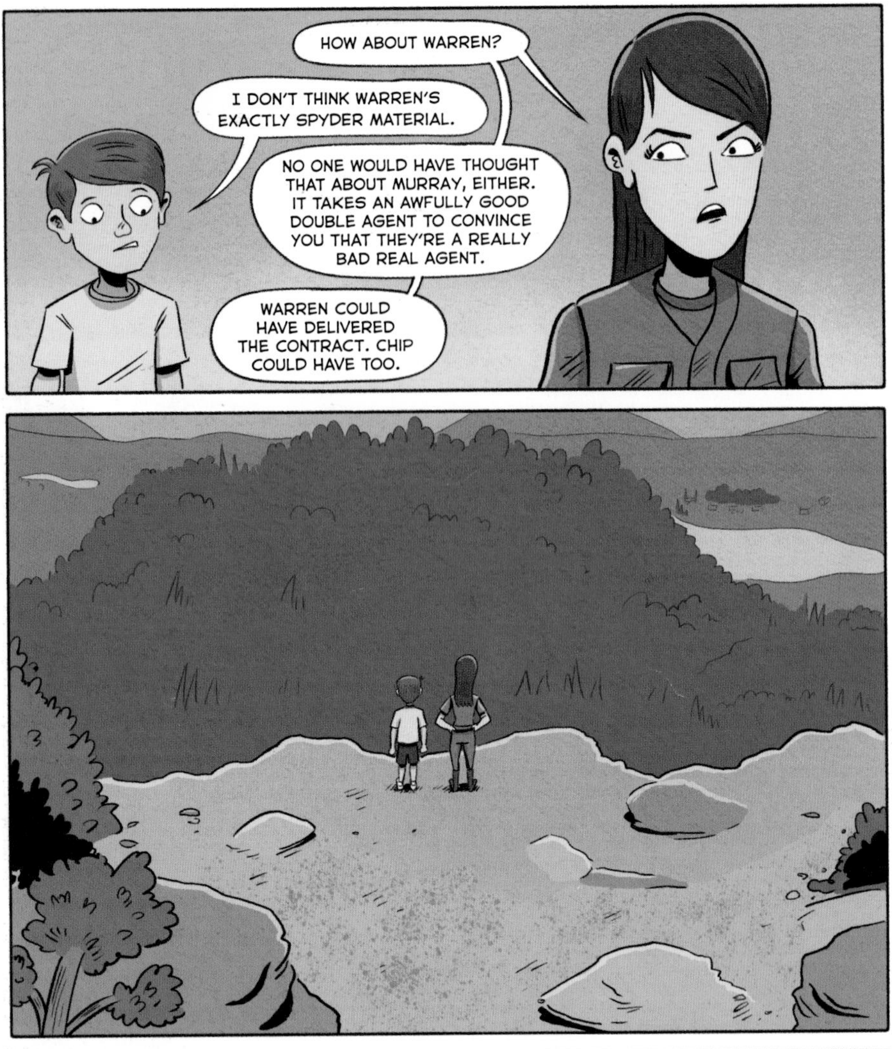
HOW ABOUT WARREN?
I DON'T THINK WARREN'S EXACTLY SPYDER MATERIAL.
NO ONE WOULD HAVE THOUGHT THAT ABOUT MURRAY, EITHER. IT TAKES AN AWFULLY GOOD DOUBLE AGENT TO CONVINCE YOU THAT THEY'RE A REALLY BAD REAL AGENT.
WARREN COULD HAVE DELIVERED THE CONTRACT. CHIP COULD HAVE TOO.
HOW ARE WE SUPPOSED TO GET DOWN?

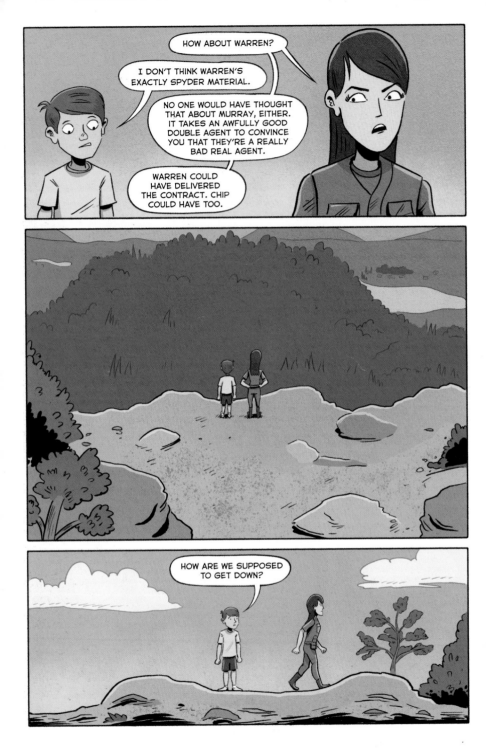

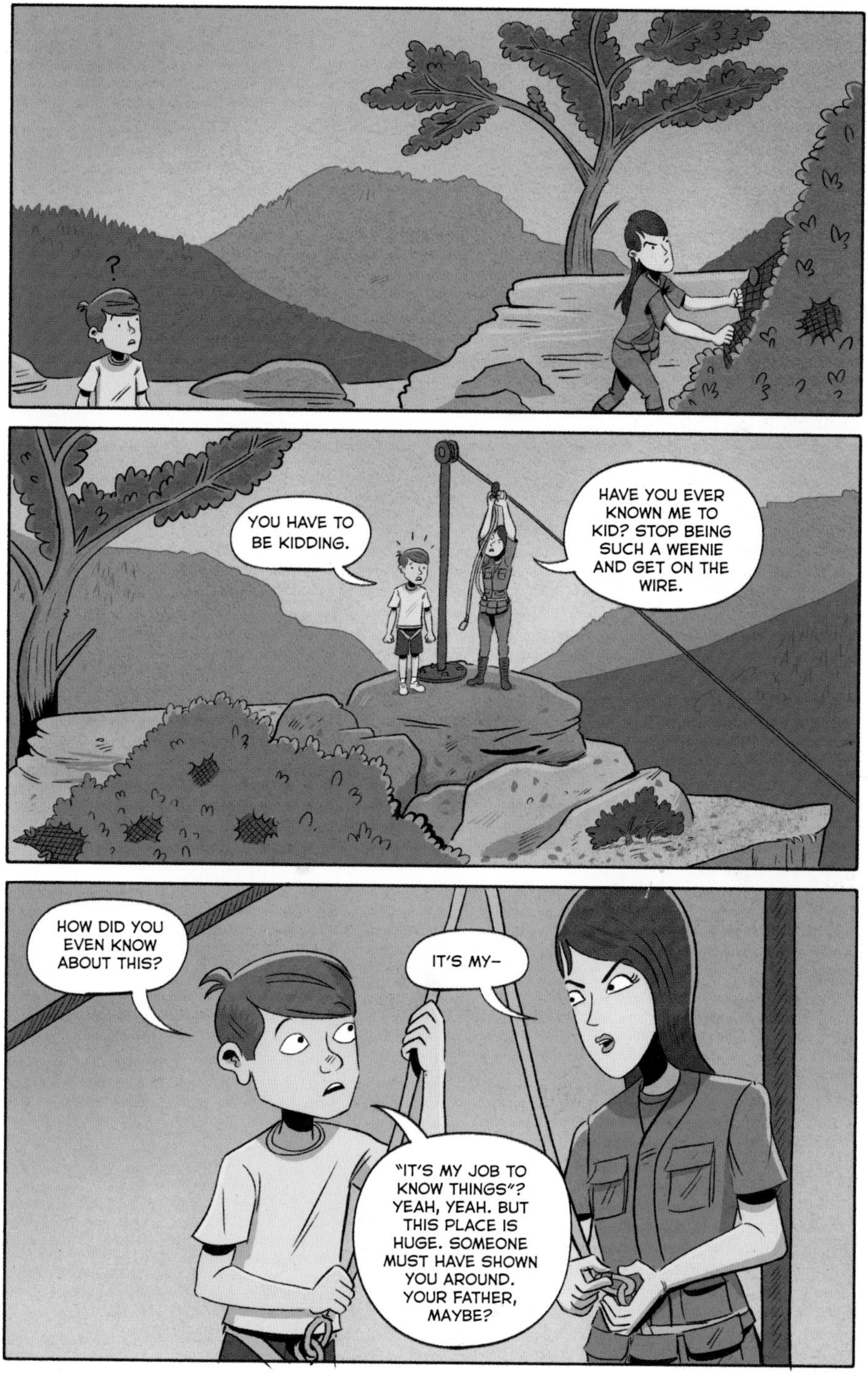
?
YOU HAVE TO BE KIDDING.
HAVE YOU EVER KNOWN ME TO KID? STOP BEING SUCH A WEENIE AND GET ON THE WIRE.
HOW DID YOU EVEN KNOW ABOUT THIS?
IT'S MY–
"IT'S MY JOB TO KNOW THINGS"? YEAH, YEAH. BUT THIS PLACE IS HUGE. SOMEONE MUST HAVE SHOWN YOU AROUND. YOUR FATHER, MAYBE?

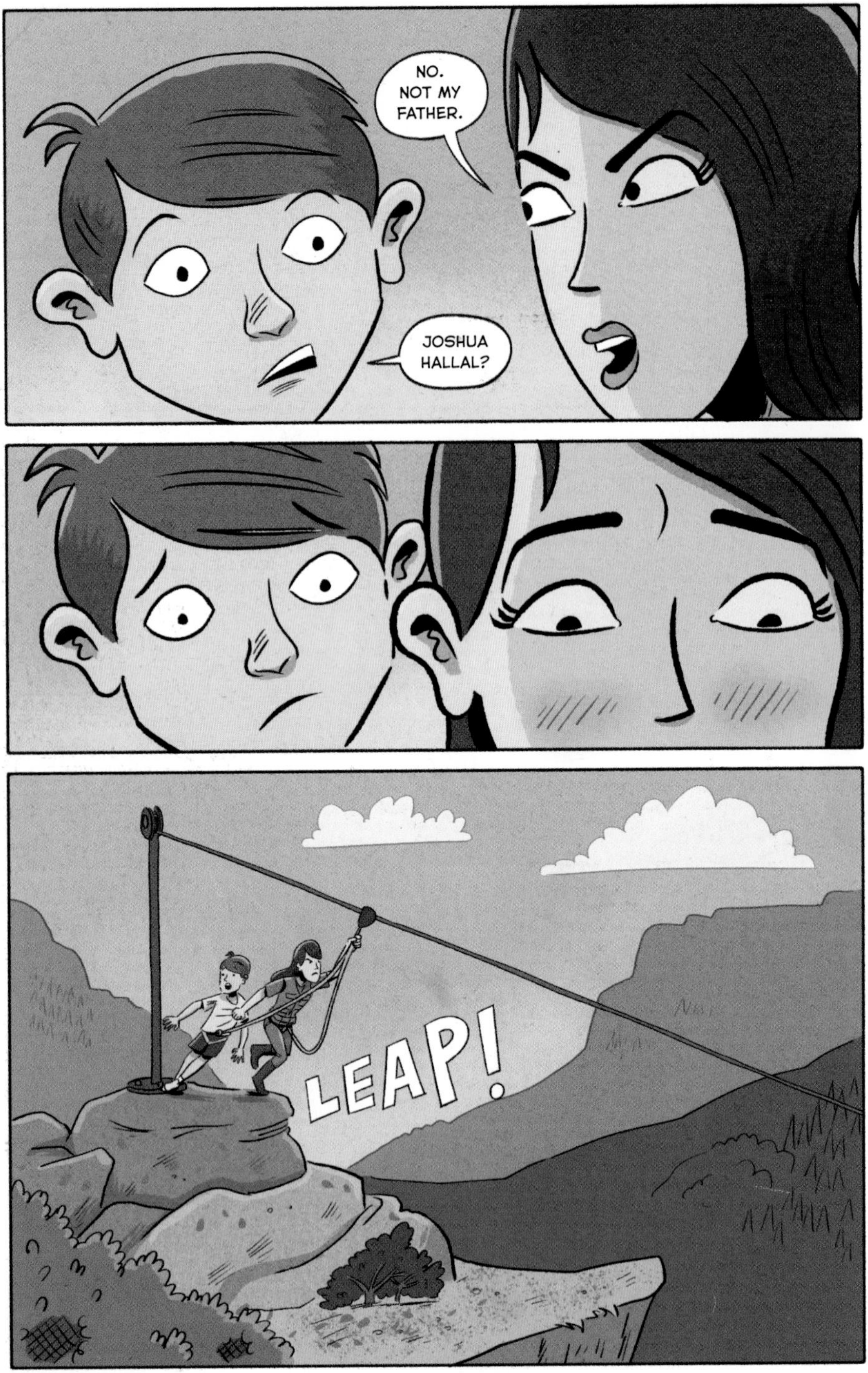
NO. NOT MY FATHER.
JOSHUA HALLAL?
LEAP!

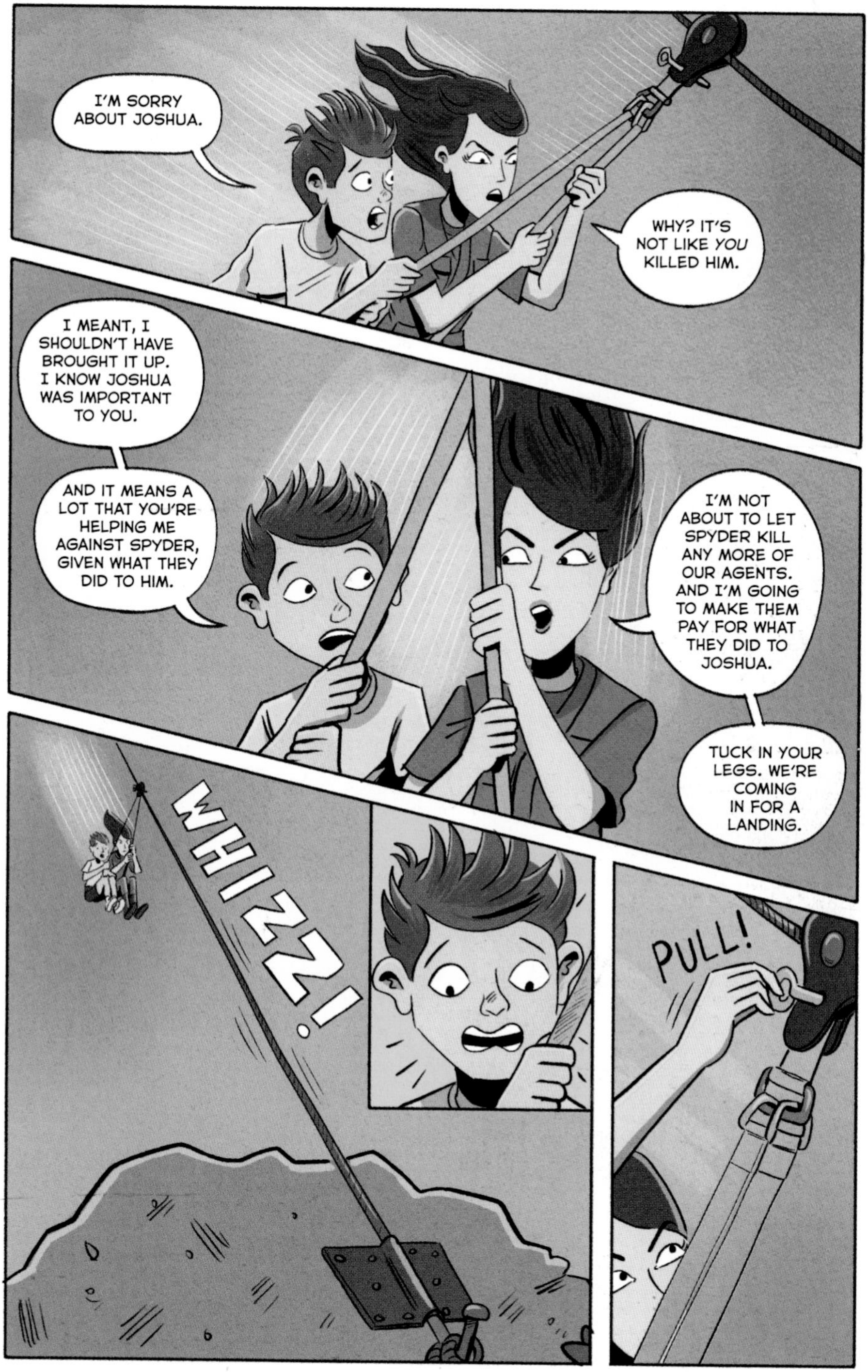
I'M SORRY ABOUT JOSHUA.
WHY? IT'S NOT LIKE *YOU* KILLED HIM.
I MEANT, I SHOULDN'T HAVE BROUGHT IT UP. I KNOW JOSHUA WAS IMPORTANT TO YOU.
AND IT MEANS A LOT THAT YOU'RE HELPING ME AGAINST SPYDER, GIVEN WHAT THEY DID TO HIM.
I'M NOT ABOUT TO LET SPYDER KILL ANY MORE OF OUR AGENTS. AND I'M GOING TO MAKE THEM PAY FOR WHAT THEY DID TO JOSHUA.
TUCK IN YOUR LEGS. WE'RE COMING IN FOR A LANDING.
WHIZZ!
PULL!

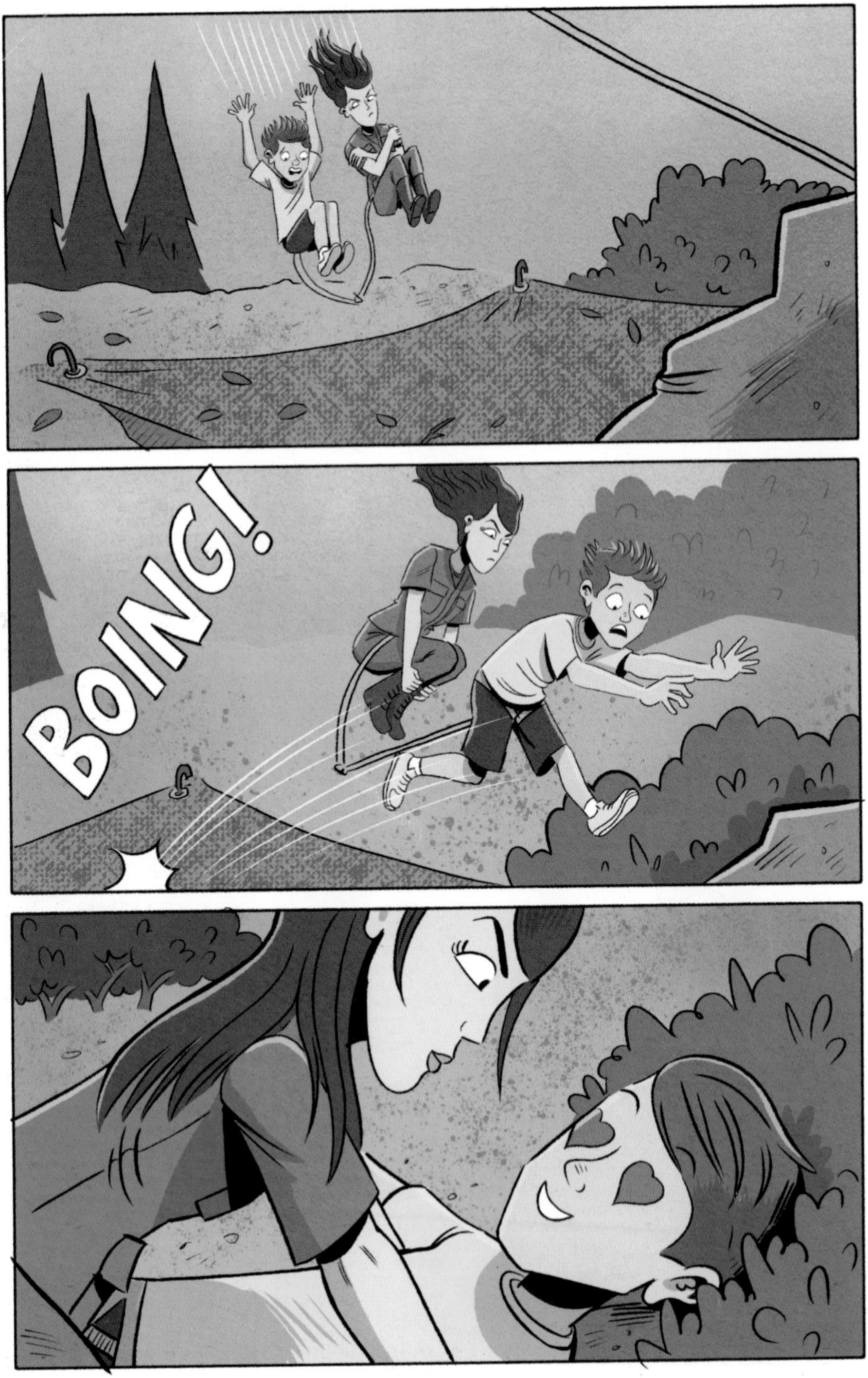
BOING!

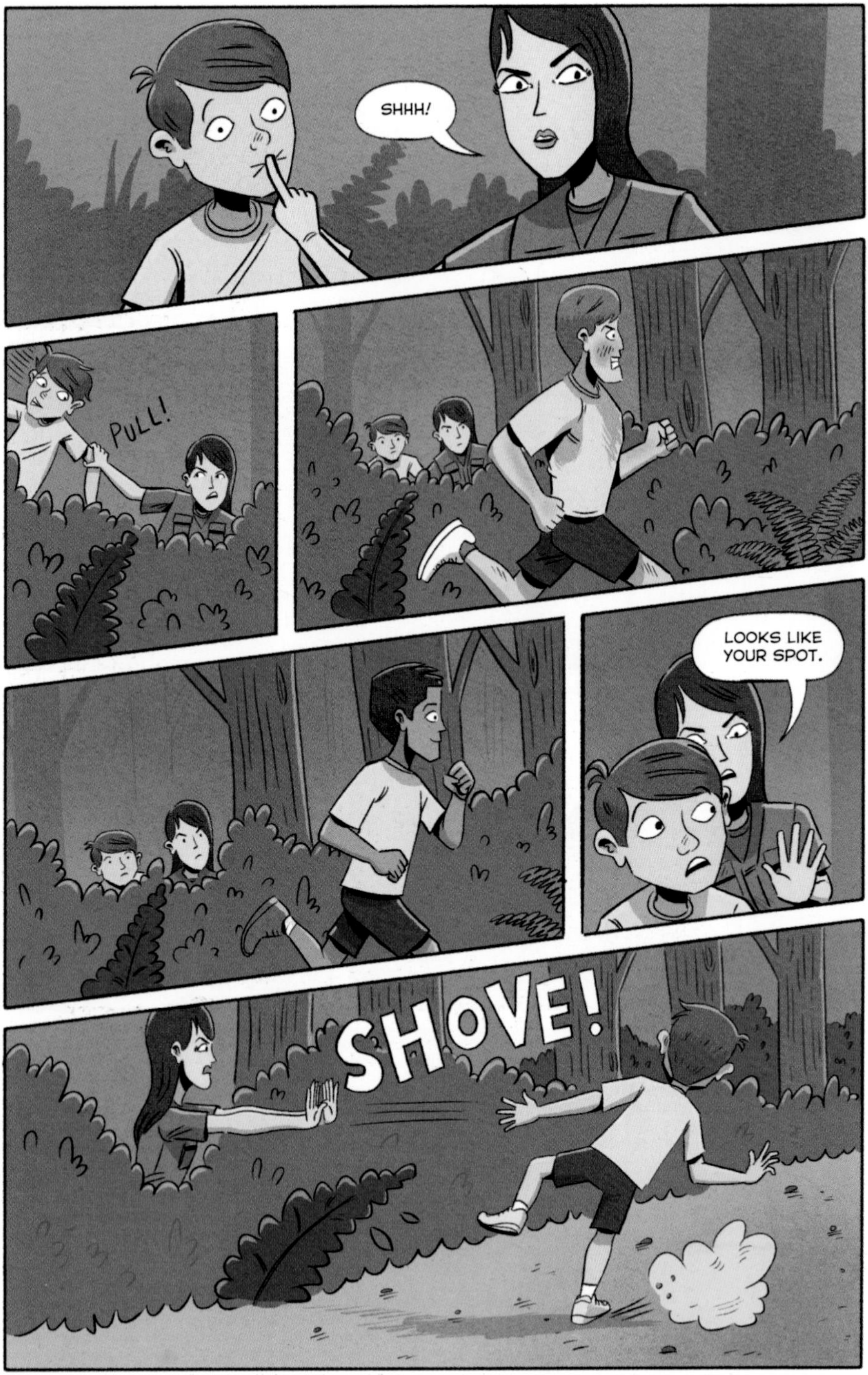
SHHH!
PULL!
LOOKS LIKE YOUR SPOT.
SHOVE!

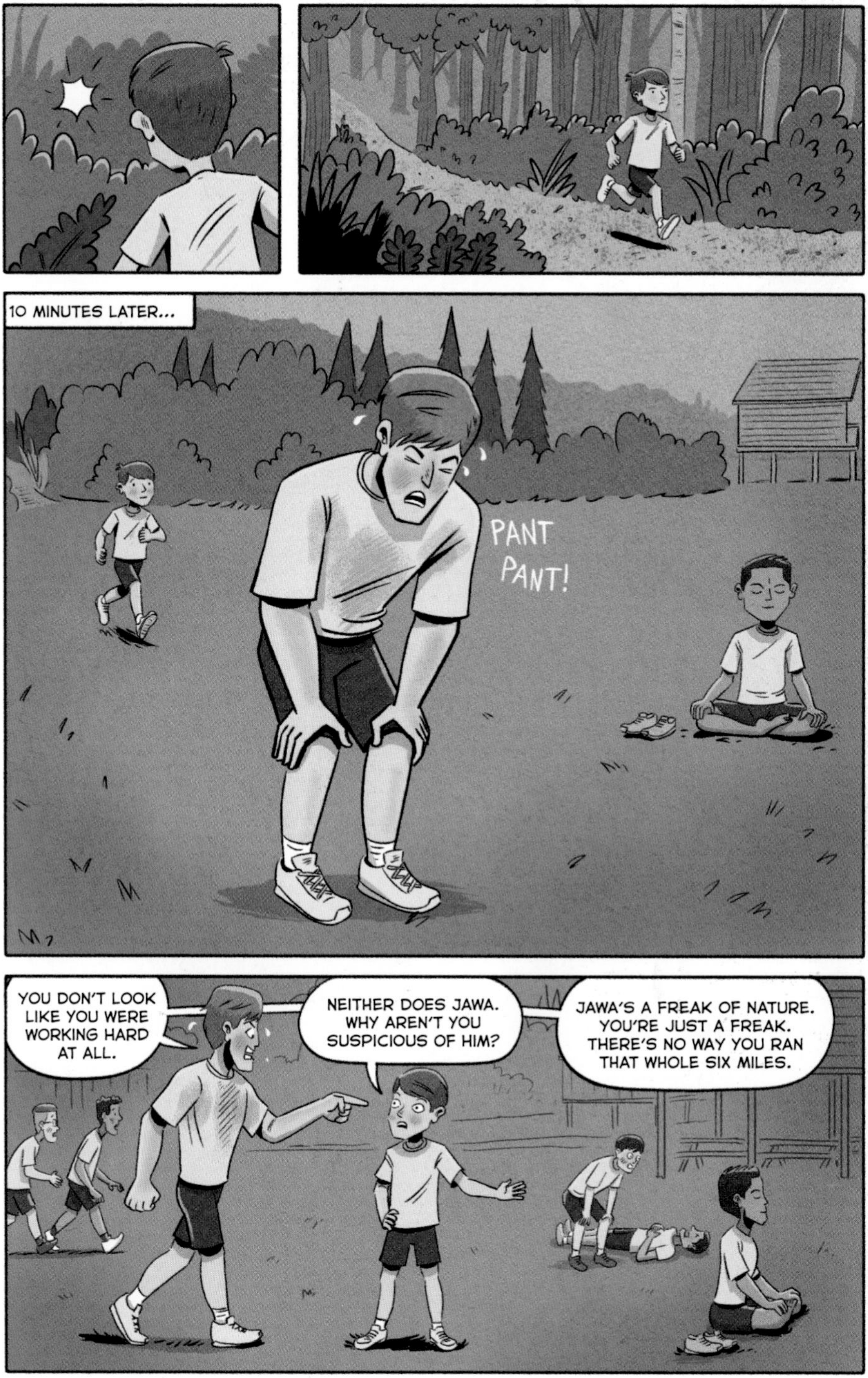
10 MINUTES LATER...
PANT
PANT!
YOU DON'T LOOK LIKE YOU WERE WORKING HARD AT ALL.
NEITHER DOES JAWA. WHY AREN'T YOU SUSPICIOUS OF HIM?
JAWA'S A FREAK OF NATURE. YOU'RE JUST A FREAK. THERE'S NO WAY YOU RAN THAT WHOLE SIX MILES.

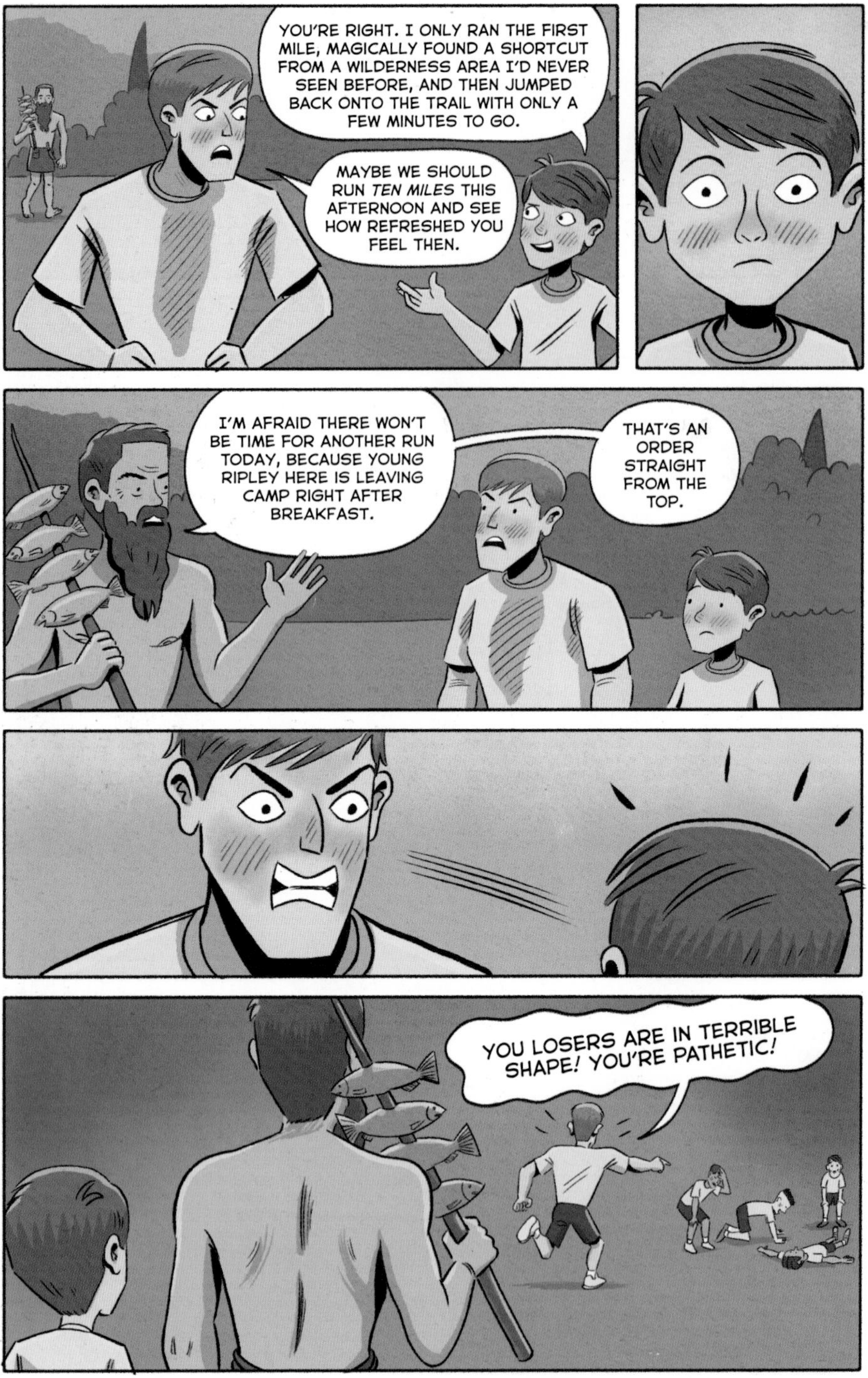
YOU'RE RIGHT. I ONLY RAN THE FIRST MILE, MAGICALLY FOUND A SHORTCUT FROM A WILDERNESS AREA I'D NEVER SEEN BEFORE, AND THEN JUMPED BACK ONTO THE TRAIL WITH ONLY A FEW MINUTES TO GO.
MAYBE WE SHOULD RUN *TEN MILES* THIS AFTERNOON AND SEE HOW REFRESHED YOU FEEL THEN.
I'M AFRAID THERE WON'T BE TIME FOR ANOTHER RUN TODAY, BECAUSE YOUNG RIPLEY HERE IS LEAVING CAMP RIGHT AFTER BREAKFAST.
THAT'S AN ORDER STRAIGHT FROM THE TOP.
YOU LOSERS ARE IN TERRIBLE SHAPE! YOU'RE PATHETIC!

101

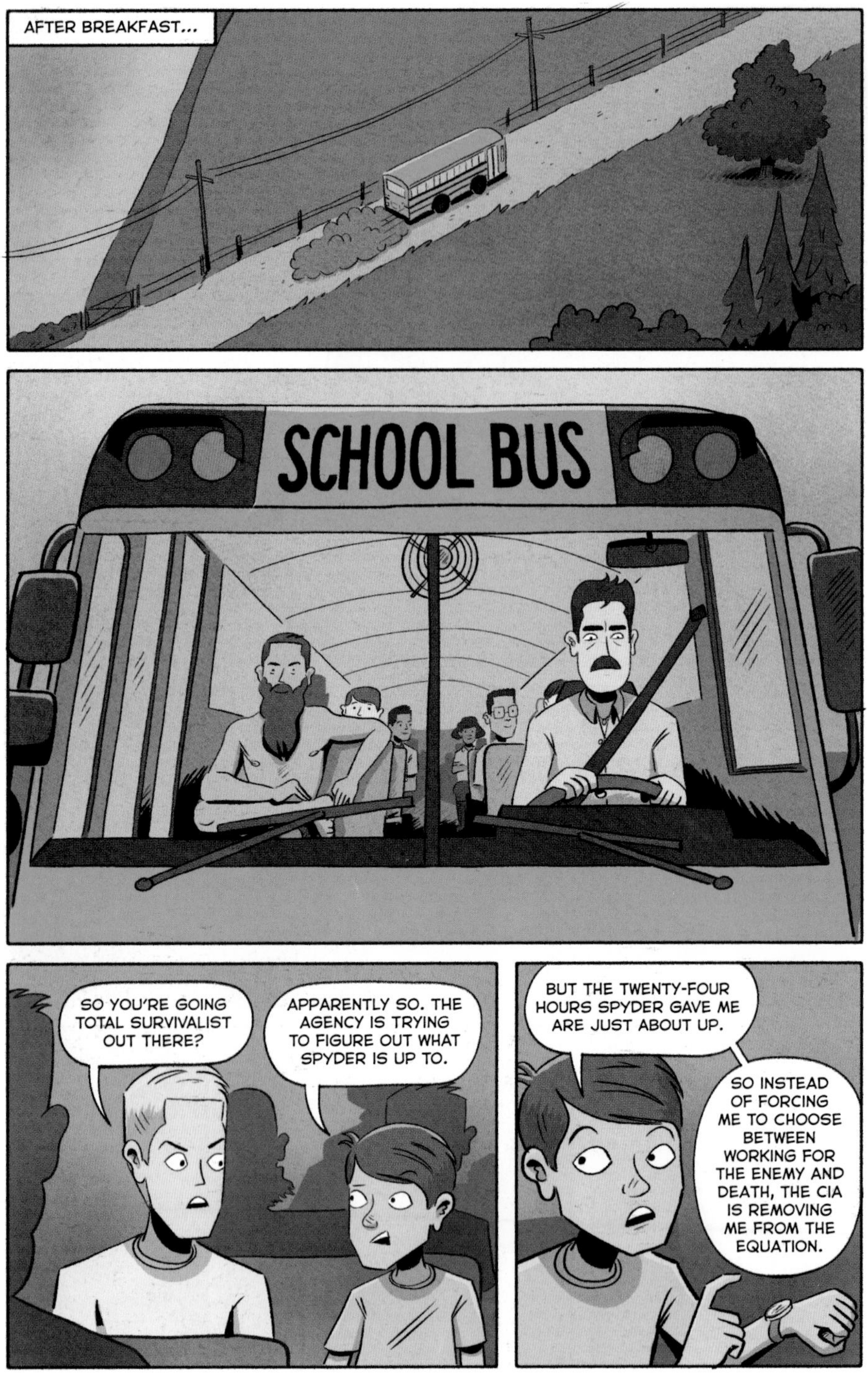
AFTER BREAKFAST...
SCHOOL BUS
SO YOU'RE GOING TOTAL SURVIVALIST OUT THERE?
APPARENTLY SO. THE AGENCY IS TRYING TO FIGURE OUT WHAT SPYDER IS UP TO.
BUT THE TWENTY-FOUR HOURS SPYDER GAVE ME ARE JUST ABOUT UP.
SO INSTEAD OF FORCING ME TO CHOOSE BETWEEN WORKING FOR THE ENEMY AND DEATH, THE CIA IS REMOVING ME FROM THE EQUATION.

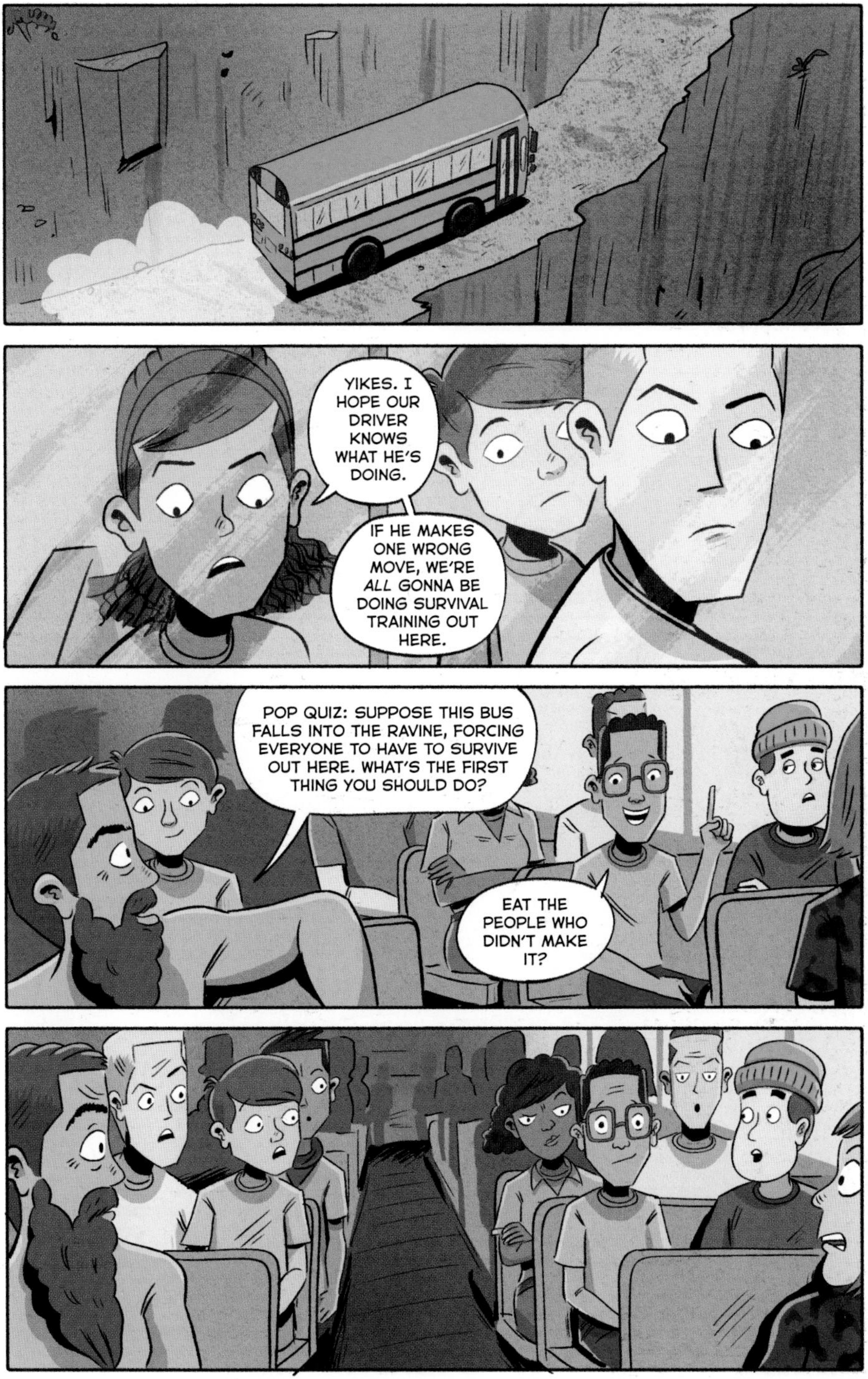
YIKES. I HOPE OUR DRIVER KNOWS WHAT HE'S DOING.
IF HE MAKES ONE WRONG MOVE, WE'RE *ALL* GONNA BE DOING SURVIVAL TRAINING OUT HERE.
POP QUIZ: SUPPOSE THIS BUS FALLS INTO THE RAVINE, FORCING EVERYONE TO HAVE TO SURVIVE OUT HERE. WHAT'S THE FIRST THING YOU SHOULD DO?
EAT THE PEOPLE WHO DIDN'T MAKE IT?

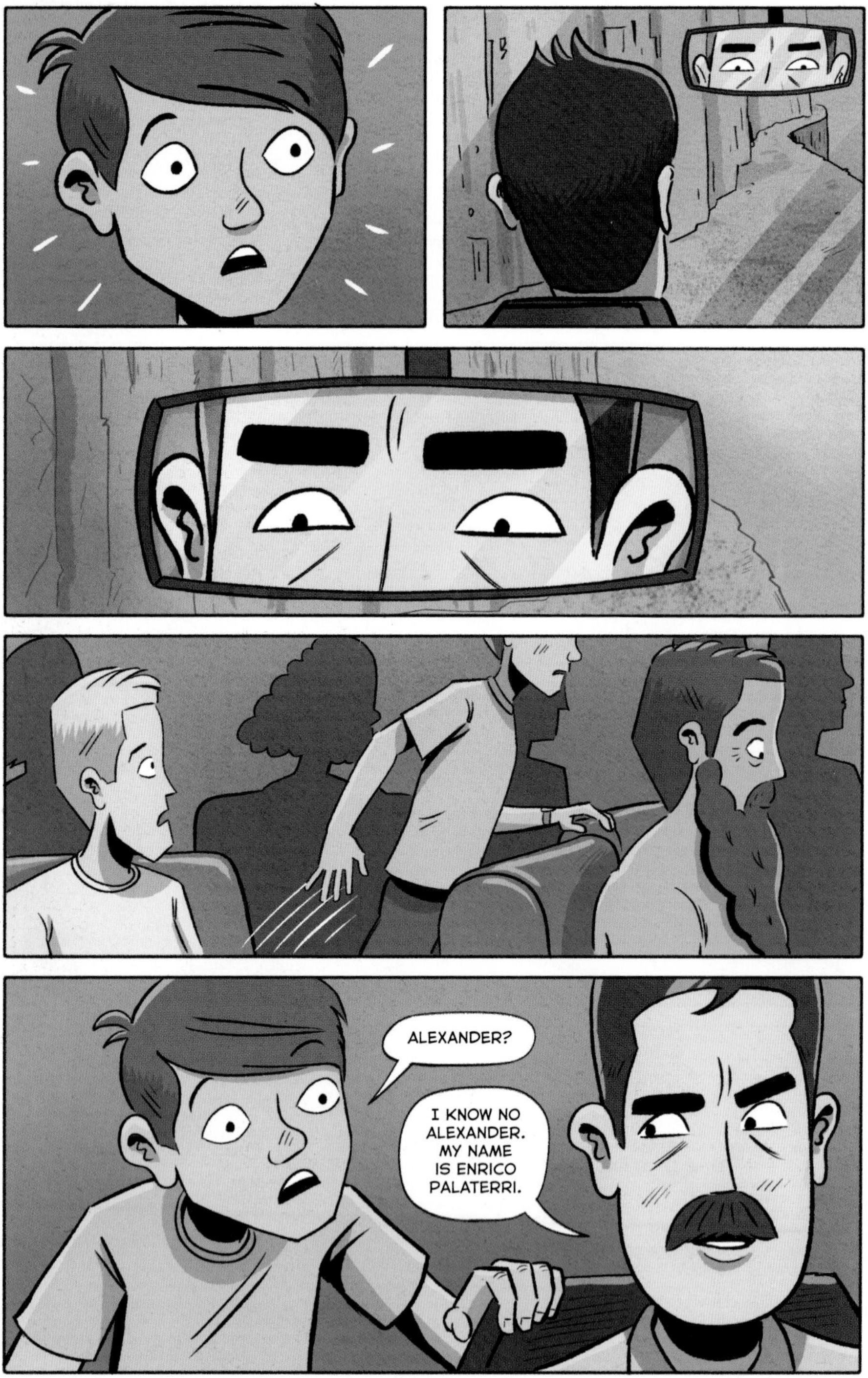
ALEXANDER?
I KNOW NO ALEXANDER. MY NAME IS ENRICO PALATERRI.

105

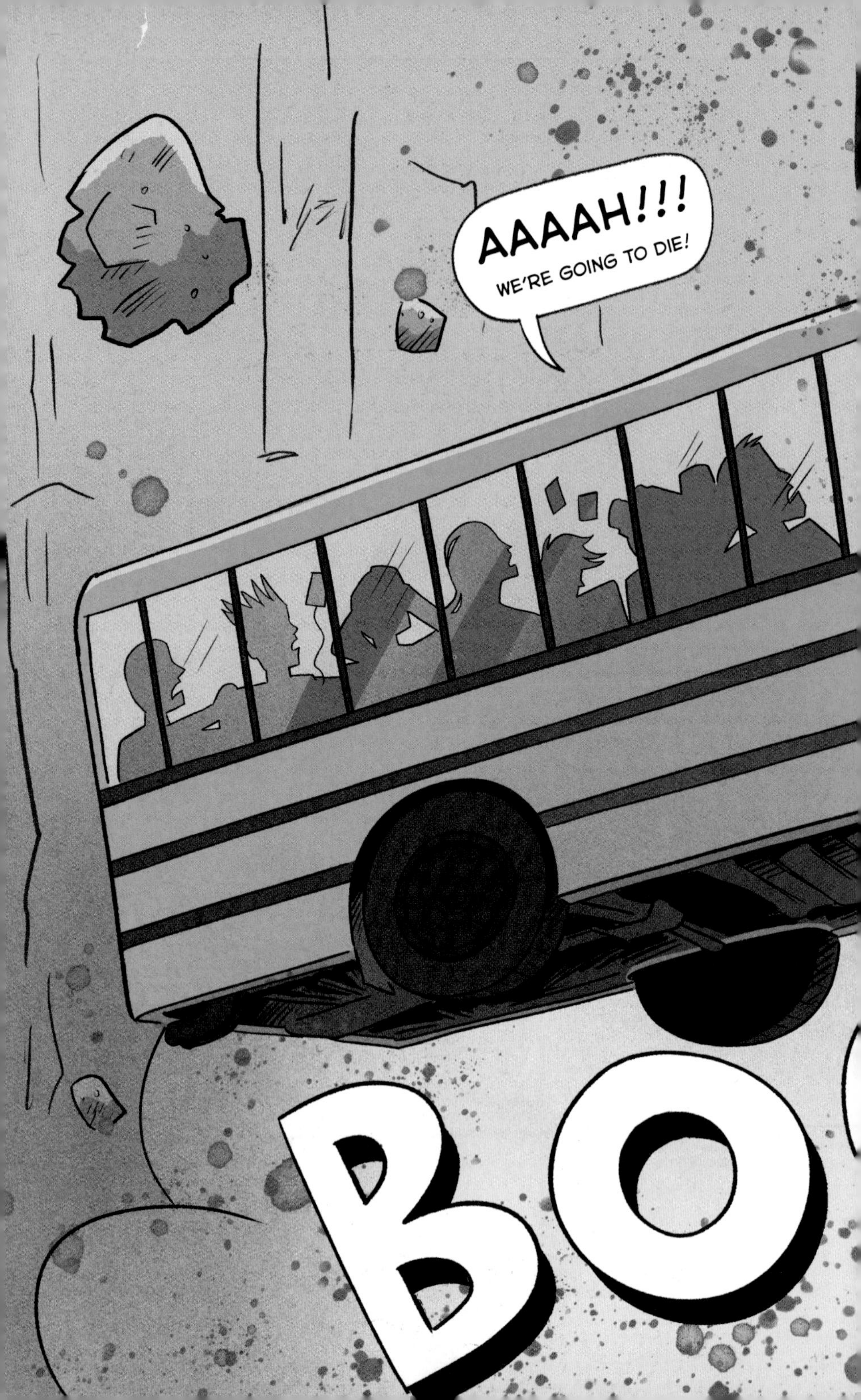
AAAAH!!!
WE'RE GOING TO DIE!
BO

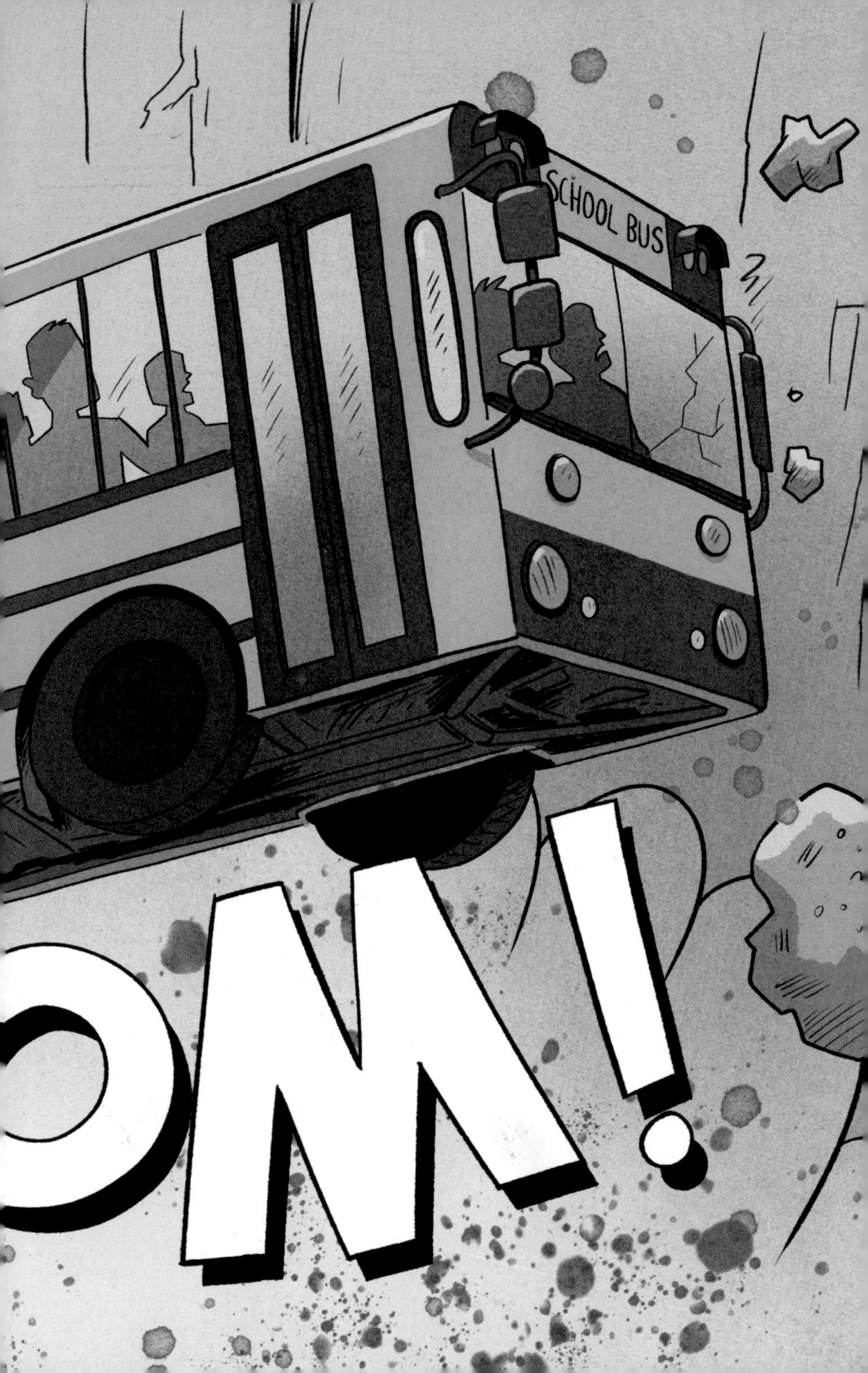
SCHOOL BUS
OM!

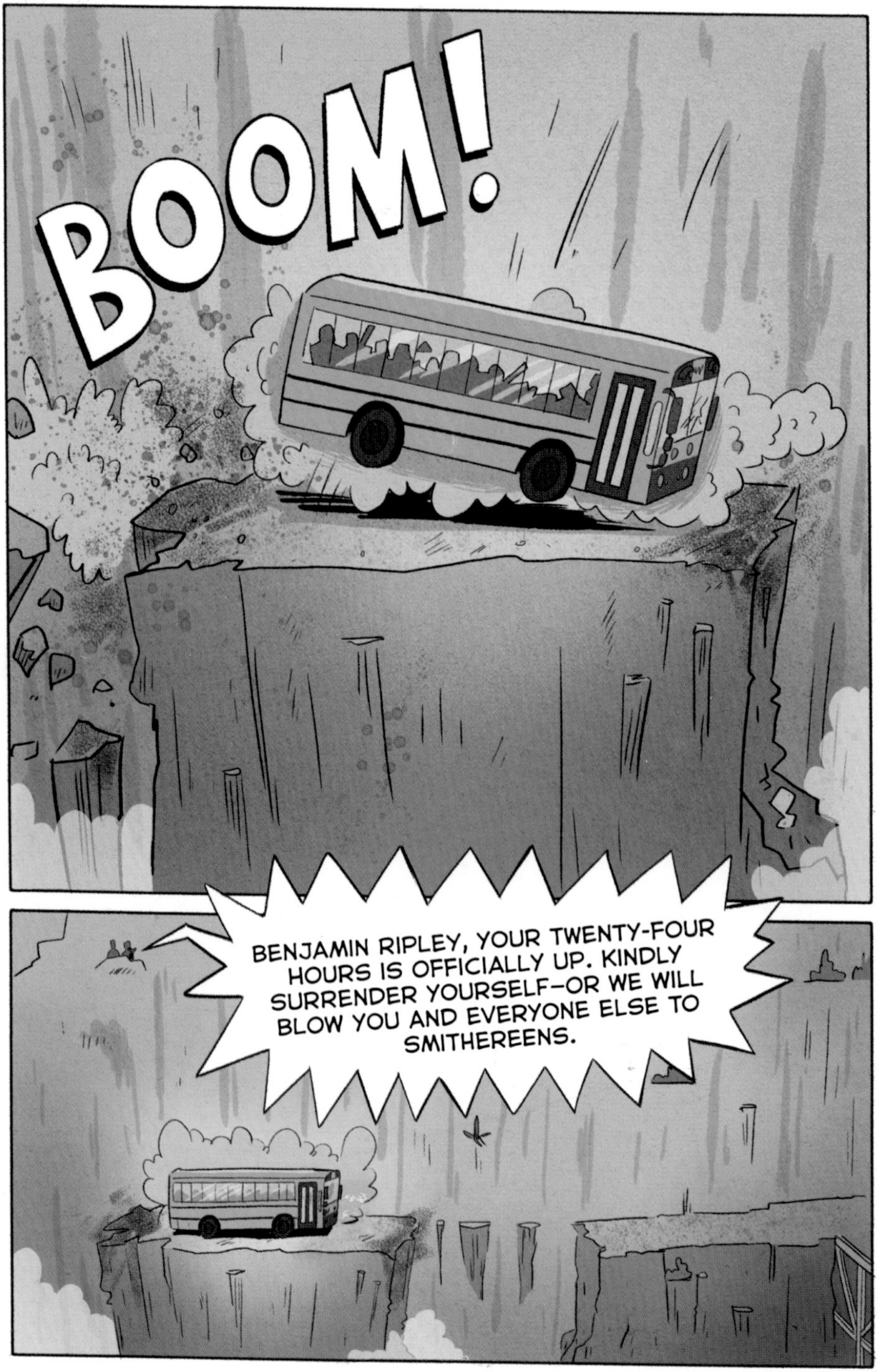
BOOM!
BENJAMIN RIPLEY, YOUR TWENTY-FOUR HOURS IS OFFICIALLY UP. KINDLY SURRENDER YOURSELF—OR WE WILL BLOW YOU AND EVERYONE ELSE TO SMITHEREENS.

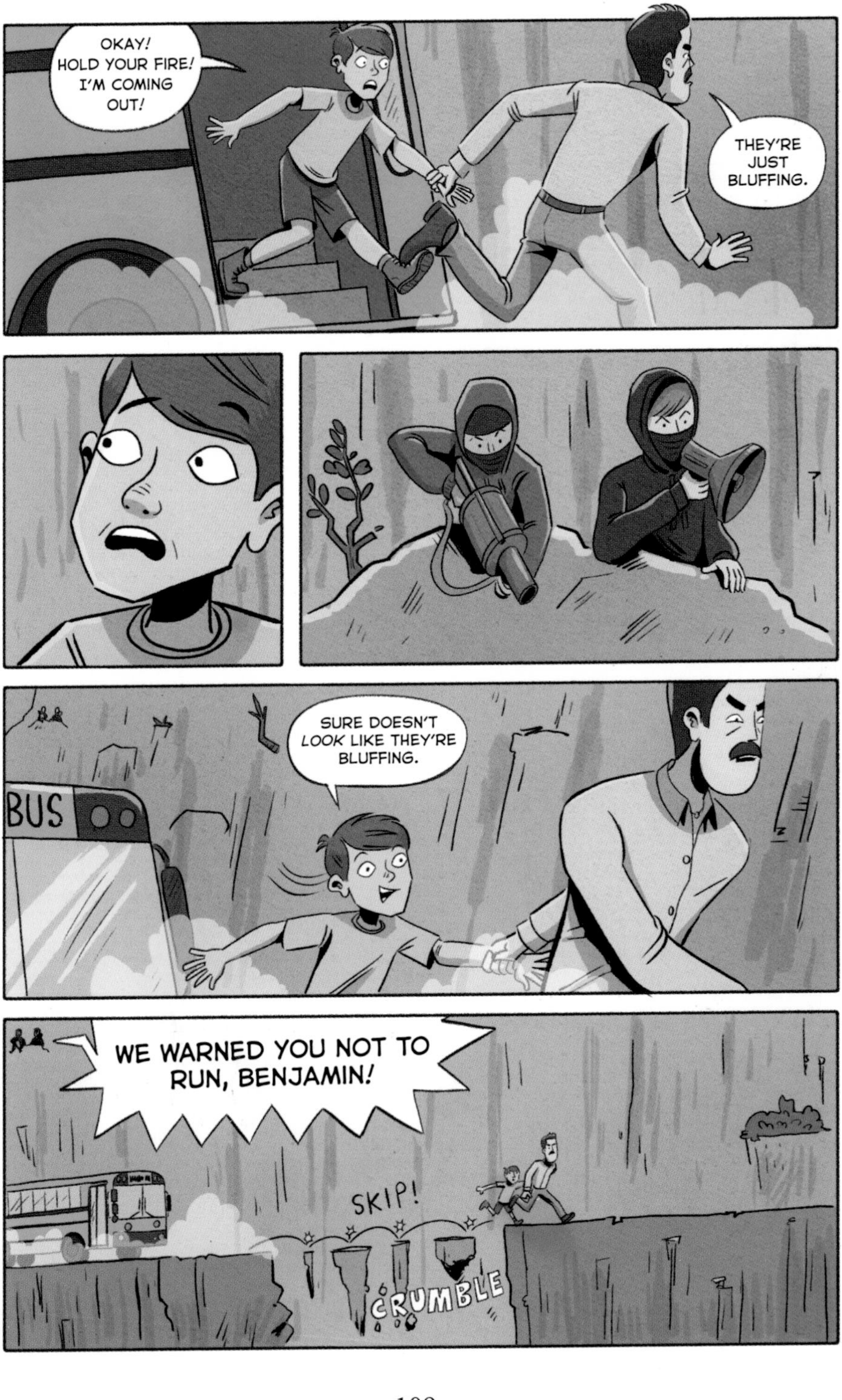
OKAY! HOLD YOUR FIRE! I'M COMING OUT!
THEY'RE JUST BLUFFING.
SURE DOESN'T *LOOK* LIKE THEY'RE BLUFFING.
BUS
WE WARNED YOU NOT TO RUN, BENJAMIN!
SKIP!
CRUMBLE

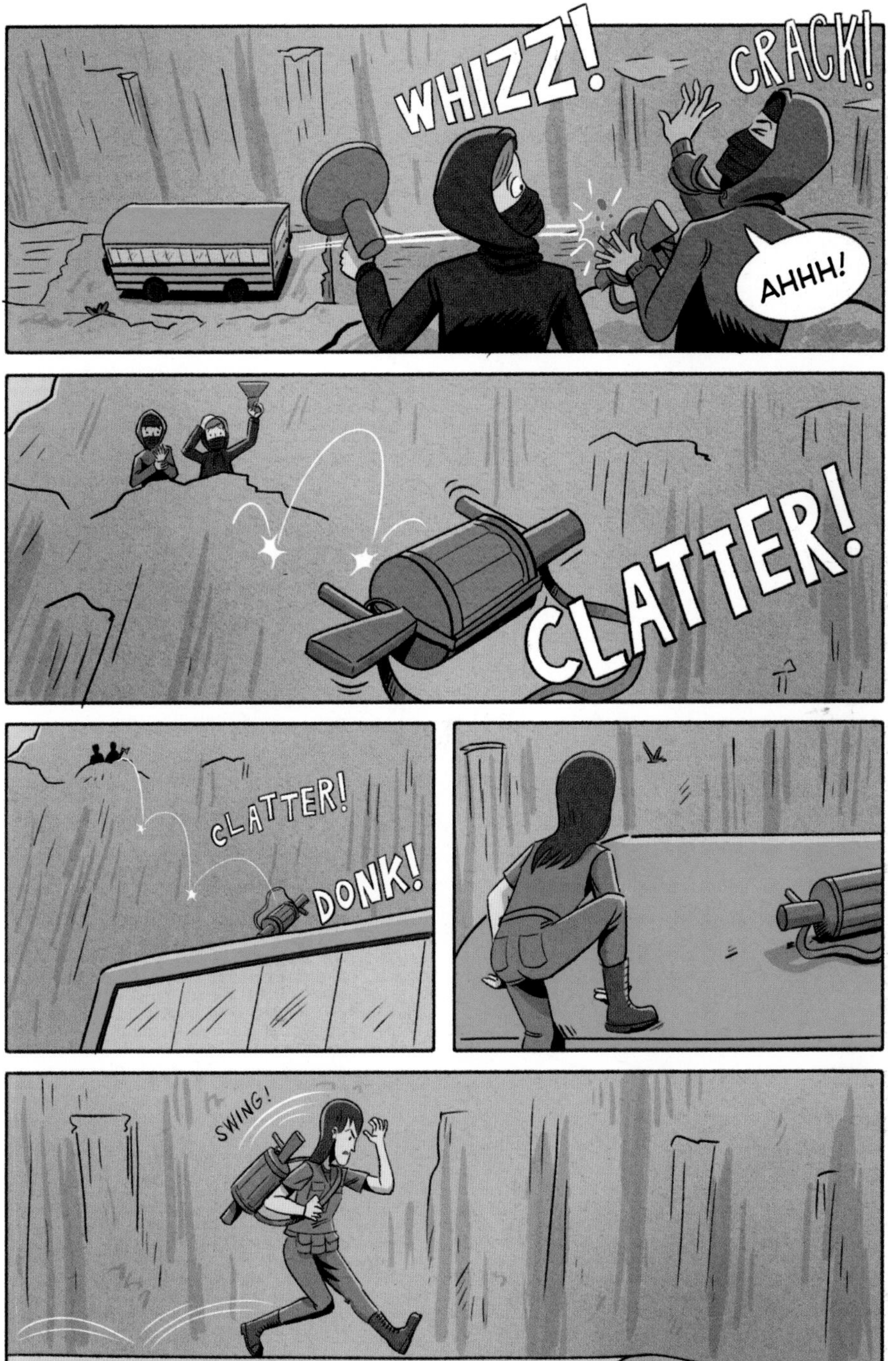
WHIZZ!
CRACK!
AHHH!
CLATTER!
CLATTER!
DONK!
SWING!
SCHOOL BUS

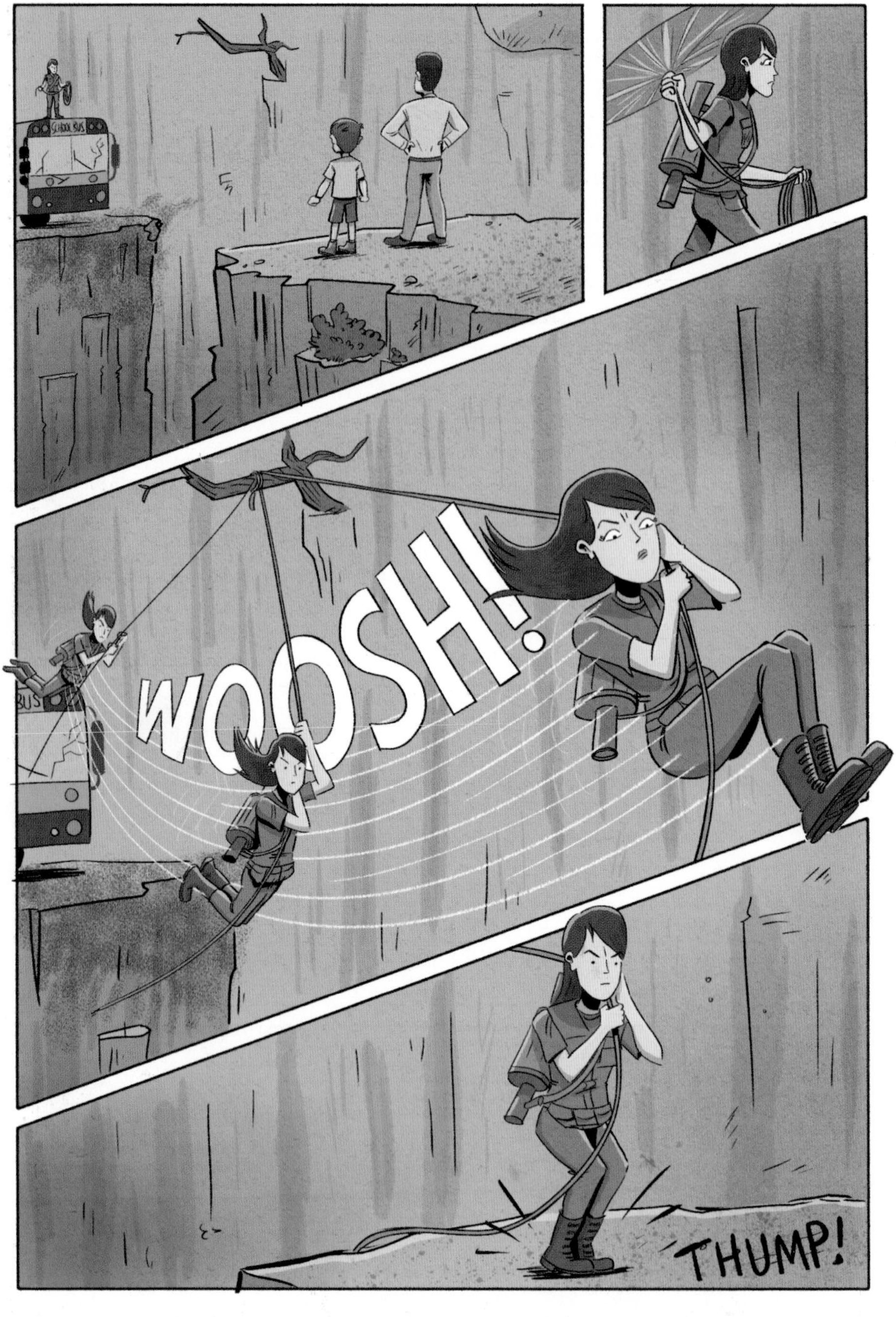
SCHOOL BUS
BUS
WOOSH!
THUMP!

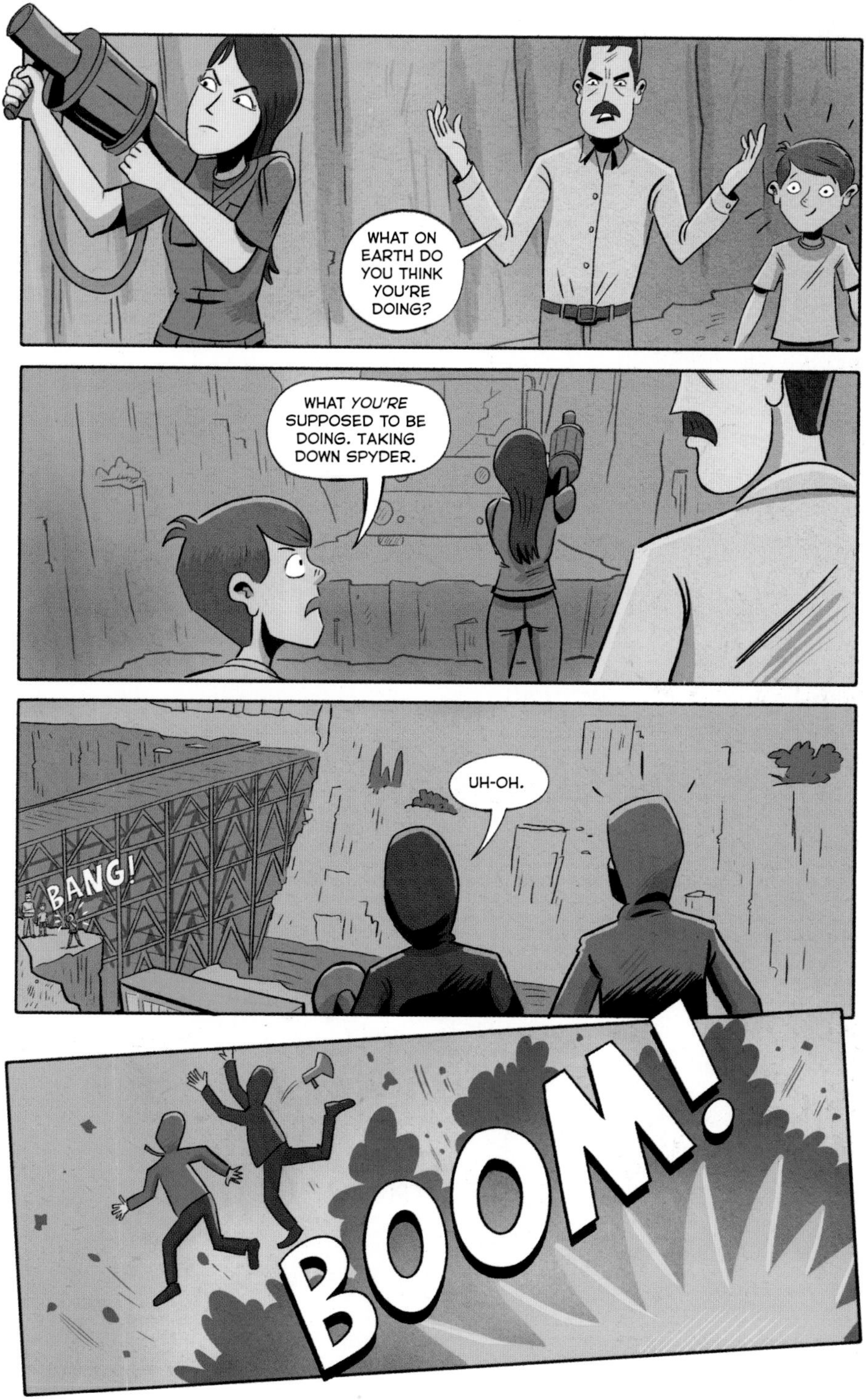
WHAT ON EARTH DO YOU THINK YOU'RE DOING?
WHAT *YOU'RE* SUPPOSED TO BE DOING. TAKING DOWN SPYDER.
UH-OH.
BANG!
BOOM!

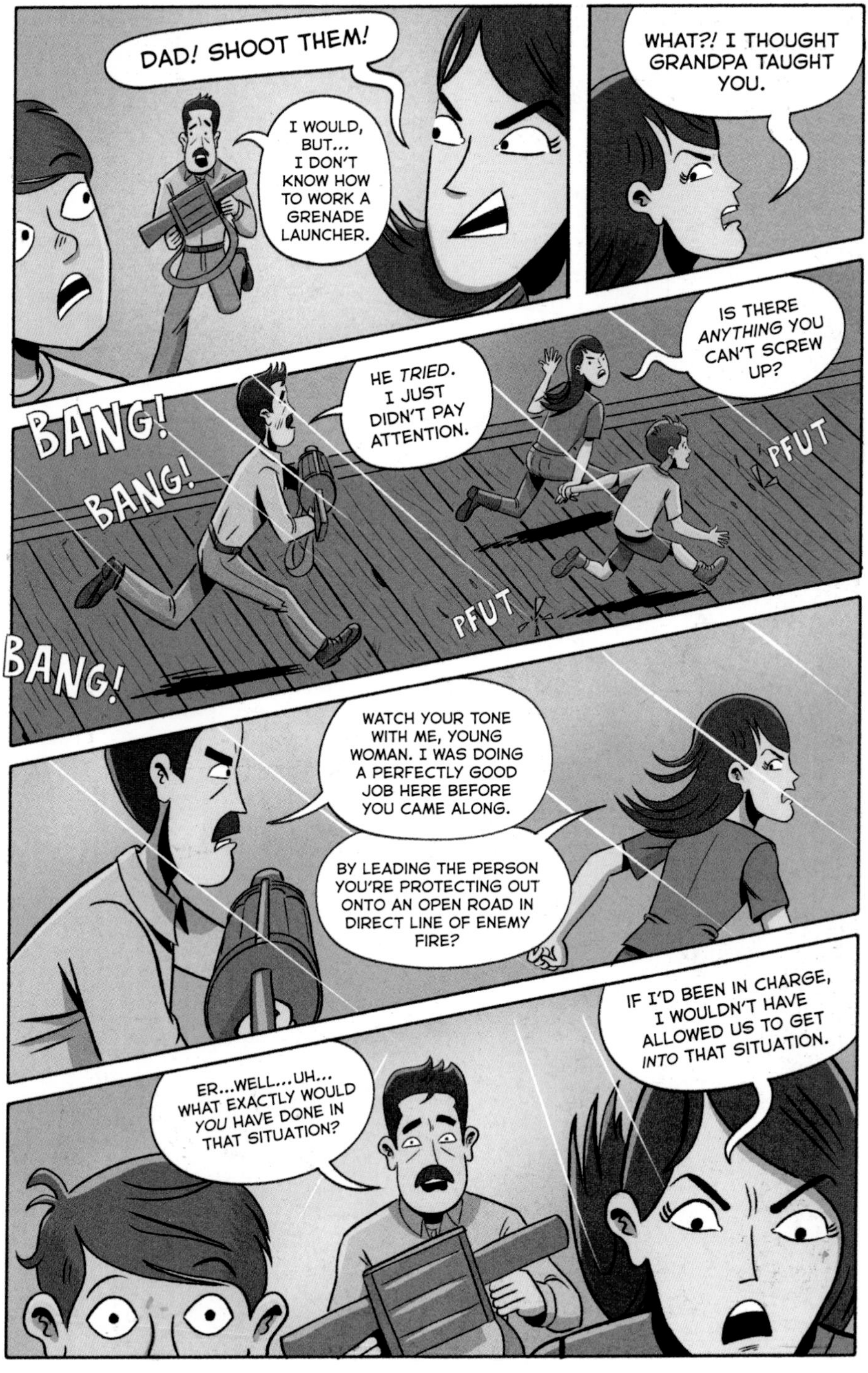
DAD! SHOOT THEM!
I WOULD, BUT... I DON'T KNOW HOW TO WORK A GRENADE LAUNCHER.
WHAT?! I THOUGHT GRANDPA TAUGHT YOU.
BANG!
BANG!
HE *TRIED*. I JUST DIDN'T PAY ATTENTION.
IS THERE *ANYTHING* YOU CAN'T SCREW UP?
PFUT
PFUT
BANG!
WATCH YOUR TONE WITH ME, YOUNG WOMAN. I WAS DOING A PERFECTLY GOOD JOB HERE BEFORE YOU CAME ALONG.
BY LEADING THE PERSON YOU'RE PROTECTING OUT ONTO AN OPEN ROAD IN DIRECT LINE OF ENEMY FIRE?
IF I'D BEEN IN CHARGE, I WOULDN'T HAVE ALLOWED US TO GET *INTO* THAT SITUATION.
ER...WELL...UH... WHAT EXACTLY WOULD *YOU* HAVE DONE IN THAT SITUATION?

116

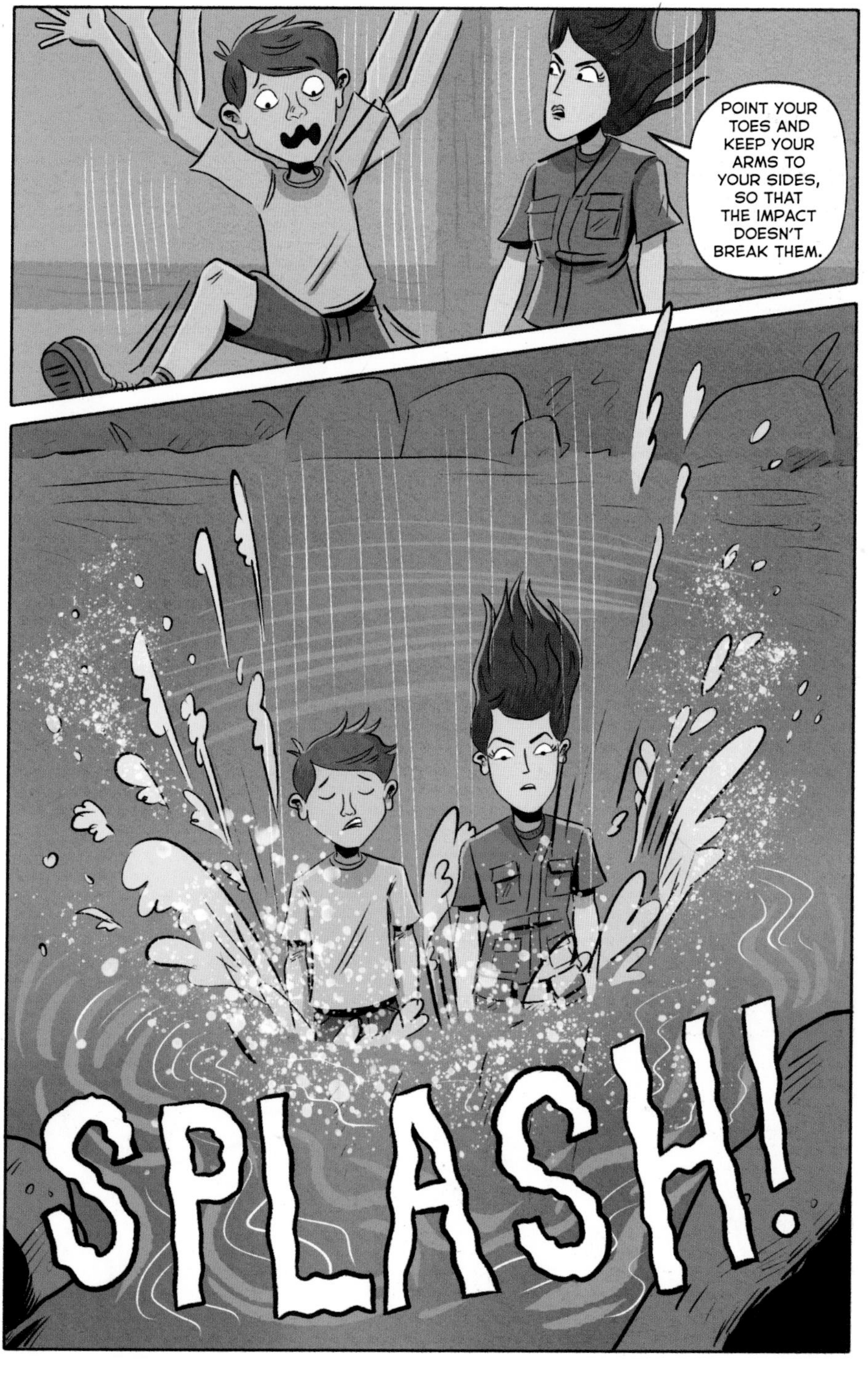
POINT YOUR TOES AND KEEP YOUR ARMS TO YOUR SIDES, SO THAT THE IMPACT DOESN'T BREAK THEM.
SPLASH!

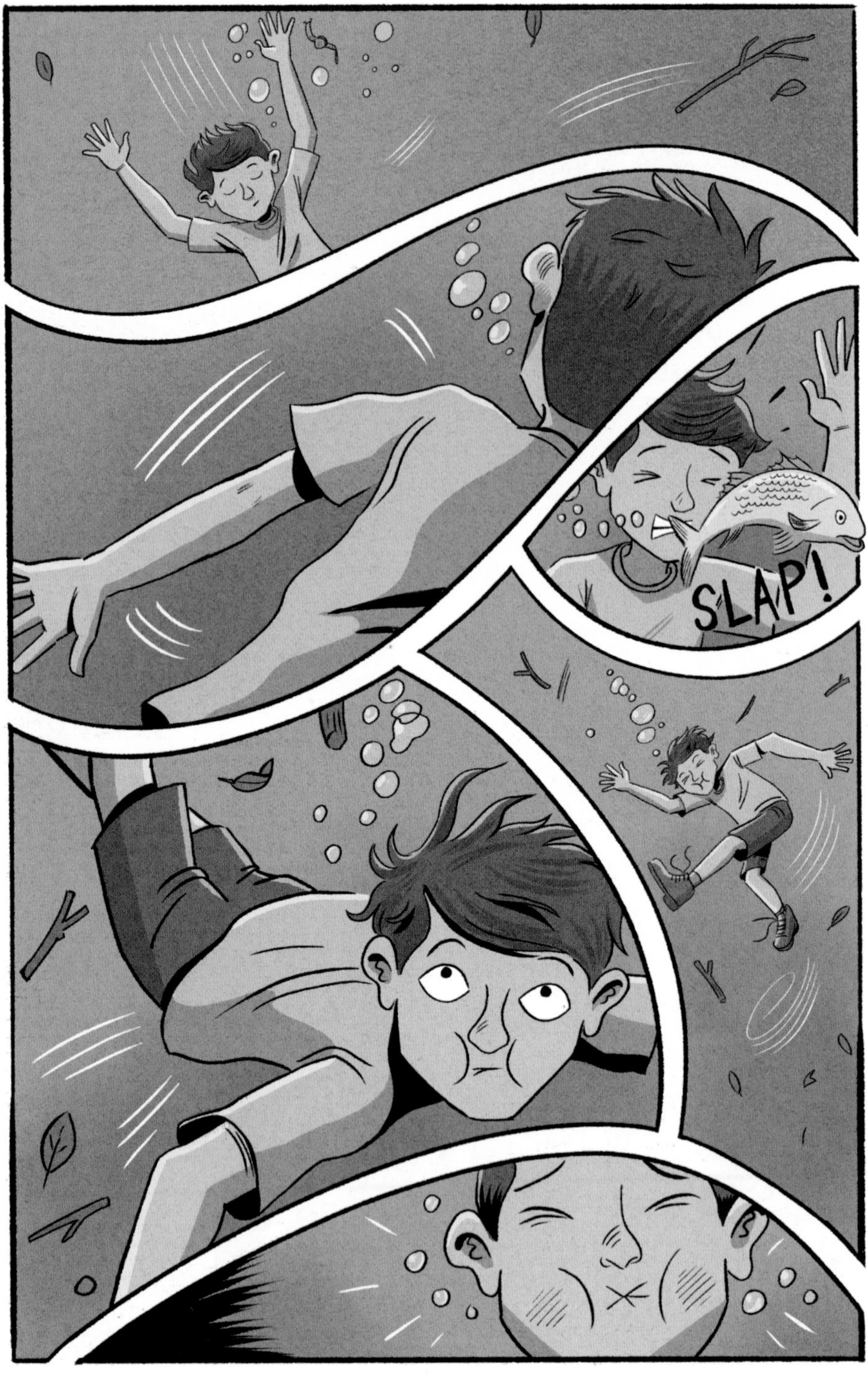
SLAP!

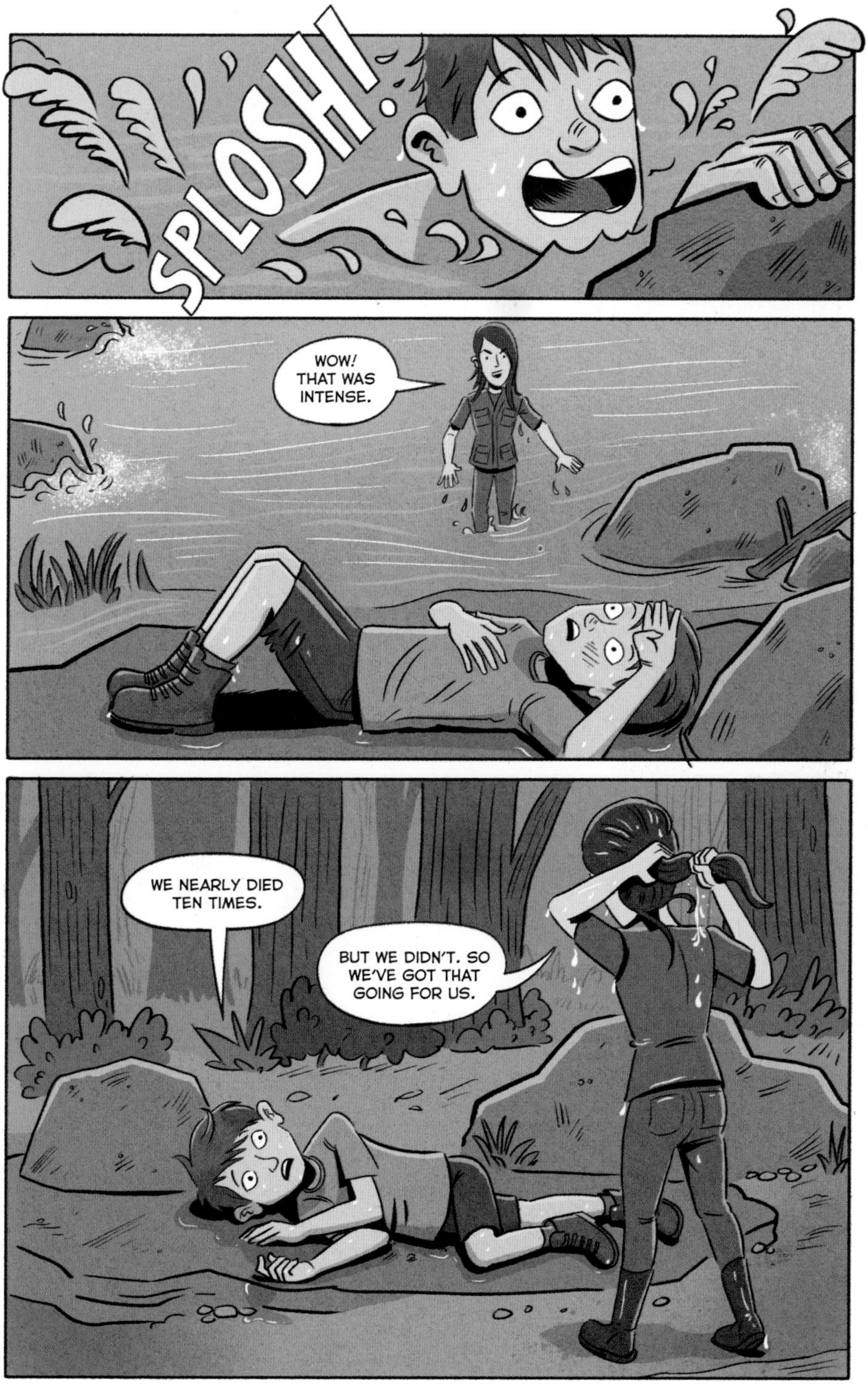
SPLOSH!
WOW! THAT WAS INTENSE.
WE NEARLY DIED TEN TIMES.
BUT WE DIDN'T. SO WE'VE GOT THAT GOING FOR US.

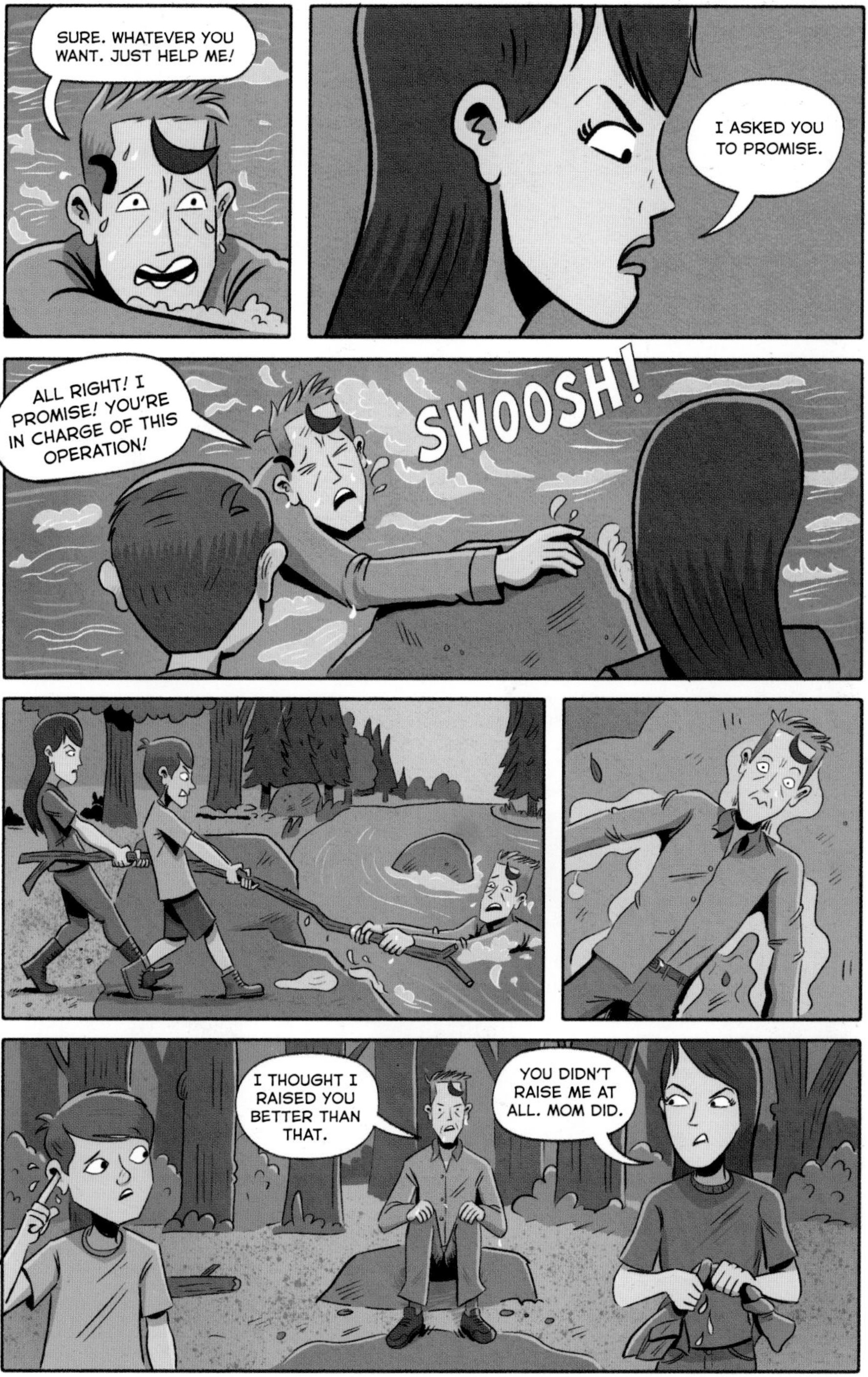
SURE. WHATEVER YOU WANT. JUST HELP ME!
I ASKED YOU TO PROMISE.
ALL RIGHT! I PROMISE! YOU'RE IN CHARGE OF THIS OPERATION!
SWOOSH!
I THOUGHT I RAISED YOU BETTER THAN THAT.
YOU DIDN'T RAISE ME AT ALL. MOM DID.

122

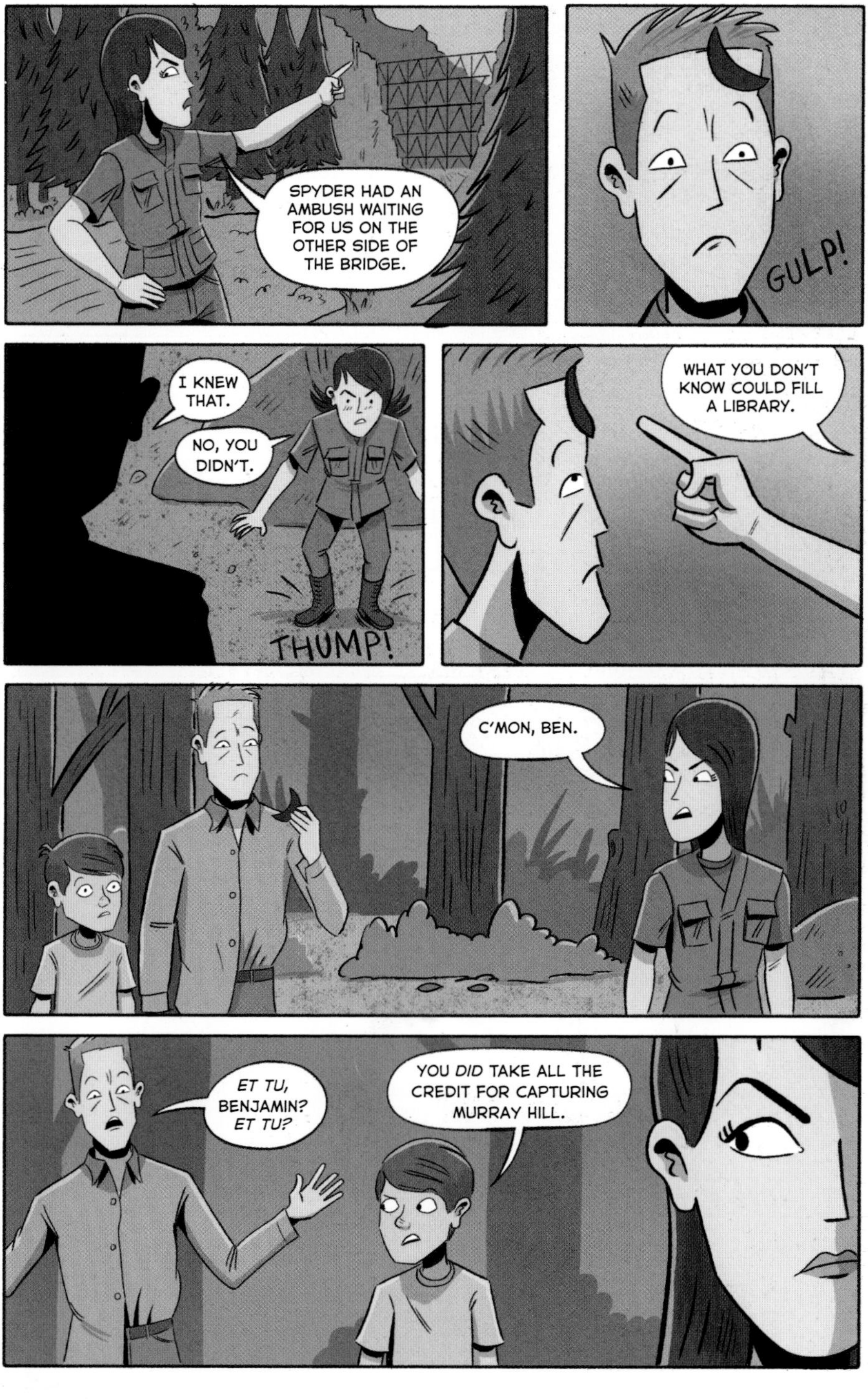
SPYDER HAD AN AMBUSH WAITING FOR US ON THE OTHER SIDE OF THE BRIDGE.
GULP!
I KNEW THAT.
NO, YOU DIDN'T.
THUMP!
WHAT YOU DON'T KNOW COULD FILL A LIBRARY.
C'MON, BEN.
ET TU, BENJAMIN? ET TU?
YOU DID TAKE ALL THE CREDIT FOR CAPTURING MURRAY HILL.

125

127

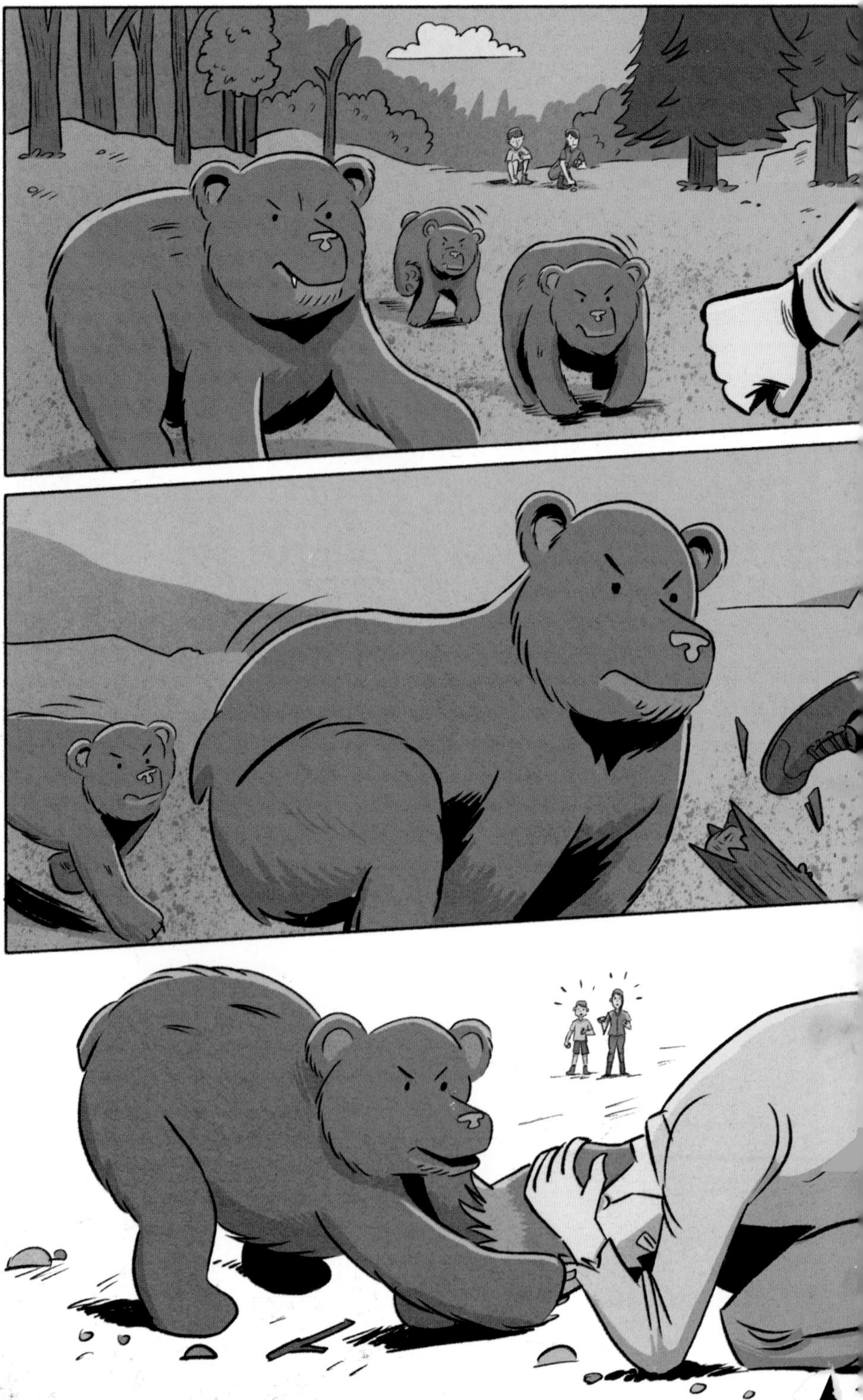

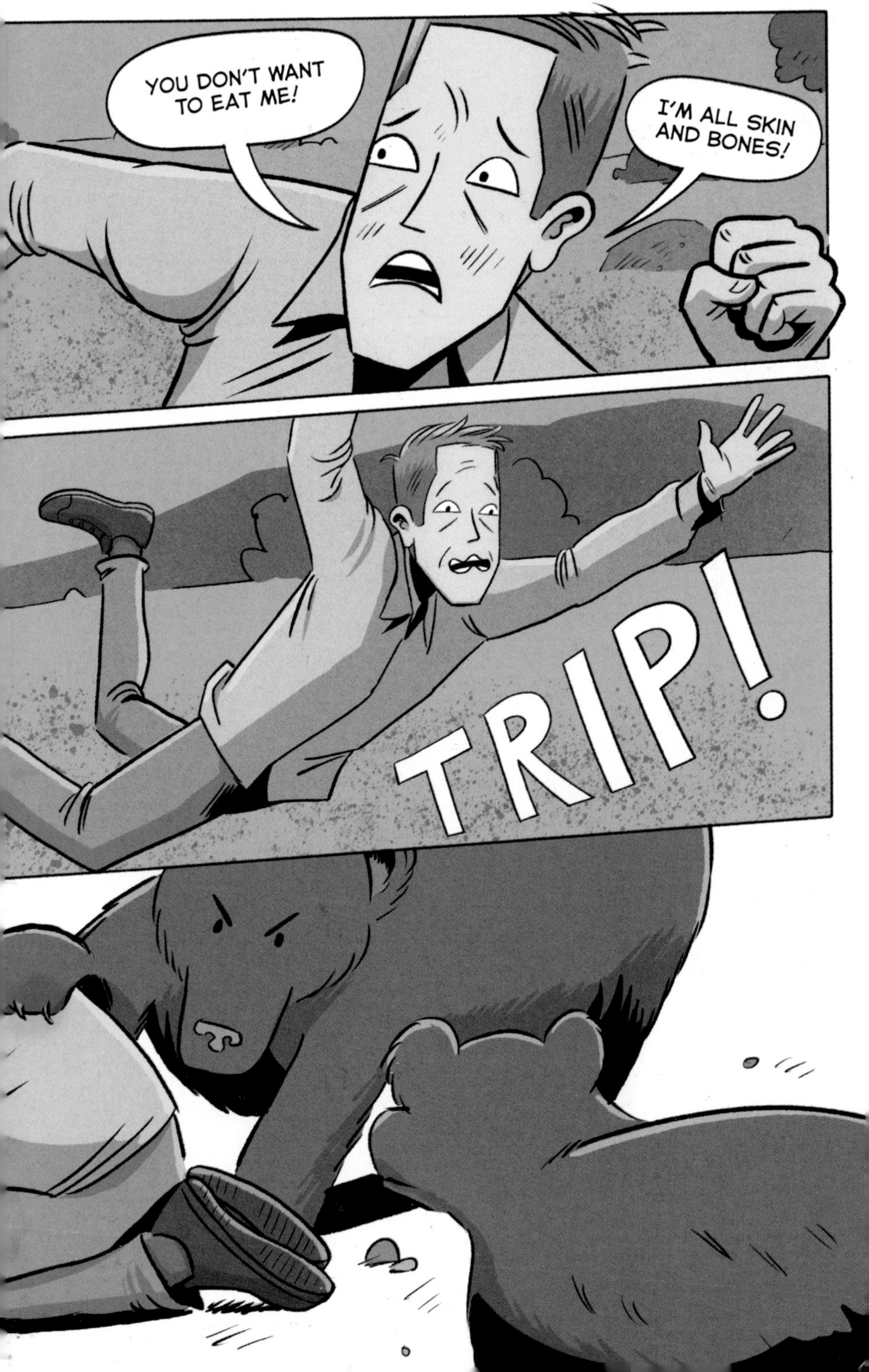
YOU DON'T WANT TO EAT ME!
I'M ALL SKIN AND BONES!
TRIP!

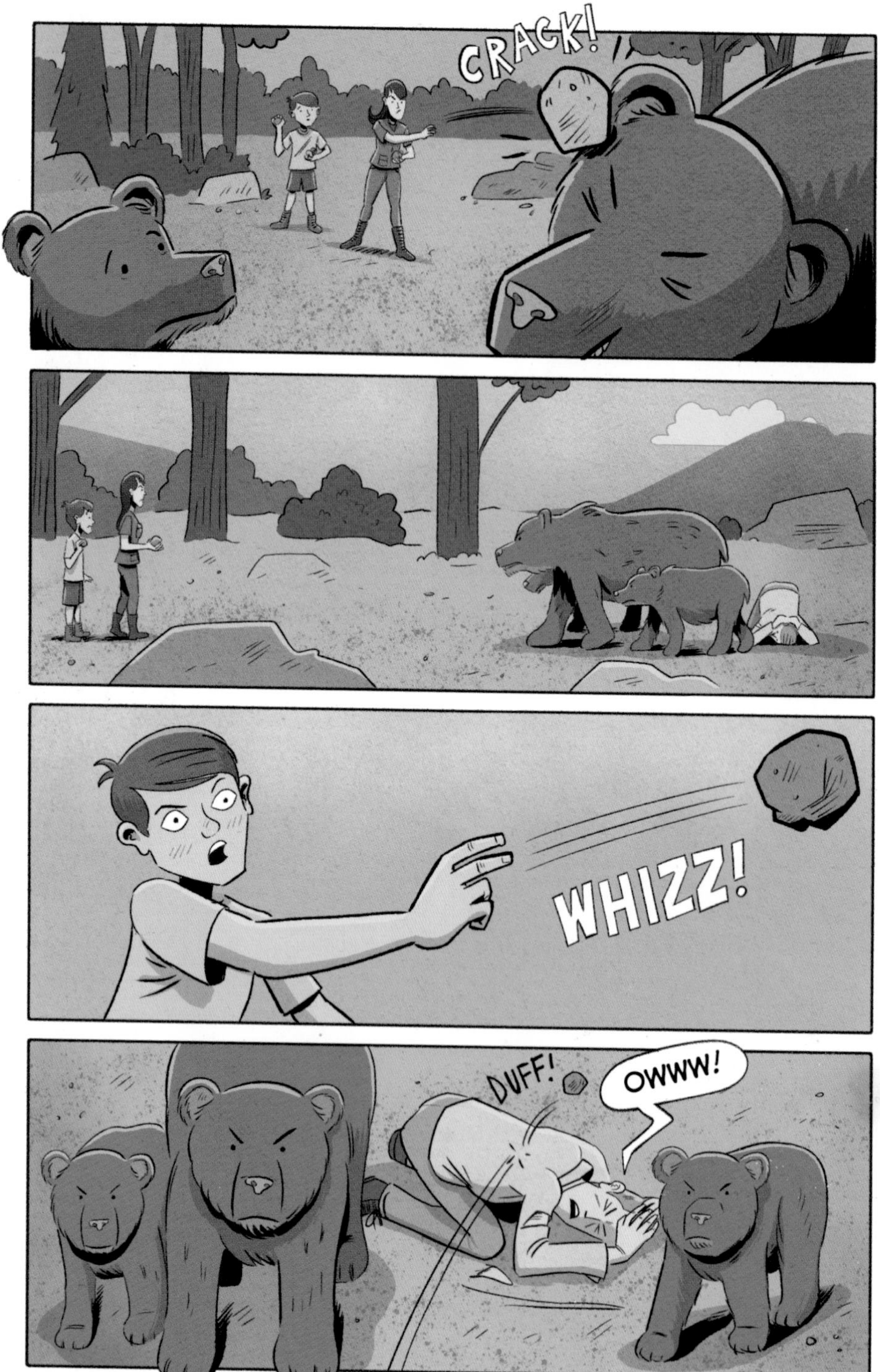
CRACK!
WHIZZ!
DUFF!
OWWW!

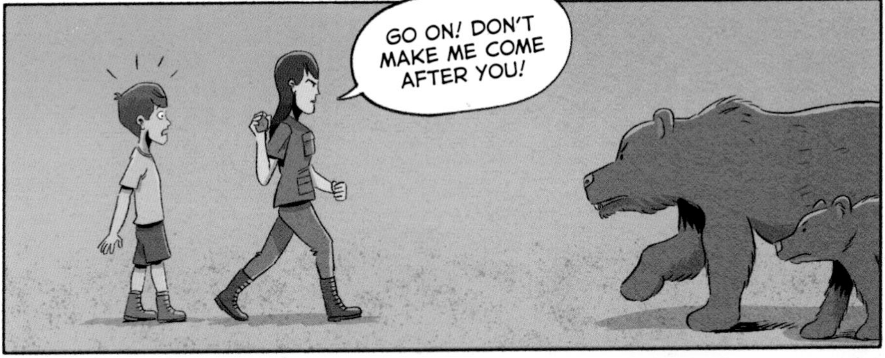
GO ON! DON'T MAKE ME COME AFTER YOU!

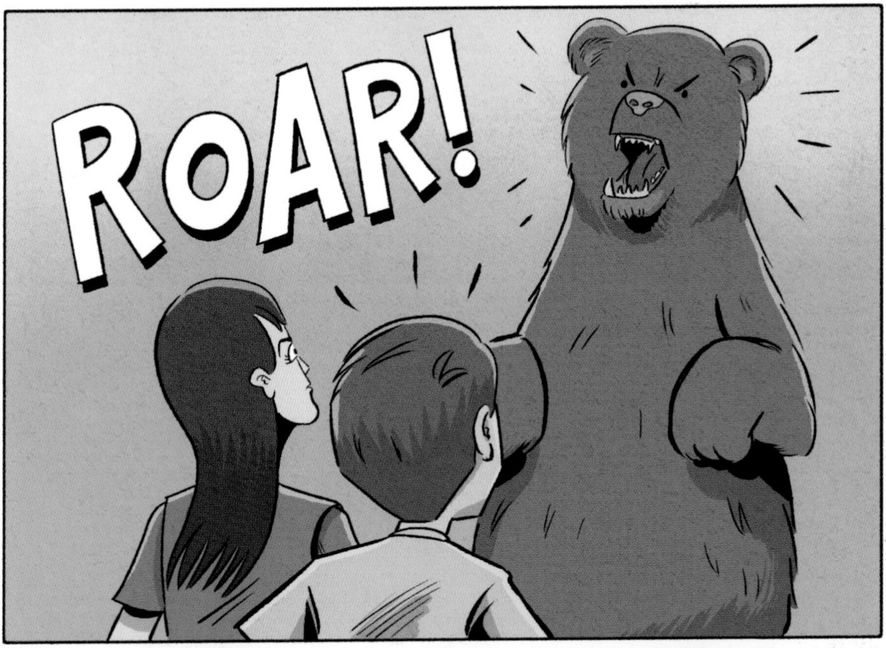
ROAR!

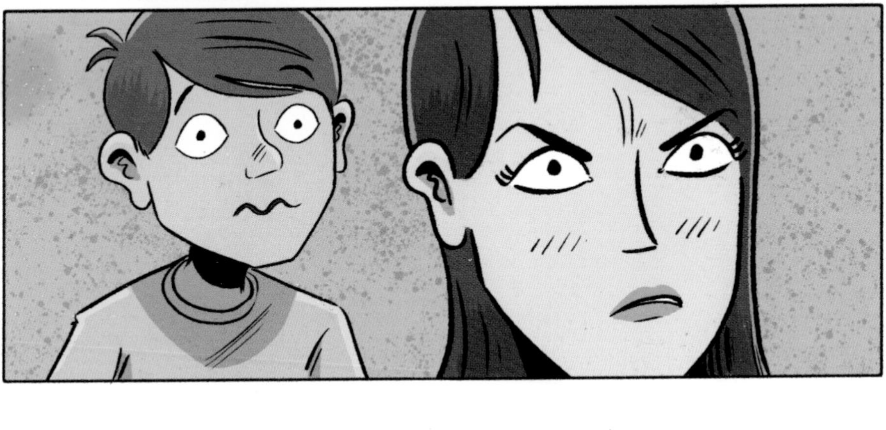

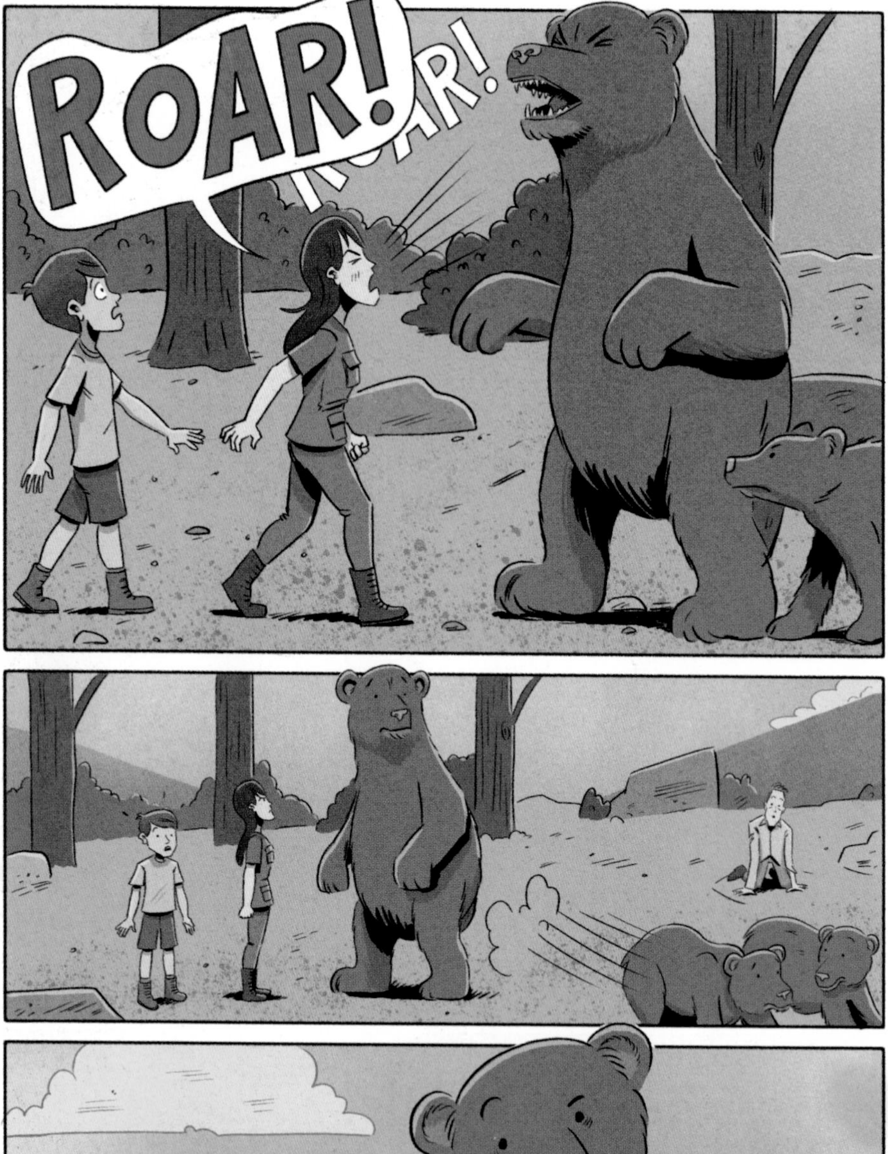
ROAR!

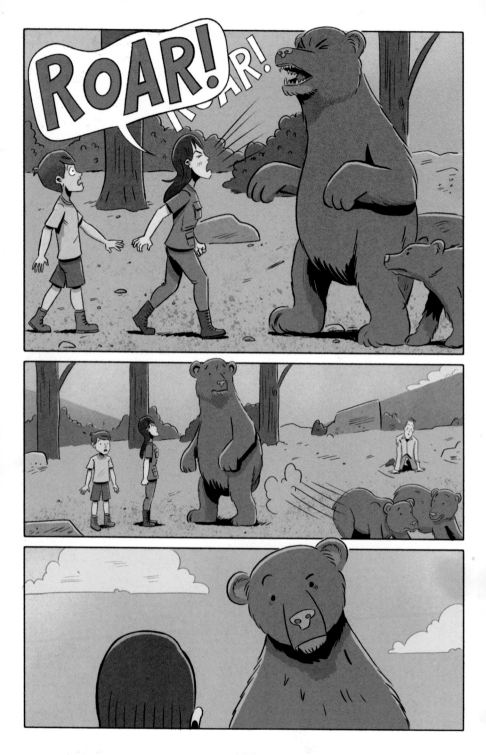

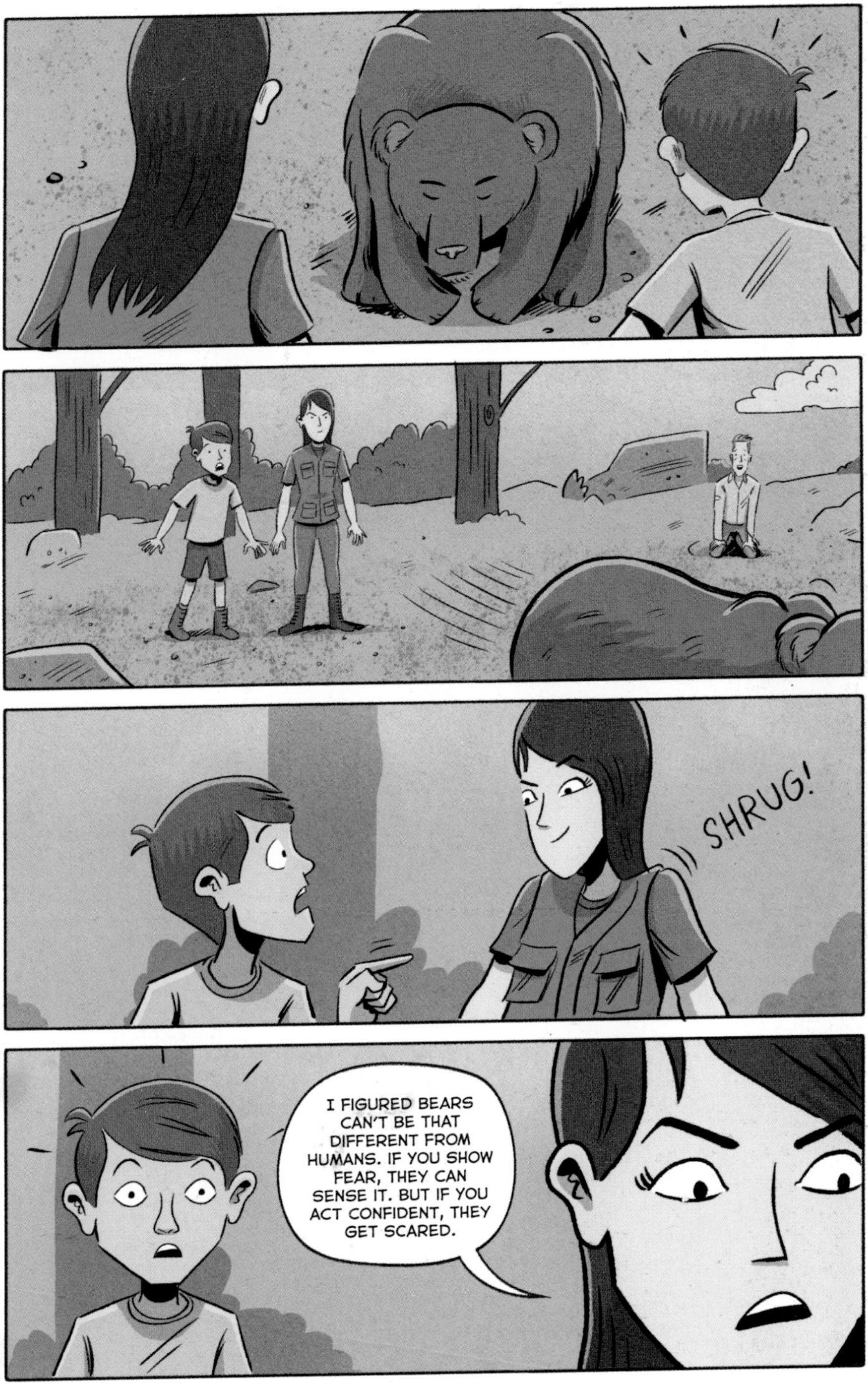
SHRUG!
I FIGURED BEARS CAN'T BE THAT DIFFERENT FROM HUMANS. IF YOU SHOW FEAR, THEY CAN SENSE IT. BUT IF YOU ACT CONFIDENT, THEY GET SCARED.

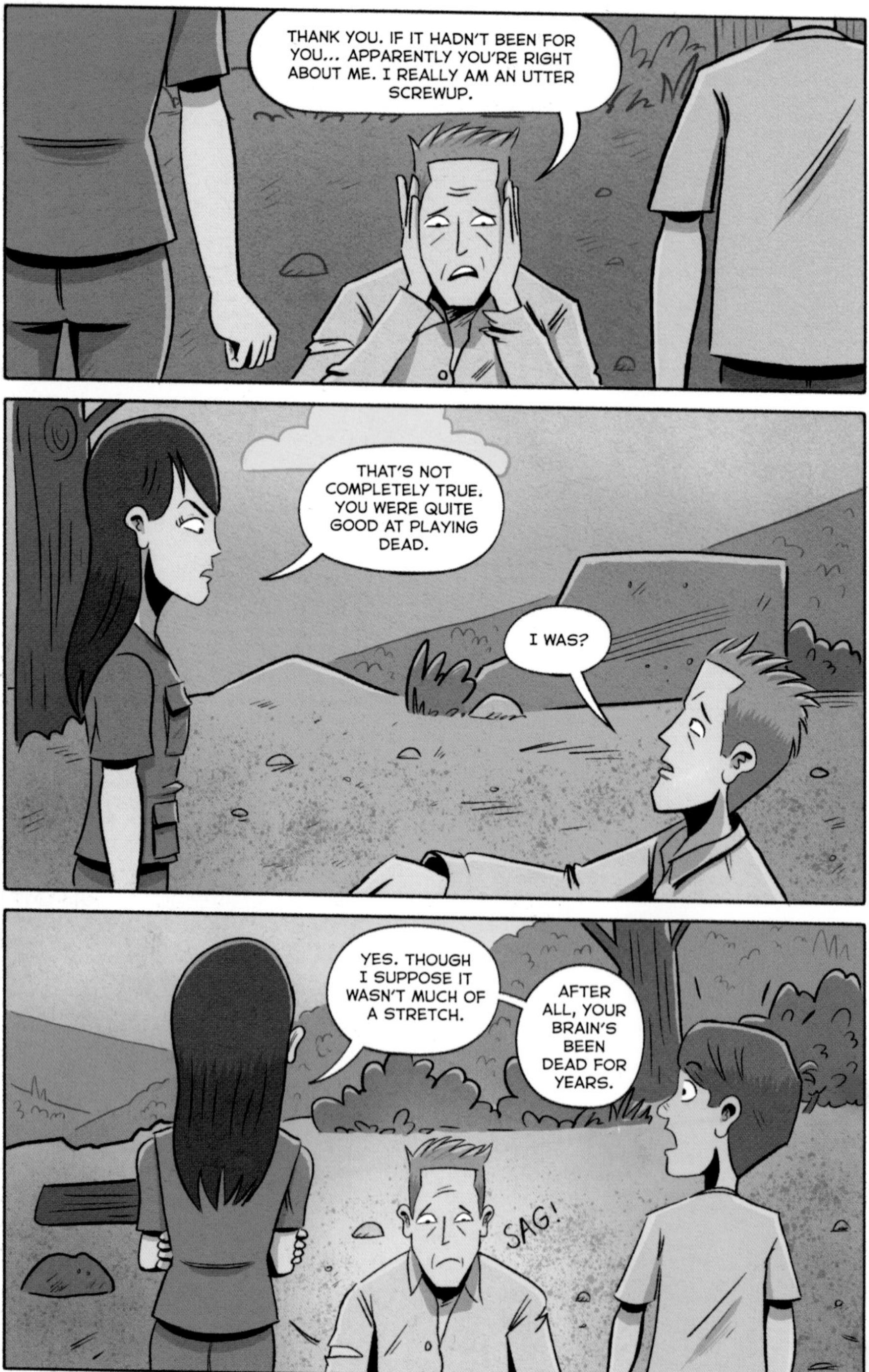
THANK YOU. IF IT HADN'T BEEN FOR YOU... APPARENTLY YOU'RE RIGHT ABOUT ME. I REALLY AM AN UTTER SCREWUP.
THAT'S NOT COMPLETELY TRUE. YOU WERE QUITE GOOD AT PLAYING DEAD.
I WAS?
YES. THOUGH I SUPPOSE IT WASN'T MUCH OF A STRETCH.
AFTER ALL, YOUR BRAIN'S BEEN DEAD FOR YEARS.
SAG!

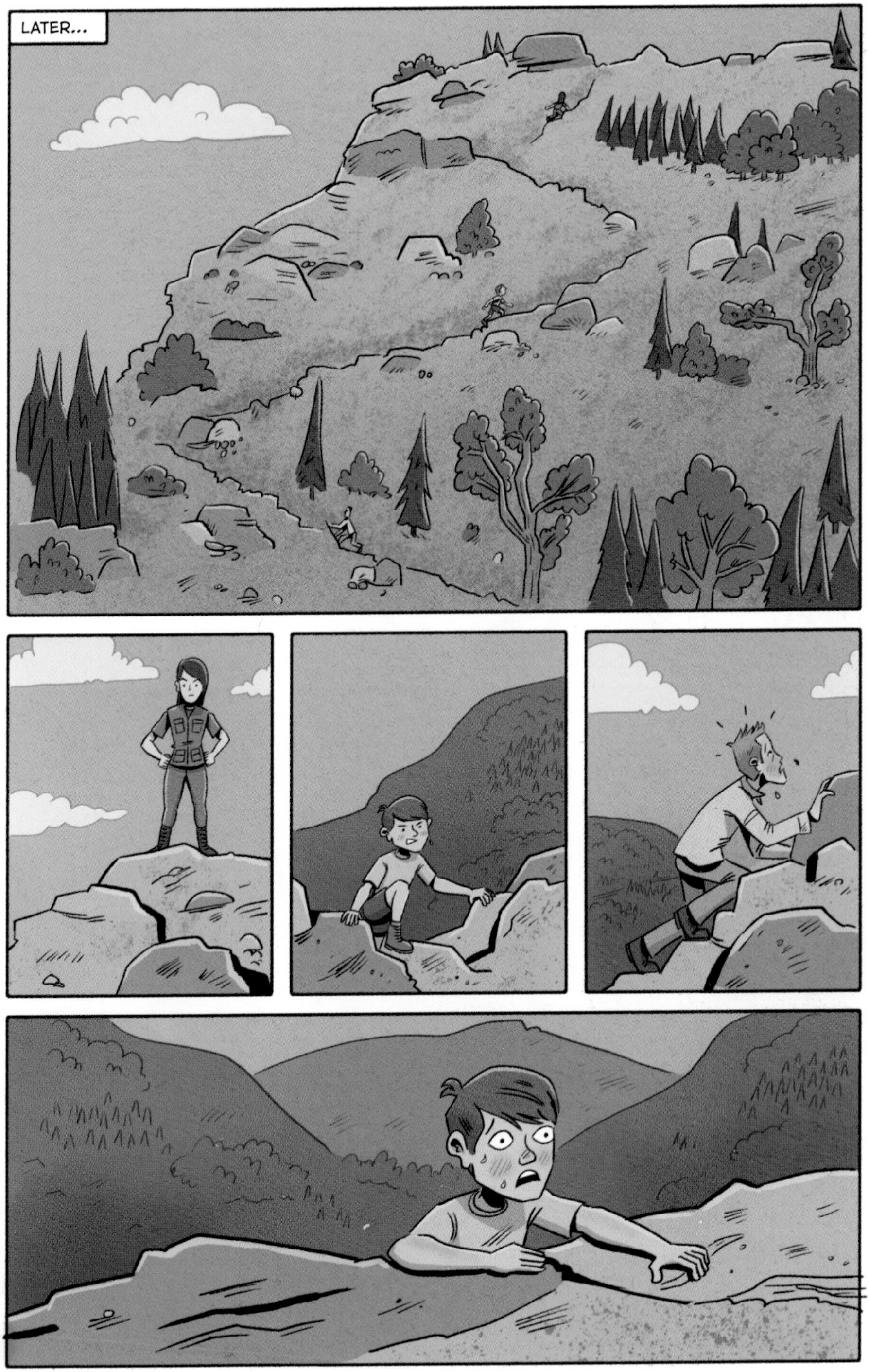
LATER...

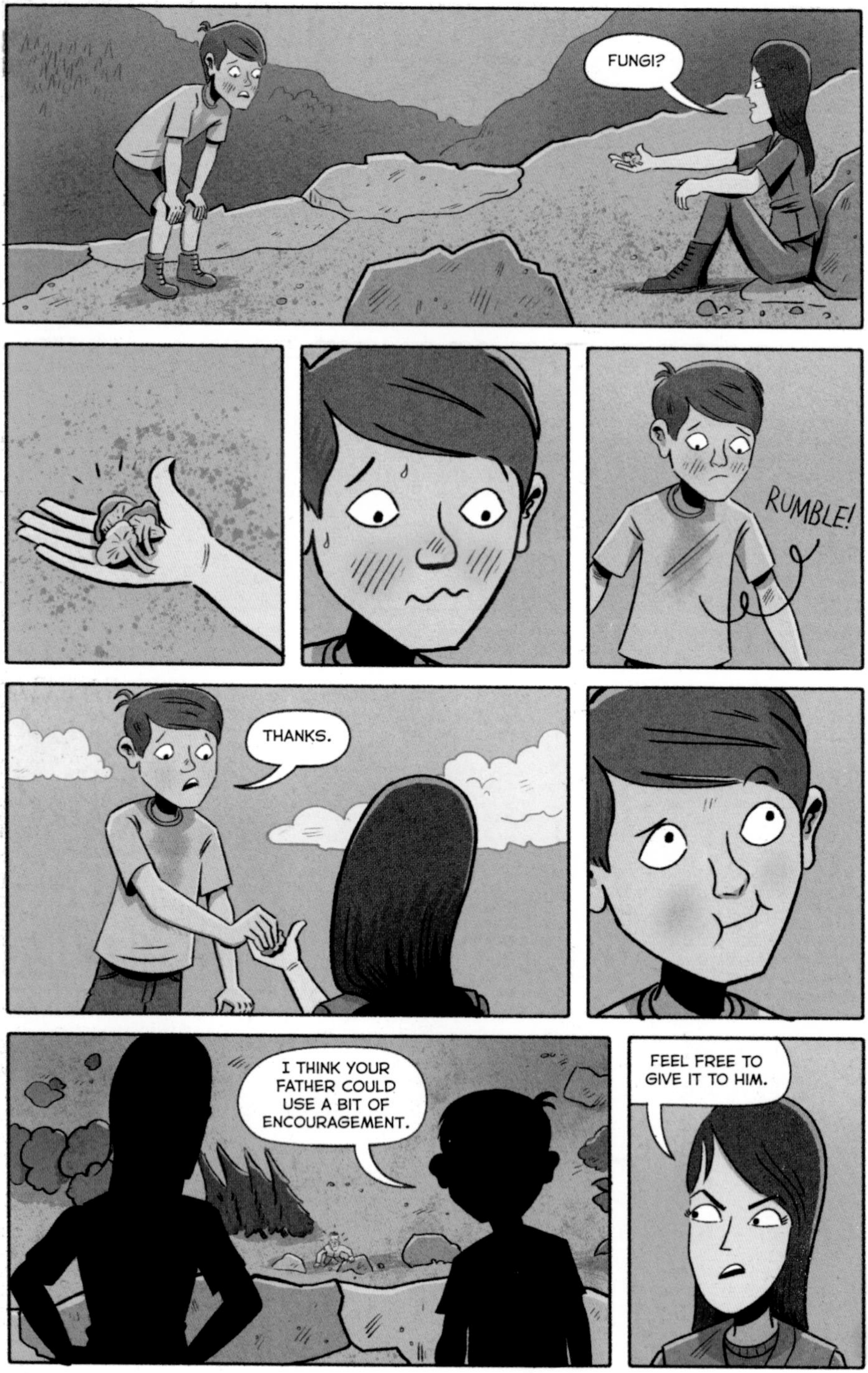
FUNGI?
RUMBLE!
THANKS.
I THINK YOUR FATHER COULD USE A BIT OF ENCOURAGEMENT.
FEEL FREE TO GIVE IT TO HIM.

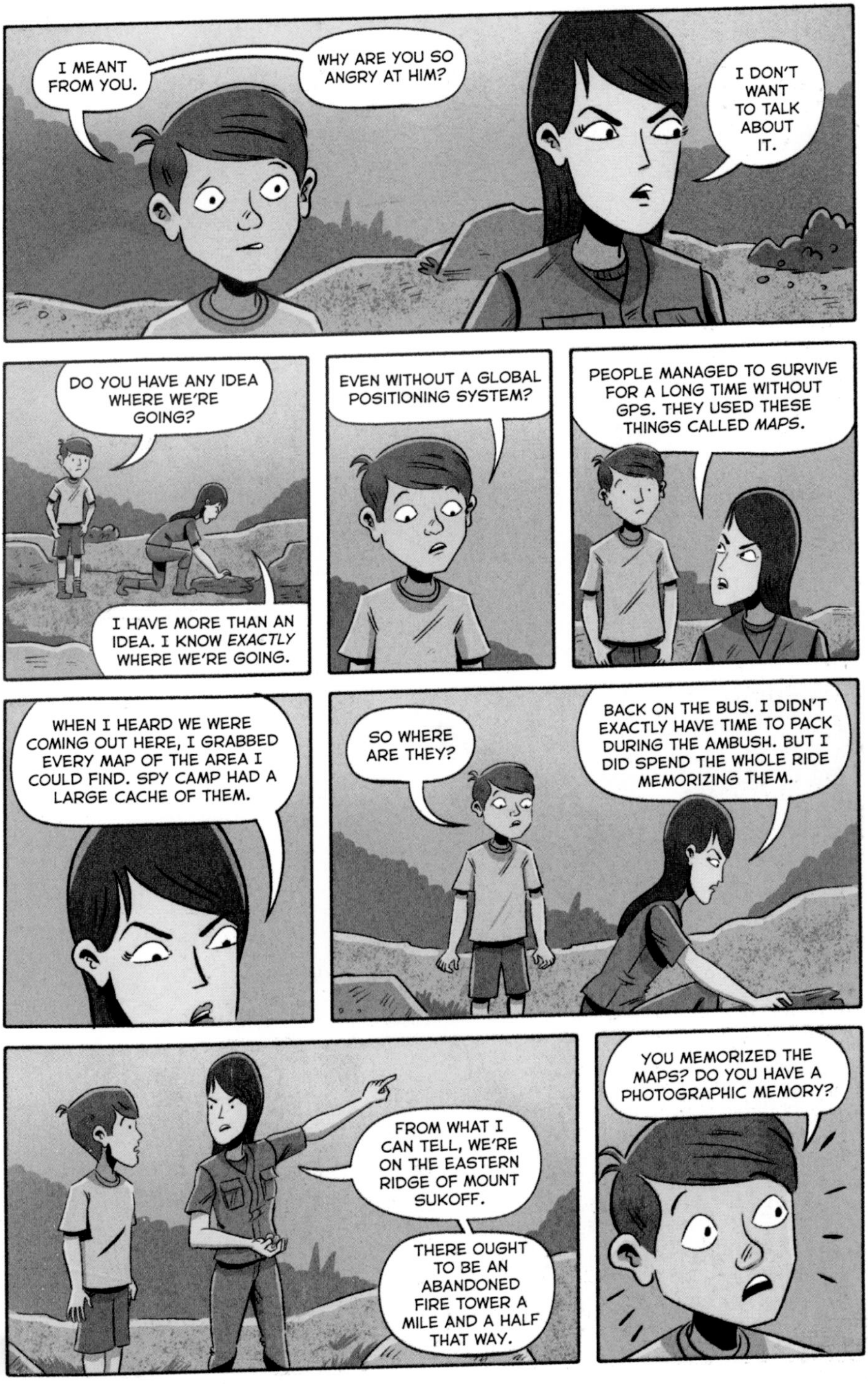
I MEANT FROM YOU.
WHY ARE YOU SO ANGRY AT HIM?
I DON'T WANT TO TALK ABOUT IT.
DO YOU HAVE ANY IDEA WHERE WE'RE GOING?
I HAVE MORE THAN AN IDEA. I KNOW *EXACTLY* WHERE WE'RE GOING.
EVEN WITHOUT A GLOBAL POSITIONING SYSTEM?
PEOPLE MANAGED TO SURVIVE FOR A LONG TIME WITHOUT GPS. THEY USED THESE THINGS CALLED *MAPS*.
WHEN I HEARD WE WERE COMING OUT HERE, I GRABBED EVERY MAP OF THE AREA I COULD FIND. SPY CAMP HAD A LARGE CACHE OF THEM.
SO WHERE ARE THEY?
BACK ON THE BUS. I DIDN'T EXACTLY HAVE TIME TO PACK DURING THE AMBUSH. BUT I DID SPEND THE WHOLE RIDE MEMORIZING THEM.
FROM WHAT I CAN TELL, WE'RE ON THE EASTERN RIDGE OF MOUNT SUKOFF.
THERE OUGHT TO BE AN ABANDONED FIRE TOWER A MILE AND A HALF THAT WAY.
YOU MEMORIZED THE MAPS? DO YOU HAVE A PHOTOGRAPHIC MEMORY?

141

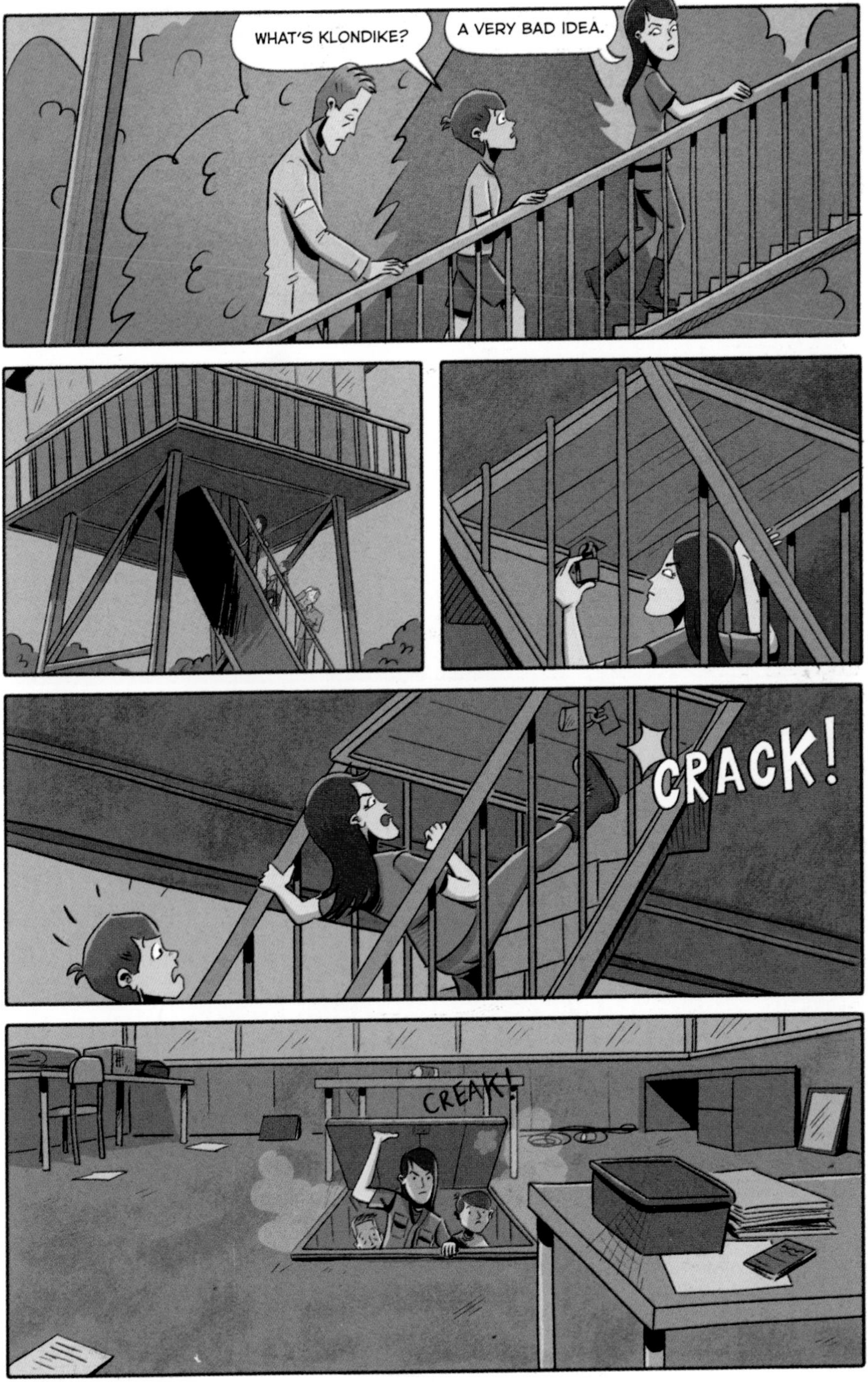
WHAT'S KLONDIKE?
A VERY BAD IDEA.
CRACK!
CREAK!

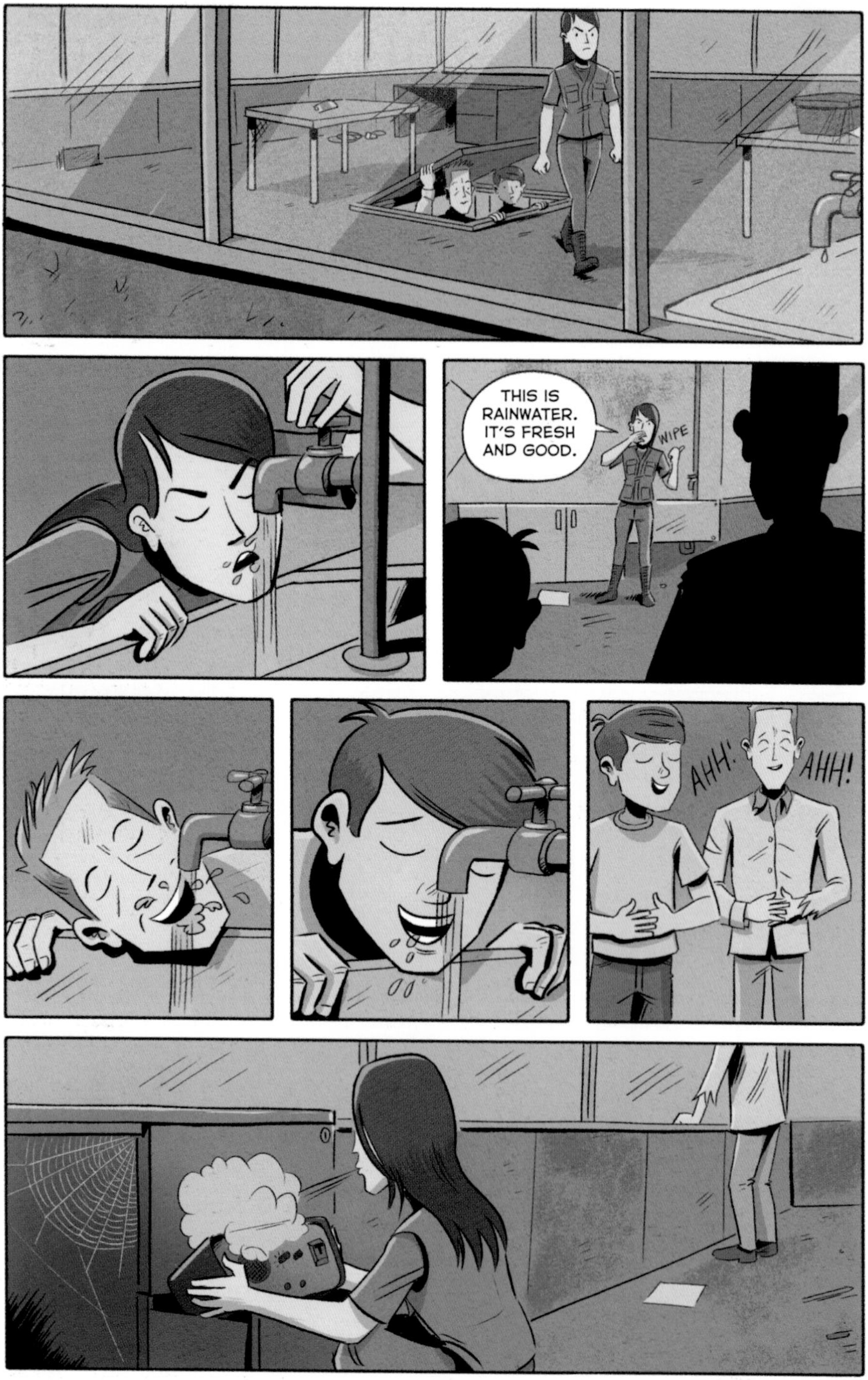
THIS IS RAINWATER. IT'S FRESH AND GOOD.
WIPE
AHH!
AHH!

148

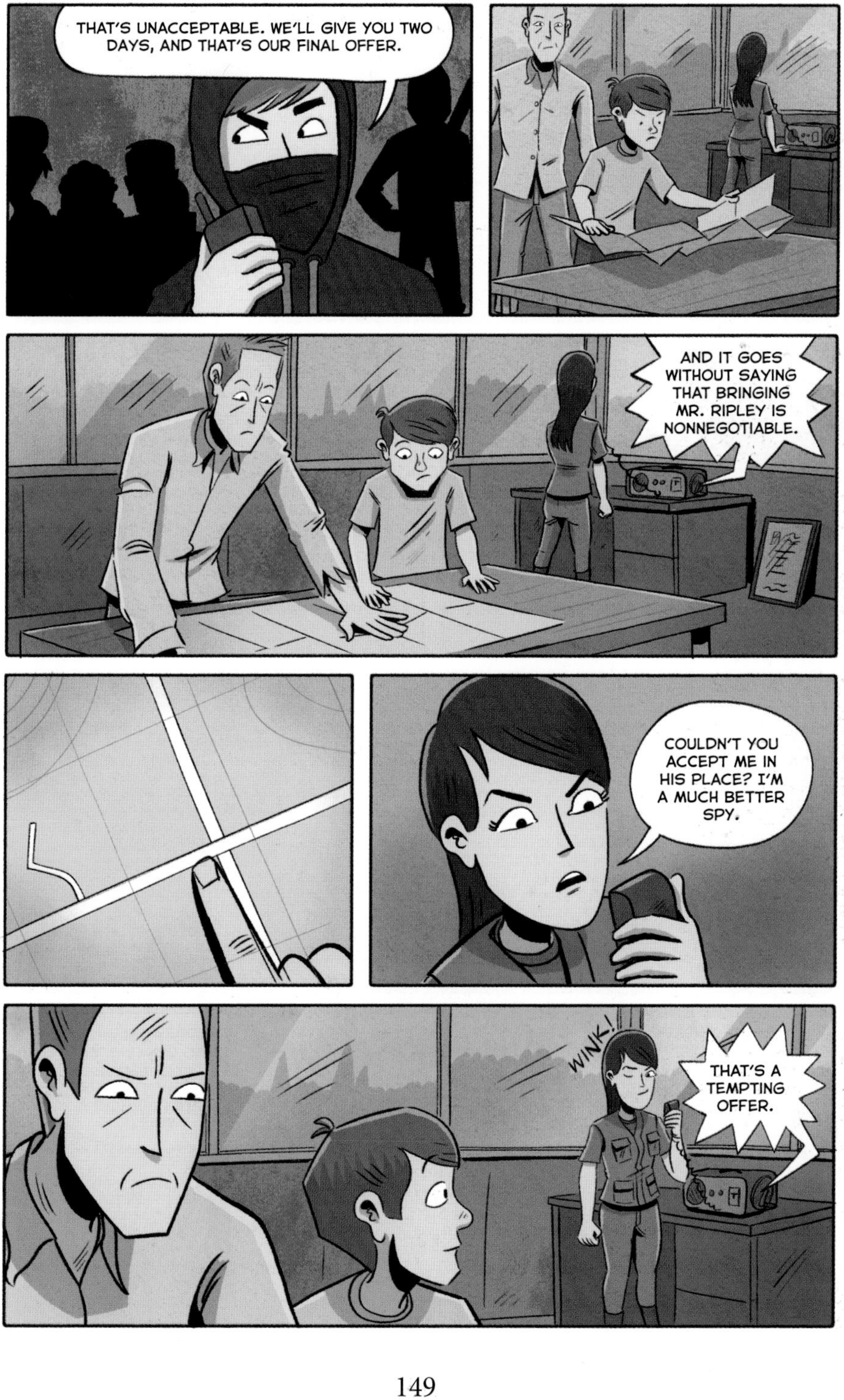
THAT'S UNACCEPTABLE. WE'LL GIVE YOU TWO DAYS, AND THAT'S OUR FINAL OFFER.
AND IT GOES WITHOUT SAYING THAT BRINGING MR. RIPLEY IS NONNEGOTIABLE.
COULDN'T YOU ACCEPT ME IN HIS PLACE? I'M A MUCH BETTER SPY.
WINK!
THAT'S A TEMPTING OFFER.

151

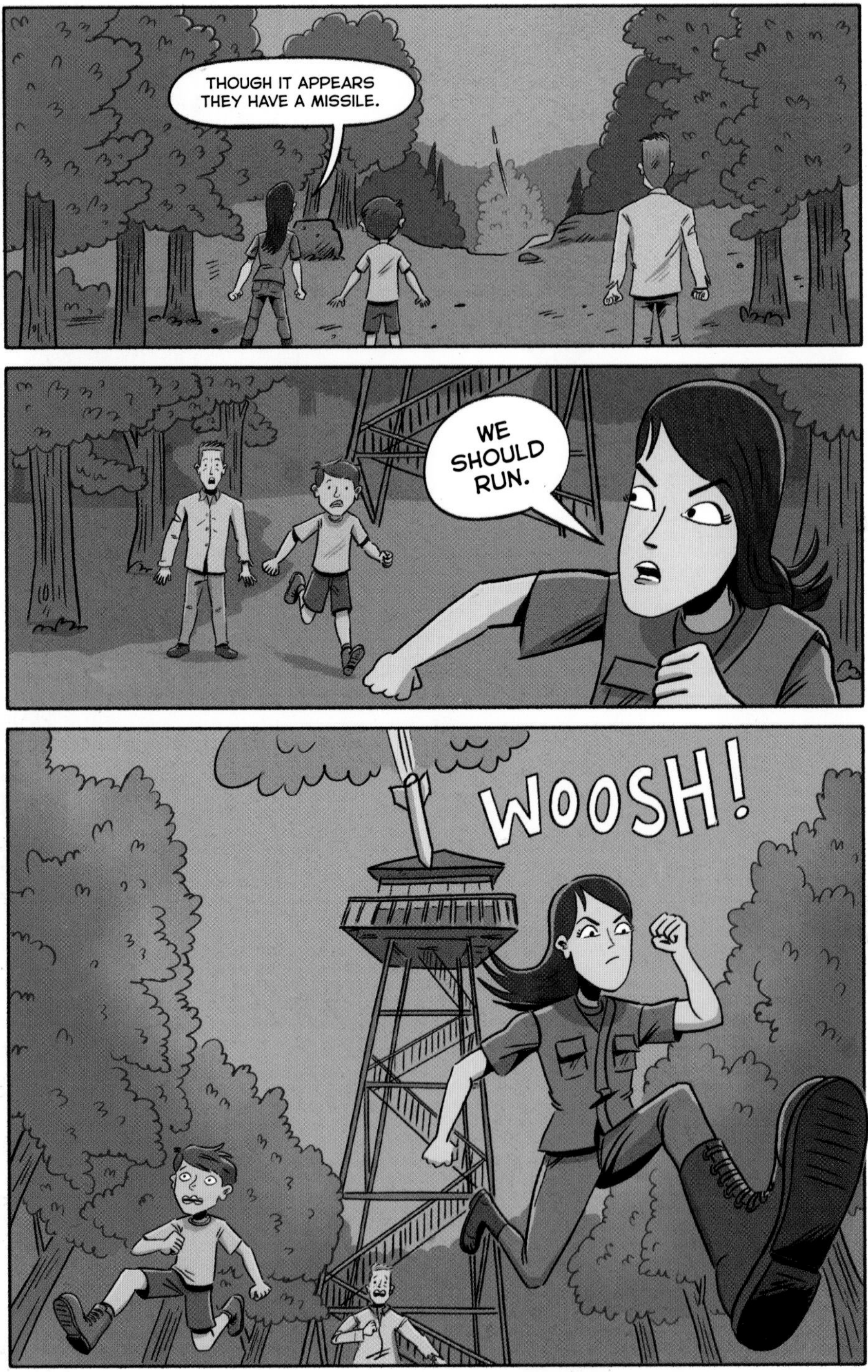
THOUGH IT APPEARS THEY HAVE A MISSILE.
WE SHOULD RUN.
WOOSH!

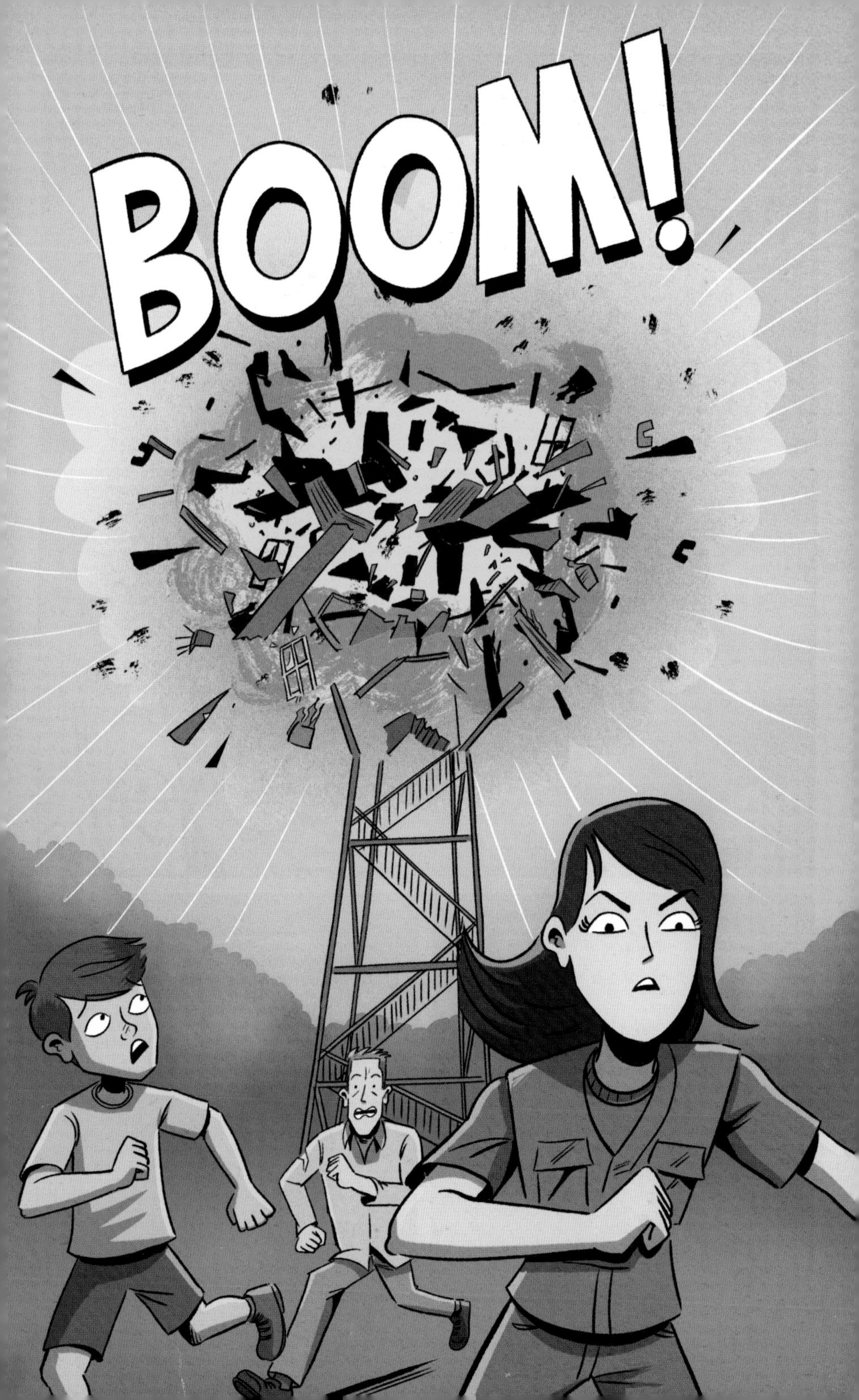
BOOM!

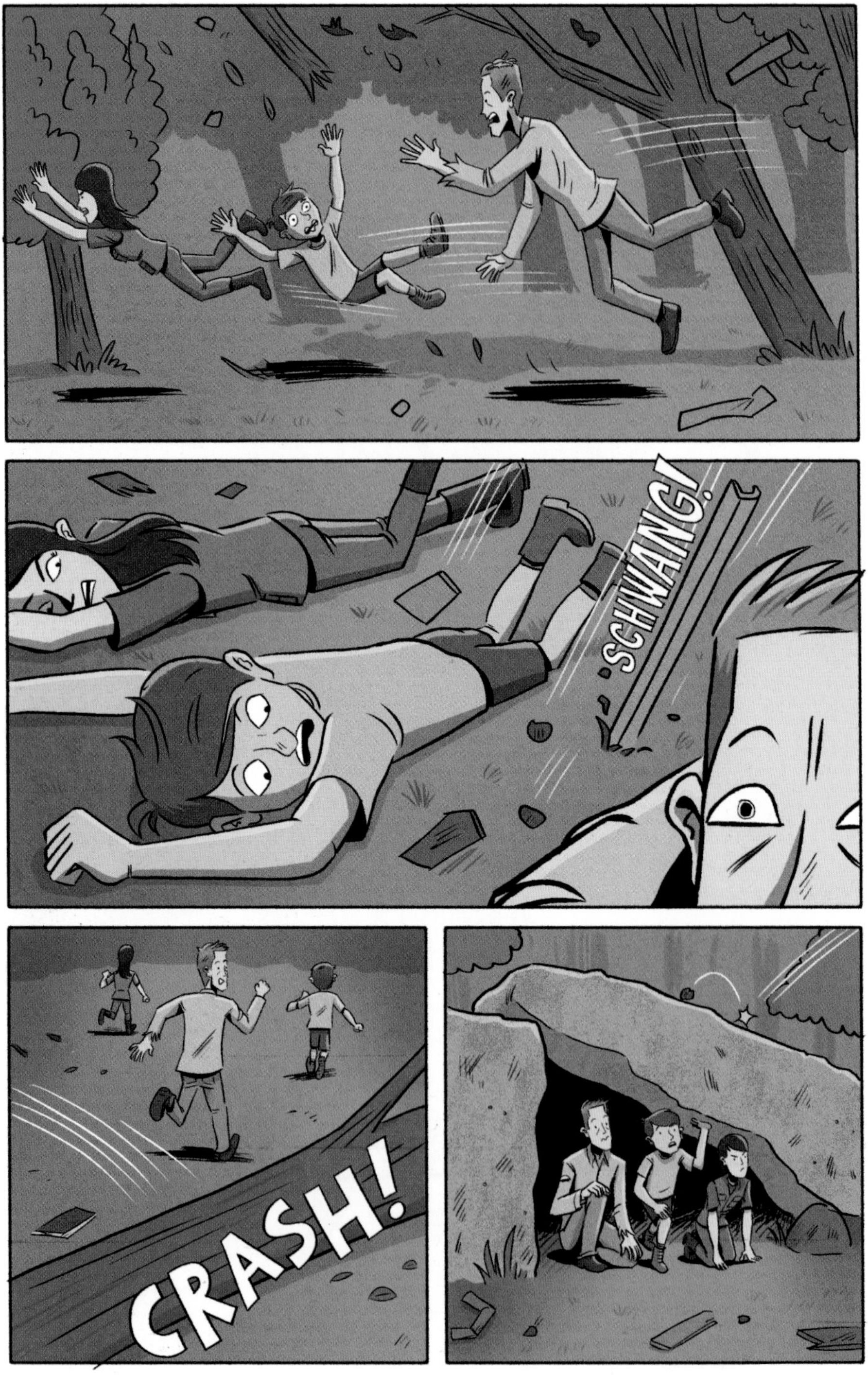
SCHWANG!
CRASH!

155

158

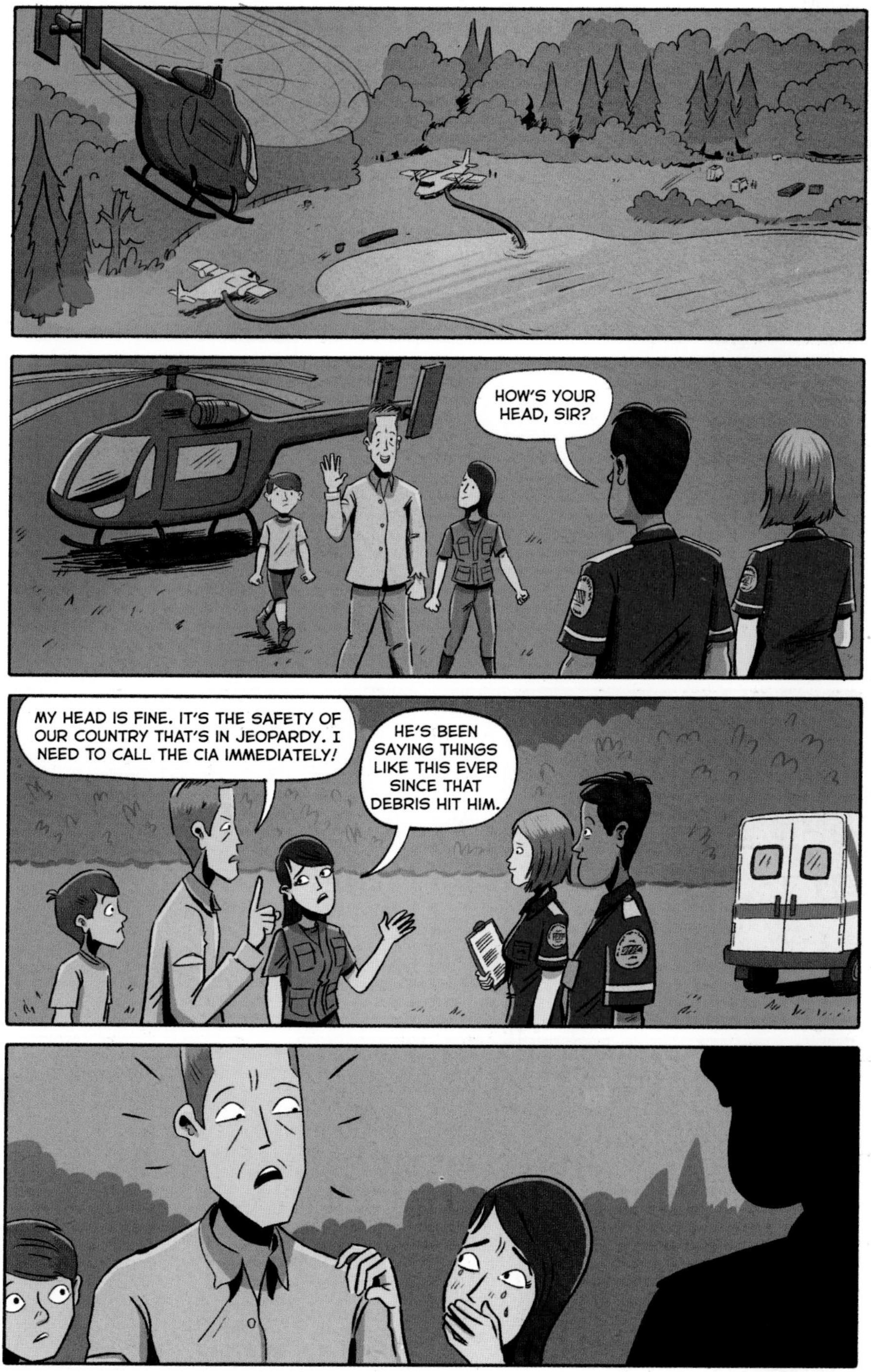
HOW'S YOUR HEAD, SIR?
MY HEAD IS FINE. IT'S THE SAFETY OF OUR COUNTRY THAT'S IN JEOPARDY. I NEED TO CALL THE CIA IMMEDIATELY!
HE'S BEEN SAYING THINGS LIKE THIS EVER SINCE THAT DEBRIS HIT HIM.

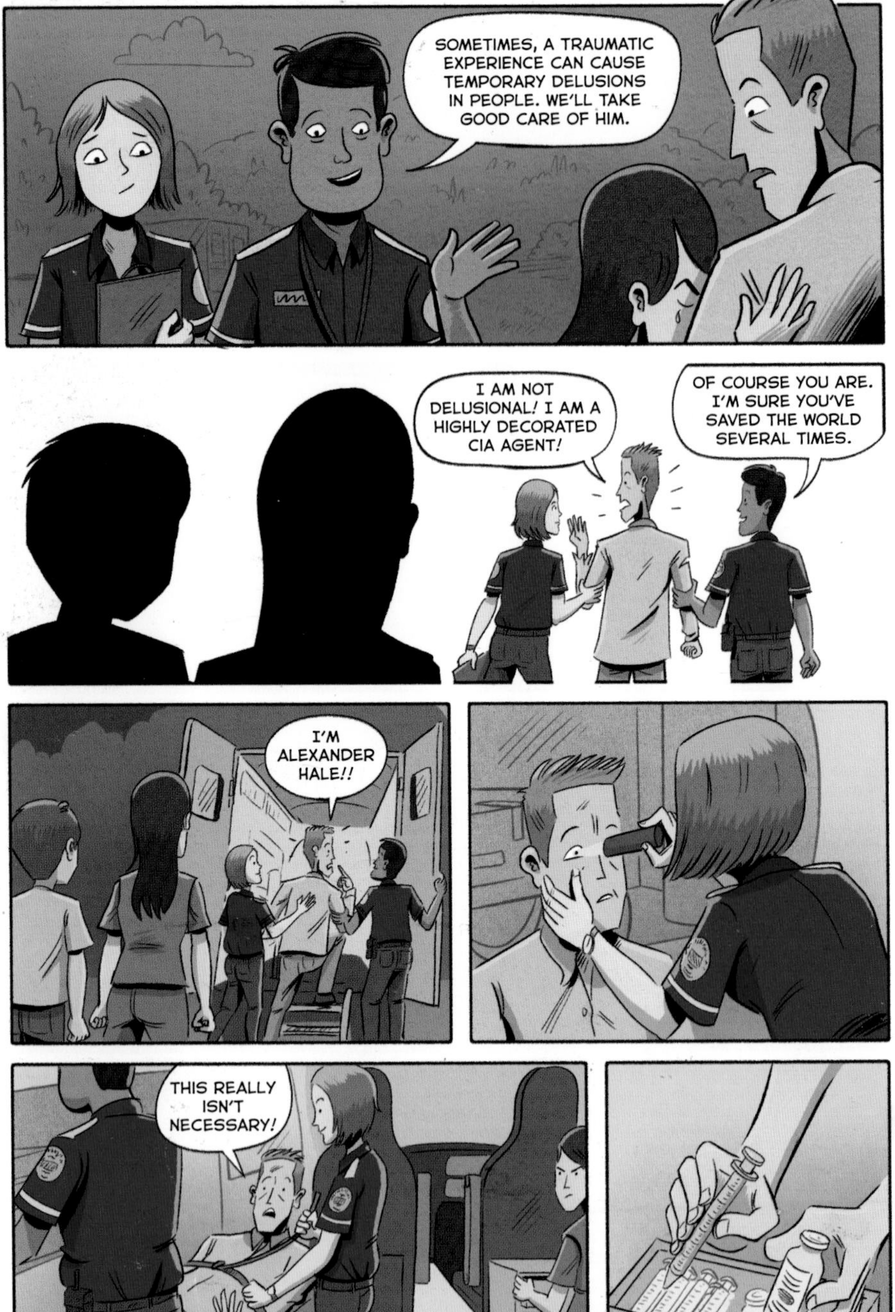
SOMETIMES, A TRAUMATIC EXPERIENCE CAN CAUSE TEMPORARY DELUSIONS IN PEOPLE. WE'LL TAKE GOOD CARE OF HIM.
I AM NOT DELUSIONAL! I AM A HIGHLY DECORATED CIA AGENT!
OF COURSE YOU ARE. I'M SURE YOU'VE SAVED THE WORLD SEVERAL TIMES.
I'M ALEXANDER HALE!!
THIS REALLY ISN'T NECESSARY!

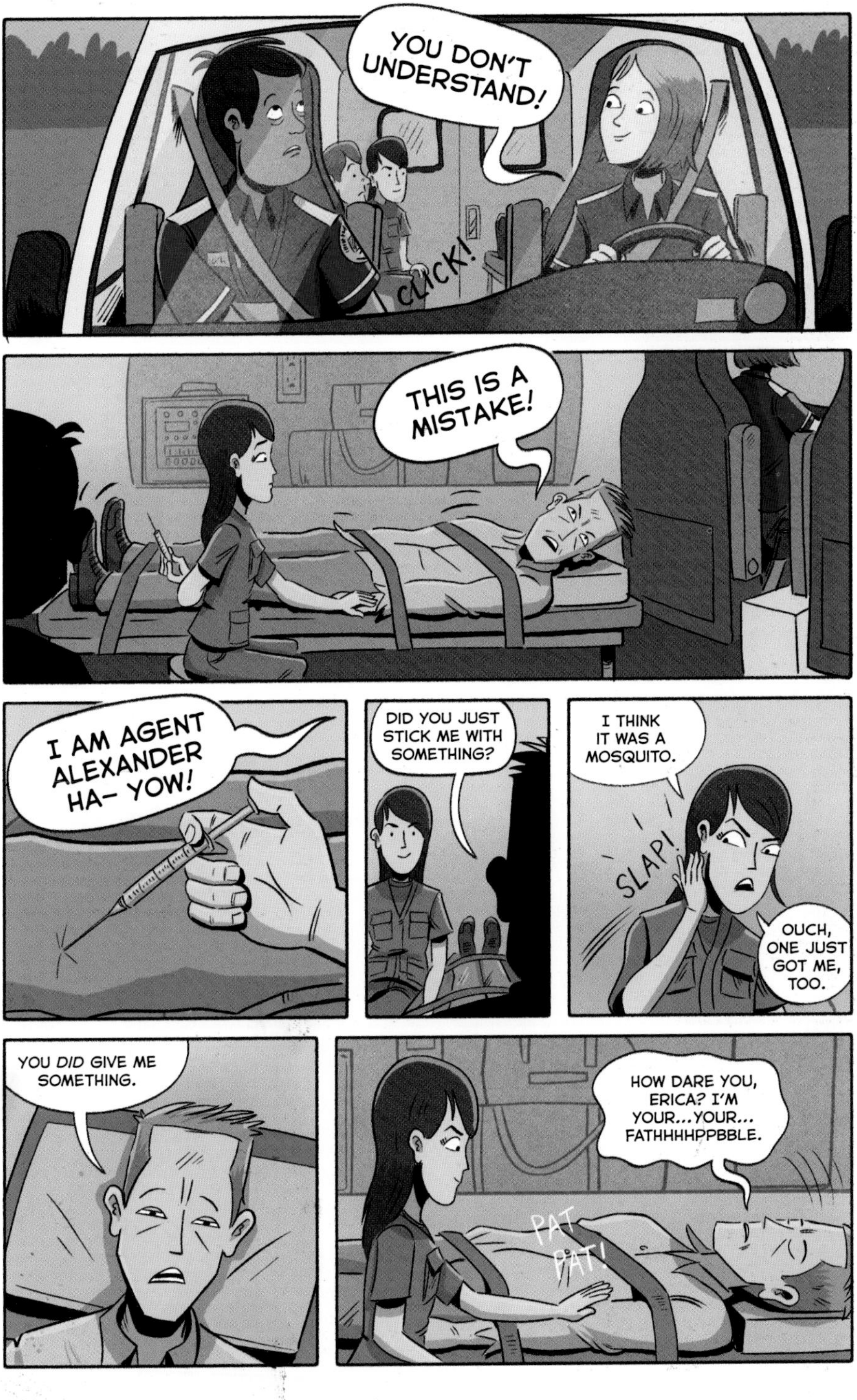
YOU DON'T UNDERSTAND!
CLICK!
THIS IS A MISTAKE!
I AM AGENT ALEXANDER HA– YOW!
DID YOU JUST STICK ME WITH SOMETHING?
I THINK IT WAS A MOSQUITO.
SLAP!
OUCH, ONE JUST GOT ME, TOO.
YOU *DID* GIVE ME SOMETHING.
HOW DARE YOU, ERICA? I'M YOUR...YOUR... FATHHHHPPBBLE.
PAT PAT!

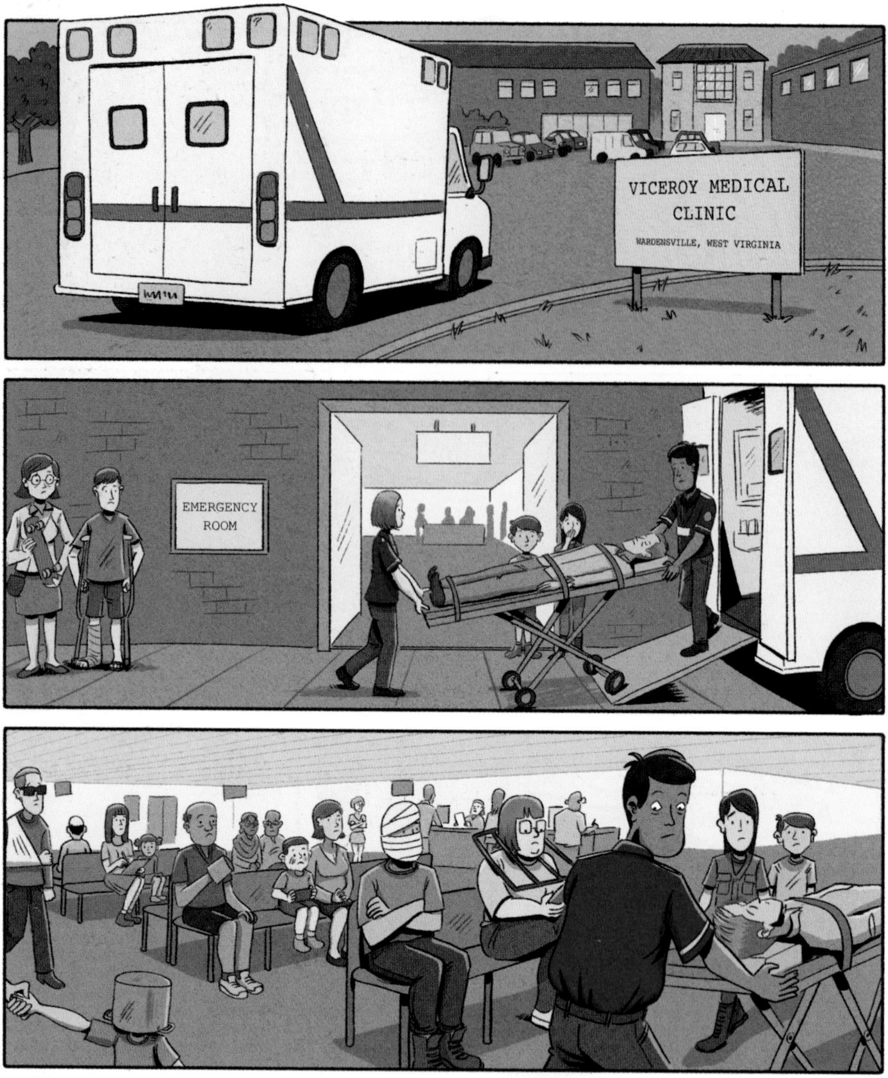
VICEROY MEDICAL CLINIC
WARDENSVILLE, WEST VIRGINIA
EMERGENCY ROOM
IT'S ALWAYS LIKE THIS AT THE BEGINNING OF SUMMER VACATION.
IS THIS YOUR FATHER?
YES...
I'M ALEXANDURBLE PURBLE...HUP!
WILL HE BE OKAY?

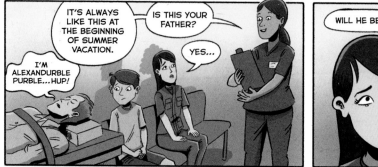

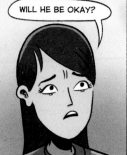

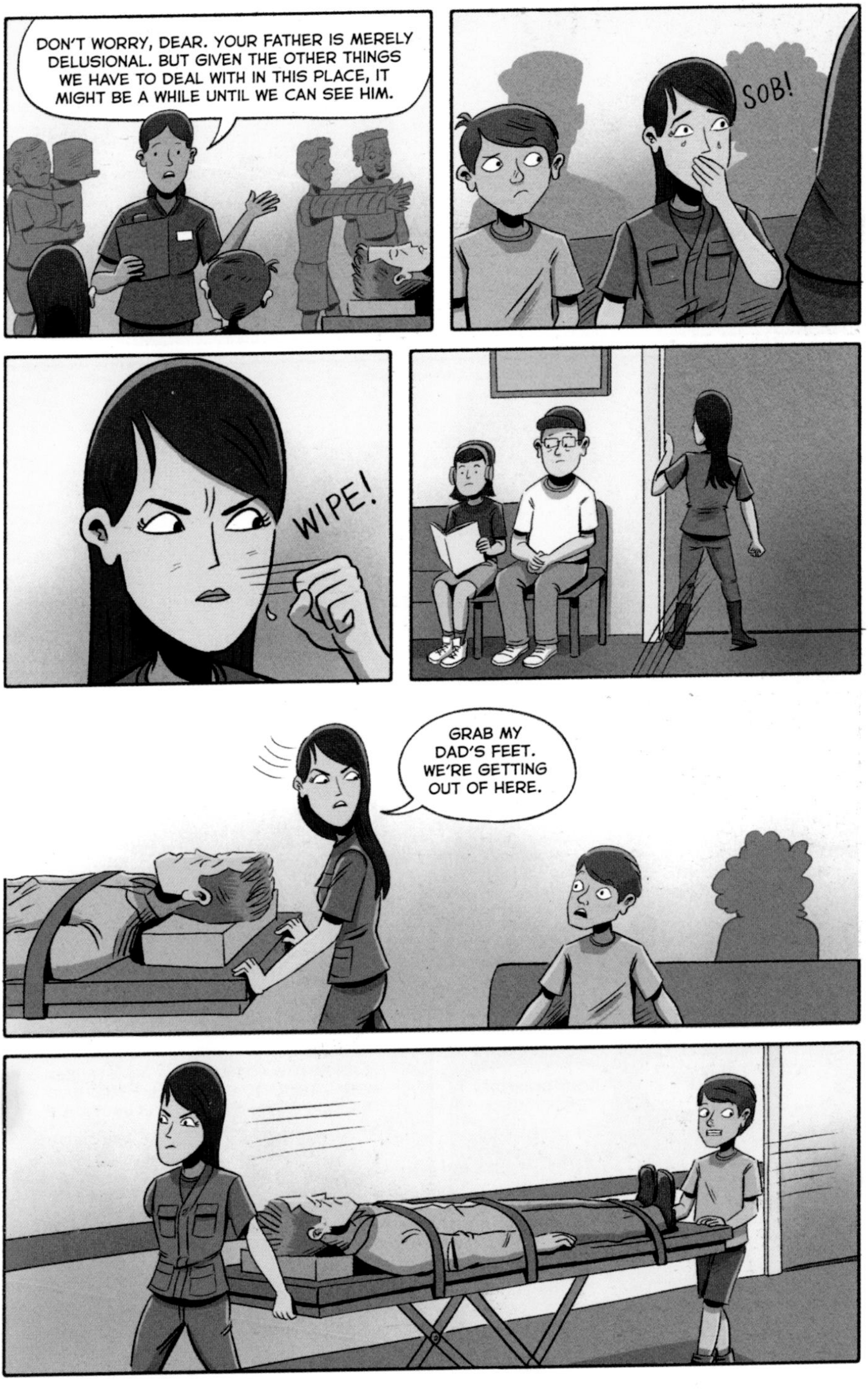
DON'T WORRY, DEAR. YOUR FATHER IS MERELY DELUSIONAL. BUT GIVEN THE OTHER THINGS WE HAVE TO DEAL WITH IN THIS PLACE, IT MIGHT BE A WHILE UNTIL WE CAN SEE HIM.
SOB!
WIPE!
GRAB MY DAD'S FEET. WE'RE GETTING OUT OF HERE.

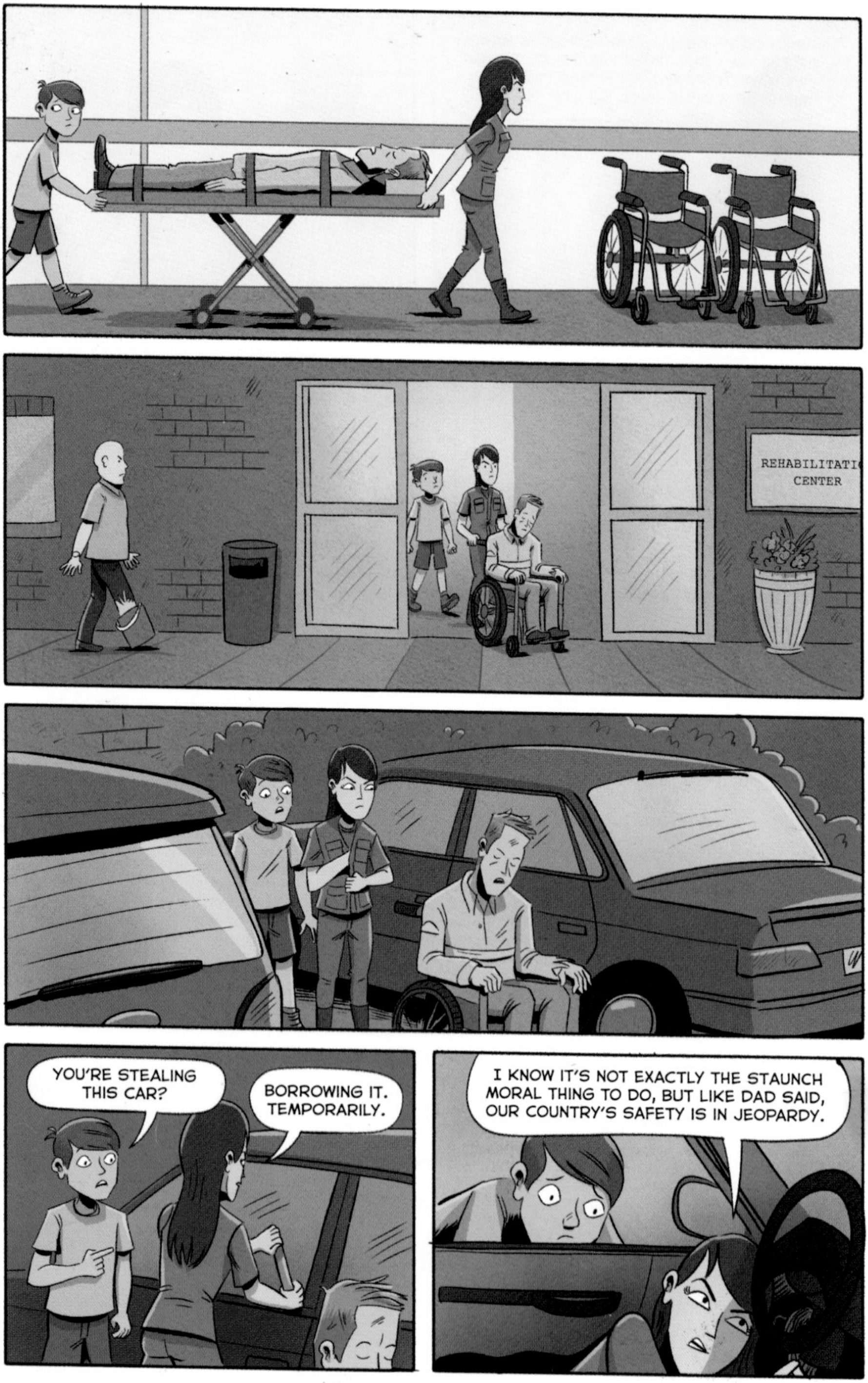
REHABILITATI
CENTER
YOU'RE STEALING THIS CAR?
BORROWING IT. TEMPORARILY.
I KNOW IT'S NOT EXACTLY THE STAUNCH MORAL THING TO DO, BUT LIKE DAD SAID, OUR COUNTRY'S SAFETY IS IN JEOPARDY.

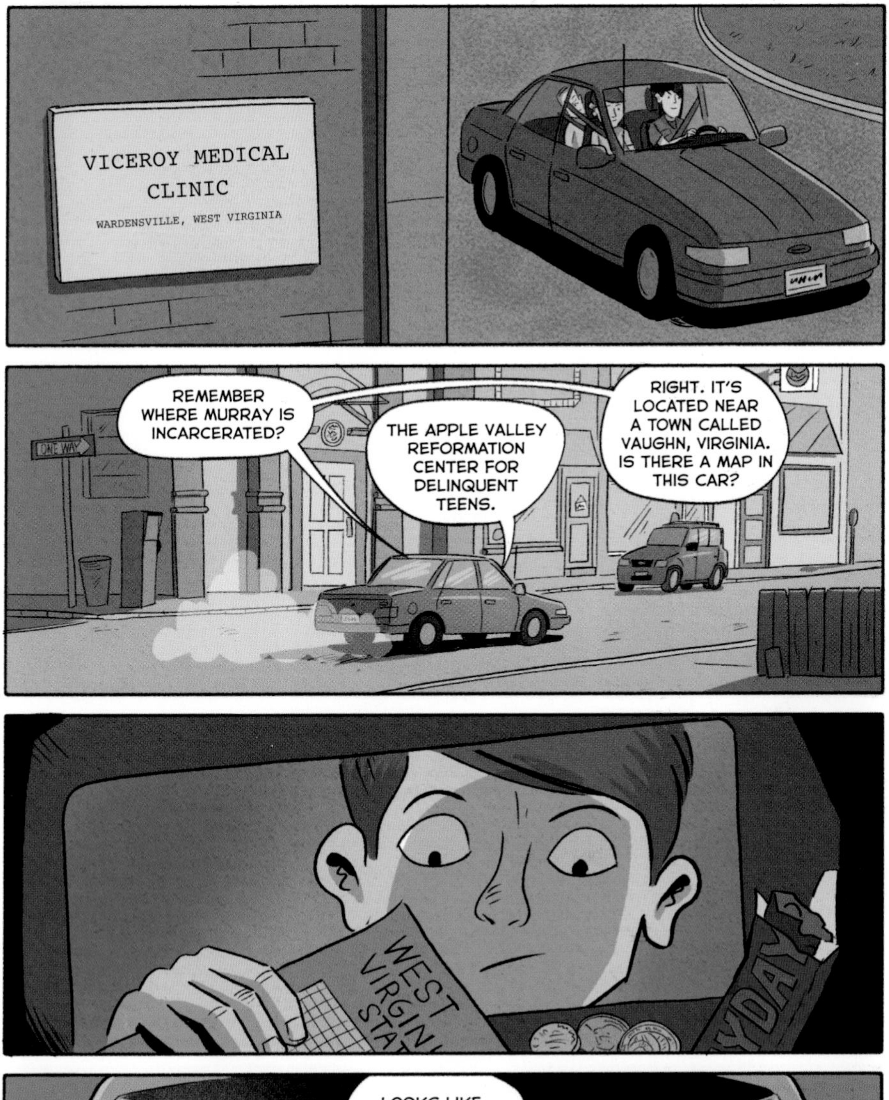
VICEROY MEDICAL CLINIC
WARDENSVILLE, WEST VIRGINIA
ONE WAY
REMEMBER WHERE MURRAY IS INCARCERATED?
THE APPLE VALLEY REFORMATION CENTER FOR DELINQUENT TEENS.
RIGHT. IT'S LOCATED NEAR A TOWN CALLED VAUGHN, VIRGINIA. IS THERE A MAP IN THIS CAR?
LOOKS LIKE IT'S ABOUT AN HOUR AWAY.
ZZZZZ

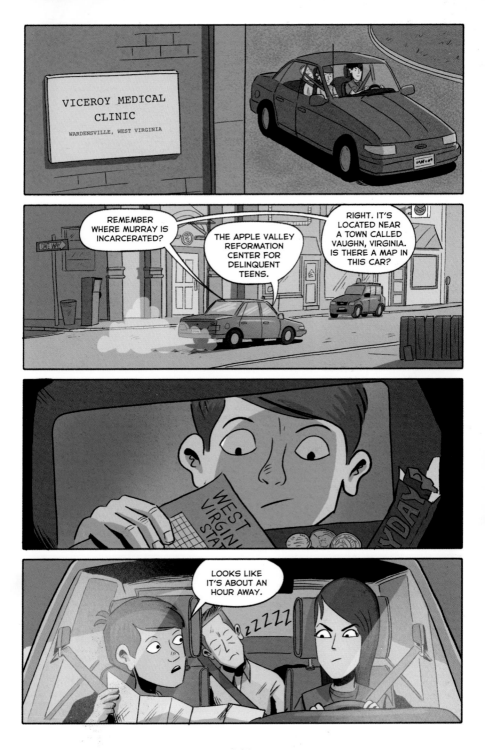

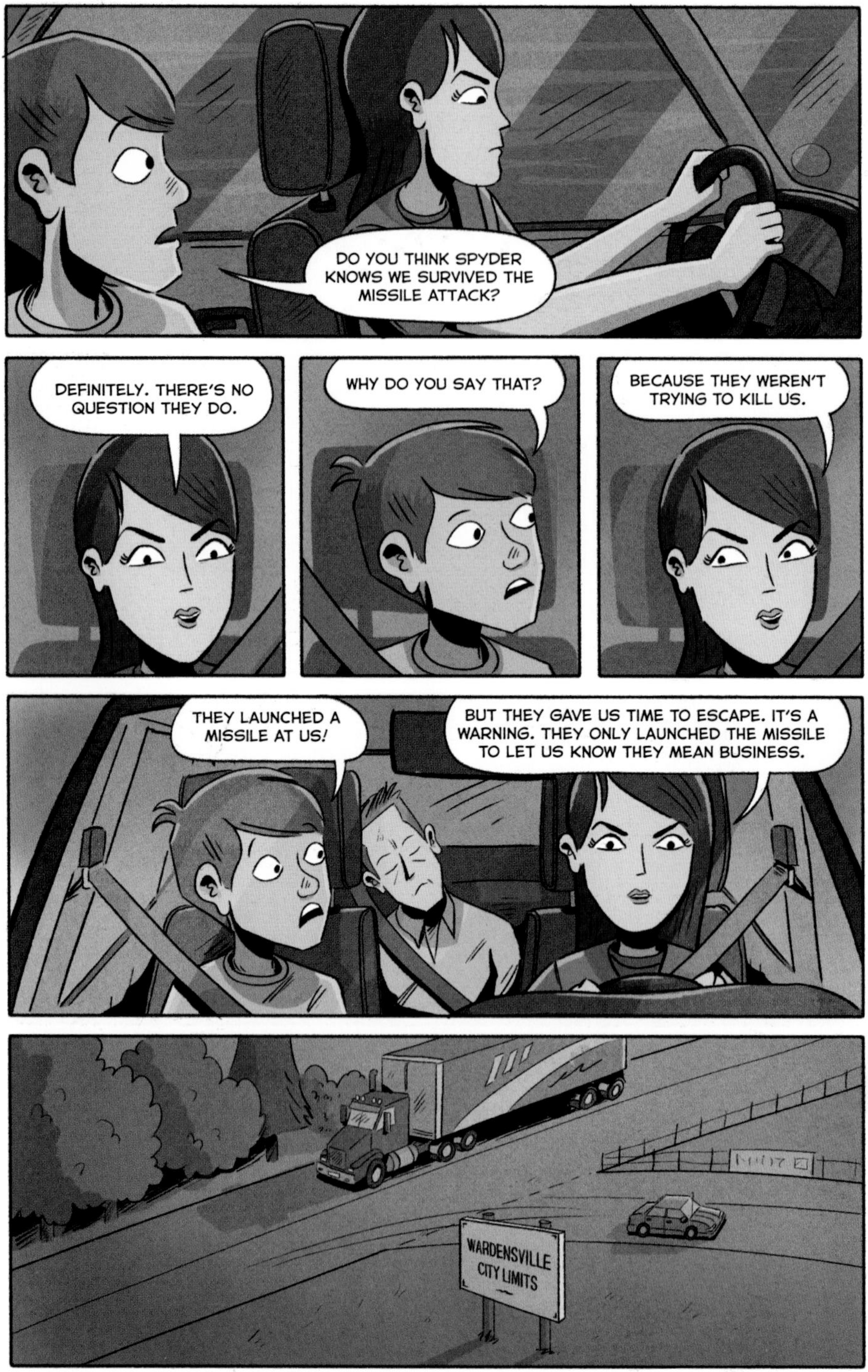

DO YOU THINK SPYDER KNOWS WE SURVIVED THE MISSILE ATTACK?
DEFINITELY. THERE'S NO QUESTION THEY DO.
WHY DO YOU SAY THAT?
BECAUSE THEY WEREN'T TRYING TO KILL US.
THEY LAUNCHED A MISSILE AT US!
BUT THEY GAVE US TIME TO ESCAPE. IT'S A WARNING. THEY ONLY LAUNCHED THE MISSILE TO LET US KNOW THEY MEAN BUSINESS.
WARDENSVILLE CITY LIMITS

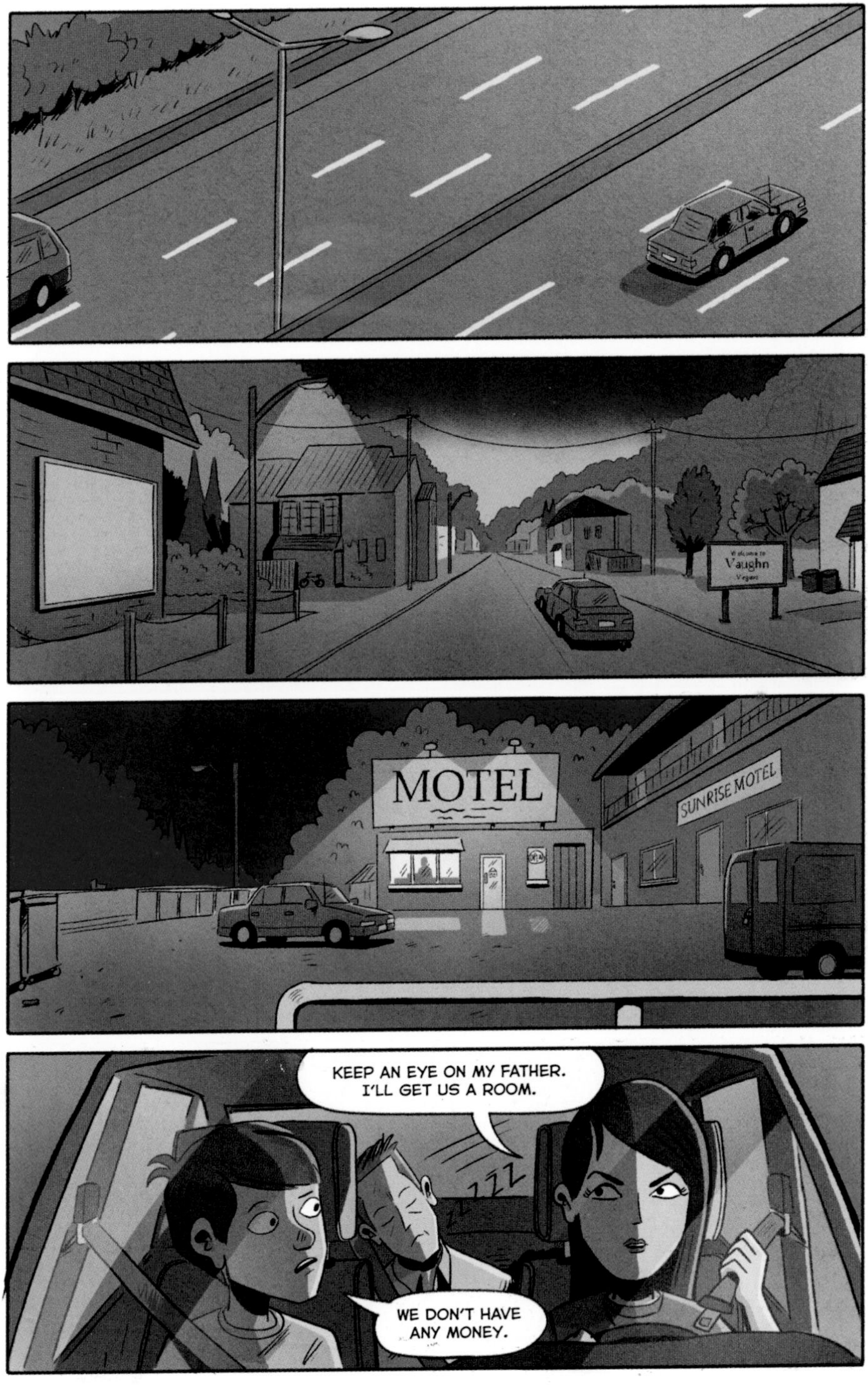
Vaughn
MOTEL
SUNRISE MOTEL
KEEP AN EYE ON MY FATHER. I'LL GET US A ROOM.
ZZZ
WE DON'T HAVE ANY MONEY.

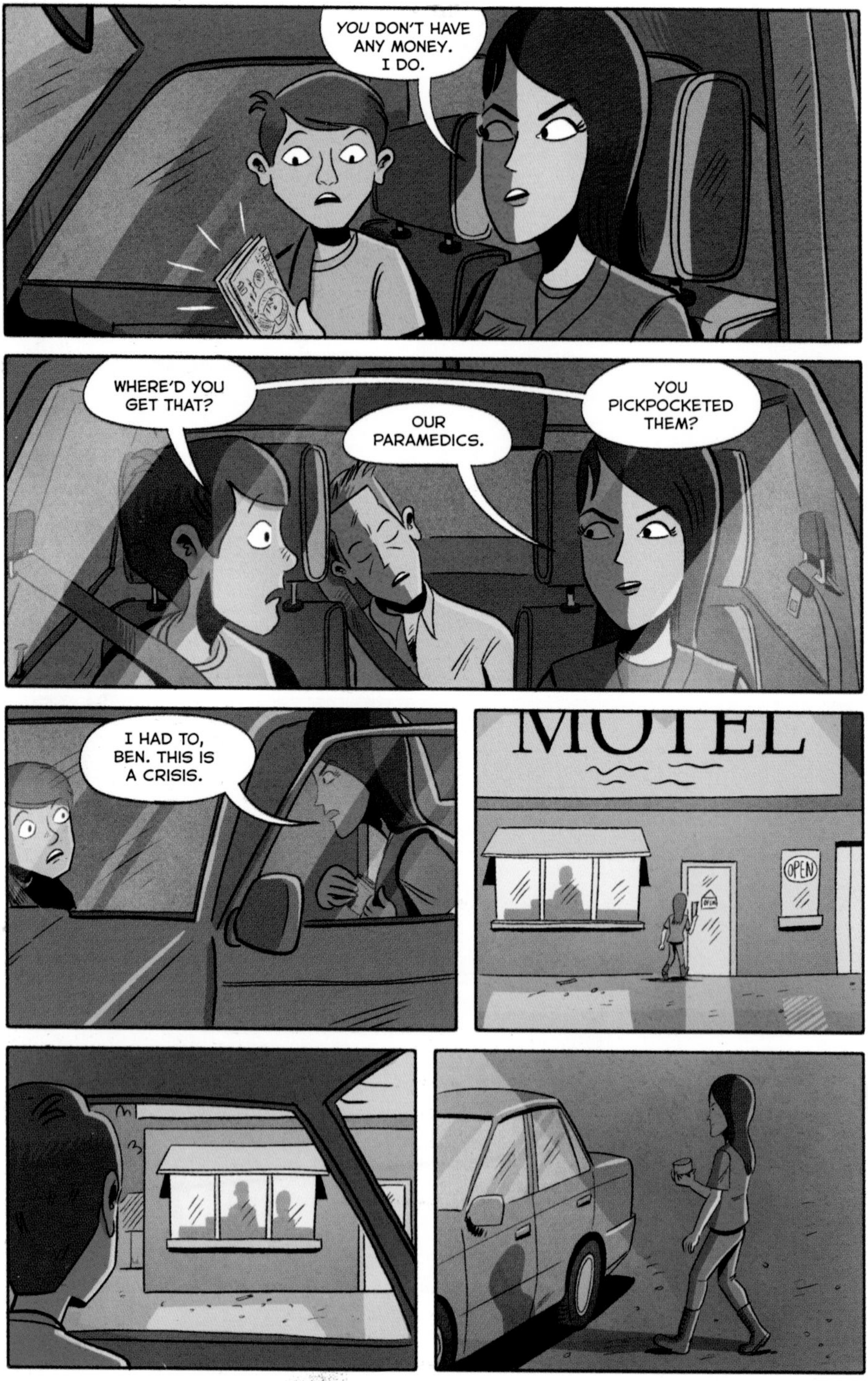
YOU DON'T HAVE ANY MONEY. I DO.
WHERE'D YOU GET THAT?
OUR PARAMEDICS.
YOU PICKPOCKETED THEM?
I HAD TO, BEN. THIS IS A CRISIS.
MOTEL
OPEN

171

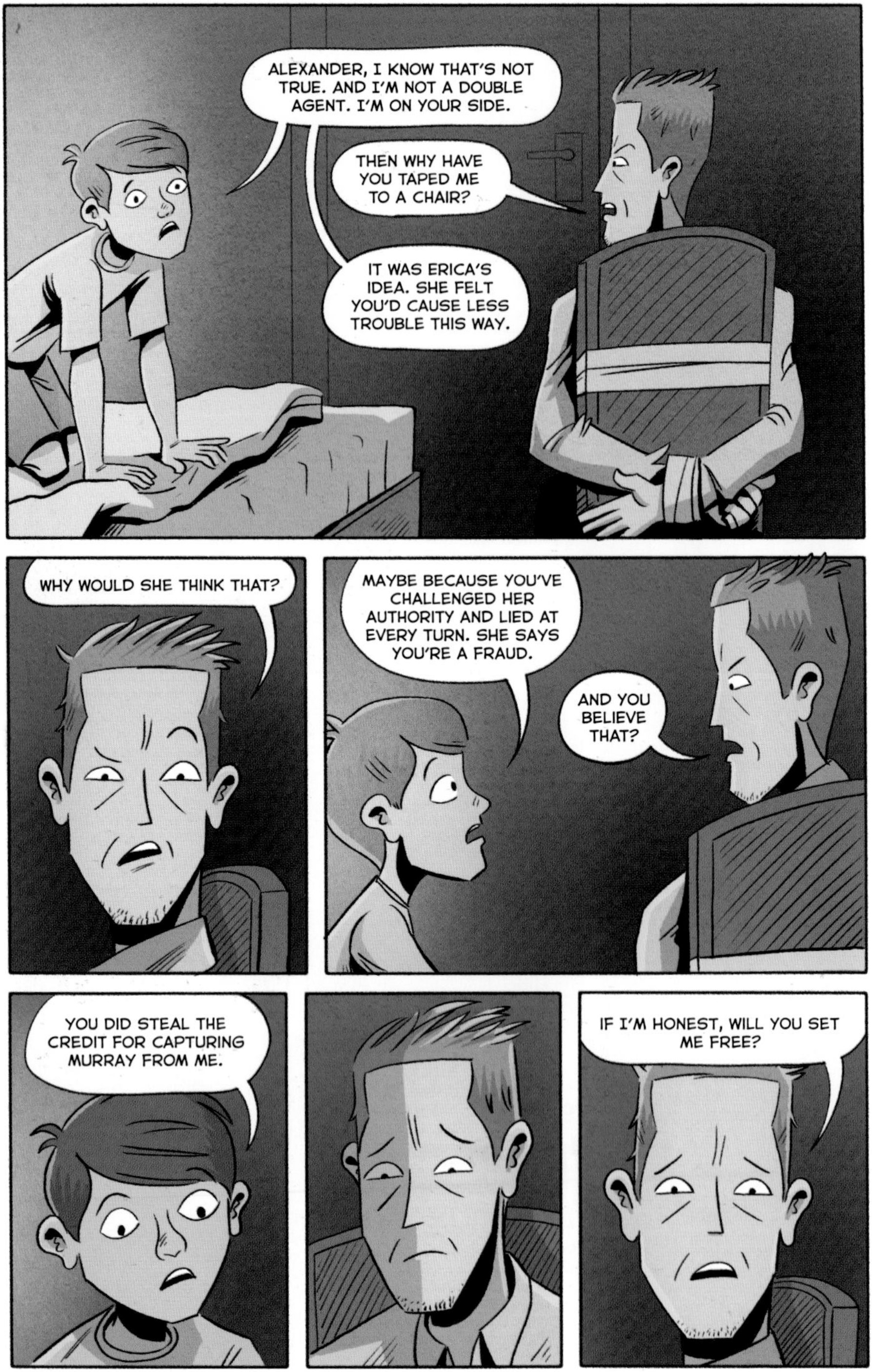
ALEXANDER, I KNOW THAT'S NOT TRUE. AND I'M NOT A DOUBLE AGENT. I'M ON YOUR SIDE.
THEN WHY HAVE YOU TAPED ME TO A CHAIR?
IT WAS ERICA'S IDEA. SHE FELT YOU'D CAUSE LESS TROUBLE THIS WAY.
WHY WOULD SHE THINK THAT?
MAYBE BECAUSE YOU'VE CHALLENGED HER AUTHORITY AND LIED AT EVERY TURN. SHE SAYS YOU'RE A FRAUD.
AND YOU BELIEVE THAT?
YOU DID STEAL THE CREDIT FOR CAPTURING MURRAY FROM ME.
IF I'M HONEST, WILL YOU SET ME FREE?

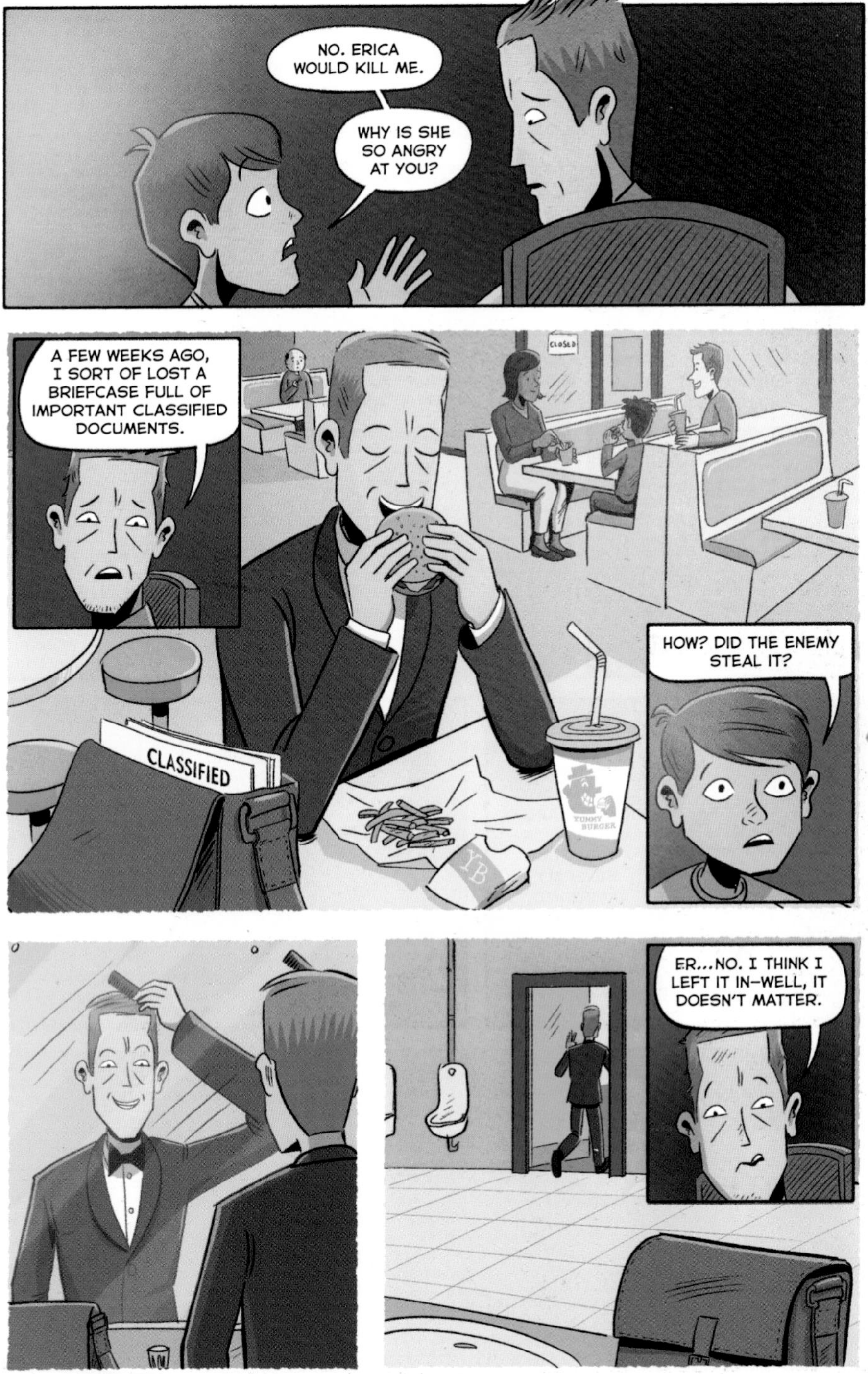
NO. ERICA WOULD KILL ME.
WHY IS SHE SO ANGRY AT YOU?
A FEW WEEKS AGO, I SORT OF LOST A BRIEFCASE FULL OF IMPORTANT CLASSIFIED DOCUMENTS.
CLOSED
CLASSIFIED
YUMMY BURGER
YB
HOW? DID THE ENEMY STEAL IT?
ER...NO. I THINK I LEFT IT IN—WELL, IT DOESN'T MATTER.

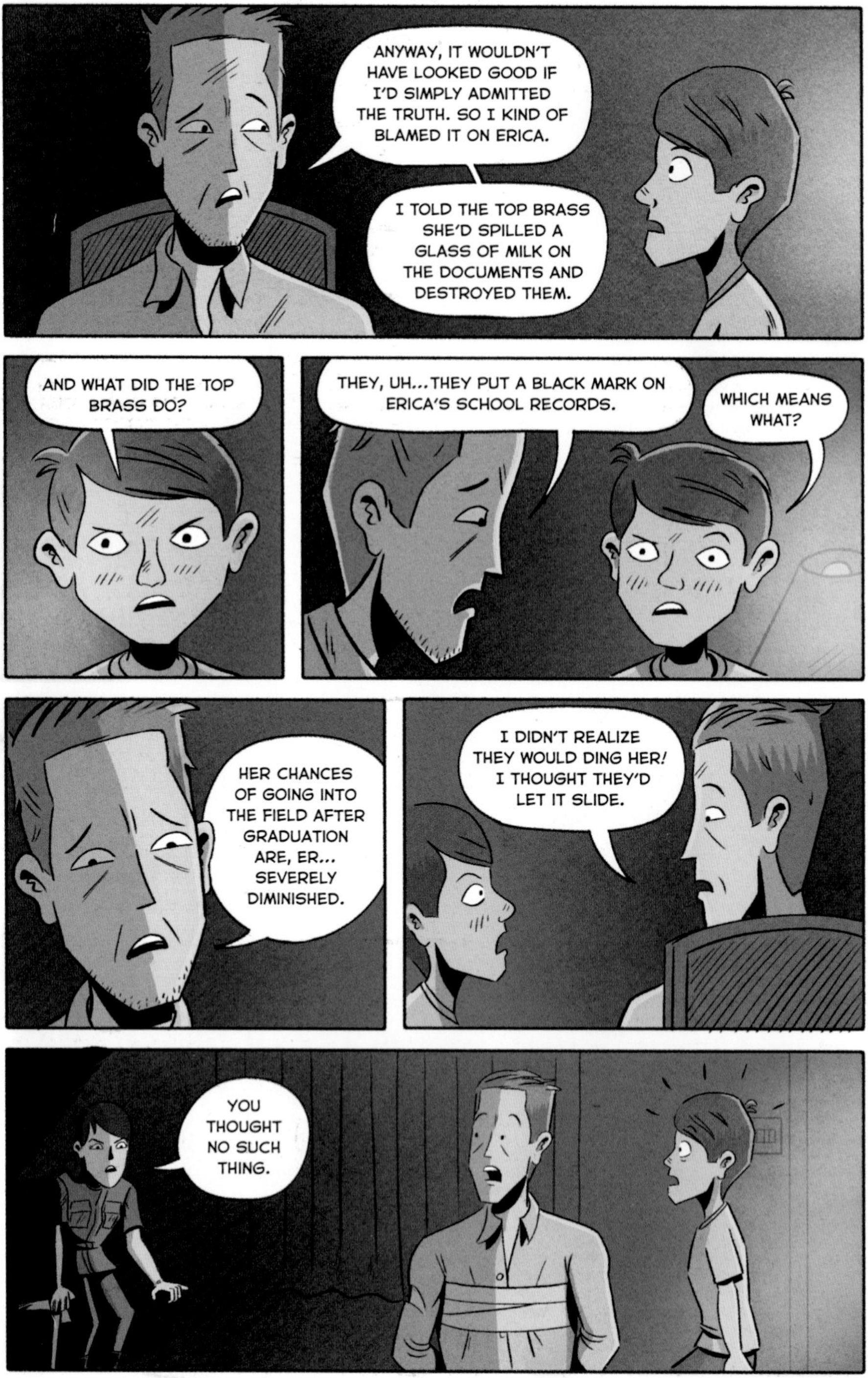
ANYWAY, IT WOULDN'T HAVE LOOKED GOOD IF I'D SIMPLY ADMITTED THE TRUTH. SO I KIND OF BLAMED IT ON ERICA.
I TOLD THE TOP BRASS SHE'D SPILLED A GLASS OF MILK ON THE DOCUMENTS AND DESTROYED THEM.
AND WHAT DID THE TOP BRASS DO?
THEY, UH...THEY PUT A BLACK MARK ON ERICA'S SCHOOL RECORDS.
WHICH MEANS WHAT?
HER CHANCES OF GOING INTO THE FIELD AFTER GRADUATION ARE, ER... SEVERELY DIMINISHED.
I DIDN'T REALIZE THEY WOULD DING HER! I THOUGHT THEY'D LET IT SLIDE.
YOU THOUGHT NO SUCH THING.

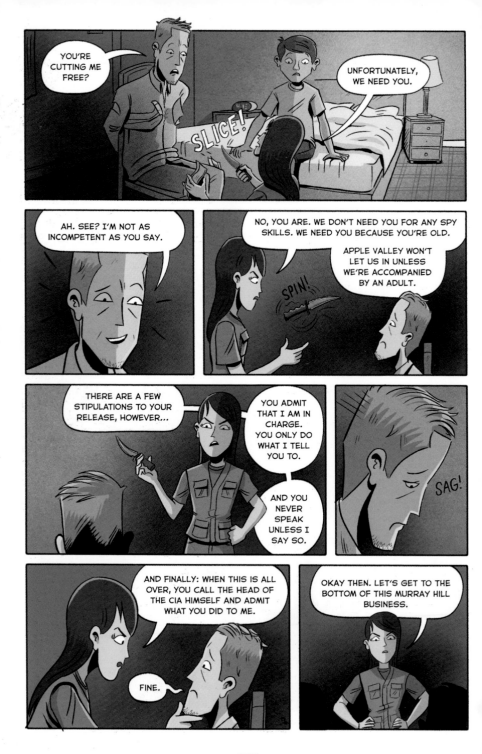

176

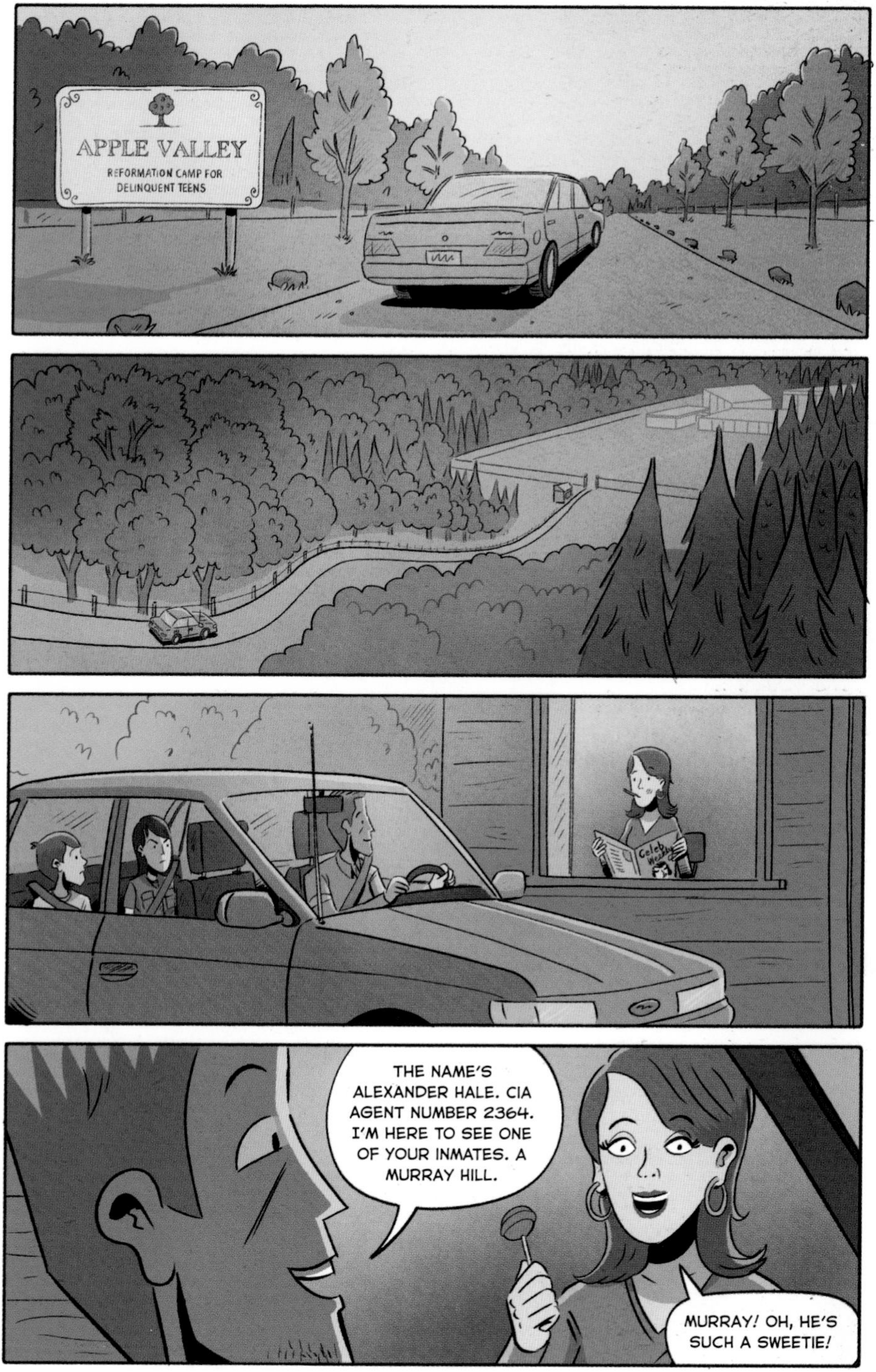
APPLE VALLEY
REFORMATION CAMP FOR DELINQUENT TEENS
THE NAME'S ALEXANDER HALE. CIA AGENT NUMBER 2364. I'M HERE TO SEE ONE OF YOUR INMATES. A MURRAY HILL.
MURRAY! OH, HE'S SUCH A SWEETIE!

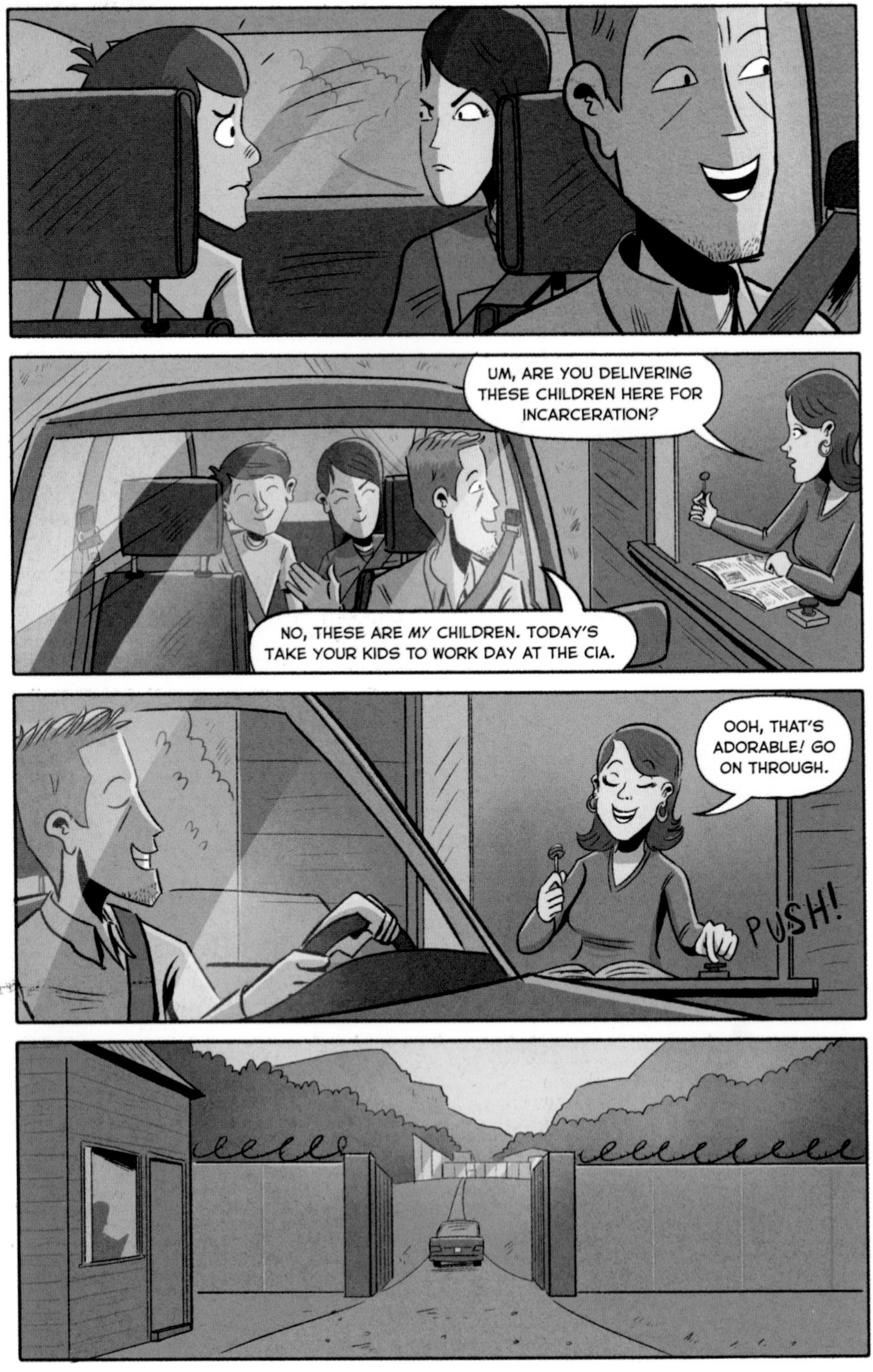
UM, ARE YOU DELIVERING THESE CHILDREN HERE FOR INCARCERATION?
NO, THESE ARE *MY* CHILDREN. TODAY'S TAKE YOUR KIDS TO WORK DAY AT THE CIA.
OOH, THAT'S ADORABLE! GO ON THROUGH.
PUSH!

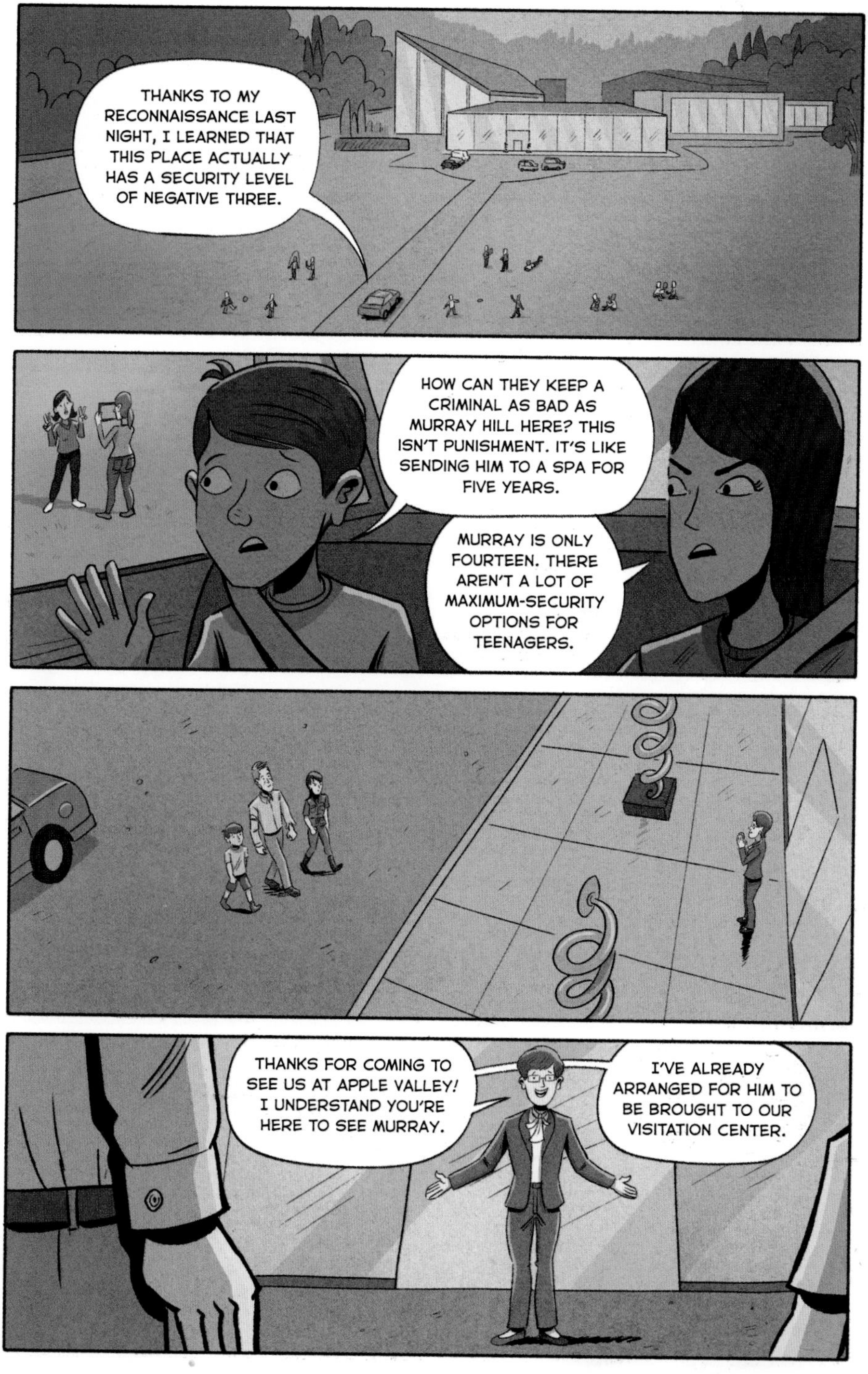
THANKS TO MY RECONNAISSANCE LAST NIGHT, I LEARNED THAT THIS PLACE ACTUALLY HAS A SECURITY LEVEL OF NEGATIVE THREE.
HOW CAN THEY KEEP A CRIMINAL AS BAD AS MURRAY HILL HERE? THIS ISN'T PUNISHMENT. IT'S LIKE SENDING HIM TO A SPA FOR FIVE YEARS.
MURRAY IS ONLY FOURTEEN. THERE AREN'T A LOT OF MAXIMUM-SECURITY OPTIONS FOR TEENAGERS.
THANKS FOR COMING TO SEE US AT APPLE VALLEY! I UNDERSTAND YOU'RE HERE TO SEE MURRAY.
I'VE ALREADY ARRANGED FOR HIM TO BE BROUGHT TO OUR VISITATION CENTER.

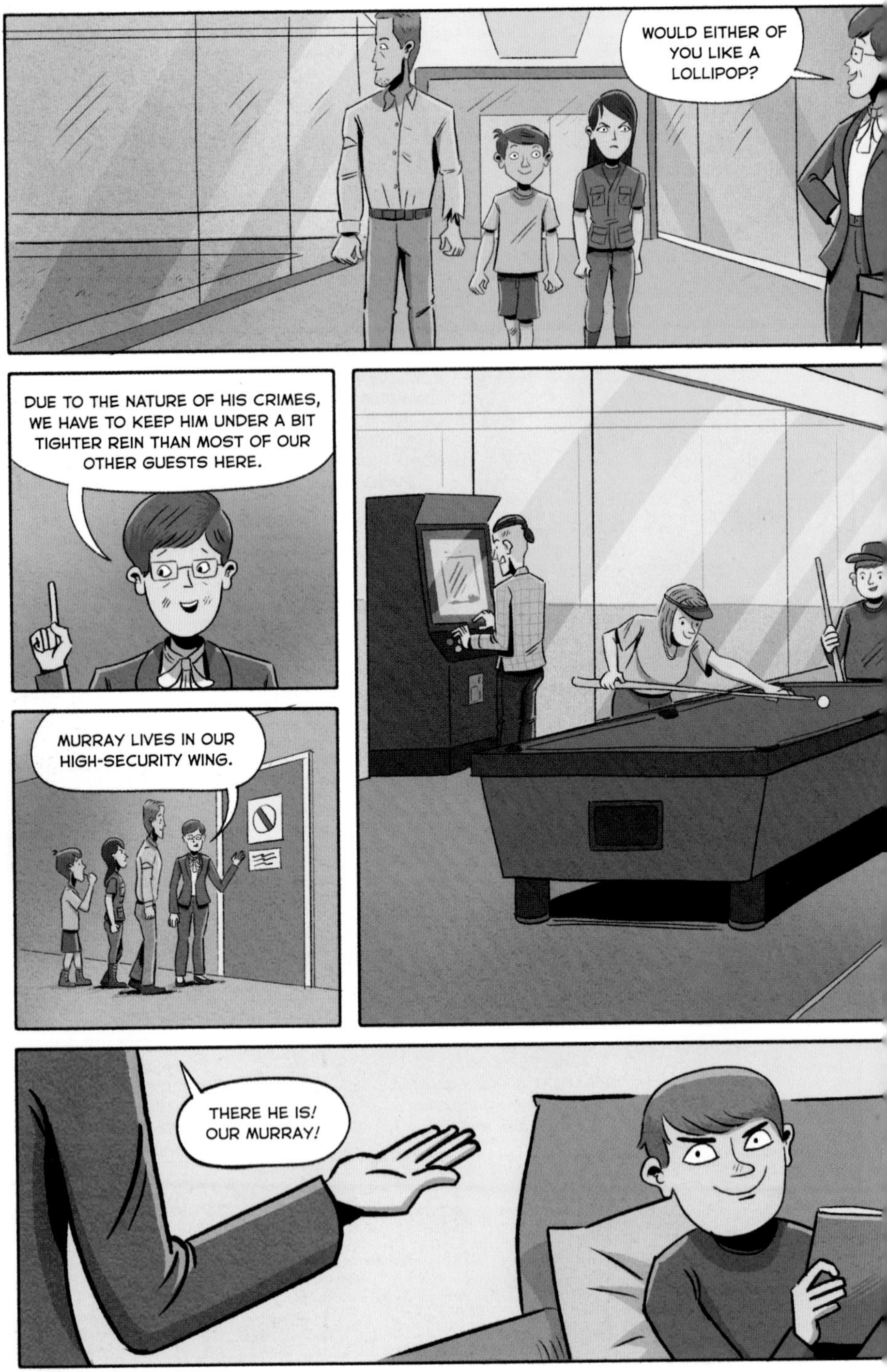
WOULD EITHER OF YOU LIKE A LOLLIPOP?
DUE TO THE NATURE OF HIS CRIMES, WE HAVE TO KEEP HIM UNDER A BIT TIGHTER REIN THAN MOST OF OUR OTHER GUESTS HERE.
MURRAY LIVES IN OUR HIGH-SECURITY WING.
THERE HE IS! OUR MURRAY!

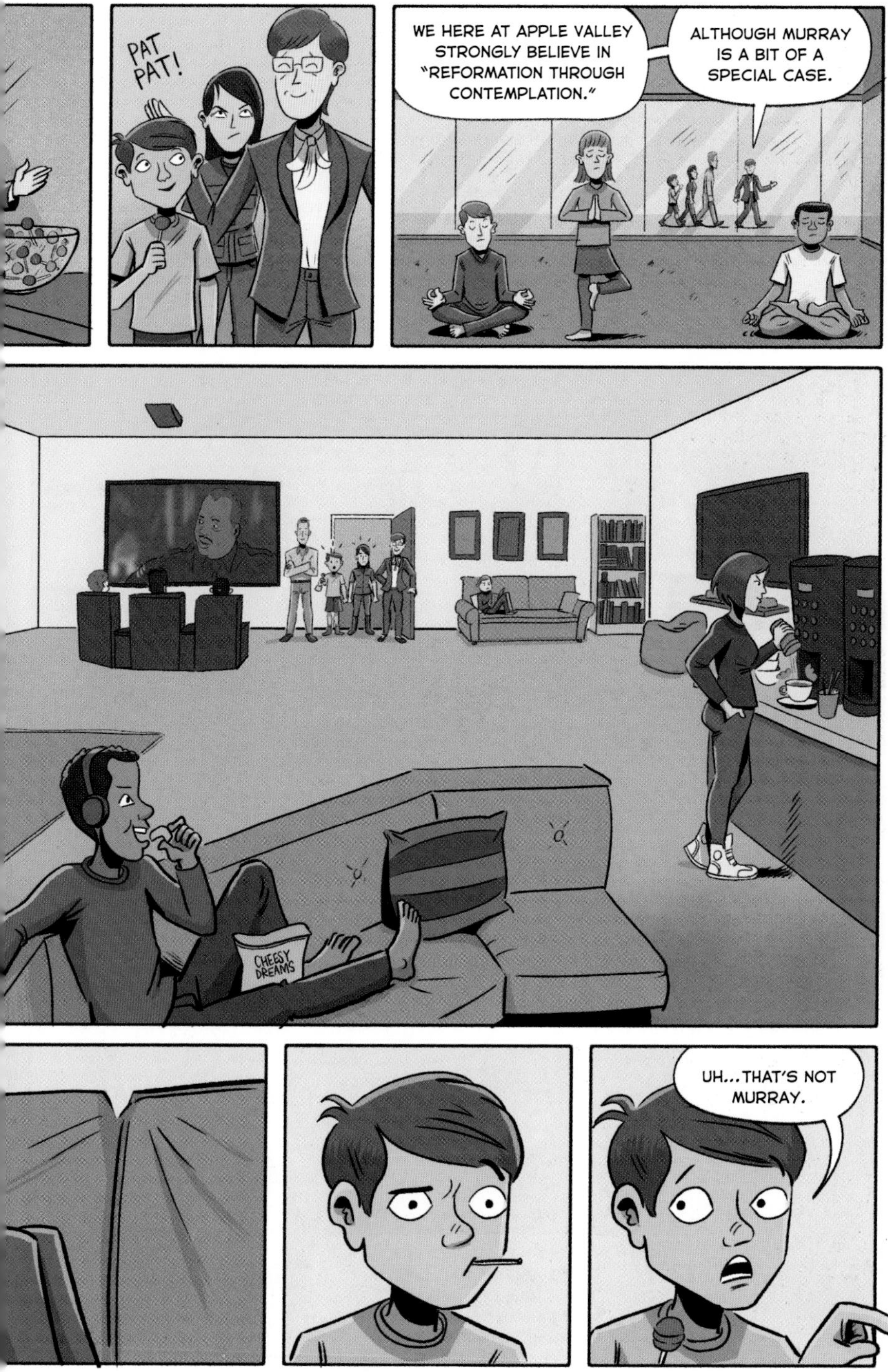
PAT PAT!
WE HERE AT APPLE VALLEY STRONGLY BELIEVE IN "REFORMATION THROUGH CONTEMPLATION."
ALTHOUGH MURRAY IS A BIT OF A SPECIAL CASE.
CHEESY DREAMS
UH...THAT'S NOT MURRAY.

182

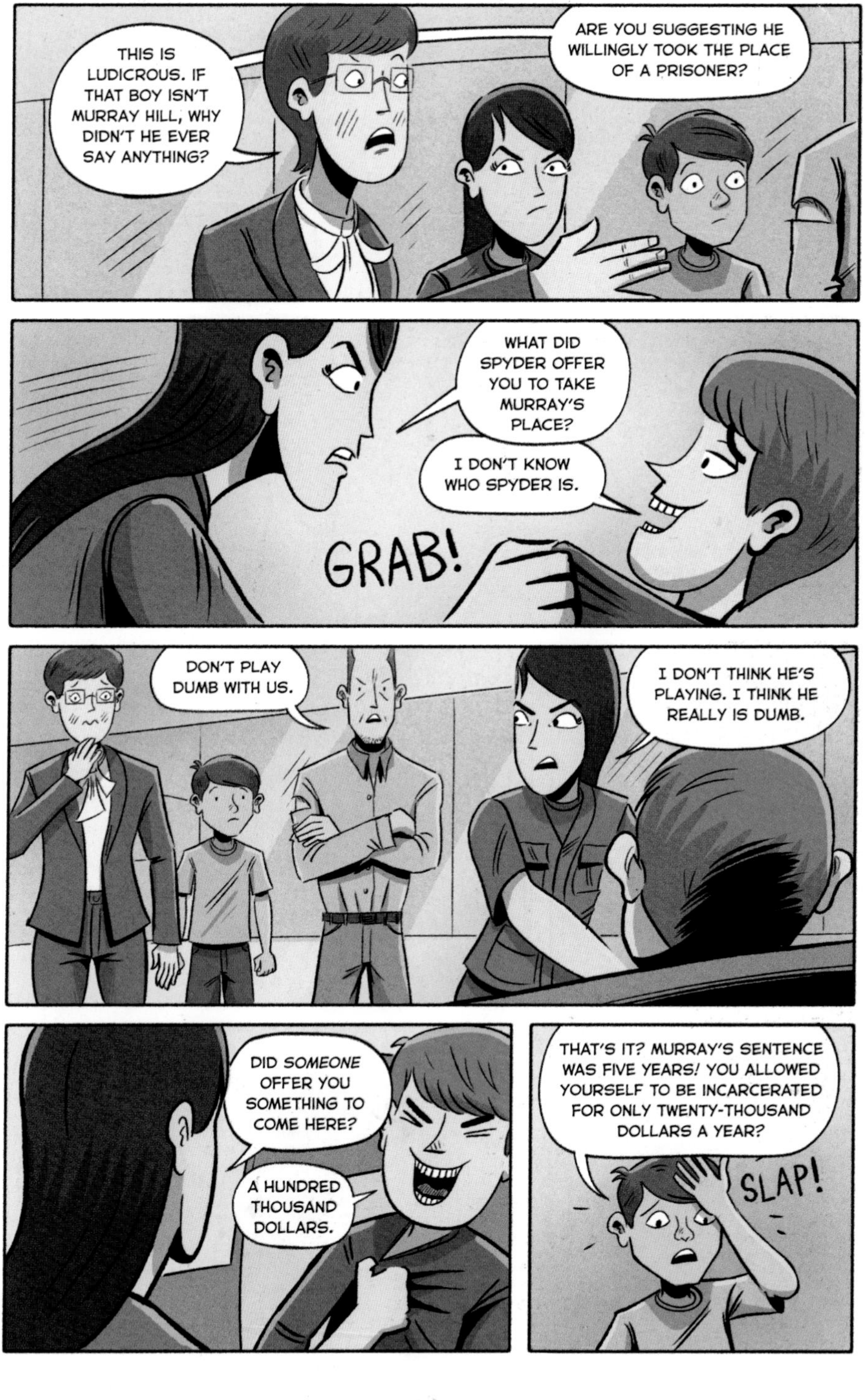
THIS IS LUDICROUS. IF THAT BOY ISN'T MURRAY HILL, WHY DIDN'T HE EVER SAY ANYTHING?
ARE YOU SUGGESTING HE WILLINGLY TOOK THE PLACE OF A PRISONER?
WHAT DID SPYDER OFFER YOU TO TAKE MURRAY'S PLACE?
I DON'T KNOW WHO SPYDER IS.
GRAB!
DON'T PLAY DUMB WITH US.
I DON'T THINK HE'S PLAYING. I THINK HE REALLY IS DUMB.
DID *SOMEONE* OFFER YOU SOMETHING TO COME HERE?
A HUNDRED THOUSAND DOLLARS.
THAT'S IT? MURRAY'S SENTENCE WAS FIVE YEARS! YOU ALLOWED YOURSELF TO BE INCARCERATED FOR ONLY TWENTY-THOUSAND DOLLARS A YEAR?
SLAP!

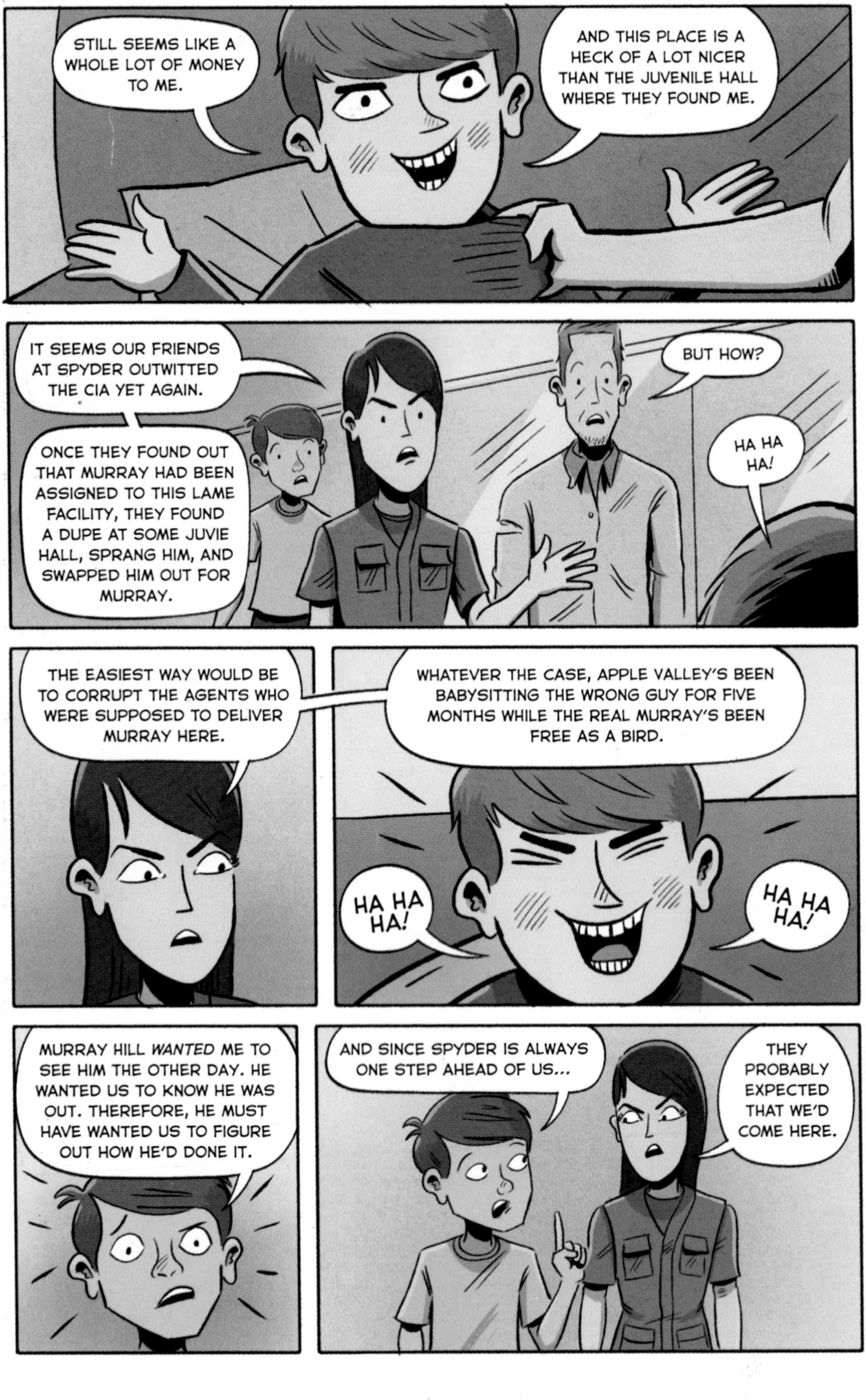
STILL SEEMS LIKE A WHOLE LOT OF MONEY TO ME.
AND THIS PLACE IS A HECK OF A LOT NICER THAN THE JUVENILE HALL WHERE THEY FOUND ME.
IT SEEMS OUR FRIENDS AT SPYDER OUTWITTED THE CIA YET AGAIN.
ONCE THEY FOUND OUT THAT MURRAY HAD BEEN ASSIGNED TO THIS LAME FACILITY, THEY FOUND A DUPE AT SOME JUVIE HALL, SPRANG HIM, AND SWAPPED HIM OUT FOR MURRAY.
BUT HOW?
HA HA HA!
THE EASIEST WAY WOULD BE TO CORRUPT THE AGENTS WHO WERE SUPPOSED TO DELIVER MURRAY HERE.
WHATEVER THE CASE, APPLE VALLEY'S BEEN BABYSITTING THE WRONG GUY FOR FIVE MONTHS WHILE THE REAL MURRAY'S BEEN FREE AS A BIRD.
HA HA HA!
HA HA HA!
MURRAY HILL *WANTED* ME TO SEE HIM THE OTHER DAY. HE WANTED US TO KNOW HE WAS OUT. THEREFORE, HE MUST HAVE WANTED US TO FIGURE OUT HOW HE'D DONE IT.
AND SINCE SPYDER IS ALWAYS ONE STEP AHEAD OF US...
THEY PROBABLY EXPECTED THAT WE'D COME HERE.

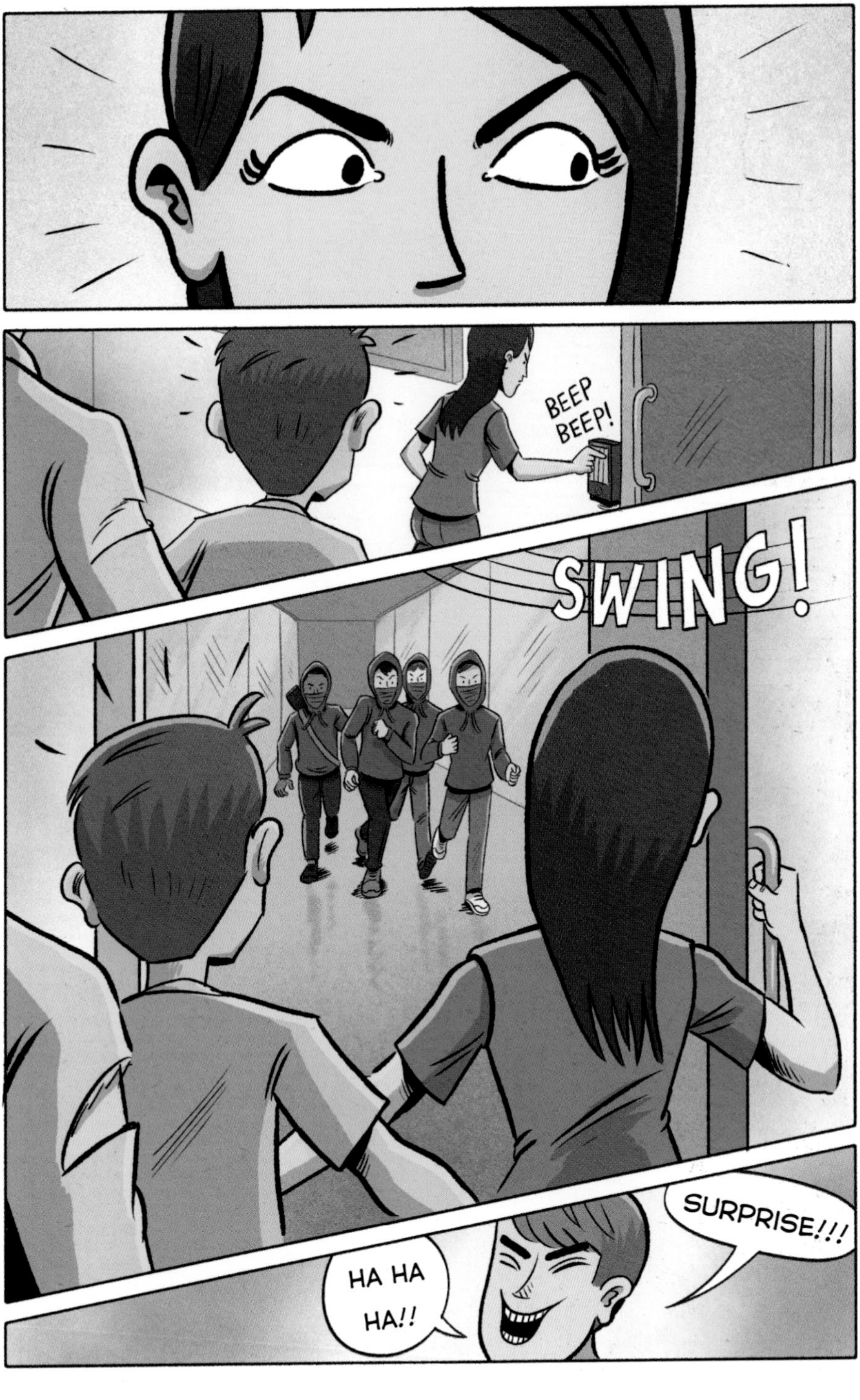
BEEP BEEP!
SWING!
HA HA HA!!
SURPRISE!!!

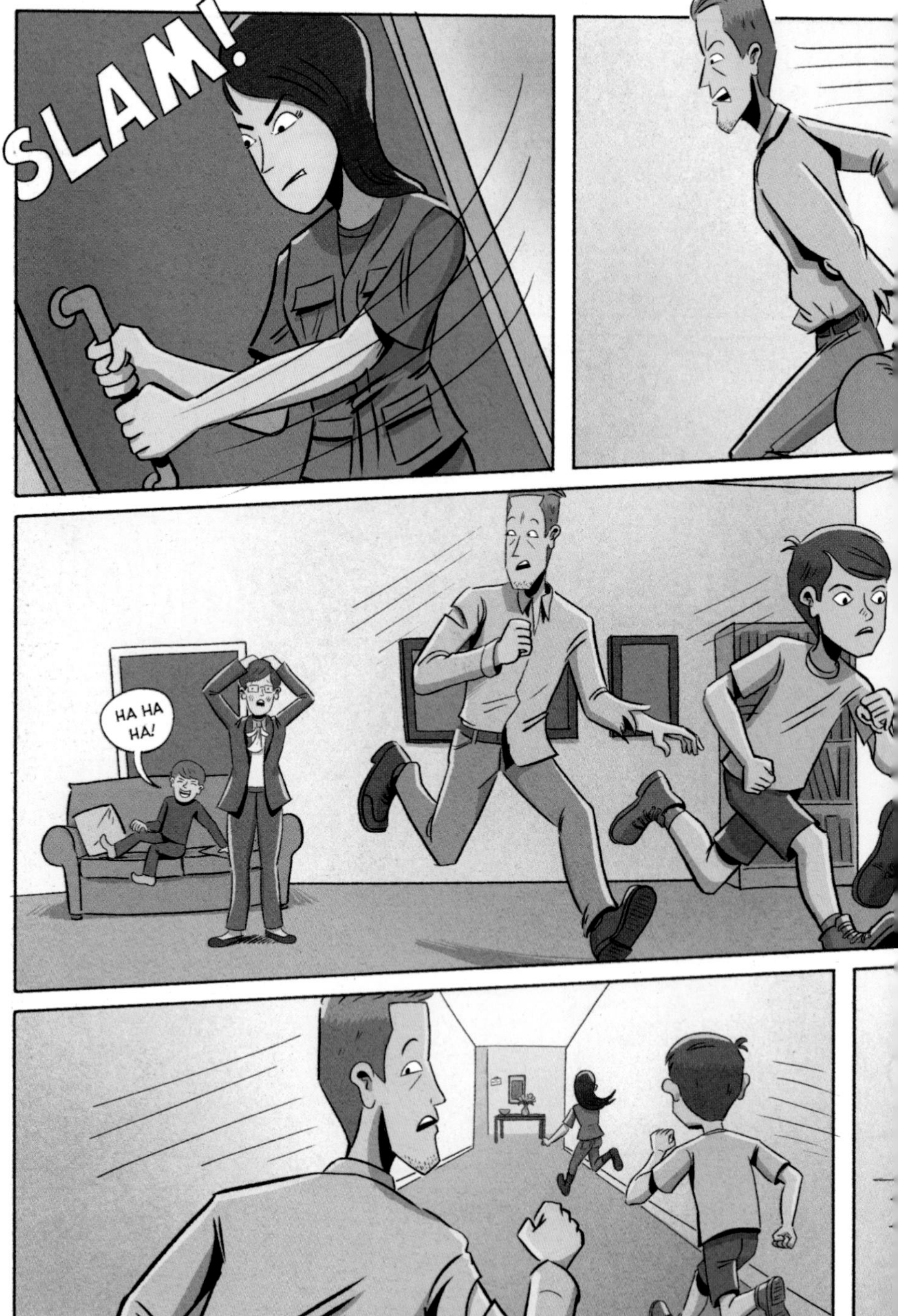
SLAM!
HA HA HA!

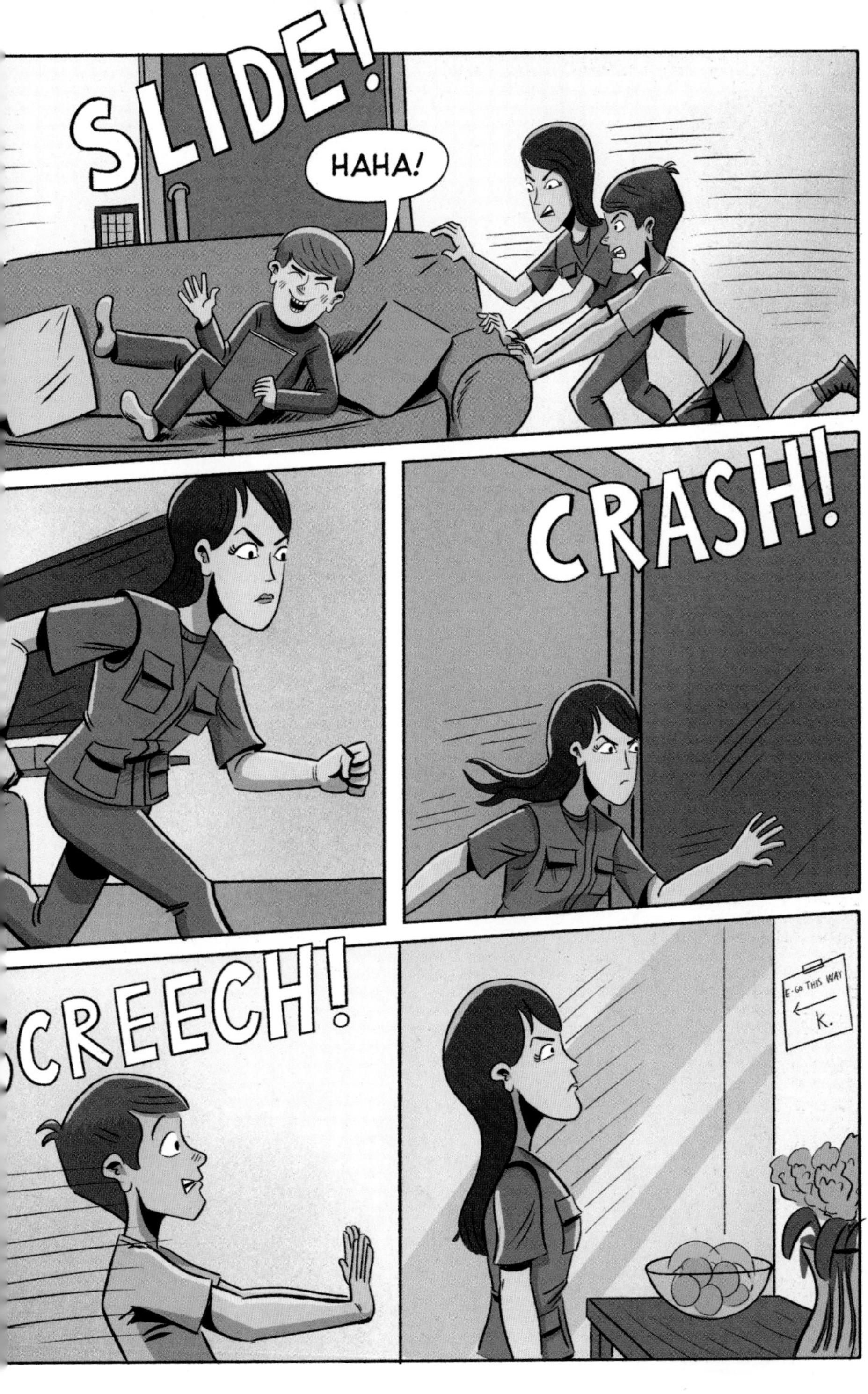
SLIDE!
HAHA!
CRASH!
SCREECH!
E-GO THIS WAY
K.

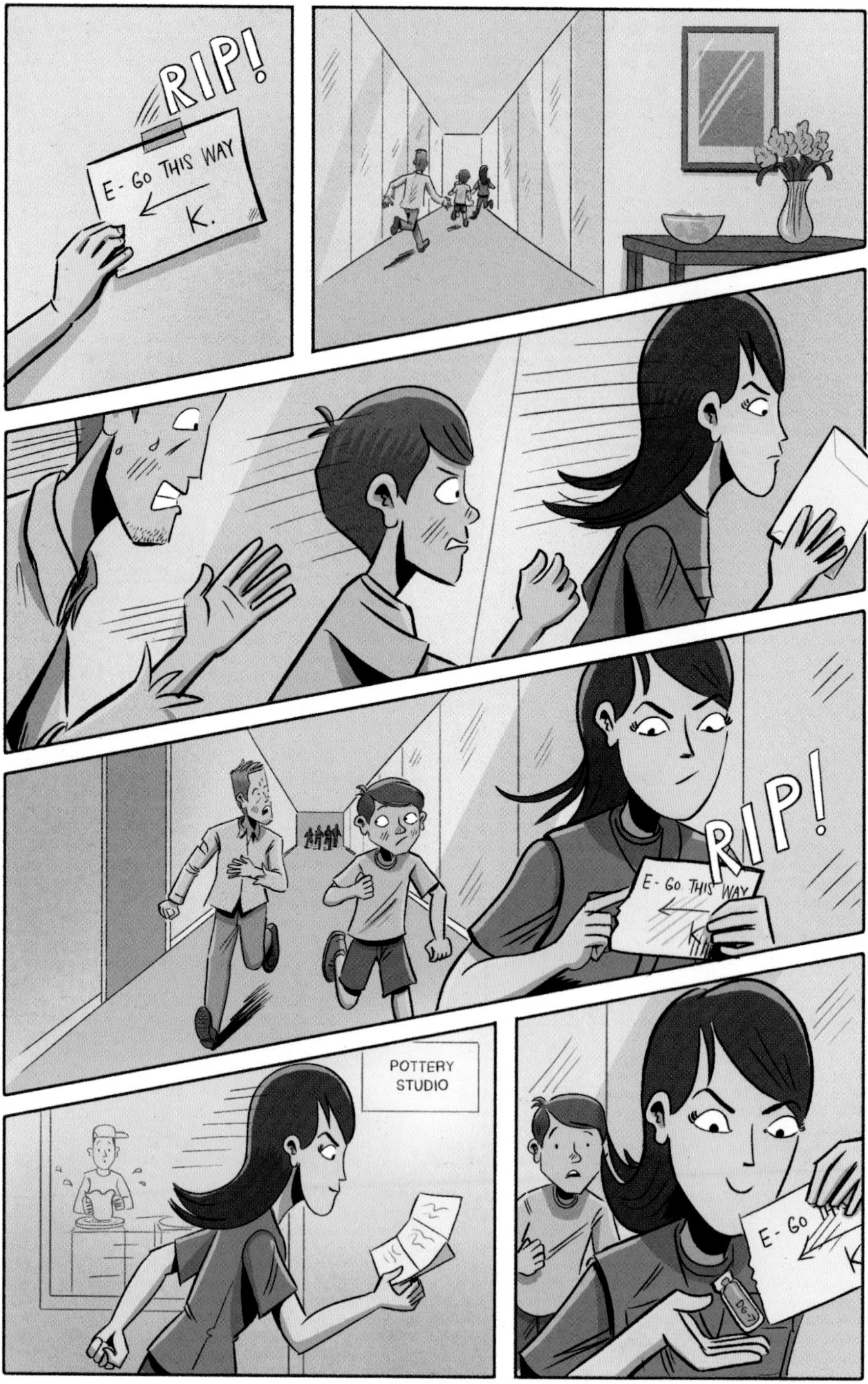
RIP!
E - GO THIS WAY
K.
RIP!
E - GO THIS WAY
K
POTTERY STUDIO
E - GO
K

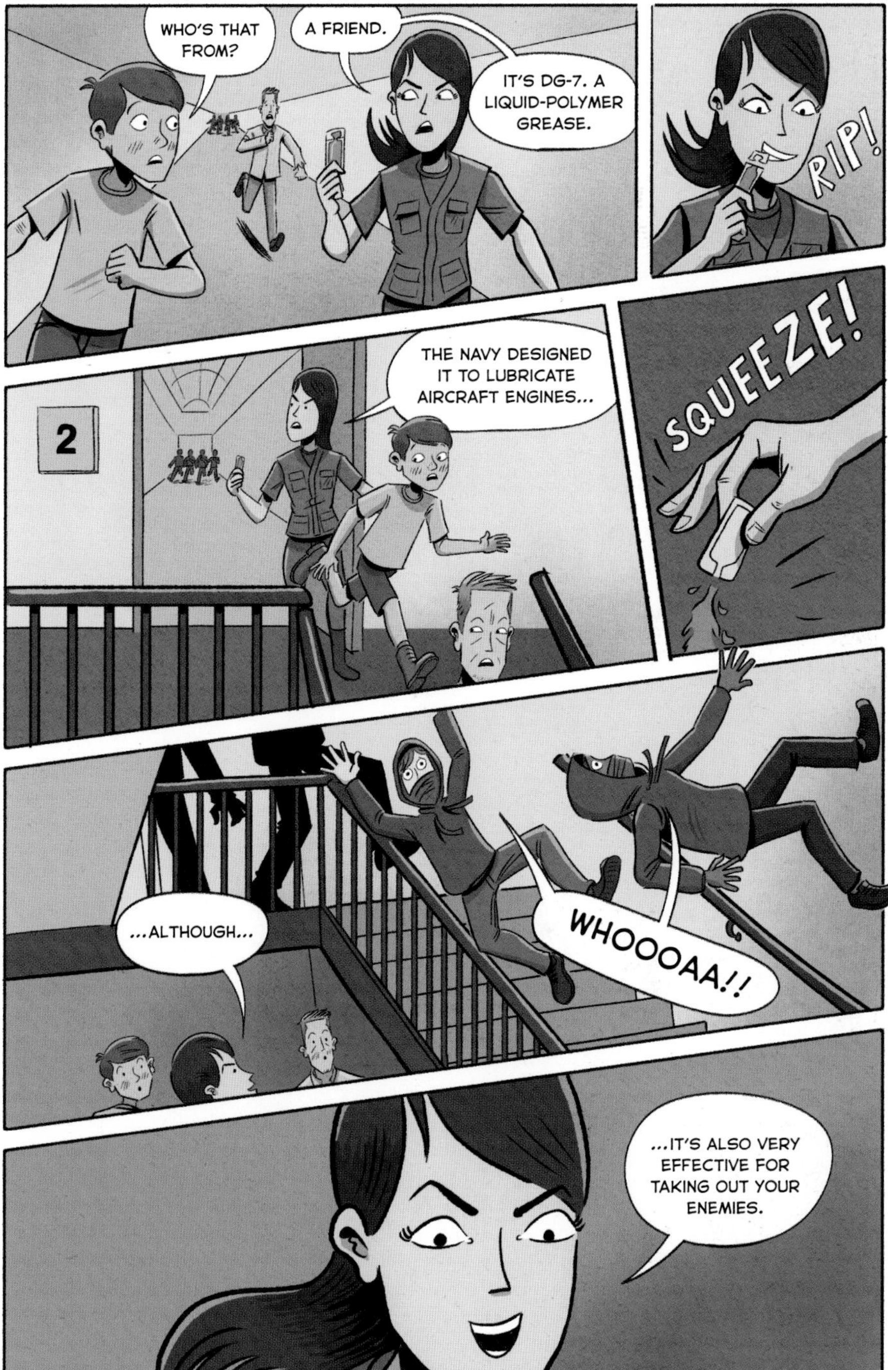
WHO'S THAT FROM?
A FRIEND.
IT'S DG-7. A LIQUID-POLYMER GREASE.
RIP!
THE NAVY DESIGNED IT TO LUBRICATE AIRCRAFT ENGINES...
2
SQUEEZE!
...ALTHOUGH...
WHOOOAA!!
...IT'S ALSO VERY EFFECTIVE FOR TAKING OUT YOUR ENEMIES.

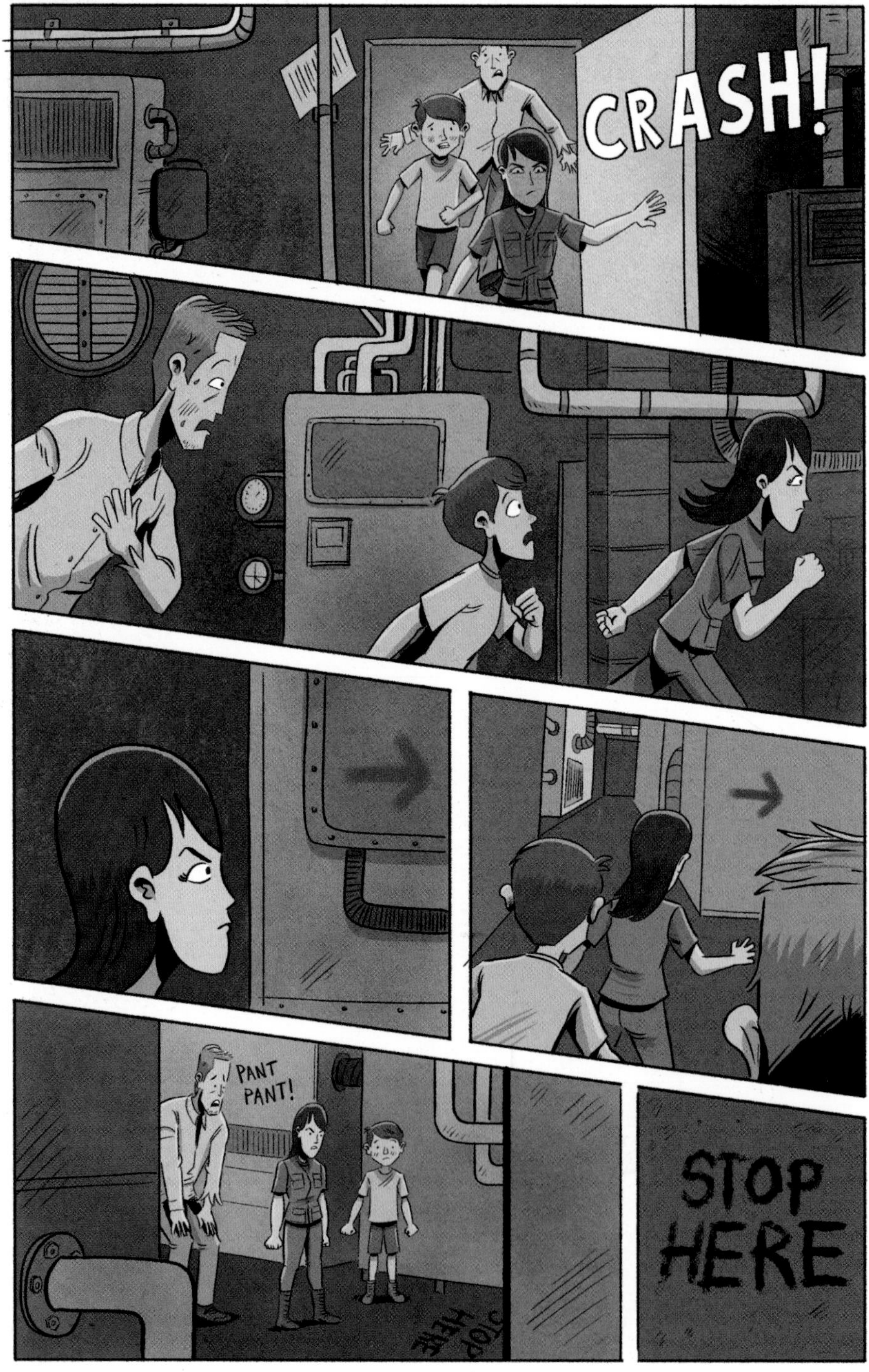
CRASH!
PANT
PANT!
STOP
HERE
STOP
HERE

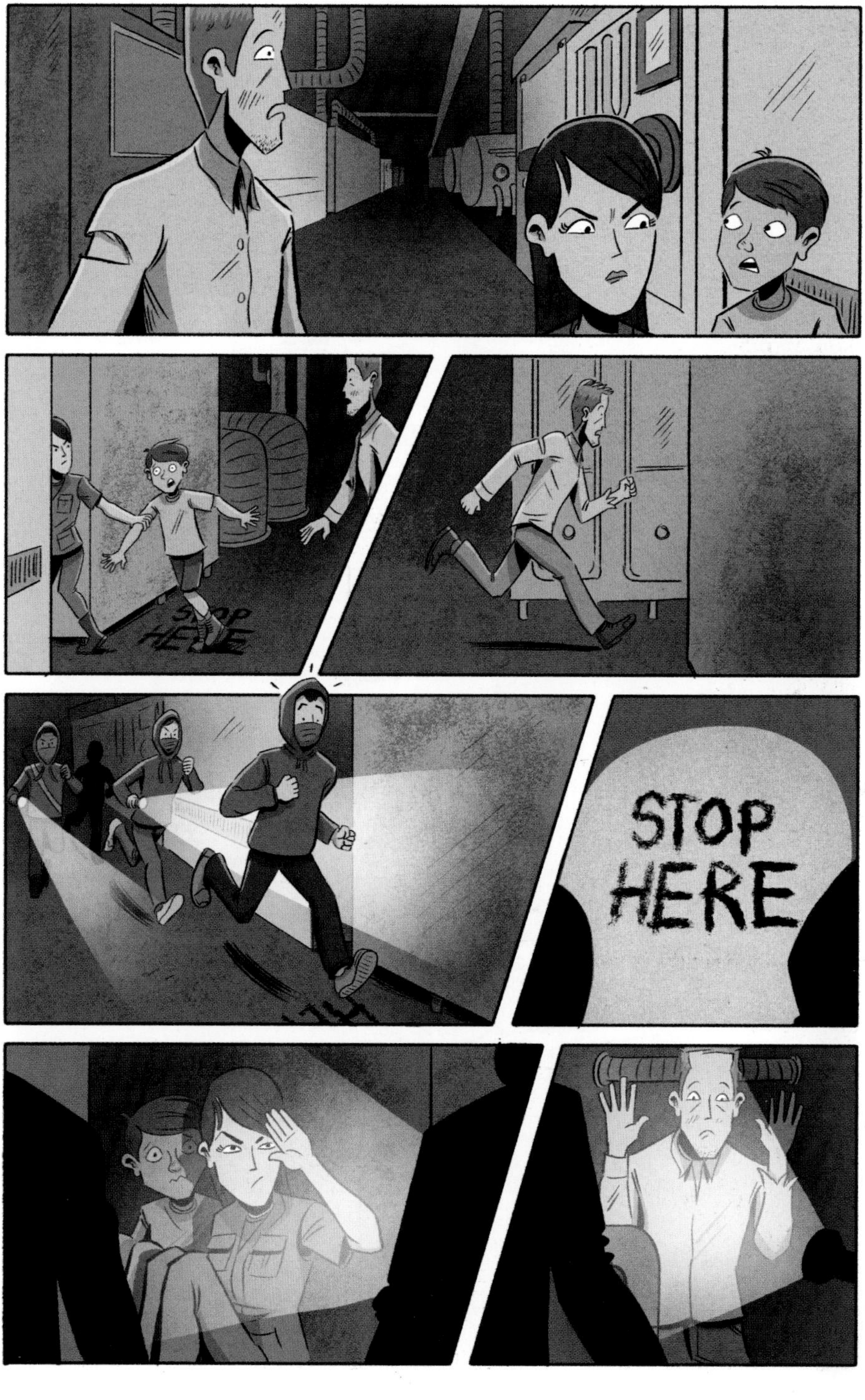

STOP HERE
STOP HERE

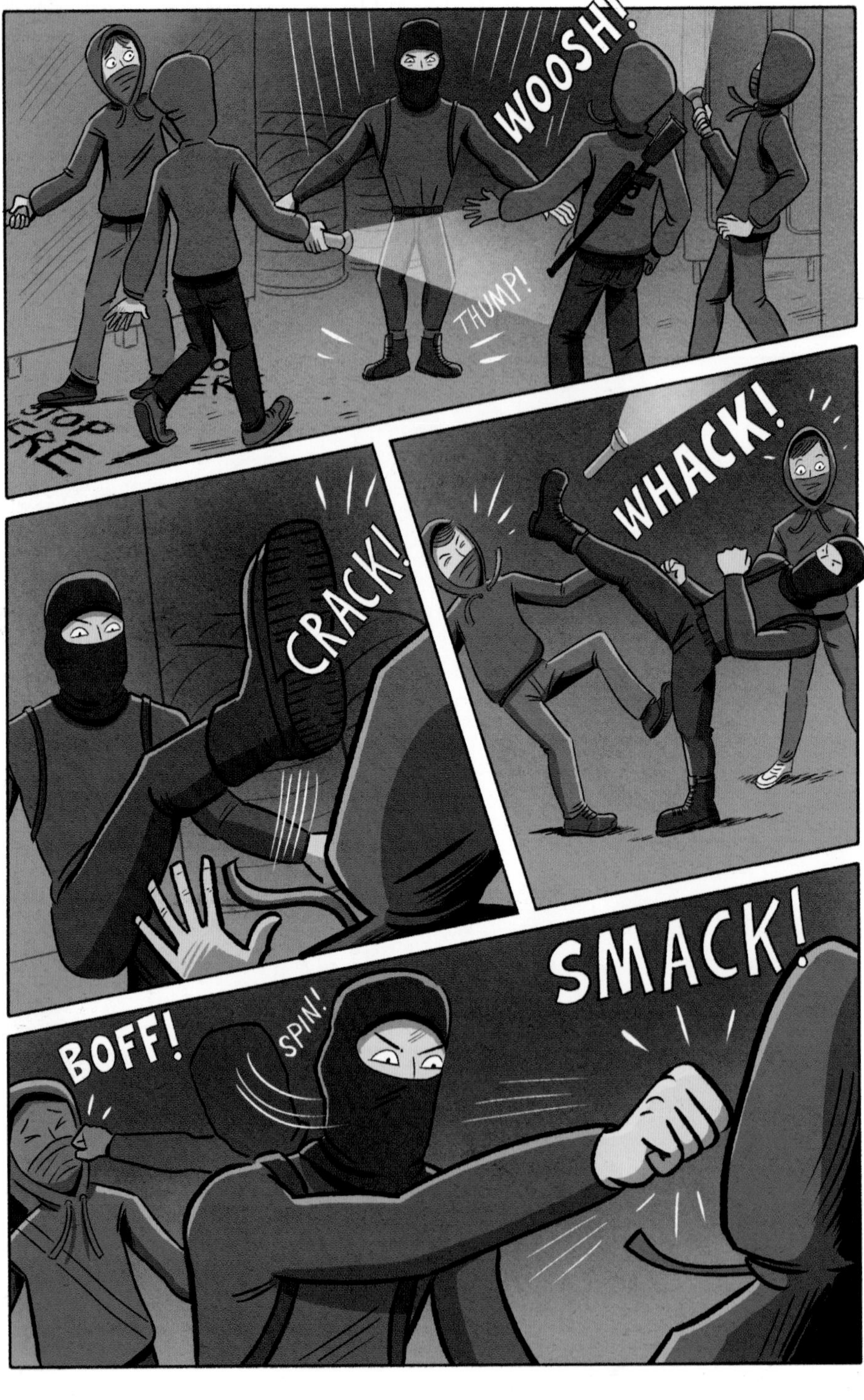
WOOSH!
THUMP!
STOP
ERE
CRACK!
WHACK!
SMACK!
BOFF!
SPIN!

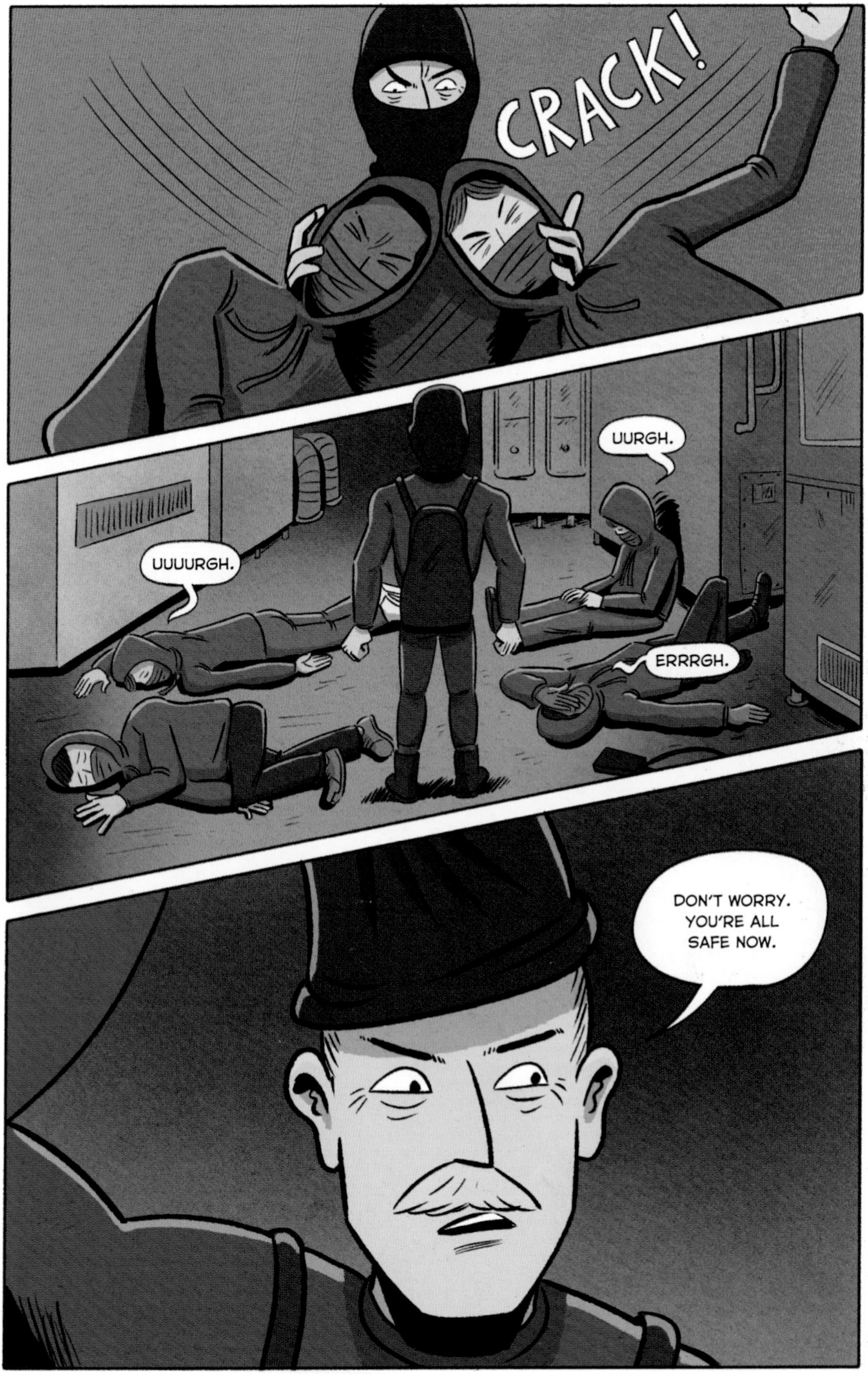
CRACK!
UURGH.
UUUURGH.
ERRRGH.
DON'T WORRY.
YOU'RE ALL
SAFE NOW.

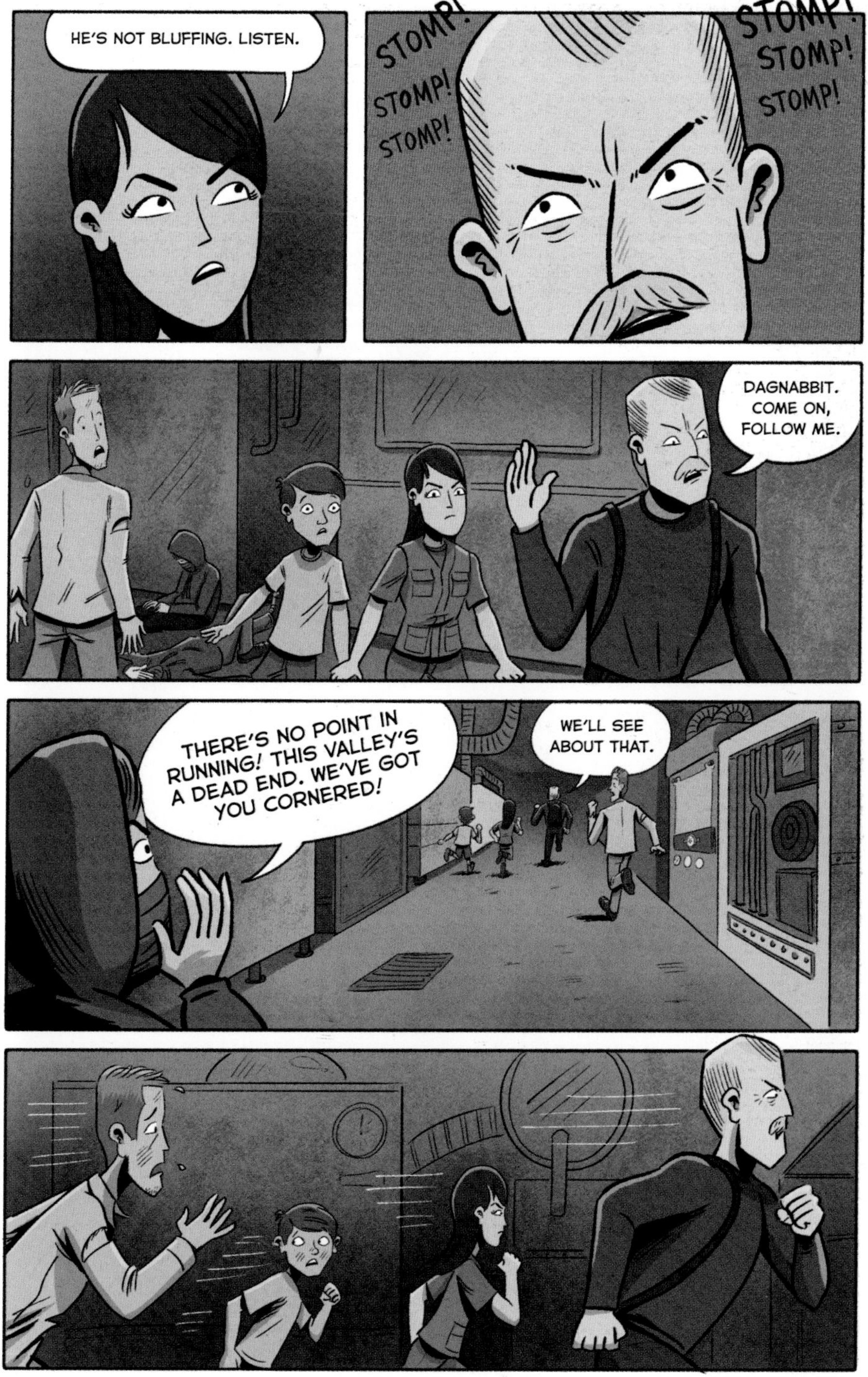
HE'S NOT BLUFFING. LISTEN.
STOMP!
STOMP!
STOMP!
STOMP!
STOMP!
STOMP!
DAGNABBIT. COME ON, FOLLOW ME.
THERE'S NO POINT IN RUNNING! THIS VALLEY'S A DEAD END. WE'VE GOT YOU CORNERED!
WE'LL SEE ABOUT THAT.

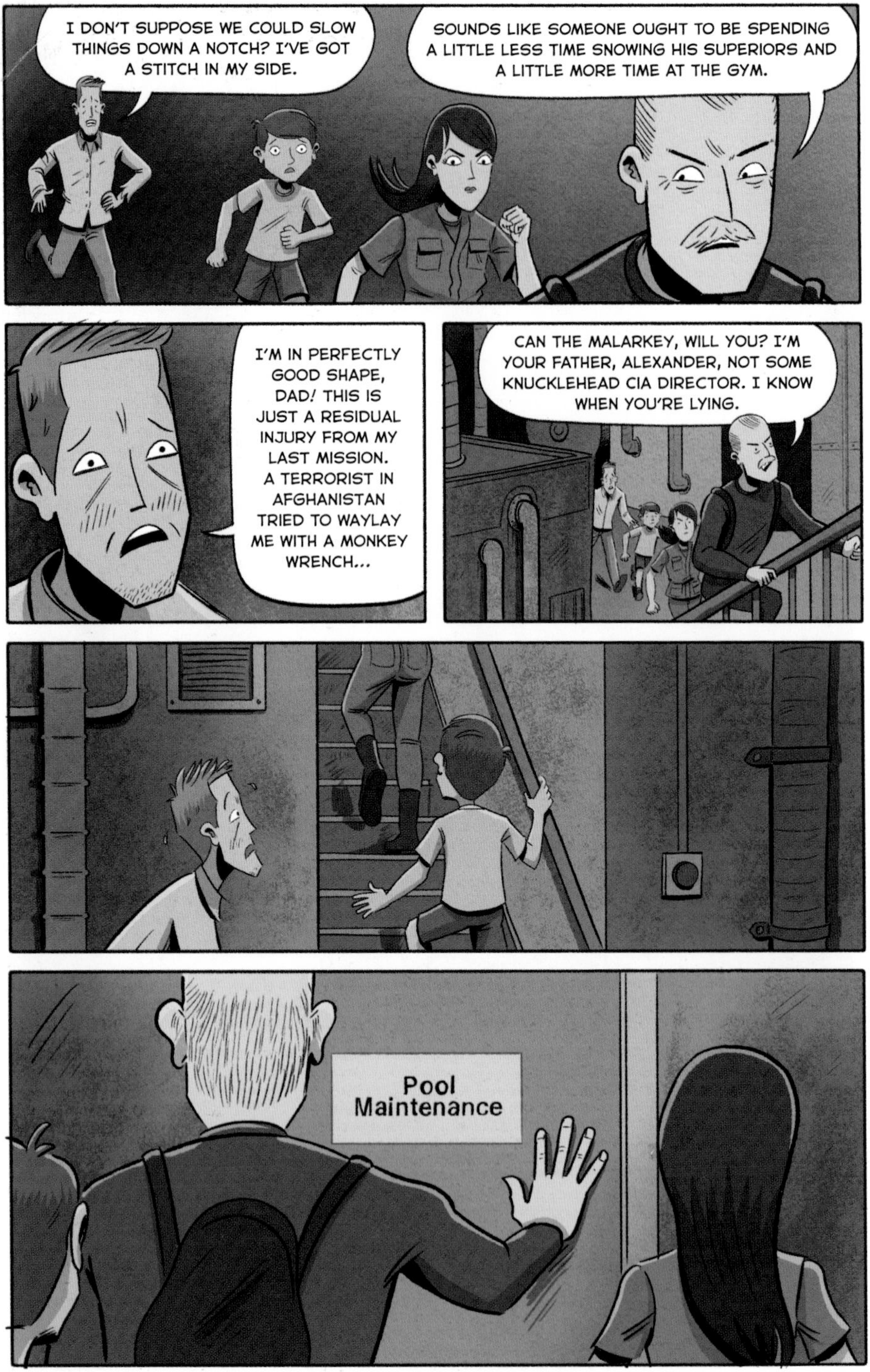
I DON'T SUPPOSE WE COULD SLOW THINGS DOWN A NOTCH? I'VE GOT A STITCH IN MY SIDE.
SOUNDS LIKE SOMEONE OUGHT TO BE SPENDING A LITTLE LESS TIME SNOWING HIS SUPERIORS AND A LITTLE MORE TIME AT THE GYM.
I'M IN PERFECTLY GOOD SHAPE, DAD! THIS IS JUST A RESIDUAL INJURY FROM MY LAST MISSION. A TERRORIST IN AFGHANISTAN TRIED TO WAYLAY ME WITH A MONKEY WRENCH...
CAN THE MALARKEY, WILL YOU? I'M YOUR FATHER, ALEXANDER, NOT SOME KNUCKLEHEAD CIA DIRECTOR. I KNOW WHEN YOU'RE LYING.
Pool
Maintenance

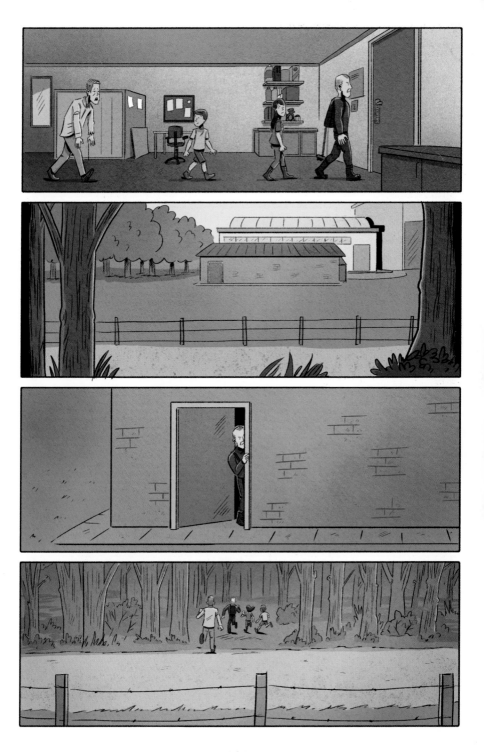

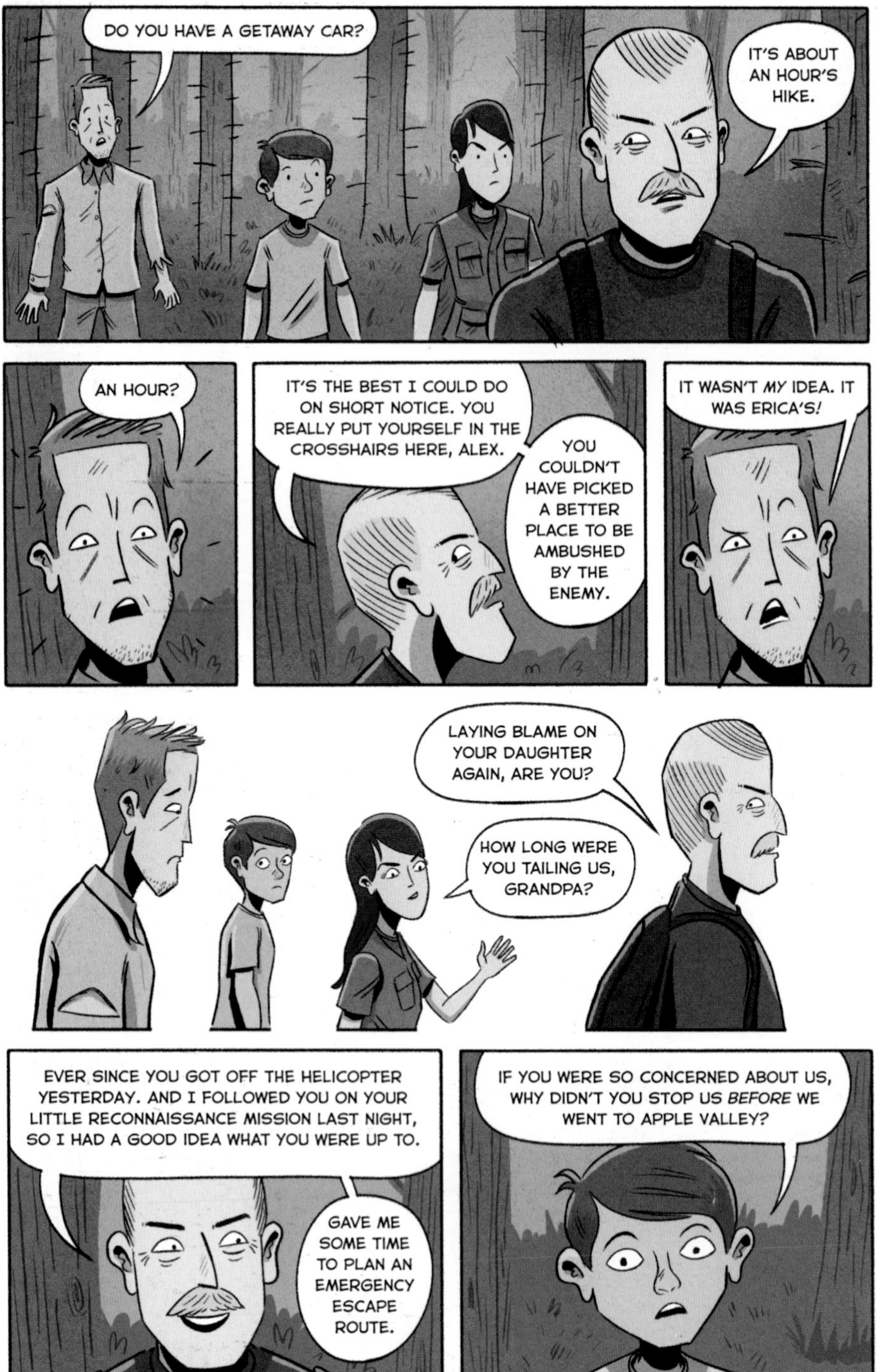
DO YOU HAVE A GETAWAY CAR?
IT'S ABOUT AN HOUR'S HIKE.
AN HOUR?
IT'S THE BEST I COULD DO ON SHORT NOTICE. YOU REALLY PUT YOURSELF IN THE CROSSHAIRS HERE, ALEX.
YOU COULDN'T HAVE PICKED A BETTER PLACE TO BE AMBUSHED BY THE ENEMY.
IT WASN'T *MY* IDEA. IT WAS ERICA'S!
LAYING BLAME ON YOUR DAUGHTER AGAIN, ARE YOU?
HOW LONG WERE YOU TAILING US, GRANDPA?
EVER SINCE YOU GOT OFF THE HELICOPTER YESTERDAY. AND I FOLLOWED YOU ON YOUR LITTLE RECONNAISSANCE MISSION LAST NIGHT, SO I HAD A GOOD IDEA WHAT YOU WERE UP TO.
GAVE ME SOME TIME TO PLAN AN EMERGENCY ESCAPE ROUTE.
IF YOU WERE SO CONCERNED ABOUT US, WHY DIDN'T YOU STOP US *BEFORE* WE WENT TO APPLE VALLEY?

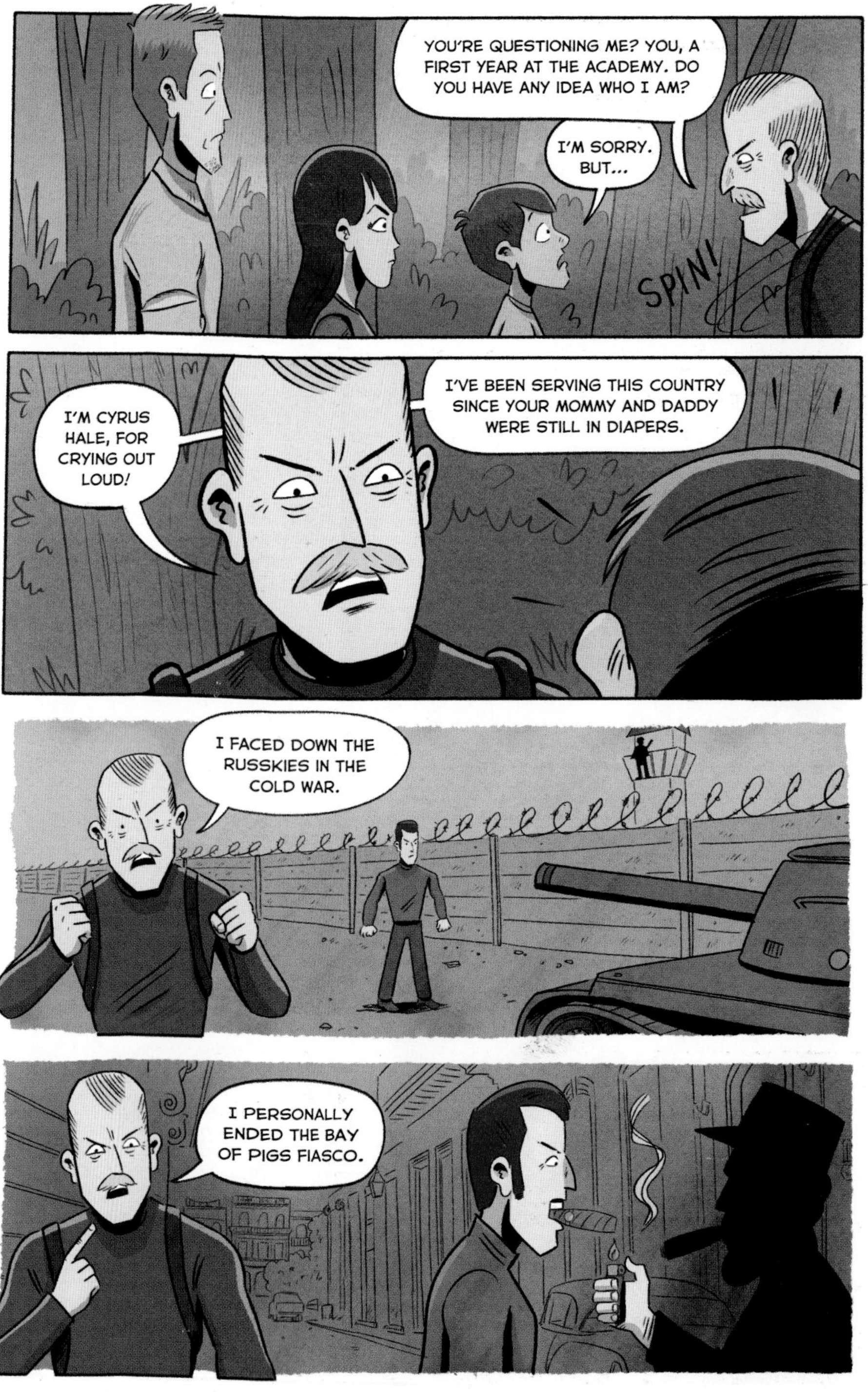
YOU'RE QUESTIONING ME? YOU, A FIRST YEAR AT THE ACADEMY. DO YOU HAVE ANY IDEA WHO I AM?
I'M SORRY. BUT...
SPIN!
I'M CYRUS HALE, FOR CRYING OUT LOUD!
I'VE BEEN SERVING THIS COUNTRY SINCE YOUR MOMMY AND DADDY WERE STILL IN DIAPERS.
I FACED DOWN THE RUSSKIES IN THE COLD WAR.
I PERSONALLY ENDED THE BAY OF PIGS FIASCO.

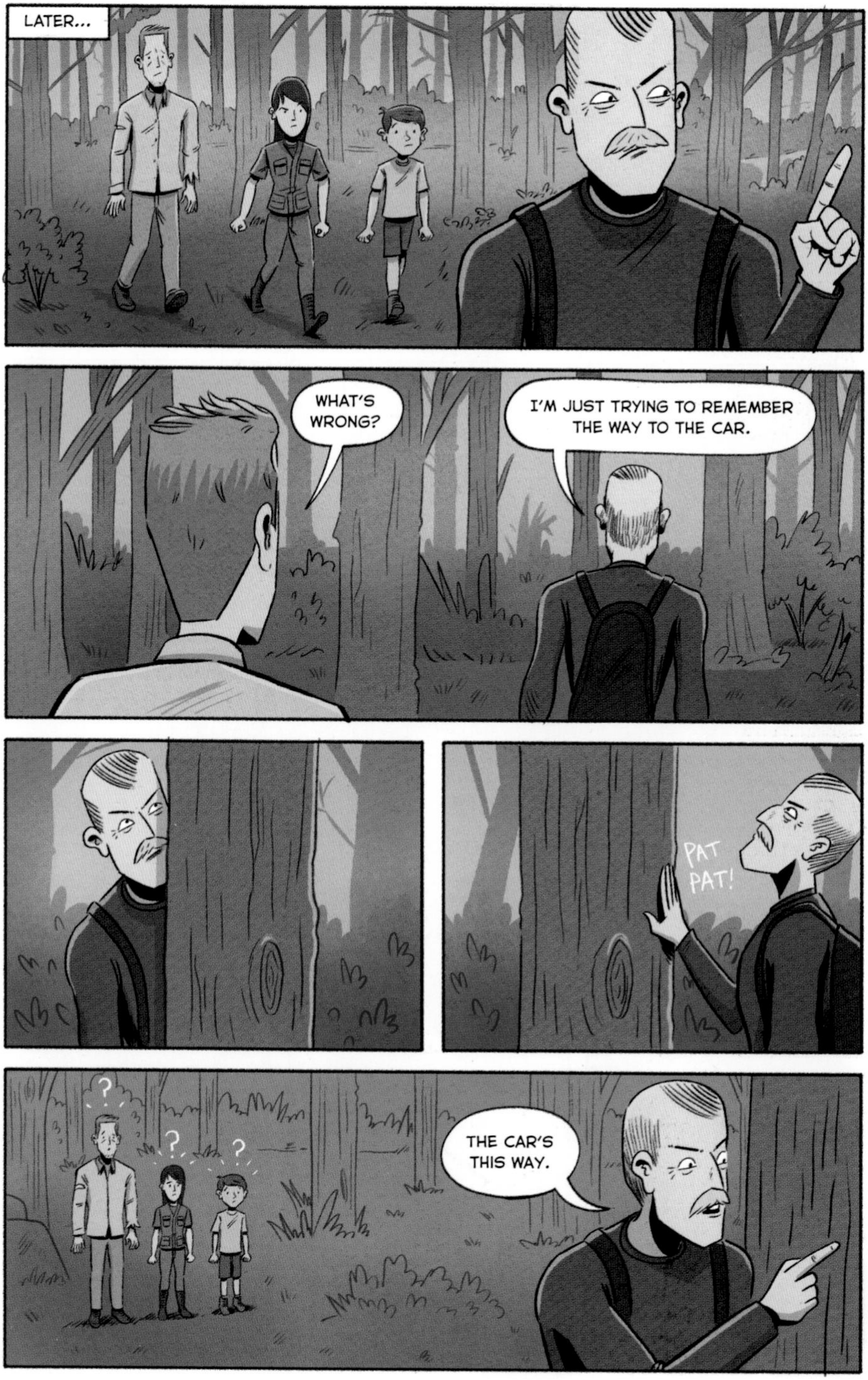
LATER...
WHAT'S WRONG?
I'M JUST TRYING TO REMEMBER THE WAY TO THE CAR.
PAT PAT!
?
?
?
THE CAR'S THIS WAY.

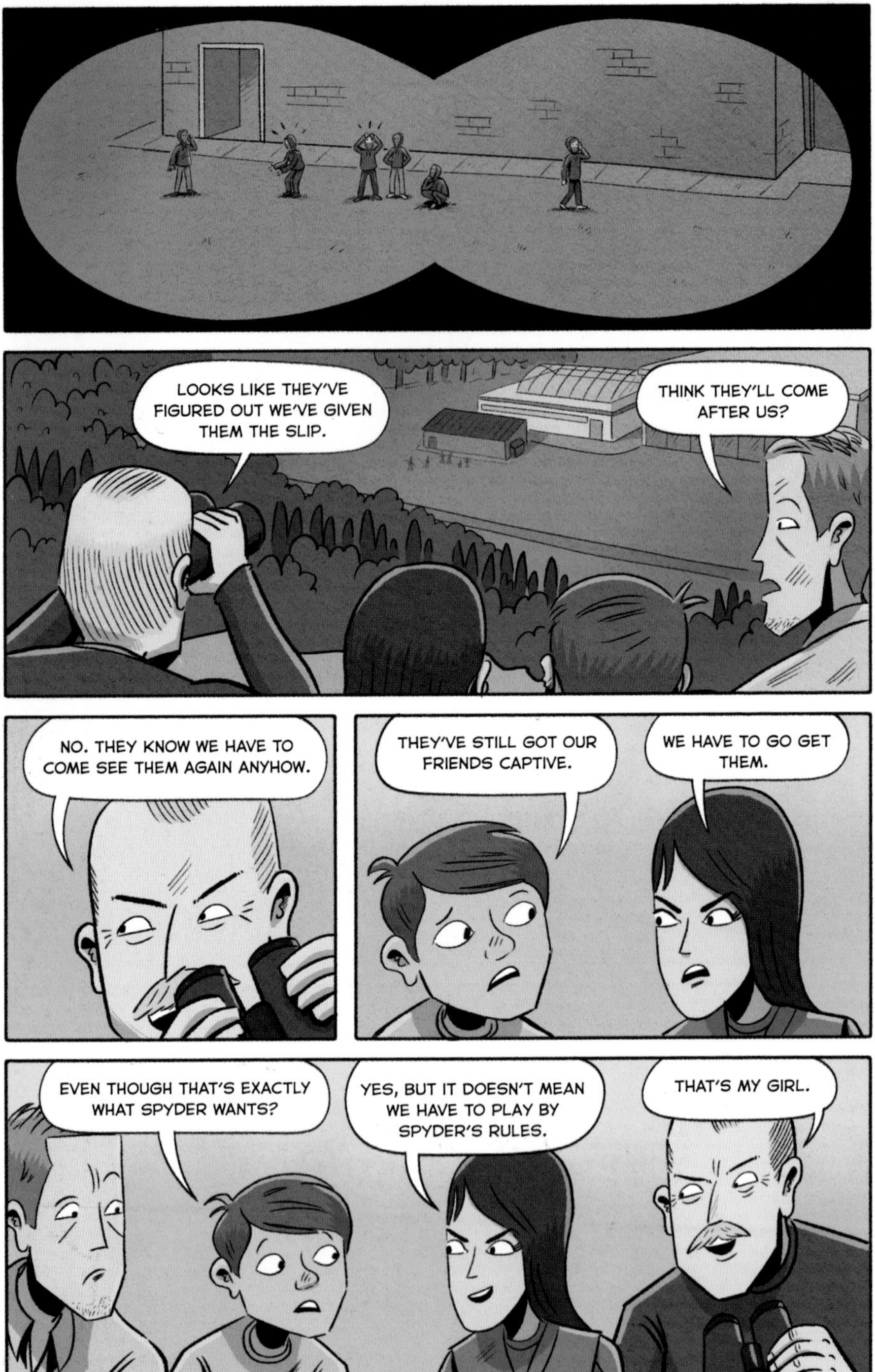
LOOKS LIKE THEY'VE FIGURED OUT WE'VE GIVEN THEM THE SLIP.
THINK THEY'LL COME AFTER US?
NO. THEY KNOW WE HAVE TO COME SEE THEM AGAIN ANYHOW.
THEY'VE STILL GOT OUR FRIENDS CAPTIVE.
WE HAVE TO GO GET THEM.
EVEN THOUGH THAT'S EXACTLY WHAT SPYDER WANTS?
YES, BUT IT DOESN'T MEAN WE HAVE TO PLAY BY SPYDER'S RULES.
THAT'S MY GIRL.

205

207

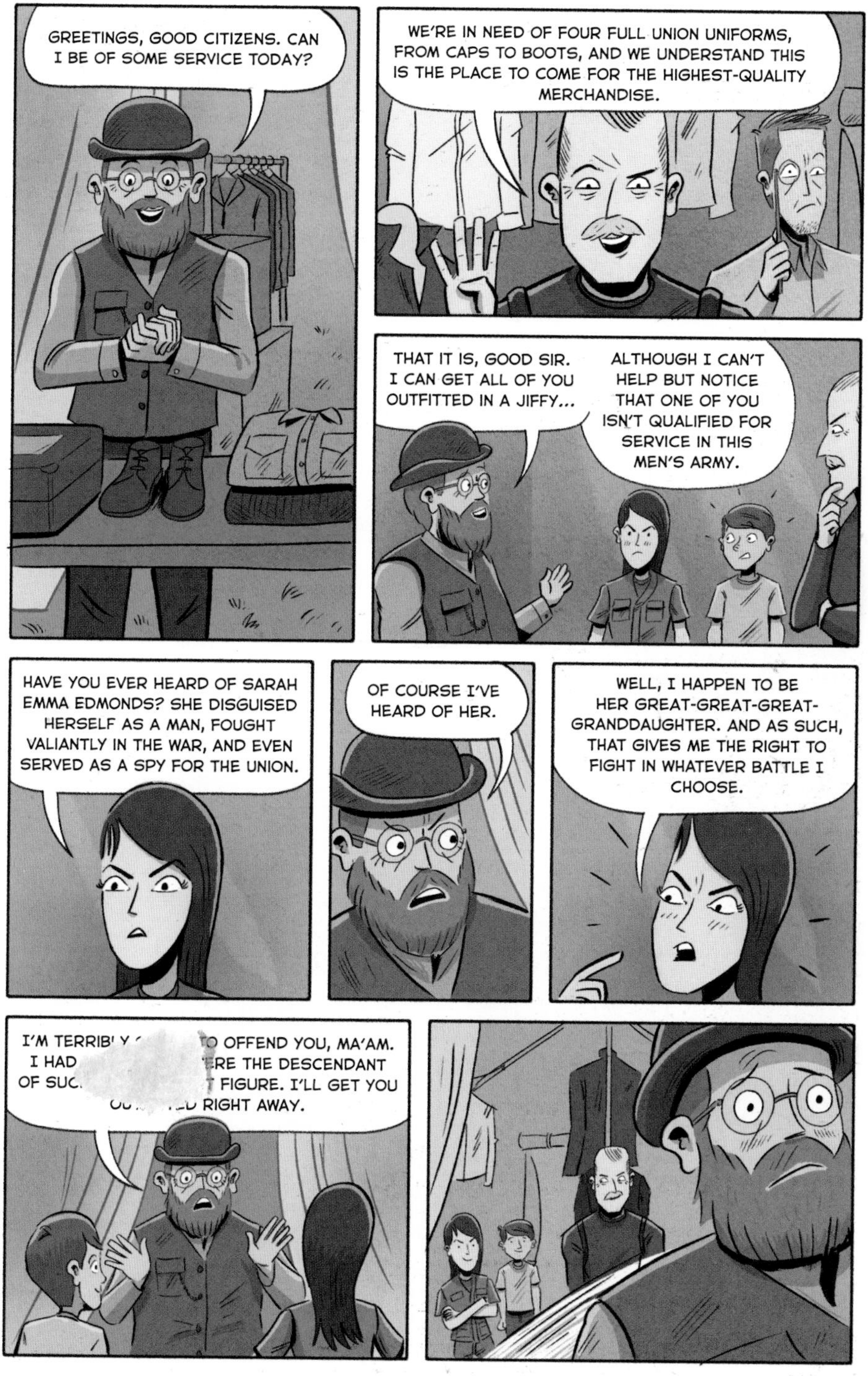
GREETINGS, GOOD CITIZENS. CAN I BE OF SOME SERVICE TODAY?
WE'RE IN NEED OF FOUR FULL UNION UNIFORMS, FROM CAPS TO BOOTS, AND WE UNDERSTAND THIS IS THE PLACE TO COME FOR THE HIGHEST-QUALITY MERCHANDISE.
THAT IT IS, GOOD SIR. I CAN GET ALL OF YOU OUTFITTED IN A JIFFY...
ALTHOUGH I CAN'T HELP BUT NOTICE THAT ONE OF YOU ISN'T QUALIFIED FOR SERVICE IN THIS MEN'S ARMY.
HAVE YOU EVER HEARD OF SARAH EMMA EDMONDS? SHE DISGUISED HERSELF AS A MAN, FOUGHT VALIANTLY IN THE WAR, AND EVEN SERVED AS A SPY FOR THE UNION.
OF COURSE I'VE HEARD OF HER.
WELL, I HAPPEN TO BE HER GREAT-GREAT-GREAT-GRANDDAUGHTER. AND AS SUCH, THAT GIVES ME THE RIGHT TO FIGHT IN WHATEVER BATTLE I CHOOSE.
I'M TERRIBL TO OFFEND YOU, MA'AM. I HAD ERE THE DESCENDANT OF SUC T FIGURE. I'LL GET YOU RIGHT AWAY.

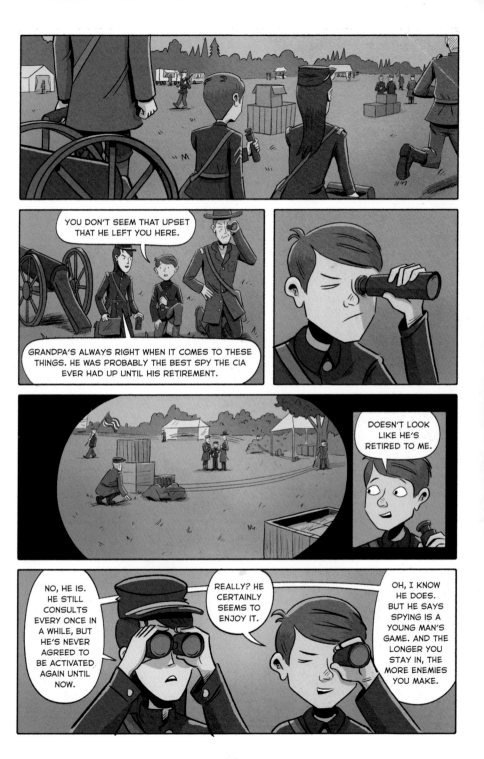

220

221

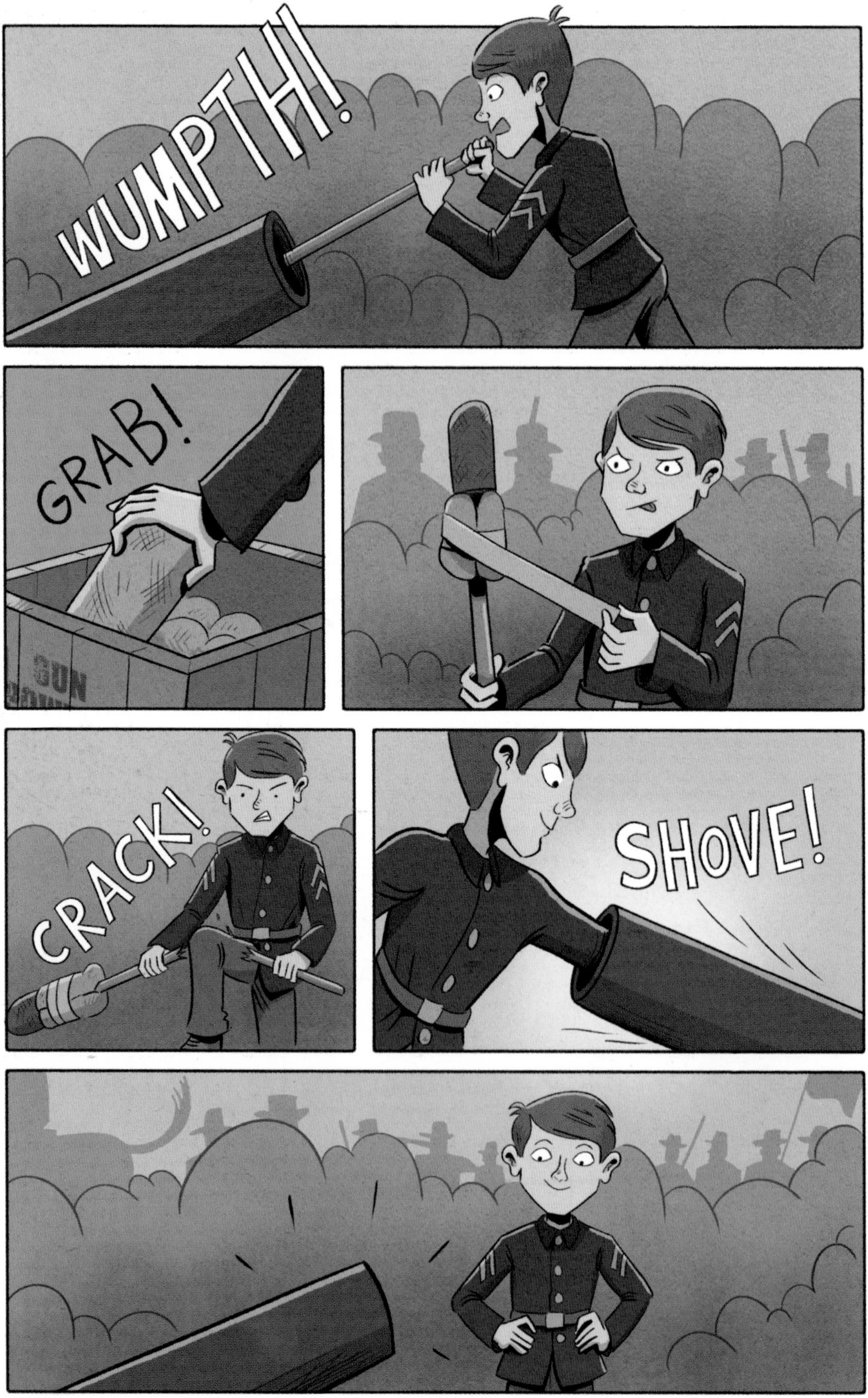
WUMPTH!
GRAB!
GUN
CRACK!
SHOVE!

223

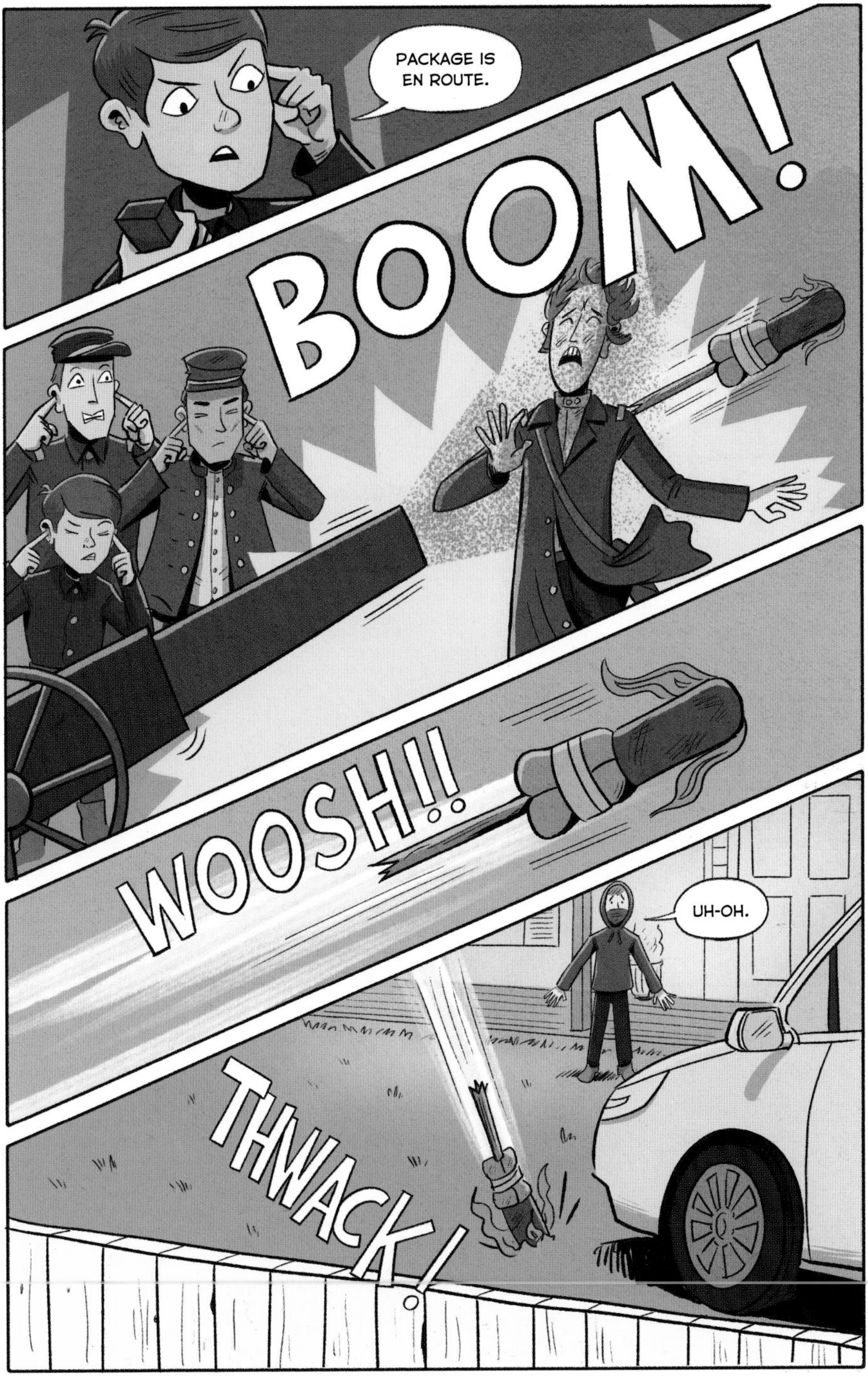
PACKAGE IS EN ROUTE.
BOOM!
WOOSH!!
UH-OH.
THWACK!

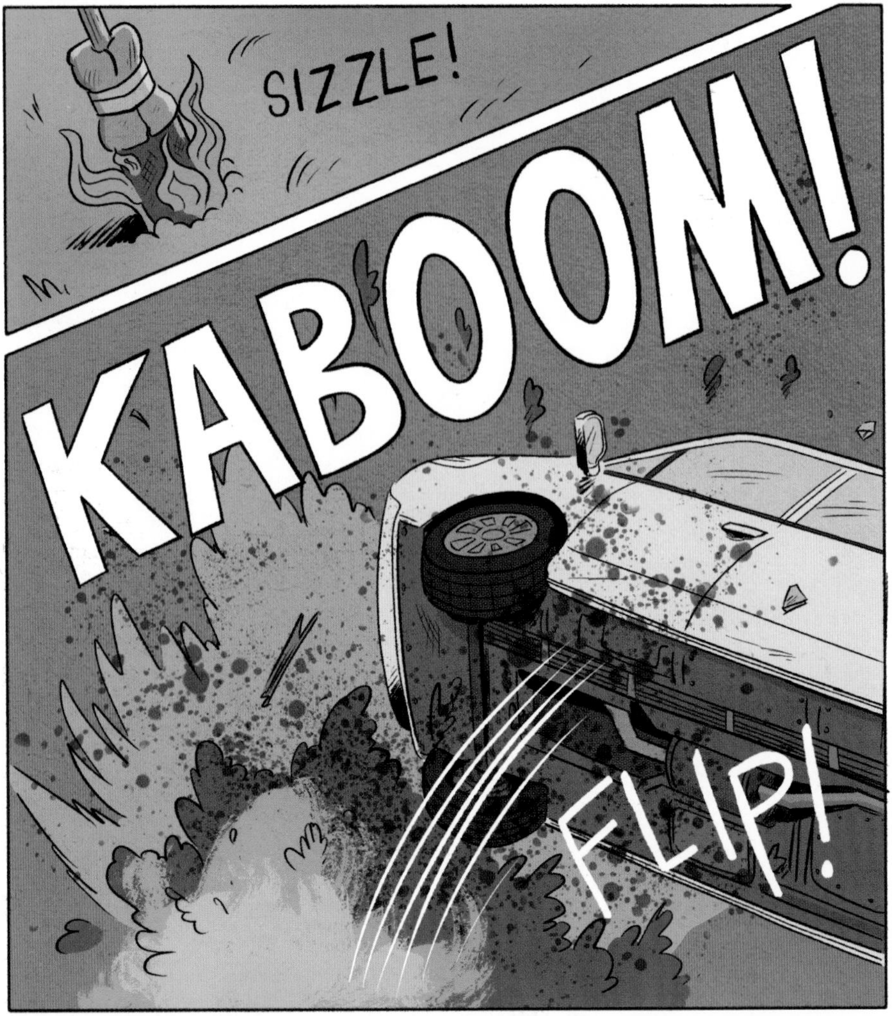
SIZZLE!
KABOOM!
FLIP!

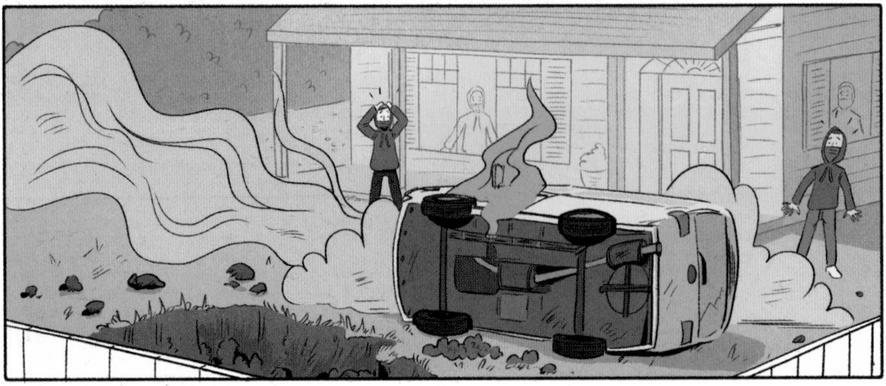

227

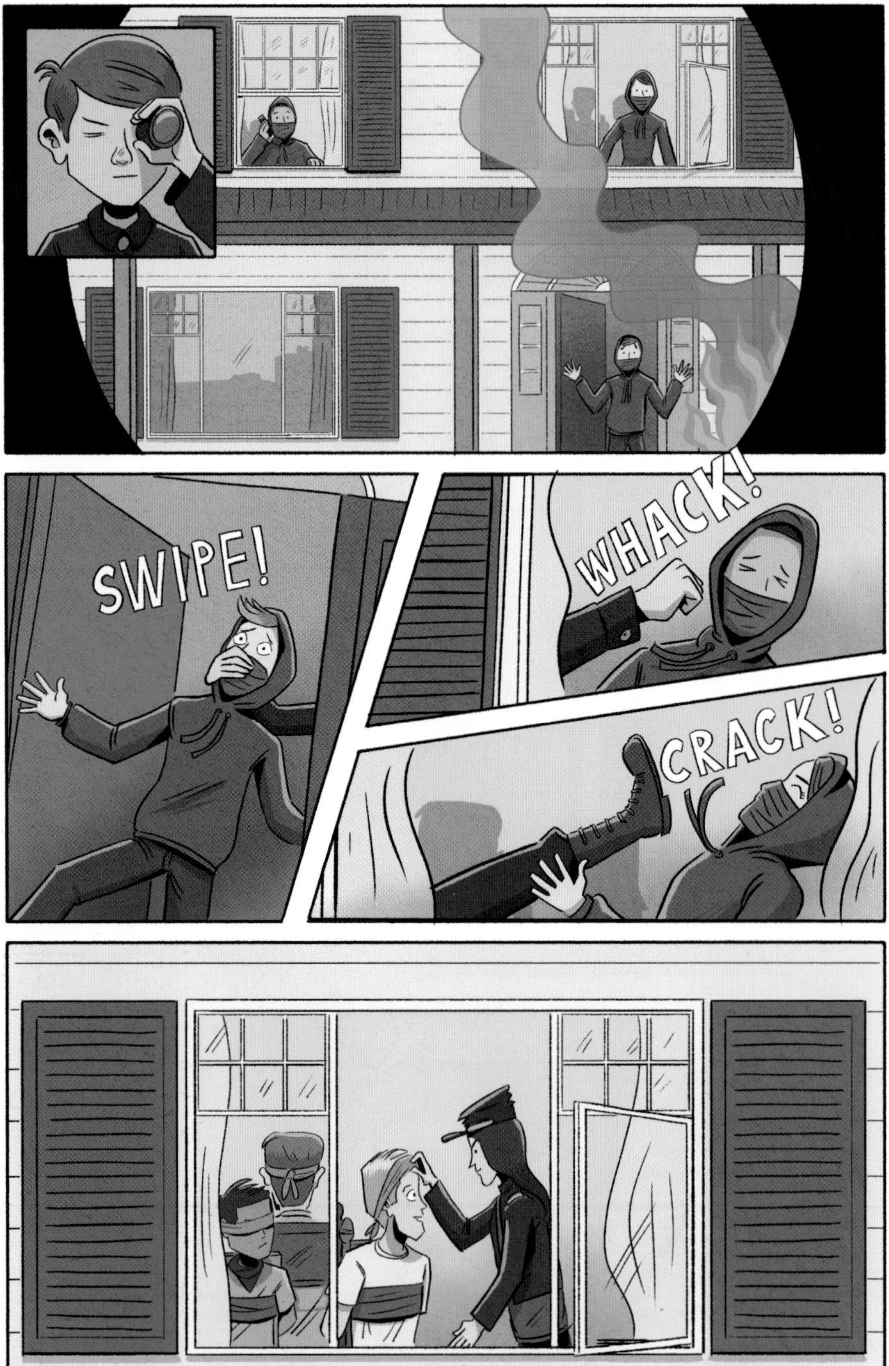
SWIPE!
WHACK!
CRACK!

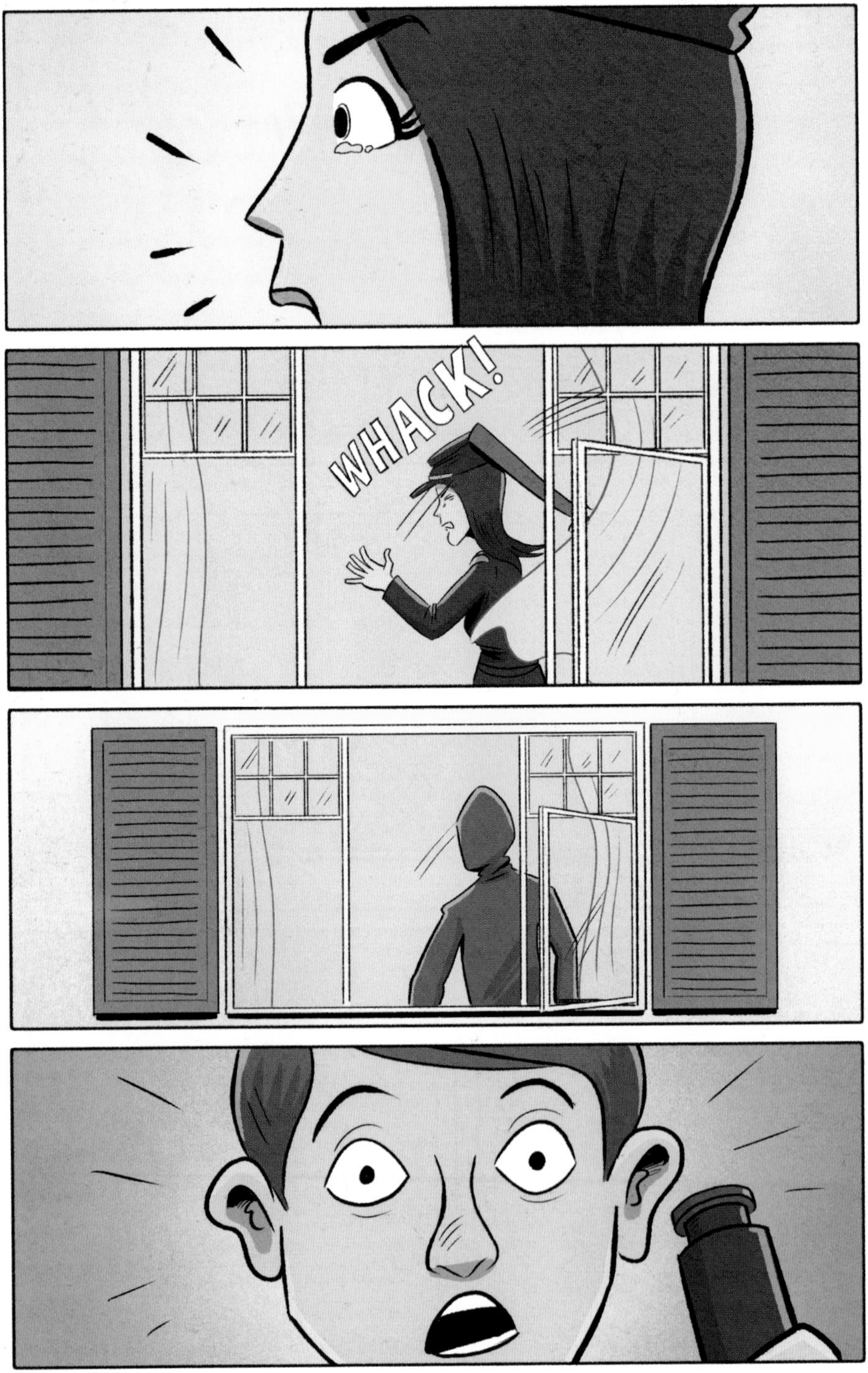
WHACK!

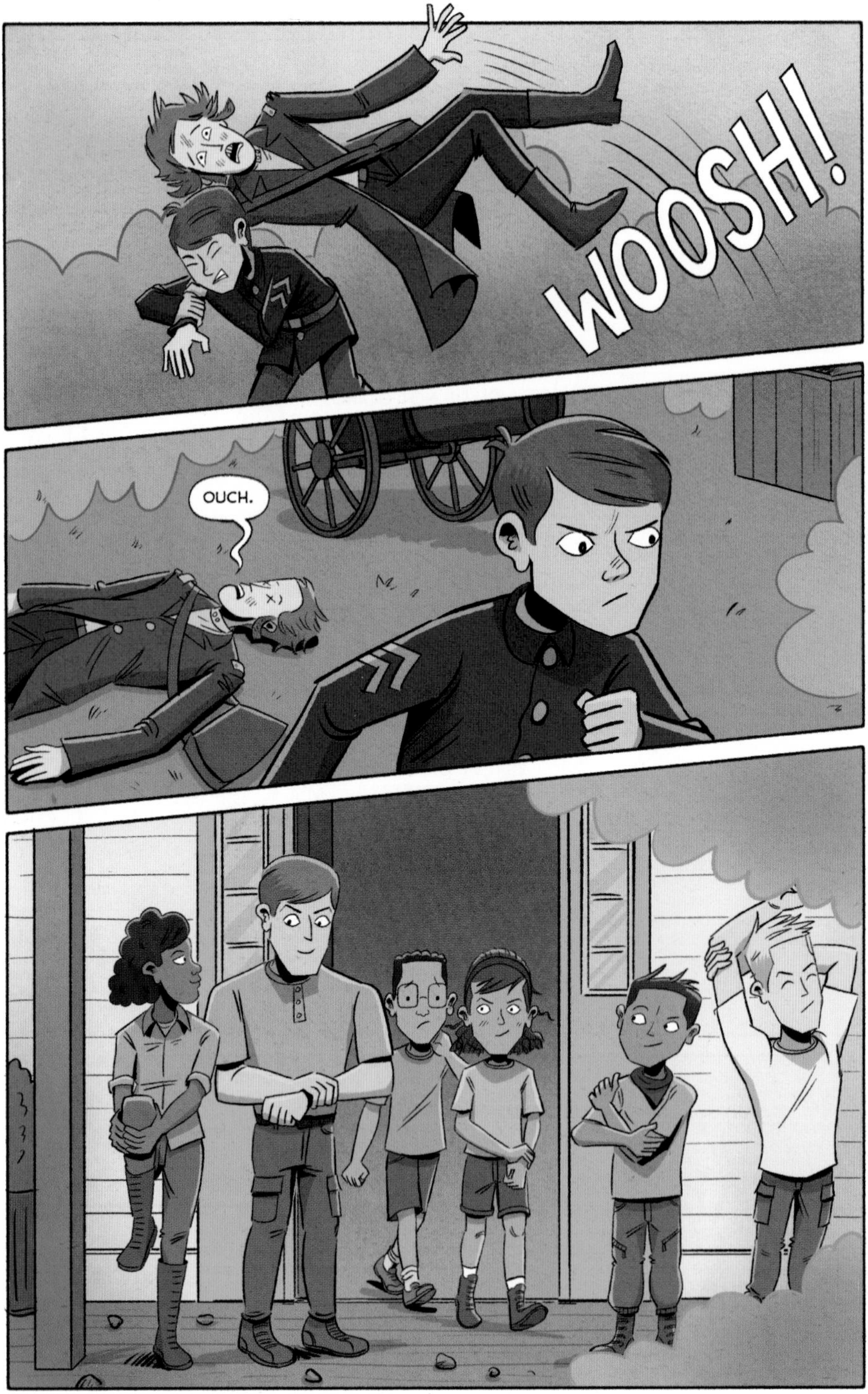
WOOSH!
OUCH.

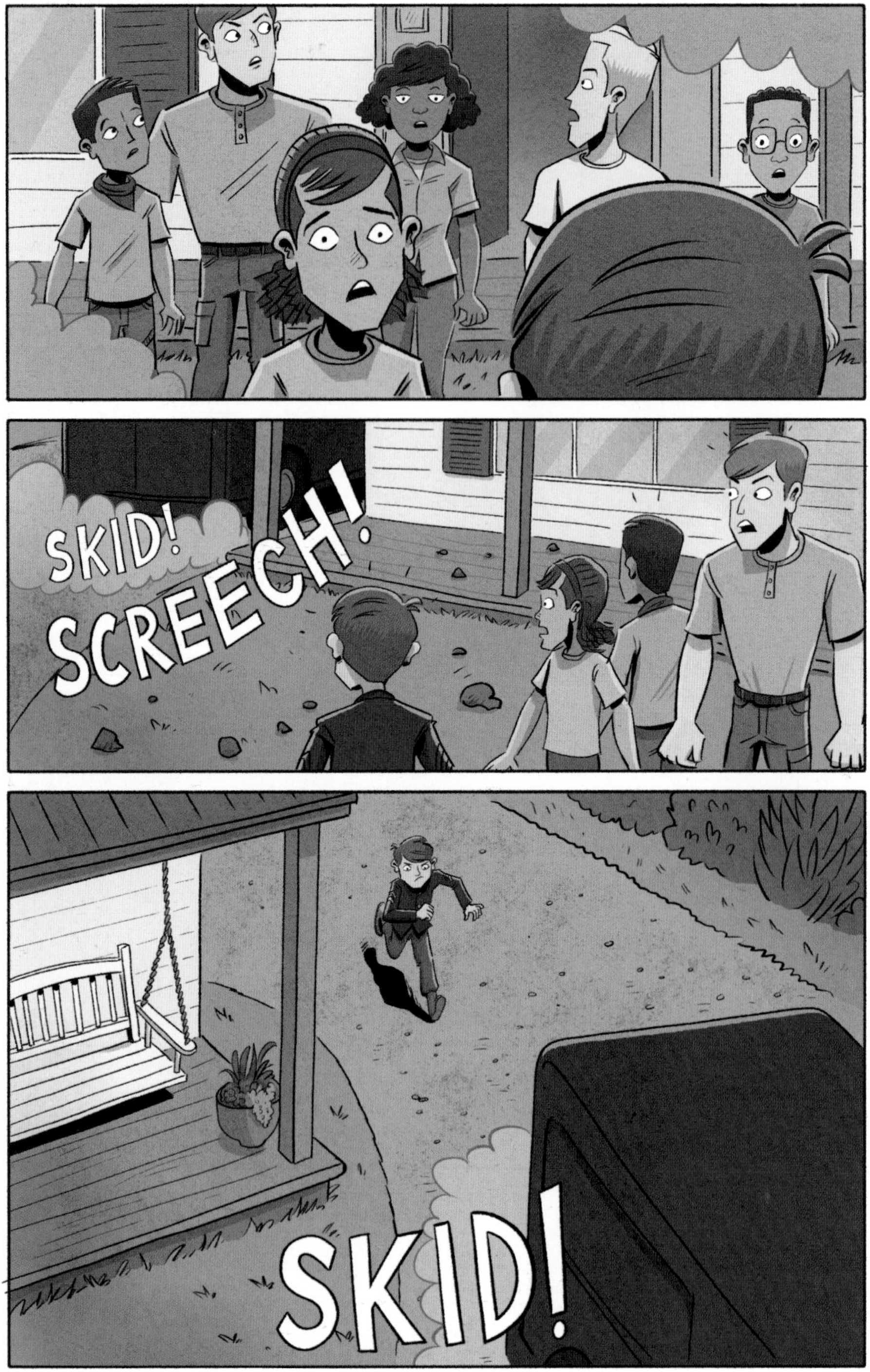
SKID!
SCREECH!
SKID!

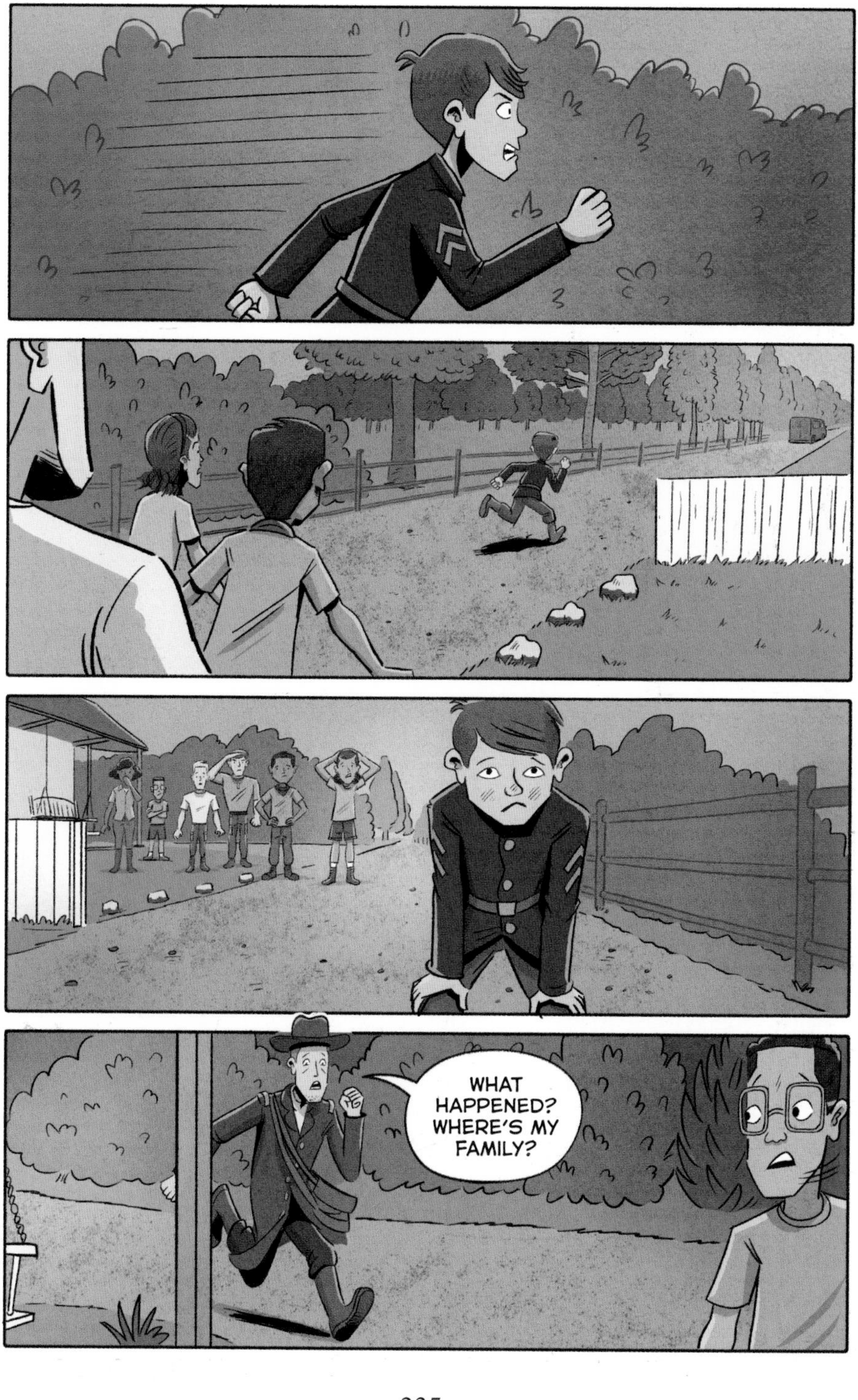
WHAT HAPPENED? WHERE'S MY FAMILY?

236

237

238

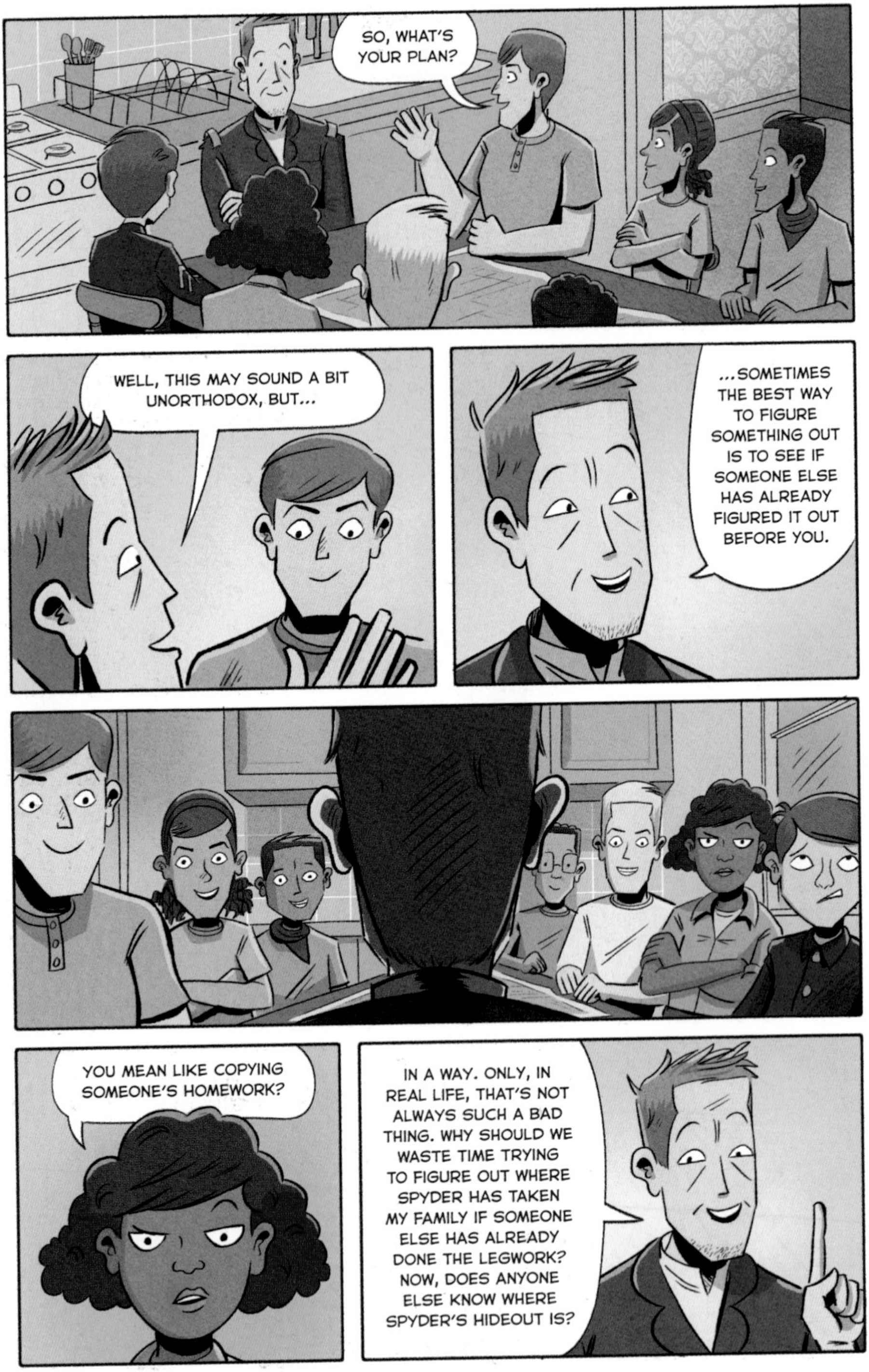
SO, WHAT'S YOUR PLAN?
WELL, THIS MAY SOUND A BIT UNORTHODOX, BUT...
...SOMETIMES THE BEST WAY TO FIGURE SOMETHING OUT IS TO SEE IF SOMEONE ELSE HAS ALREADY FIGURED IT OUT BEFORE YOU.
YOU MEAN LIKE COPYING SOMEONE'S HOMEWORK?
IN A WAY. ONLY, IN REAL LIFE, THAT'S NOT ALWAYS SUCH A BAD THING. WHY SHOULD WE WASTE TIME TRYING TO FIGURE OUT WHERE SPYDER HAS TAKEN MY FAMILY IF SOMEONE ELSE HAS ALREADY DONE THE LEGWORK? NOW, DOES ANYONE ELSE KNOW WHERE SPYDER'S HIDEOUT IS?

244

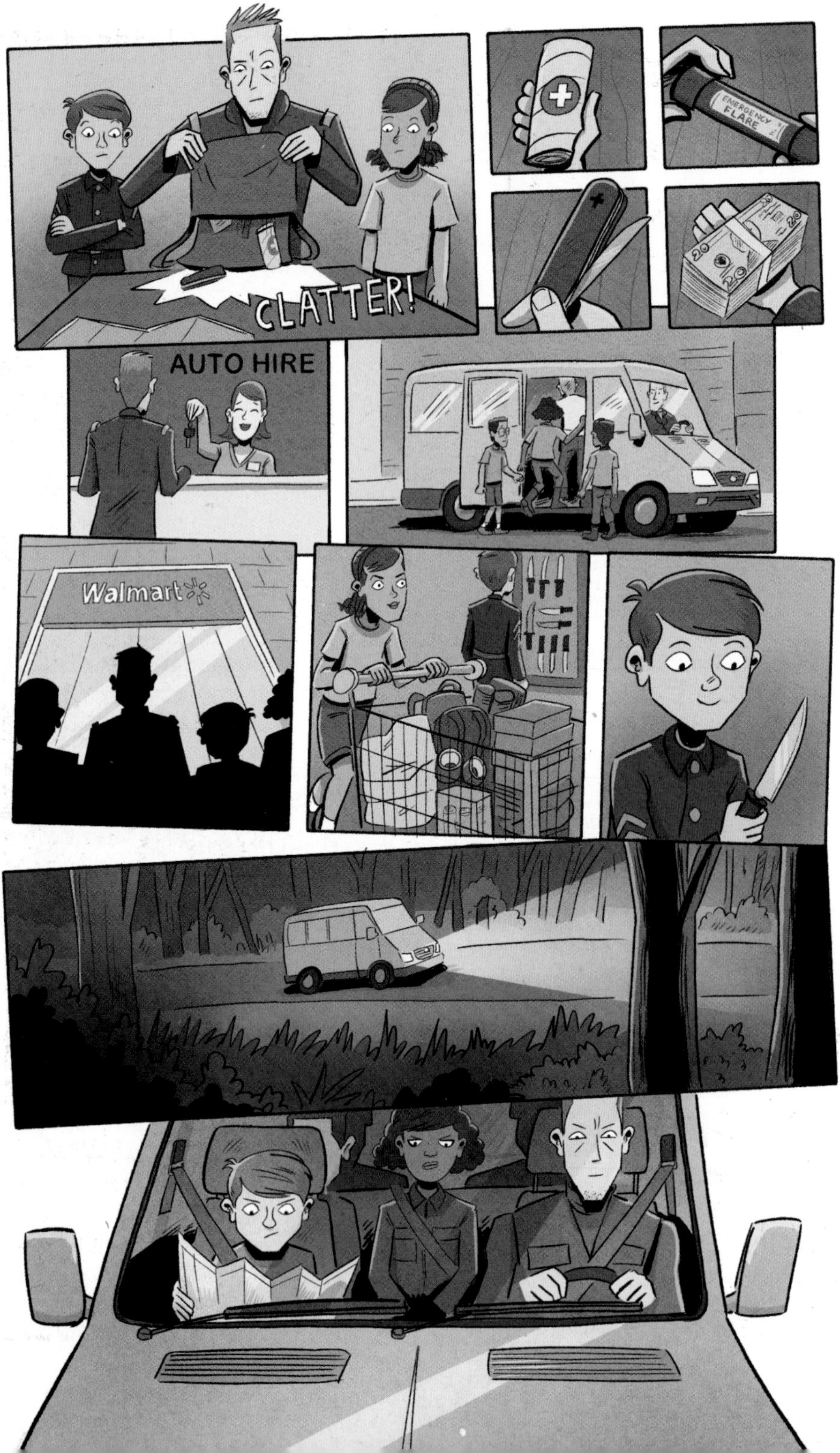

CLATTER!
EMERGENCY FLARE
AUTO HIRE
Walmart

SPLOSH!

DIP!

JUST GET BEHIND YOUR TARGET AND CLAP THIS OVER THEIR NOSE AND MOUTH.

WHAT IS IT?

SNIFF SNIFF!

SIGH!

SLAM!

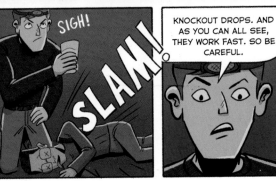

KNOCKOUT DROPS. AND AS YOU CAN ALL SEE, THEY WORK FAST. SO BE CAREFUL.

248

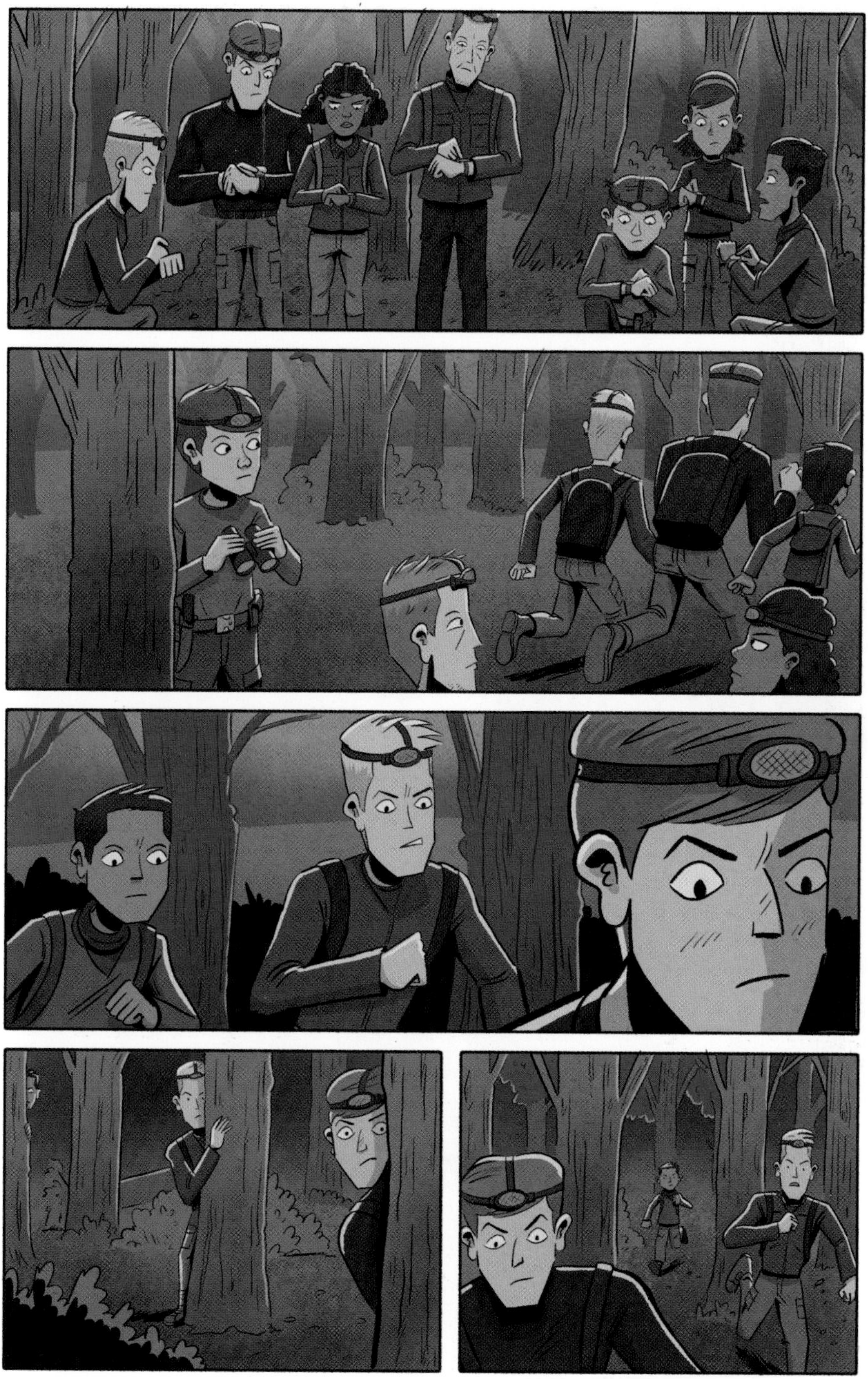

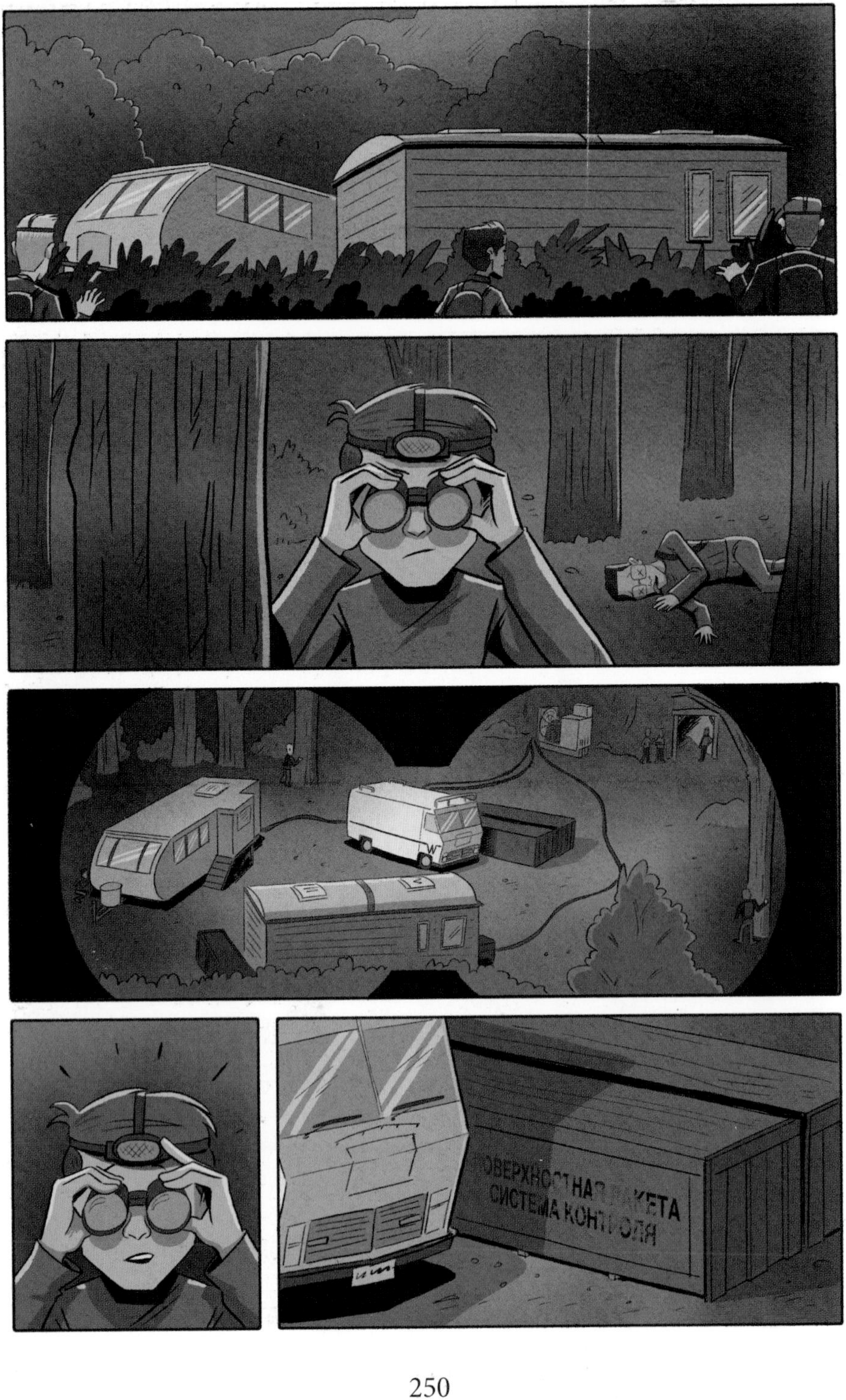
ОВЕРХНОСТНА КЕТА
СИСТЕМА КОНТ ОЛЯ

SO *THAT'S* WHAT THEY WANT WITH HIM.

WHAT DO YOU MEAN?

THE GLOBAL POSITIONING SYSTEM WAS DEVELOPED BY THE DEPARTMENT OF DEFENSE IN THE 1970S.

MY FATHER WAS THE CIA LIAISON TO THE PROJECT. THE ORIGINAL PURPOSE OF GPS HAD NOTHING TO DO WITH GIVING EVERYONE DIRECTIONS IN THEIR CARS. IT WAS FOR THE MILITARY.

MISSILE GUIDANCE SYSTEMS.

AMONG OTHER THINGS. MY FATHER KNEW ALL ALONG THAT THE MILITARY WOULD NEVER BE ABLE TO KEEP GPS UNDER TIGHT WRAPS. EVENTUALLY, THE PUBLIC WOULD BE ABLE TO USE IT.

MY FATHER FELT THAT WOULD BE A SECURITY RISK, SO HE CONVINCED DEFENSE TO PURPOSELY BUILD ERRORS INTO THE SYSTEM...

...TO PROTECT CERTAIN LOCATIONS THAT MIGHT BE TARGETED BY TERRORISTS.

BUT YOUR FATHER KNOWS THE ACTUAL COORDINATES FOR THOSE PLACES?

BUT NOW, SPYDER CAN MAKE HIM GIVE THEM UP.

YES. HE FELT IT WAS TOO DANGEROUS TO RECORD THEM ANYWHERE. SO HE MEMORIZED THEM.

I'M AFRAID SO. IF THEY HAD ONLY CAPTURED MY FATHER, HE'D NEVER GIVE UP THE INFORMATION.

252

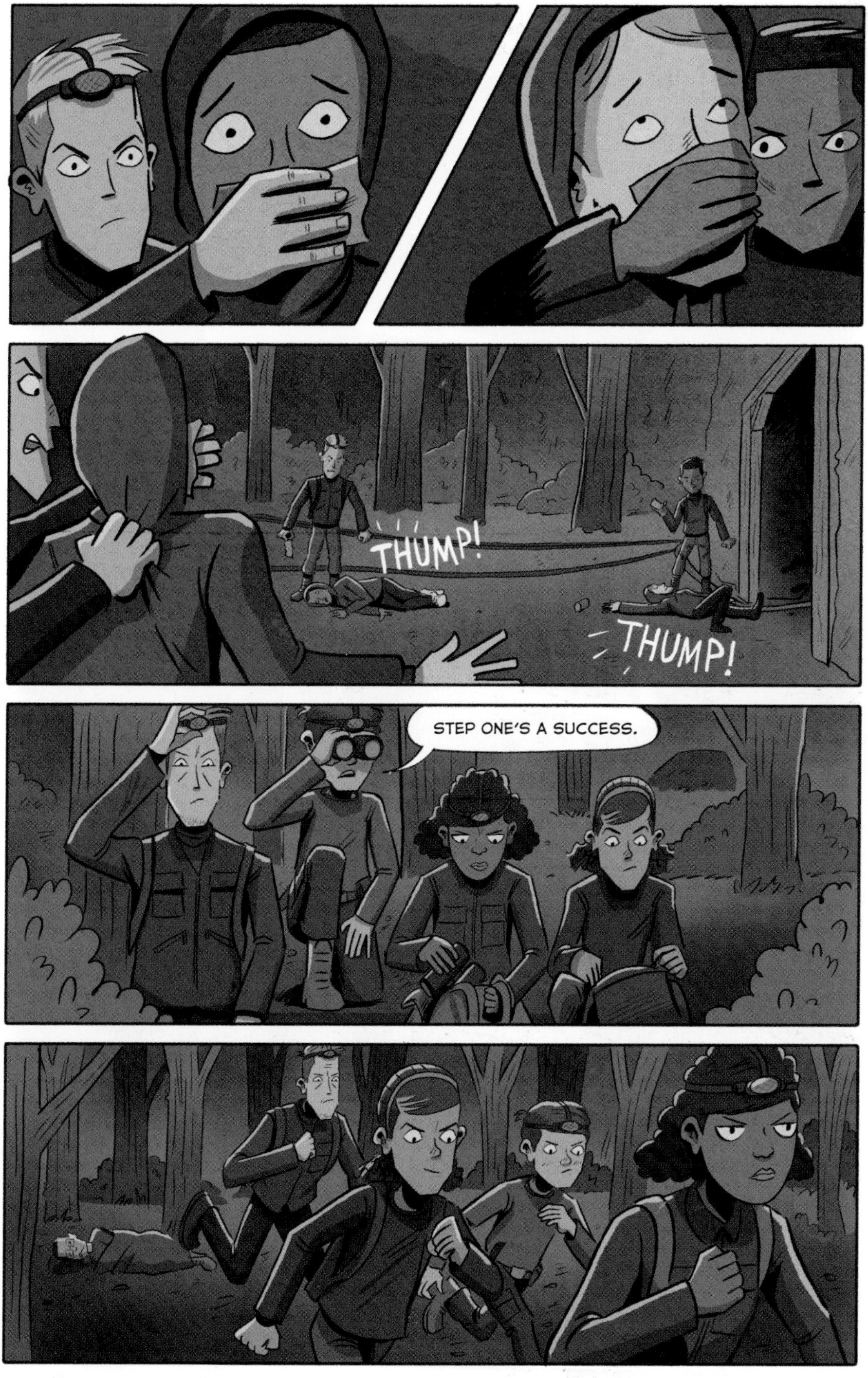
THUMP!
THUMP!
STEP ONE'S A SUCCESS.

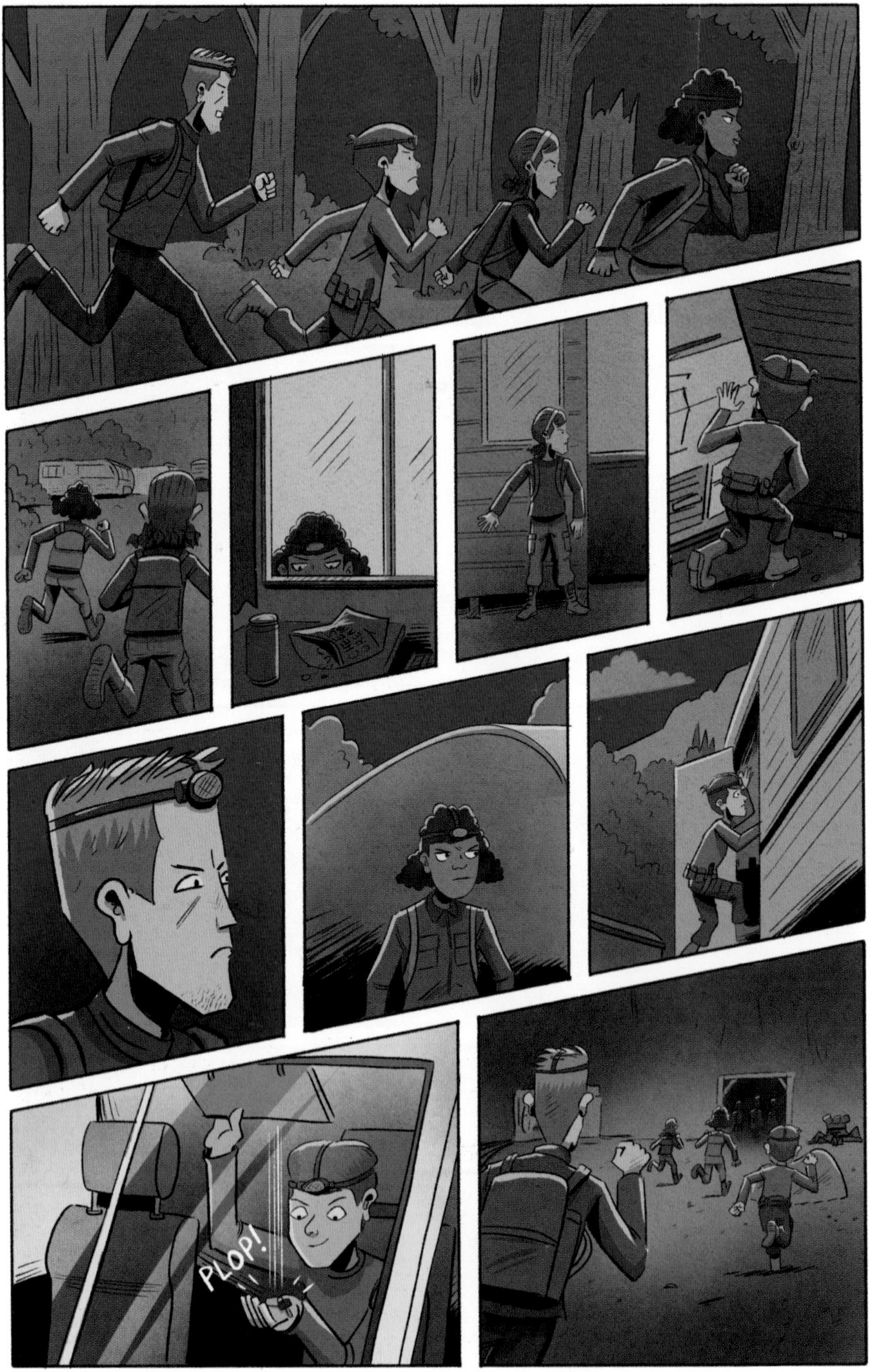
PLOP!

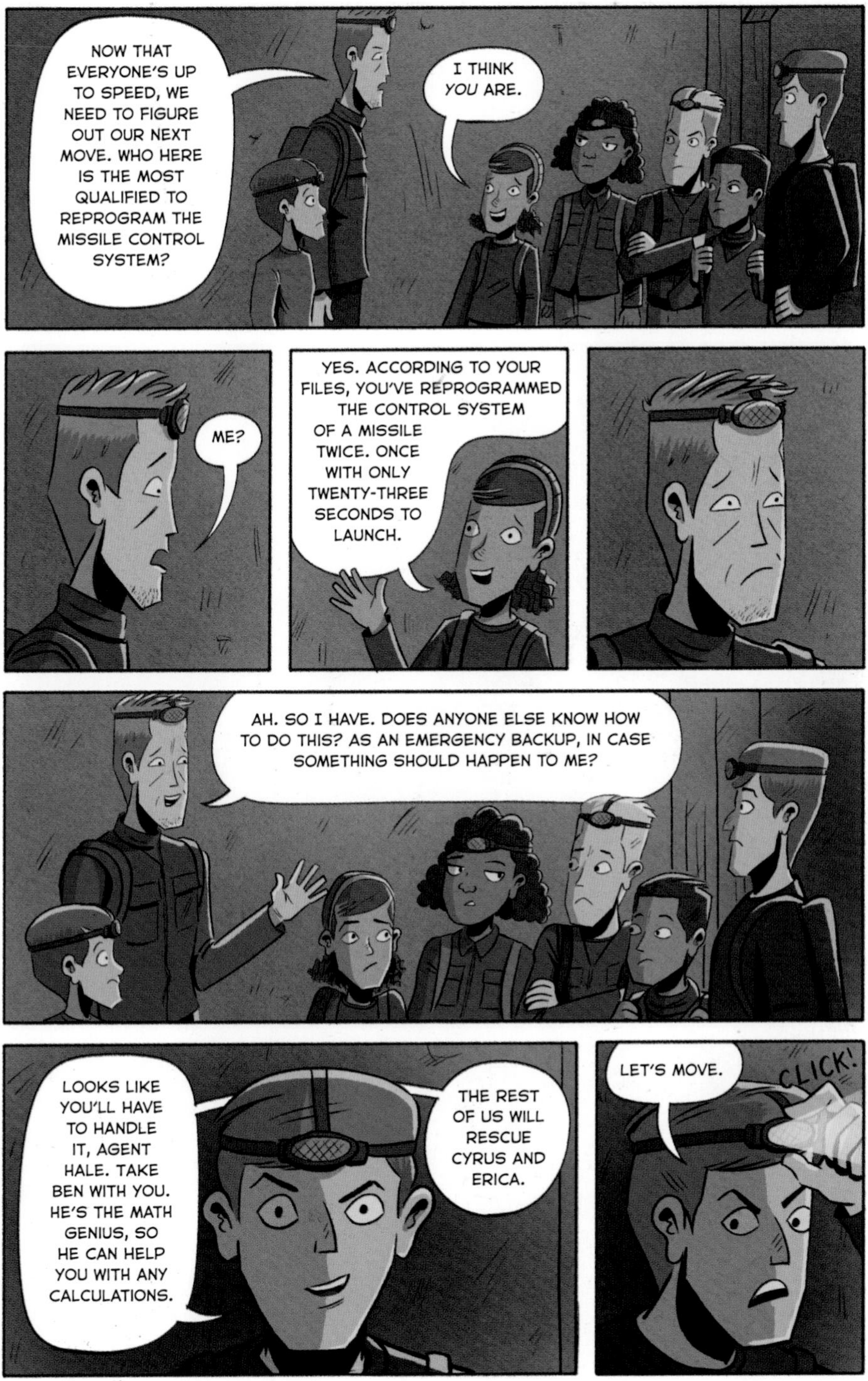
NOW THAT EVERYONE'S UP TO SPEED, WE NEED TO FIGURE OUT OUR NEXT MOVE. WHO HERE IS THE MOST QUALIFIED TO REPROGRAM THE MISSILE CONTROL SYSTEM?
I THINK *YOU* ARE.
ME?
YES. ACCORDING TO YOUR FILES, YOU'VE REPROGRAMMED THE CONTROL SYSTEM OF A MISSILE TWICE. ONCE WITH ONLY TWENTY-THREE SECONDS TO LAUNCH.
AH. SO I HAVE. DOES ANYONE ELSE KNOW HOW TO DO THIS? AS AN EMERGENCY BACKUP, IN CASE SOMETHING SHOULD HAPPEN TO ME?
LOOKS LIKE YOU'LL HAVE TO HANDLE IT, AGENT HALE. TAKE BEN WITH YOU. HE'S THE MATH GENIUS, SO HE CAN HELP YOU WITH ANY CALCULATIONS.
THE REST OF US WILL RESCUE CYRUS AND ERICA.
LET'S MOVE.
CLICK!

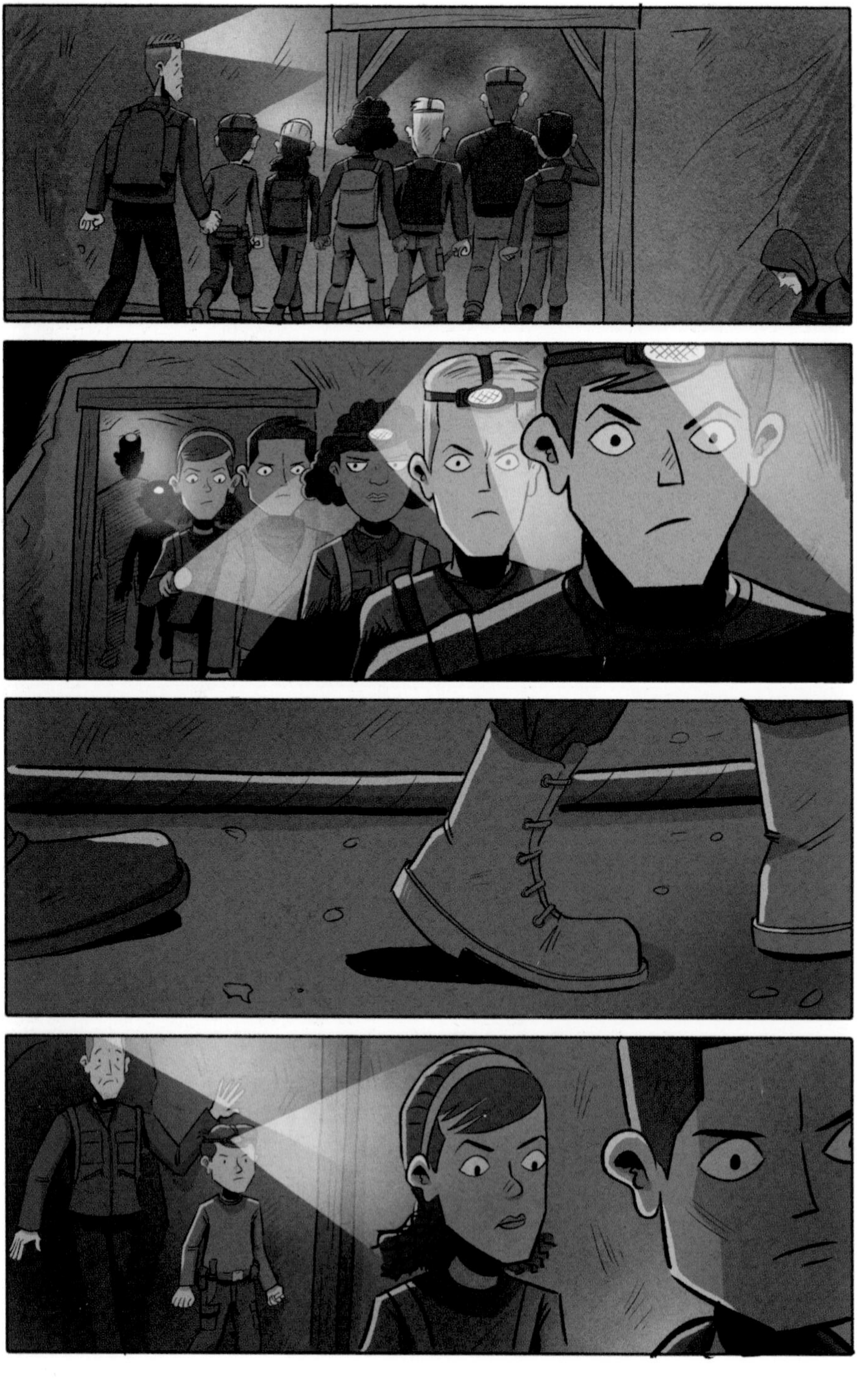

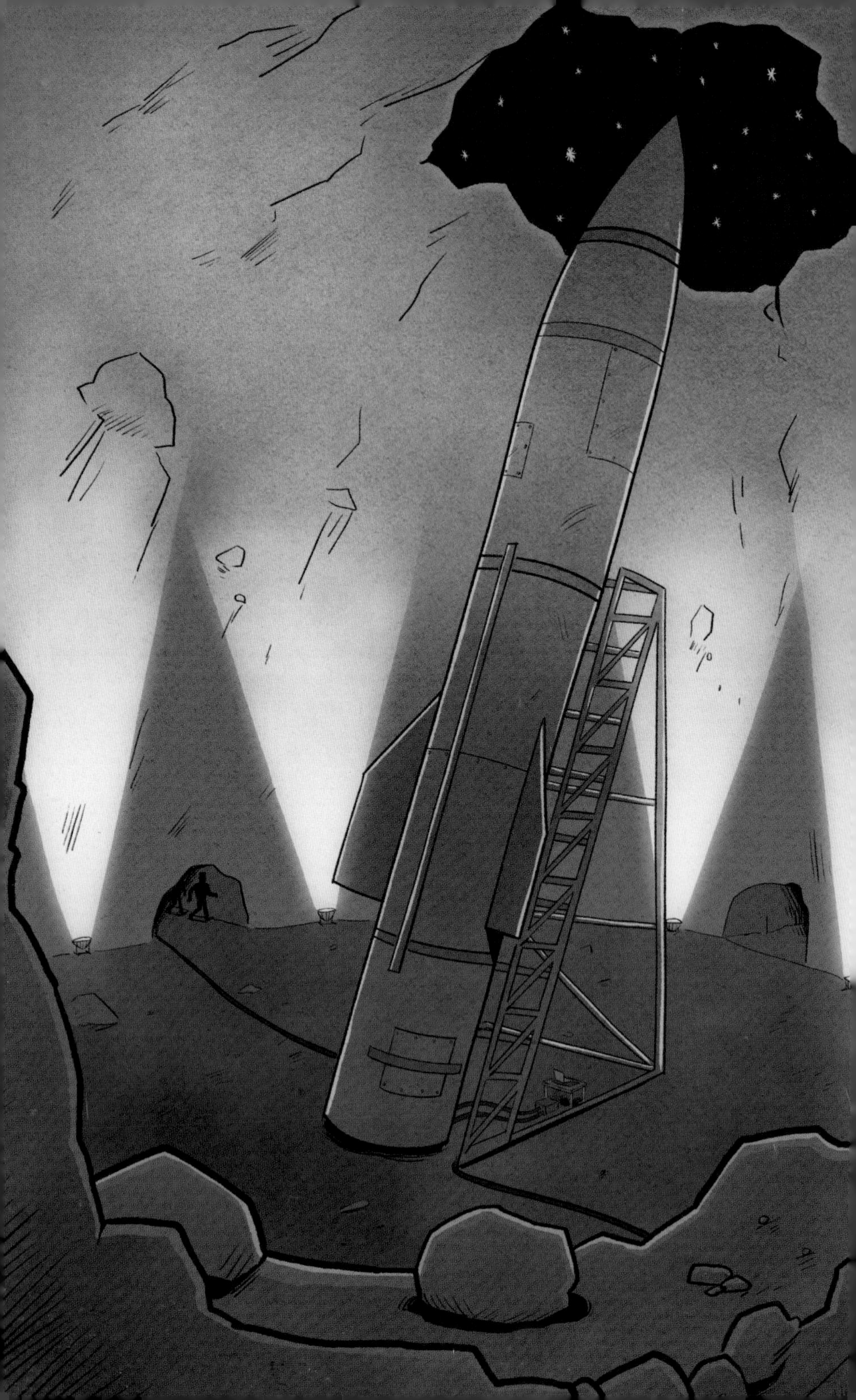

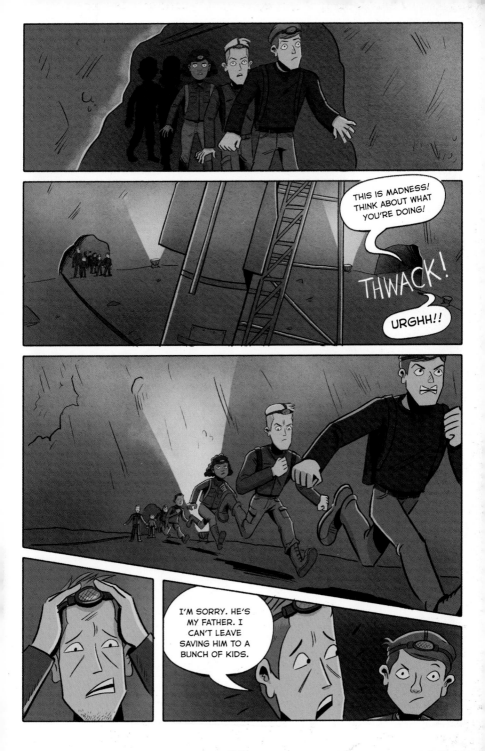

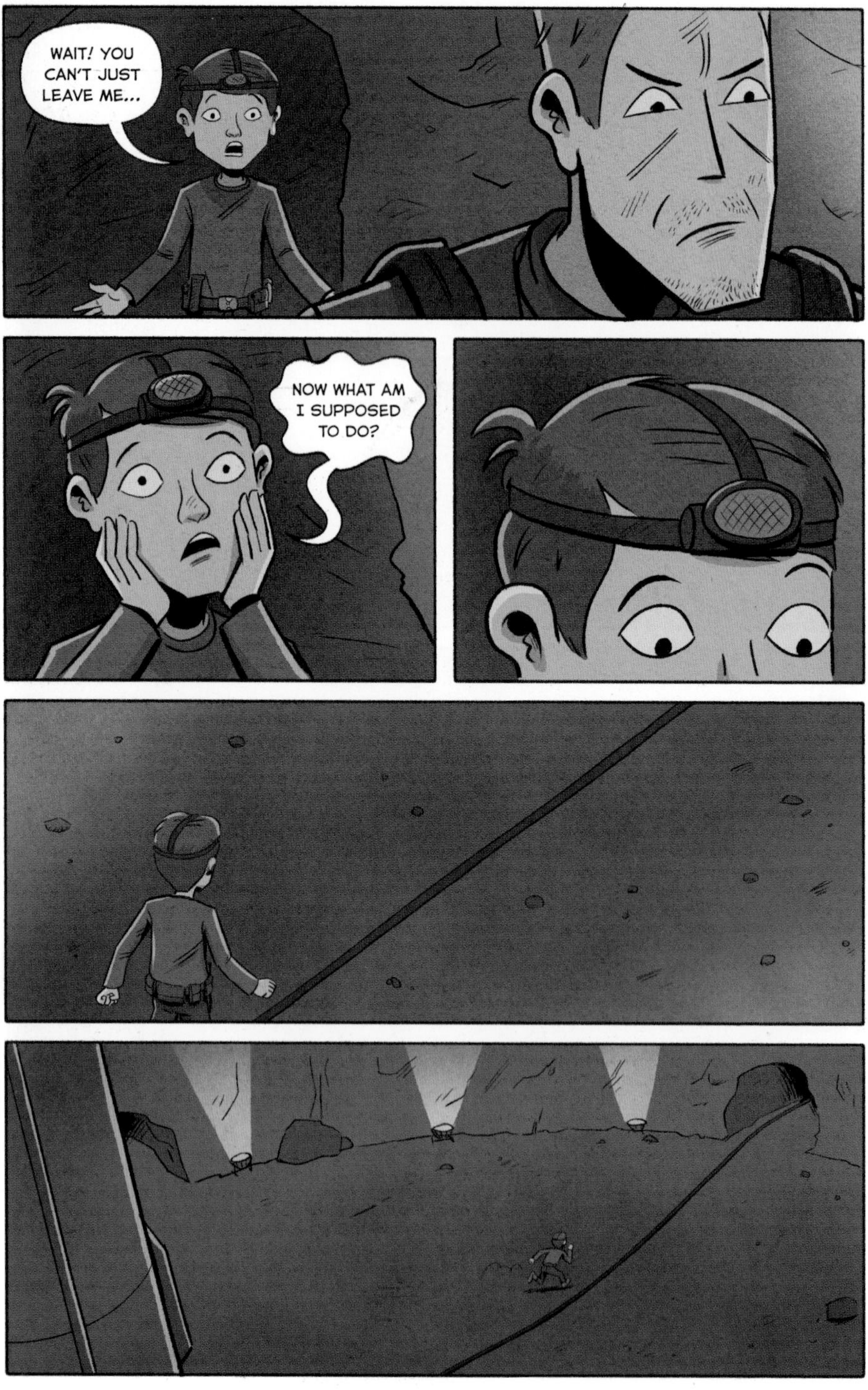
WAIT! YOU CAN'T JUST LEAVE ME...
NOW WHAT AM I SUPPOSED TO DO?

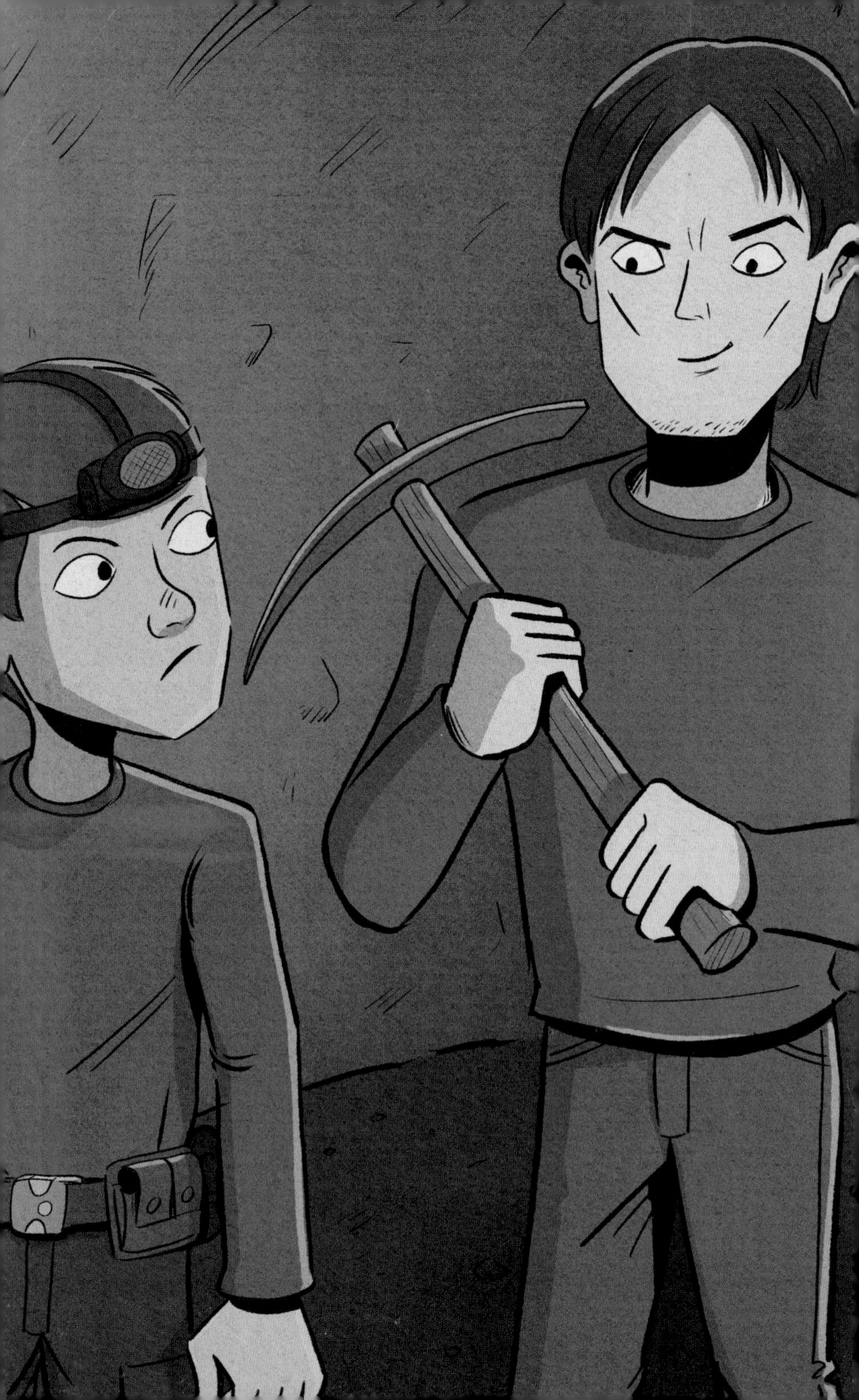

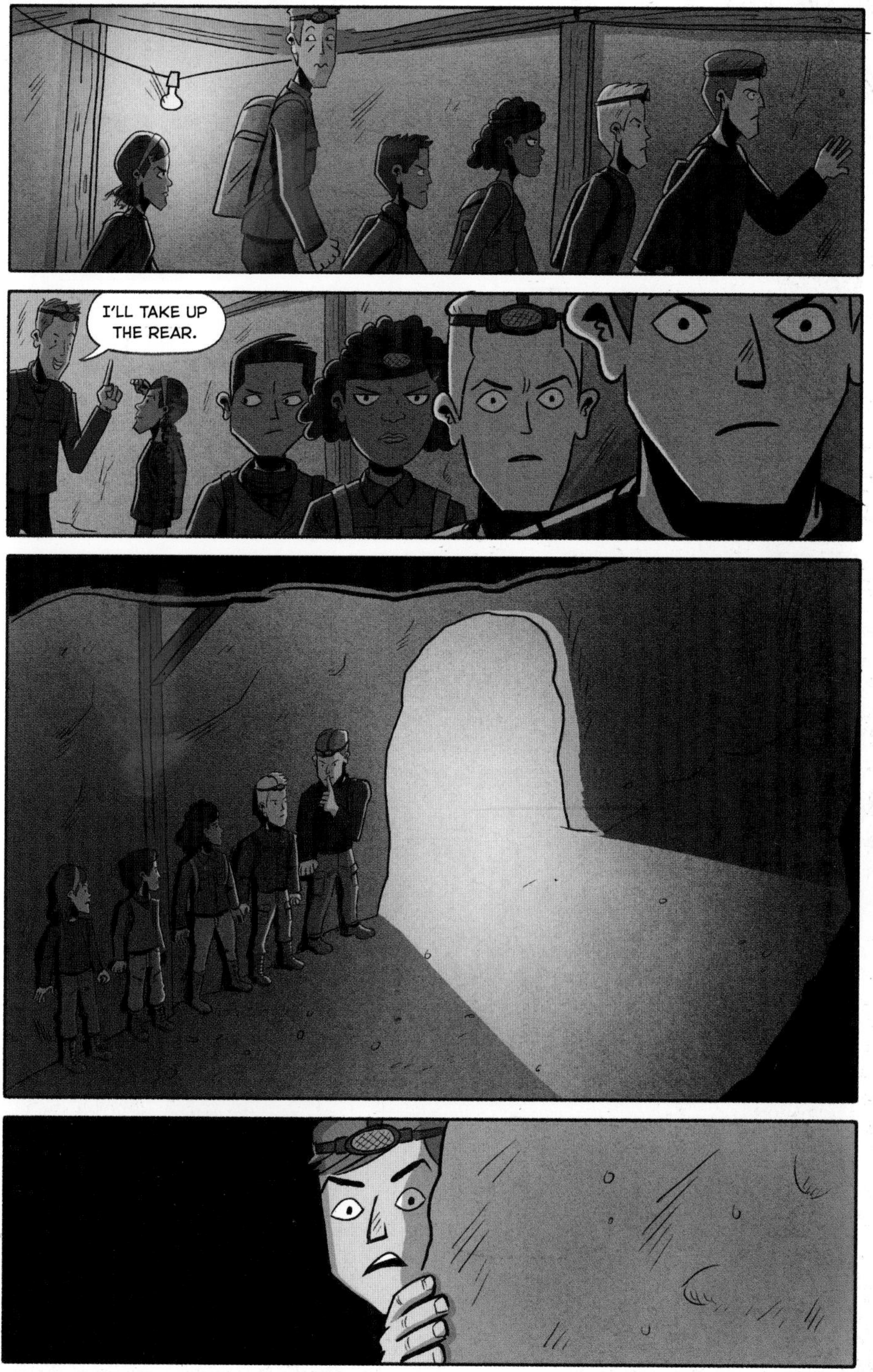
I'LL TAKE UP THE REAR.

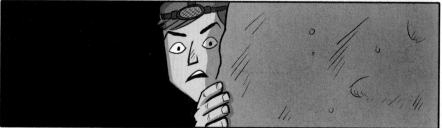

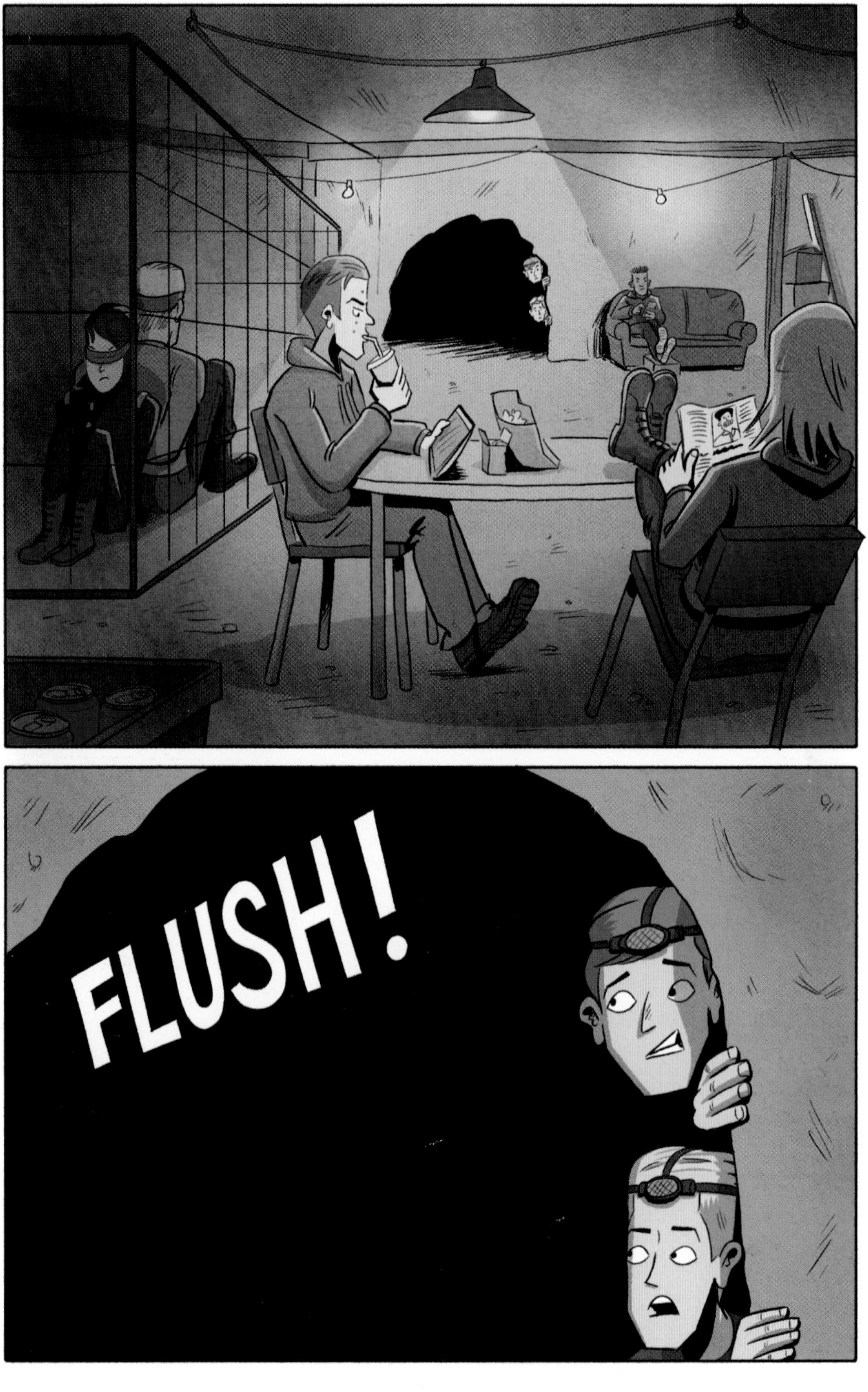
FLUSH!

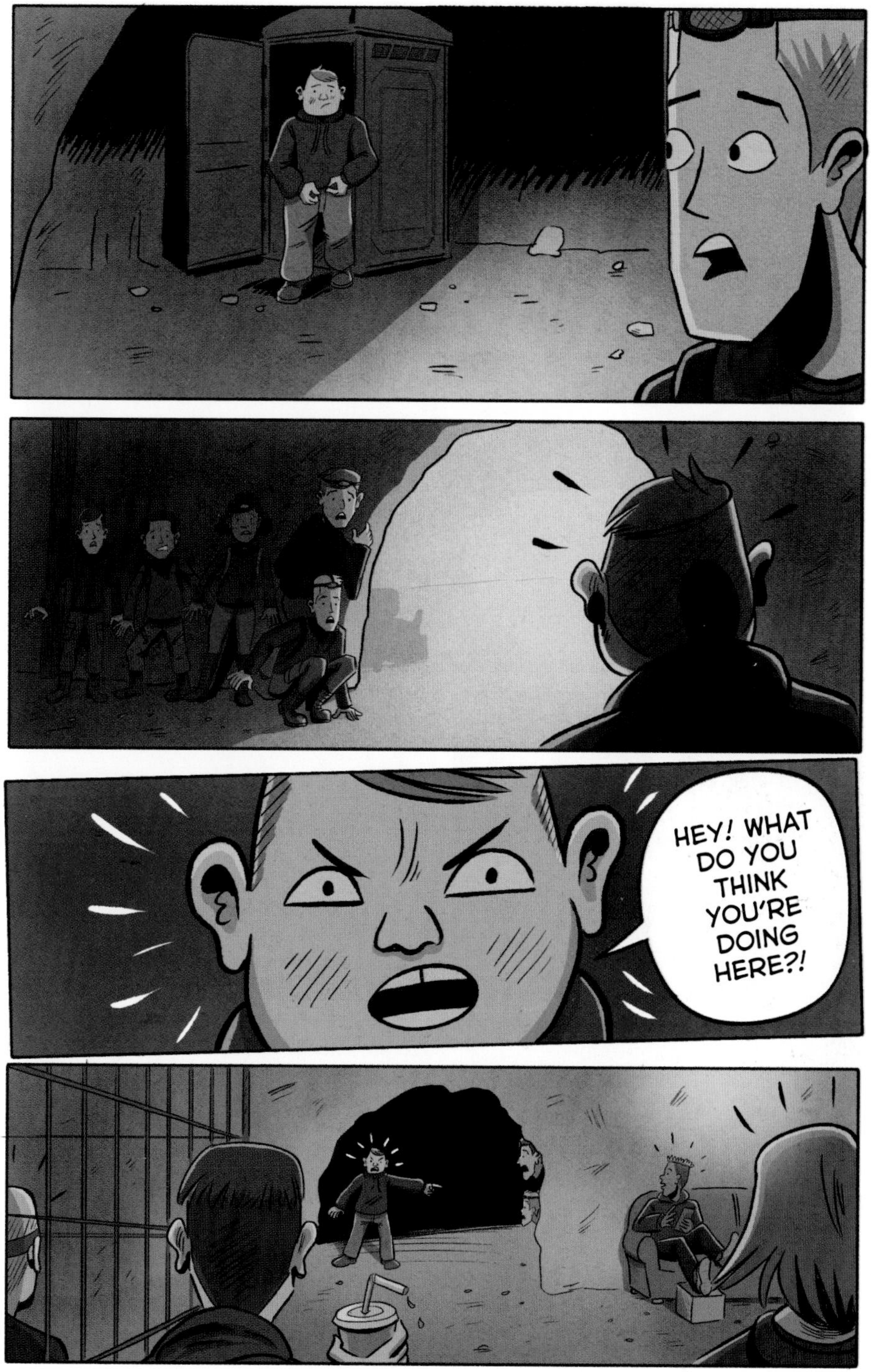
HEY! WHAT DO YOU THINK YOU'RE DOING HERE?!

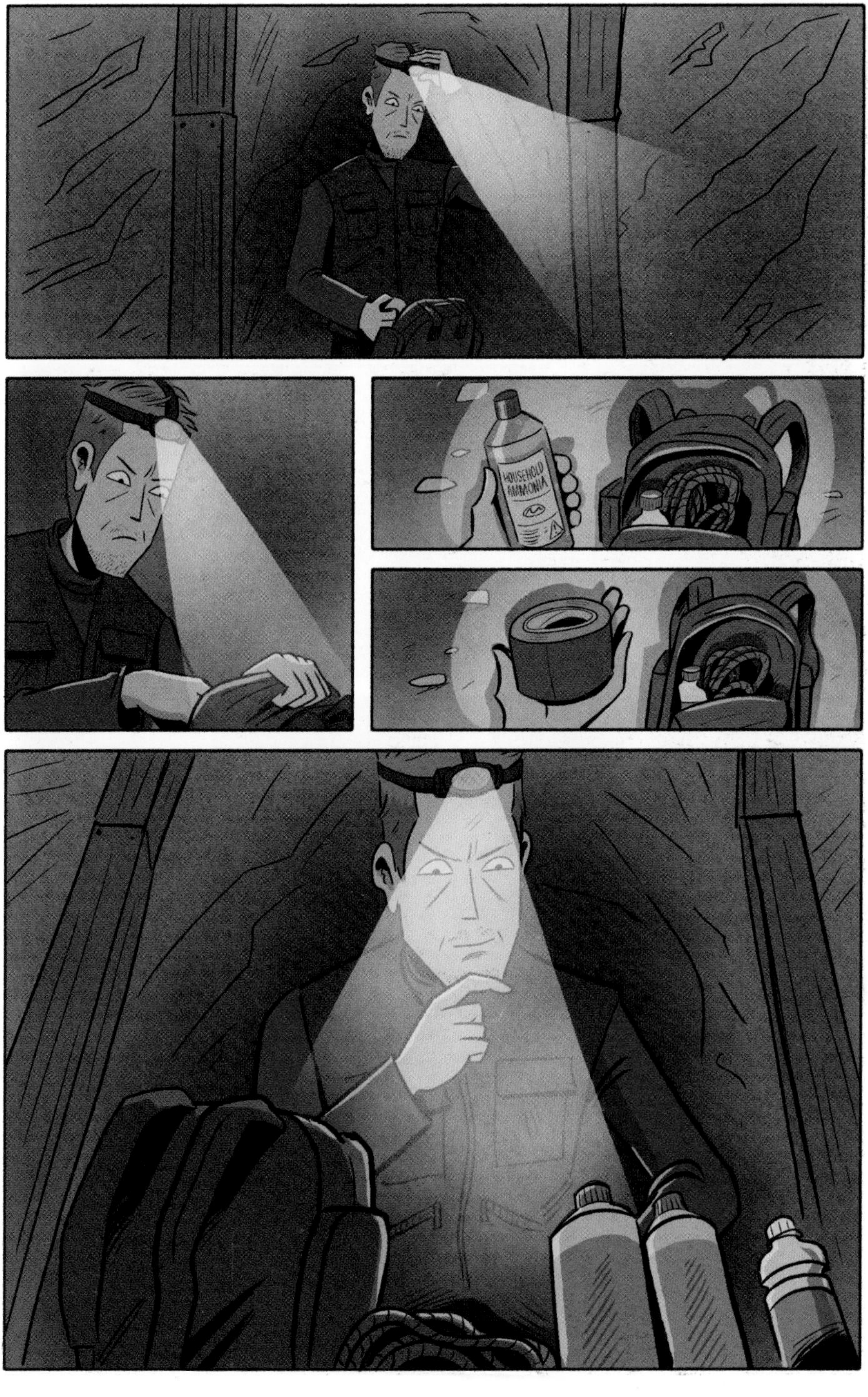
HOUSEHOLD AMMONIA

**DROP YOUR WEAPONS.**

**HOW DID YOU KNOW IT WAS ME?**

**THE WHOLE TIME WE'VE BEEN UP AGAINST YOU, EVERYONE ASSUMED WE HAD ANOTHER MOLE INSIDE THE SCHOOL. BUT WHOEVER IT WAS OBVIOUSLY KNEW FAR MORE THAN MOST STUDENTS.**

**THEY'D HAVE TO KNOW SPY SCHOOL AND SPY CAMP AS WELL AS ERICA—AND SHE LEARNED A LOT OF THAT INFORMATION FROM YOU.**

**SO IT OCCURRED TO ME, IF SPYDER COULD DELIVER SOMEONE WHO WASN'T MURRAY TO APPLE VALLEY WITHOUT ANYONE NOTICING, THEY COULD EASILY HAVE HELPED YOU FAKE YOUR OWN DEATH.**

**THAT'S SOME NICE DEDUCTIVE WORK.**

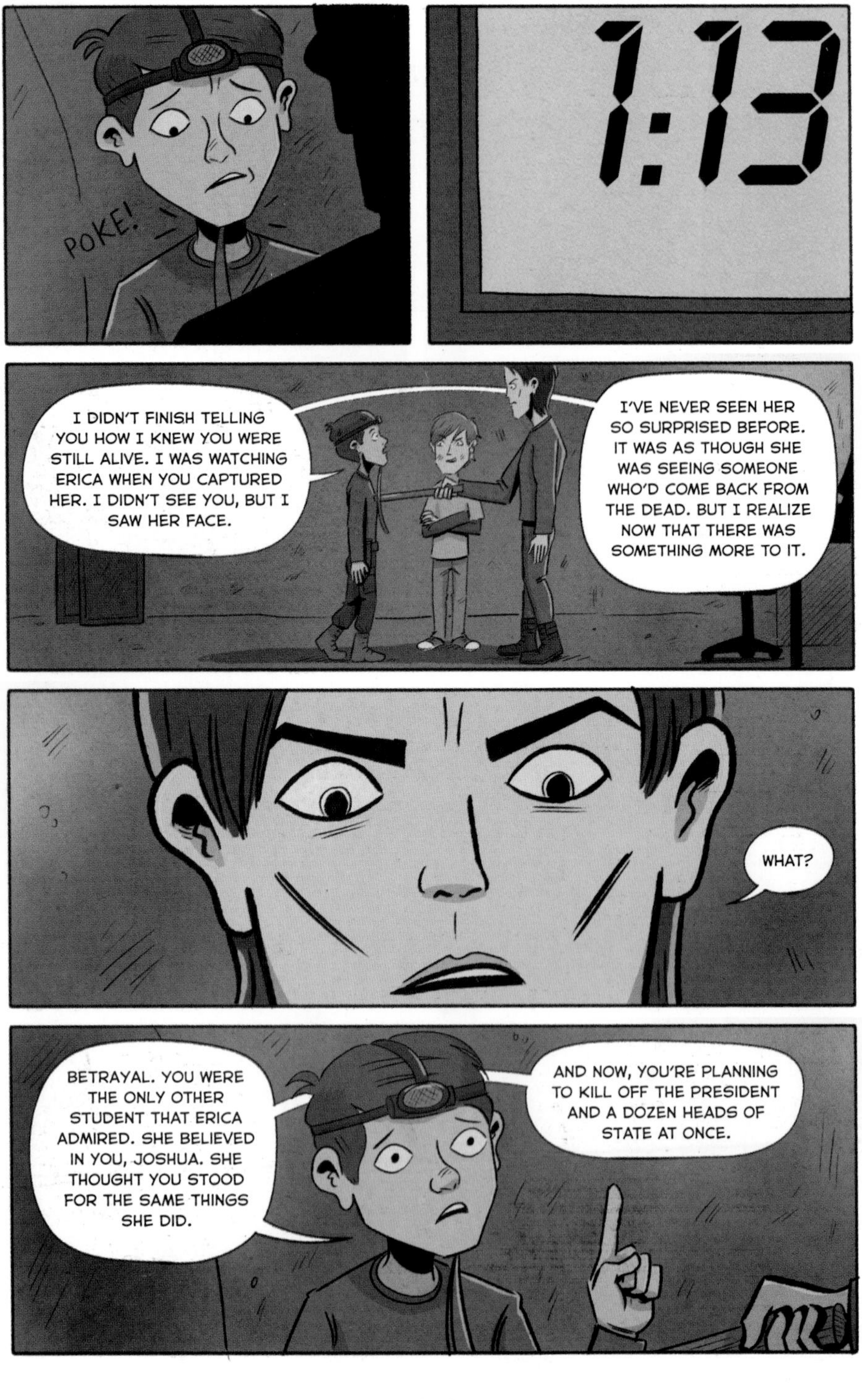
POKE!
1:13
I DIDN'T FINISH TELLING YOU HOW I KNEW YOU WERE STILL ALIVE. I WAS WATCHING ERICA WHEN YOU CAPTURED HER. I DIDN'T SEE YOU, BUT I SAW HER FACE.
I'VE NEVER SEEN HER SO SURPRISED BEFORE. IT WAS AS THOUGH SHE WAS SEEING SOMEONE WHO'D COME BACK FROM THE DEAD. BUT I REALIZE NOW THAT THERE WAS SOMETHING MORE TO IT.
WHAT?
BETRAYAL. YOU WERE THE ONLY OTHER STUDENT THAT ERICA ADMIRED. SHE BELIEVED IN YOU, JOSHUA. SHE THOUGHT YOU STOOD FOR THE SAME THINGS SHE DID.
AND NOW, YOU'RE PLANNING TO KILL OFF THE PRESIDENT AND A DOZEN HEADS OF STATE AT ONCE.

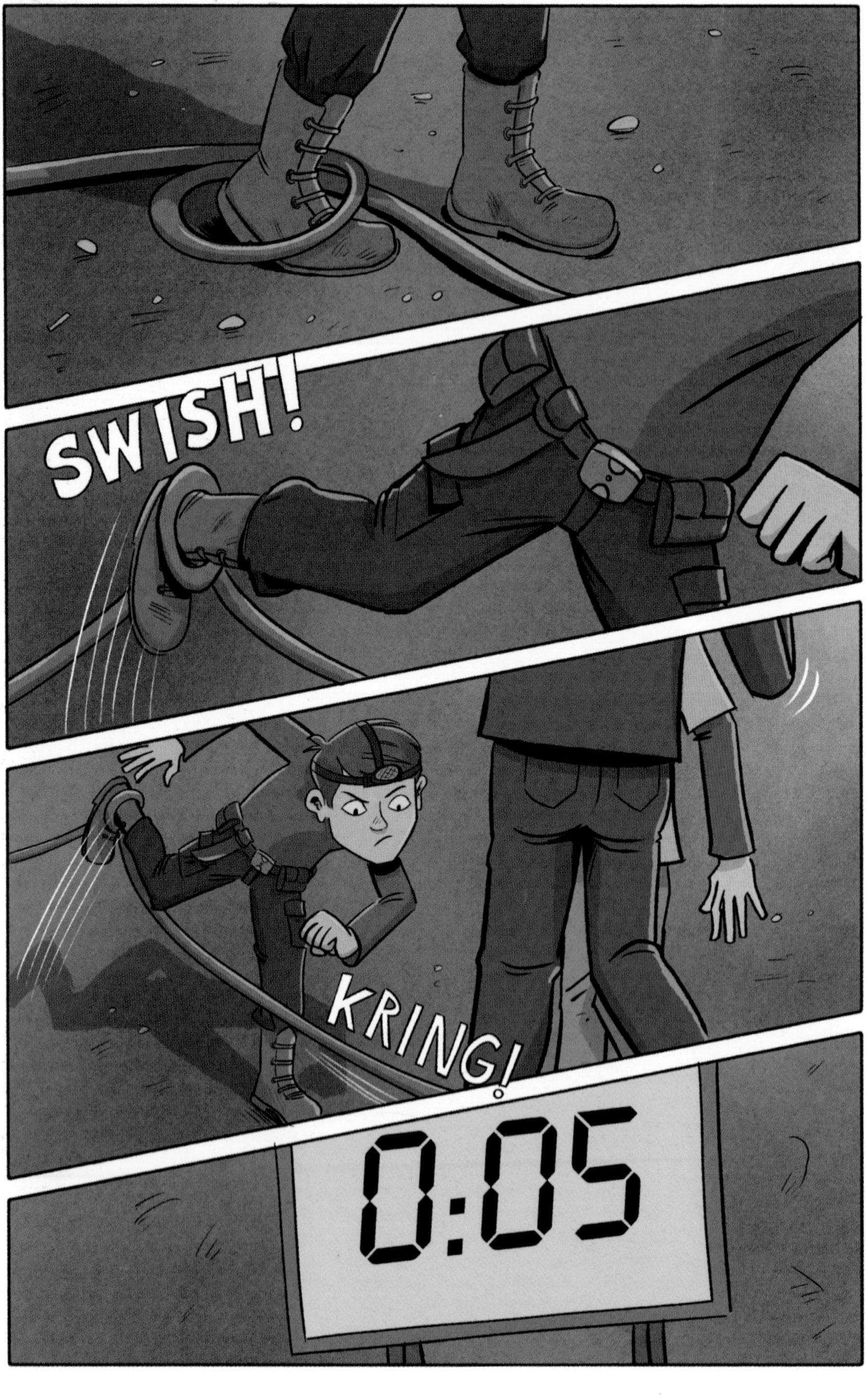
SWISH!
KRING!
0:05

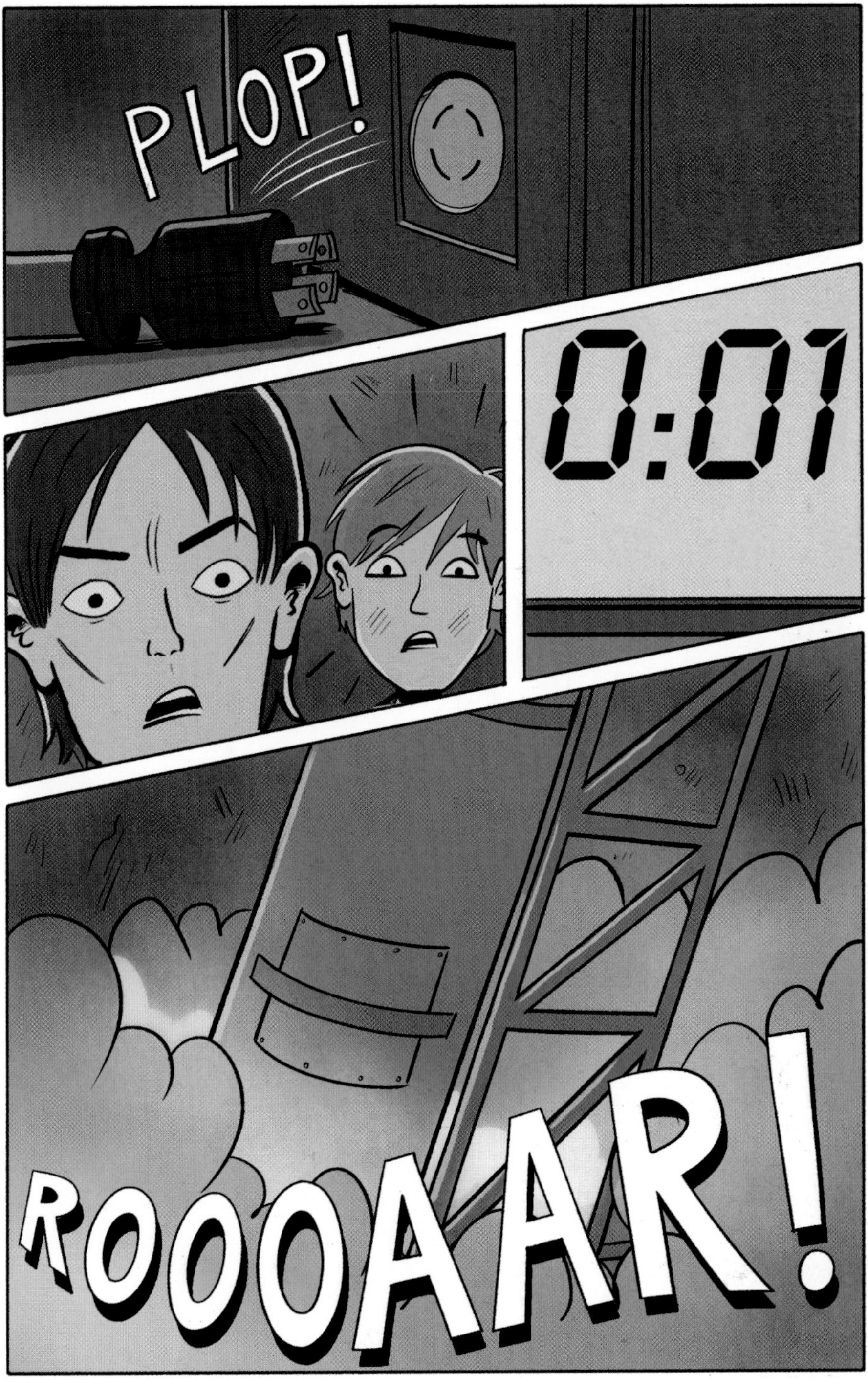
PLOP!
0:01
ROOOAAR!

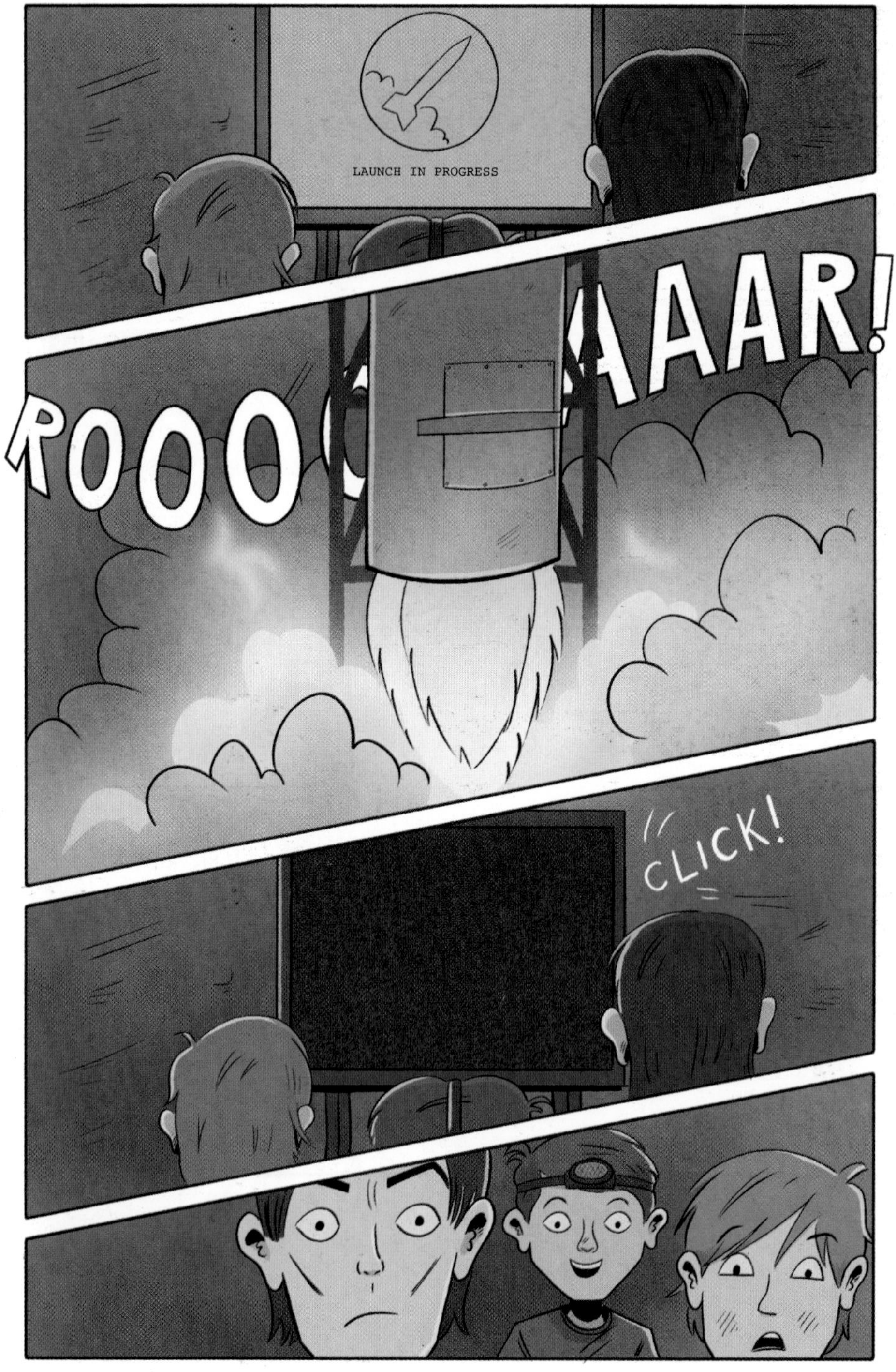
LAUNCH IN PROGRESS
ROOO
AAAR!
CLICK!

279

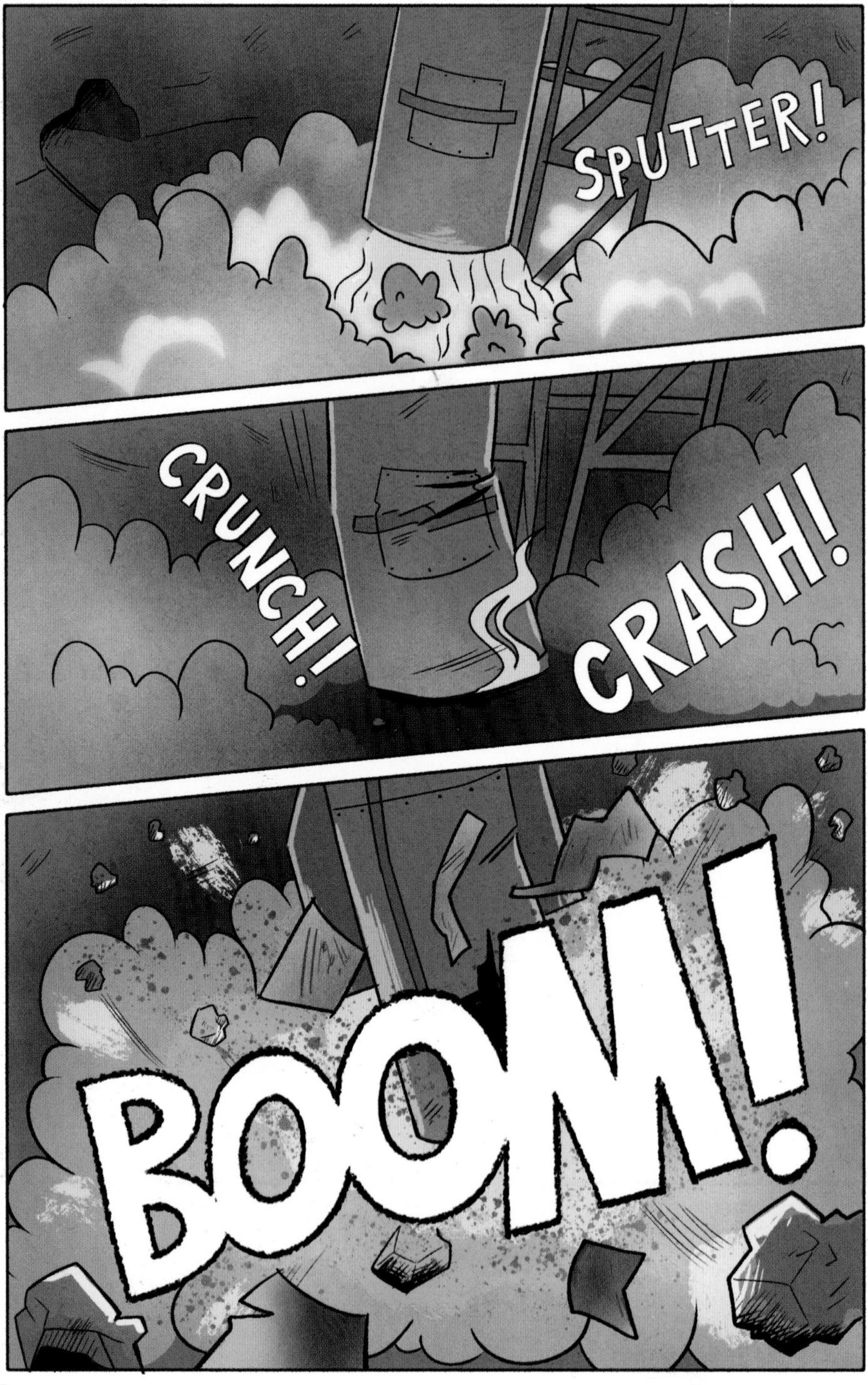
SPUTTER!
CRUNCH!
CRASH!
BOOM!

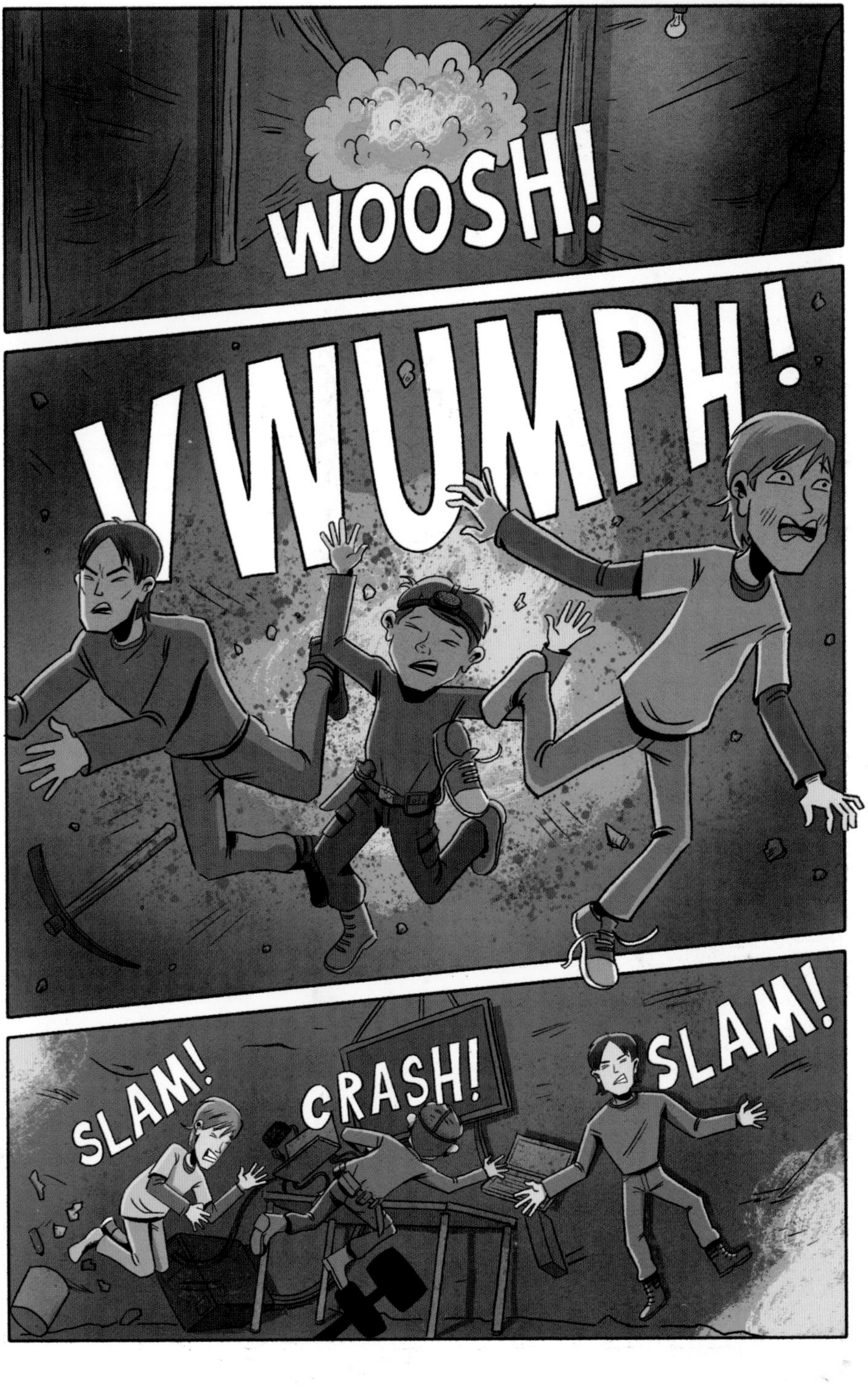
WOOSH!
VWUMPH!
SLAM!
CRASH!
SLAM!

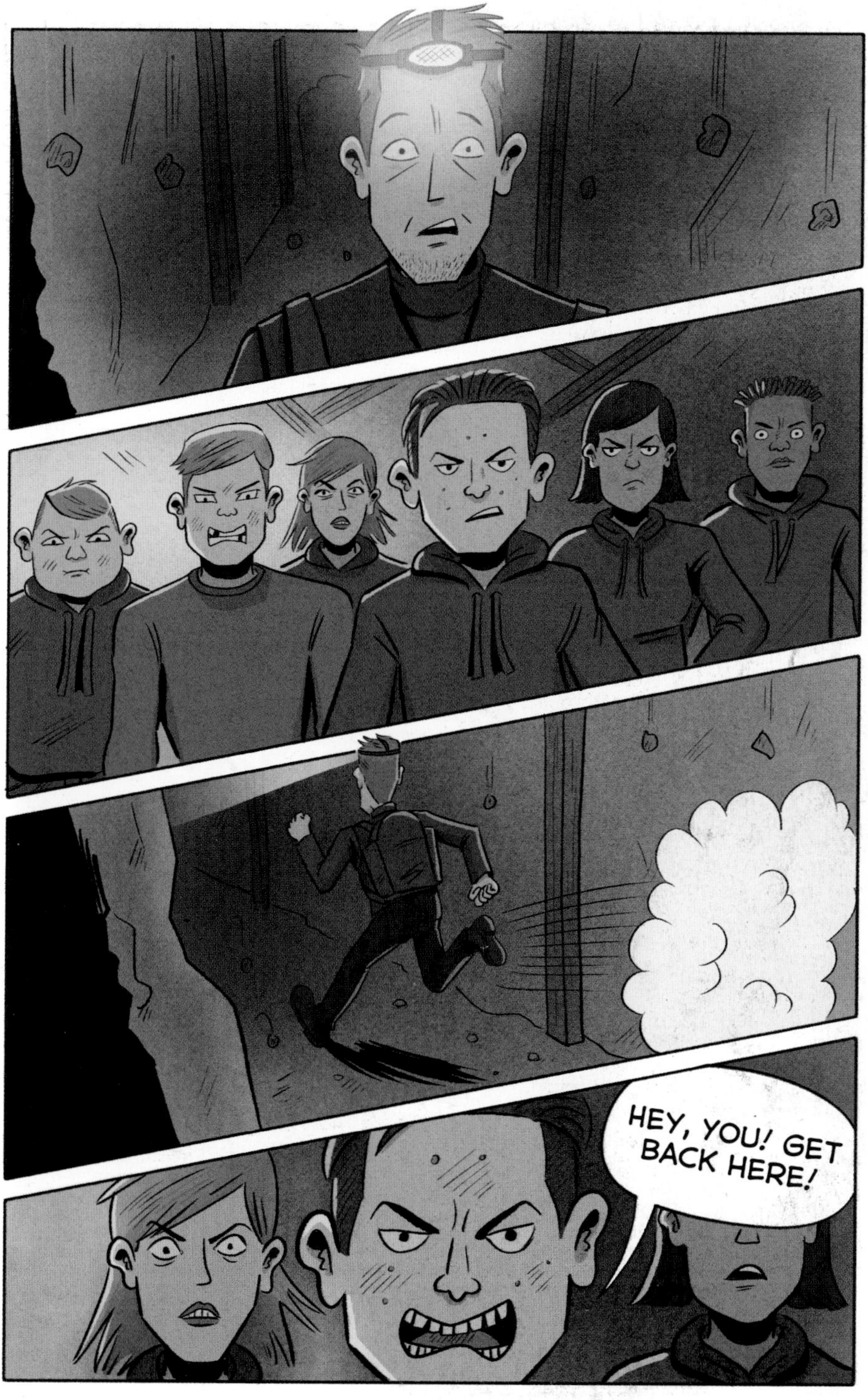
HEY, YOU! GET BACK HERE!

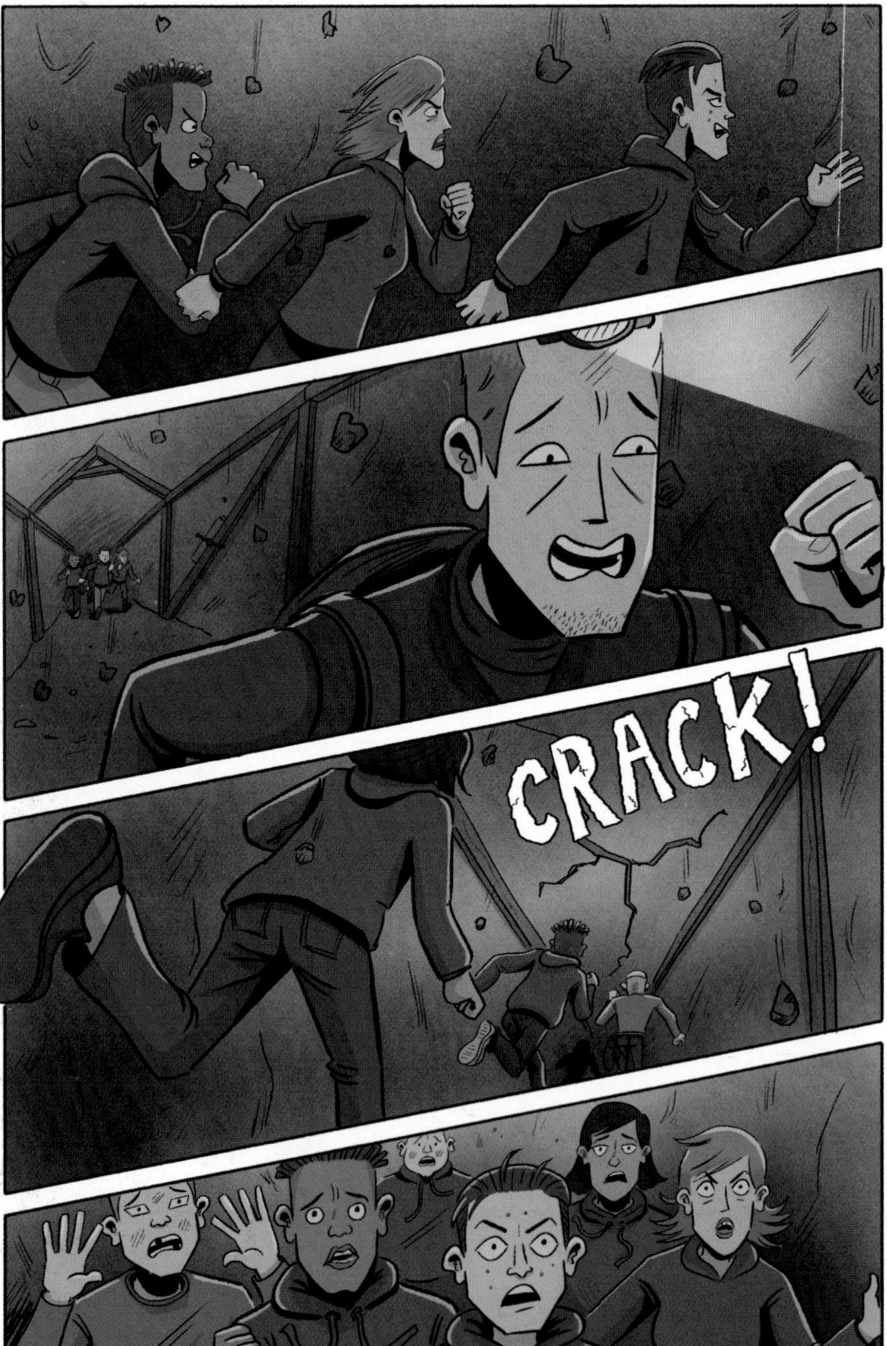
CRACK!

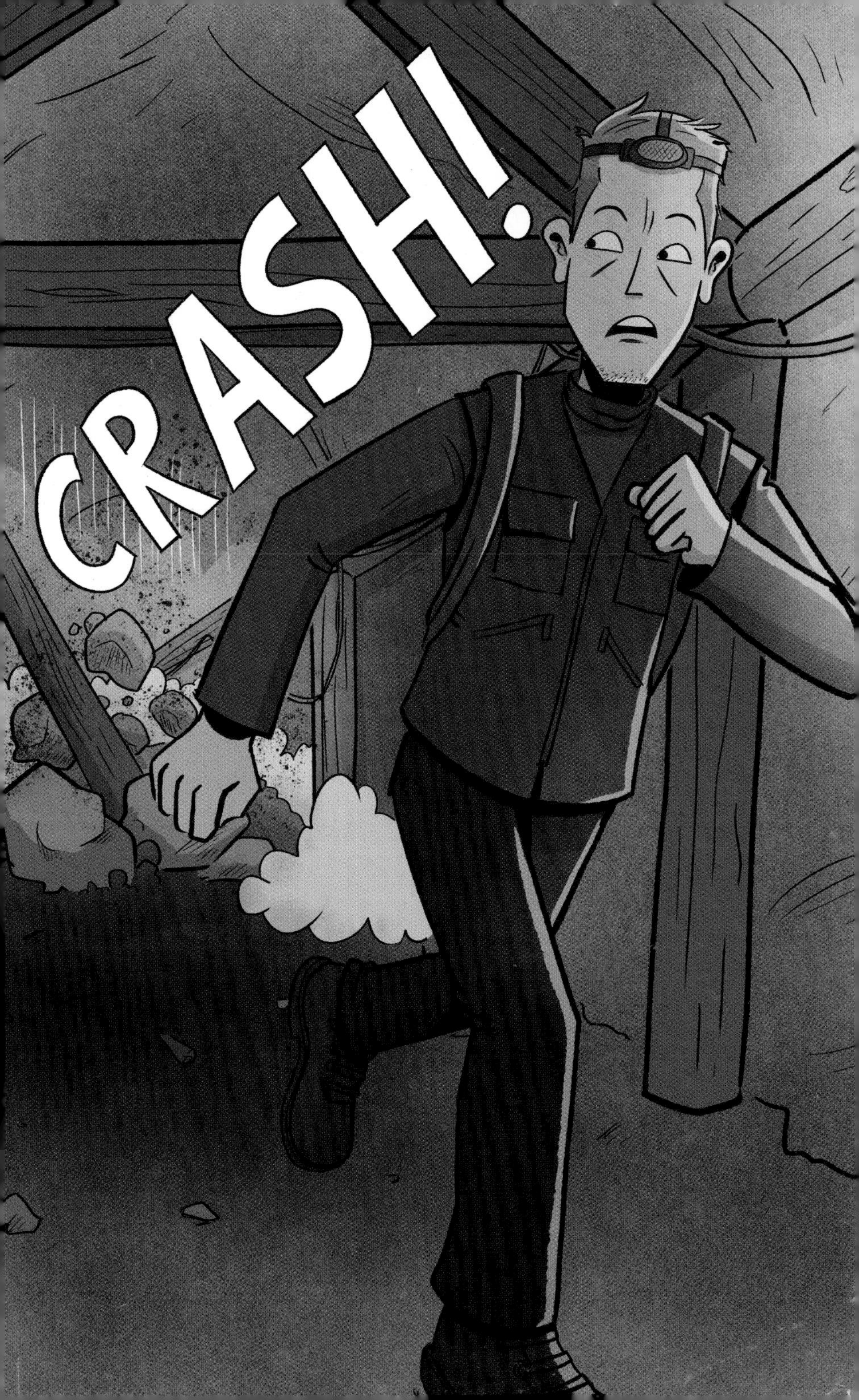
CRASH!

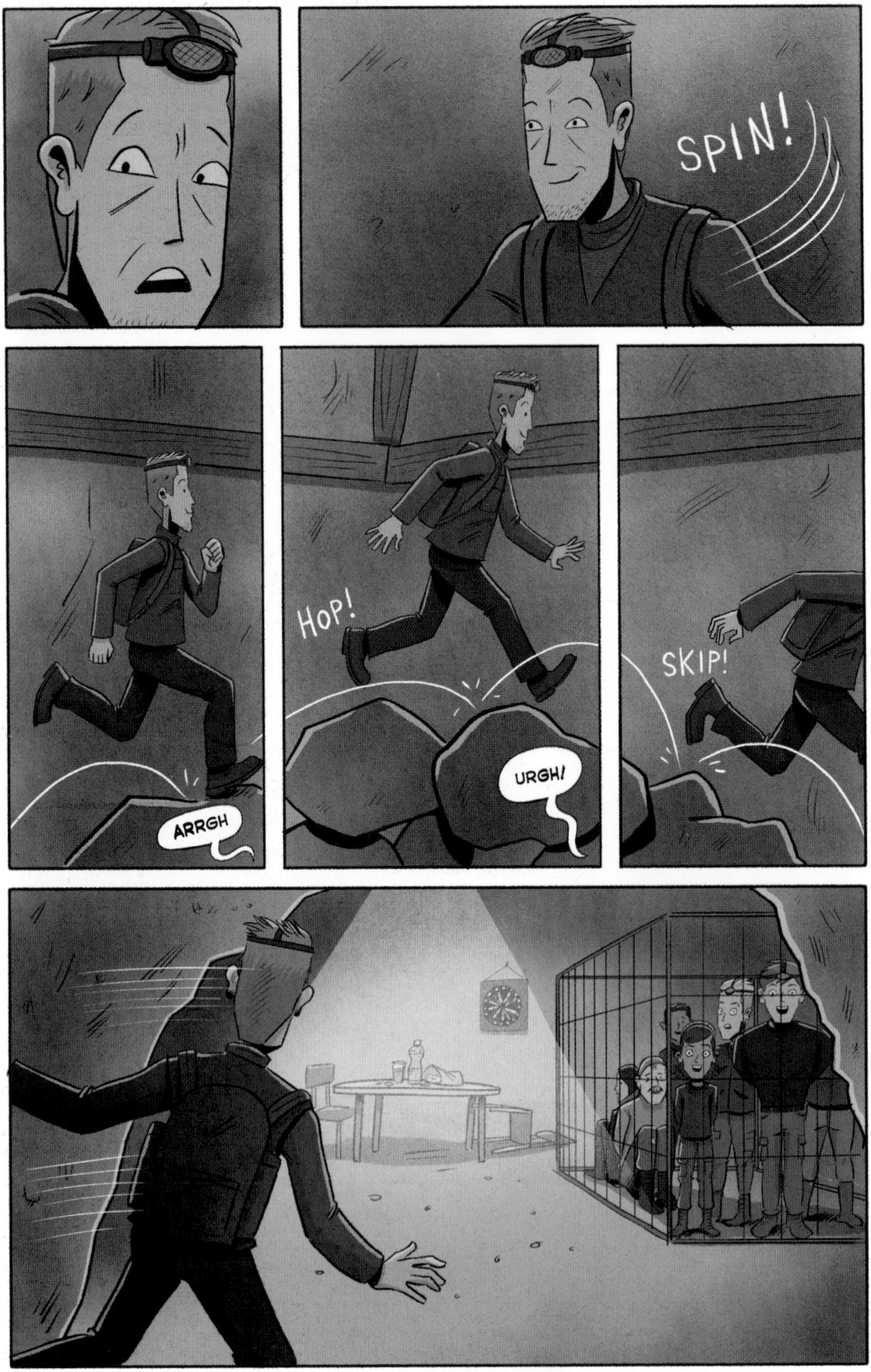
SPIN!
ARRGH
HOP!
URGH!
SKIP!

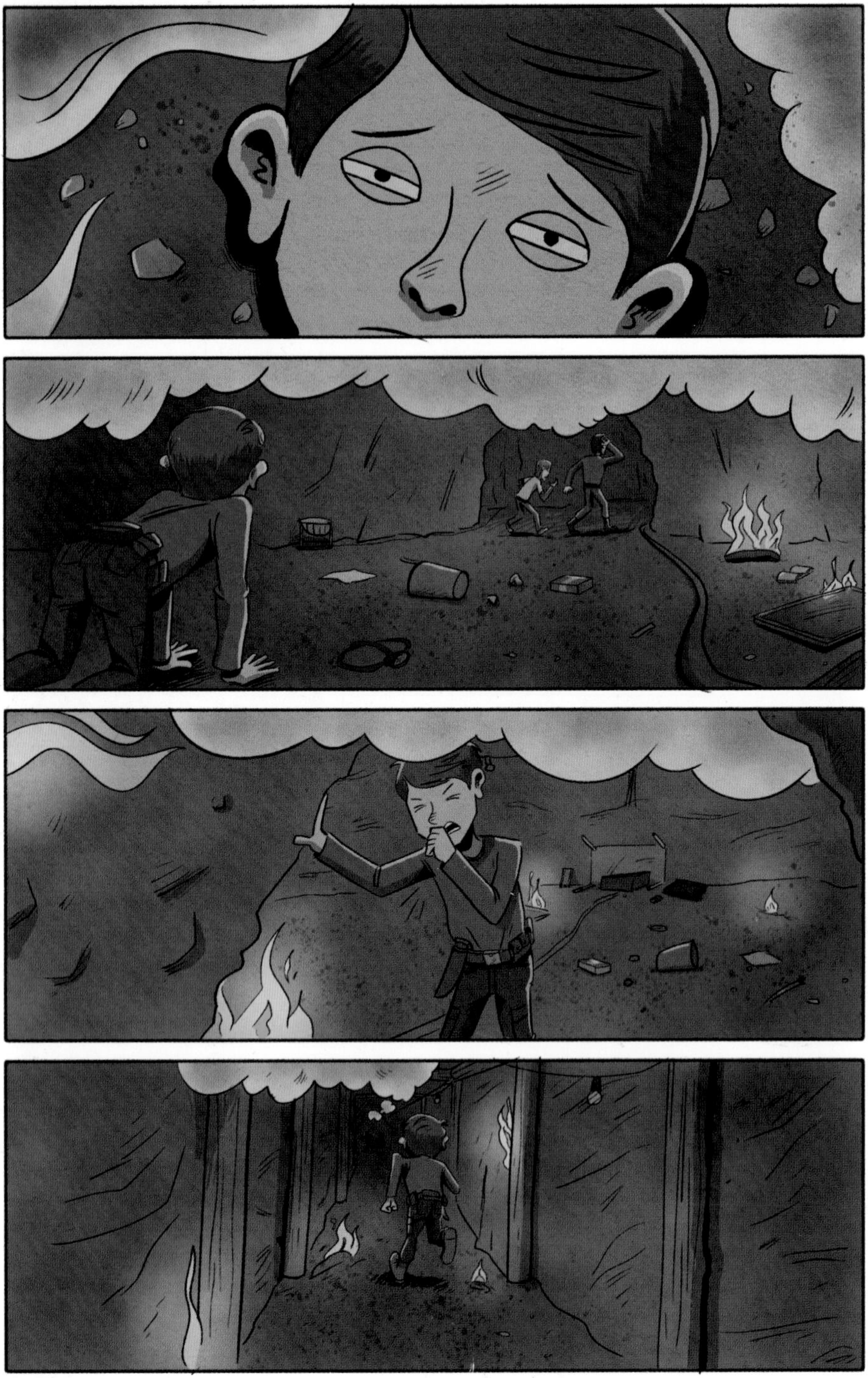

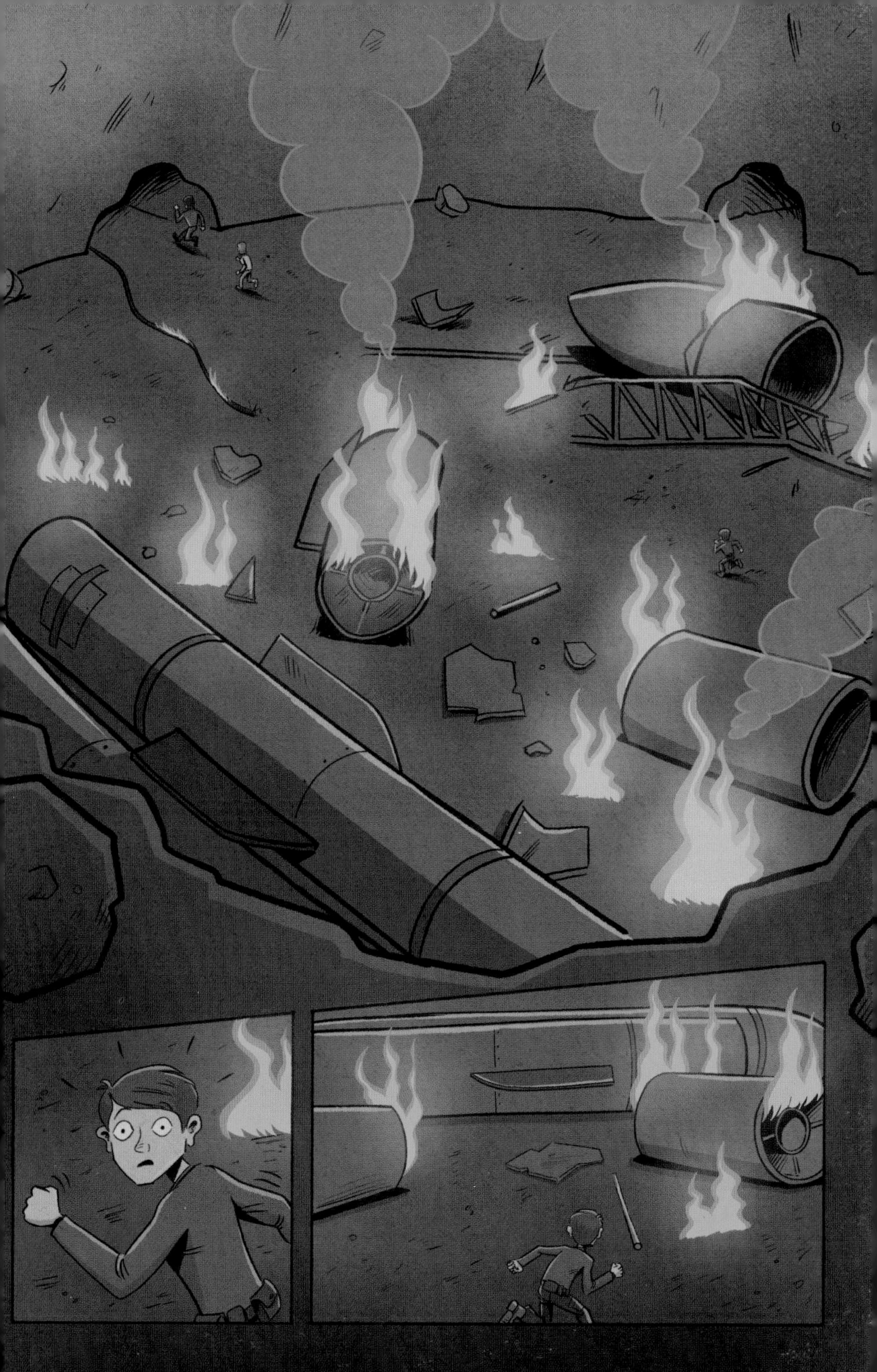

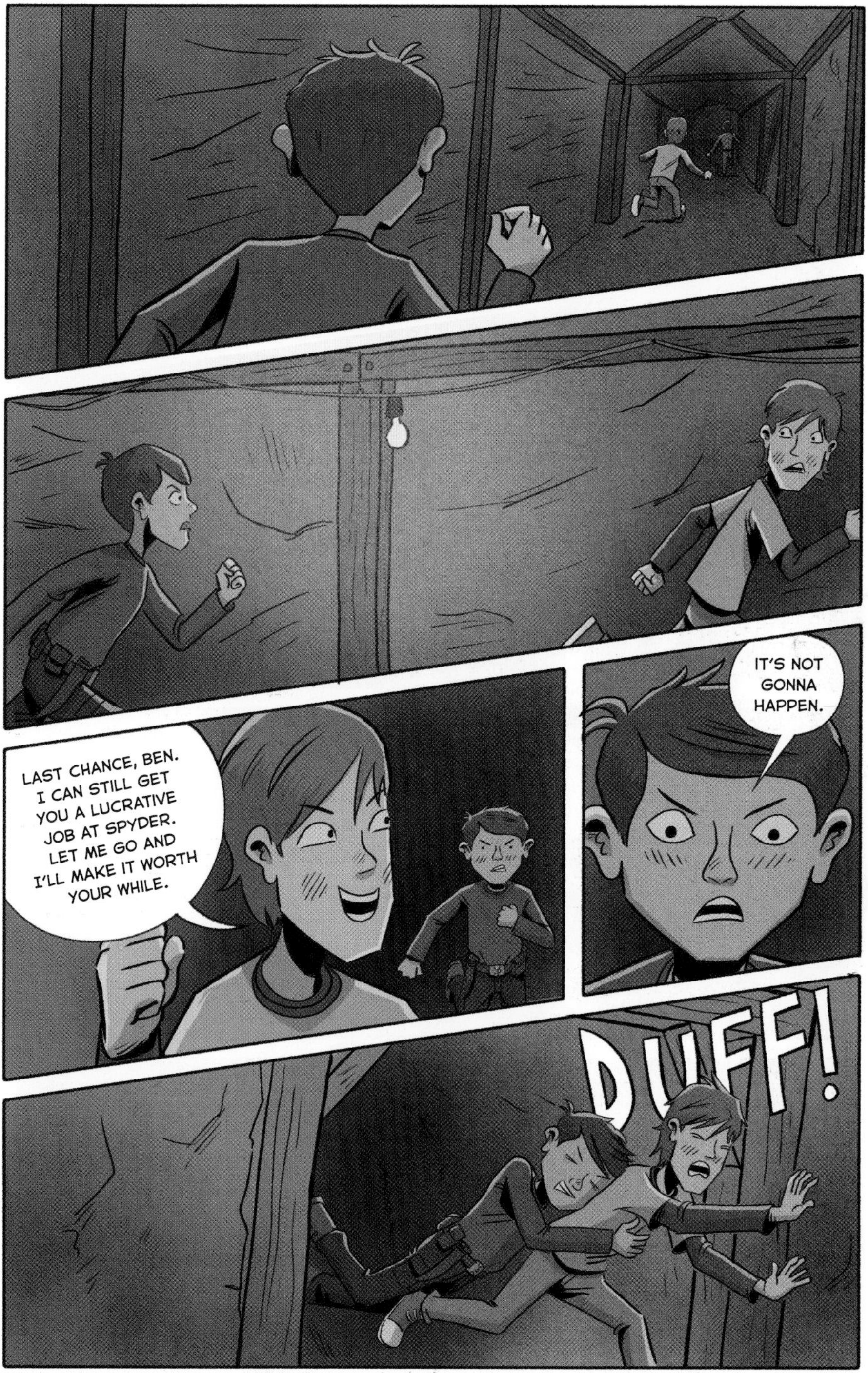
LAST CHANCE, BEN. I CAN STILL GET YOU A LUCRATIVE JOB AT SPYDER. LET ME GO AND I'LL MAKE IT WORTH YOUR WHILE.
IT'S NOT GONNA HAPPEN.
DUFF!

293

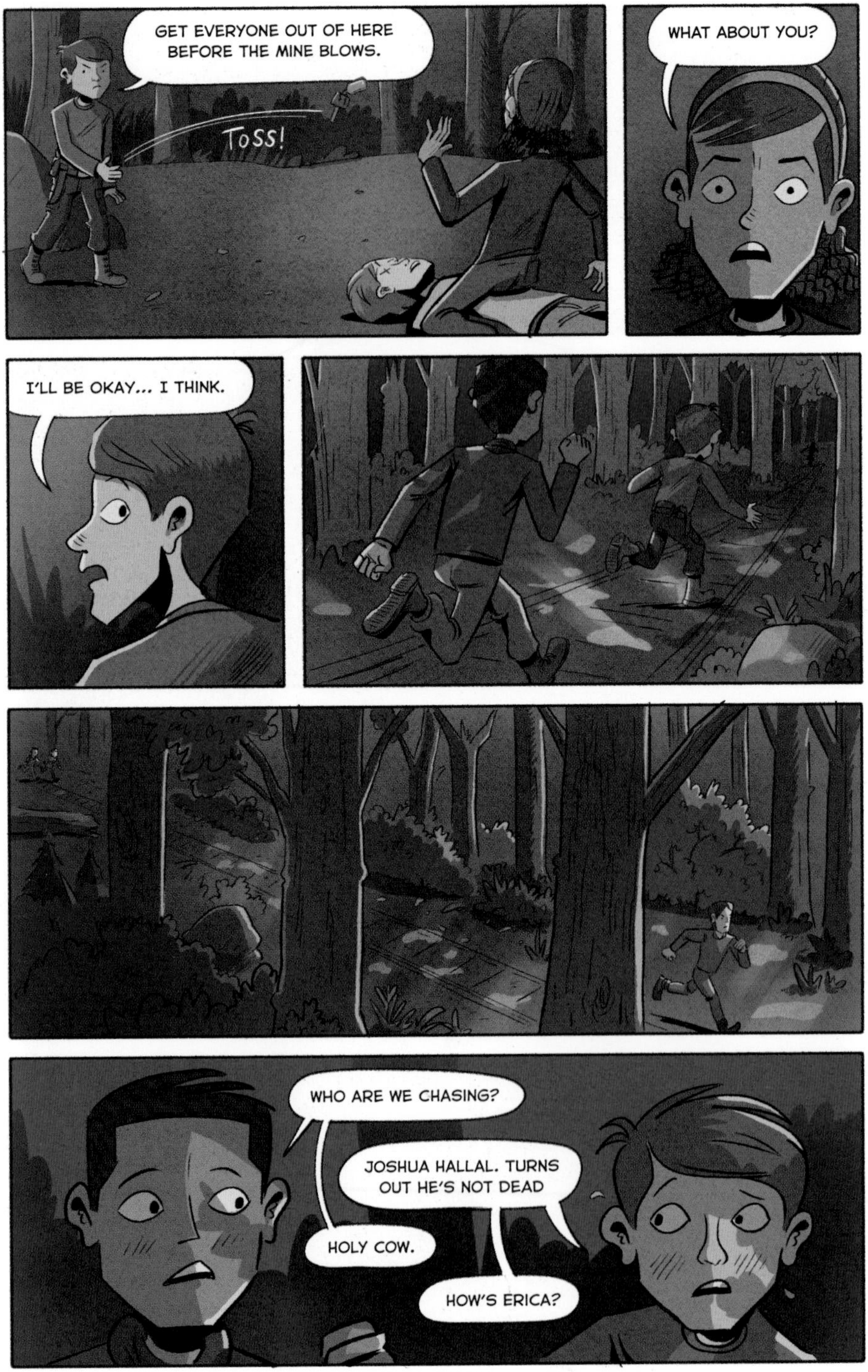
GET EVERYONE OUT OF HERE BEFORE THE MINE BLOWS.
TOSS!
WHAT ABOUT YOU?
I'LL BE OKAY... I THINK.
WHO ARE WE CHASING?
JOSHUA HALLAL. TURNS OUT HE'S NOT DEAD
HOLY COW.
HOW'S ERICA?

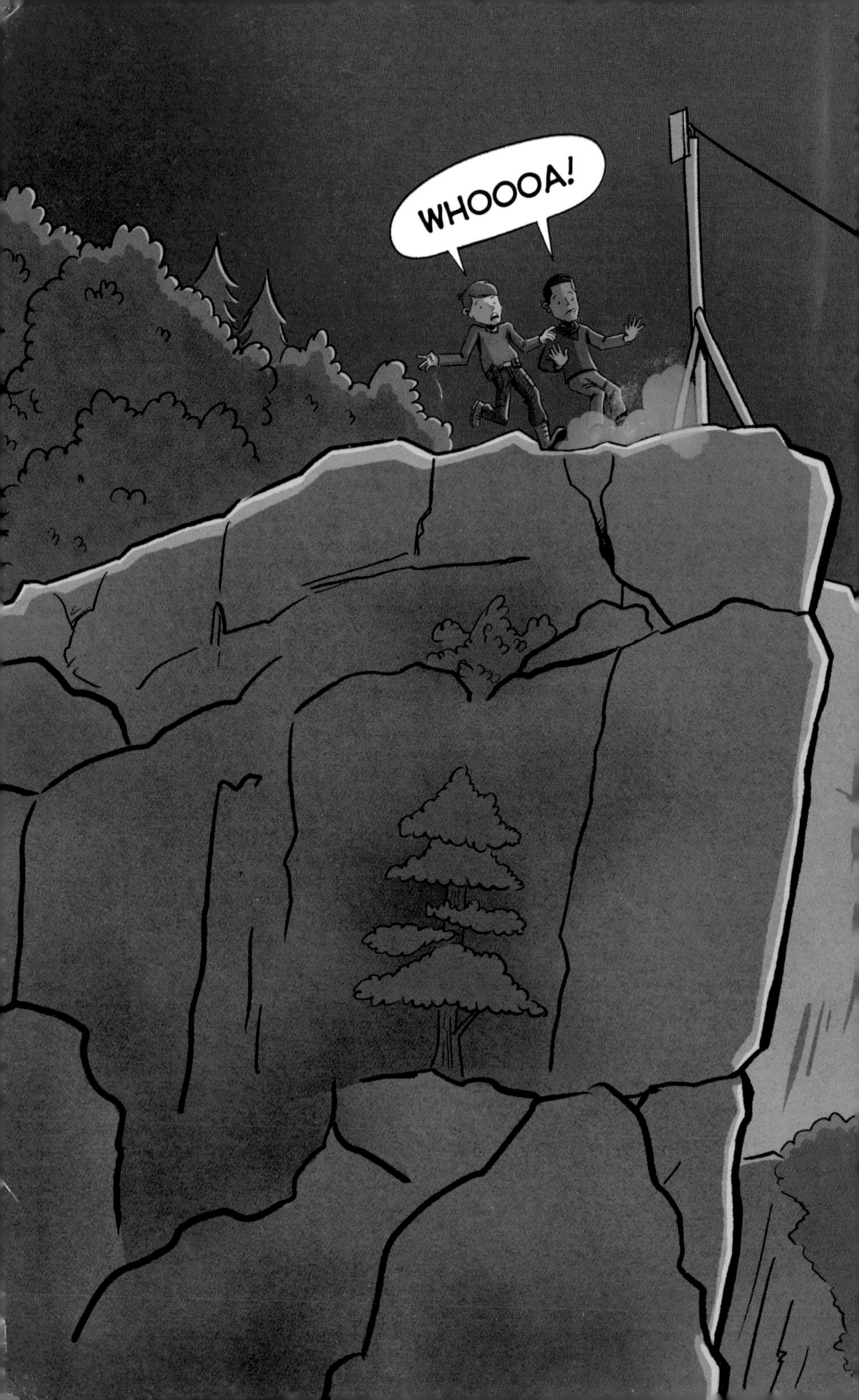
WHOOOA!

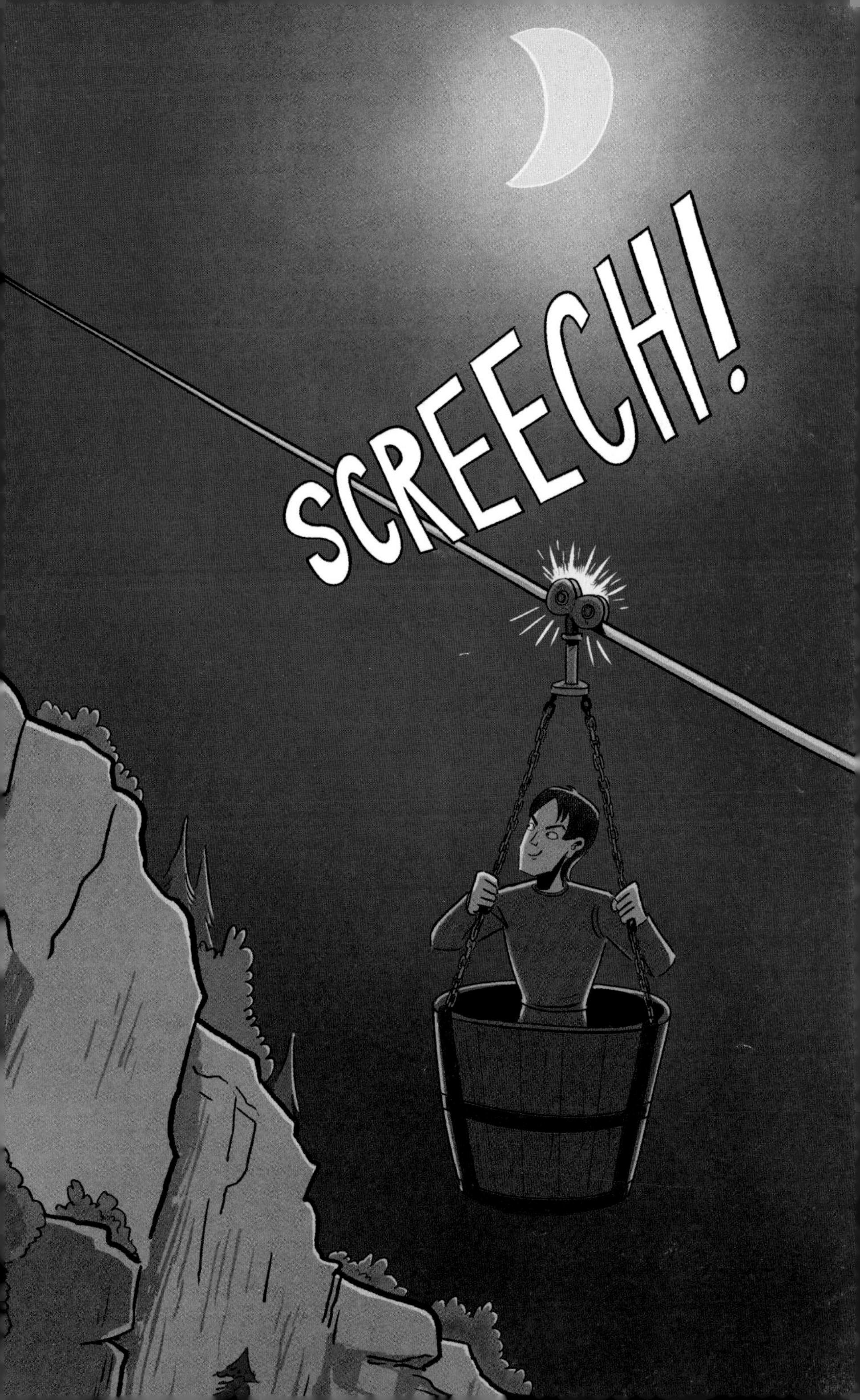
SCREECH!

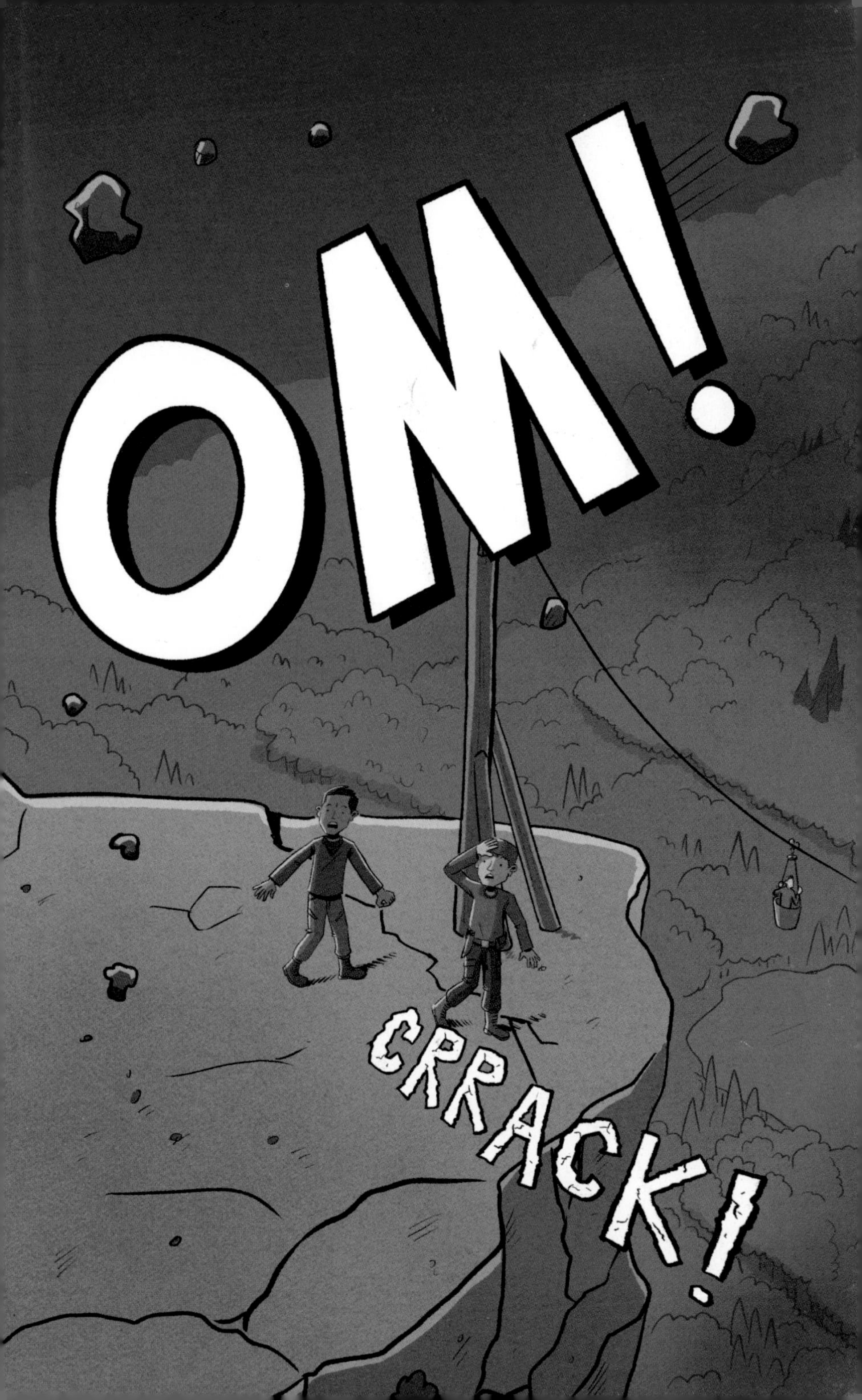
OM!
CRRACK!

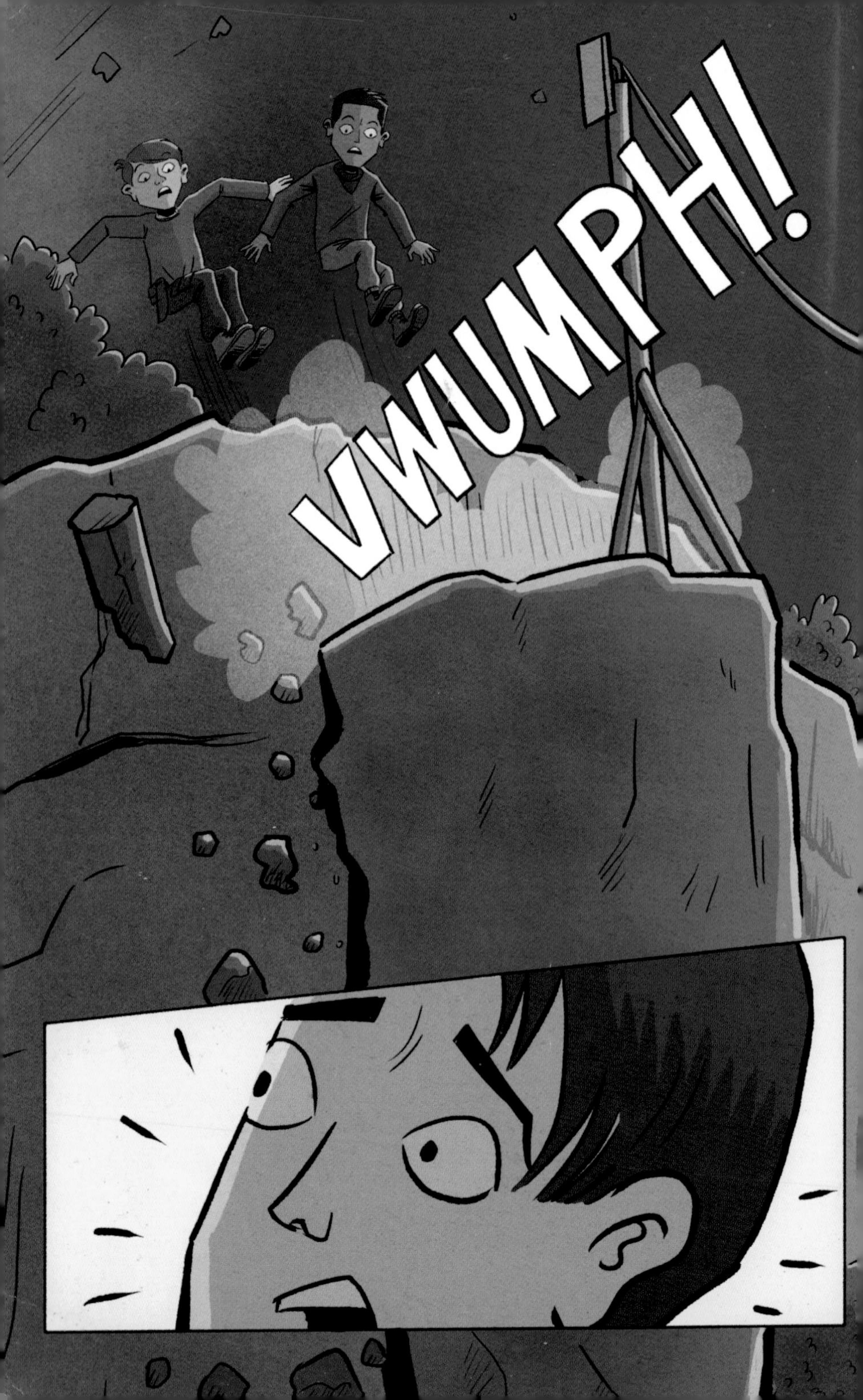
VWUMPH!

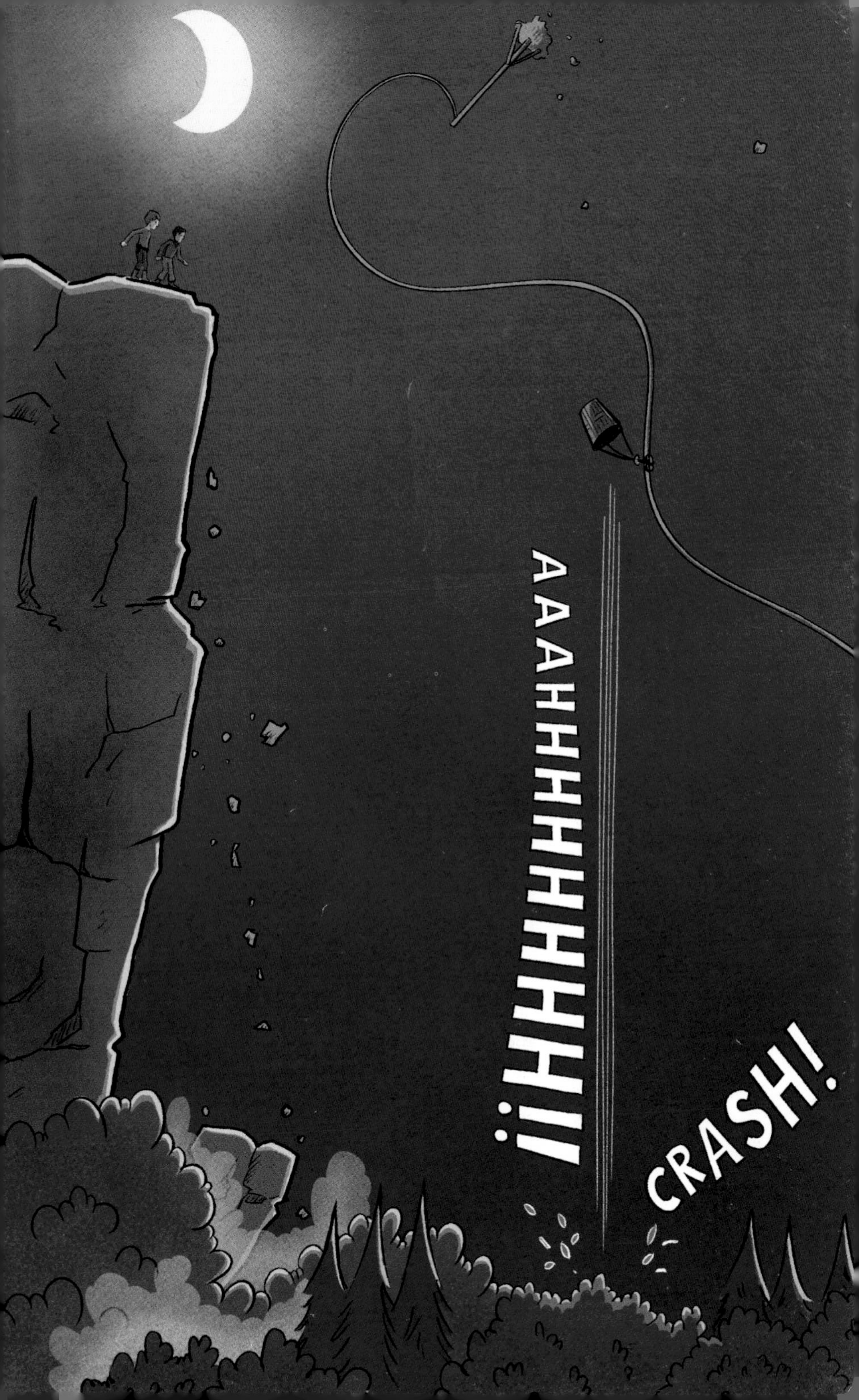
AAAHHHHHHHH!!
CRASH!

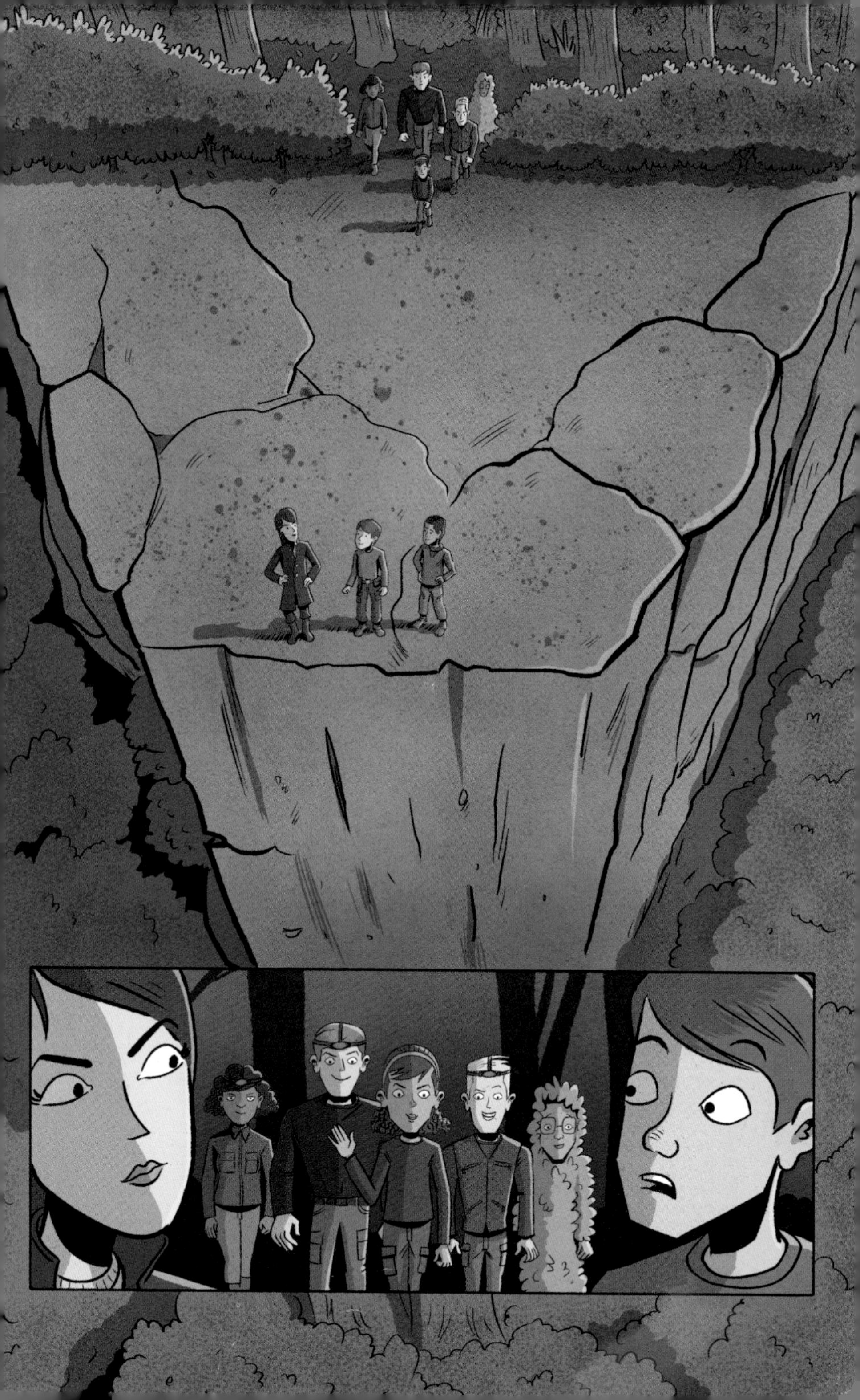

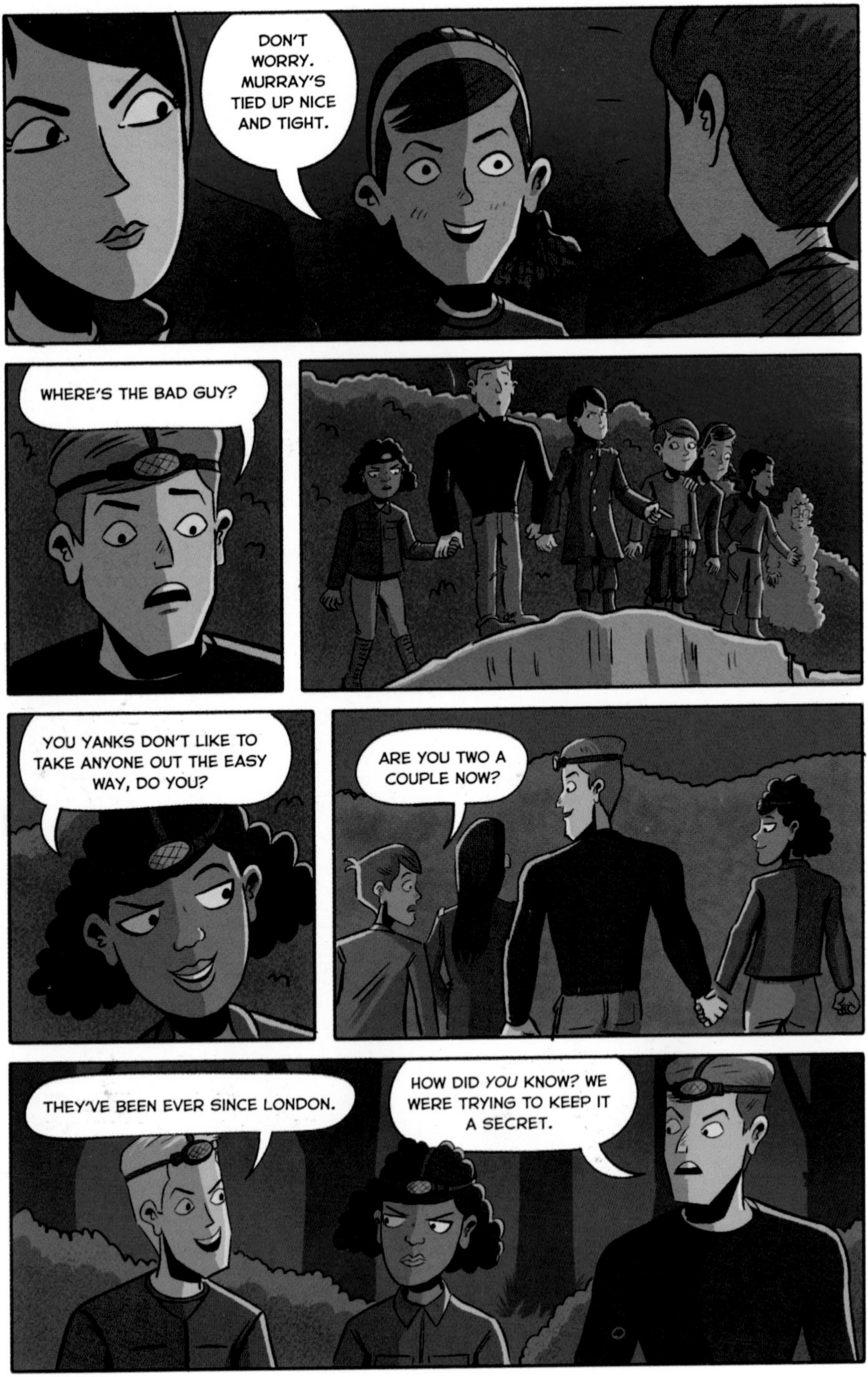
DON'T WORRY. MURRAY'S TIED UP NICE AND TIGHT.
WHERE'S THE BAD GUY?
YOU YANKS DON'T LIKE TO TAKE ANYONE OUT THE EASY WAY, DO YOU?
ARE YOU TWO A COUPLE NOW?
THEY'VE BEEN EVER SINCE LONDON.
HOW DID *YOU* KNOW? WE WERE TRYING TO KEEP IT A SECRET.

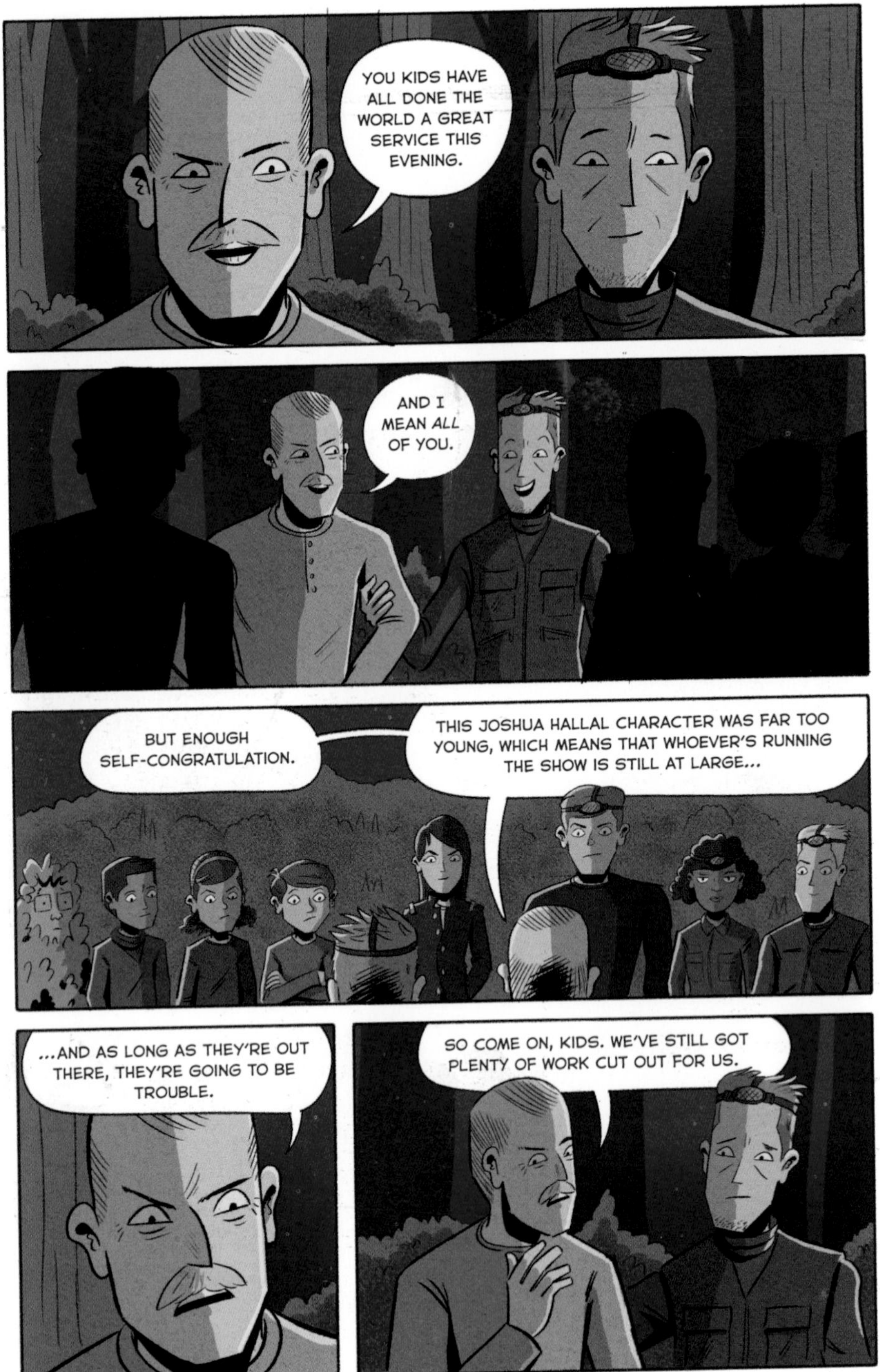
YOU KIDS HAVE ALL DONE THE WORLD A GREAT SERVICE THIS EVENING.
AND I MEAN *ALL* OF YOU.
BUT ENOUGH SELF-CONGRATULATION.
THIS JOSHUA HALLAL CHARACTER WAS FAR TOO YOUNG, WHICH MEANS THAT WHOEVER'S RUNNING THE SHOW IS STILL AT LARGE...
...AND AS LONG AS THEY'RE OUT THERE, THEY'RE GOING TO BE TROUBLE.
SO COME ON, KIDS. WE'VE STILL GOT PLENTY OF WORK CUT OUT FOR US.

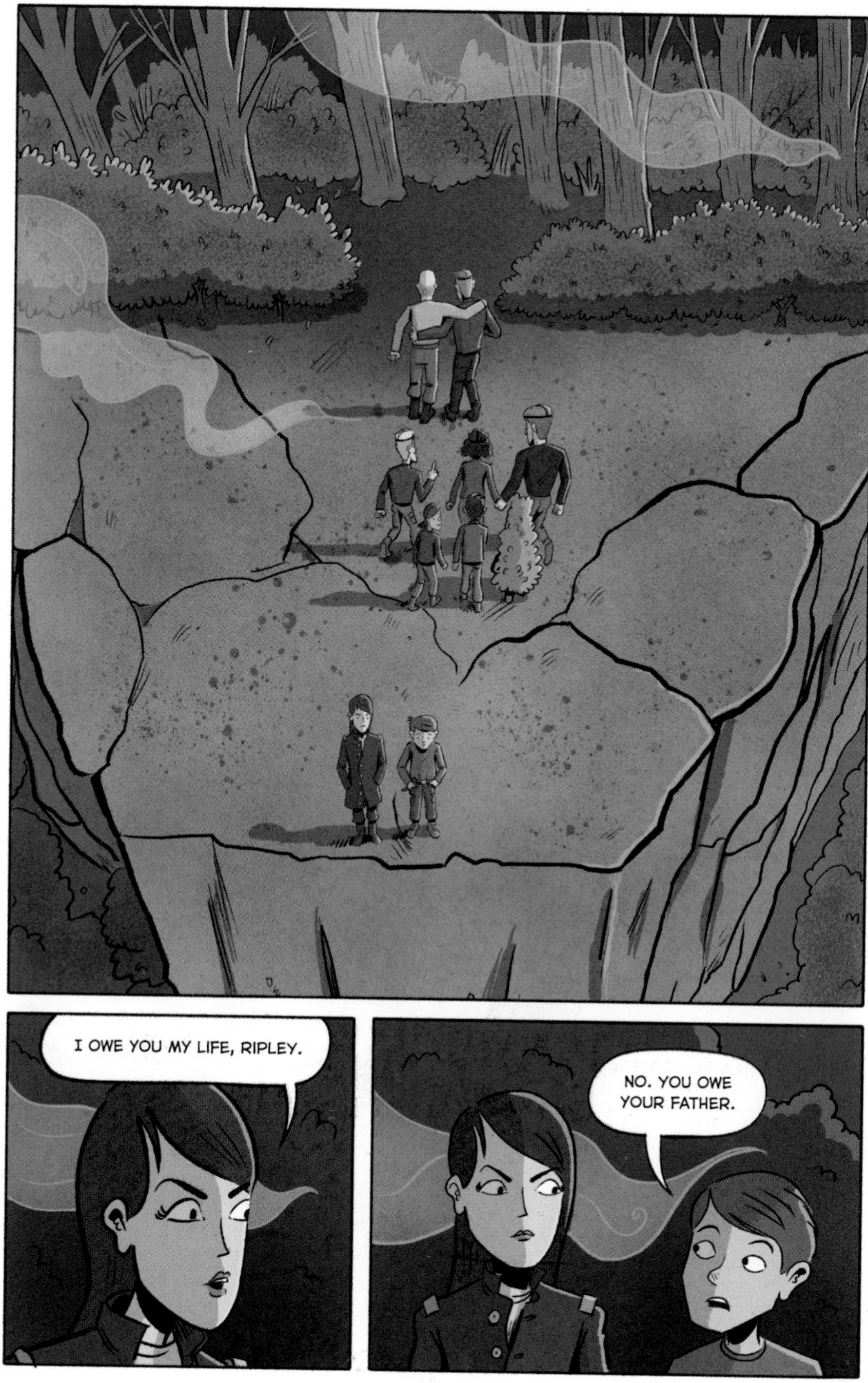
I OWE YOU MY LIFE, RIPLEY.
NO. YOU OWE YOUR FATHER.

308

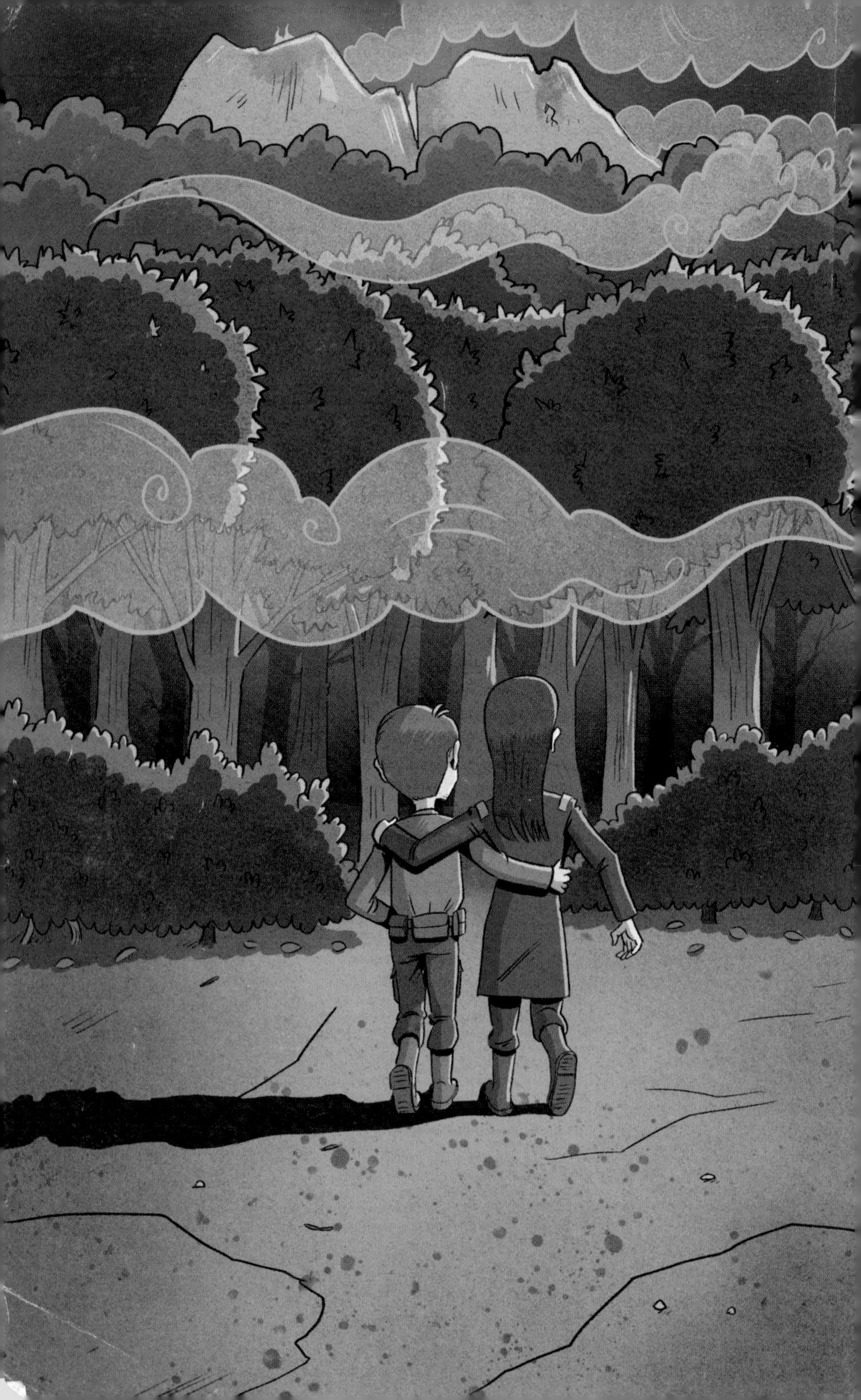

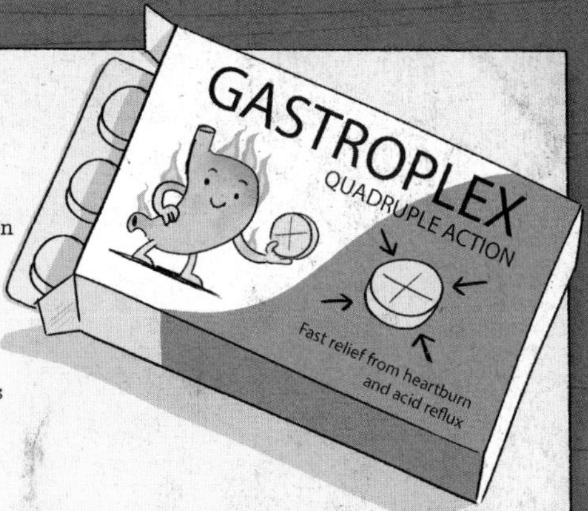
GASTROPLEX
QUADRUPLE ACTION
Fast relief from heartburn
and acid reflux

From:
Office of Intelligence Coordination
The White House
Washington, DC

To:
[redacted]
Director of Internal Investigations
CIA Headquarters
Langley, Virginia

Classified Documents Enclosed
Security Level AA2
For Your Eyes Only

After reading the enclosed transcript, it is evident that we need to [redacted] immediately. No expense must be spared to root out any agents within the CIA who are secretly working for SPYDER. To that end, I recommend [redacted]

In addition, we must step up our efforts to determine the identities of the leadership of SPYDER before said organization can wreak any more havoc. To that end, I recommend that Benjamin Ripley be [redacted], though he need not be informed of this until necessary. Agent [redacted], aka [redacted] suggests that young Mr. Ripley may even be of further use against SPYDER, perhaps in Operation Deadly Weasel.

Finally, there is the issue of Erica Hale. Obviously, the black mark placed on her record was a mistake. It ought to be expunged and, given her impressive skill set, Ms. Hale should be [redacted] against SPYDER.

These actions need to take place immediately, if not sooner. SPYDER is obviously a great threat to our national security that, if unchecked, may prove the end of our intelligence community—if not our great nation—once and for all.

Hope to see you at the White House barbecue this weekend.

[redacted]
Director of Covert Affairs

# Acknowledgments

Once again, I am indebted to the incredibly talented Anjan Sarkar for his tireless work on this project. This isn't just a graphic novel, folks. It's a work of art. To that end, I also have to thank the equally incredibly talented Lucy Ruth Cummins and Krista Vitola for shepherding this project, as well as all the other fine folks at Simon & Schuster: Justin Chanda, Erin Toller, Beth Parker, Roberta Stout, Kendra Levin, Alyza Liu, Anne Zafian, Lisa Moraleda, Jenica Nasworthy, Chrissy Noh, Ashley Mitchell, Brendon MacDonald, Nadia Almahdi, Christina Pecorale, Victor Iannone, Emily Hutton, Emily Ritter, Theresa Pang, Dainese Santos, Chava Wolin, Tom Daly, and Michelle Leo. Plus my amazing agent, Jennifer Joel.

Thanks are also due to my fellow authors (and support group): Sarah Mlynowski, Rose Brock, James Ponti, Julie Buxbaum, Max Brallier, Gordon Korman, Christina Soontornvat, Karina Yan Glaser, Alyson Gerber, and Julia Devillers.

This project wouldn't have happened without the exceptional contributions of Caroline Curran. And I couldn't get anything done these days without my fantastic assistant, Emma Chanen.

On the home front, thanks (and much love) to Ronald and Jane Gibbs; Suzanne, Darragh, and Ciara Howard; and finally, Dashiell and Violet, the best kids any parent could ever ask for.